Macbeth

THE GRAPHIC NOVEL
William Shakespeare

Script by John McDonald

Adapted by Brigit Viney

LUCENT BOOKS
A part of Gale, Cengage Learning

GALE
CENGAGE Learning

Detroit • New York • San Francisco • New Haven, Conn • Waterville, Maine • London

Macbeth: The Graphic Novel
William Shakespeare
Script by John McDonald
Adapted by Brigit Viney

> For permission to use material from this text or product,
> submit all requests online at **cengage.com/permissions**
>
> Further permissions questions can be emailed to
> **permissionrequest@cengage.com**

Lucent Books
27500 Drake Rd.
Farmington Hills, MI 48331

ISBN-13: 978-1-4205-0373-9
ISBN-10: 1-4205-0373-1

Library of Congress Control Number: 2010924000

Published in association with Classical Comics Ltd.

Images on pages 3 & 6 reproduced with the kind permission
of the Trustees of the National Library of Scotland.
© National Library of Scotland.

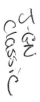

Printed in the United States of America
1 2 3 4 5 6 7 14 13 12 11 10

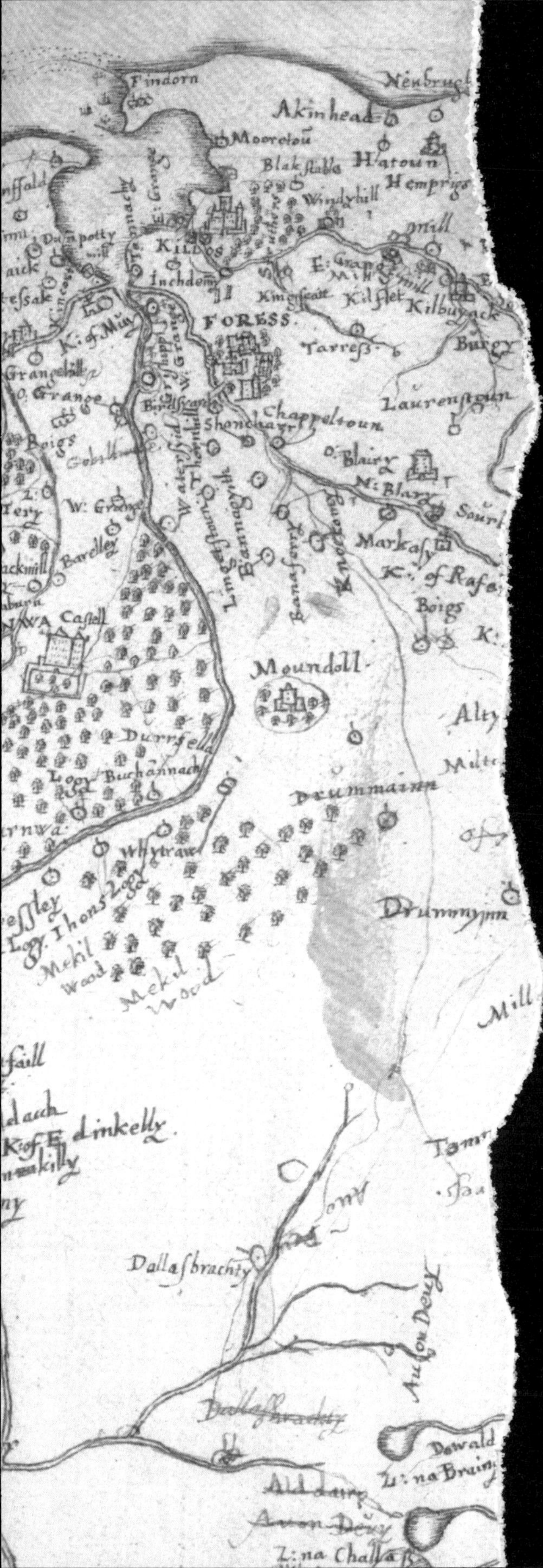
Findorn
Akinhead
Moorclou
Blakstable
Hatoun
Hemprigs
Windyhill
Kildos
Inchdom
FORESS
Tarress
Laurenstoun
Chappeltoun
Shondharry
Markasy
Boigs
Moundall
Durrfell
Logy Buchannach
Drummainn
Whytrave
Drummynin
Mekil Wood
Mill
Edinkelly
Dallasbrachty
Aucon Dery
Dowald
Aldeary
Avon Dery

Contents

Characters

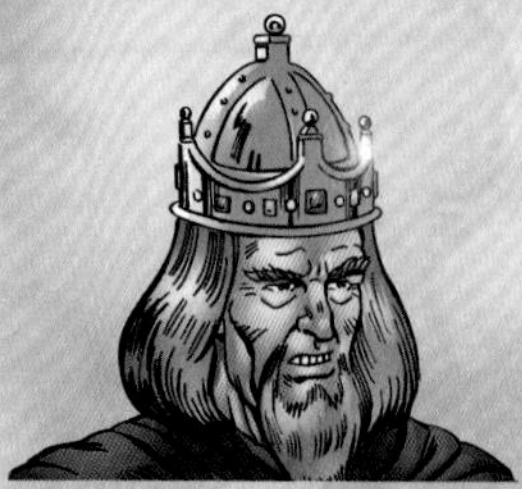

Duncan
King of Scotland

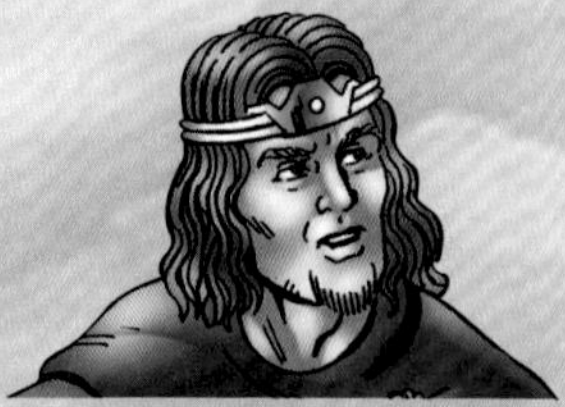

Malcolm
Son of Duncan

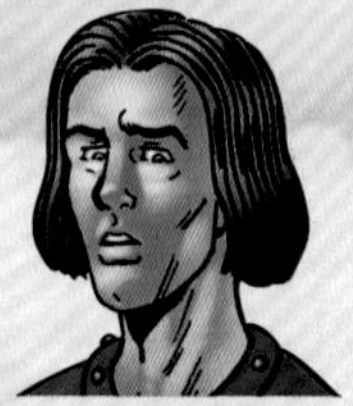

Donalbain
Son of Duncan

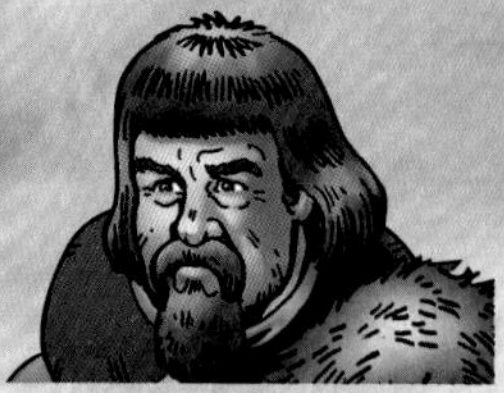

Macduff
*Scottish **Nobleman***

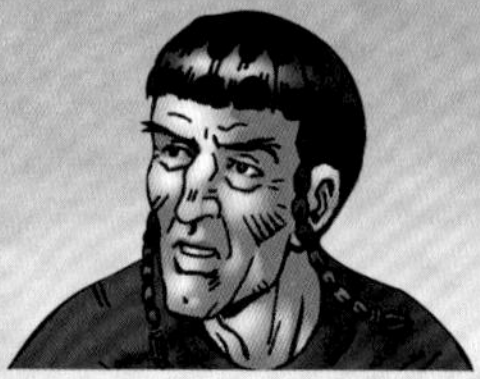

Lenox
*Scottish **Nobleman***

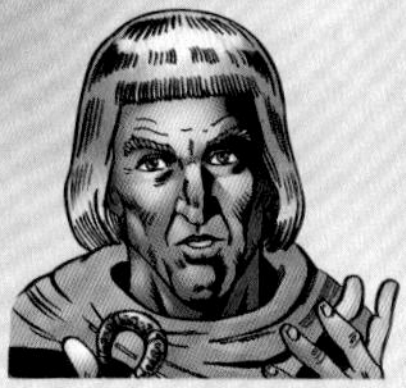

Rosse
*Scottish **Nobleman***

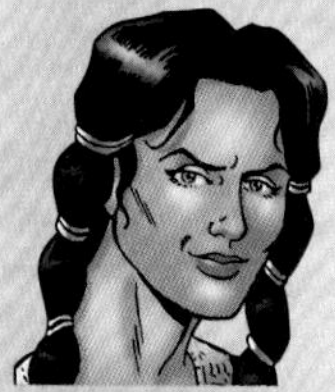

Lady Macbeth
Wife of Macbeth

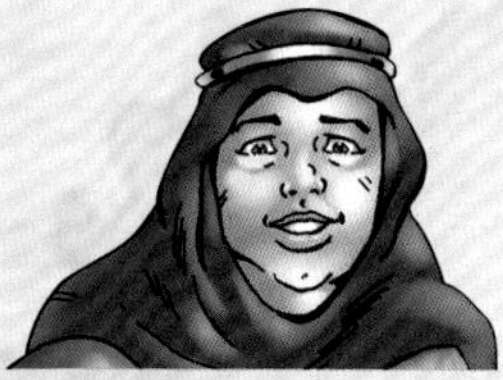

Lady Macduff
Wife of Macduff

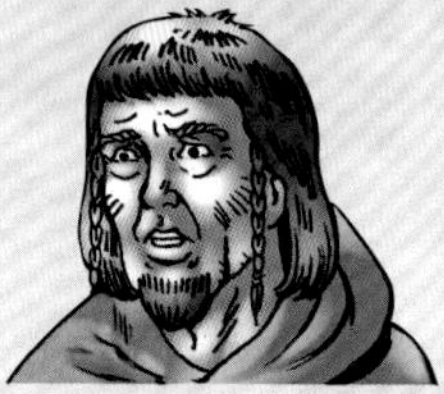

Siward
*Leader of the English **Army***

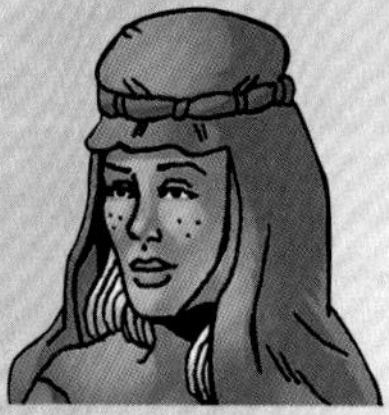

A lady who ***serves***
Lady Macbeth

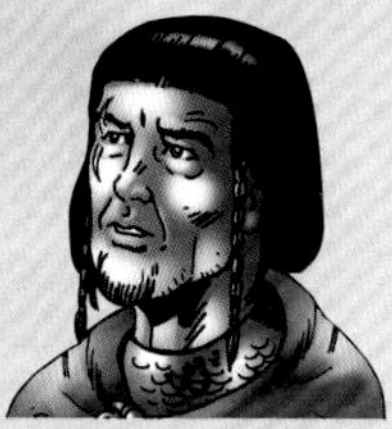

Seyton
*A man who **serves** Macbeth*

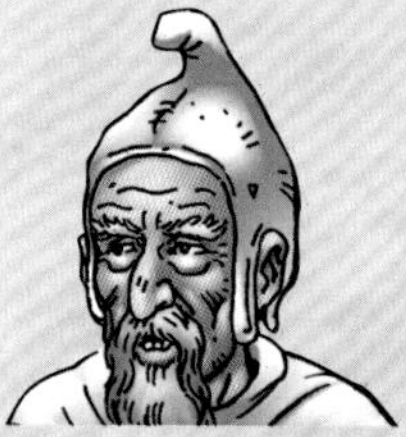

An English Doctor

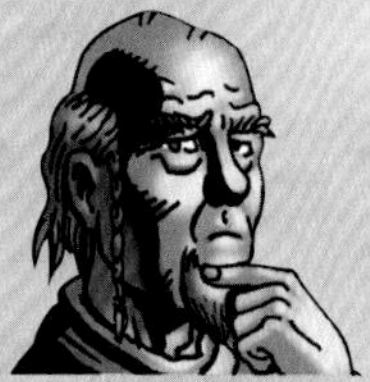

A Scottish Doctor

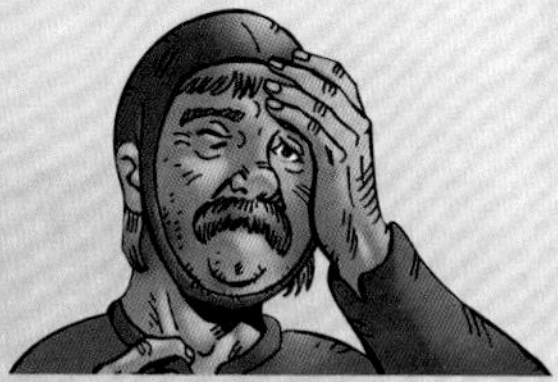

A **Porter**

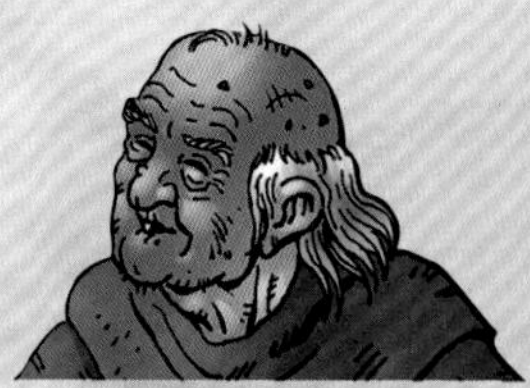

An Old Man

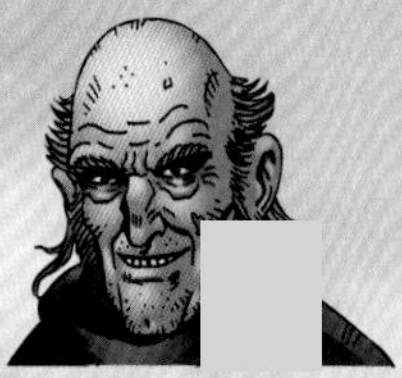

First Murderer

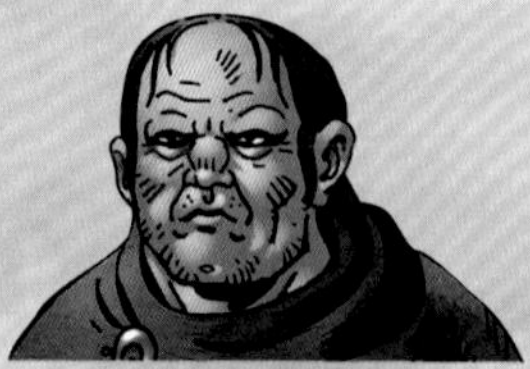

Second Murderer

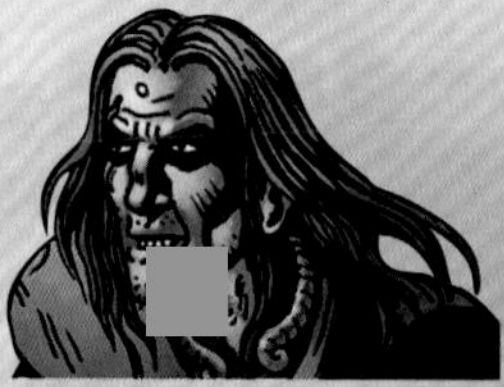

Third Murderer

Characters

Macbeth
A leader in the King's Army

Banquo
A leader in the King's Army

The Ghost of Banquo

Menteth
Scottish Nobleman

Angus
Scottish Nobleman

Cathness
Scottish Nobleman

Young Siward
Son of Siward

Fleance
Son of Banquo

Boy
Son of Macduff

First Witch

Second Witch

Third Witch

Hecate
The "Queen" Witch

and **Lords,** Ladies,
Officers, Soldiers,
Messengers, Ghosts,
and **Spirits.**

5

Introduction

It is Scotland in the year 1040.

King Duncan has **ruled** the land for six years, since the death of his grandfather. He is a good king, but Scotland is not a peaceful country. It has been divided in two for centuries. **Vikings** live in the north, and **Saxons** live in the south. Each small group of **Vikings** or **Saxons** has its own strong leader who is a great fighter.

Now that Duncan is king, all the different groups have a chance to come together and form a single nation. However some leaders do not welcome this. They want to remain independent, and they continue to fight against Duncan. Sometimes they are joined by groups of fighters from Ireland and Norway. Some of them would even like to be King of Scotland themselves.

Duncan sends a powerful **army** to fight against these groups who do not accept him as king. The **army** is led by a number of **noblemen** who are experienced soldiers. The greatest and most trusted of these is King Duncan's **cousin.** This is the **Thane** of Glamis, whose name is …

… Macbeth.

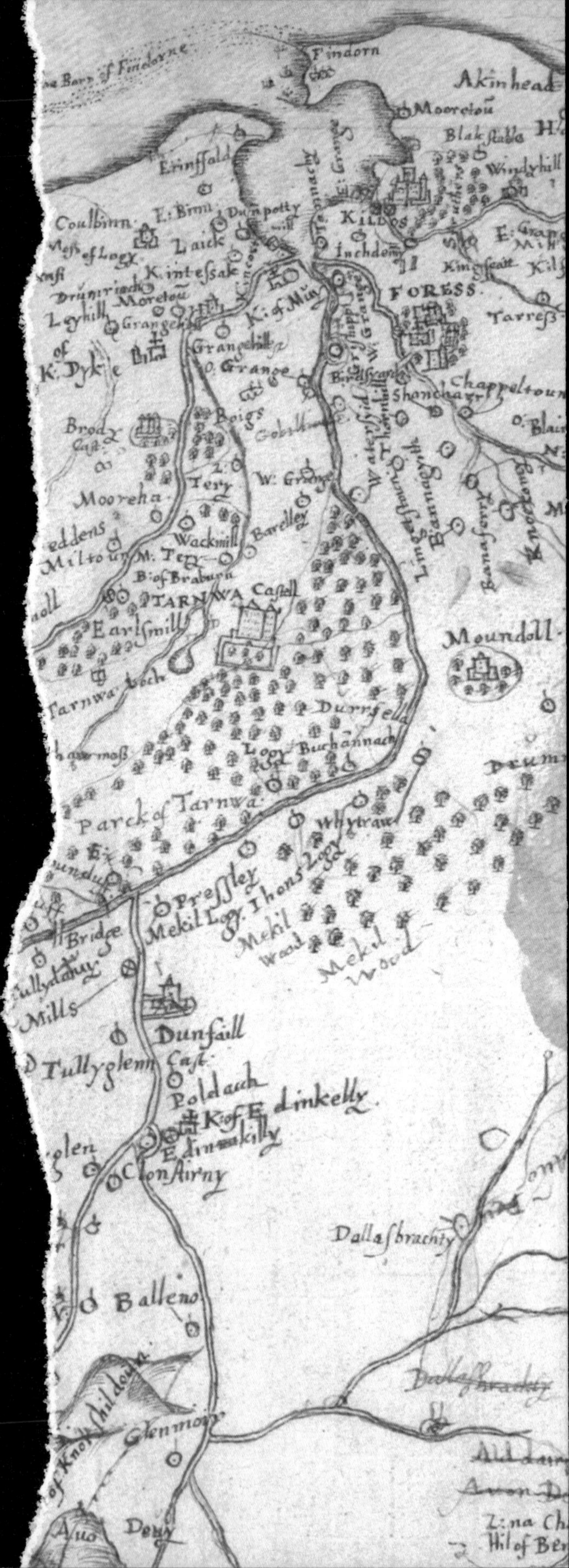

Findorn
FORESS
Chappeltoun
Earlsmill
Wackmill
TARNWA Castell
Moundoll
Park of Tarnwa
Dunfaill
Dallasbrachty

Macbeth

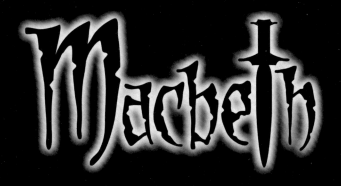

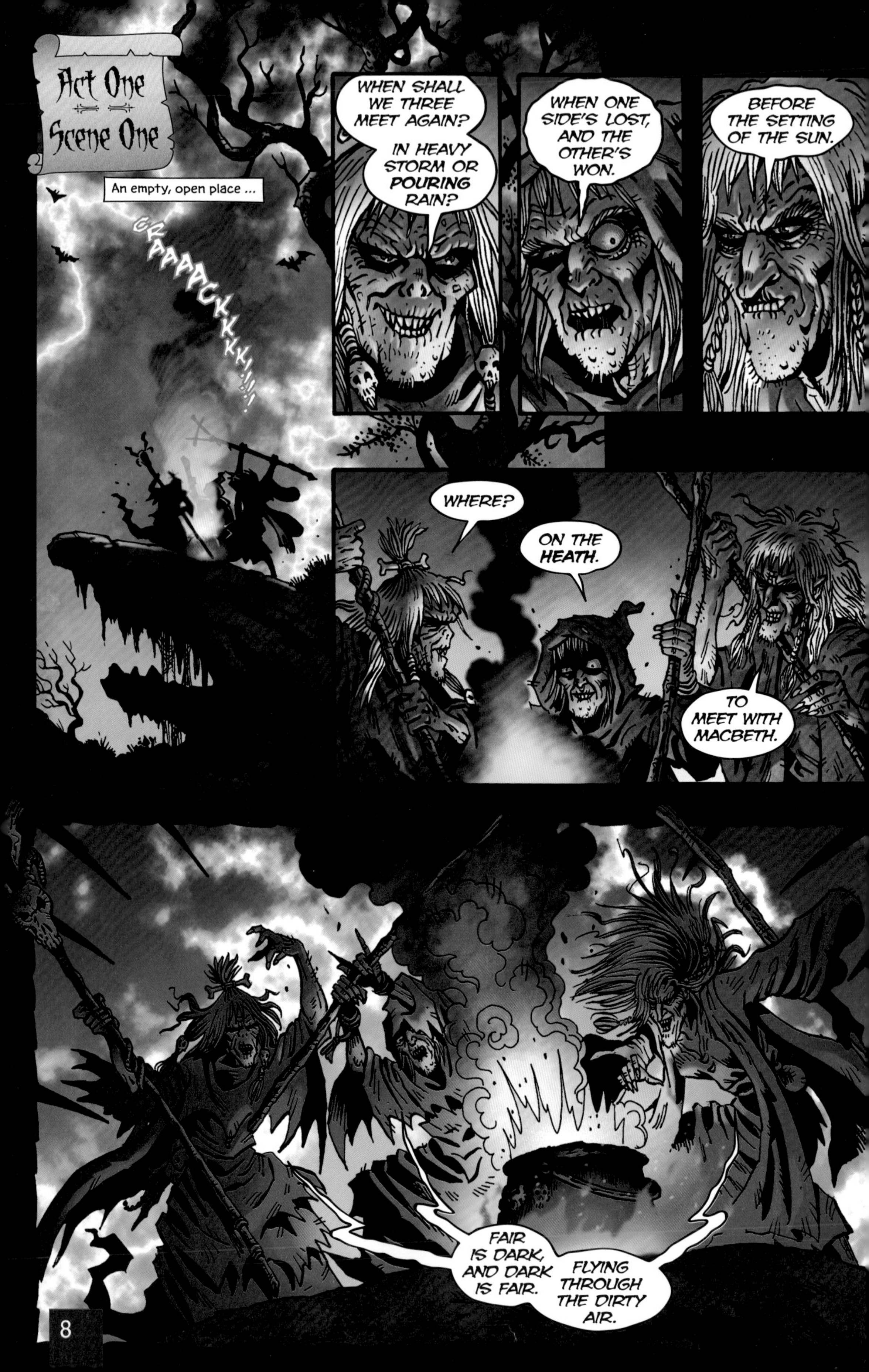

Act One
Scene One
An empty, open place ...
CRAAAACKKKK!!!!
WHEN SHALL WE THREE MEET AGAIN?
IN HEAVY STORM OR POURING RAIN?
WHEN ONE SIDE'S LOST, AND THE OTHER'S WON.
BEFORE THE SETTING OF THE SUN.
WHERE?
ON THE HEATH.
TO MEET WITH MACBETH.
FAIR IS DARK, AND DARK IS FAIR.
FLYING THROUGH THE DIRTY AIR.

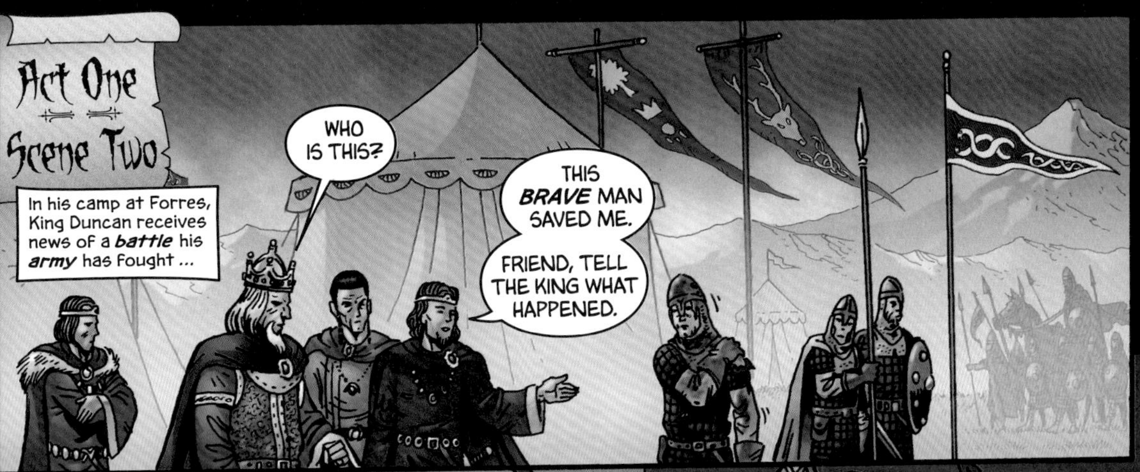
Act One
Scene Two
In his camp at Forres, King Duncan receives news of a *battle* his *army* has fought ...
WHO IS THIS?
THIS *BRAVE* MAN SAVED ME.
FRIEND, TELL THE KING WHAT HAPPENED.

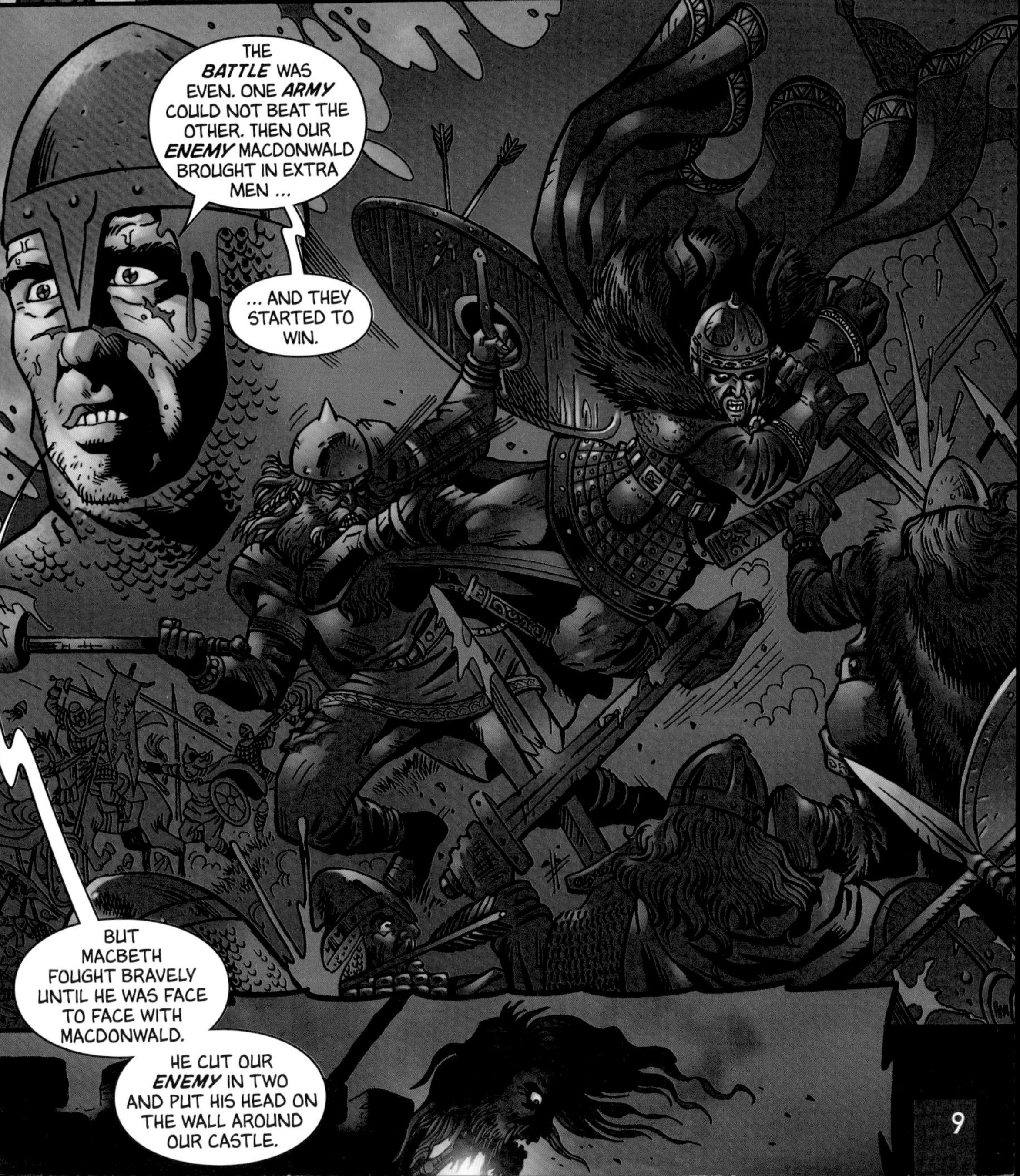
THE *BATTLE* WAS EVEN. ONE *ARMY* COULD NOT BEAT THE OTHER. THEN OUR *ENEMY* MACDONWALD BROUGHT IN EXTRA MEN ...
... AND THEY STARTED TO WIN.
BUT MACBETH FOUGHT BRAVELY UNTIL HE WAS FACE TO FACE WITH MACDONWALD.
HE CUT OUR *ENEMY* IN TWO AND PUT HIS HEAD ON THE WALL AROUND OUR CASTLE.

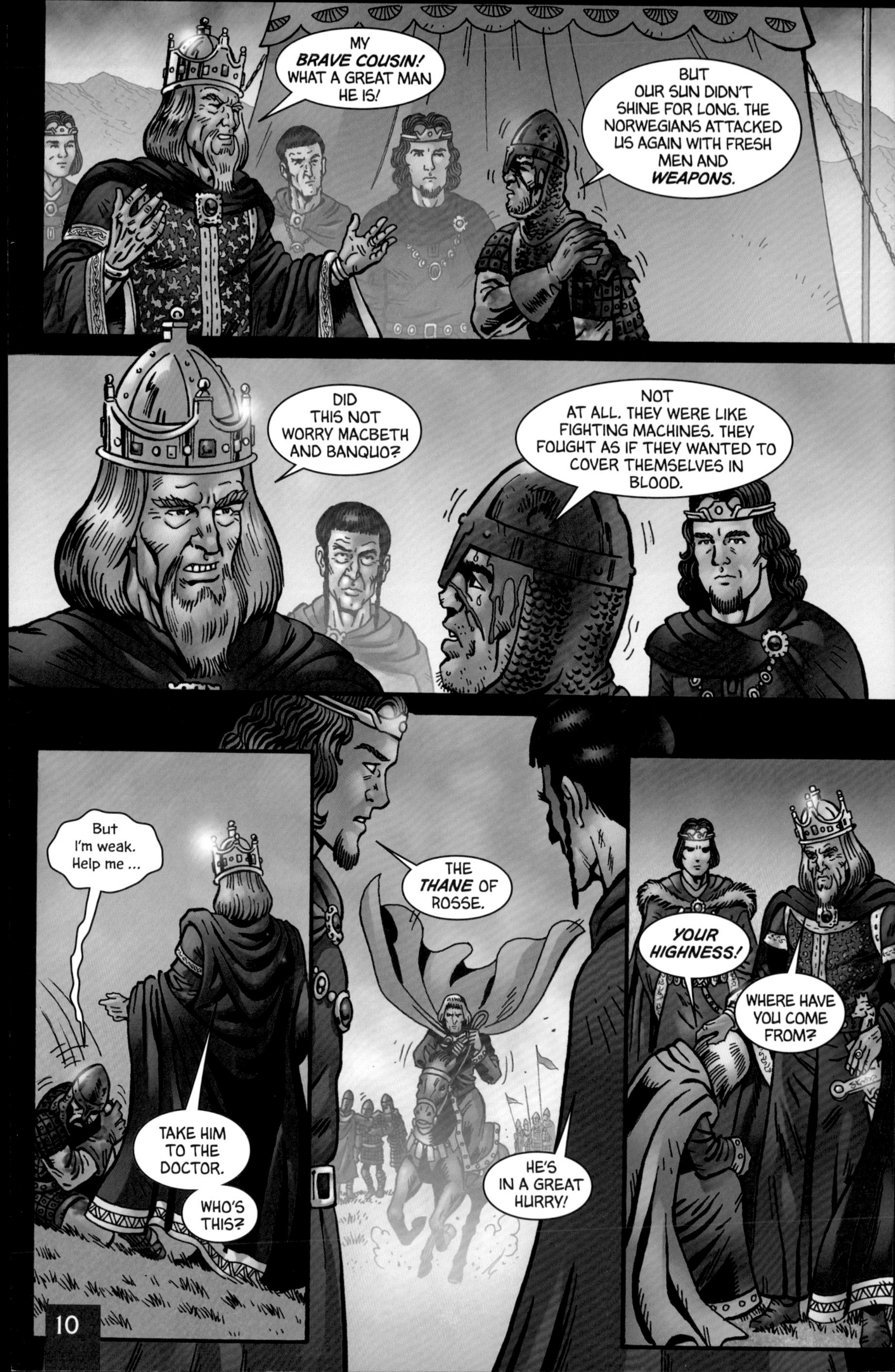

MY BRAVE COUSIN! WHAT A GREAT MAN HE IS!
BUT OUR SUN DIDN'T SHINE FOR LONG. THE NORWEGIANS ATTACKED US AGAIN WITH FRESH MEN AND WEAPONS.
DID THIS NOT WORRY MACBETH AND BANQUO?
NOT AT ALL. THEY WERE LIKE FIGHTING MACHINES. THEY FOUGHT AS IF THEY WANTED TO COVER THEMSELVES IN BLOOD.
But I'm weak. Help me ...
TAKE HIM TO THE DOCTOR.
WHO'S THIS?
THE THANE OF ROSSE.
HE'S IN A GREAT HURRY!
YOUR HIGHNESS!
WHERE HAVE YOU COME FROM?

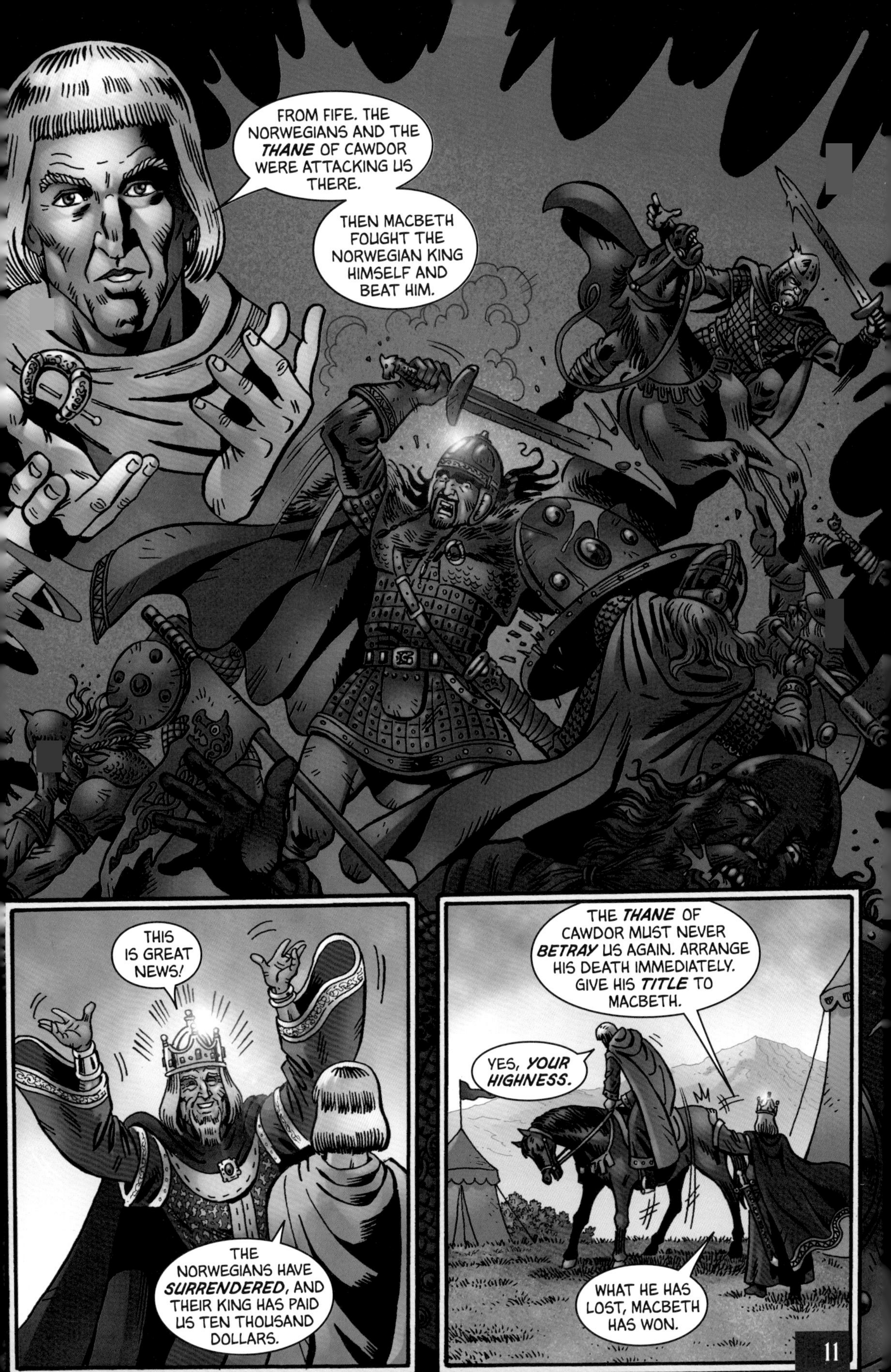
FROM FIFE. THE NORWEGIANS AND THE THANE OF CAWDOR WERE ATTACKING US THERE.
THEN MACBETH FOUGHT THE NORWEGIAN KING HIMSELF AND BEAT HIM.
THIS IS GREAT NEWS!
THE NORWEGIANS HAVE SURRENDERED, AND THEIR KING HAS PAID US TEN THOUSAND DOLLARS.
THE THANE OF CAWDOR MUST NEVER BETRAY US AGAIN. ARRANGE HIS DEATH IMMEDIATELY. GIVE HIS TITLE TO MACBETH.
YES, YOUR HIGHNESS.
WHAT HE HAS LOST, MACBETH HAS WON.

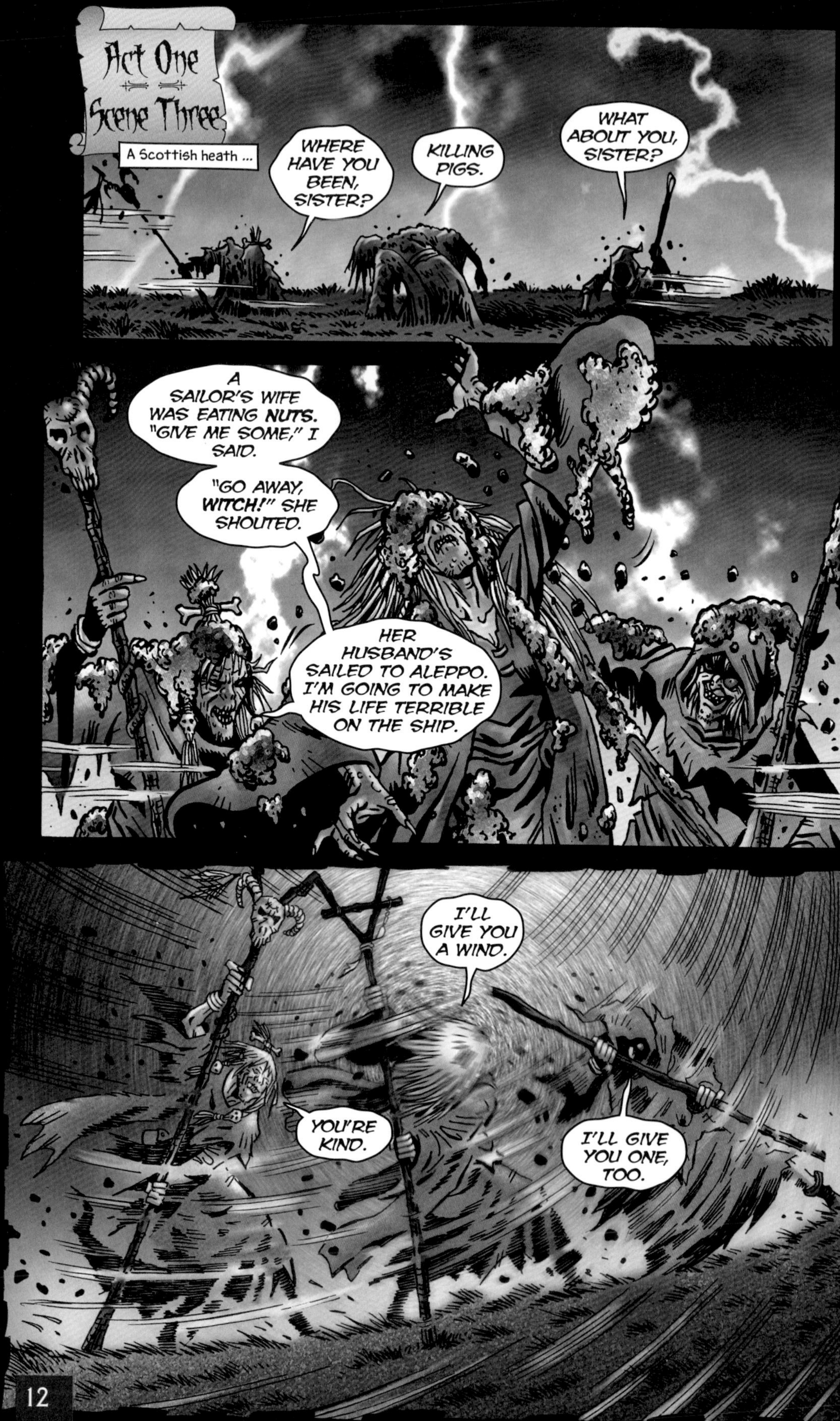
Act One
Scene Three
A Scottish heath ...
WHERE HAVE YOU BEEN, SISTER?
KILLING PIGS.
WHAT ABOUT YOU, SISTER?
A SAILOR'S WIFE WAS EATING NUTS. "GIVE ME SOME," I SAID.
"GO AWAY, WITCH!" SHE SHOUTED.
HER HUSBAND'S SAILED TO ALEPPO. I'M GOING TO MAKE HIS LIFE TERRIBLE ON THE SHIP.
I'LL GIVE YOU A WIND.
YOU'RE KIND.
I'LL GIVE YOU ONE, TOO.

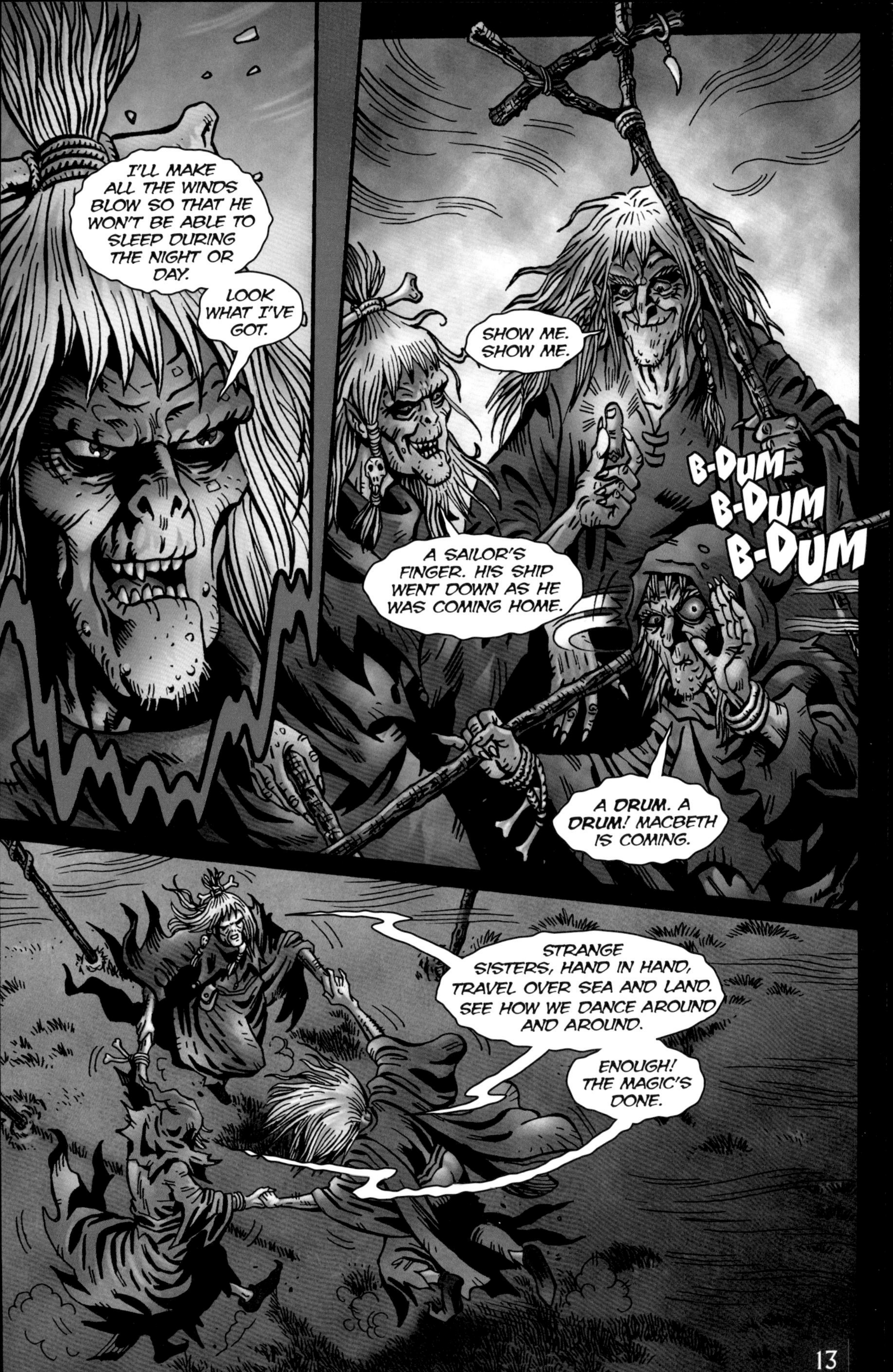
I'LL MAKE ALL THE WINDS BLOW SO THAT HE WON'T BE ABLE TO SLEEP DURING THE NIGHT OR DAY.
LOOK WHAT I'VE GOT.
SHOW ME. SHOW ME.
A SAILOR'S FINGER. HIS SHIP WENT DOWN AS HE WAS COMING HOME.
B-DUM B-DUM B-DUM
A DRUM. A DRUM! MACBETH IS COMING.
STRANGE SISTERS, HAND IN HAND, TRAVEL OVER SEA AND LAND. SEE HOW WE DANCE AROUND AND AROUND.
ENOUGH! THE MAGIC'S DONE.

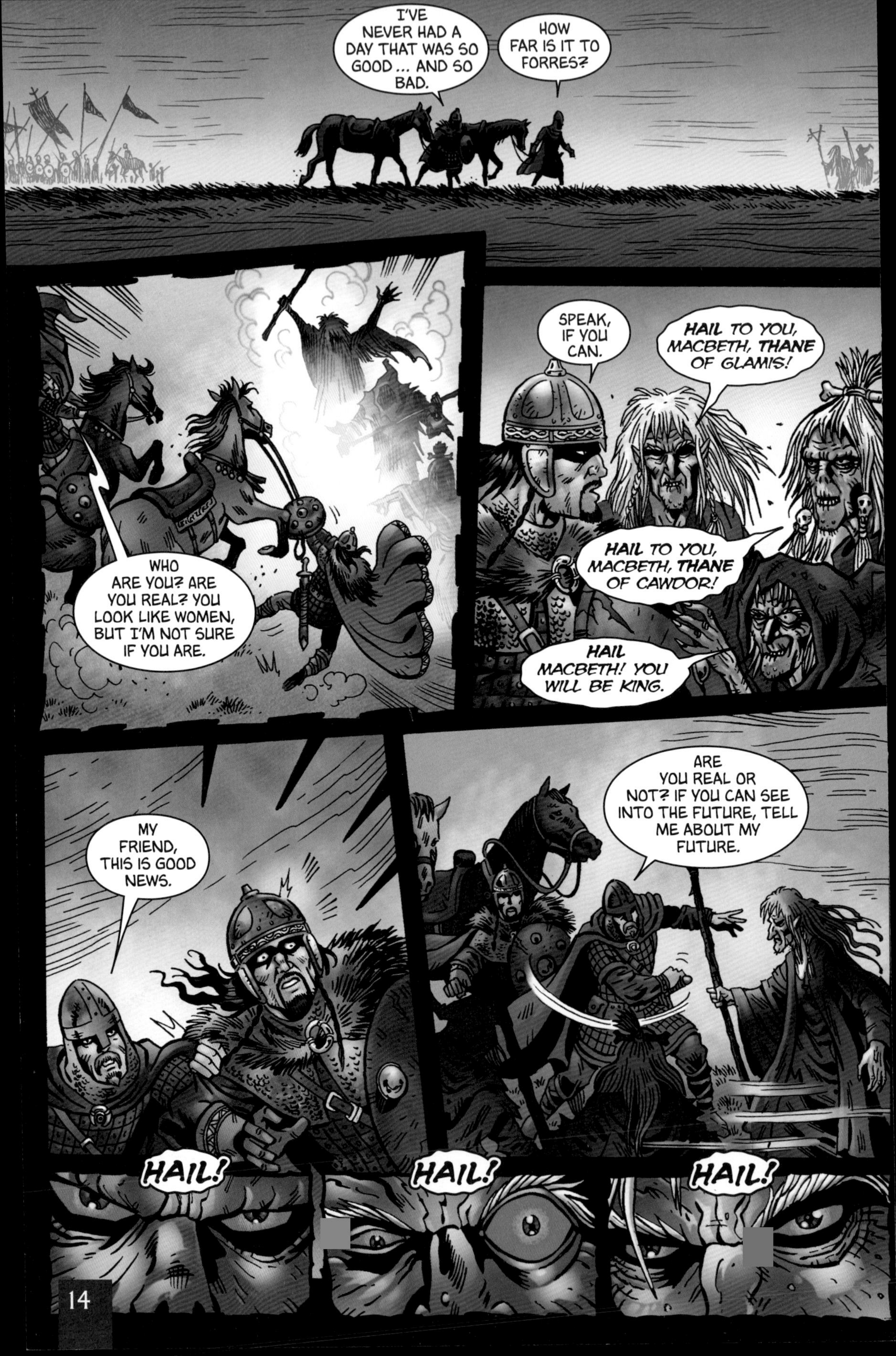

I'VE NEVER HAD A DAY THAT WAS SO GOOD ... AND SO BAD.
HOW FAR IS IT TO FORRES?
WHO ARE YOU? ARE YOU REAL? YOU LOOK LIKE WOMEN, BUT I'M NOT SURE IF YOU ARE.
SPEAK, IF YOU CAN.
HAIL TO YOU, MACBETH, THANE OF GLAMIS!
HAIL TO YOU, MACBETH, THANE OF CAWDOR!
HAIL MACBETH! YOU WILL BE KING.
MY FRIEND, THIS IS GOOD NEWS.
ARE YOU REAL OR NOT? IF YOU CAN SEE INTO THE FUTURE, TELL ME ABOUT MY FUTURE.
HAIL!
HAIL!
HAIL!

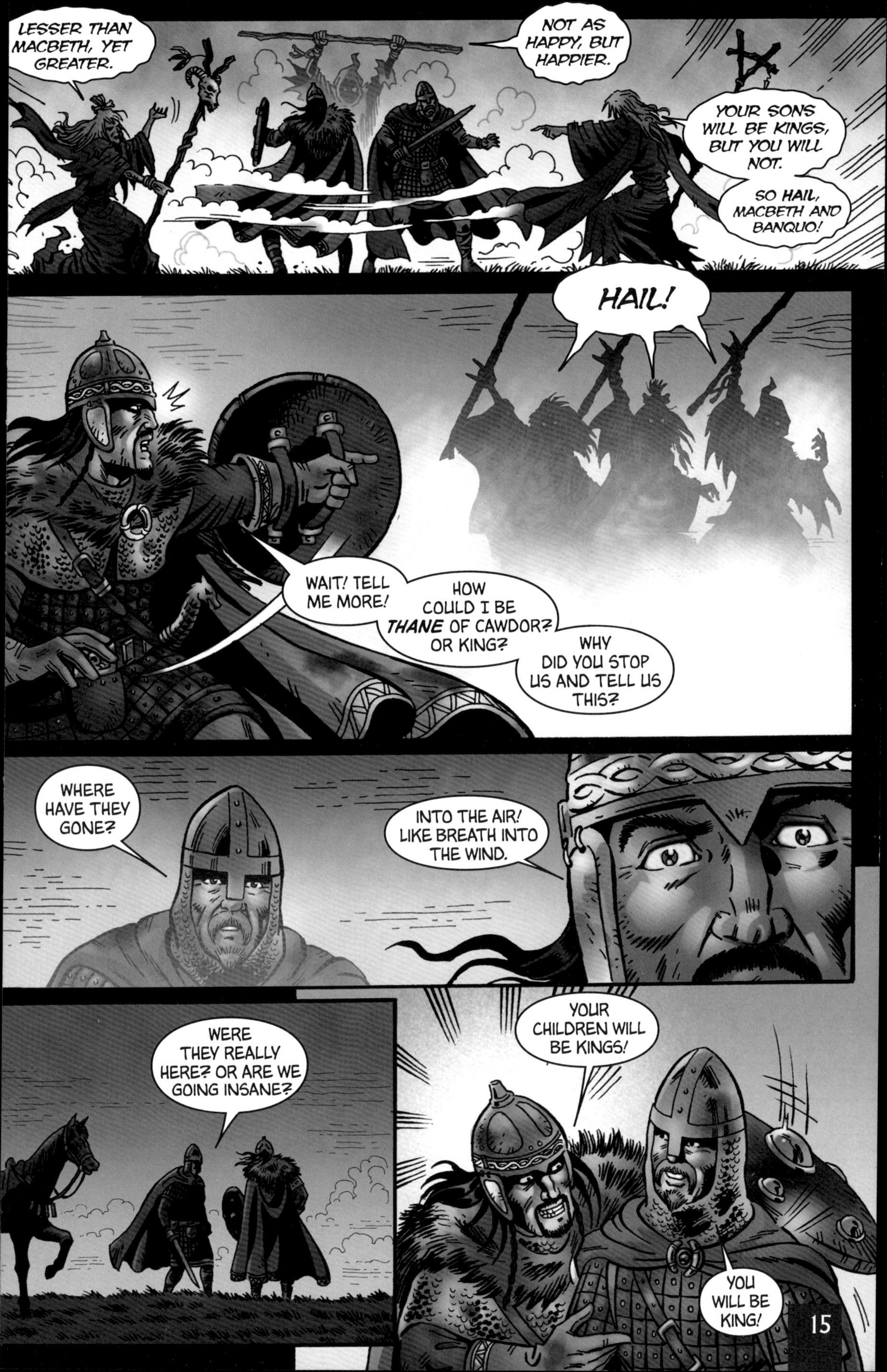
LESSER THAN MACBETH, YET GREATER.
NOT AS HAPPY, BUT HAPPIER.
YOUR SONS WILL BE KINGS, BUT YOU WILL NOT.
SO HAIL, MACBETH AND BANQUO!
HAIL!
WAIT! TELL ME MORE!
HOW COULD I BE THANE OF CAWDOR? OR KING?
WHY DID YOU STOP US AND TELL US THIS?
WHERE HAVE THEY GONE?
INTO THE AIR! LIKE BREATH INTO THE WIND.
WERE THEY REALLY HERE? OR ARE WE GOING INSANE?
YOUR CHILDREN WILL BE KINGS!
YOU WILL BE KING!

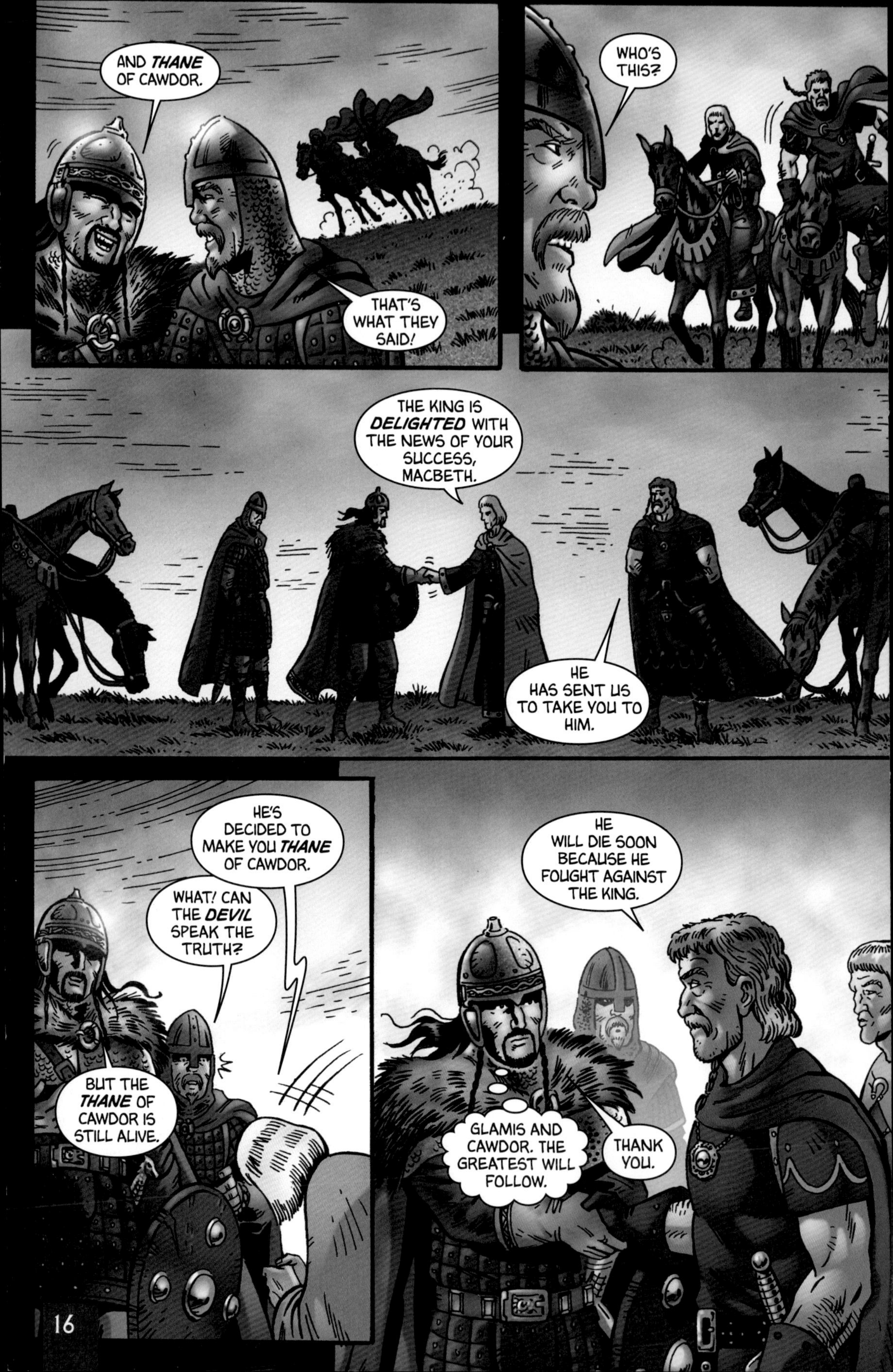
AND THANE OF CAWDOR.
THAT'S WHAT THEY SAID!
WHO'S THIS?
THE KING IS DELIGHTED WITH THE NEWS OF YOUR SUCCESS, MACBETH.
HE HAS SENT US TO TAKE YOU TO HIM.
HE'S DECIDED TO MAKE YOU THANE OF CAWDOR.
WHAT! CAN THE DEVIL SPEAK THE TRUTH?
BUT THE THANE OF CAWDOR IS STILL ALIVE.
HE WILL DIE SOON BECAUSE HE FOUGHT AGAINST THE KING.
GLAMIS AND CAWDOR. THE GREATEST WILL FOLLOW.
THANK YOU.

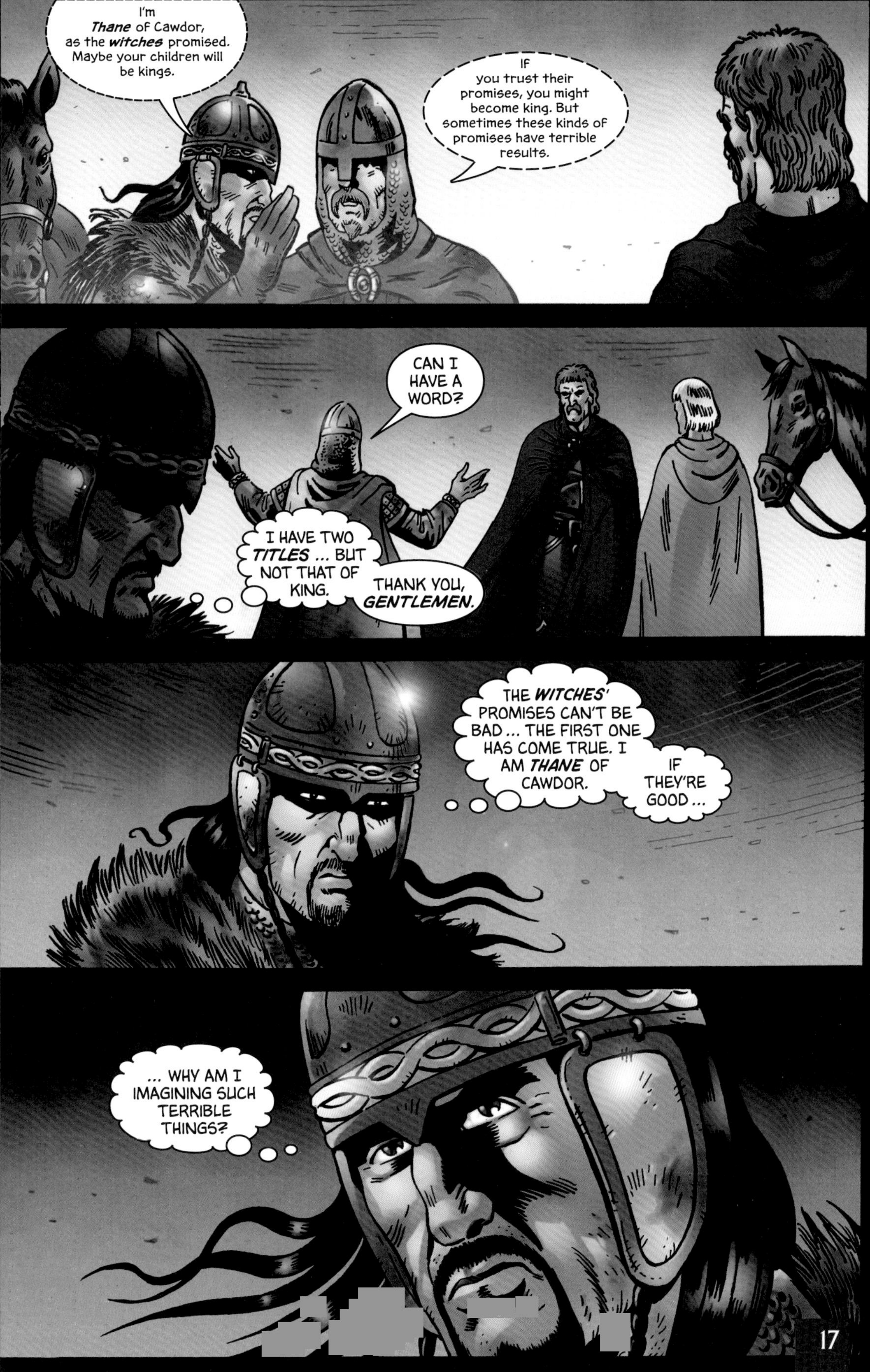
I'm *Thane* of Cawdor, as the *witches* promised. Maybe your children will be kings.
IF you trust their promises, you might become king. But sometimes these kinds of promises have terrible results.
CAN I HAVE A WORD?
I HAVE TWO *TITLES* ... BUT NOT THAT OF KING.
THANK YOU, *GENTLEMEN.*
THE *WITCHES'* PROMISES CAN'T BE BAD ... THE FIRST ONE HAS COME TRUE. I AM *THANE* OF CAWDOR.
IF THEY'RE GOOD ...
... WHY AM I IMAGINING SUCH TERRIBLE THINGS?

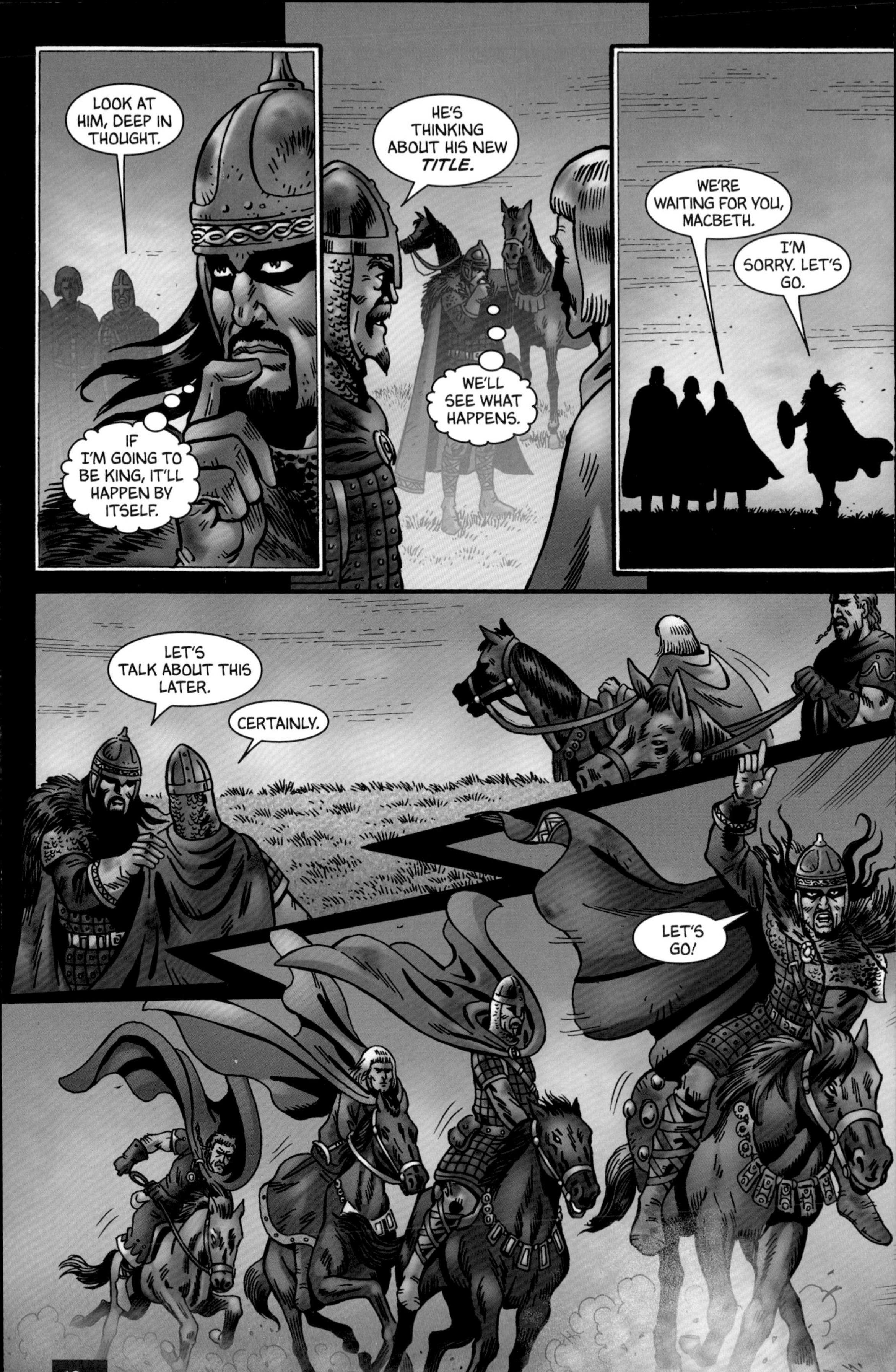
LOOK AT HIM, DEEP IN THOUGHT.
IF I'M GOING TO BE KING, IT'LL HAPPEN BY ITSELF.
HE'S THINKING ABOUT HIS NEW *TITLE.*
WE'LL SEE WHAT HAPPENS.
WE'RE WAITING FOR YOU, MACBETH.
I'M SORRY. LET'S GO.
LET'S TALK ABOUT THIS LATER.
CERTAINLY.
LET'S GO!

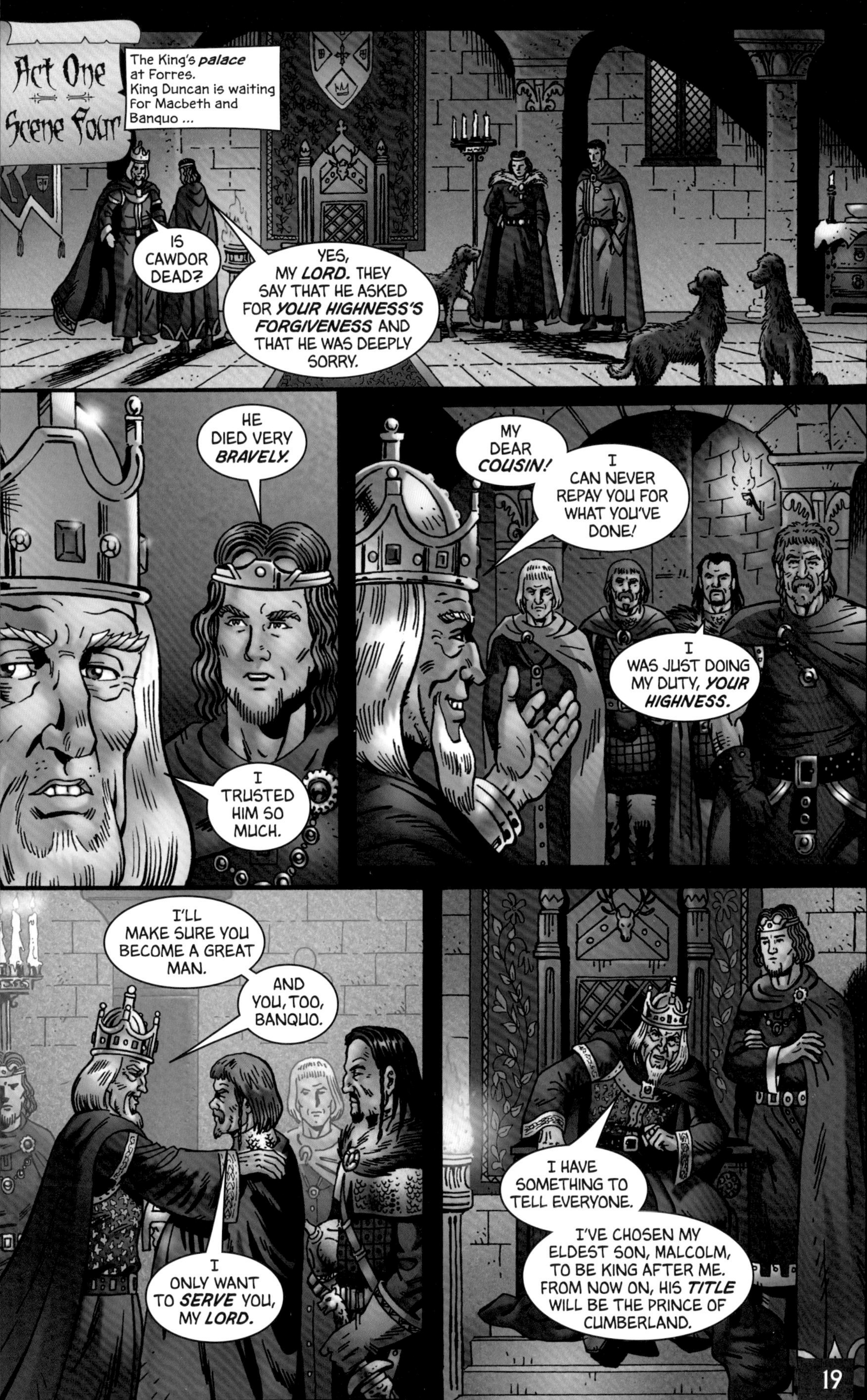
Act One
Scene Four
The King's palace at Forres. King Duncan is waiting for Macbeth and Banquo ...
IS CAWDOR DEAD?
YES, MY LORD. THEY SAY THAT HE ASKED FOR YOUR HIGHNESS'S FORGIVENESS AND THAT HE WAS DEEPLY SORRY.
HE DIED VERY BRAVELY.
I TRUSTED HIM SO MUCH.
MY DEAR COUSIN!
I CAN NEVER REPAY YOU FOR WHAT YOU'VE DONE!
I WAS JUST DOING MY DUTY, YOUR HIGHNESS.
I'LL MAKE SURE YOU BECOME A GREAT MAN.
AND YOU, TOO, BANQUO.
I ONLY WANT TO SERVE YOU, MY LORD.
I HAVE SOMETHING TO TELL EVERYONE.
I'VE CHOSEN MY ELDEST SON, MALCOLM, TO BE KING AFTER ME. FROM NOW ON, HIS TITLE WILL BE THE PRINCE OF CUMBERLAND.

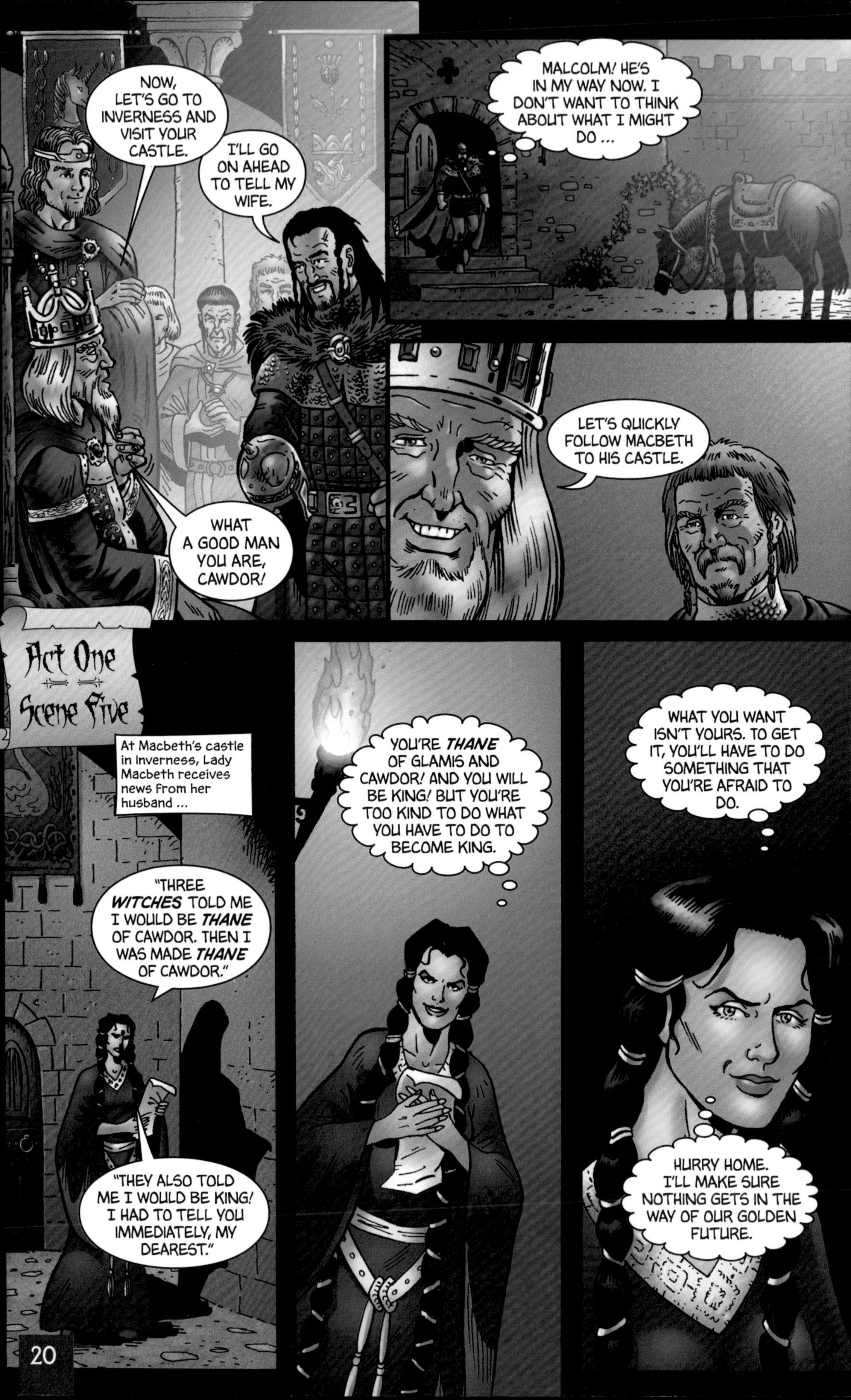
NOW, LET'S GO TO INVERNESS AND VISIT YOUR CASTLE.
I'LL GO ON AHEAD TO TELL MY WIFE.
WHAT A GOOD MAN YOU ARE, CAWDOR!
MALCOLM! HE'S IN MY WAY NOW. I DON'T WANT TO THINK ABOUT WHAT I MIGHT DO ...
LET'S QUICKLY FOLLOW MACBETH TO HIS CASTLE.
Act One
Scene Five
At Macbeth's castle in Inverness, Lady Macbeth receives news from her husband ...
"THREE WITCHES TOLD ME I WOULD BE THANE OF CAWDOR. THEN I WAS MADE THANE OF CAWDOR."
"THEY ALSO TOLD ME I WOULD BE KING! I HAD TO TELL YOU IMMEDIATELY, MY DEAREST."
YOU'RE THANE OF GLAMIS AND CAWDOR! AND YOU WILL BE KING! BUT YOU'RE TOO KIND TO DO WHAT YOU HAVE TO DO TO BECOME KING.
WHAT YOU WANT ISN'T YOURS. TO GET IT, YOU'LL HAVE TO DO SOMETHING THAT YOU'RE AFRAID TO DO.
HURRY HOME. I'LL MAKE SURE NOTHING GETS IN THE WAY OF OUR GOLDEN FUTURE.

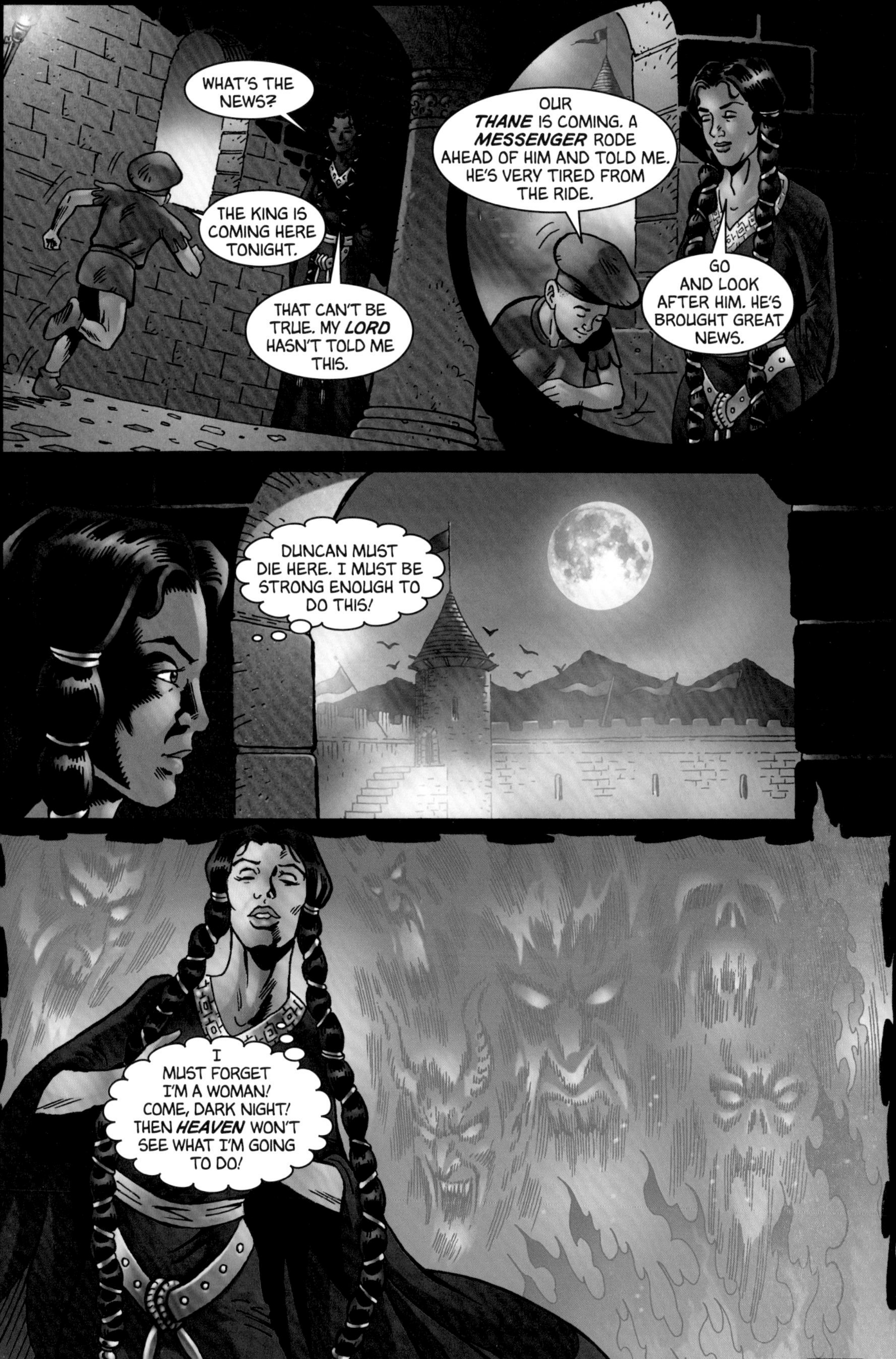
WHAT'S THE NEWS?
THE KING IS COMING HERE TONIGHT.
THAT CAN'T BE TRUE. MY LORD HASN'T TOLD ME THIS.
OUR THANE IS COMING. A MESSENGER RODE AHEAD OF HIM AND TOLD ME. HE'S VERY TIRED FROM THE RIDE.
GO AND LOOK AFTER HIM. HE'S BROUGHT GREAT NEWS.
DUNCAN MUST DIE HERE. I MUST BE STRONG ENOUGH TO DO THIS!
I MUST FORGET I'M A WOMAN! COME, DARK NIGHT! THEN HEAVEN WON'T SEE WHAT I'M GOING TO DO!

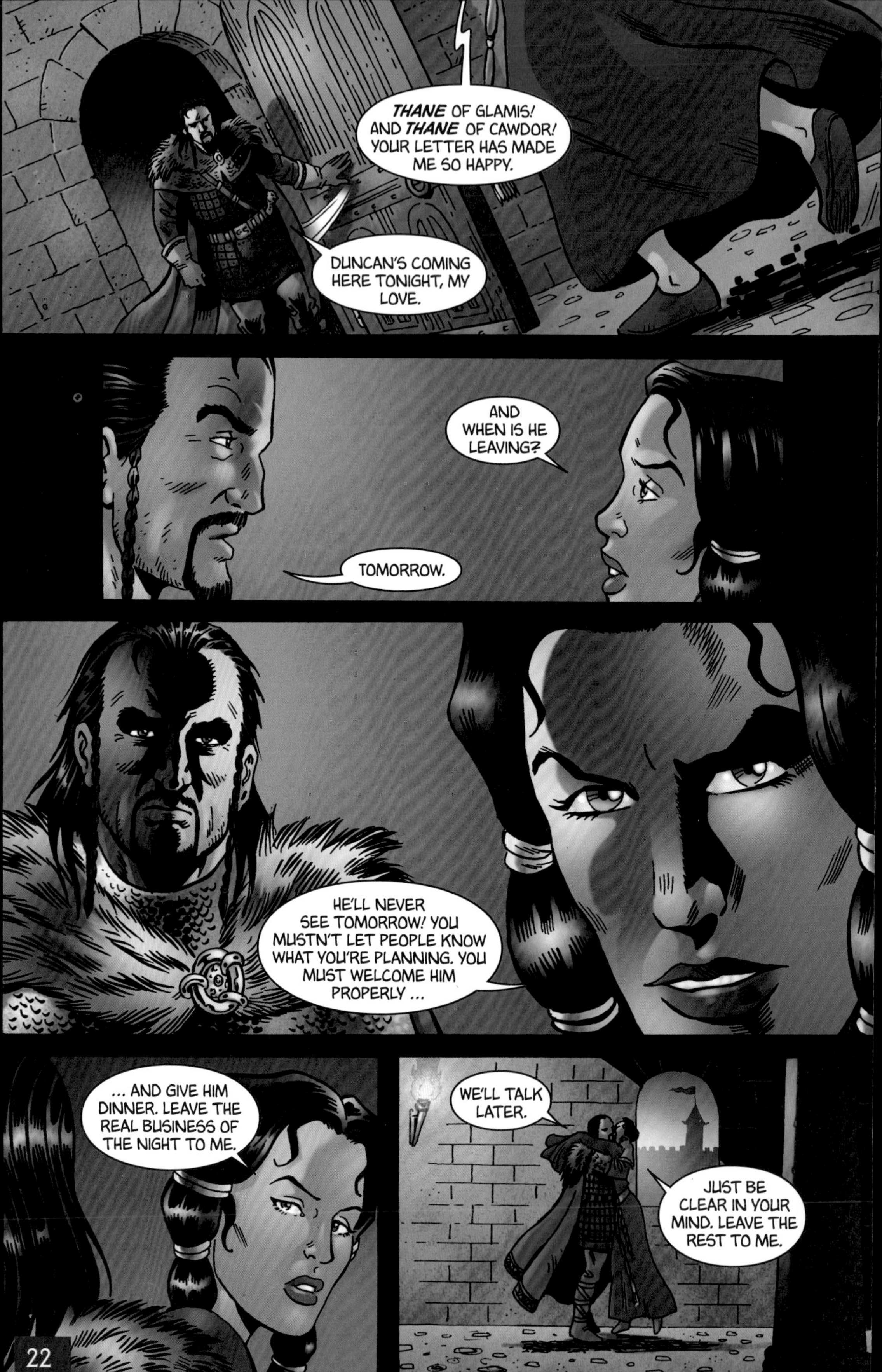
THANE OF GLAMIS! AND THANE OF CAWDOR! YOUR LETTER HAS MADE ME SO HAPPY.
DUNCAN'S COMING HERE TONIGHT, MY LOVE.
AND WHEN IS HE LEAVING?
TOMORROW.
HE'LL NEVER SEE TOMORROW! YOU MUSTN'T LET PEOPLE KNOW WHAT YOU'RE PLANNING. YOU MUST WELCOME HIM PROPERLY ...
... AND GIVE HIM DINNER. LEAVE THE REAL BUSINESS OF THE NIGHT TO ME.
WE'LL TALK LATER.
JUST BE CLEAR IN YOUR MIND. LEAVE THE REST TO ME.

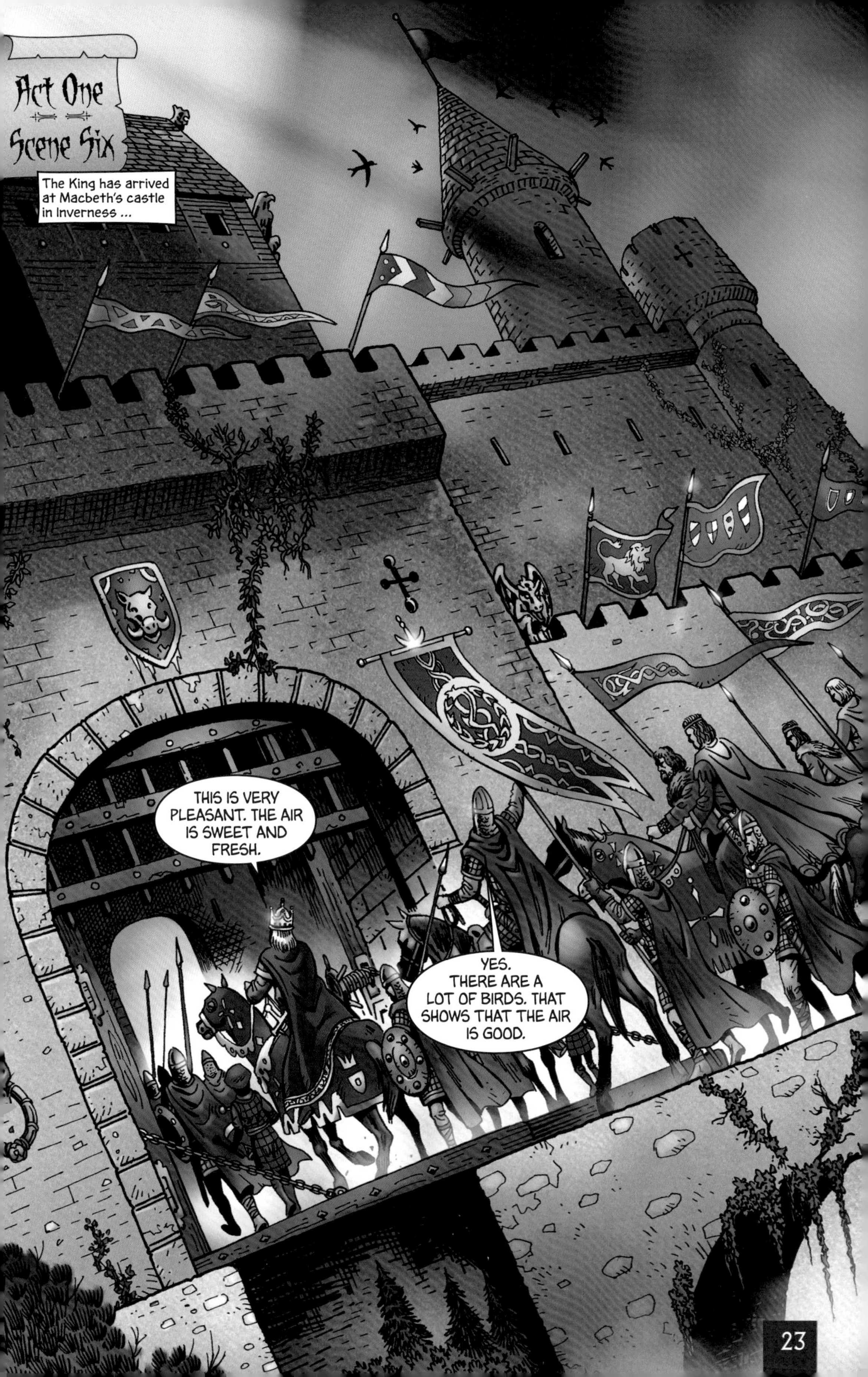

Act One
Scene Six
The King has arrived at Macbeth's castle in Inverness ...
THIS IS VERY PLEASANT. THE AIR IS SWEET AND FRESH.
YES. THERE ARE A LOT OF BIRDS. THAT SHOWS THAT THE AIR IS GOOD.

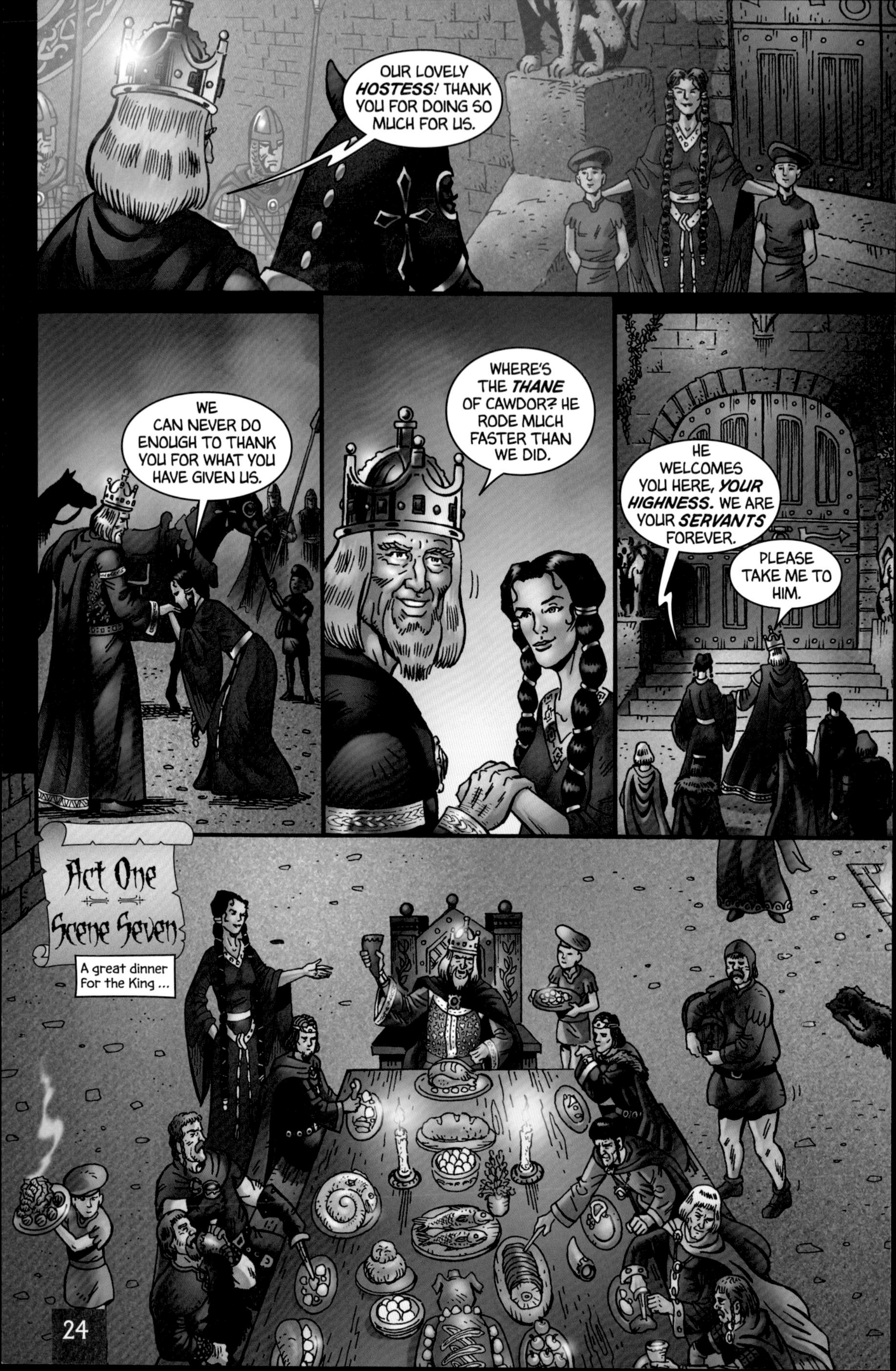
OUR LOVELY HOSTESS! THANK YOU FOR DOING SO MUCH FOR US.
WE CAN NEVER DO ENOUGH TO THANK YOU FOR WHAT YOU HAVE GIVEN US.
WHERE'S THE THANE OF CAWDOR? HE RODE MUCH FASTER THAN WE DID.
HE WELCOMES YOU HERE, YOUR HIGHNESS. WE ARE YOUR SERVANTS FOREVER.
PLEASE TAKE ME TO HIM.
Act One
Scene Seven
A great dinner for the King ...

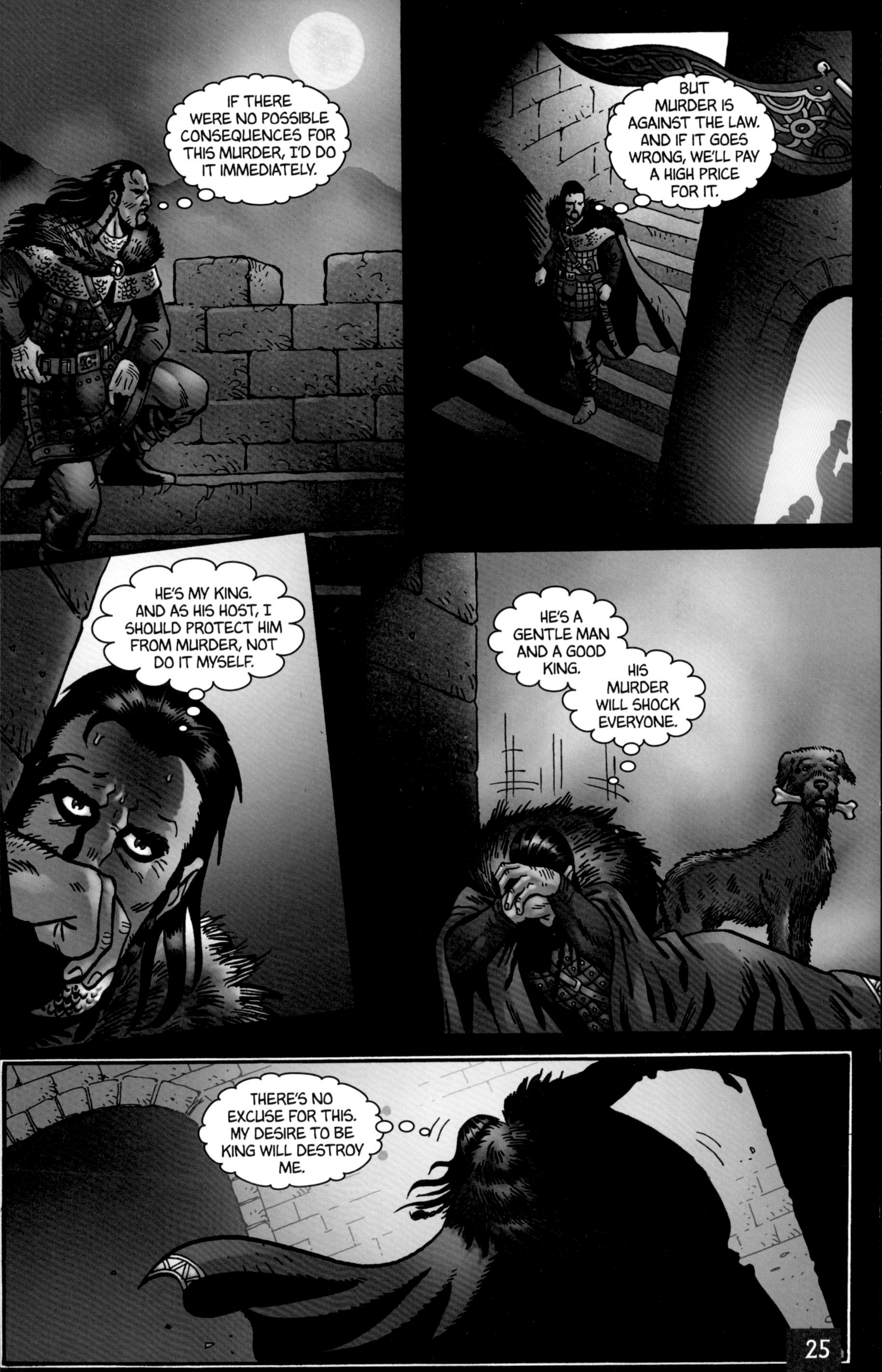
IF THERE WERE NO POSSIBLE CONSEQUENCES FOR THIS MURDER, I'D DO IT IMMEDIATELY.
BUT MURDER IS AGAINST THE LAW. AND IF IT GOES WRONG, WE'LL PAY A HIGH PRICE FOR IT.
HE'S MY KING. AND AS HIS HOST, I SHOULD PROTECT HIM FROM MURDER, NOT DO IT MYSELF.
HE'S A GENTLE MAN AND A GOOD KING.
HIS MURDER WILL SHOCK EVERYONE.
THERE'S NO EXCUSE FOR THIS. MY DESIRE TO BE KING WILL DESTROY ME.

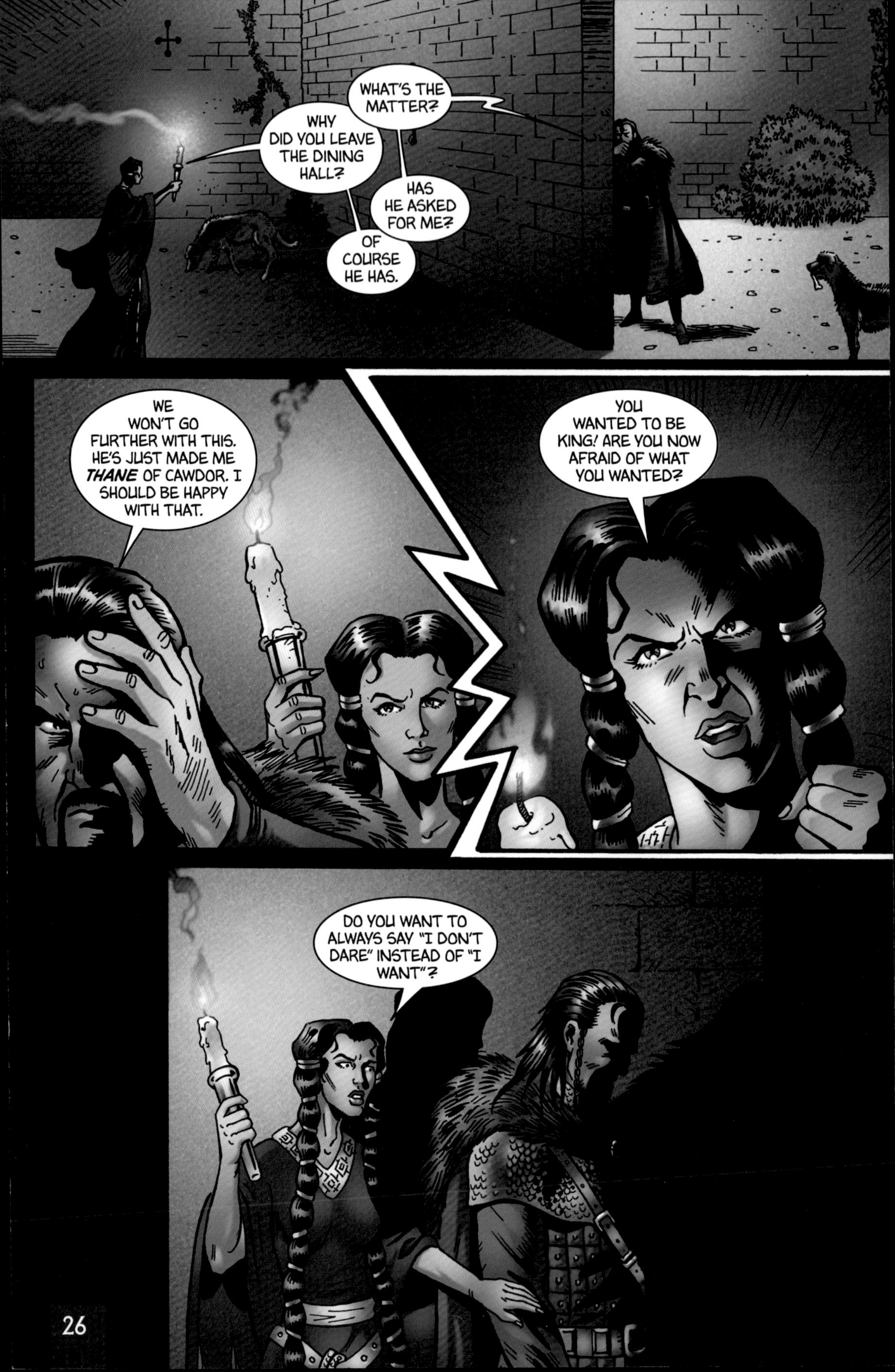

WHY DID YOU LEAVE THE DINING HALL?
WHAT'S THE MATTER?
HAS HE ASKED FOR ME?
OF COURSE HE HAS.
WE WON'T GO FURTHER WITH THIS. HE'S JUST MADE ME ***THANE*** OF CAWDOR. I SHOULD BE HAPPY WITH THAT.
YOU WANTED TO BE KING! ARE YOU NOW AFRAID OF WHAT YOU WANTED?
DO YOU WANT TO ALWAYS SAY "I DON'T DARE" INSTEAD OF "I WANT"?

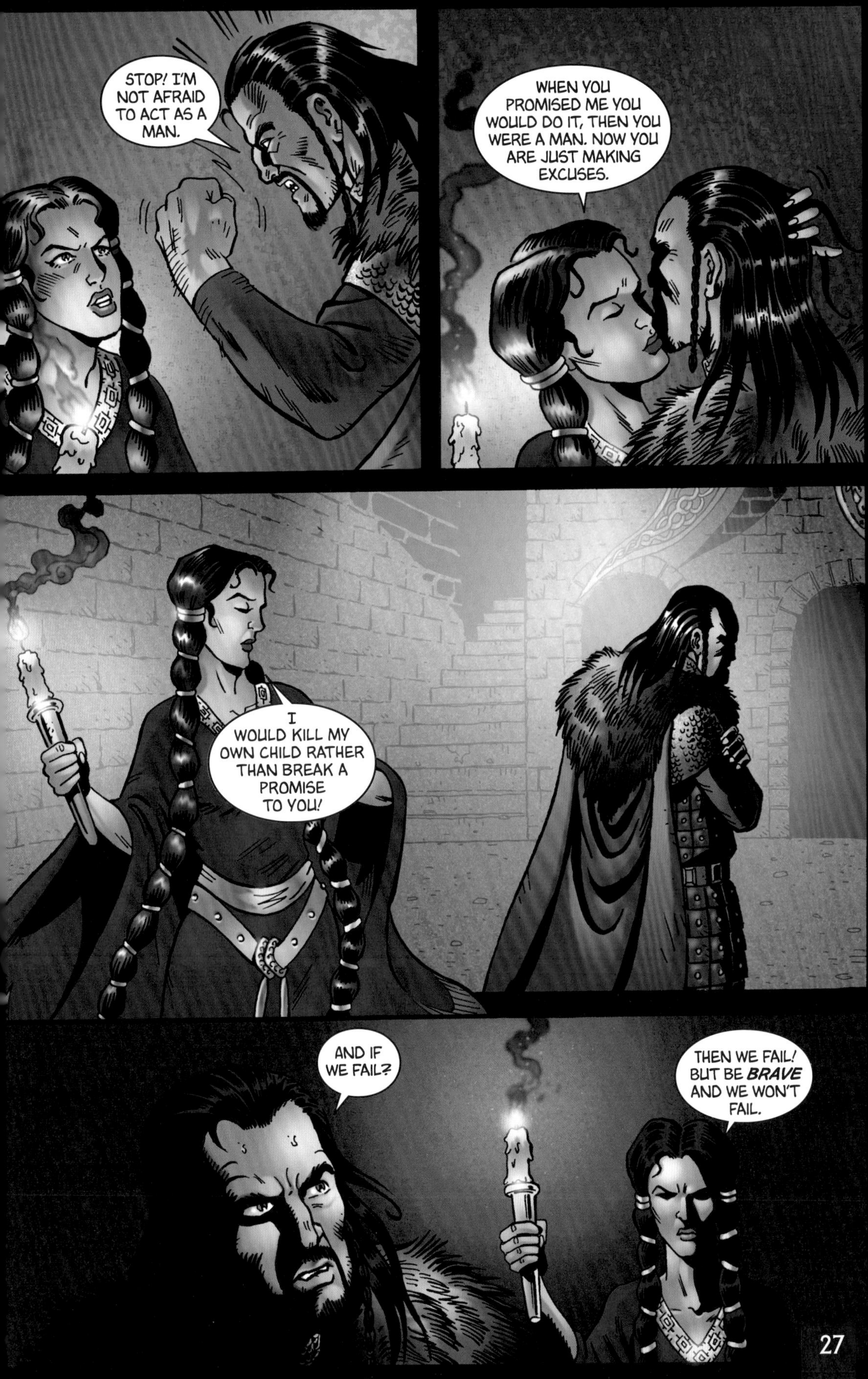
STOP! I'M NOT AFRAID TO ACT AS A MAN.
WHEN YOU PROMISED ME YOU WOULD DO IT, THEN YOU WERE A MAN. NOW YOU ARE JUST MAKING EXCUSES.
I WOULD KILL MY OWN CHILD RATHER THAN BREAK A PROMISE TO YOU!
AND IF WE FAIL?
THEN WE FAIL! BUT BE *BRAVE* AND WE WON'T FAIL.

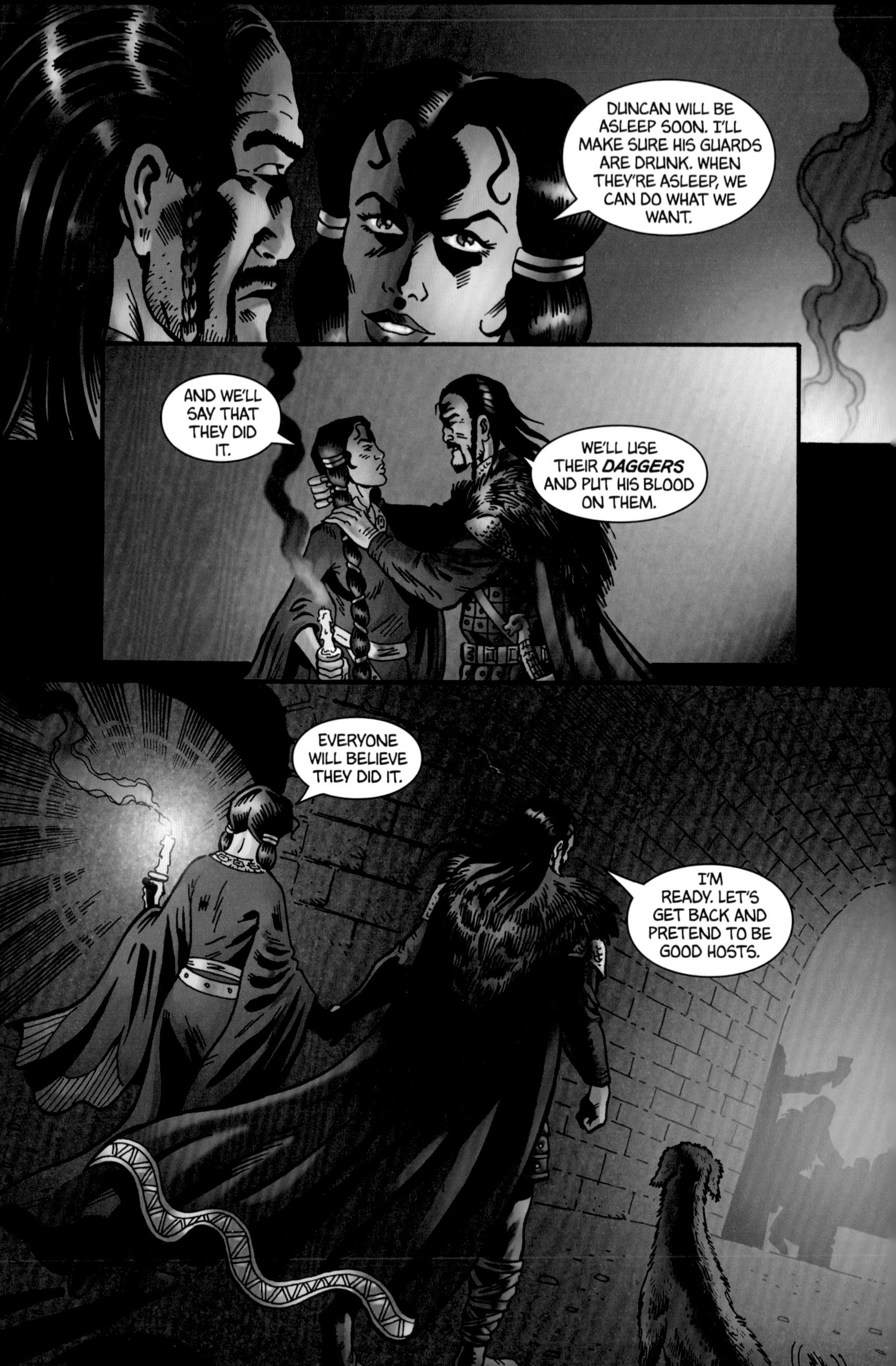
DUNCAN WILL BE ASLEEP SOON. I'LL MAKE SURE HIS GUARDS ARE DRUNK. WHEN THEY'RE ASLEEP, WE CAN DO WHAT WE WANT.
AND WE'LL SAY THAT THEY DID IT.
WE'LL USE THEIR *DAGGERS* AND PUT HIS BLOOD ON THEM.
EVERYONE WILL BELIEVE THEY DID IT.
I'M READY. LET'S GET BACK AND PRETEND TO BE GOOD HOSTS.

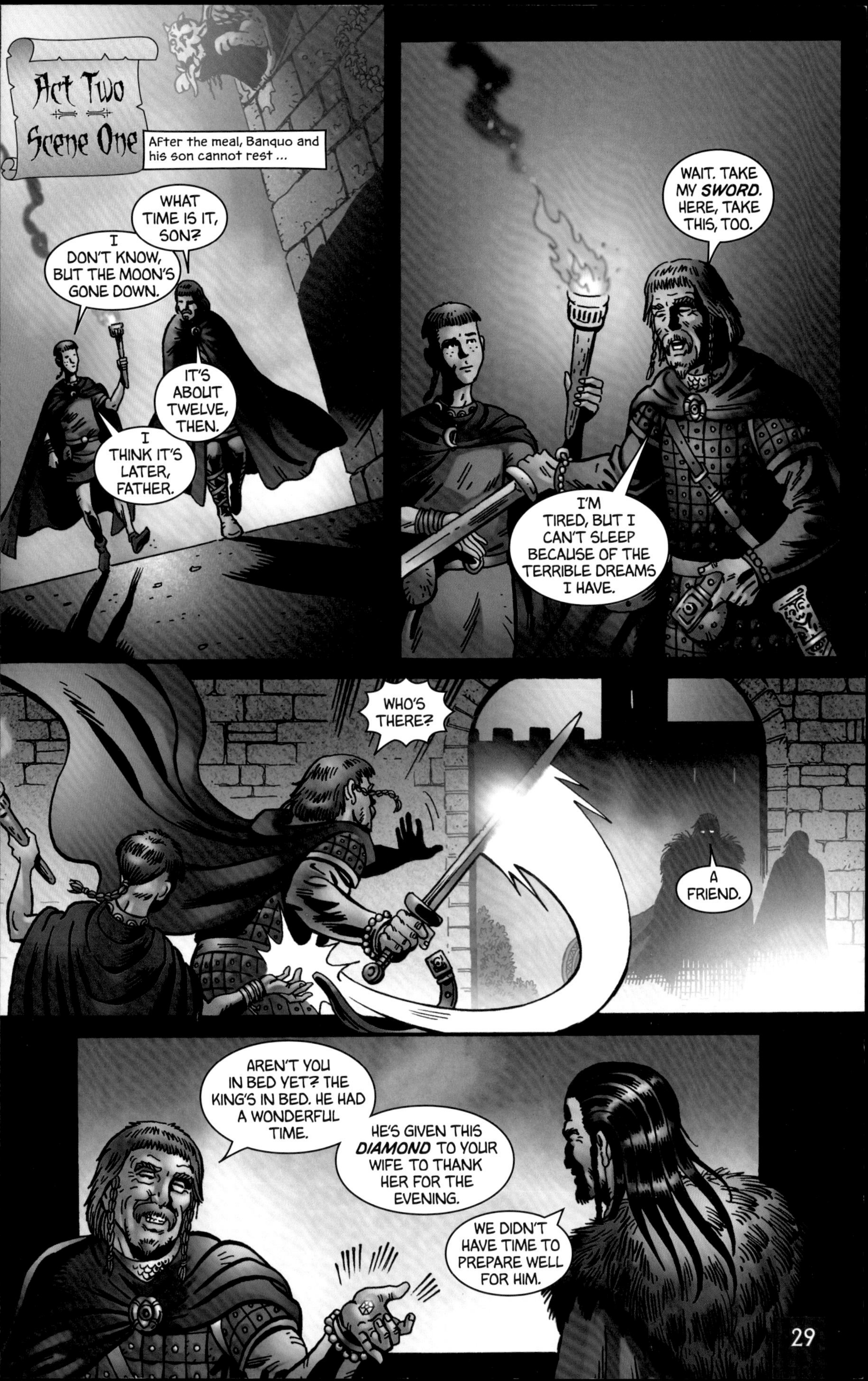
Act Two
Scene One
After the meal, Banquo and his son cannot rest ...
WHAT TIME IS IT, SON?
I DON'T KNOW, BUT THE MOON'S GONE DOWN.
IT'S ABOUT TWELVE, THEN.
I THINK IT'S LATER, FATHER.
WAIT. TAKE MY *SWORD*. HERE, TAKE THIS, TOO.
I'M TIRED, BUT I CAN'T SLEEP BECAUSE OF THE TERRIBLE DREAMS I HAVE.
WHO'S THERE?
A FRIEND.
AREN'T YOU IN BED YET? THE KING'S IN BED. HE HAD A WONDERFUL TIME.
HE'S GIVEN THIS *DIAMOND* TO YOUR WIFE TO THANK HER FOR THE EVENING.
WE DIDN'T HAVE TIME TO PREPARE WELL FOR HIM.

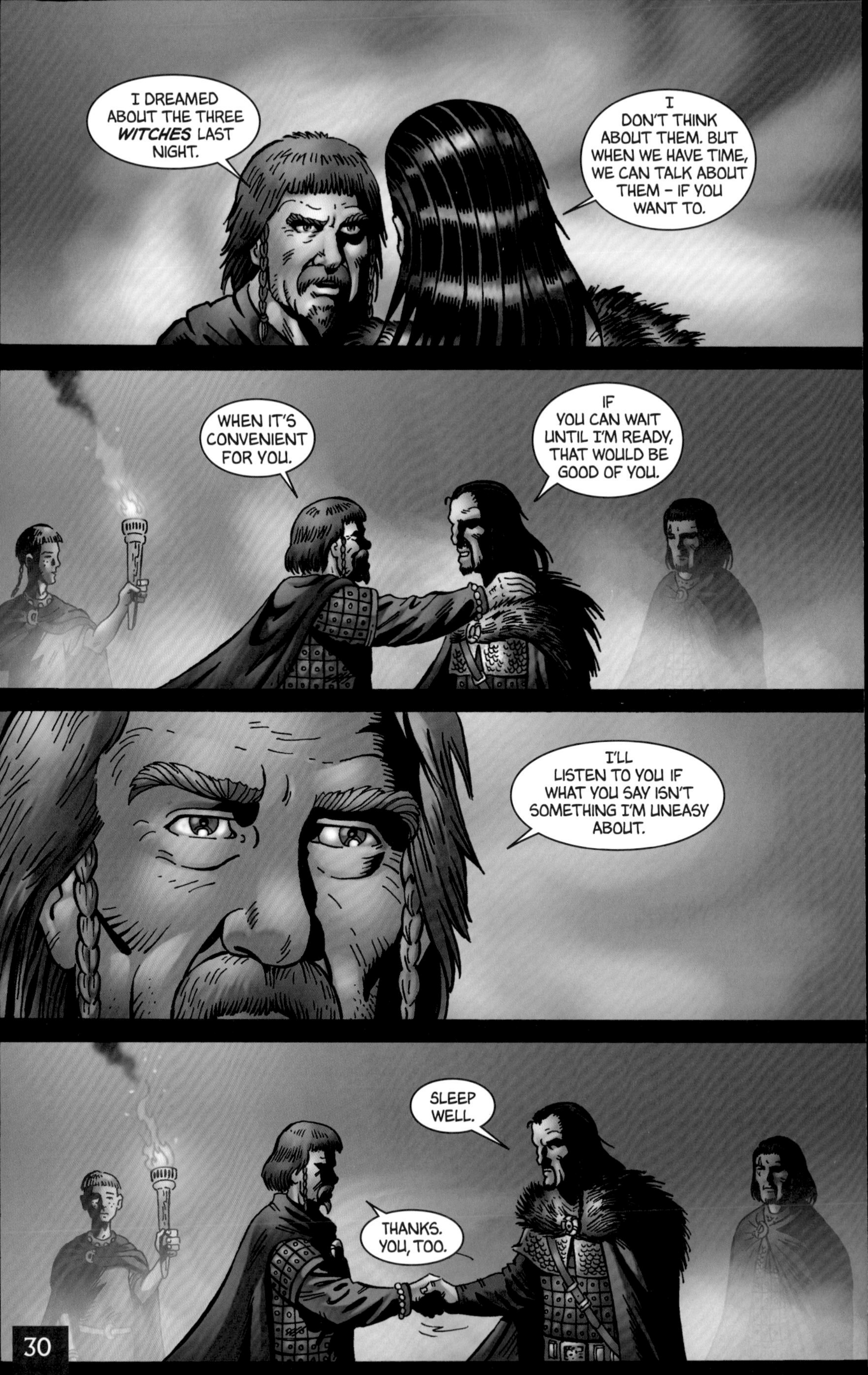
I DREAMED ABOUT THE THREE *WITCHES* LAST NIGHT.
I DON'T THINK ABOUT THEM. BUT WHEN WE HAVE TIME, WE CAN TALK ABOUT THEM – IF YOU WANT TO.
WHEN IT'S CONVENIENT FOR YOU.
IF YOU CAN WAIT UNTIL I'M READY, THAT WOULD BE GOOD OF YOU.
I'LL LISTEN TO YOU IF WHAT YOU SAY ISN'T SOMETHING I'M UNEASY ABOUT.
SLEEP WELL.
THANKS. YOU, TOO.

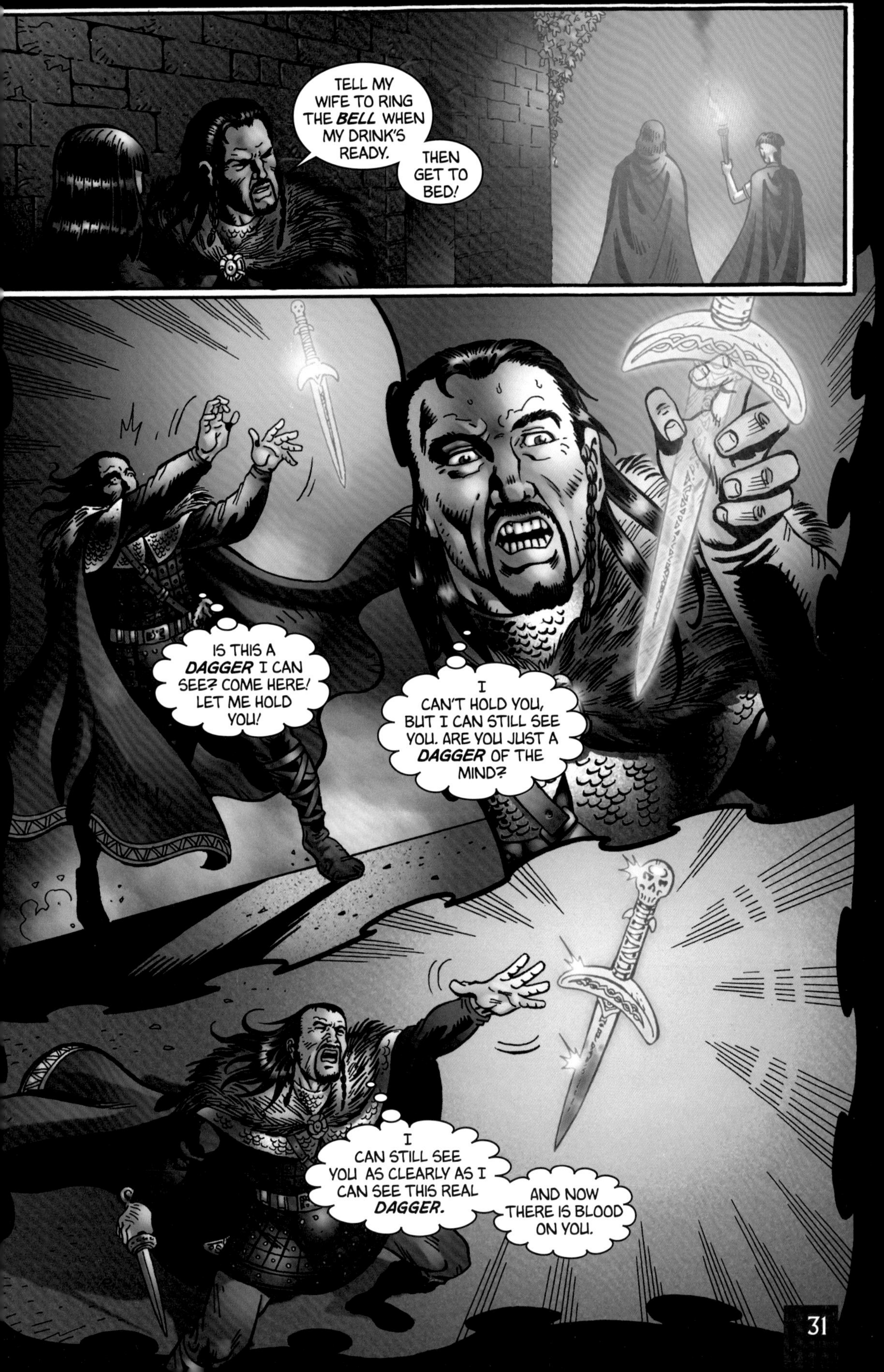
TELL MY WIFE TO RING THE **BELL** WHEN MY DRINK'S READY.
THEN GET TO BED!
IS THIS A **DAGGER** I CAN SEE? COME HERE! LET ME HOLD YOU!
I CAN'T HOLD YOU, BUT I CAN STILL SEE YOU. ARE YOU JUST A **DAGGER** OF THE MIND?
I CAN STILL SEE YOU AS CLEARLY AS I CAN SEE THIS REAL **DAGGER.**
AND NOW THERE IS BLOOD ON YOU.

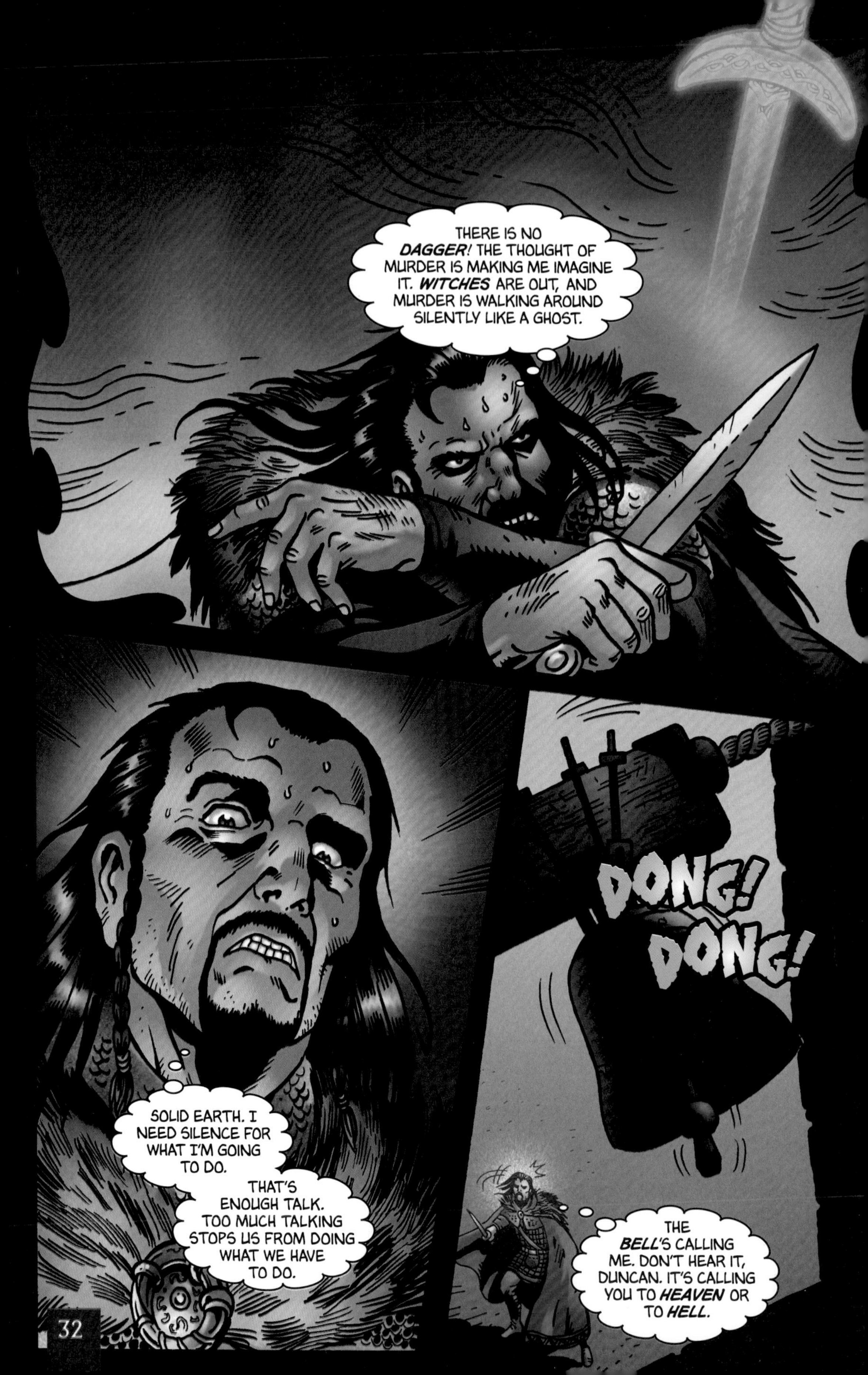
THERE IS NO DAGGER! THE THOUGHT OF MURDER IS MAKING ME IMAGINE IT. WITCHES ARE OUT, AND MURDER IS WALKING AROUND SILENTLY LIKE A GHOST.
SOLID EARTH. I NEED SILENCE FOR WHAT I'M GOING TO DO.
THAT'S ENOUGH TALK. TOO MUCH TALKING STOPS US FROM DOING WHAT WE HAVE TO DO.
DONG! DONG!
THE BELL'S CALLING ME. DON'T HEAR IT, DUNCAN. IT'S CALLING YOU TO HEAVEN OR TO HELL.

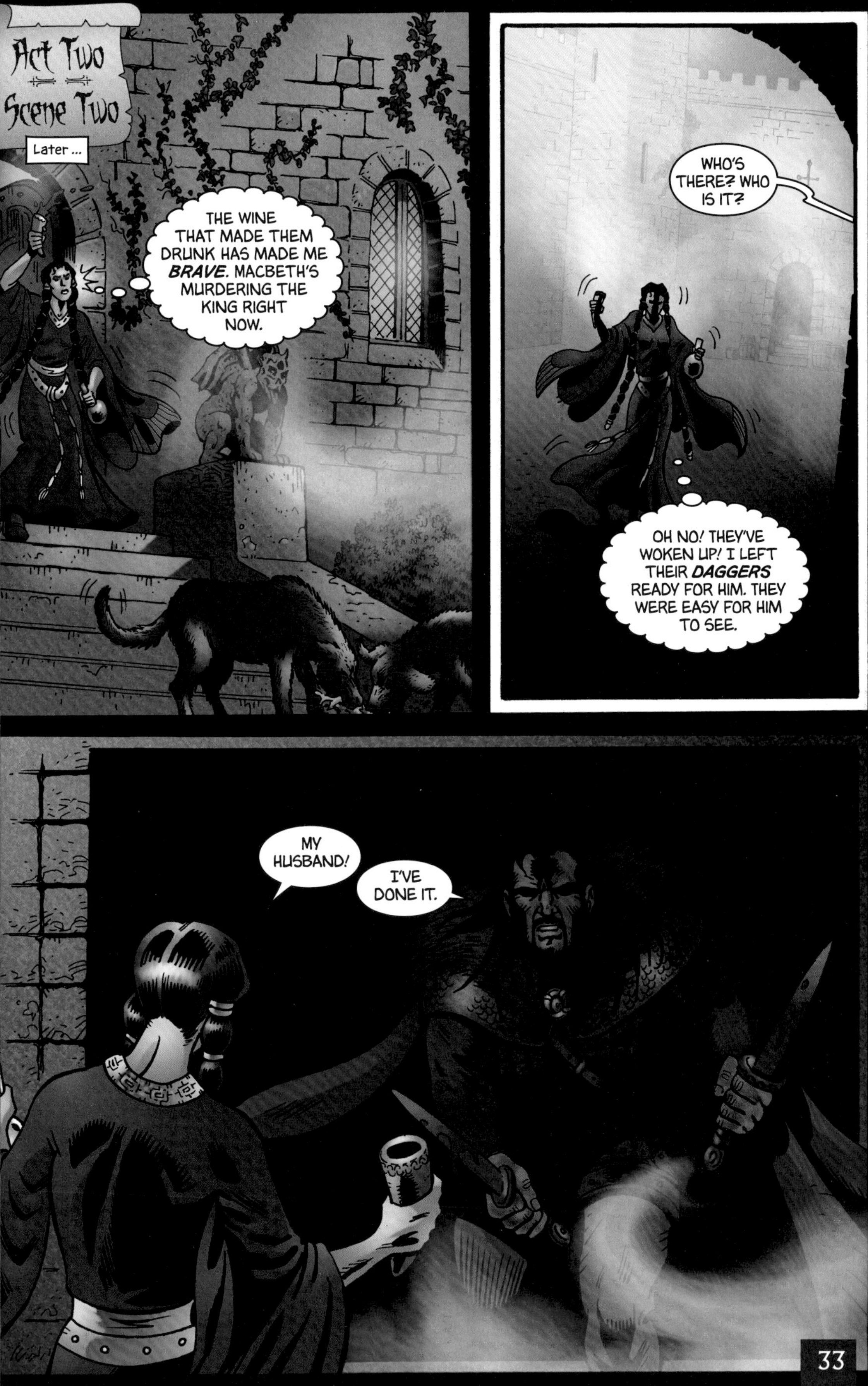
Act Two
Scene Two
Later ...
THE WINE THAT MADE THEM DRUNK HAS MADE ME *BRAVE*. MACBETH'S MURDERING THE KING RIGHT NOW.
WHO'S THERE? WHO IS IT?
OH NO! THEY'VE WOKEN UP! I LEFT THEIR *DAGGERS* READY FOR HIM. THEY WERE EASY FOR HIM TO SEE.
MY HUSBAND!
I'VE DONE IT.

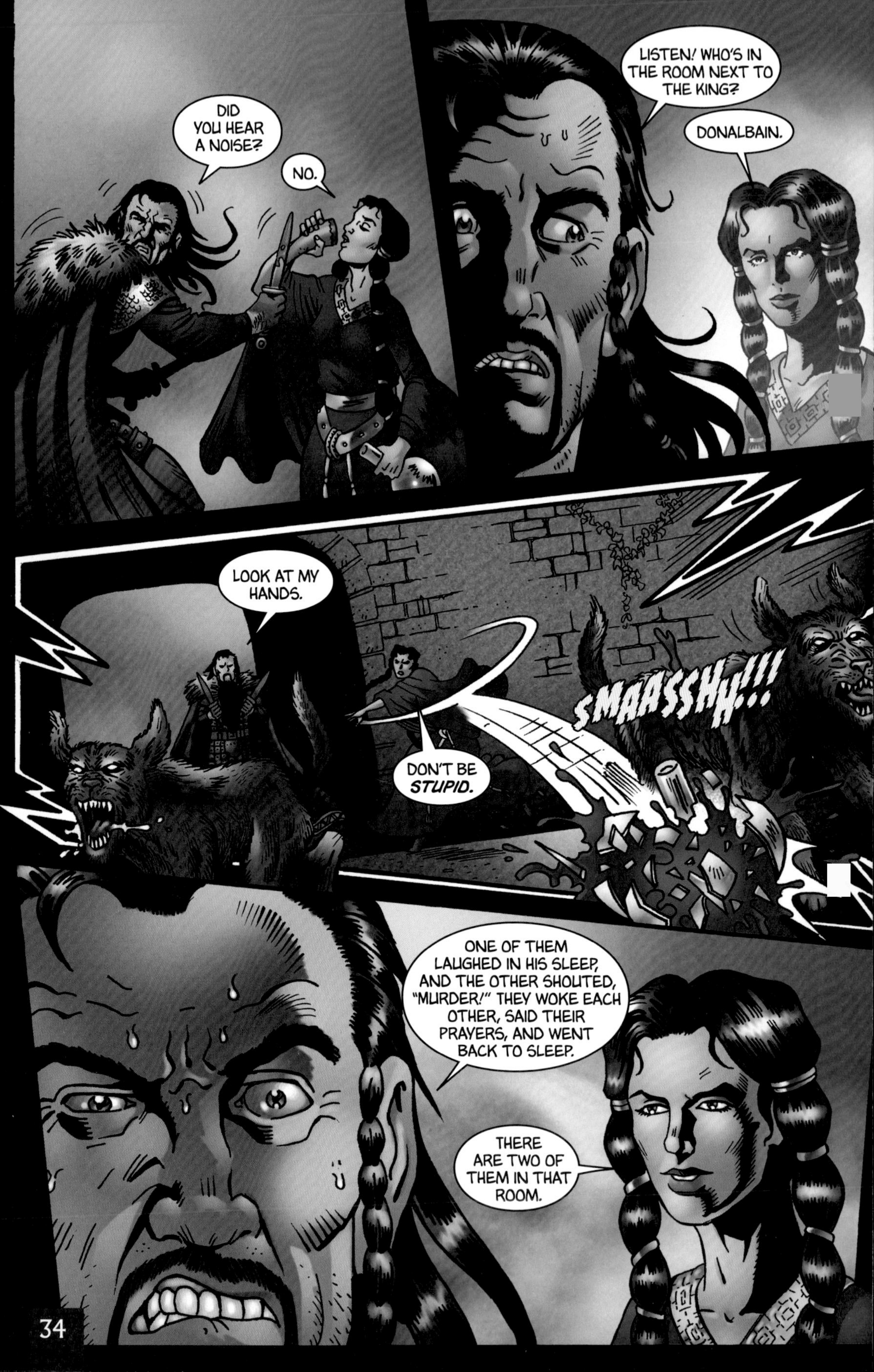
DID YOU HEAR A NOISE?
NO.
LISTEN! WHO'S IN THE ROOM NEXT TO THE KING?
DONALBAIN.
LOOK AT MY HANDS.
DON'T BE STUPID.
SMAASSHH!!!
ONE OF THEM LAUGHED IN HIS SLEEP, AND THE OTHER SHOUTED, "MURDER!" THEY WOKE EACH OTHER, SAID THEIR PRAYERS, AND WENT BACK TO SLEEP.
THERE ARE TWO OF THEM IN THAT ROOM.

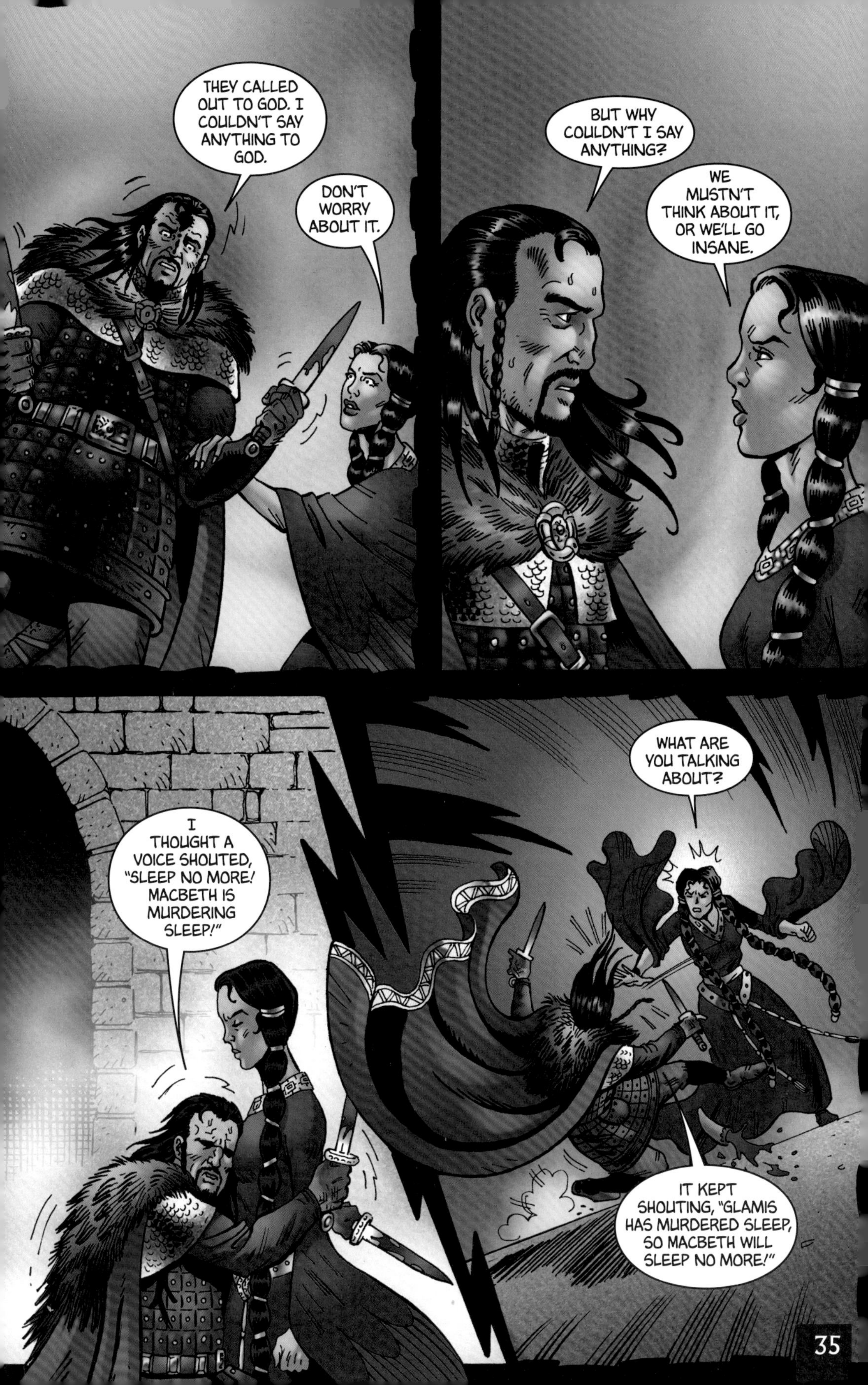
THEY CALLED OUT TO GOD. I COULDN'T SAY ANYTHING TO GOD.
DON'T WORRY ABOUT IT.
BUT WHY COULDN'T I SAY ANYTHING?
WE MUSTN'T THINK ABOUT IT, OR WE'LL GO INSANE.
I THOUGHT A VOICE SHOUTED, "SLEEP NO MORE! MACBETH IS MURDERING SLEEP!"
WHAT ARE YOU TALKING ABOUT?
IT KEPT SHOUTING, "GLAMIS HAS MURDERED SLEEP, SO MACBETH WILL SLEEP NO MORE!"

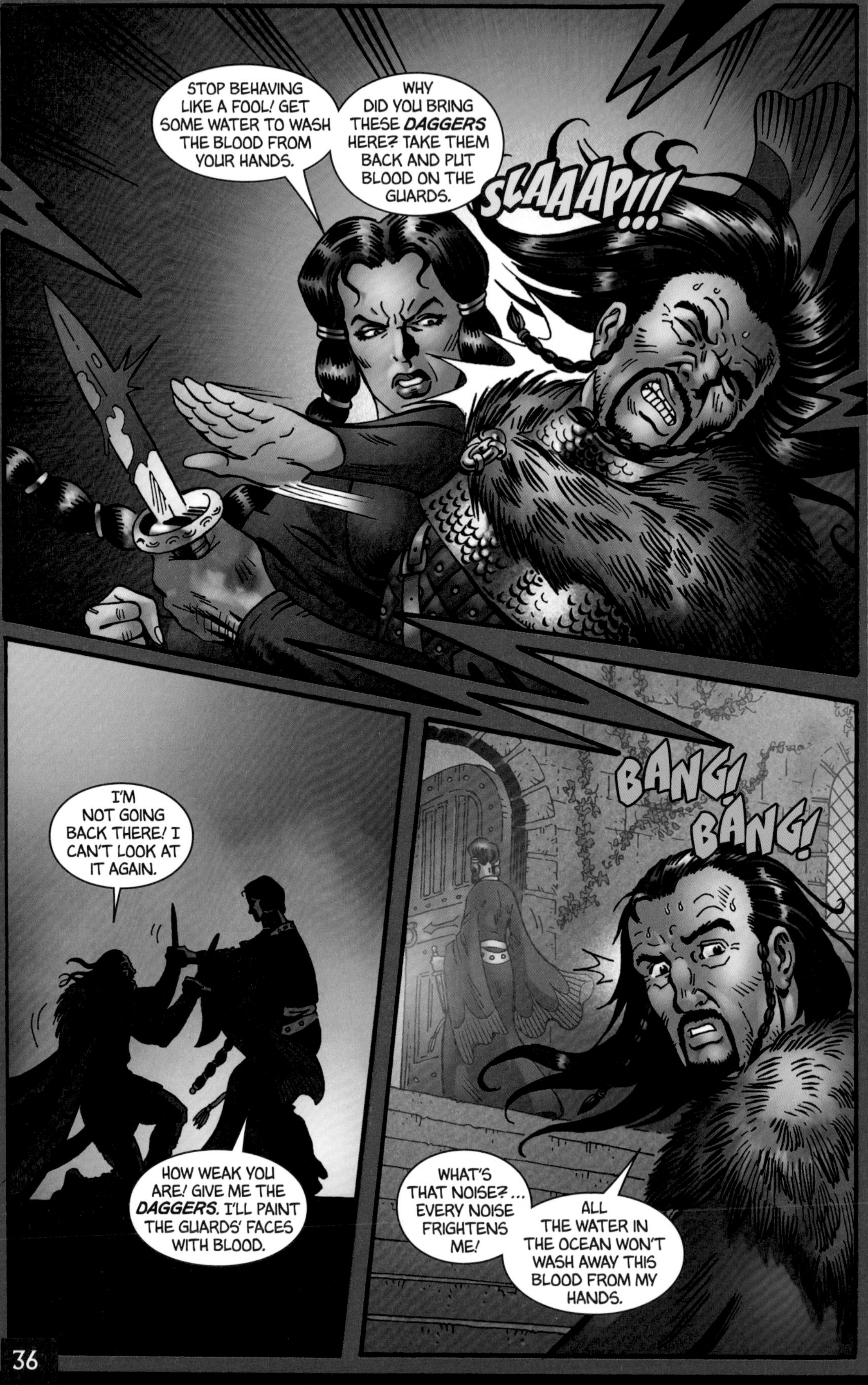
STOP BEHAVING LIKE A FOOL! GET SOME WATER TO WASH THE BLOOD FROM YOUR HANDS.
WHY DID YOU BRING THESE DAGGERS HERE? TAKE THEM BACK AND PUT BLOOD ON THE GUARDS.
SLAAAP!!!
I'M NOT GOING BACK THERE! I CAN'T LOOK AT IT AGAIN.
HOW WEAK YOU ARE! GIVE ME THE DAGGERS. I'LL PAINT THE GUARDS' FACES WITH BLOOD.
BANG! BANG!
WHAT'S THAT NOISE? ... EVERY NOISE FRIGHTENS ME!
ALL THE WATER IN THE OCEAN WON'T WASH AWAY THIS BLOOD FROM MY HANDS.

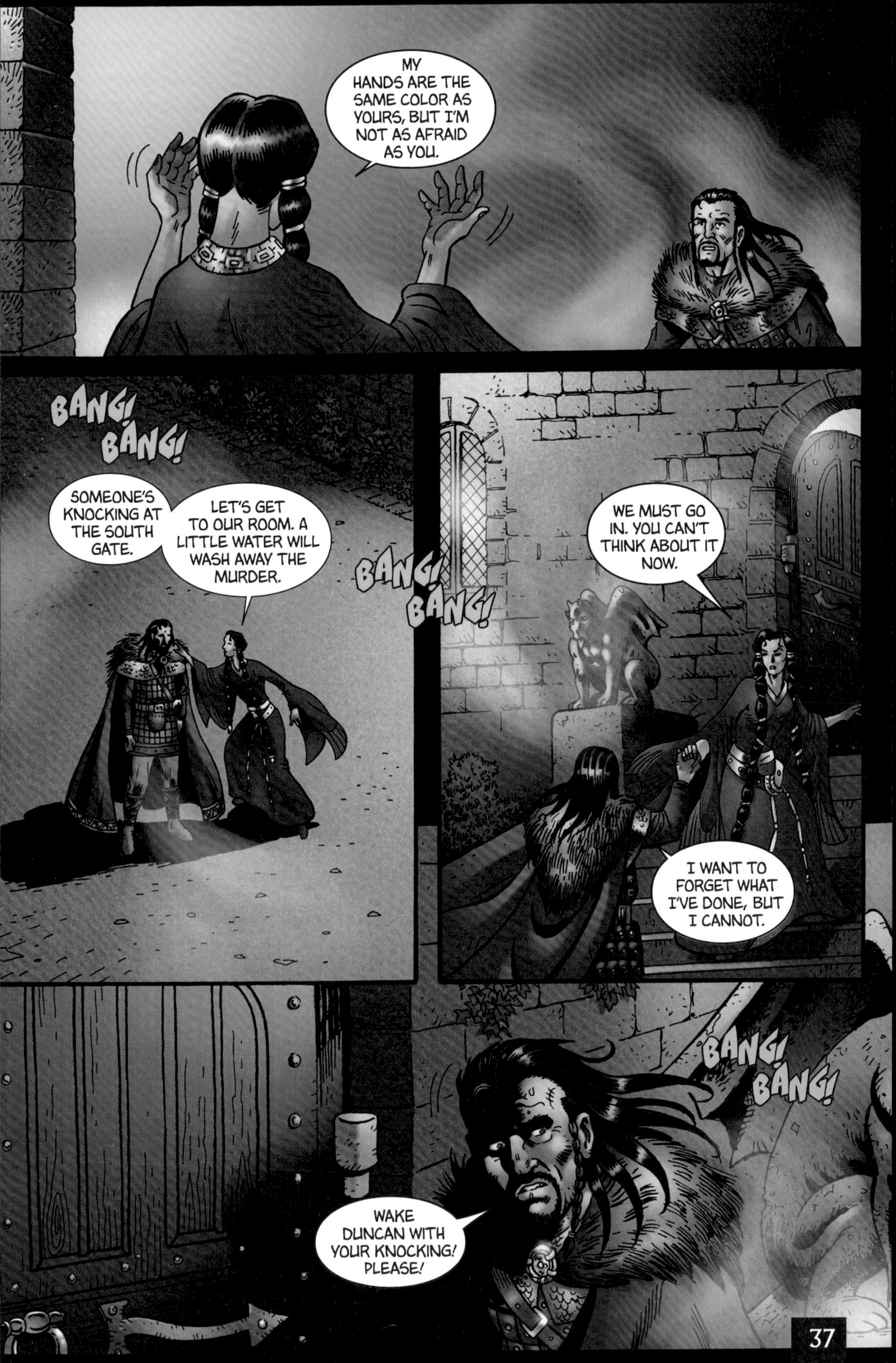
MY HANDS ARE THE SAME COLOR AS YOURS, BUT I'M NOT AS AFRAID AS YOU.
BANG! BANG!
SOMEONE'S KNOCKING AT THE SOUTH GATE.
LET'S GET TO OUR ROOM. A LITTLE WATER WILL WASH AWAY THE MURDER.
BANG! BANG!
WE MUST GO IN. YOU CAN'T THINK ABOUT IT NOW.
I WANT TO FORGET WHAT I'VE DONE, BUT I CANNOT.
BANG! BANG!
WAKE DUNCAN WITH YOUR KNOCKING! PLEASE!

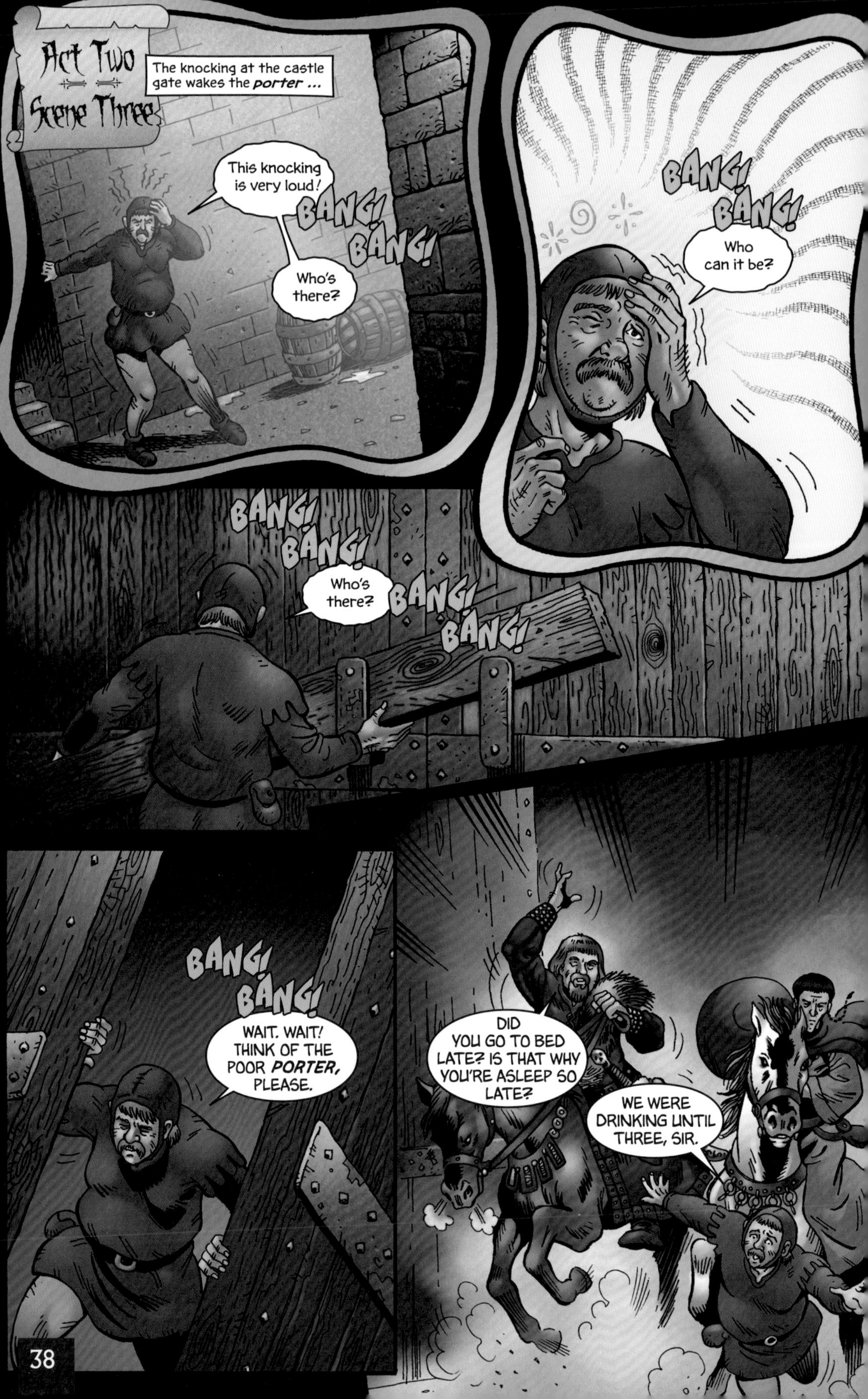
Act Two
Scene Three
The knocking at the castle gate wakes the *porter* ...
This knocking is very loud!
BANG! BANG!
Who's there?
BANG! BANG!
Who can it be?
BANG! BANG!
Who's there?
BANG! BANG!
BANG! BANG!
WAIT. WAIT! THINK OF THE POOR *PORTER,* PLEASE.
DID YOU GO TO BED LATE? IS THAT WHY YOU'RE ASLEEP SO LATE?
WE WERE DRINKING UNTIL THREE, SIR.

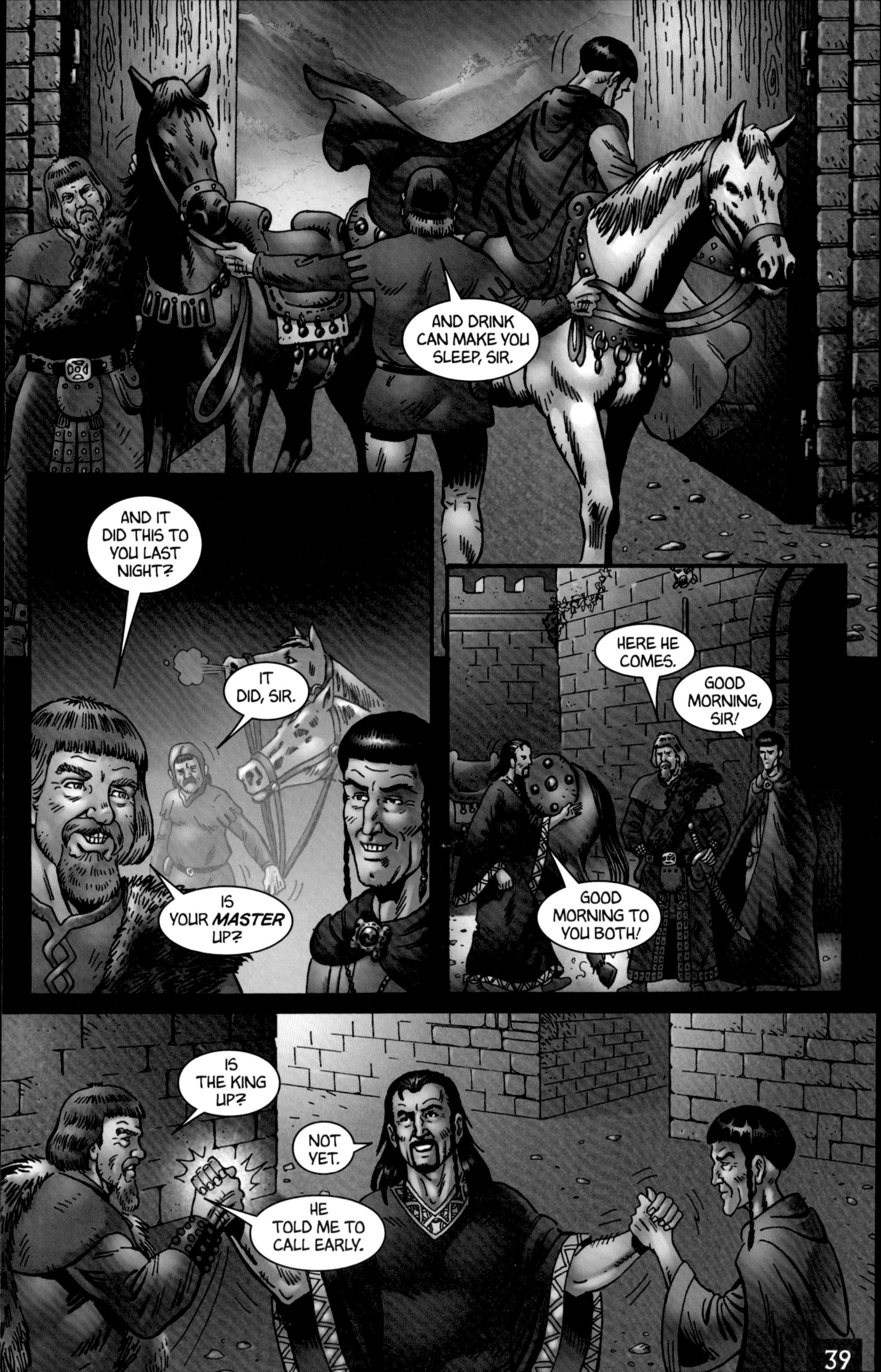
AND DRINK CAN MAKE YOU SLEEP, SIR.
AND IT DID THIS TO YOU LAST NIGHT?
IT DID, SIR.
IS YOUR MASTER UP?
HERE HE COMES.
GOOD MORNING, SIR!
GOOD MORNING TO YOU BOTH!
IS THE KING UP?
NOT YET.
HE TOLD ME TO CALL EARLY.

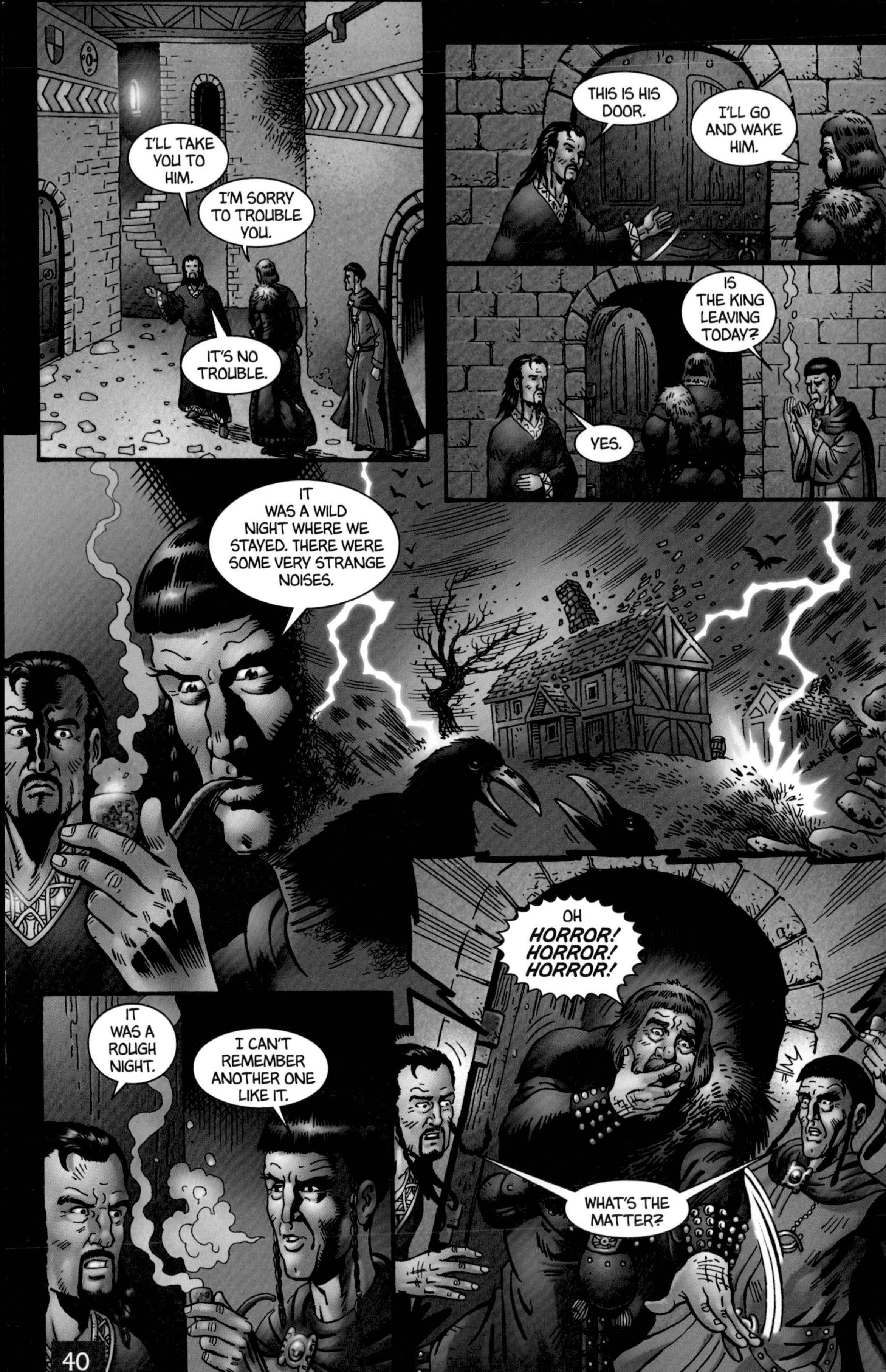
I'LL TAKE YOU TO HIM.
I'M SORRY TO TROUBLE YOU.
IT'S NO TROUBLE.
THIS IS HIS DOOR.
I'LL GO AND WAKE HIM.
IS THE KING LEAVING TODAY?
YES.
IT WAS A WILD NIGHT WHERE WE STAYED. THERE WERE SOME VERY STRANGE NOISES.
IT WAS A ROUGH NIGHT.
I CAN'T REMEMBER ANOTHER ONE LIKE IT.
OH HORROR! HORROR! HORROR!
WHAT'S THE MATTER?

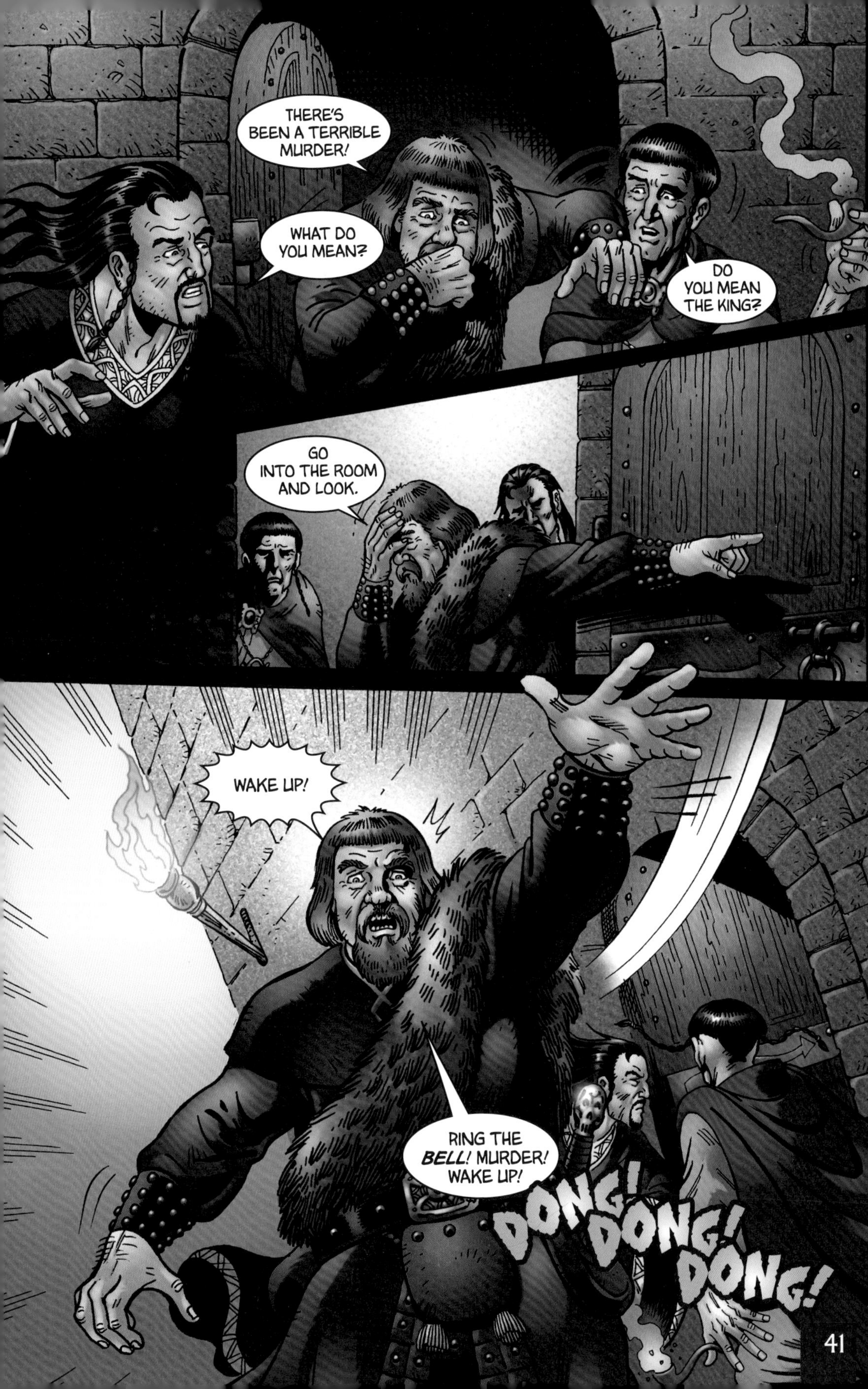
THERE'S BEEN A TERRIBLE MURDER!
WHAT DO YOU MEAN?
DO YOU MEAN THE KING?
GO INTO THE ROOM AND LOOK.
WAKE UP!
RING THE BELL! MURDER! WAKE UP!
DONG! DONG! DONG!

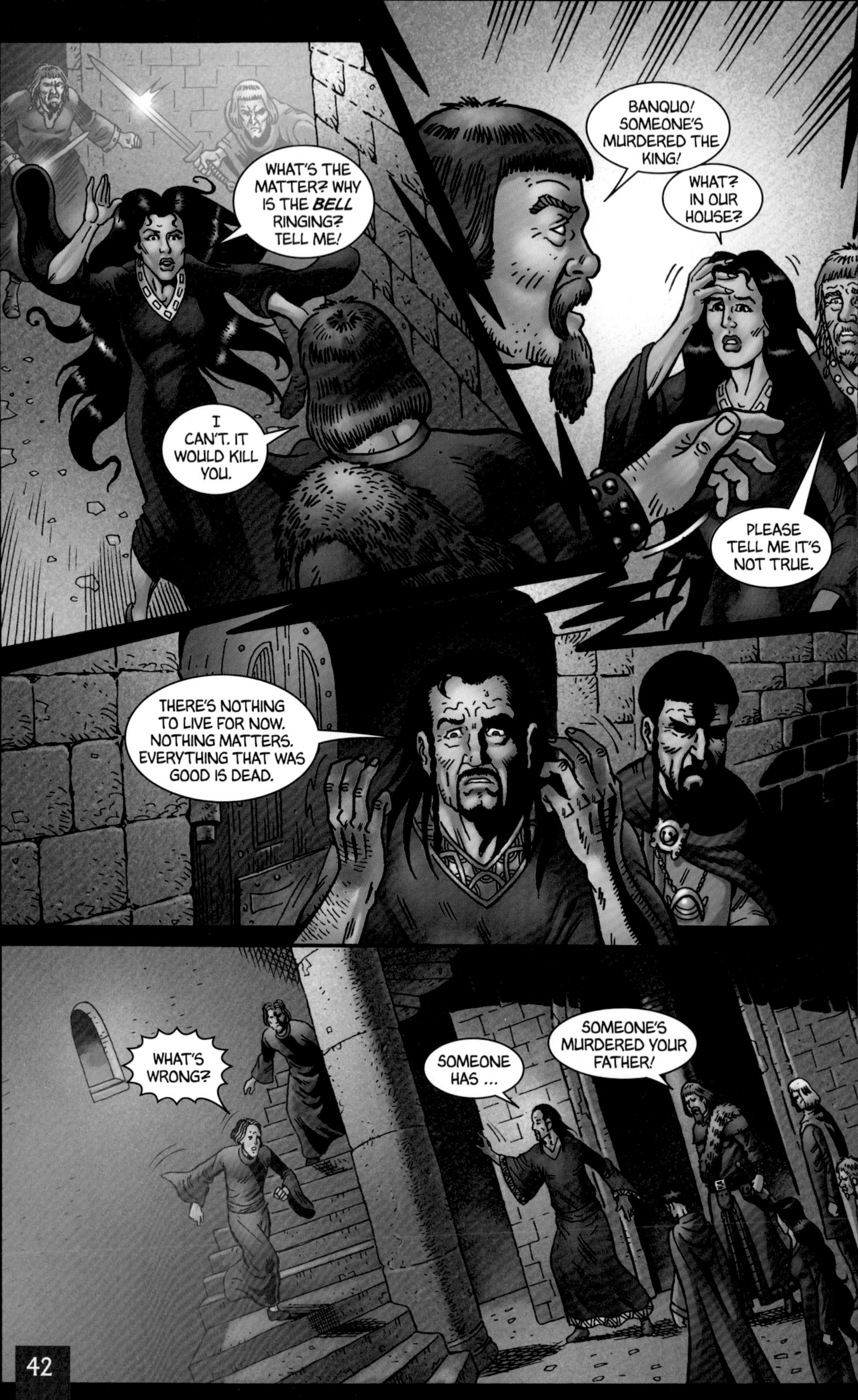
WHAT'S THE MATTER? WHY IS THE BELL RINGING? TELL ME!
I CAN'T. IT WOULD KILL YOU.
BANQUO! SOMEONE'S MURDERED THE KING!
WHAT? IN OUR HOUSE?
PLEASE TELL ME IT'S NOT TRUE.
THERE'S NOTHING TO LIVE FOR NOW. NOTHING MATTERS. EVERYTHING THAT WAS GOOD IS DEAD.
WHAT'S WRONG?
SOMEONE HAS ...
SOMEONE'S MURDERED YOUR FATHER!

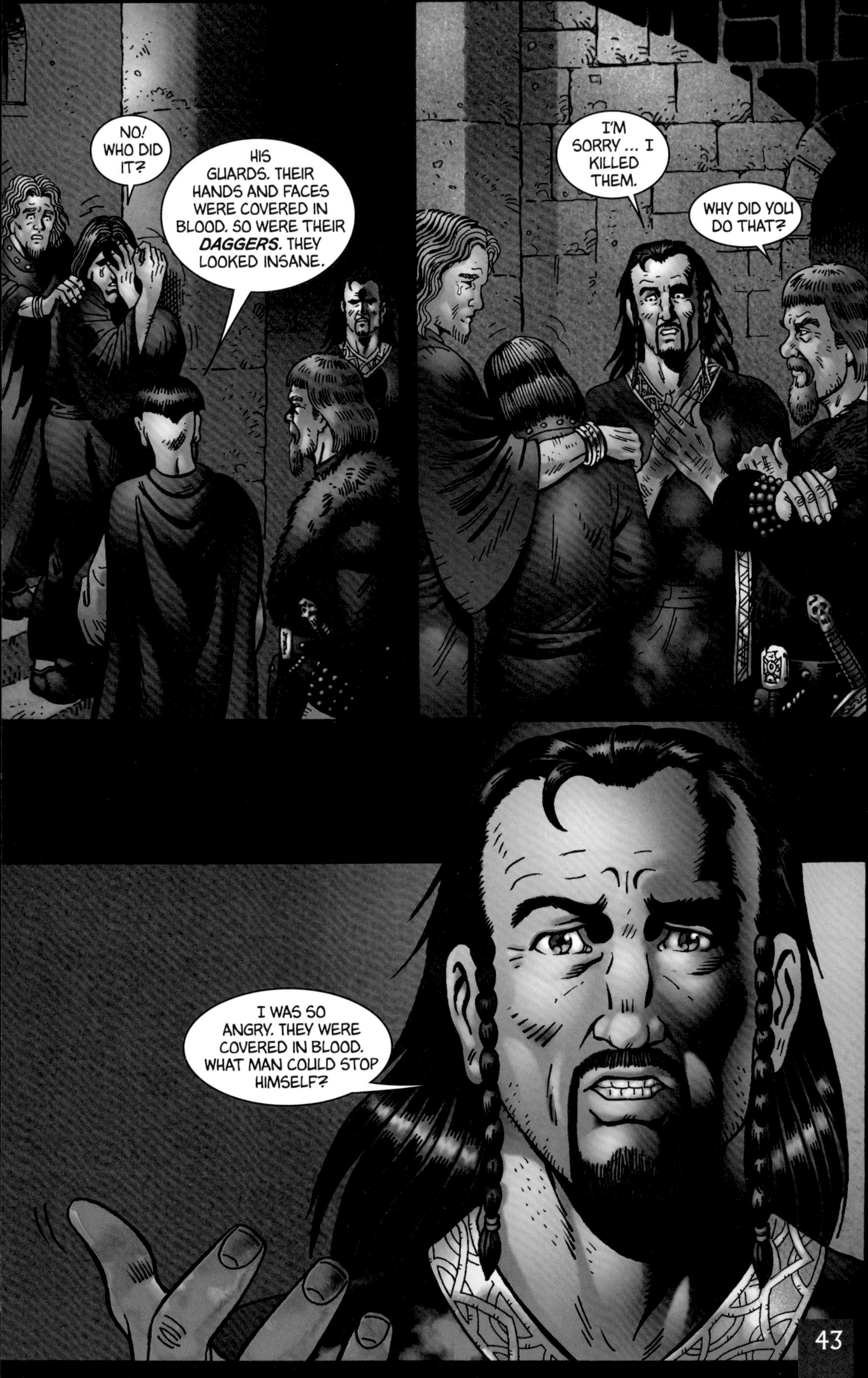
NO! WHO DID IT?
HIS GUARDS. THEIR HANDS AND FACES WERE COVERED IN BLOOD. SO WERE THEIR *DAGGERS.* THEY LOOKED INSANE.
I'M SORRY ... I KILLED THEM.
WHY DID YOU DO THAT?
I WAS SO ANGRY. THEY WERE COVERED IN BLOOD. WHAT MAN COULD STOP HIMSELF?

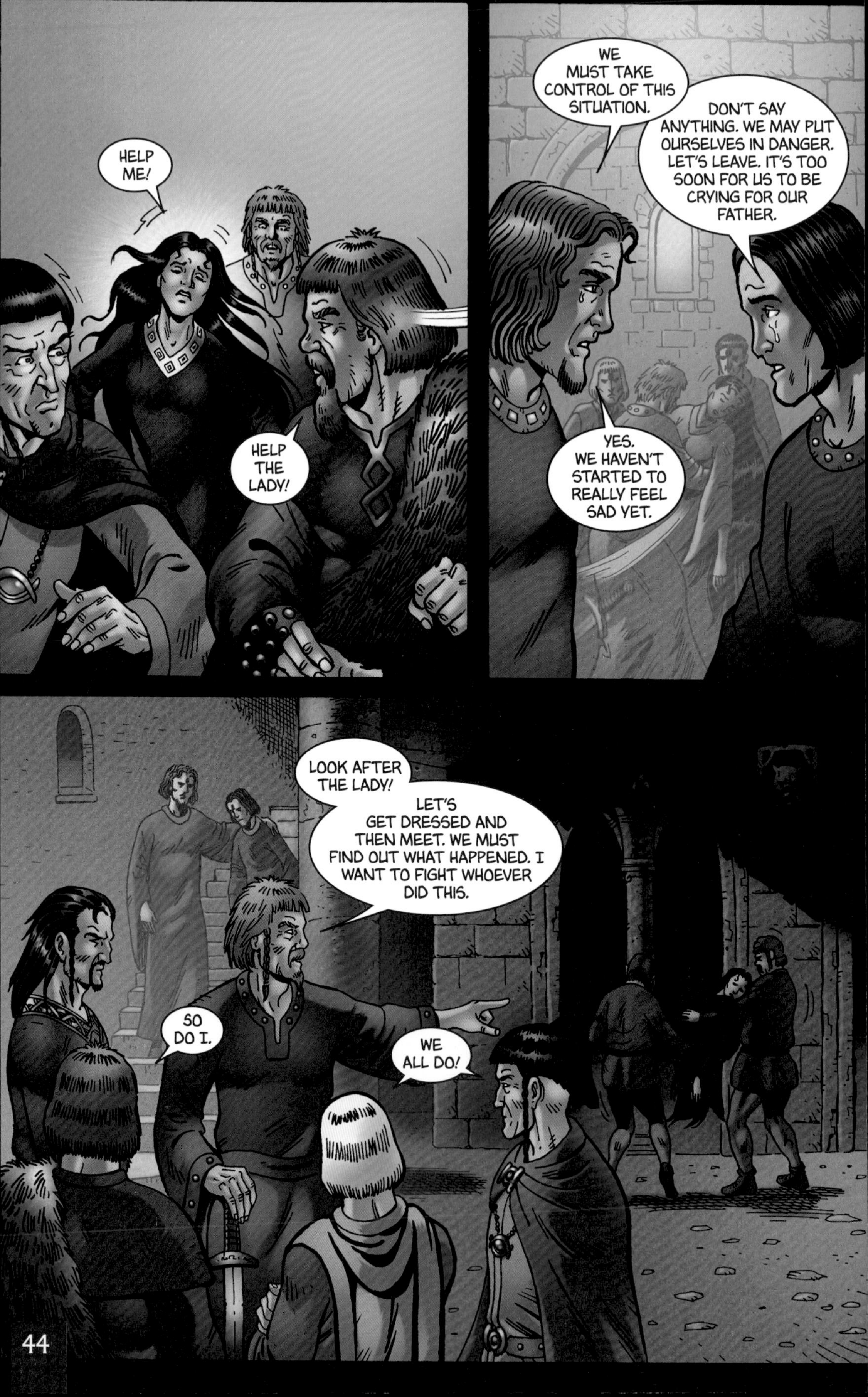
HELP ME!
HELP THE LADY!
WE MUST TAKE CONTROL OF THIS SITUATION.
DON'T SAY ANYTHING. WE MAY PUT OURSELVES IN DANGER. LET'S LEAVE. IT'S TOO SOON FOR US TO BE CRYING FOR OUR FATHER.
YES. WE HAVEN'T STARTED TO REALLY FEEL SAD YET.
LOOK AFTER THE LADY!
LET'S GET DRESSED AND THEN MEET. WE MUST FIND OUT WHAT HAPPENED. I WANT TO FIGHT WHOEVER DID THIS.
SO DO I.
WE ALL DO!

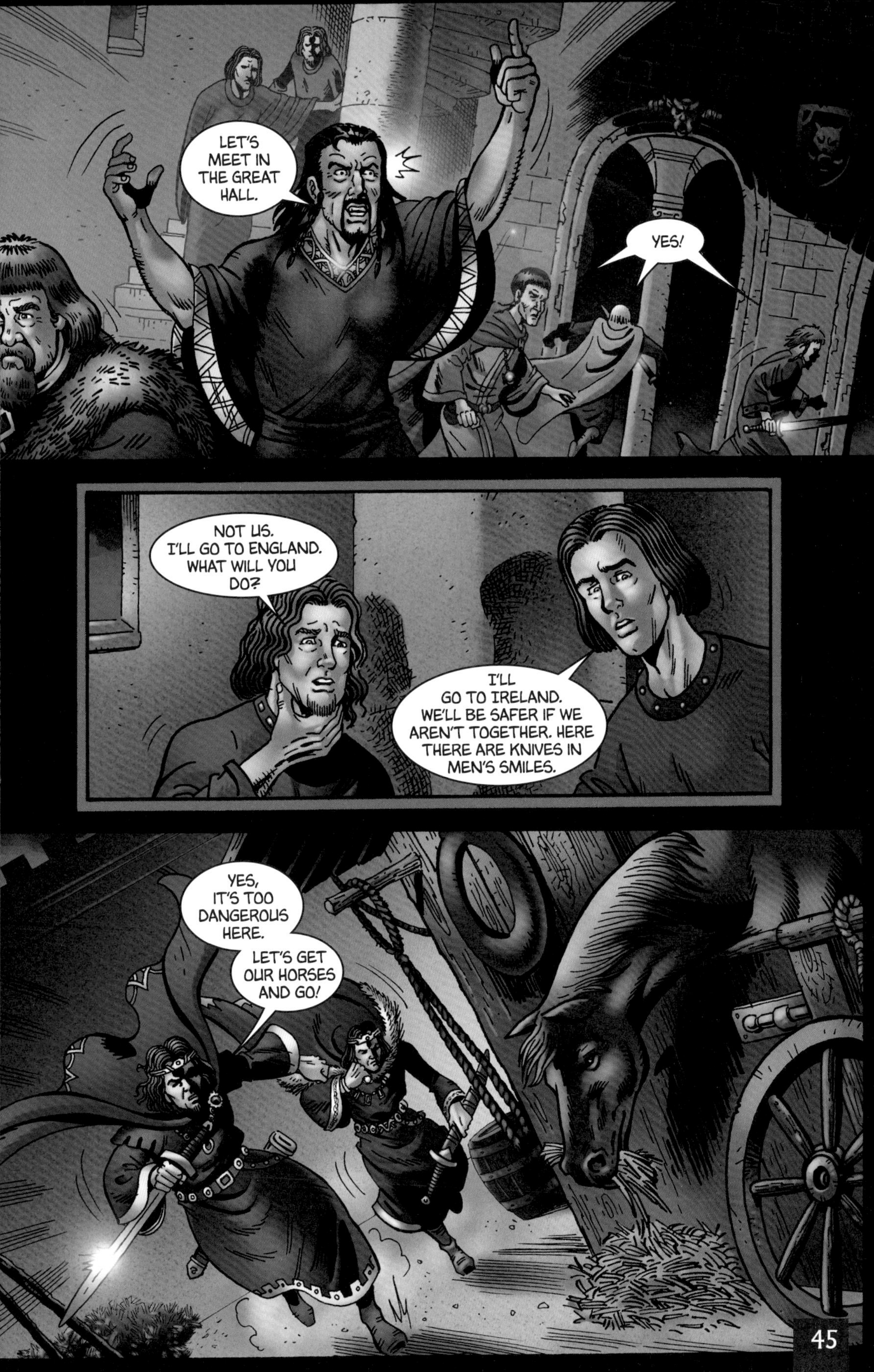
LET'S MEET IN THE GREAT HALL.
YES!
NOT US. I'LL GO TO ENGLAND. WHAT WILL YOU DO?
I'LL GO TO IRELAND. WE'LL BE SAFER IF WE AREN'T TOGETHER. HERE THERE ARE KNIVES IN MEN'S SMILES.
YES, IT'S TOO DANGEROUS HERE.
LET'S GET OUR HORSES AND GO!

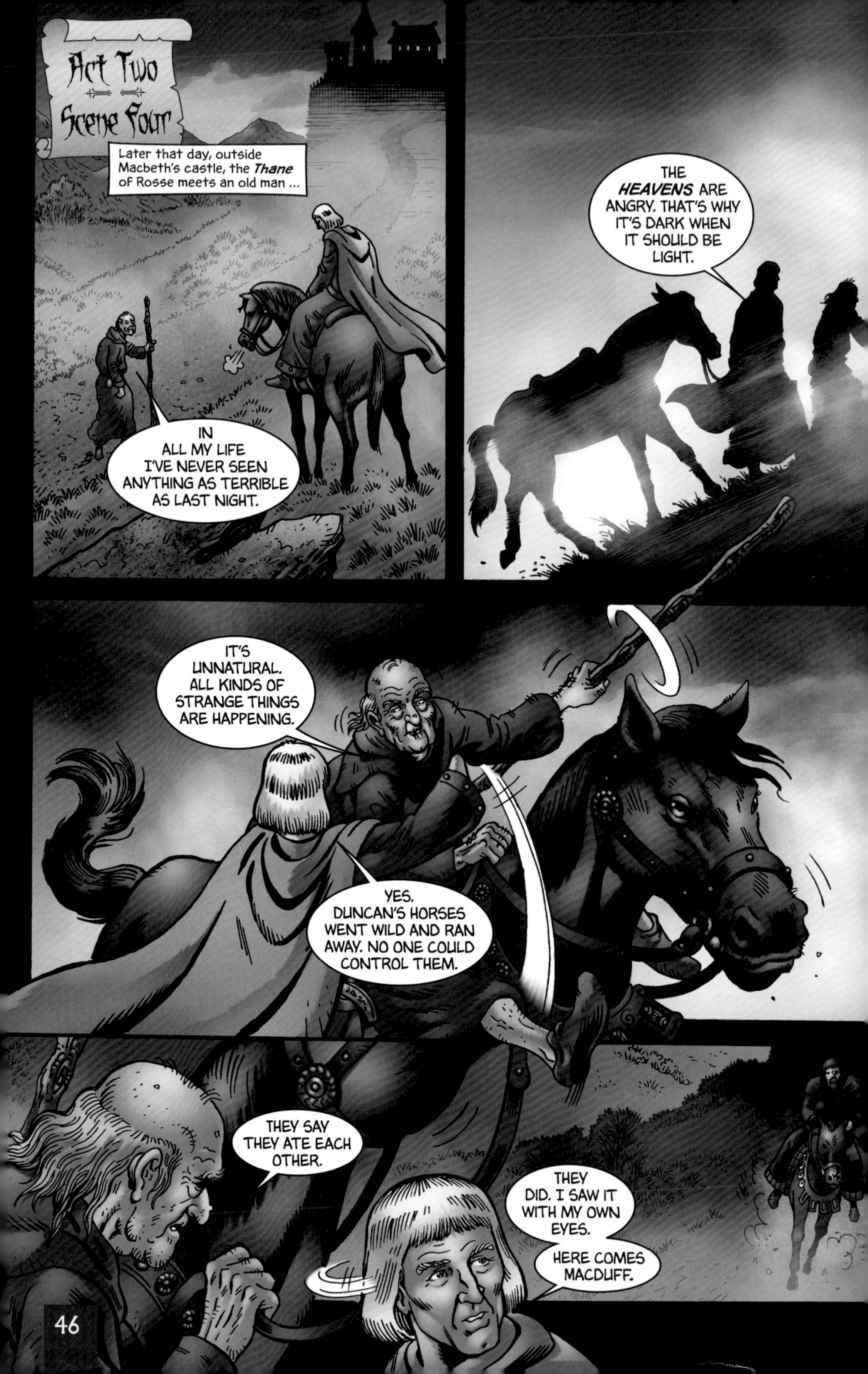
Act Two
Scene Four
Later that day, outside Macbeth's castle, the *Thane* of Rosse meets an old man ...
IN ALL MY LIFE I'VE NEVER SEEN ANYTHING AS TERRIBLE AS LAST NIGHT.
THE *HEAVENS* ARE ANGRY. THAT'S WHY IT'S DARK WHEN IT SHOULD BE LIGHT.
IT'S UNNATURAL. ALL KINDS OF STRANGE THINGS ARE HAPPENING.
YES. DUNCAN'S HORSES WENT WILD AND RAN AWAY. NO ONE COULD CONTROL THEM.
THEY SAY THEY ATE EACH OTHER.
THEY DID. I SAW IT WITH MY OWN EYES.
HERE COMES MACDUFF.

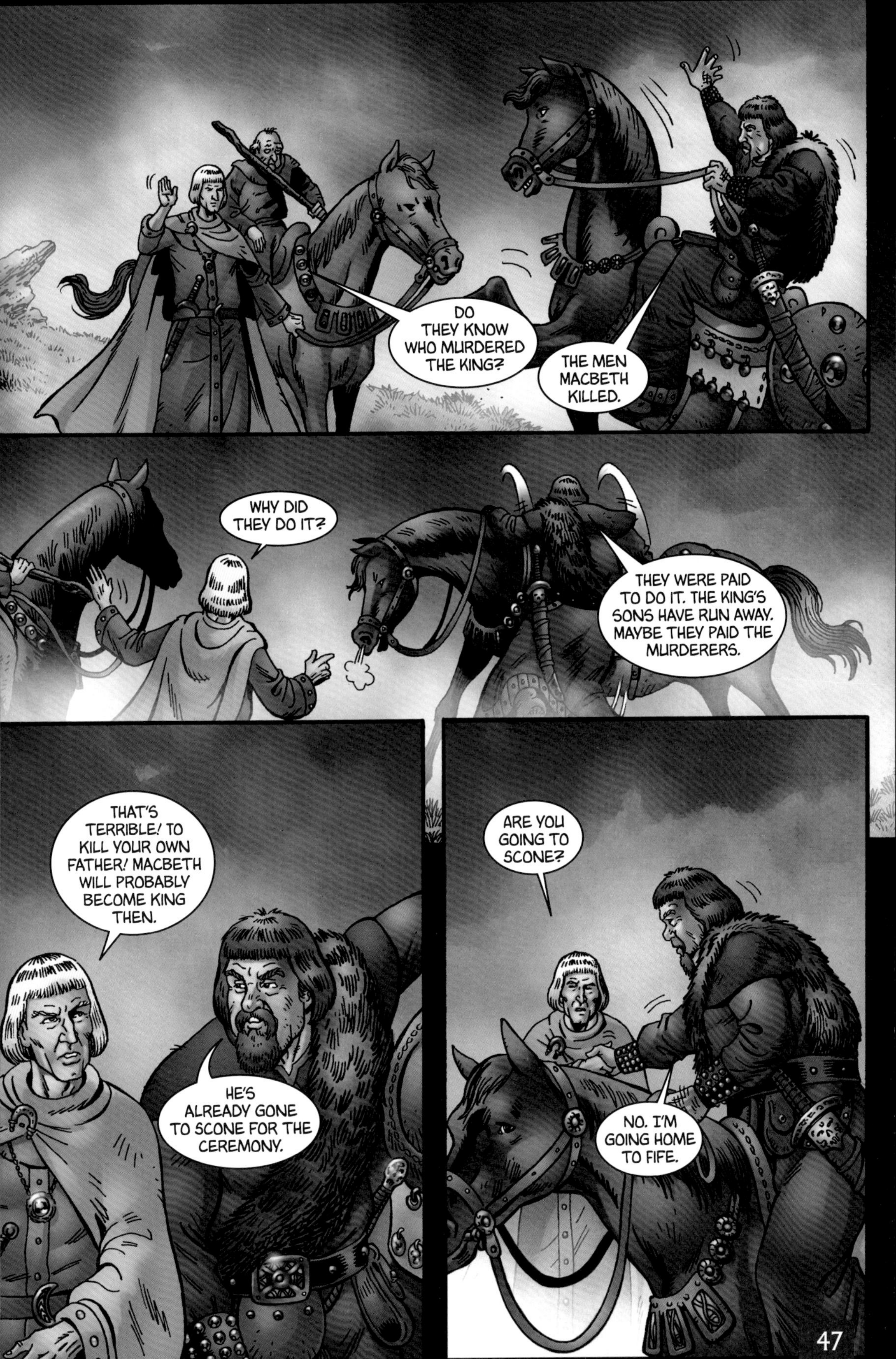
DO THEY KNOW WHO MURDERED THE KING?
THE MEN MACBETH KILLED.
WHY DID THEY DO IT?
THEY WERE PAID TO DO IT. THE KING'S SONS HAVE RUN AWAY. MAYBE THEY PAID THE MURDERERS.
THAT'S TERRIBLE! TO KILL YOUR OWN FATHER! MACBETH WILL PROBABLY BECOME KING THEN.
HE'S ALREADY GONE TO SCONE FOR THE CEREMONY.
ARE YOU GOING TO SCONE?
NO. I'M GOING HOME TO FIFE.

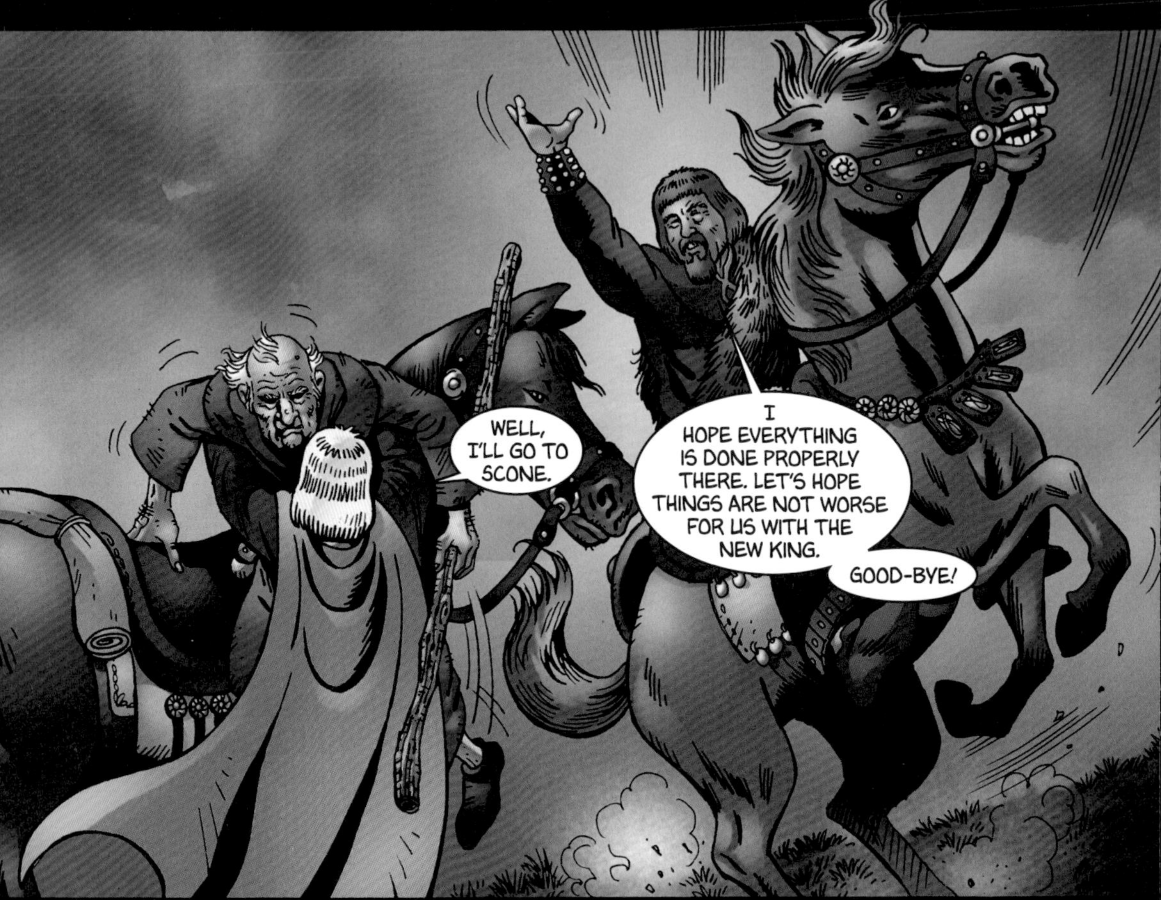
WELL, I'LL GO TO SCONE.
I HOPE EVERYTHING IS DONE PROPERLY THERE. LET'S HOPE THINGS ARE NOT WORSE FOR US WITH THE NEW KING.
GOOD-BYE!

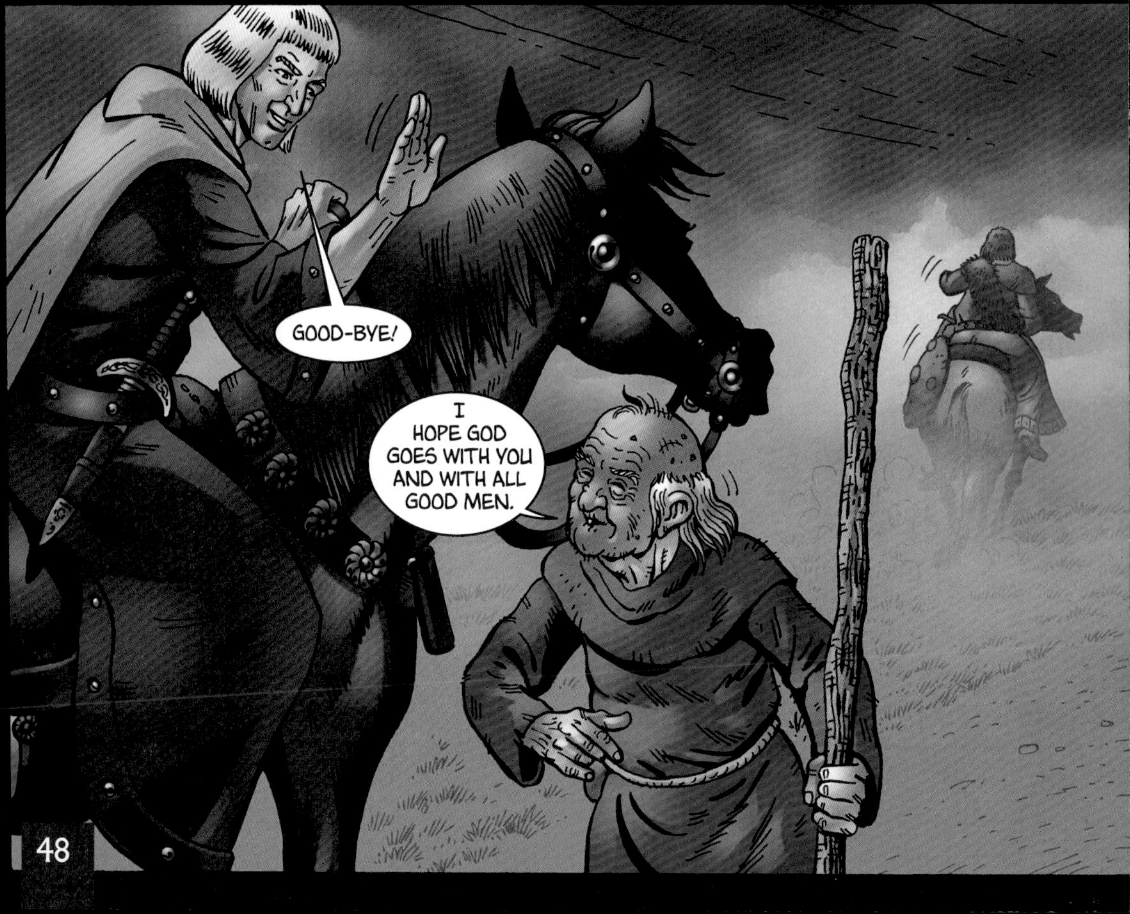
GOOD-BYE!
I HOPE GOD GOES WITH YOU AND WITH ALL GOOD MEN.

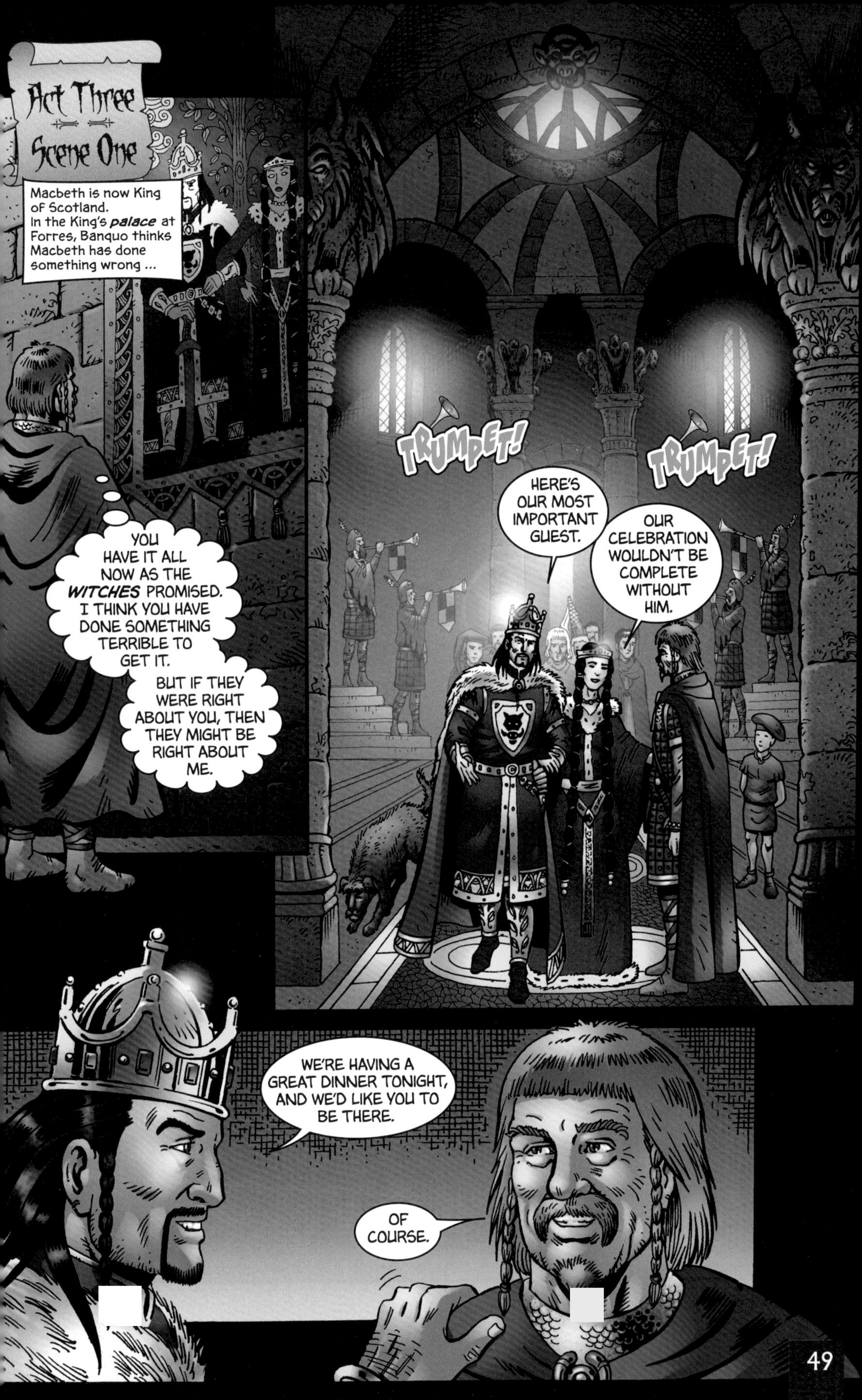
Act Three
Scene One
Macbeth is now King of Scotland. In the King's *palace* at Forres, Banquo thinks Macbeth has done something wrong ...
YOU HAVE IT ALL NOW AS THE WITCHES PROMISED. I THINK YOU HAVE DONE SOMETHING TERRIBLE TO GET IT.
BUT IF THEY WERE RIGHT ABOUT YOU, THEN THEY MIGHT BE RIGHT ABOUT ME.
TRUMPET!
TRUMPET!
HERE'S OUR MOST IMPORTANT GUEST.
OUR CELEBRATION WOULDN'T BE COMPLETE WITHOUT HIM.
WE'RE HAVING A GREAT DINNER TONIGHT, AND WE'D LIKE YOU TO BE THERE.
OF COURSE.

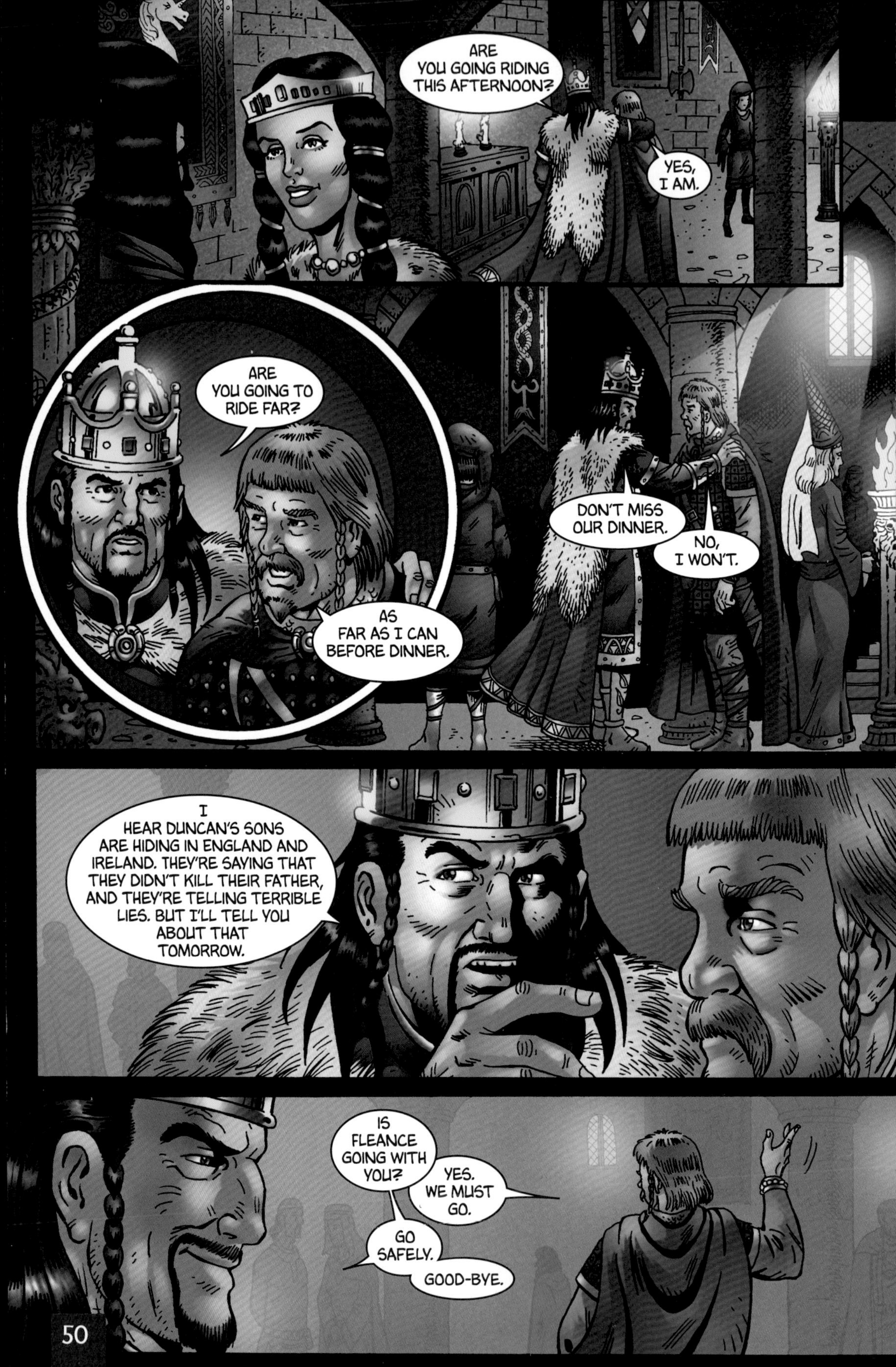
ARE YOU GOING RIDING THIS AFTERNOON?
YES, I AM.
ARE YOU GOING TO RIDE FAR?
AS FAR AS I CAN BEFORE DINNER.
DON'T MISS OUR DINNER.
NO, I WON'T.
I HEAR DUNCAN'S SONS ARE HIDING IN ENGLAND AND IRELAND. THEY'RE SAYING THAT THEY DIDN'T KILL THEIR FATHER, AND THEY'RE TELLING TERRIBLE LIES. BUT I'LL TELL YOU ABOUT THAT TOMORROW.
IS FLEANCE GOING WITH YOU?
YES. WE MUST GO.
GO SAFELY.
GOOD-BYE.

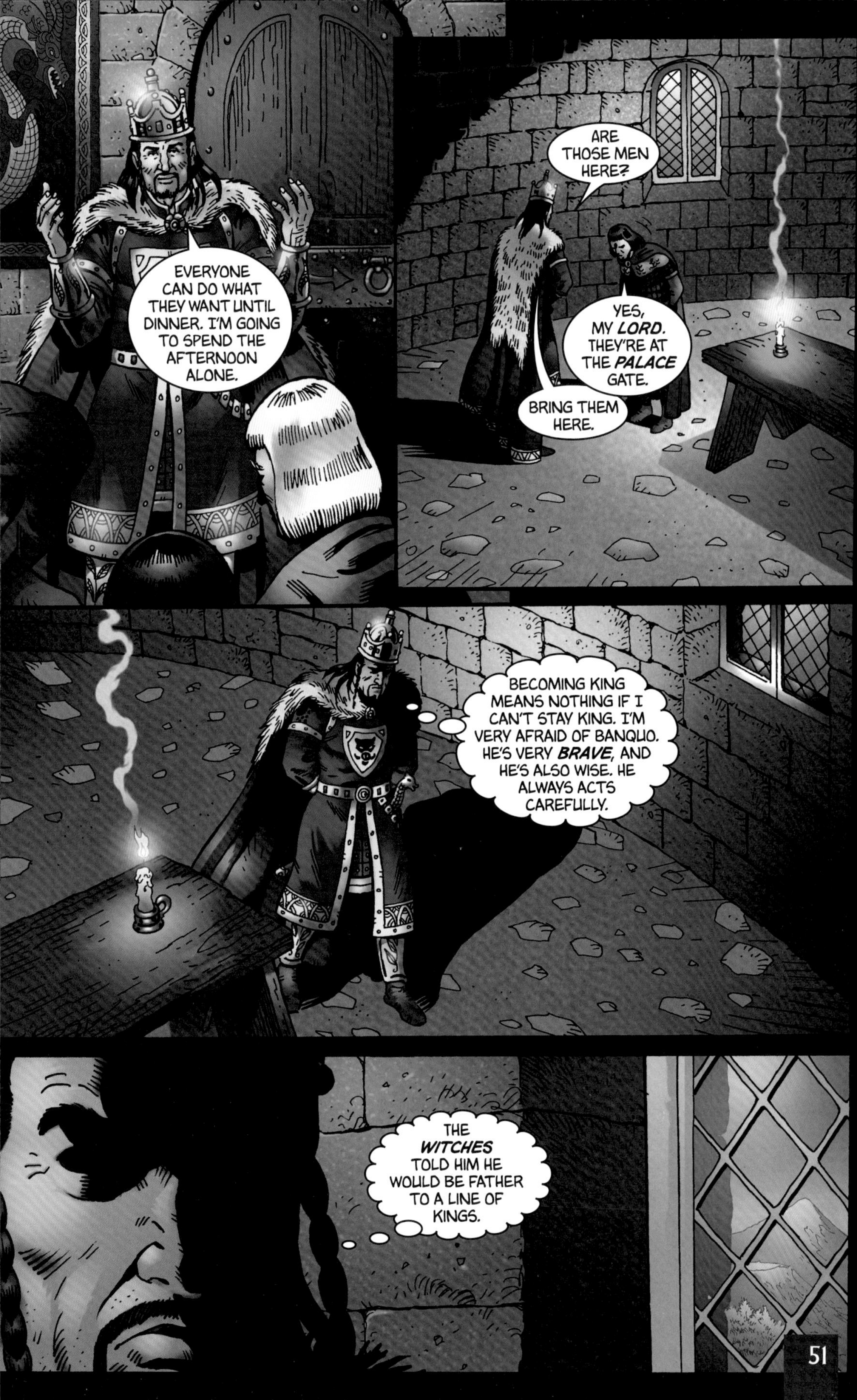
EVERYONE CAN DO WHAT THEY WANT UNTIL DINNER. I'M GOING TO SPEND THE AFTERNOON ALONE.
ARE THOSE MEN HERE?
YES, MY **LORD.** THEY'RE AT THE **PALACE** GATE.
BRING THEM HERE.
BECOMING KING MEANS NOTHING IF I CAN'T STAY KING. I'M VERY AFRAID OF BANQUO. HE'S VERY **BRAVE,** AND HE'S ALSO WISE. HE ALWAYS ACTS CAREFULLY.
THE **WITCHES** TOLD HIM HE WOULD BE FATHER TO A LINE OF KINGS.

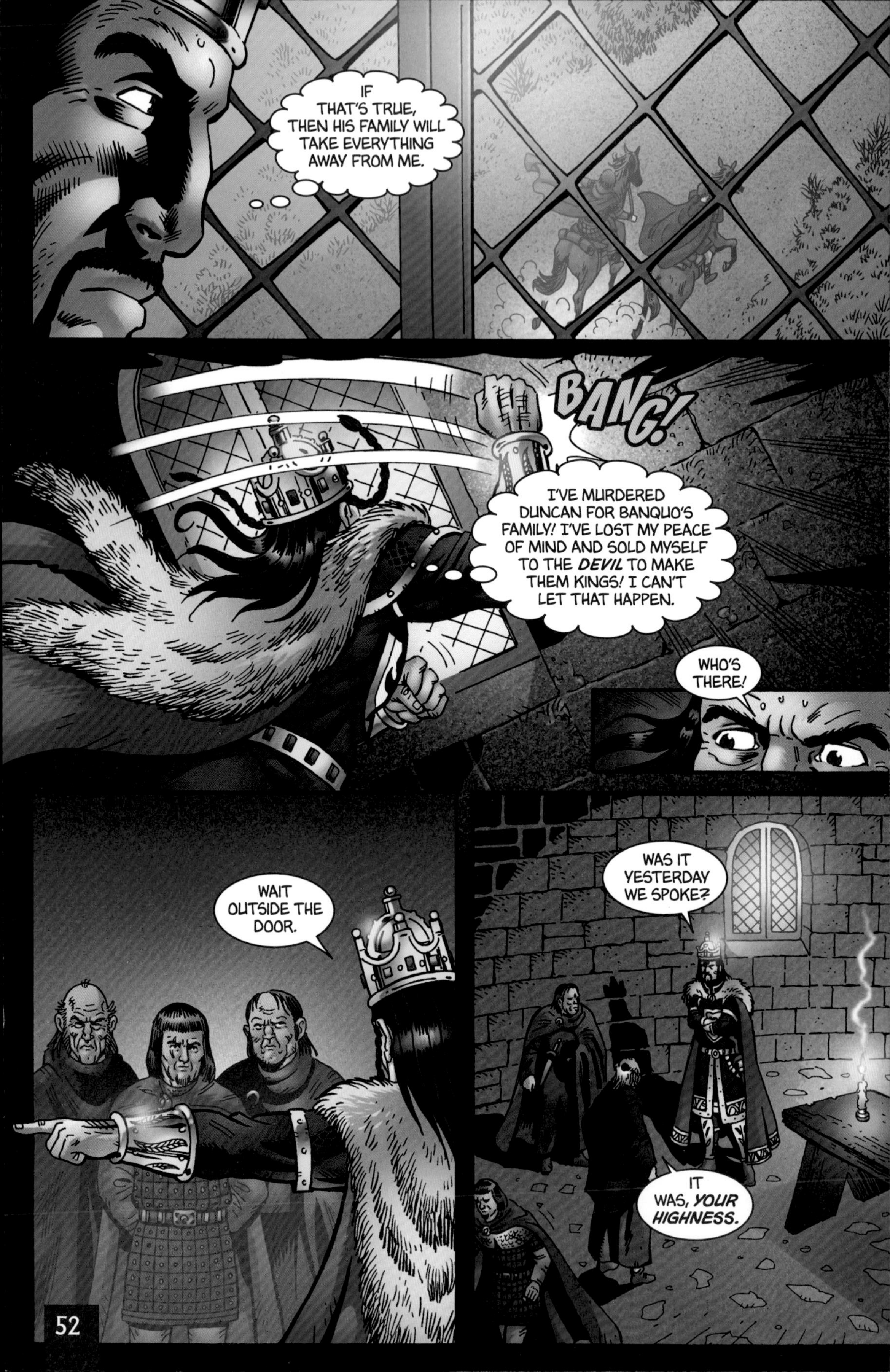
IF THAT'S TRUE, THEN HIS FAMILY WILL TAKE EVERYTHING AWAY FROM ME.
BANG!
I'VE MURDERED DUNCAN FOR BANQUO'S FAMILY! I'VE LOST MY PEACE OF MIND AND SOLD MYSELF TO THE *DEVIL* TO MAKE THEM KINGS! I CAN'T LET THAT HAPPEN.
WHO'S THERE!
WAIT OUTSIDE THE DOOR.
WAS IT YESTERDAY WE SPOKE?
IT WAS, ***YOUR HIGHNESS.***

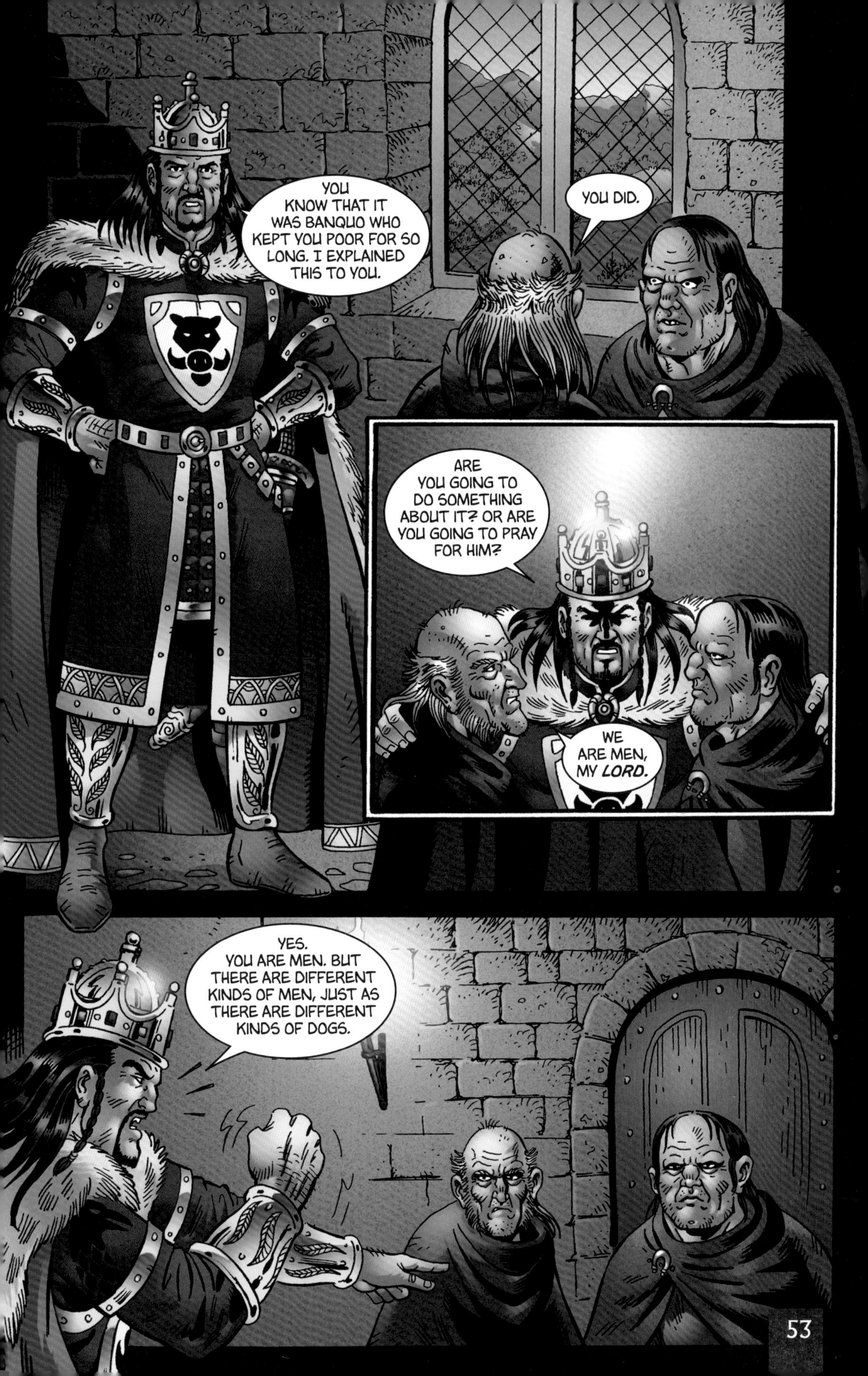
YOU KNOW THAT IT WAS BANQUO WHO KEPT YOU POOR FOR SO LONG. I EXPLAINED THIS TO YOU.
YOU DID.
ARE YOU GOING TO DO SOMETHING ABOUT IT? OR ARE YOU GOING TO PRAY FOR HIM?
WE ARE MEN, MY *LORD.*
YES. YOU ARE MEN. BUT THERE ARE DIFFERENT KINDS OF MEN, JUST AS THERE ARE DIFFERENT KINDS OF DOGS.

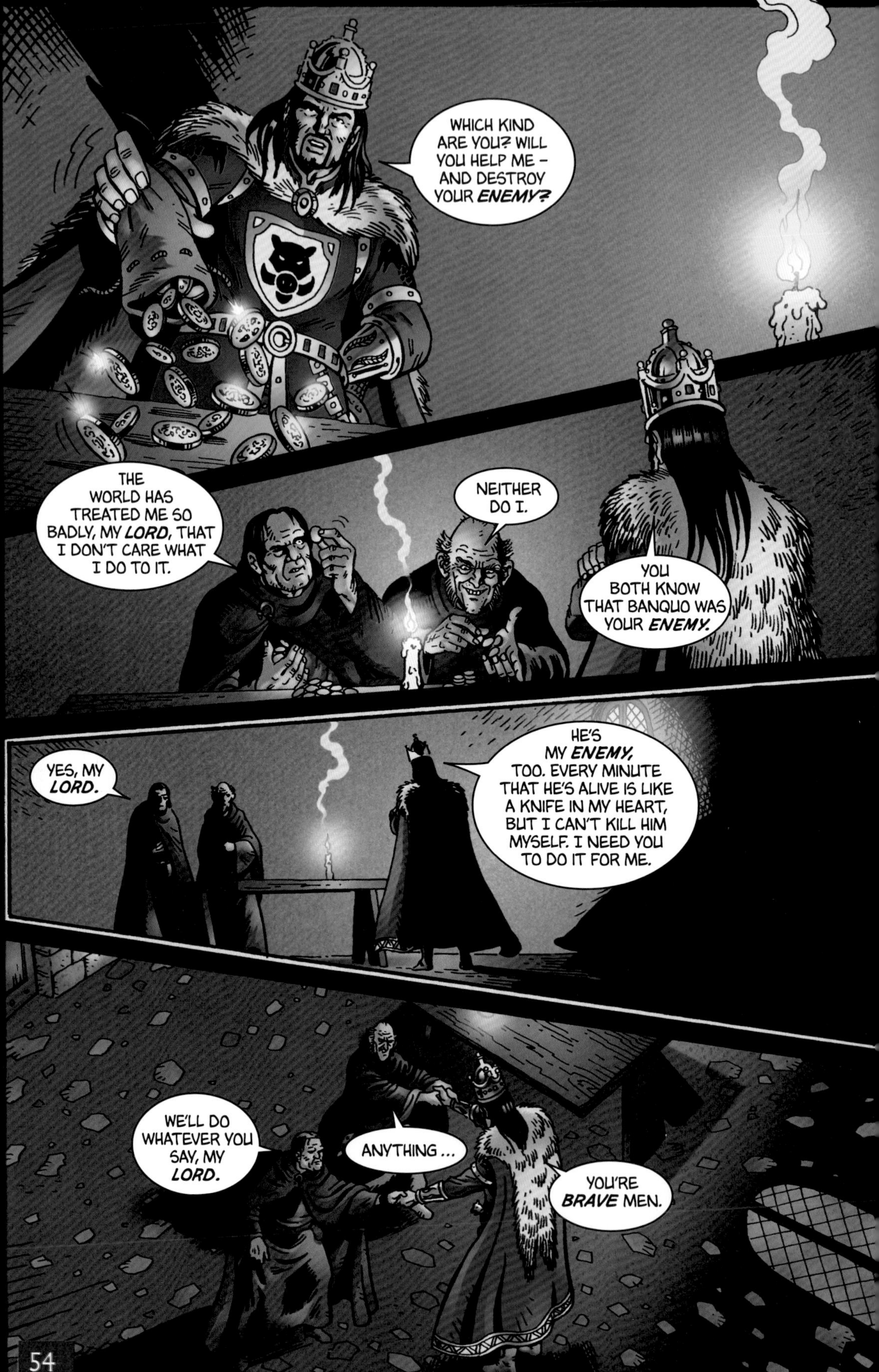

WHICH KIND ARE YOU? WILL YOU HELP ME – AND DESTROY YOUR ENEMY?
THE WORLD HAS TREATED ME SO BADLY, MY LORD, THAT I DON'T CARE WHAT I DO TO IT.
NEITHER DO I.
YOU BOTH KNOW THAT BANQUO WAS YOUR ENEMY.
YES, MY LORD.
HE'S MY ENEMY, TOO. EVERY MINUTE THAT HE'S ALIVE IS LIKE A KNIFE IN MY HEART, BUT I CAN'T KILL HIM MYSELF. I NEED YOU TO DO IT FOR ME.
WE'LL DO WHATEVER YOU SAY, MY LORD.
ANYTHING ...
YOU'RE BRAVE MEN.

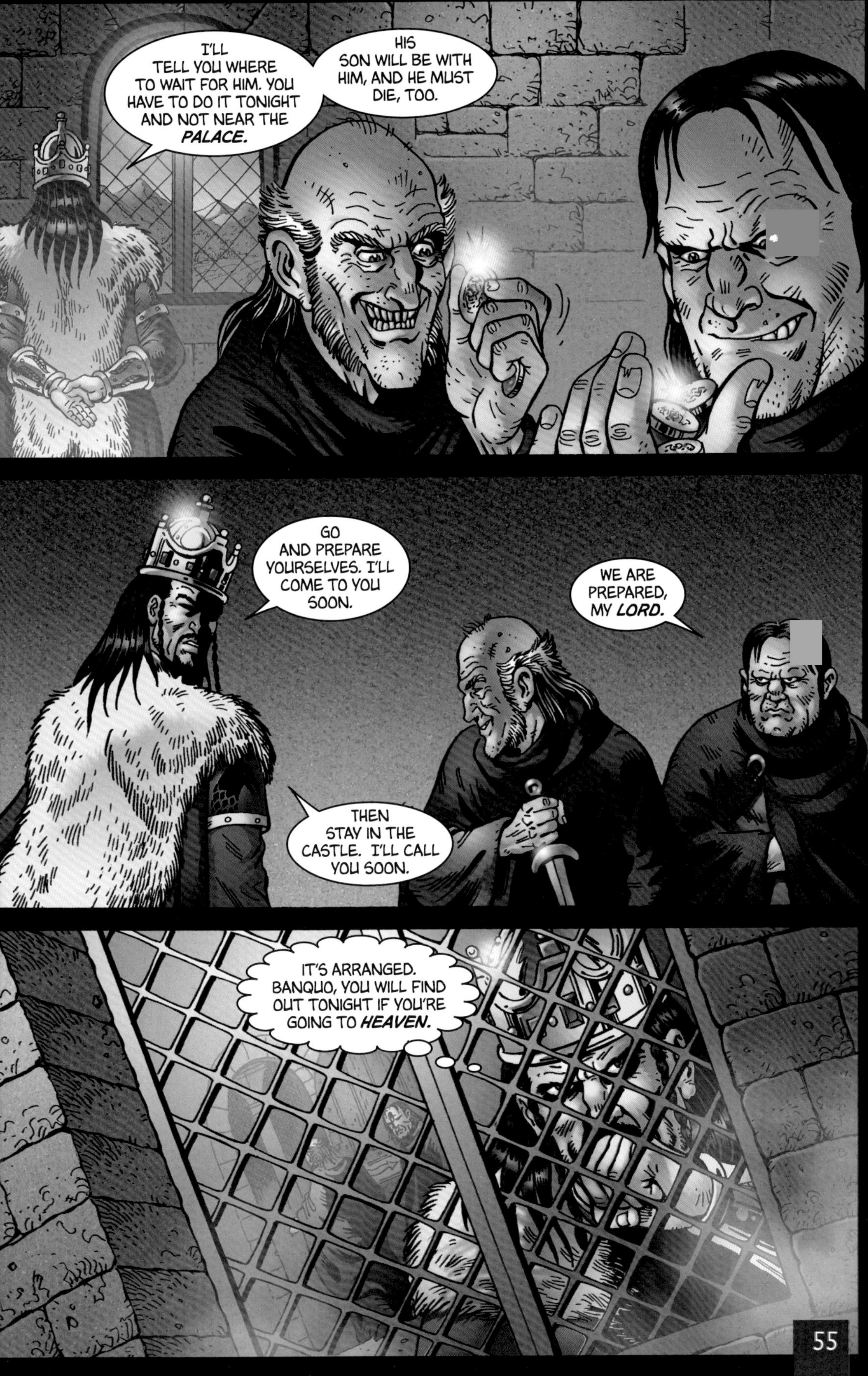
I'LL TELL YOU WHERE TO WAIT FOR HIM. YOU HAVE TO DO IT TONIGHT AND NOT NEAR THE *PALACE.*
HIS SON WILL BE WITH HIM, AND HE MUST DIE, TOO.
GO AND PREPARE YOURSELVES. I'LL COME TO YOU SOON.
WE ARE PREPARED, MY *LORD.*
THEN STAY IN THE CASTLE. I'LL CALL YOU SOON.
IT'S ARRANGED. BANQUO, YOU WILL FIND OUT TONIGHT IF YOU'RE GOING TO *HEAVEN.*

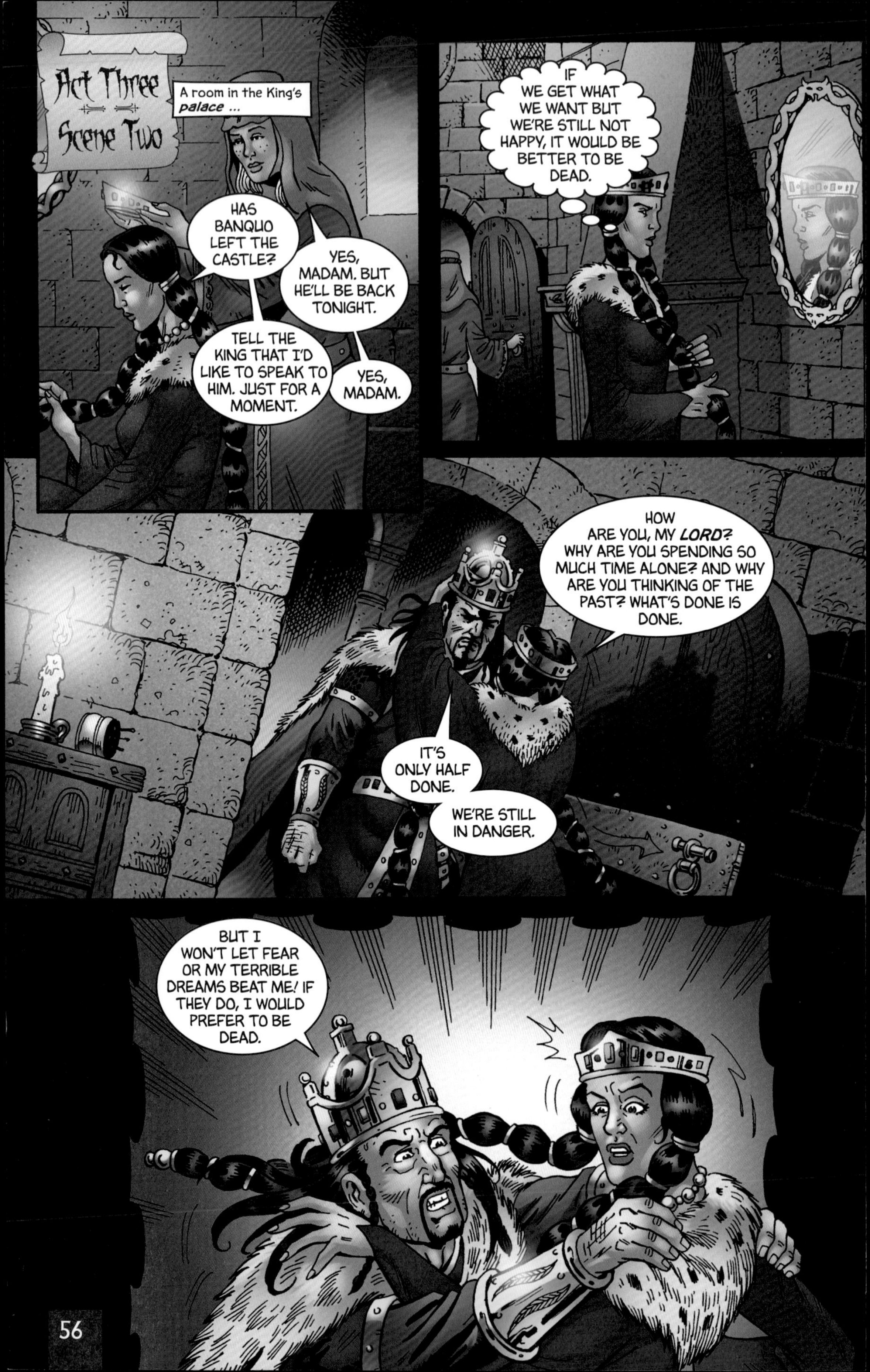
Act Three
Scene Two
A room in the King's *palace* ...
HAS BANQUO LEFT THE CASTLE?
YES, MADAM. BUT HE'LL BE BACK TONIGHT.
TELL THE KING THAT I'D LIKE TO SPEAK TO HIM. JUST FOR A MOMENT.
YES, MADAM.
IF WE GET WHAT WE WANT BUT WE'RE STILL NOT HAPPY, IT WOULD BE BETTER TO BE DEAD.
HOW ARE YOU, MY *LORD*? WHY ARE YOU SPENDING SO MUCH TIME ALONE? AND WHY ARE YOU THINKING OF THE PAST? WHAT'S DONE IS DONE.
IT'S ONLY HALF DONE.
WE'RE STILL IN DANGER.
BUT I WON'T LET FEAR OR MY TERRIBLE DREAMS BEAT ME! IF THEY DO, I WOULD PREFER TO BE DEAD.

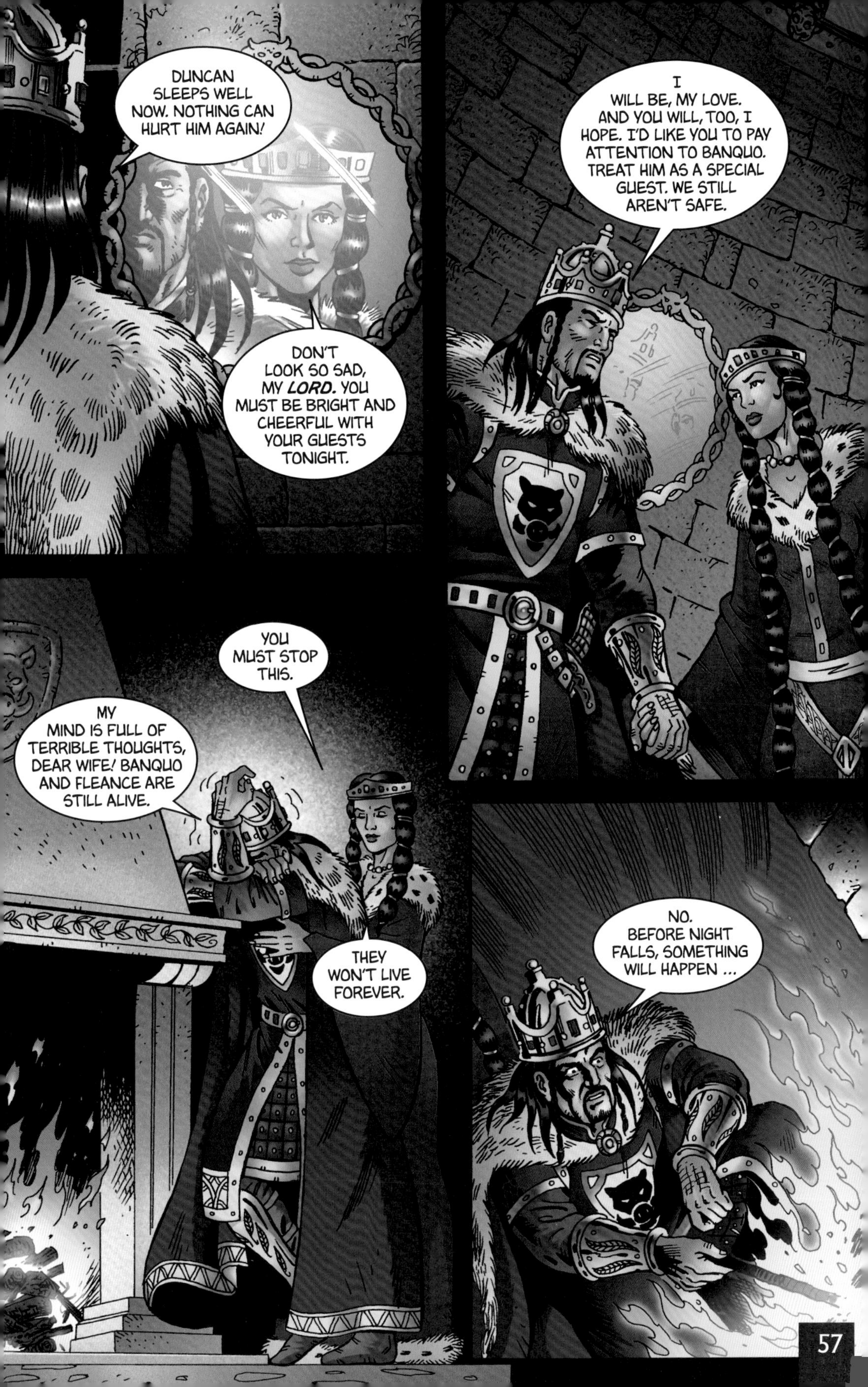
DUNCAN SLEEPS WELL NOW. NOTHING CAN HURT HIM AGAIN!
DON'T LOOK SO SAD, MY **LORD.** YOU MUST BE BRIGHT AND CHEERFUL WITH YOUR GUESTS TONIGHT.
I WILL BE, MY LOVE. AND YOU WILL, TOO, I HOPE. I'D LIKE YOU TO PAY ATTENTION TO BANQUO. TREAT HIM AS A SPECIAL GUEST. WE STILL AREN'T SAFE.
YOU MUST STOP THIS.
MY MIND IS FULL OF TERRIBLE THOUGHTS, DEAR WIFE! BANQUO AND FLEANCE ARE STILL ALIVE.
THEY WON'T LIVE FOREVER.
NO. BEFORE NIGHT FALLS, SOMETHING WILL HAPPEN ...

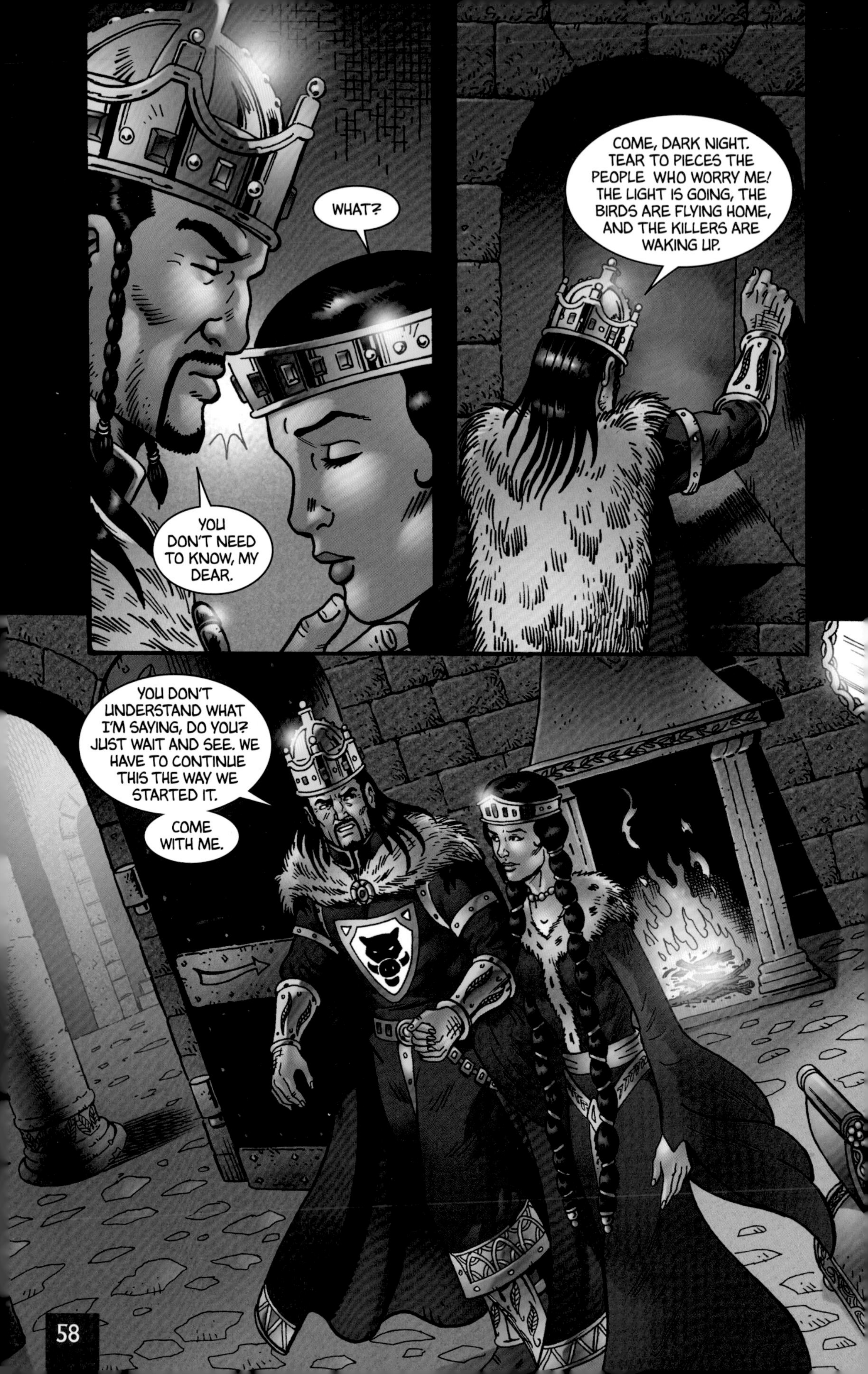
WHAT?
YOU DON'T NEED TO KNOW, MY DEAR.
COME, DARK NIGHT. TEAR TO PIECES THE PEOPLE WHO WORRY ME! THE LIGHT IS GOING, THE BIRDS ARE FLYING HOME, AND THE KILLERS ARE WAKING UP.
YOU DON'T UNDERSTAND WHAT I'M SAYING, DO YOU? JUST WAIT AND SEE. WE HAVE TO CONTINUE THIS THE WAY WE STARTED IT.
COME WITH ME.

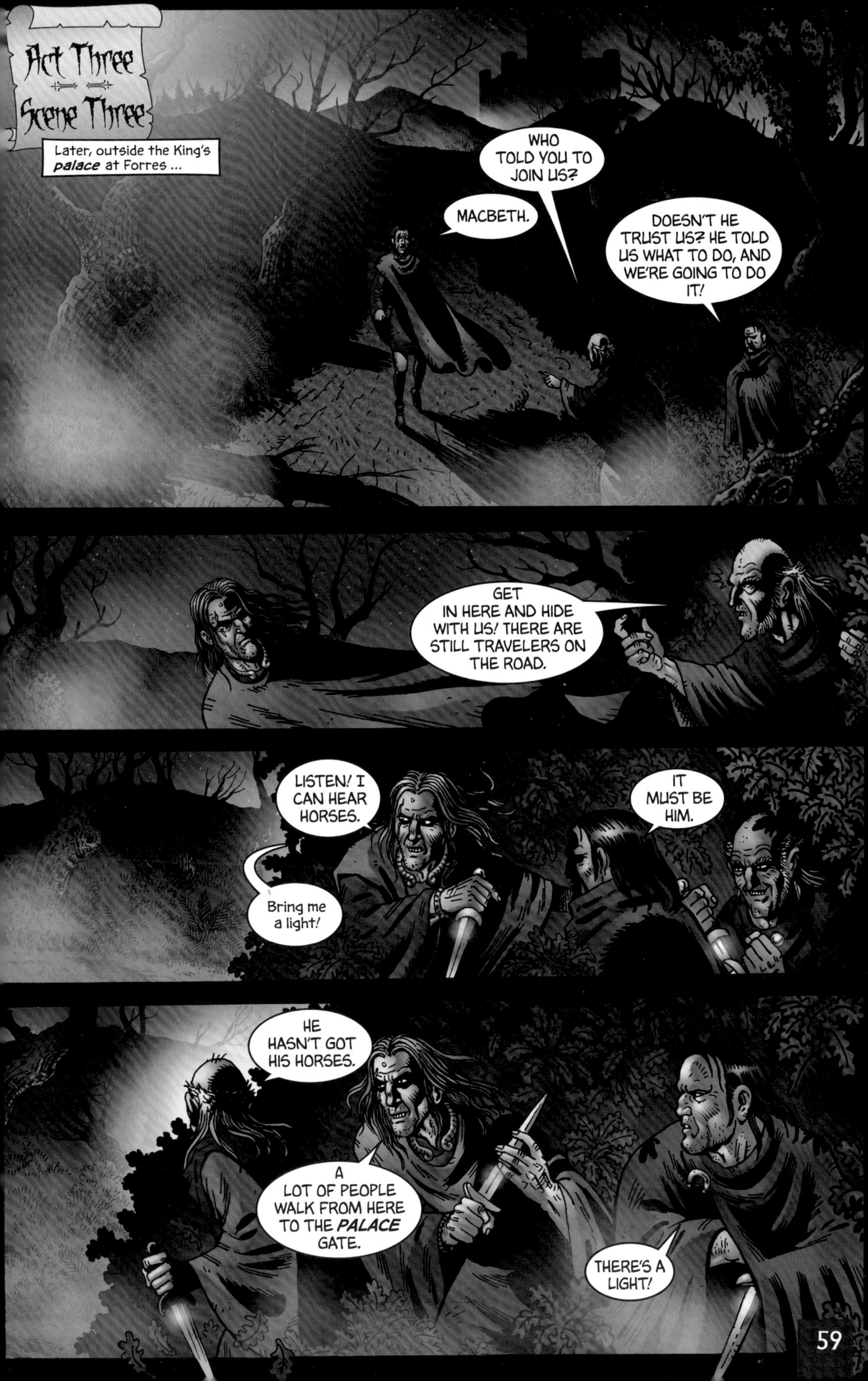
Act Three
Scene Three
Later, outside the King's *palace* at Forres ...
WHO TOLD YOU TO JOIN US?
MACBETH.
DOESN'T HE TRUST US? HE TOLD US WHAT TO DO, AND WE'RE GOING TO DO IT!
GET IN HERE AND HIDE WITH US! THERE ARE STILL TRAVELERS ON THE ROAD.
LISTEN! I CAN HEAR HORSES.
Bring me a light!
IT MUST BE HIM.
HE HASN'T GOT HIS HORSES.
A LOT OF PEOPLE WALK FROM HERE TO THE *PALACE* GATE.
THERE'S A LIGHT!

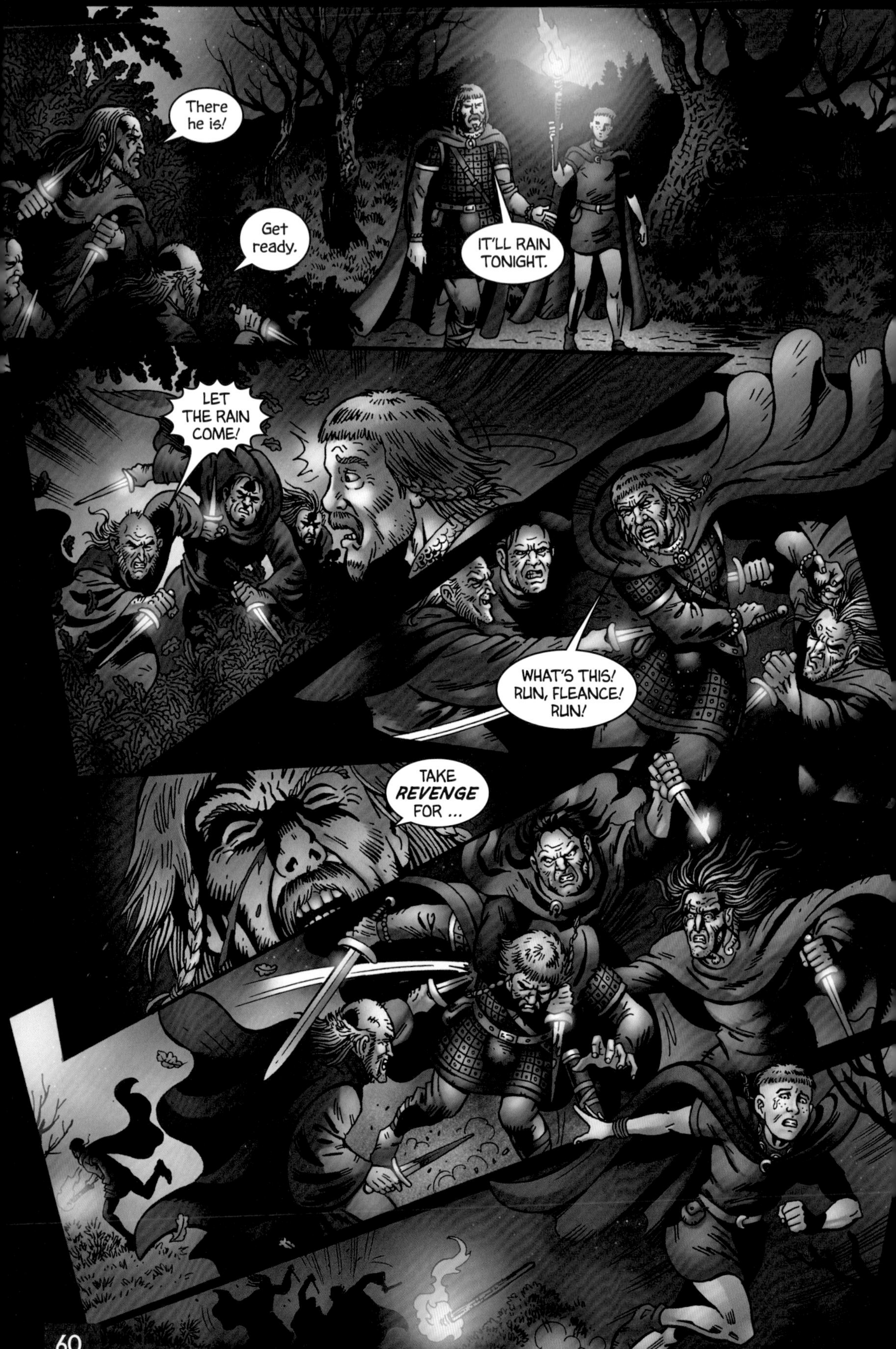
There he is!
Get ready.
IT'LL RAIN TONIGHT.
LET THE RAIN COME!
WHAT'S THIS! RUN, FLEANCE! RUN!
TAKE *REVENGE* FOR ...

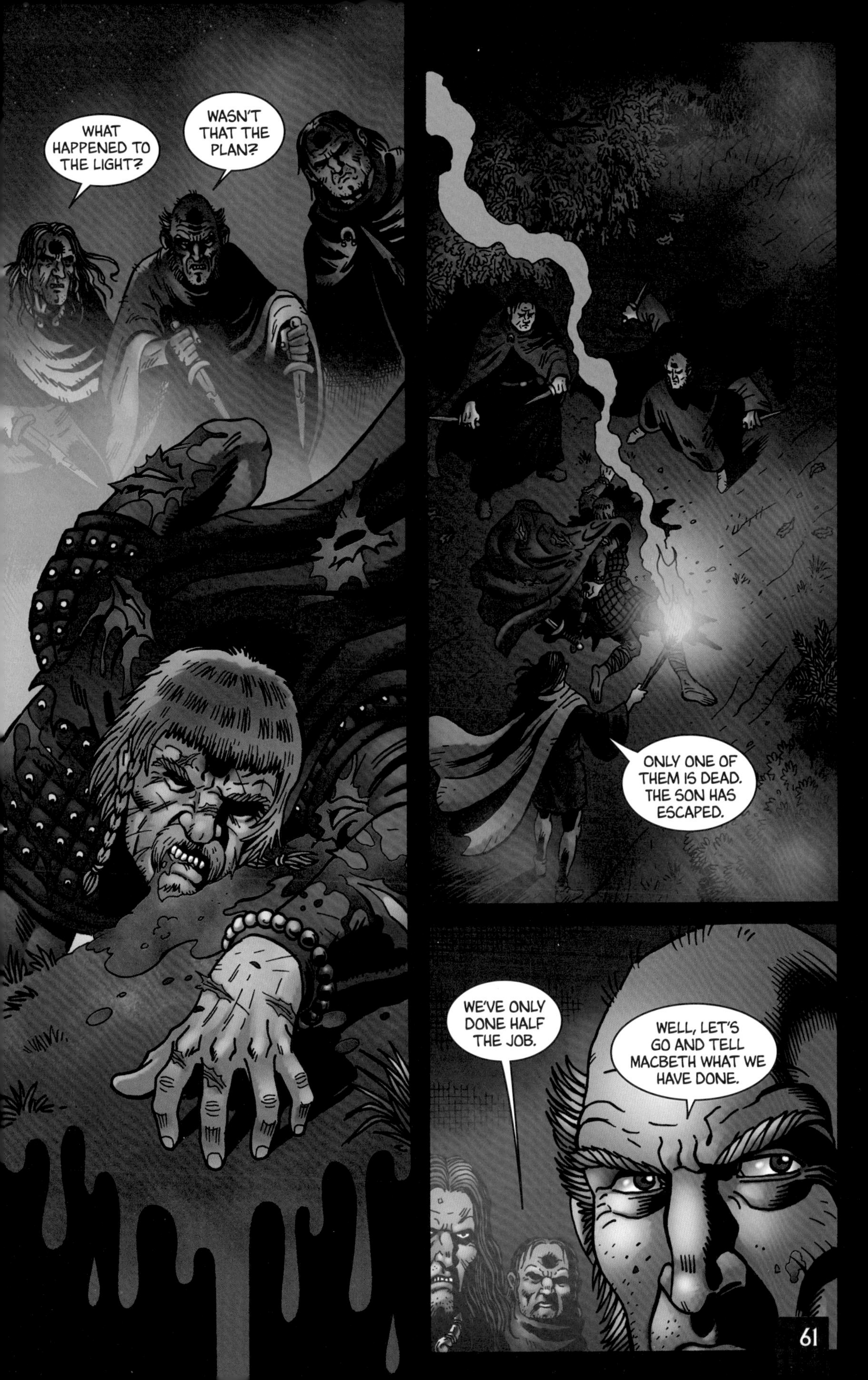
WHAT HAPPENED TO THE LIGHT?
WASN'T THAT THE PLAN?
ONLY ONE OF THEM IS DEAD. THE SON HAS ESCAPED.
WE'VE ONLY DONE HALF THE JOB.
WELL, LET'S GO AND TELL MACBETH WHAT WE HAVE DONE.

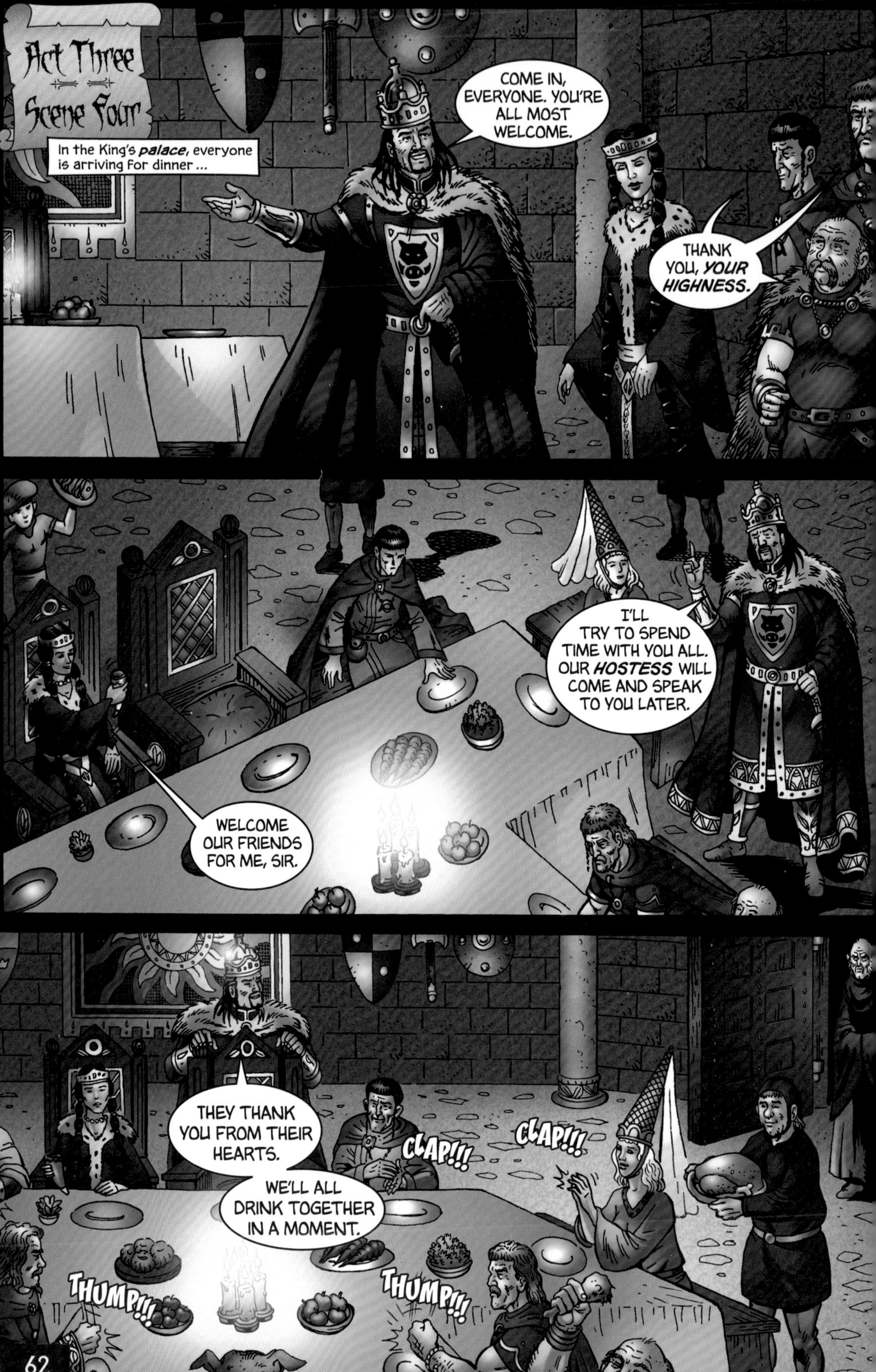
Act Three Scene Four
In the King's *palace*, everyone is arriving for dinner ...
COME IN, EVERYONE. YOU'RE ALL MOST WELCOME.
THANK YOU, *YOUR HIGHNESS.*
I'LL TRY TO SPEND TIME WITH YOU ALL. OUR *HOSTESS* WILL COME AND SPEAK TO YOU LATER.
WELCOME OUR FRIENDS FOR ME, SIR.
THEY THANK YOU FROM THEIR HEARTS.
WE'LL ALL DRINK TOGETHER IN A MOMENT.
CLAP!!!
CLAP!!!
THUMP!!!
THUMP!!!

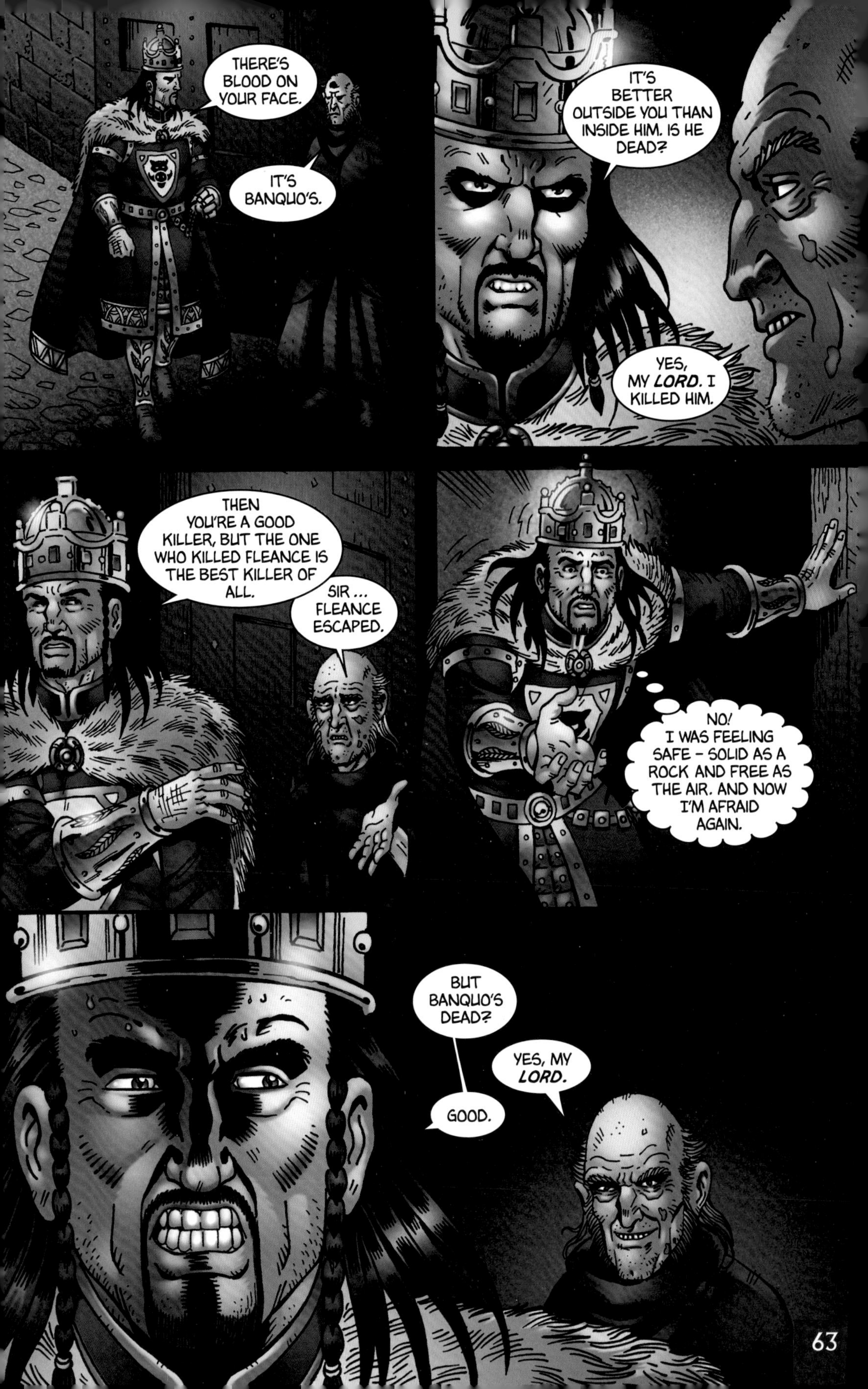
THERE'S BLOOD ON YOUR FACE.
IT'S BANQUO'S.
IT'S BETTER OUTSIDE YOU THAN INSIDE HIM. IS HE DEAD?
YES, MY **LORD.** I KILLED HIM.
THEN YOU'RE A GOOD KILLER, BUT THE ONE WHO KILLED FLEANCE IS THE BEST KILLER OF ALL.
SIR ... FLEANCE ESCAPED.
NO! I WAS FEELING SAFE – SOLID AS A ROCK AND FREE AS THE AIR. AND NOW I'M AFRAID AGAIN.
BUT BANQUO'S DEAD?
YES, MY **LORD.**
GOOD.

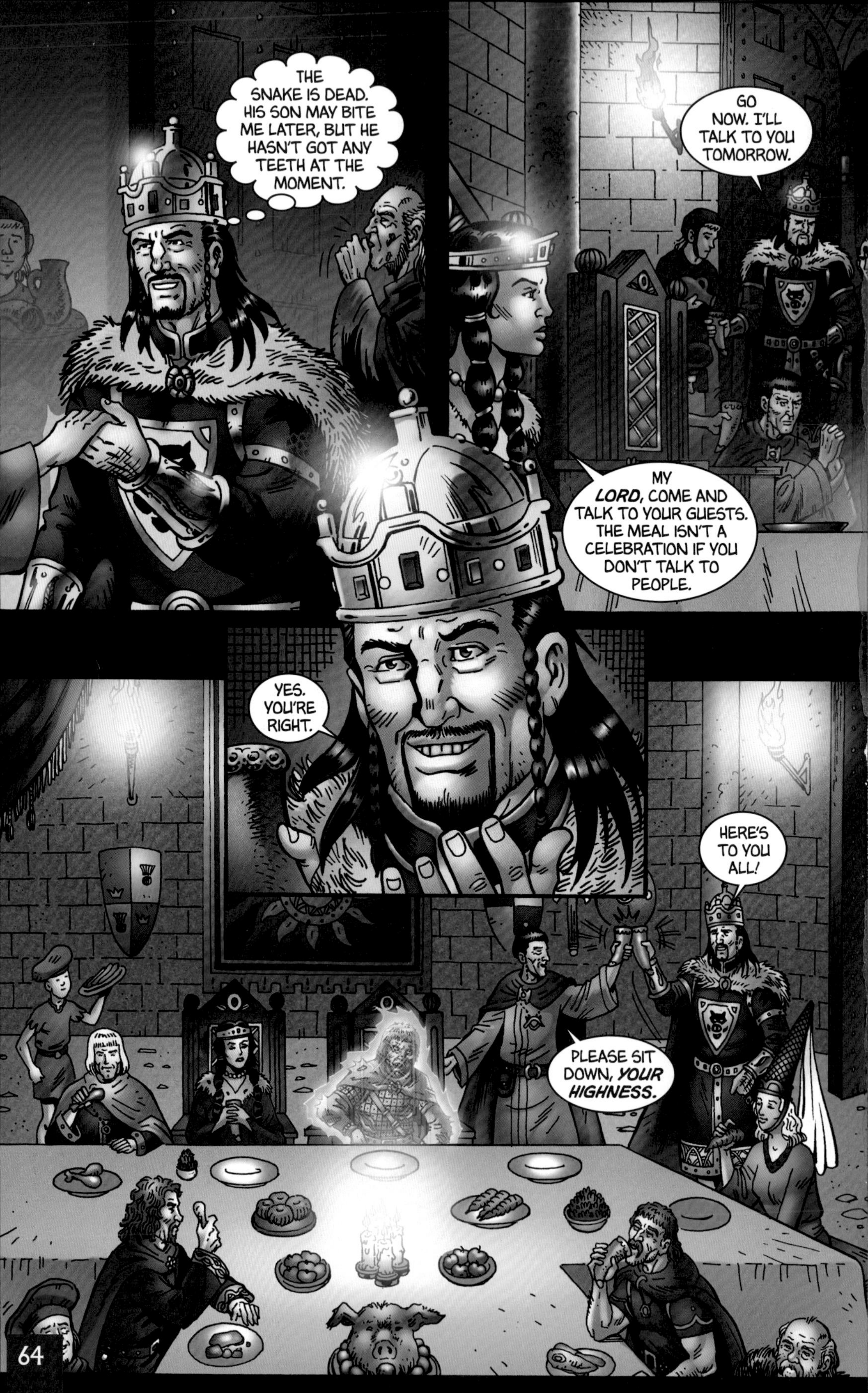
THE SNAKE IS DEAD. HIS SON MAY BITE ME LATER, BUT HE HASN'T GOT ANY TEETH AT THE MOMENT.
GO NOW. I'LL TALK TO YOU TOMORROW.
MY *LORD*, COME AND TALK TO YOUR GUESTS. THE MEAL ISN'T A CELEBRATION IF YOU DON'T TALK TO PEOPLE.
YES. YOU'RE RIGHT.
HERE'S TO YOU ALL!
PLEASE SIT DOWN, *YOUR HIGHNESS.*

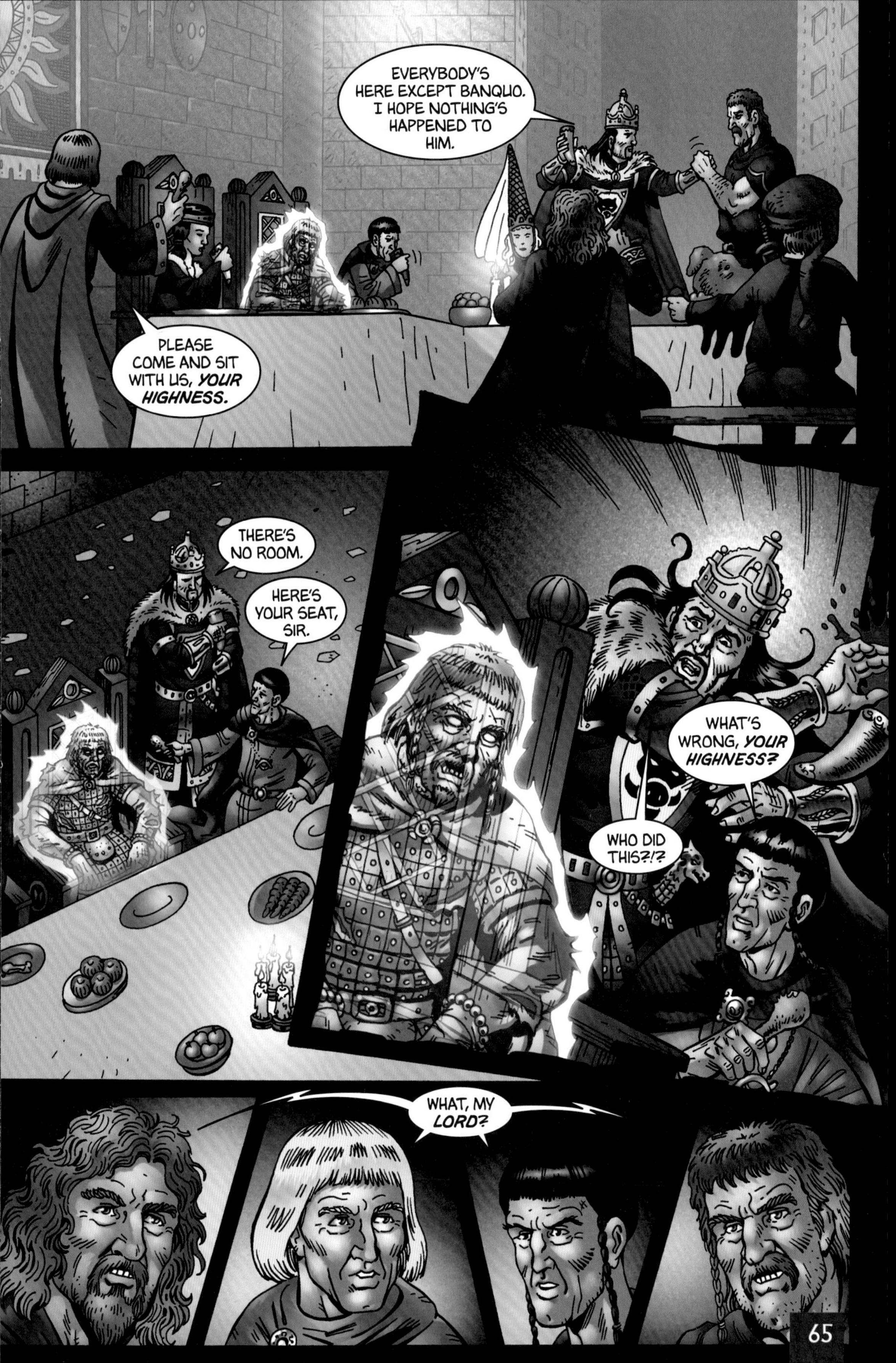
EVERYBODY'S HERE EXCEPT BANQUO. I HOPE NOTHING'S HAPPENED TO HIM.
PLEASE COME AND SIT WITH US, *YOUR HIGHNESS.*
THERE'S NO ROOM.
HERE'S YOUR SEAT, SIR.
WHAT'S WRONG, *YOUR HIGHNESS?*
WHO DID THIS?!?
WHAT, MY *LORD?*

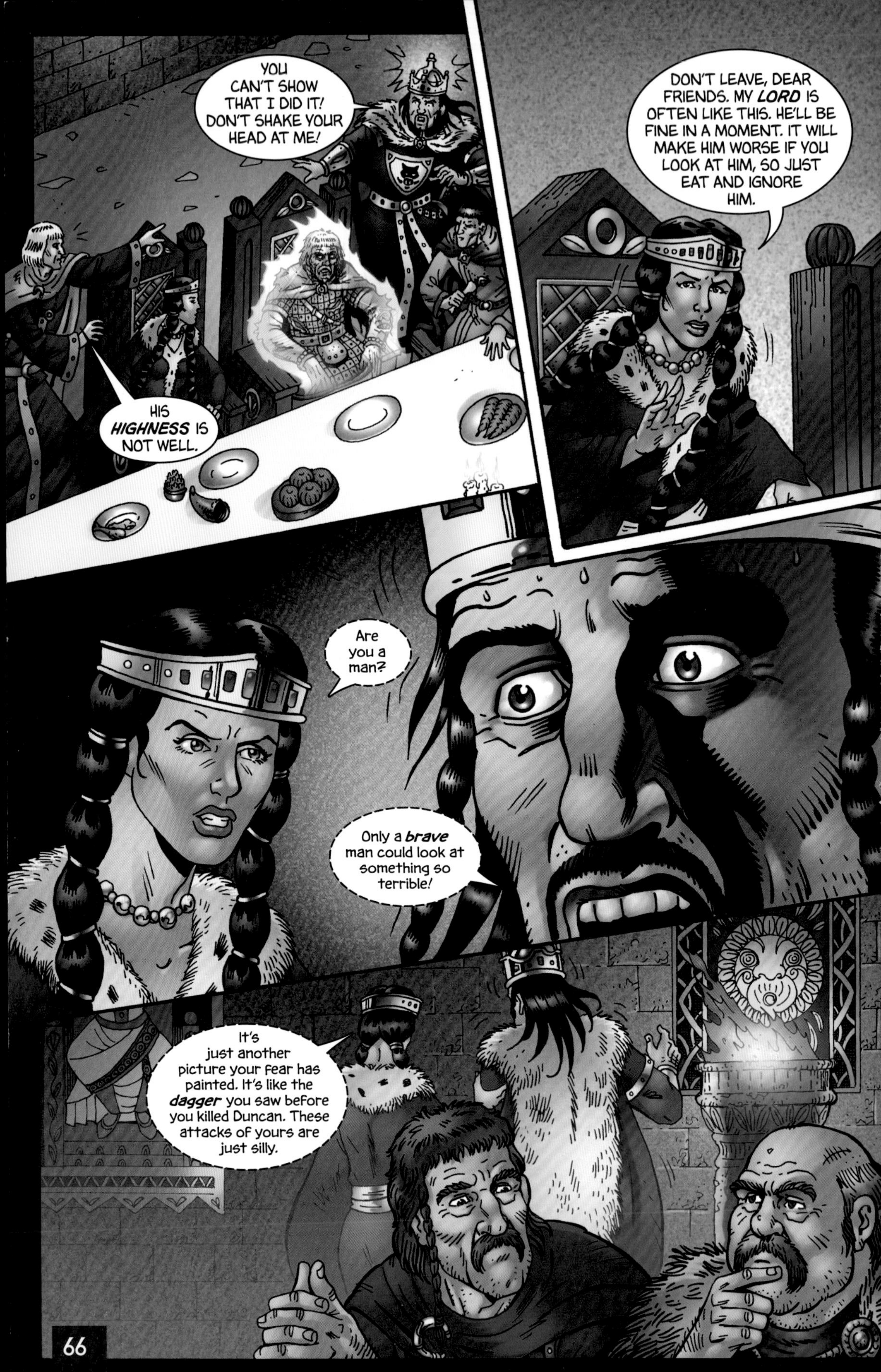

YOU CAN'T SHOW THAT I DID IT! DON'T SHAKE YOUR HEAD AT ME!
HIS *HIGHNESS* IS NOT WELL.
DON'T LEAVE, DEAR FRIENDS. MY *LORD* IS OFTEN LIKE THIS. HE'LL BE FINE IN A MOMENT. IT WILL MAKE HIM WORSE IF YOU LOOK AT HIM, SO JUST EAT AND IGNORE HIM.
Are you a man?
Only a *brave* man could look at something so terrible!
It's just another picture your fear has painted. It's like the *dagger* you saw before you killed Duncan. These attacks of yours are just silly.

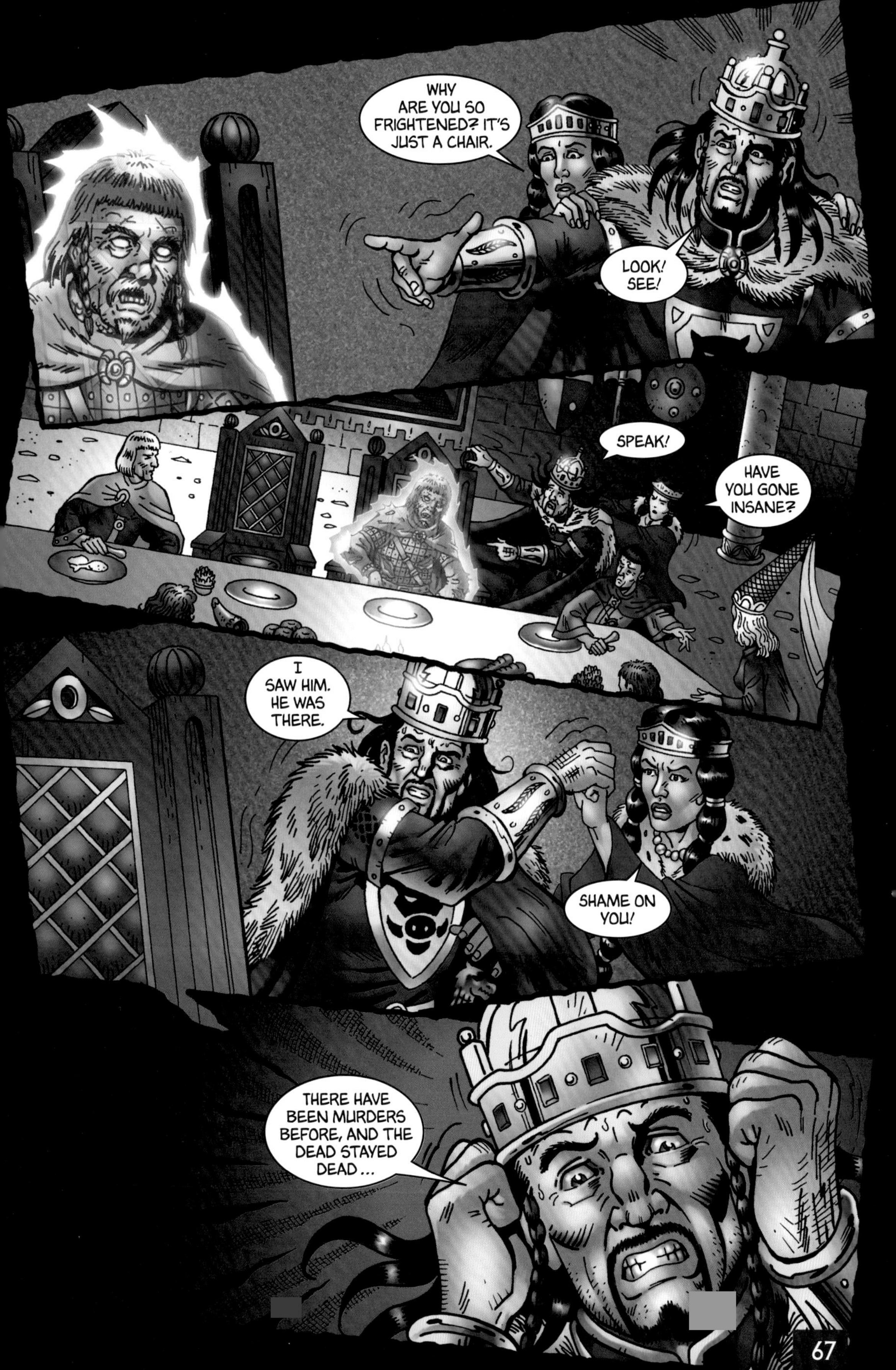
WHY ARE YOU SO FRIGHTENED? IT'S JUST A CHAIR.
LOOK! SEE!
SPEAK!
HAVE YOU GONE INSANE?
I SAW HIM. HE WAS THERE.
SHAME ON YOU!
THERE HAVE BEEN MURDERS BEFORE, AND THE DEAD STAYED DEAD ...

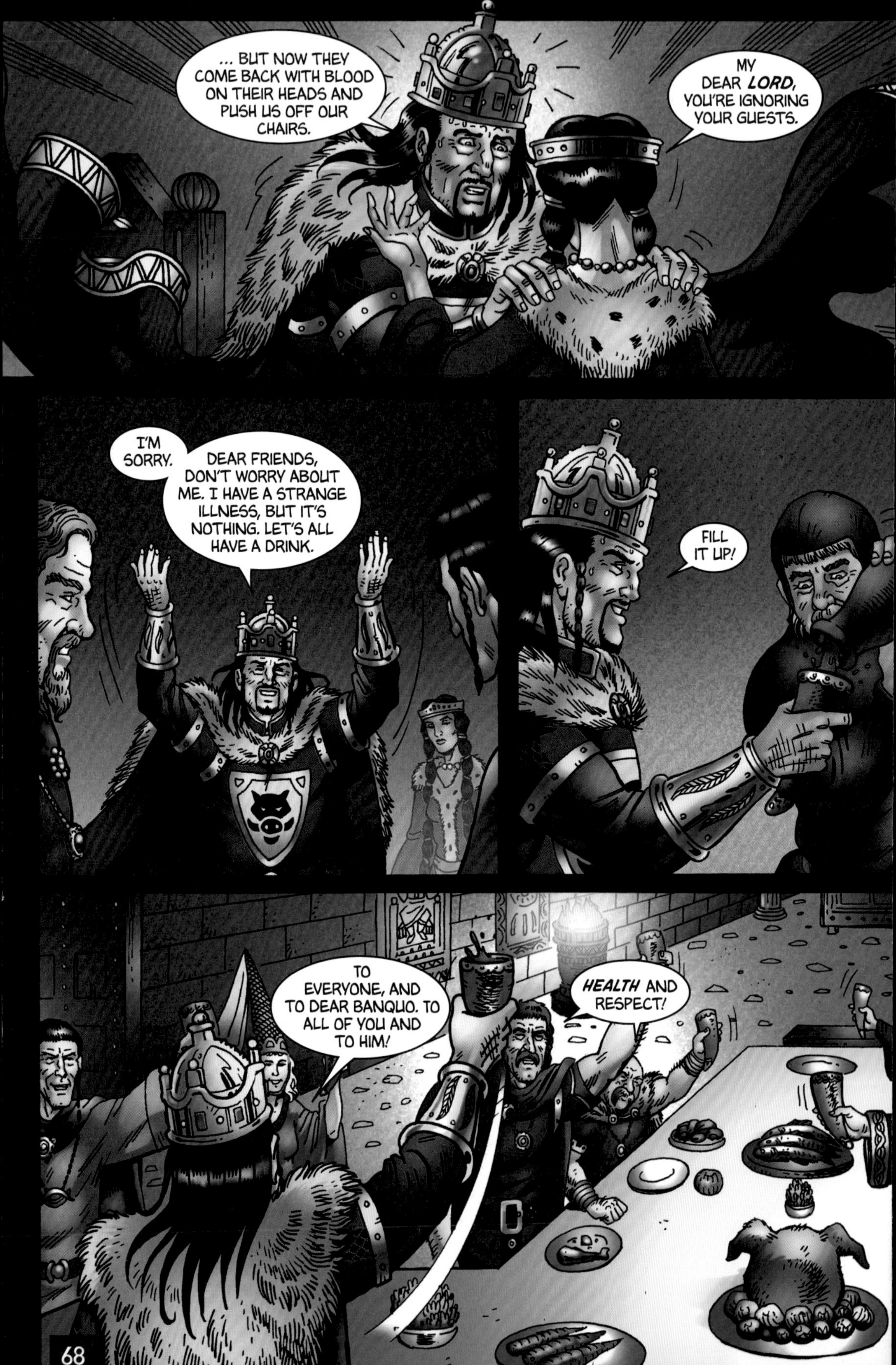
... BUT NOW THEY COME BACK WITH BLOOD ON THEIR HEADS AND PUSH US OFF OUR CHAIRS.
MY DEAR *LORD*, YOU'RE IGNORING YOUR GUESTS.
I'M SORRY.
DEAR FRIENDS, DON'T WORRY ABOUT ME. I HAVE A STRANGE ILLNESS, BUT IT'S NOTHING. LET'S ALL HAVE A DRINK.
FILL IT UP!
TO EVERYONE, AND TO DEAR BANQUO. TO ALL OF YOU AND TO HIM!
HEALTH AND RESPECT!

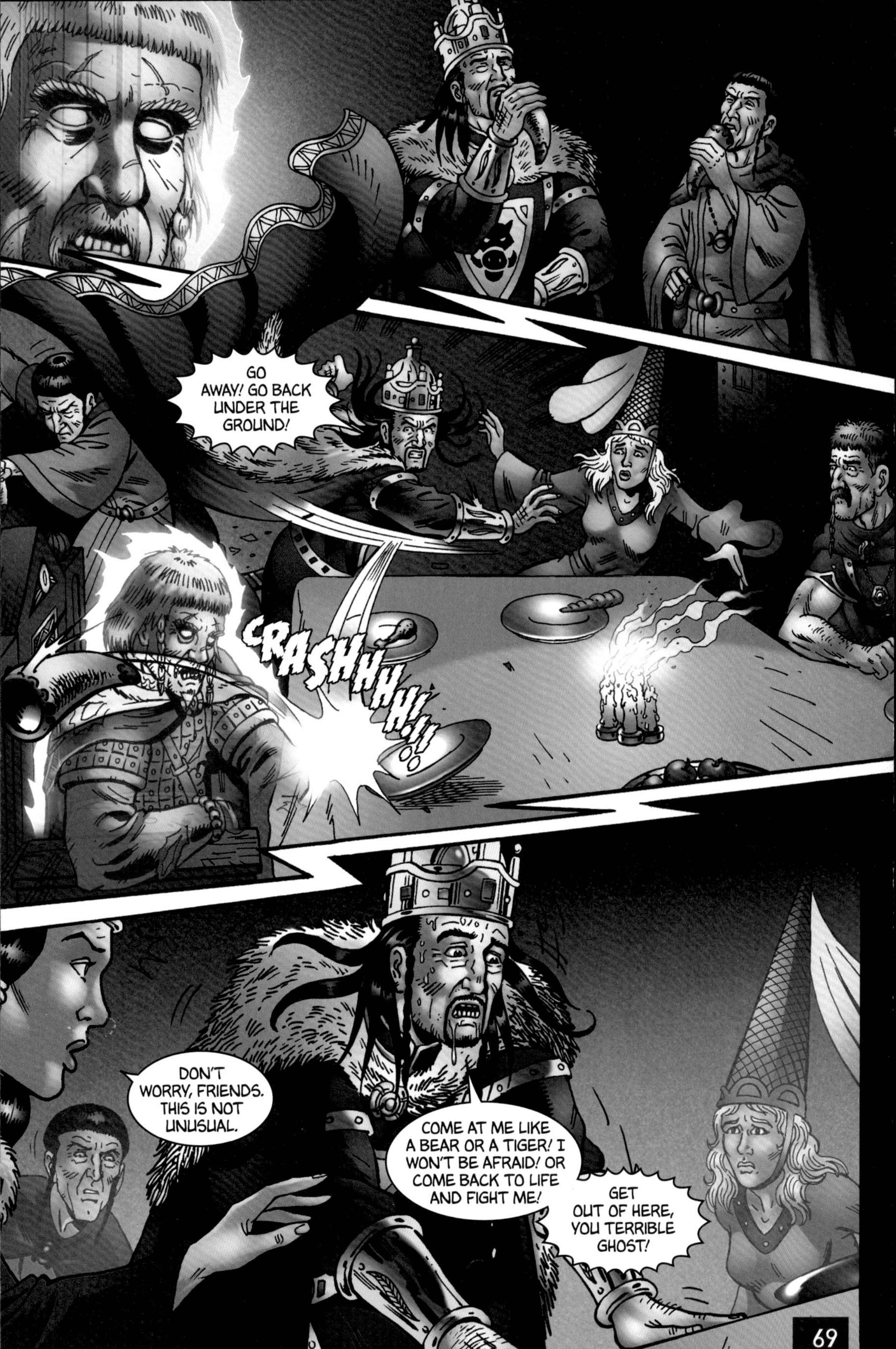
GO AWAY! GO BACK UNDER THE GROUND!
CRASHHHH!!!
DON'T WORRY, FRIENDS. THIS IS NOT UNUSUAL.
COME AT ME LIKE A BEAR OR A TIGER! I WON'T BE AFRAID! OR COME BACK TO LIFE AND FIGHT ME!
GET OUT OF HERE, YOU TERRIBLE GHOST!

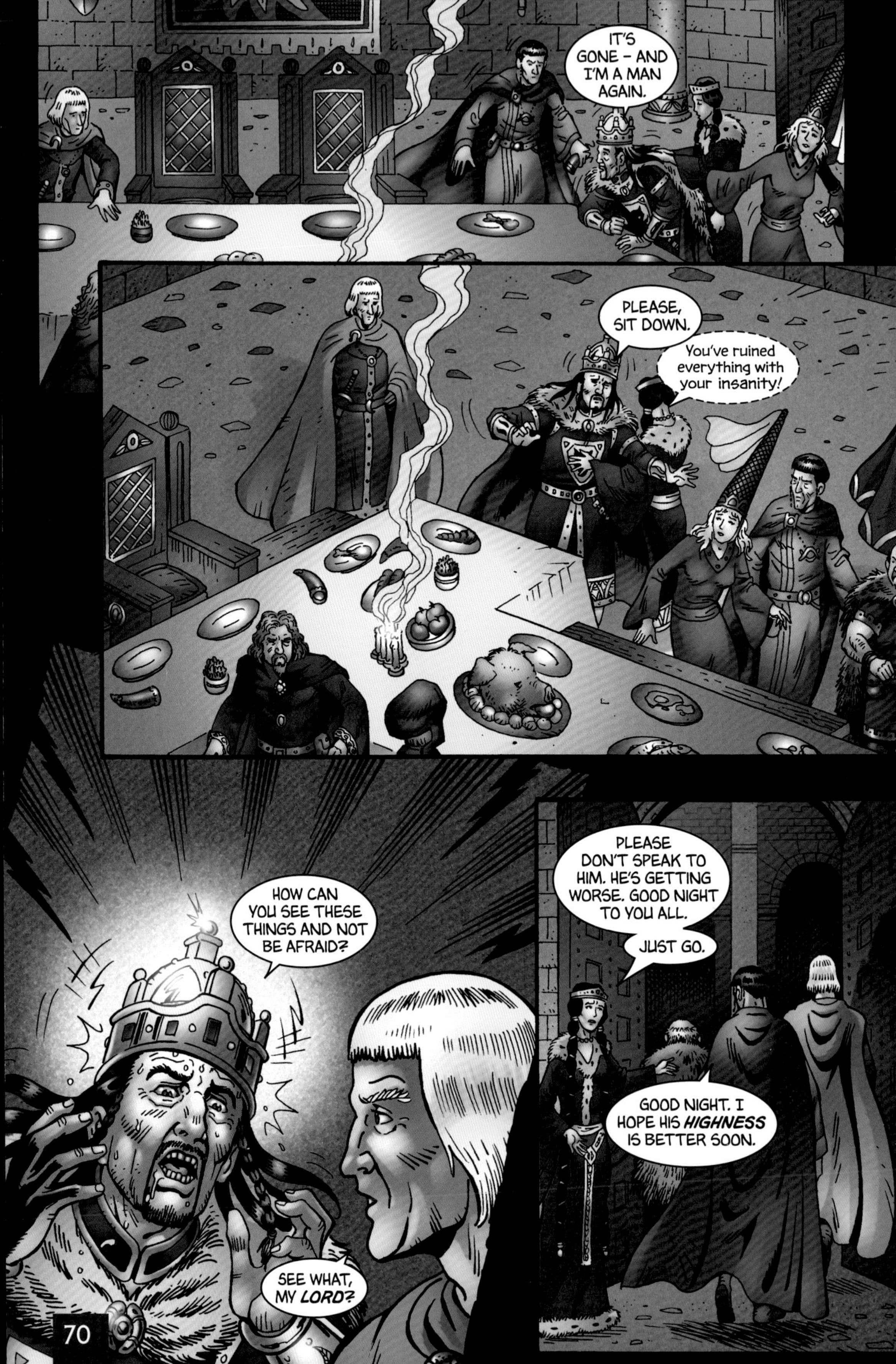
IT'S GONE – AND I'M A MAN AGAIN.
PLEASE, SIT DOWN.
You've ruined everything with your insanity!
HOW CAN YOU SEE THESE THINGS AND NOT BE AFRAID?
SEE WHAT, MY *LORD*?
PLEASE DON'T SPEAK TO HIM. HE'S GETTING WORSE. GOOD NIGHT TO YOU ALL.
JUST GO.
GOOD NIGHT. I HOPE HIS *HIGHNESS* IS BETTER SOON.

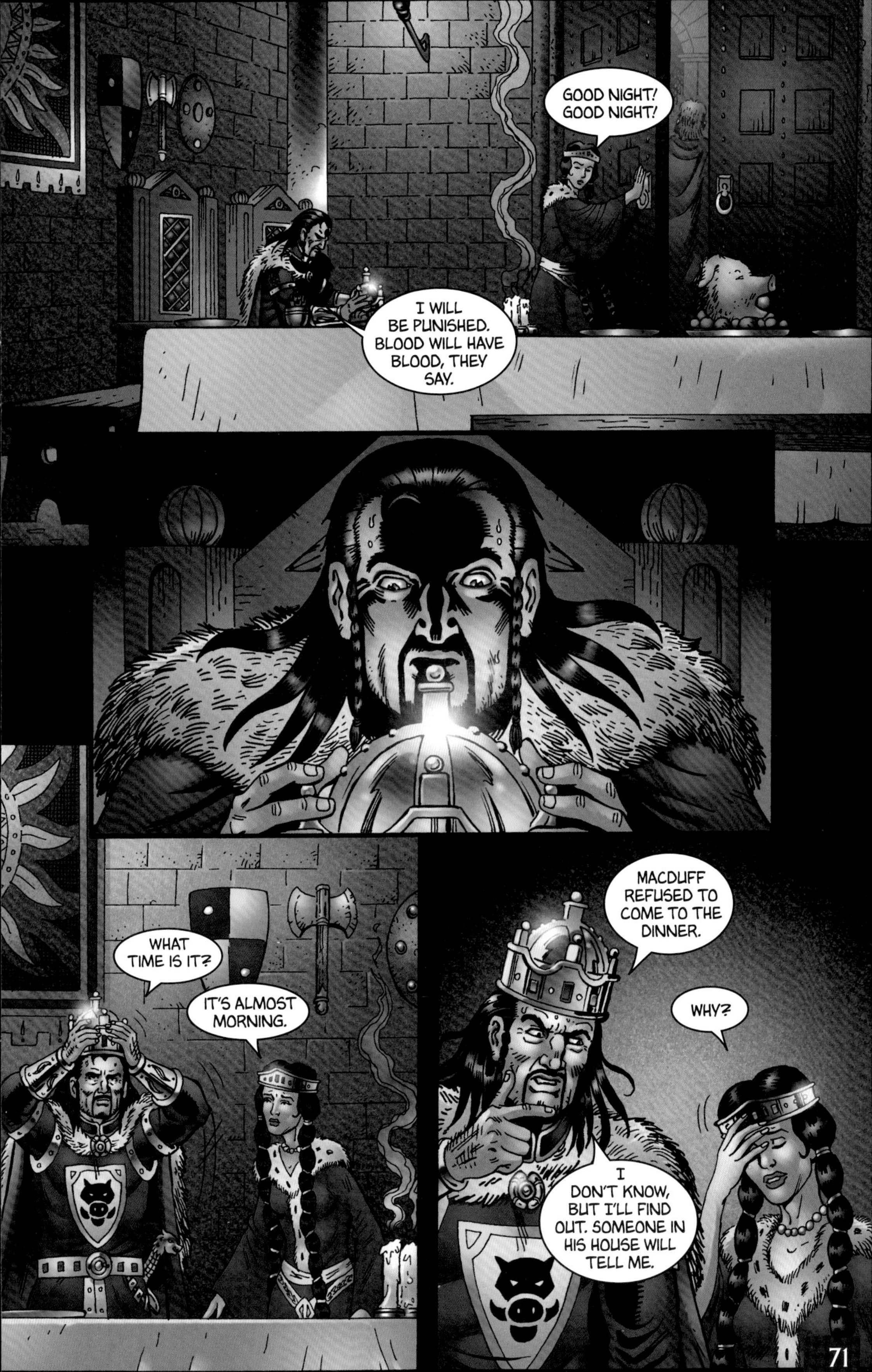
GOOD NIGHT! GOOD NIGHT!
I WILL BE PUNISHED. BLOOD WILL HAVE BLOOD, THEY SAY.
WHAT TIME IS IT?
IT'S ALMOST MORNING.
MACDUFF REFUSED TO COME TO THE DINNER.
WHY?
I DON'T KNOW, BUT I'LL FIND OUT. SOMEONE IN HIS HOUSE WILL TELL ME.

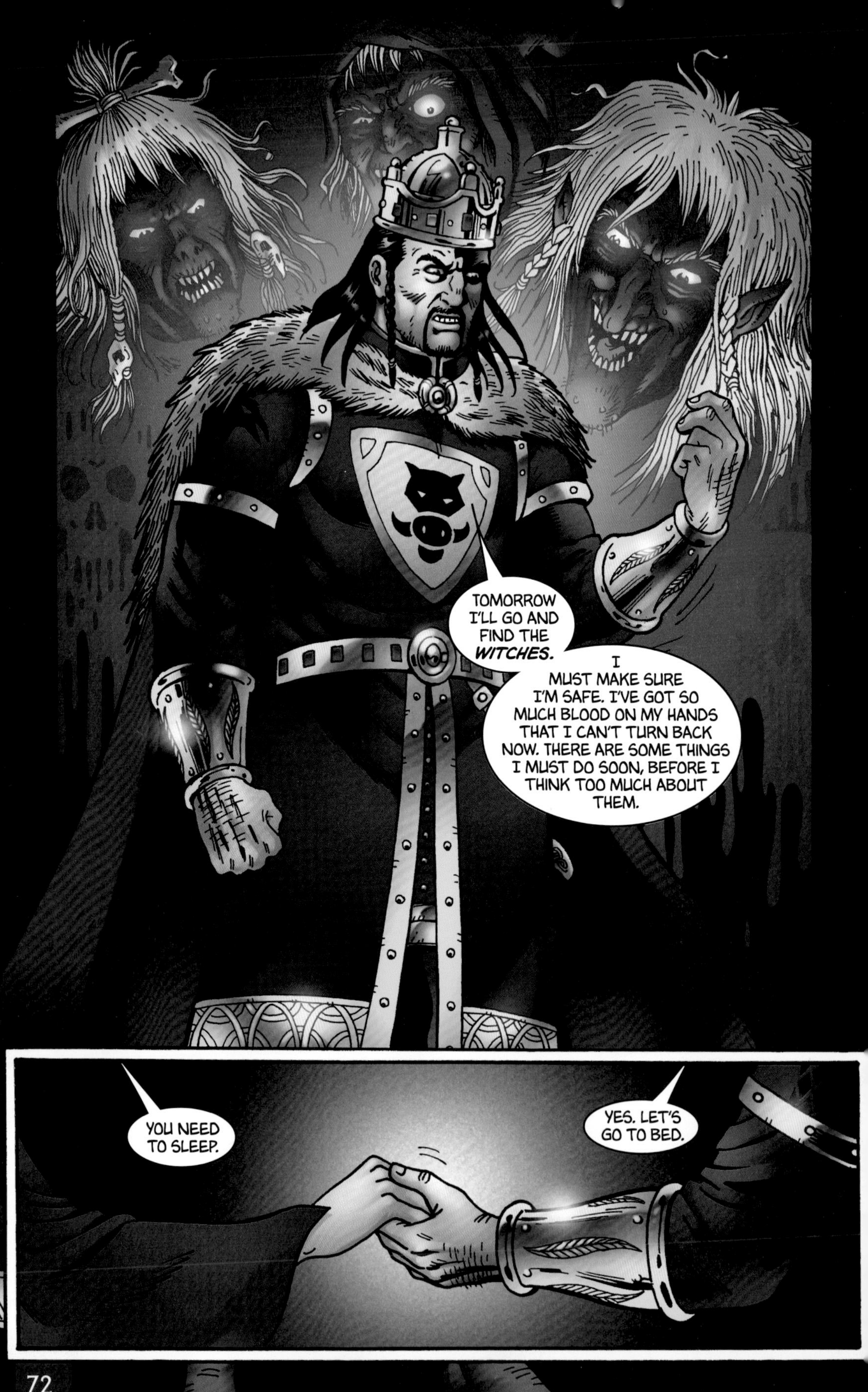
TOMORROW I'LL GO AND FIND THE *WITCHES.*
I MUST MAKE SURE I'M SAFE. I'VE GOT SO MUCH BLOOD ON MY HANDS THAT I CAN'T TURN BACK NOW. THERE ARE SOME THINGS I MUST DO SOON, BEFORE I THINK TOO MUCH ABOUT THEM.
YOU NEED TO SLEEP.
YES. LET'S GO TO BED.

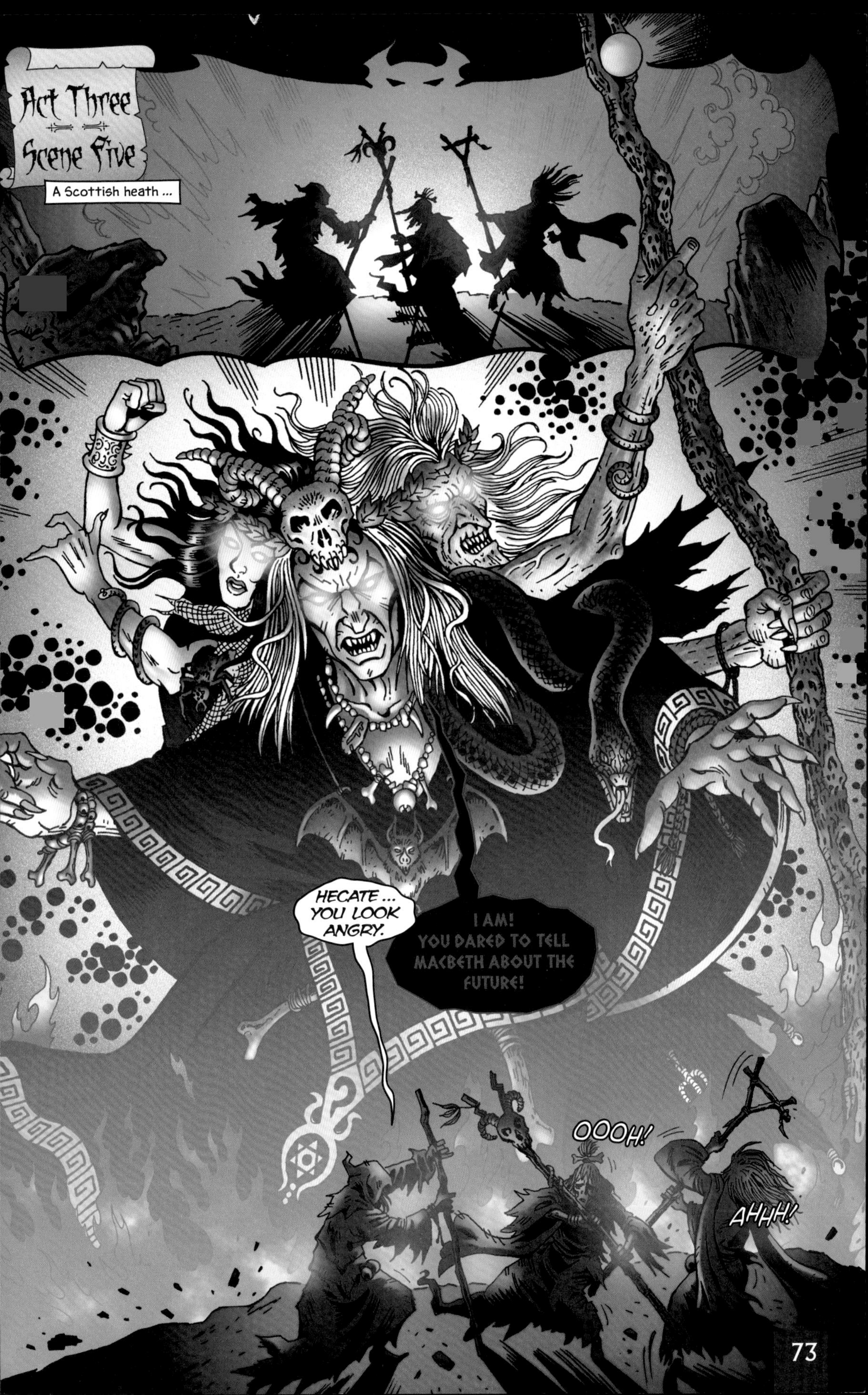
Act Three
Scene Five
A Scottish heath ...
HECATE ... YOU LOOK ANGRY.
I AM! YOU DARED TO TELL MACBETH ABOUT THE FUTURE!
OOOH!
AHHH!

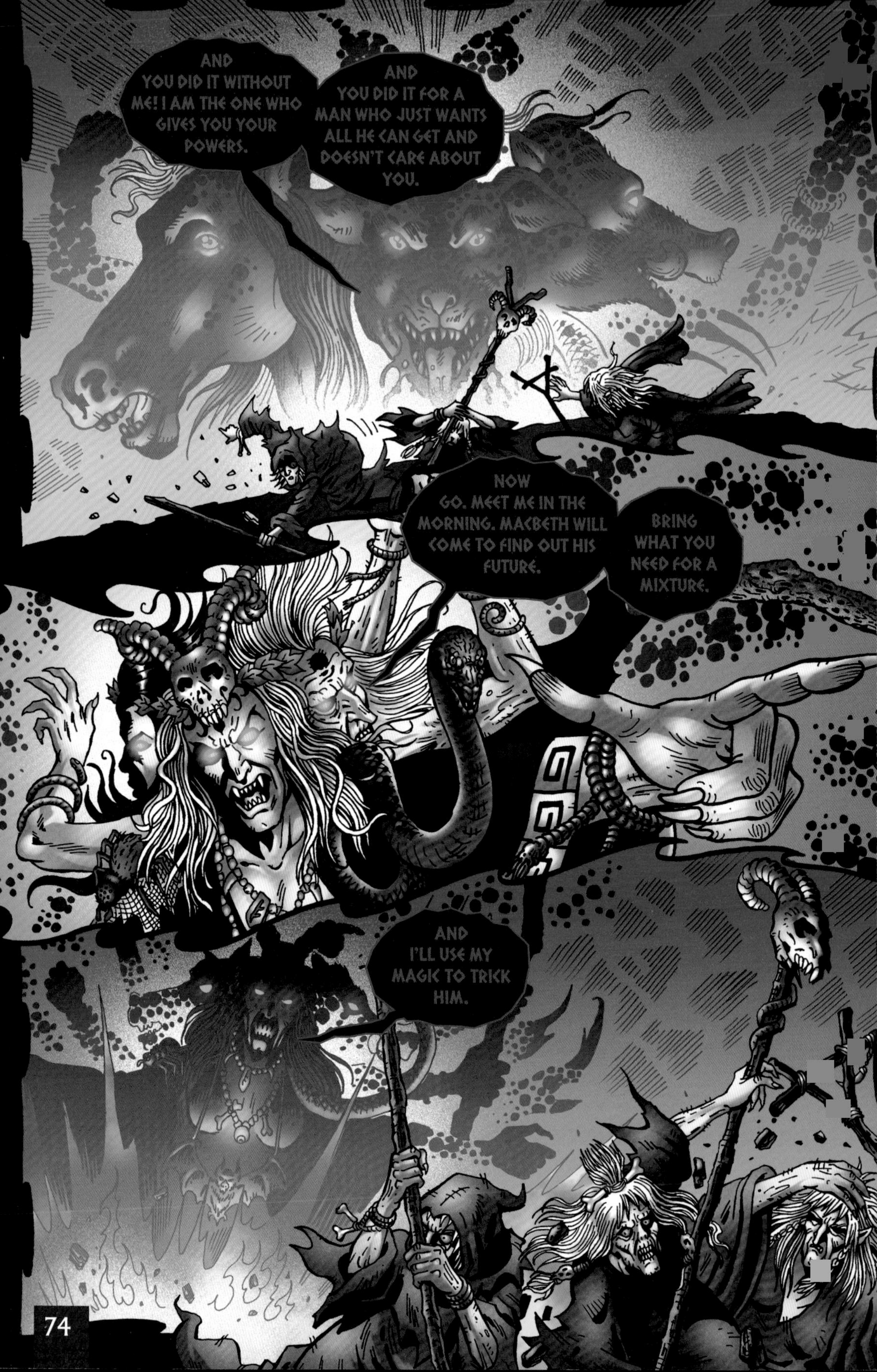
AND YOU DID IT WITHOUT ME! I AM THE ONE WHO GIVES YOU YOUR POWERS.
AND YOU DID IT FOR A MAN WHO JUST WANTS ALL HE CAN GET AND DOESN'T CARE ABOUT YOU.
NOW GO. MEET ME IN THE MORNING. MACBETH WILL COME TO FIND OUT HIS FUTURE.
BRING WHAT YOU NEED FOR A MIXTURE.
AND I'LL USE MY MAGIC TO TRICK HIM.

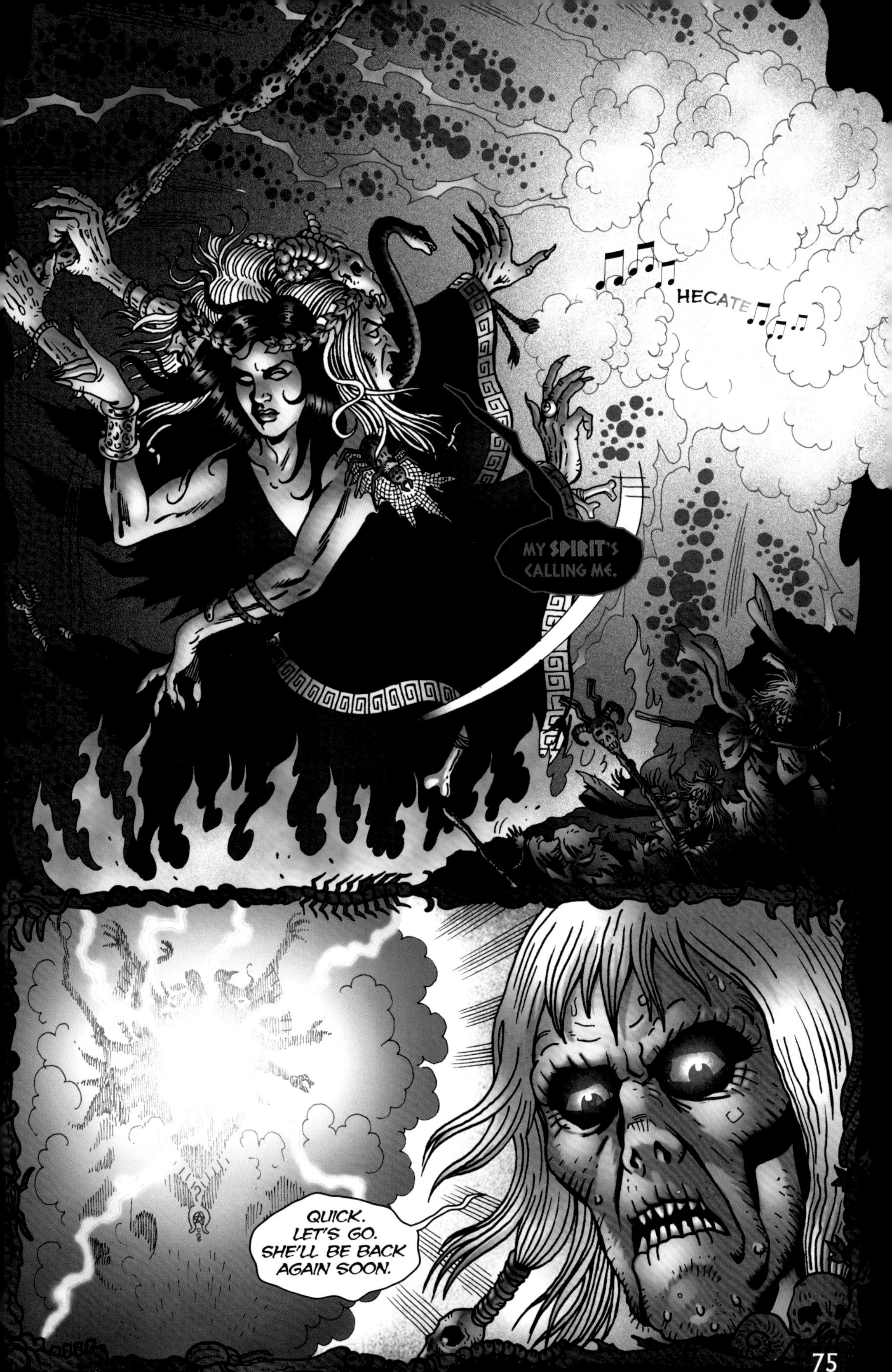
HECATE
MY SPIRIT'S CALLING ME.
QUICK. LET'S GO. SHE'LL BE BACK AGAIN SOON.

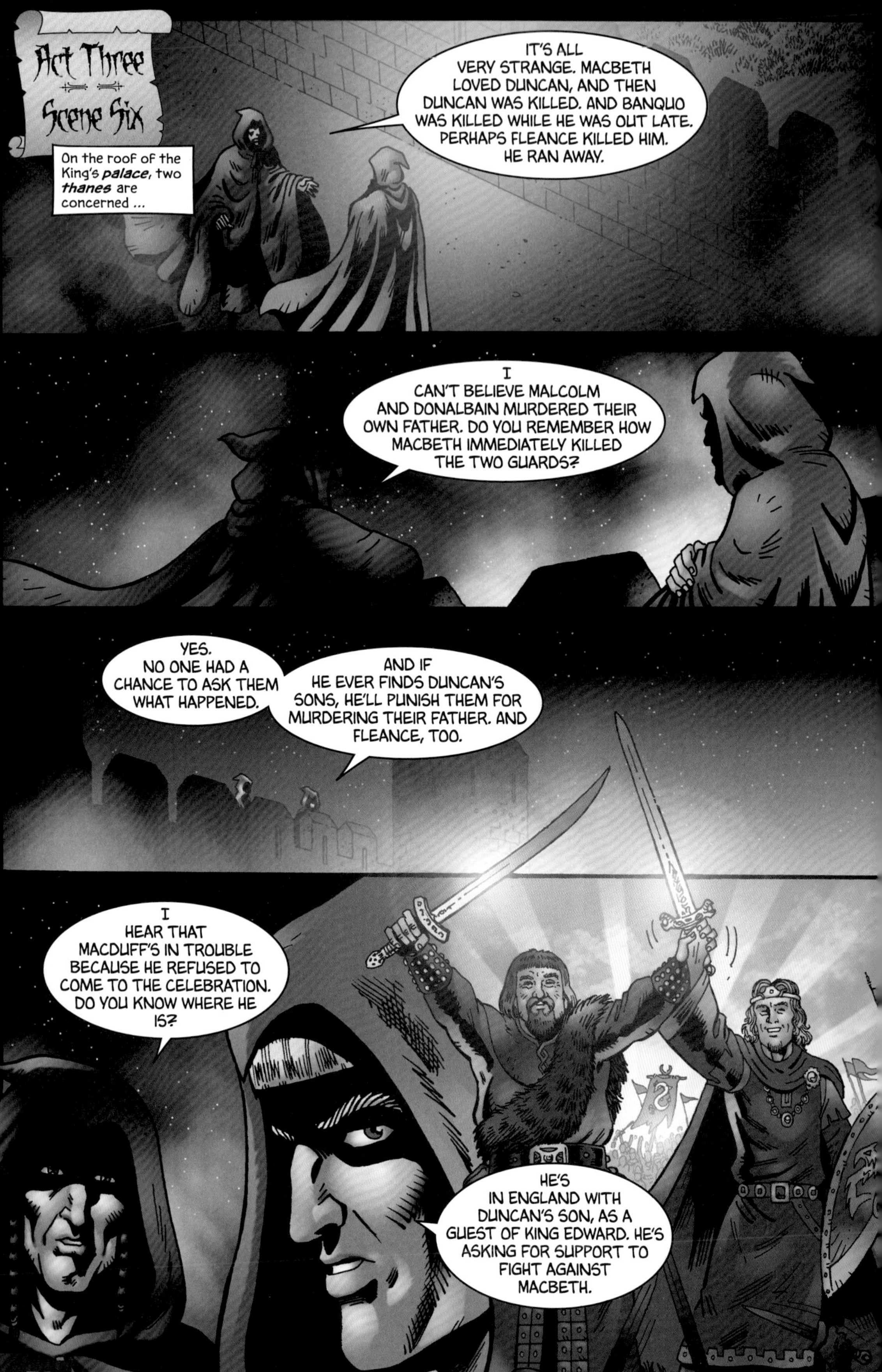
Act Three
Scene Six
On the roof of the King's *palace*, two *thanes* are concerned ...
IT'S ALL VERY STRANGE. MACBETH LOVED DUNCAN, AND THEN DUNCAN WAS KILLED. AND BANQUO WAS KILLED WHILE HE WAS OUT LATE. PERHAPS FLEANCE KILLED HIM. HE RAN AWAY.
I CAN'T BELIEVE MALCOLM AND DONALBAIN MURDERED THEIR OWN FATHER. DO YOU REMEMBER HOW MACBETH IMMEDIATELY KILLED THE TWO GUARDS?
YES. NO ONE HAD A CHANCE TO ASK THEM WHAT HAPPENED.
AND IF HE EVER FINDS DUNCAN'S SONS, HE'LL PUNISH THEM FOR MURDERING THEIR FATHER. AND FLEANCE, TOO.
I HEAR THAT MACDUFF'S IN TROUBLE BECAUSE HE REFUSED TO COME TO THE CELEBRATION. DO YOU KNOW WHERE HE IS?
HE'S IN ENGLAND WITH DUNCAN'S SON, AS A GUEST OF KING EDWARD. HE'S ASKING FOR SUPPORT TO FIGHT AGAINST MACBETH.

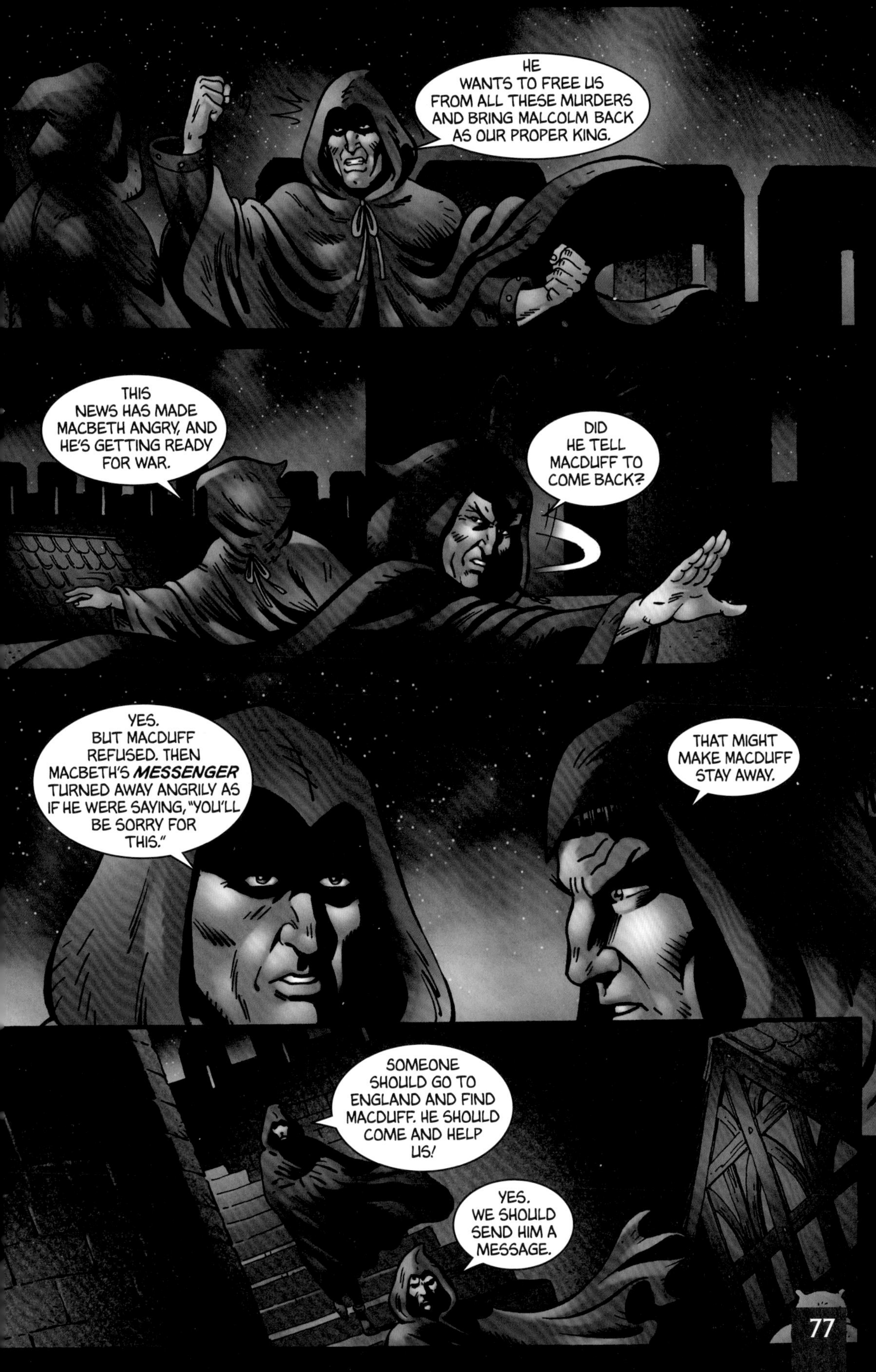
HE WANTS TO FREE US FROM ALL THESE MURDERS AND BRING MALCOLM BACK AS OUR PROPER KING.
THIS NEWS HAS MADE MACBETH ANGRY, AND HE'S GETTING READY FOR WAR.
DID HE TELL MACDUFF TO COME BACK?
YES. BUT MACDUFF REFUSED. THEN MACBETH'S *MESSENGER* TURNED AWAY ANGRILY AS IF HE WERE SAYING, "YOU'LL BE SORRY FOR THIS."
THAT MIGHT MAKE MACDUFF STAY AWAY.
SOMEONE SHOULD GO TO ENGLAND AND FIND MACDUFF. HE SHOULD COME AND HELP US!
YES. WE SHOULD SEND HIM A MESSAGE.

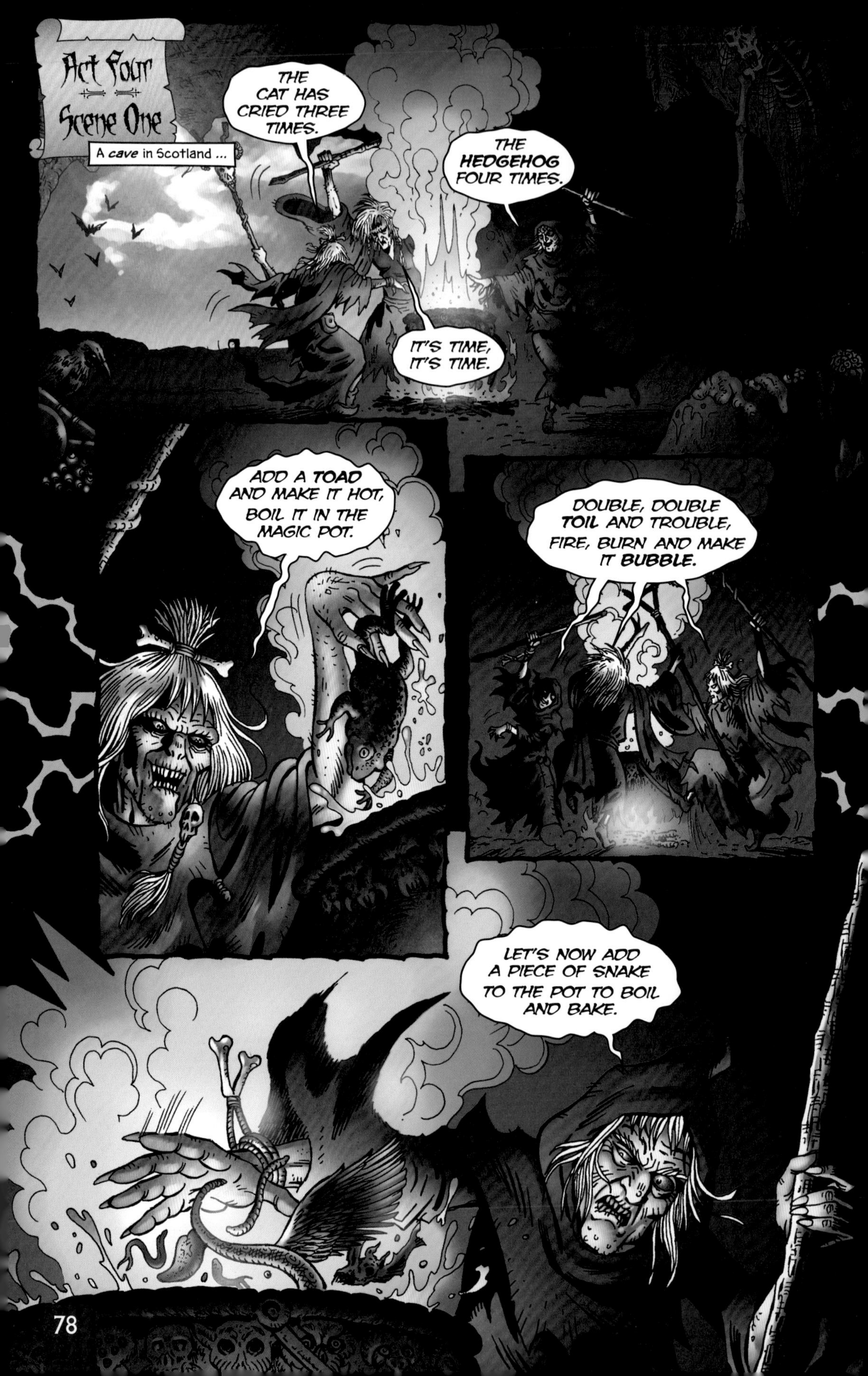
Act Four
Scene One
A *cave* in Scotland ...
THE CAT HAS CRIED THREE TIMES.
THE **HEDGEHOG** FOUR TIMES.
IT'S TIME, IT'S TIME.
ADD A **TOAD** AND MAKE IT HOT, BOIL IT IN THE MAGIC POT.
DOUBLE, DOUBLE **TOIL** AND TROUBLE, FIRE, BURN AND MAKE IT **BUBBLE.**
LET'S NOW ADD A PIECE OF SNAKE TO THE POT TO BOIL AND BAKE.

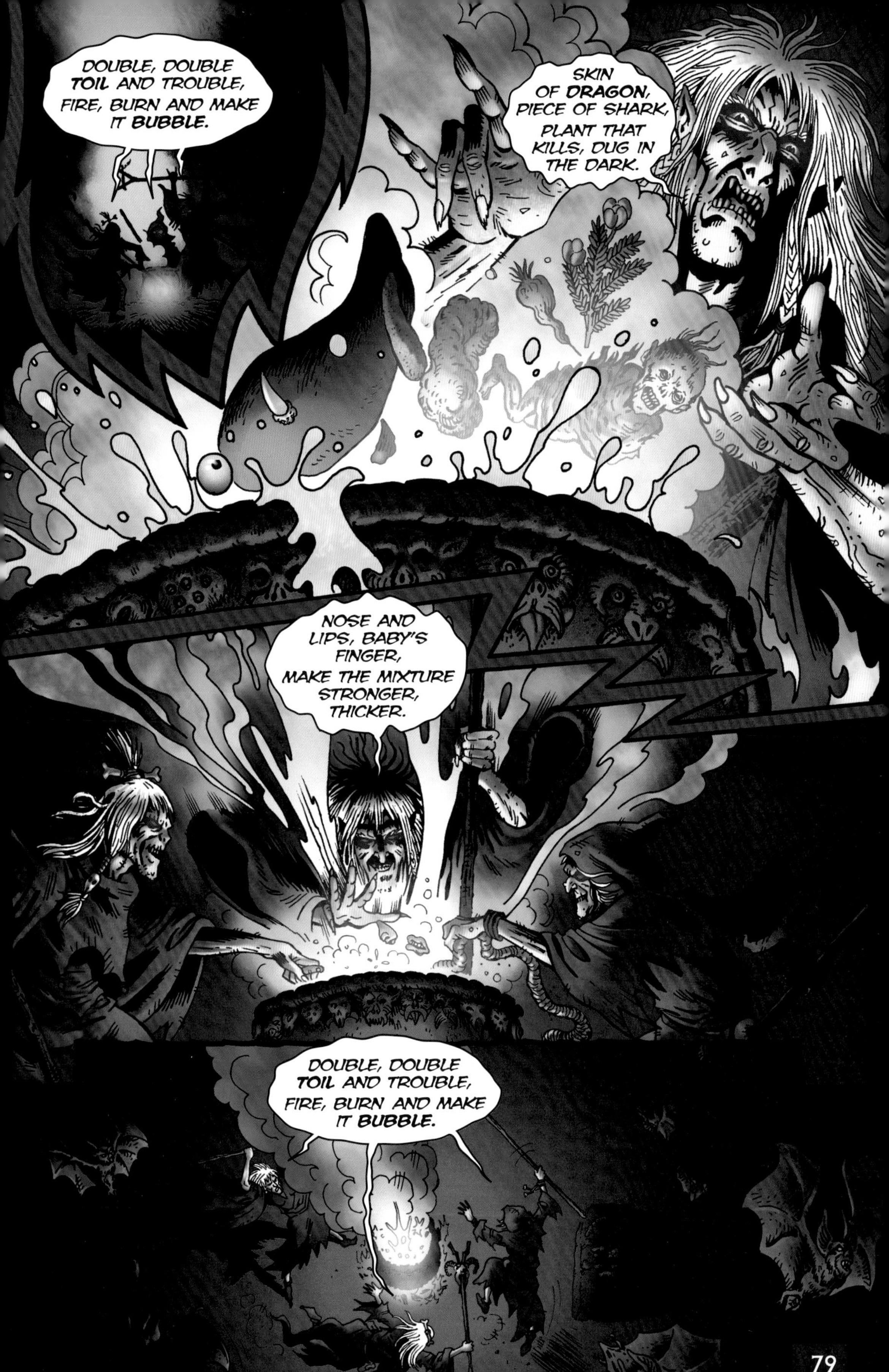
DOUBLE, DOUBLE TOIL AND TROUBLE, FIRE, BURN AND MAKE IT BUBBLE.
SKIN OF DRAGON, PIECE OF SHARK, PLANT THAT KILLS, DUG IN THE DARK.
NOSE AND LIPS, BABY'S FINGER, MAKE THE MIXTURE STRONGER, THICKER.
DOUBLE, DOUBLE TOIL AND TROUBLE, FIRE, BURN AND MAKE IT BUBBLE.

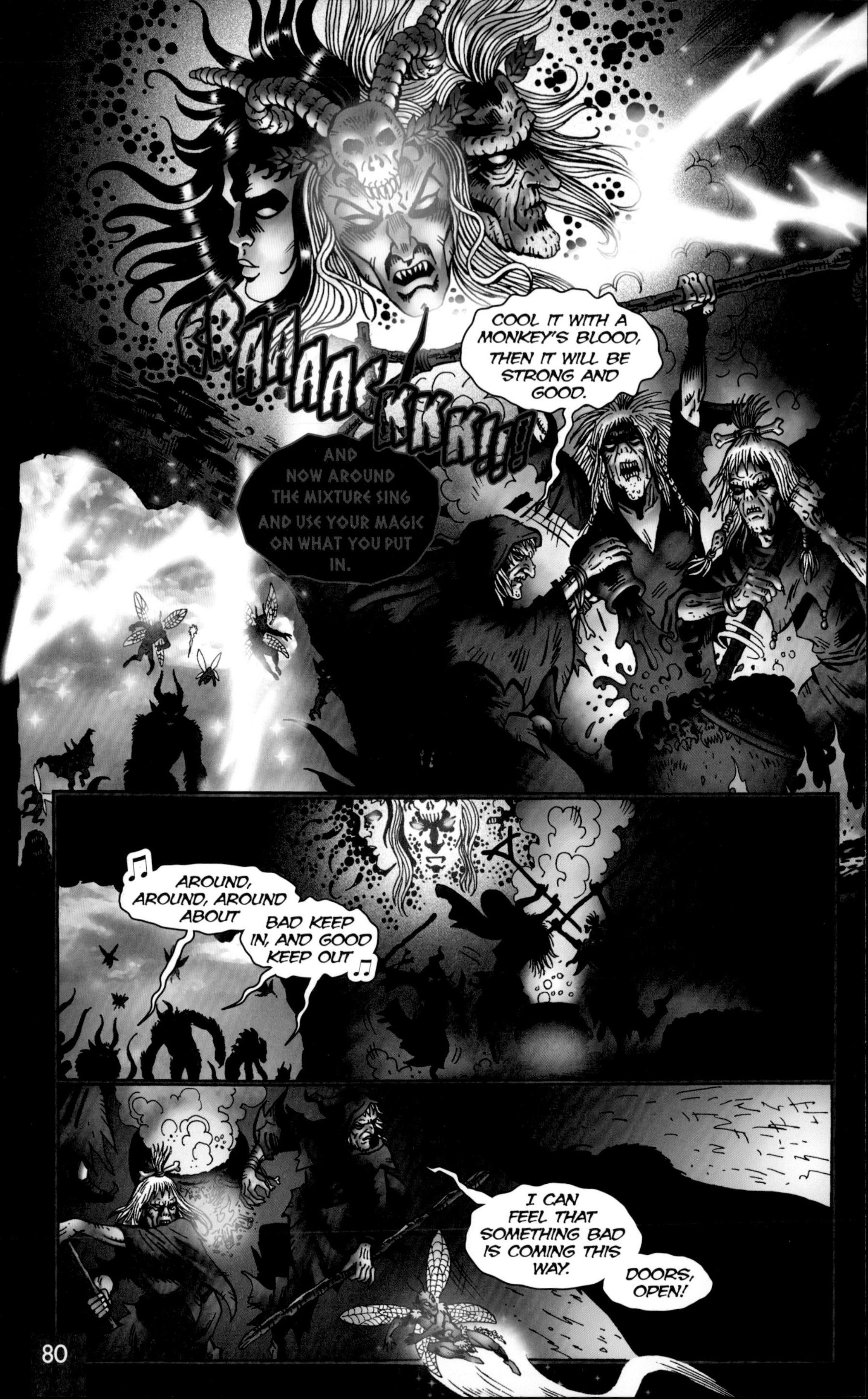
CRAAAACKKK!!!
COOL IT WITH A MONKEY'S BLOOD, THEN IT WILL BE STRONG AND GOOD.
AND NOW AROUND THE MIXTURE SING AND USE YOUR MAGIC ON WHAT YOU PUT IN.
AROUND, AROUND, AROUND ABOUT
BAD KEEP IN, AND GOOD KEEP OUT
I CAN FEEL THAT SOMETHING BAD IS COMING THIS WAY.
DOORS, OPEN!

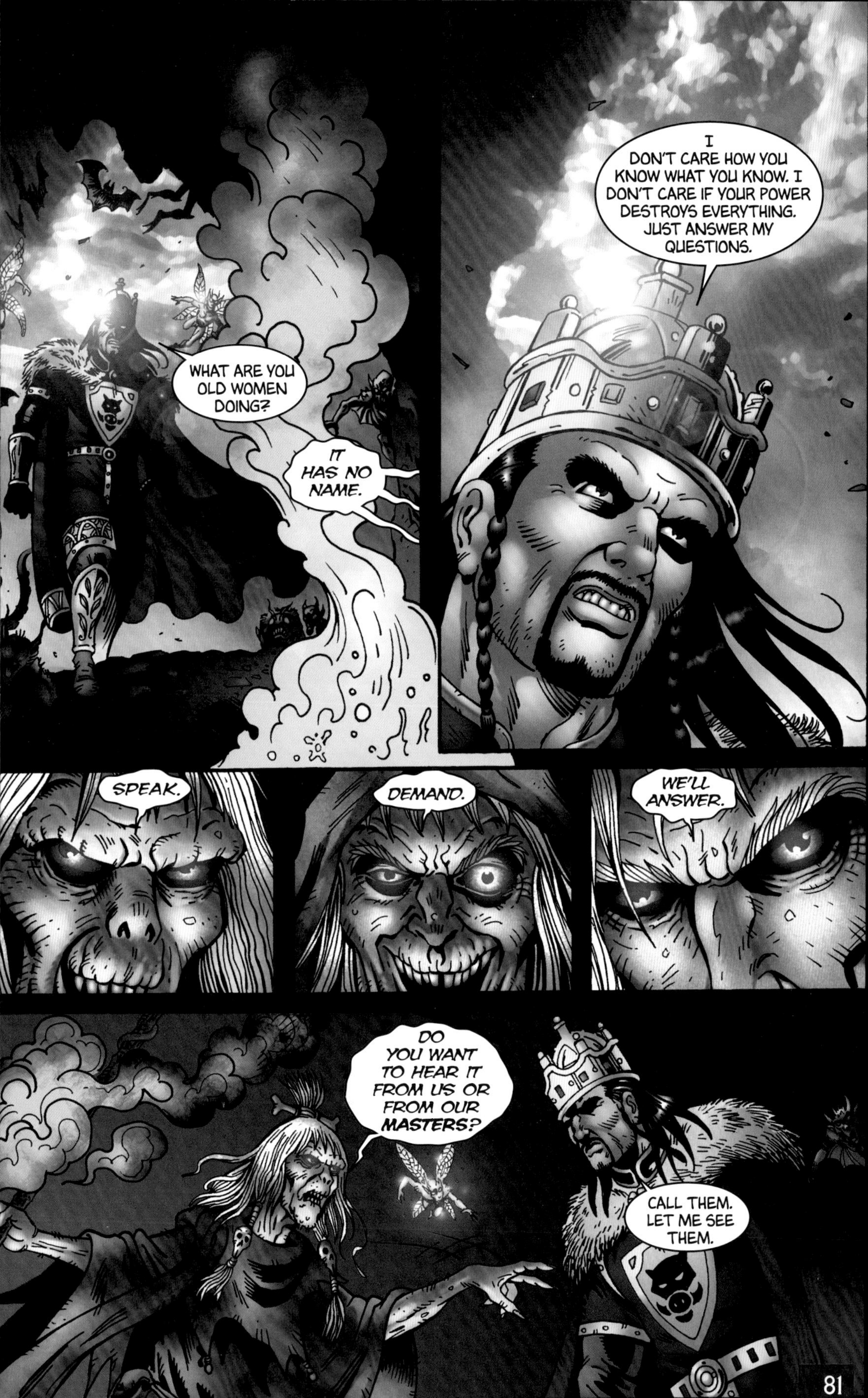
WHAT ARE YOU OLD WOMEN DOING?
IT HAS NO NAME.
I DON'T CARE HOW YOU KNOW WHAT YOU KNOW. I DON'T CARE IF YOUR POWER DESTROYS EVERYTHING. JUST ANSWER MY QUESTIONS.
SPEAK.
DEMAND.
WE'LL ANSWER.
DO YOU WANT TO HEAR IT FROM US OR FROM OUR MASTERS?
CALL THEM. LET ME SEE THEM.

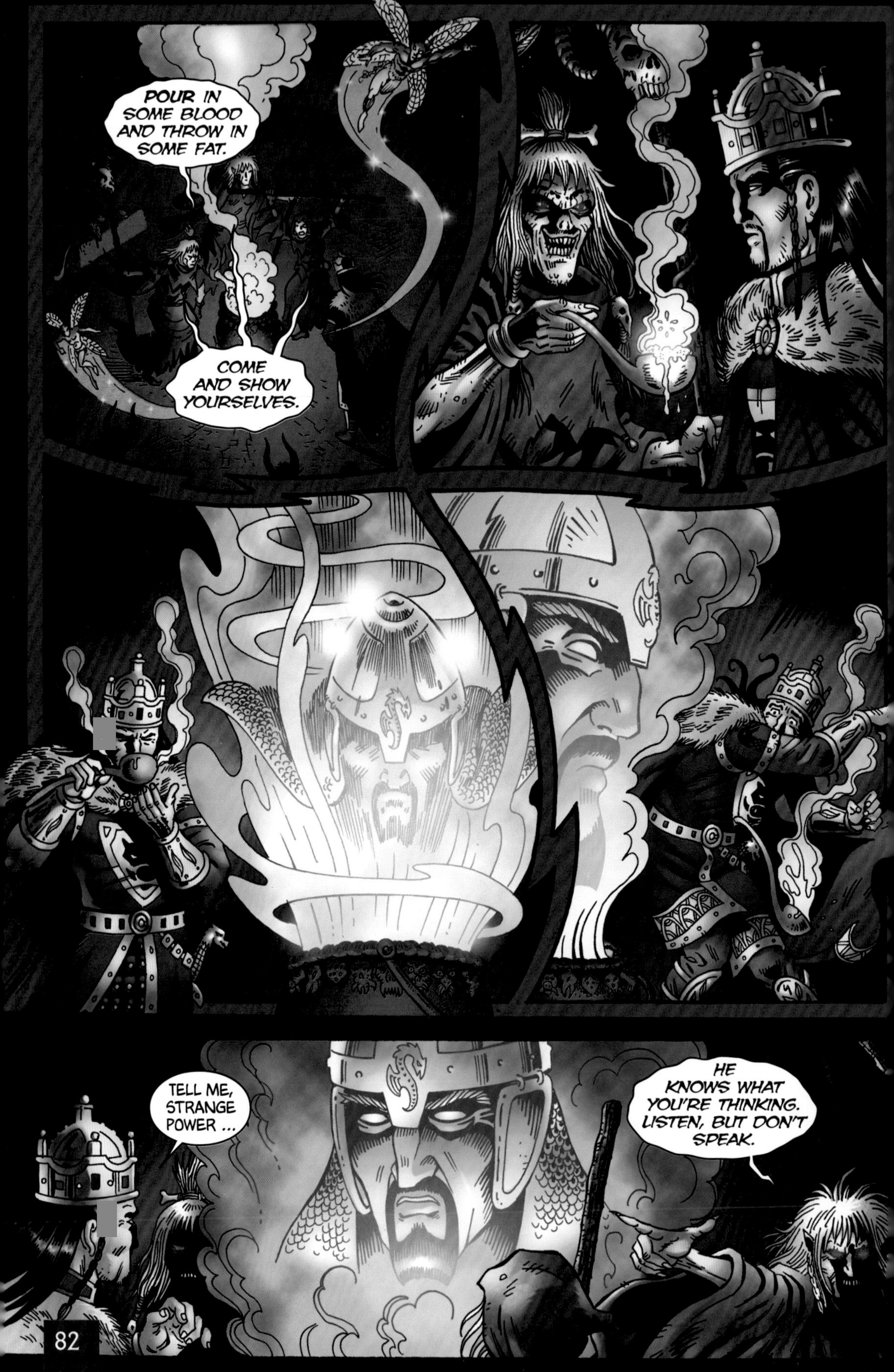
POUR IN SOME BLOOD AND THROW IN SOME FAT.
COME AND SHOW YOURSELVES.
TELL ME, STRANGE POWER ...
HE KNOWS WHAT YOU'RE THINKING. LISTEN, BUT DON'T SPEAK.

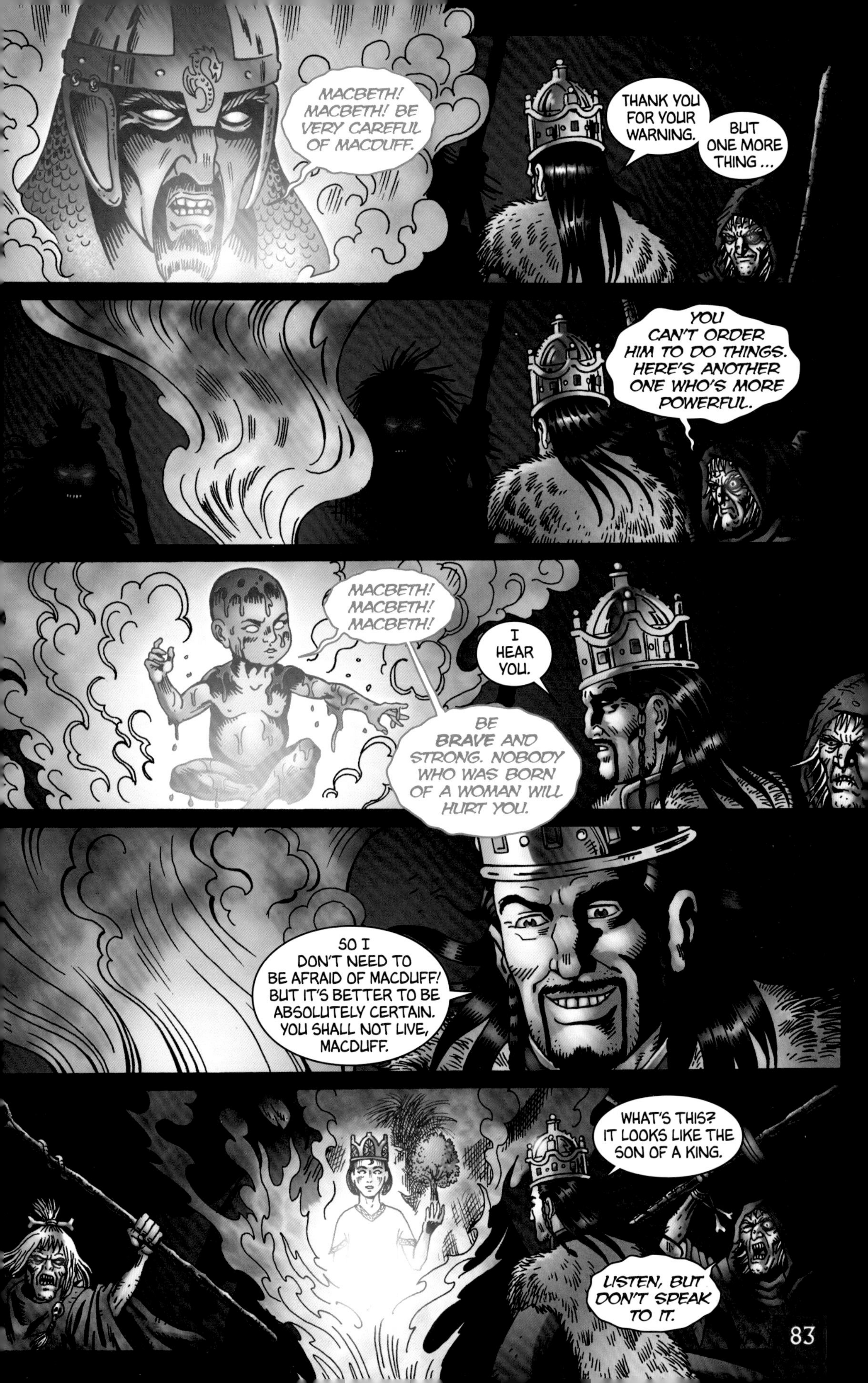
MACBETH! MACBETH! BE VERY CAREFUL OF MACDUFF.
THANK YOU FOR YOUR WARNING.
BUT ONE MORE THING ...
YOU CAN'T ORDER HIM TO DO THINGS. HERE'S ANOTHER ONE WHO'S MORE POWERFUL.
MACBETH! MACBETH! MACBETH!
I HEAR YOU.
BE BRAVE AND STRONG. NOBODY WHO WAS BORN OF A WOMAN WILL HURT YOU.
SO I DON'T NEED TO BE AFRAID OF MACDUFF! BUT IT'S BETTER TO BE ABSOLUTELY CERTAIN. YOU SHALL NOT LIVE, MACDUFF.
WHAT'S THIS? IT LOOKS LIKE THE SON OF A KING.
LISTEN, BUT DON'T SPEAK TO IT.

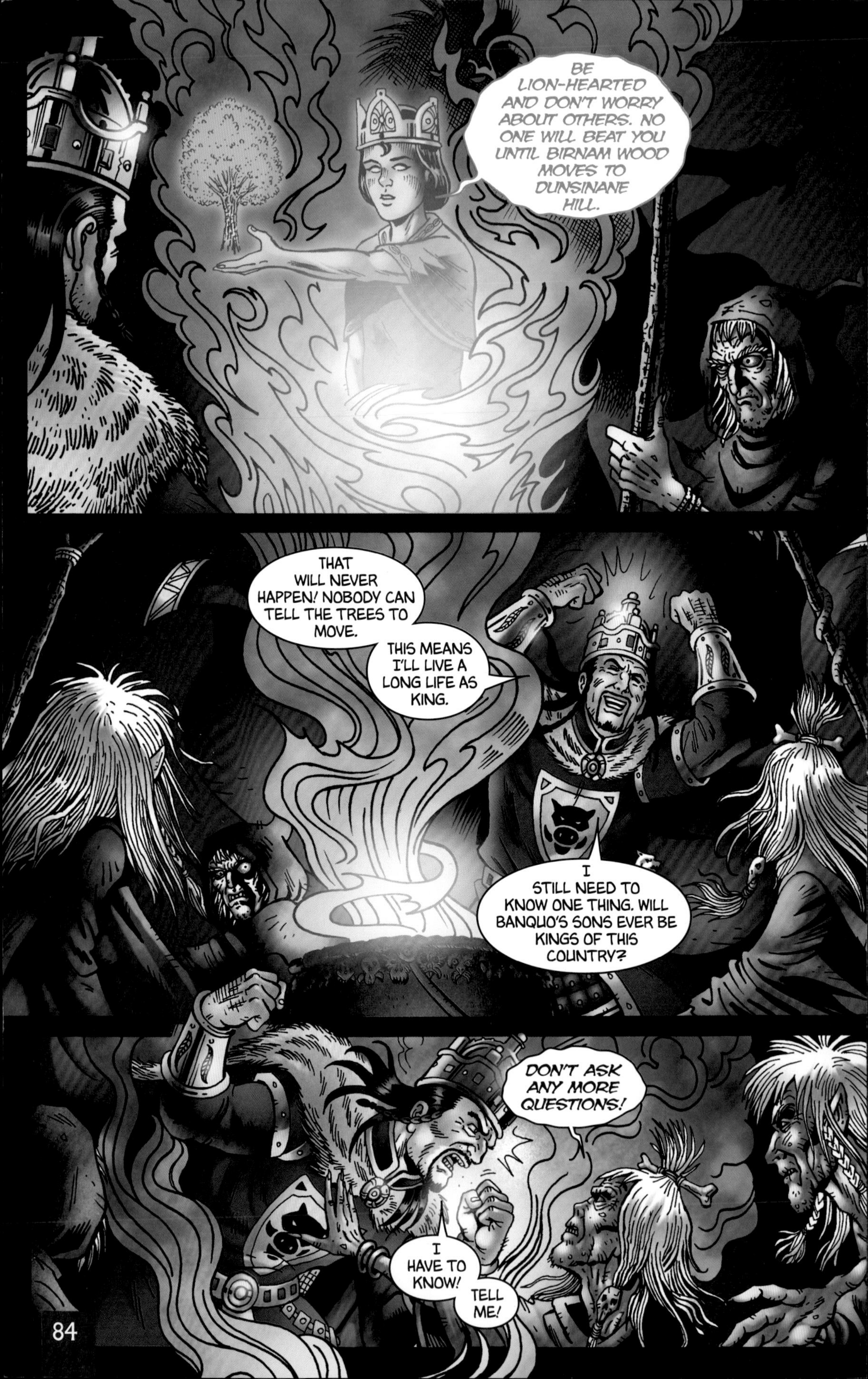
BE LION-HEARTED AND DON'T WORRY ABOUT OTHERS. NO ONE WILL BEAT YOU UNTIL BIRNAM WOOD MOVES TO DUNSINANE HILL.
THAT WILL NEVER HAPPEN! NOBODY CAN TELL THE TREES TO MOVE.
THIS MEANS I'LL LIVE A LONG LIFE AS KING.
I STILL NEED TO KNOW ONE THING. WILL BANQUO'S SONS EVER BE KINGS OF THIS COUNTRY?
DON'T ASK ANY MORE QUESTIONS!
I HAVE TO KNOW!
TELL ME!

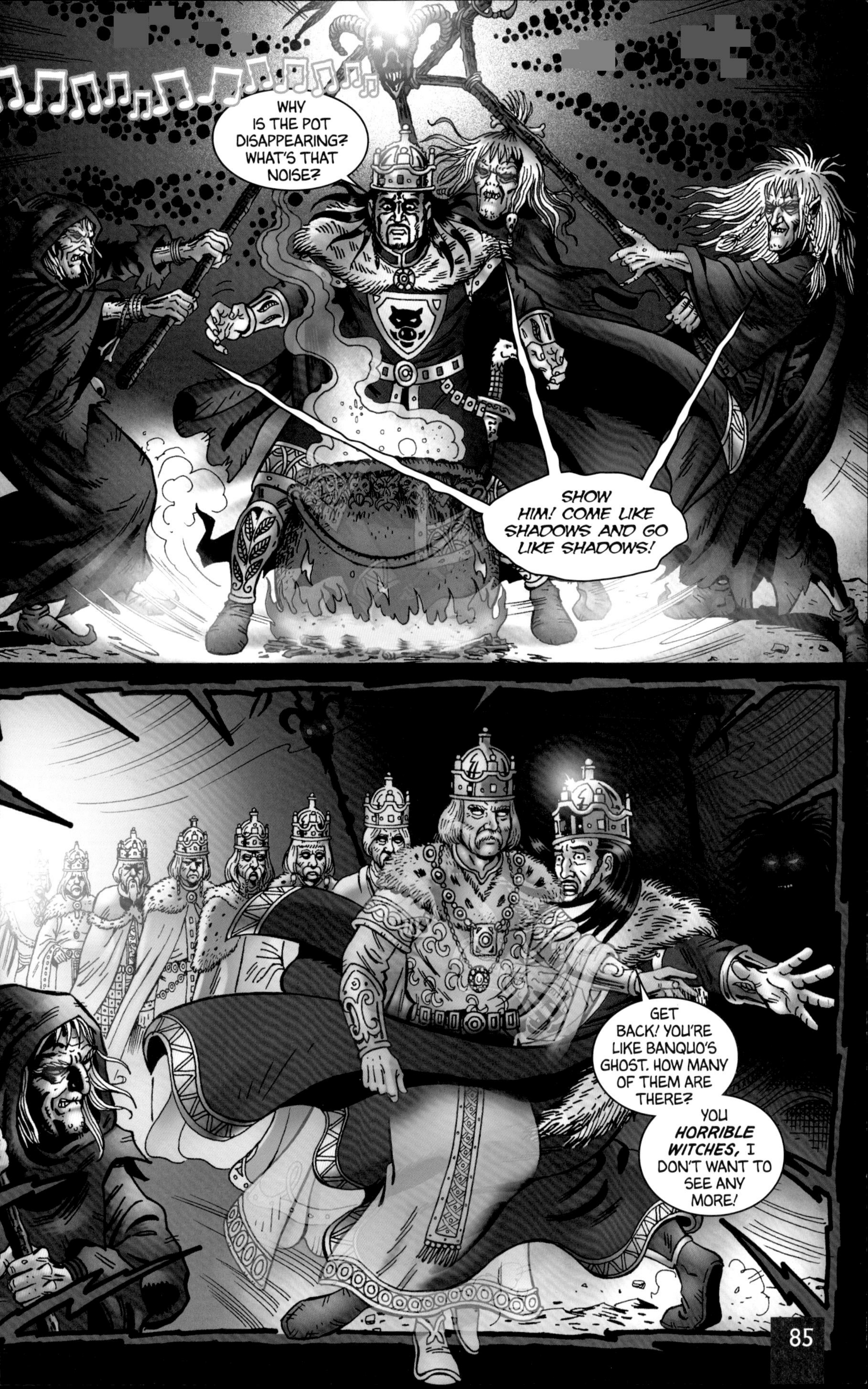
WHY IS THE POT DISAPPEARING? WHAT'S THAT NOISE?
SHOW HIM! COME LIKE SHADOWS AND GO LIKE SHADOWS!
GET BACK! YOU'RE LIKE BANQUO'S GHOST. HOW MANY OF THEM ARE THERE?
YOU **HORRIBLE WITCHES,** I DON'T WANT TO SEE ANY MORE!

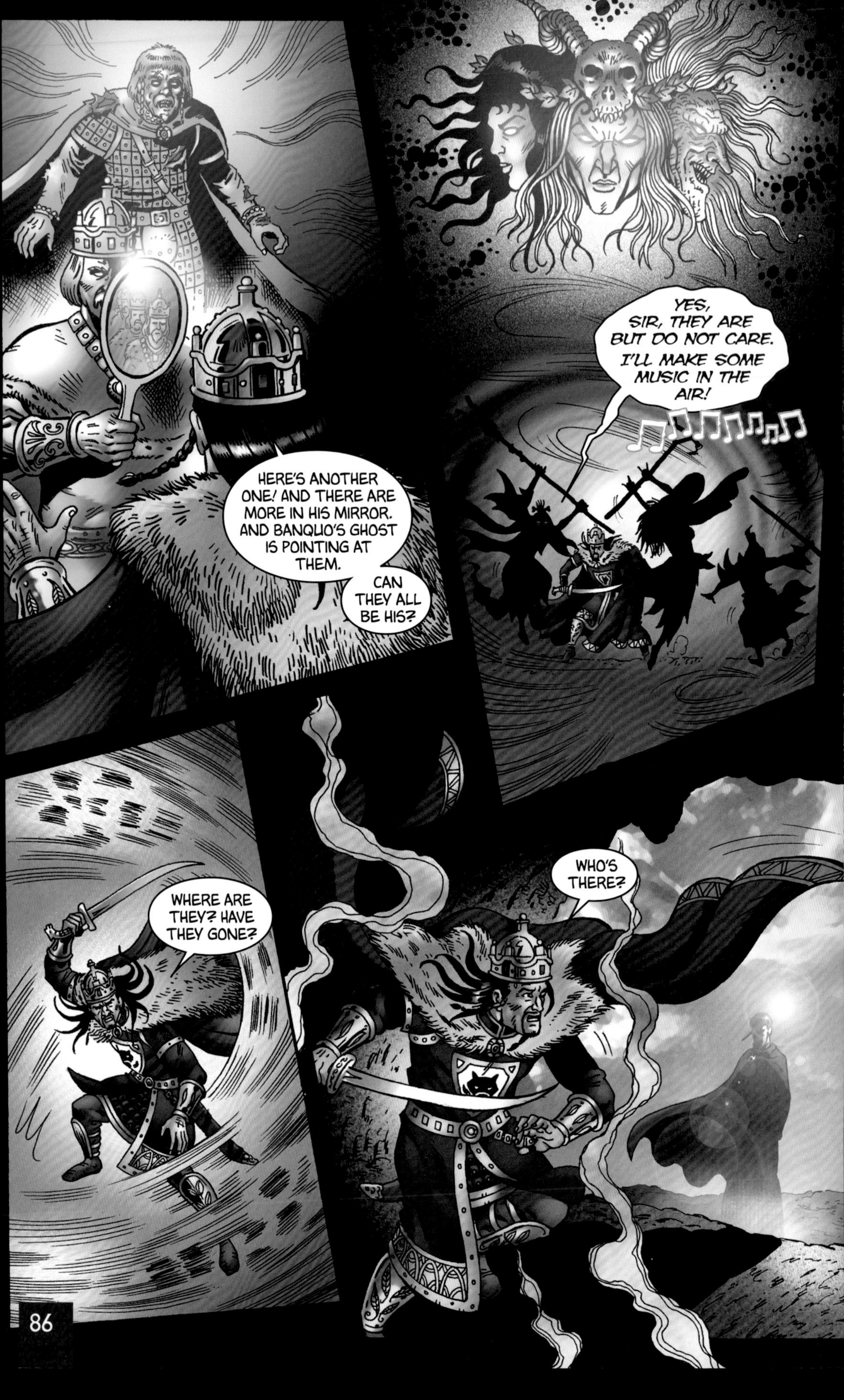
HERE'S ANOTHER ONE! AND THERE ARE MORE IN HIS MIRROR. AND BANQUO'S GHOST IS POINTING AT THEM.
CAN THEY ALL BE HIS?
YES, SIR, THEY ARE BUT DO NOT CARE. I'LL MAKE SOME MUSIC IN THE AIR!
WHERE ARE THEY? HAVE THEY GONE?
WHO'S THERE?

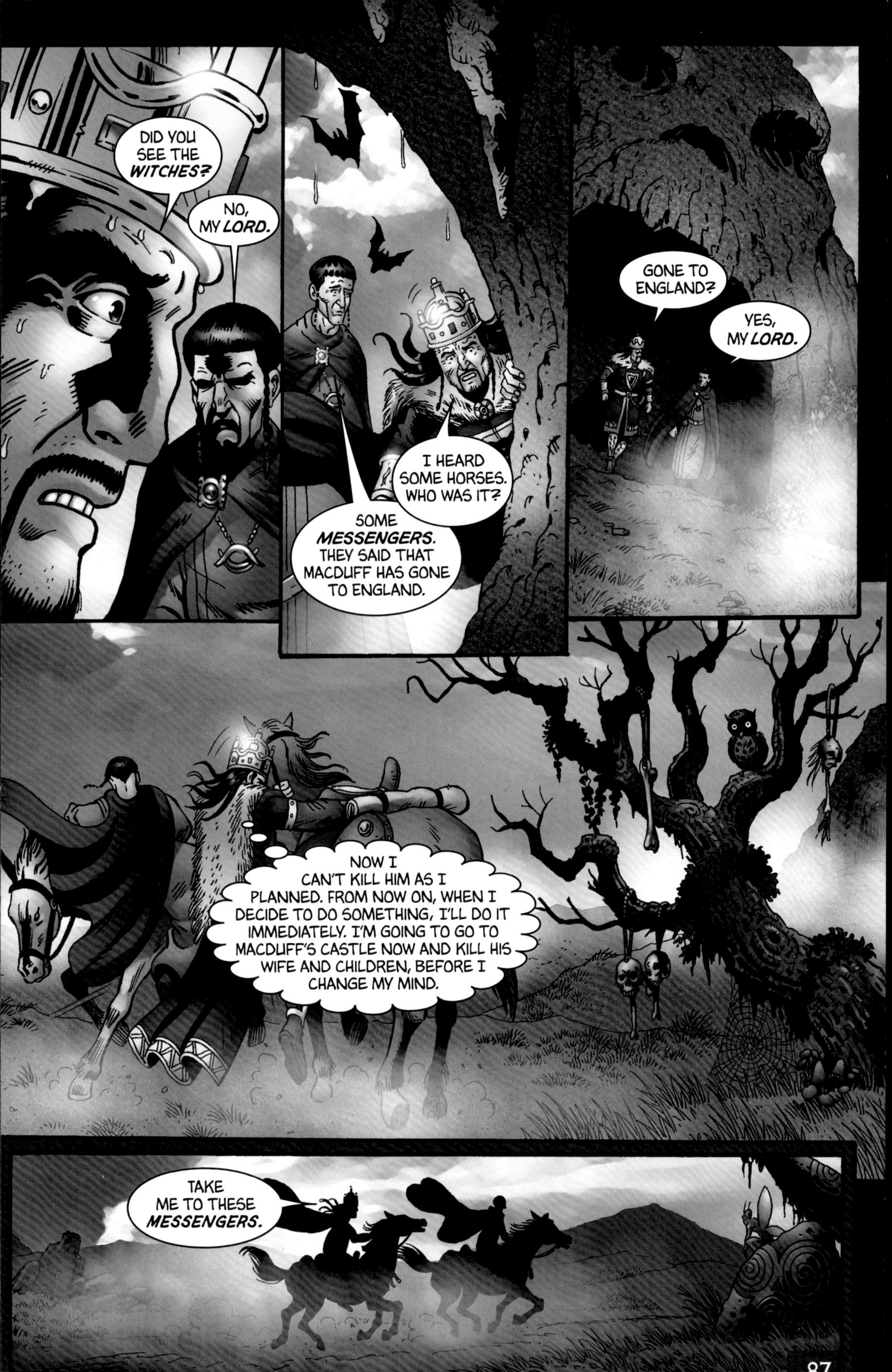

DID YOU SEE THE *WITCHES?*
NO, MY *LORD.*
I HEARD SOME HORSES. WHO WAS IT?
SOME *MESSENGERS.* THEY SAID THAT MACDUFF HAS GONE TO ENGLAND.
GONE TO ENGLAND?
YES, MY *LORD.*
NOW I CAN'T KILL HIM AS I PLANNED. FROM NOW ON, WHEN I DECIDE TO DO SOMETHING, I'LL DO IT IMMEDIATELY. I'M GOING TO GO TO MACDUFF'S CASTLE NOW AND KILL HIS WIFE AND CHILDREN, BEFORE I CHANGE MY MIND.
TAKE ME TO THESE *MESSENGERS.*

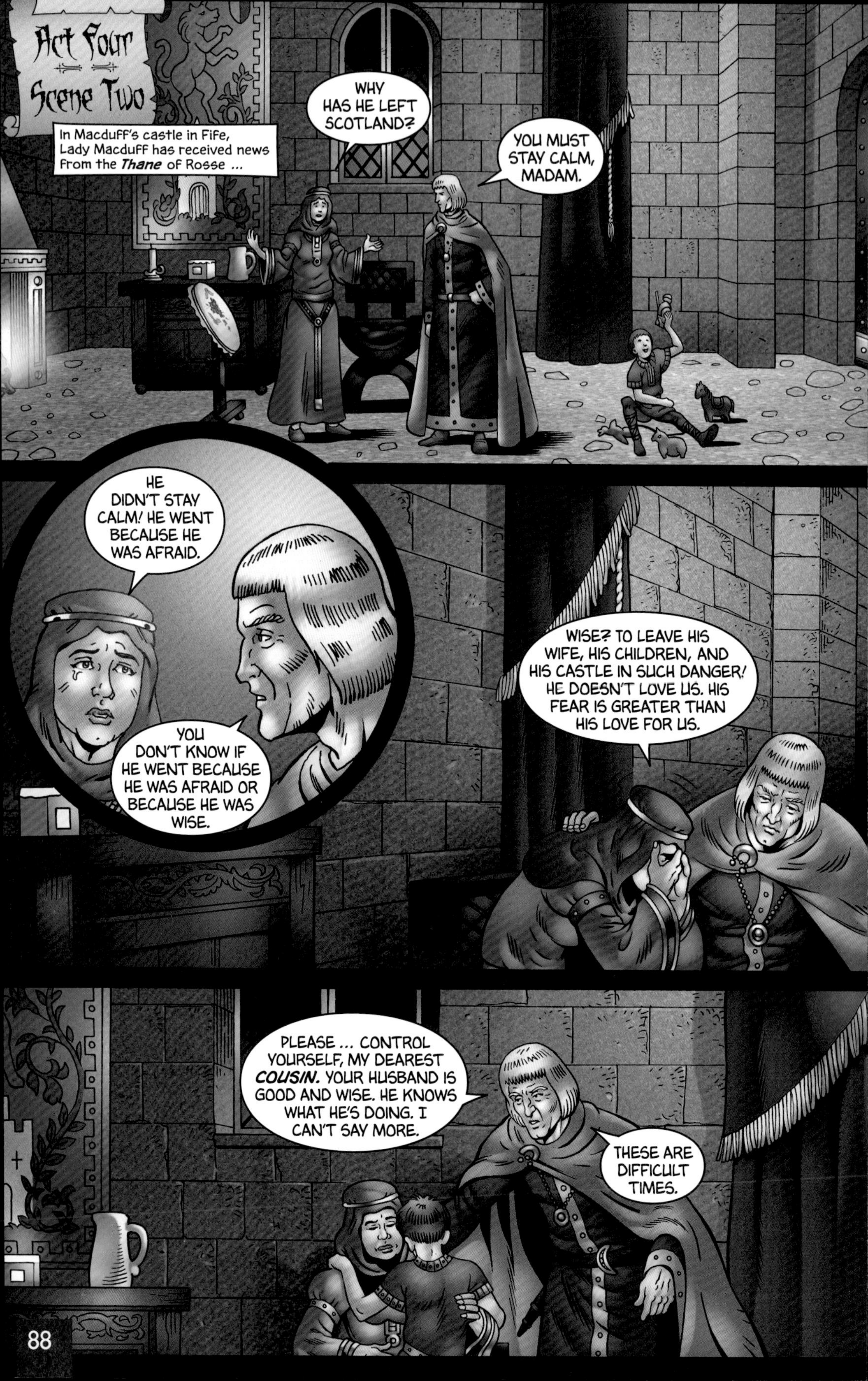

Act Four
Scene Two
In Macduff's castle in Fife, Lady Macduff has received news from the *Thane* of Rosse ...
WHY HAS HE LEFT SCOTLAND?
YOU MUST STAY CALM, MADAM.
HE DIDN'T STAY CALM! HE WENT BECAUSE HE WAS AFRAID.
YOU DON'T KNOW IF HE WENT BECAUSE HE WAS AFRAID OR BECAUSE HE WAS WISE.
WISE? TO LEAVE HIS WIFE, HIS CHILDREN, AND HIS CASTLE IN SUCH DANGER! HE DOESN'T LOVE US. HIS FEAR IS GREATER THAN HIS LOVE FOR US.
PLEASE ... CONTROL YOURSELF, MY DEAREST ***COUSIN.*** YOUR HUSBAND IS GOOD AND WISE. HE KNOWS WHAT HE'S DOING. I CAN'T SAY MORE.
THESE ARE DIFFICULT TIMES.

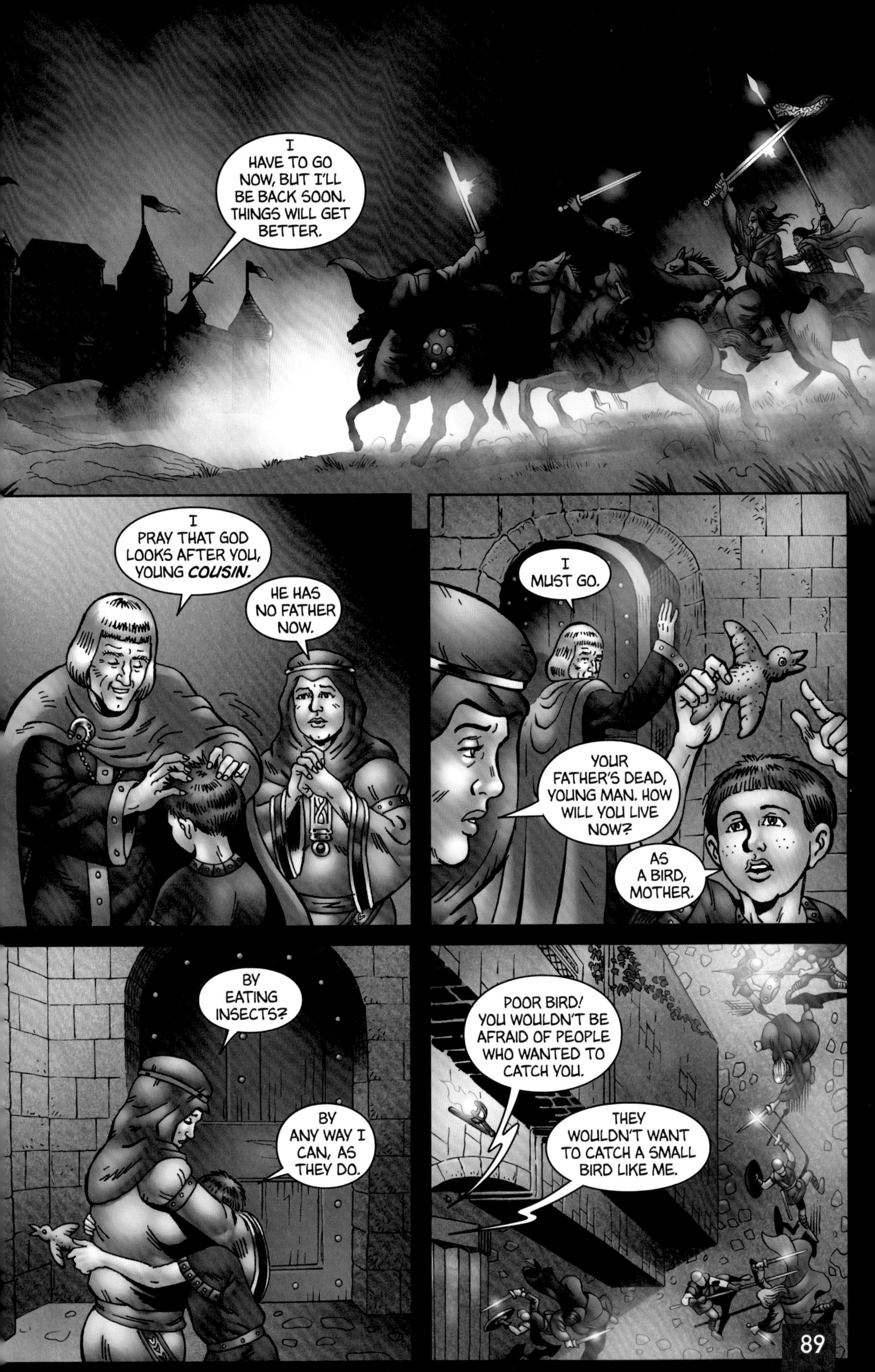
I HAVE TO GO NOW, BUT I'LL BE BACK SOON. THINGS WILL GET BETTER.
I PRAY THAT GOD LOOKS AFTER YOU, YOUNG *COUSIN.*
HE HAS NO FATHER NOW.
I MUST GO.
YOUR FATHER'S DEAD, YOUNG MAN. HOW WILL YOU LIVE NOW?
AS A BIRD, MOTHER.
BY EATING INSECTS?
BY ANY WAY I CAN, AS THEY DO.
POOR BIRD! YOU WOULDN'T BE AFRAID OF PEOPLE WHO WANTED TO CATCH YOU.
THEY WOULDN'T WANT TO CATCH A SMALL BIRD LIKE ME.

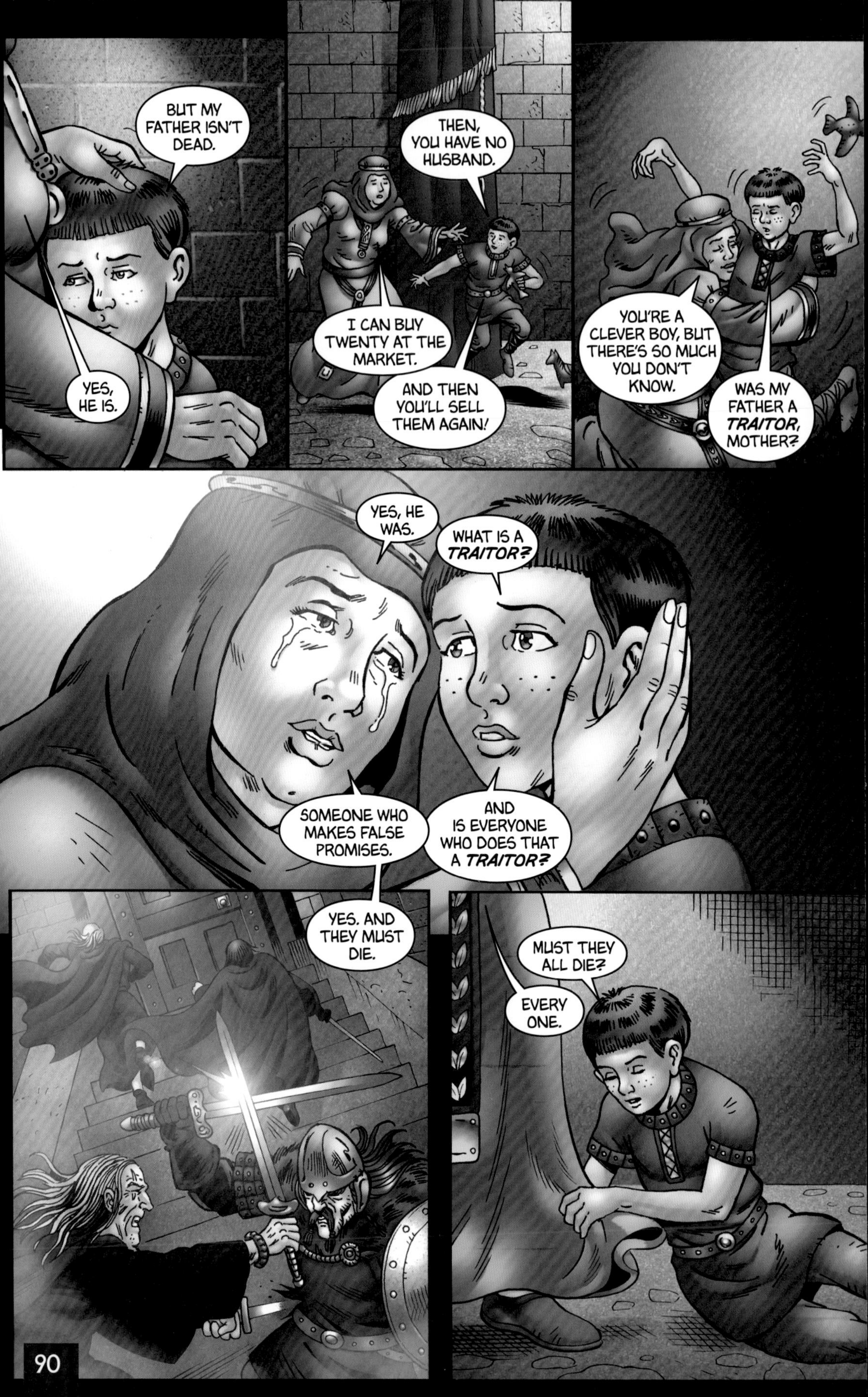

BUT MY FATHER ISN'T DEAD.
YES, HE IS.
THEN, YOU HAVE NO HUSBAND.
I CAN BUY TWENTY AT THE MARKET.
AND THEN YOU'LL SELL THEM AGAIN!
YOU'RE A CLEVER BOY, BUT THERE'S SO MUCH YOU DON'T KNOW.
WAS MY FATHER A TRAITOR, MOTHER?
YES, HE WAS.
WHAT IS A TRAITOR?
SOMEONE WHO MAKES FALSE PROMISES.
AND IS EVERYONE WHO DOES THAT A TRAITOR?
YES. AND THEY MUST DIE.
MUST THEY ALL DIE?
EVERY ONE.

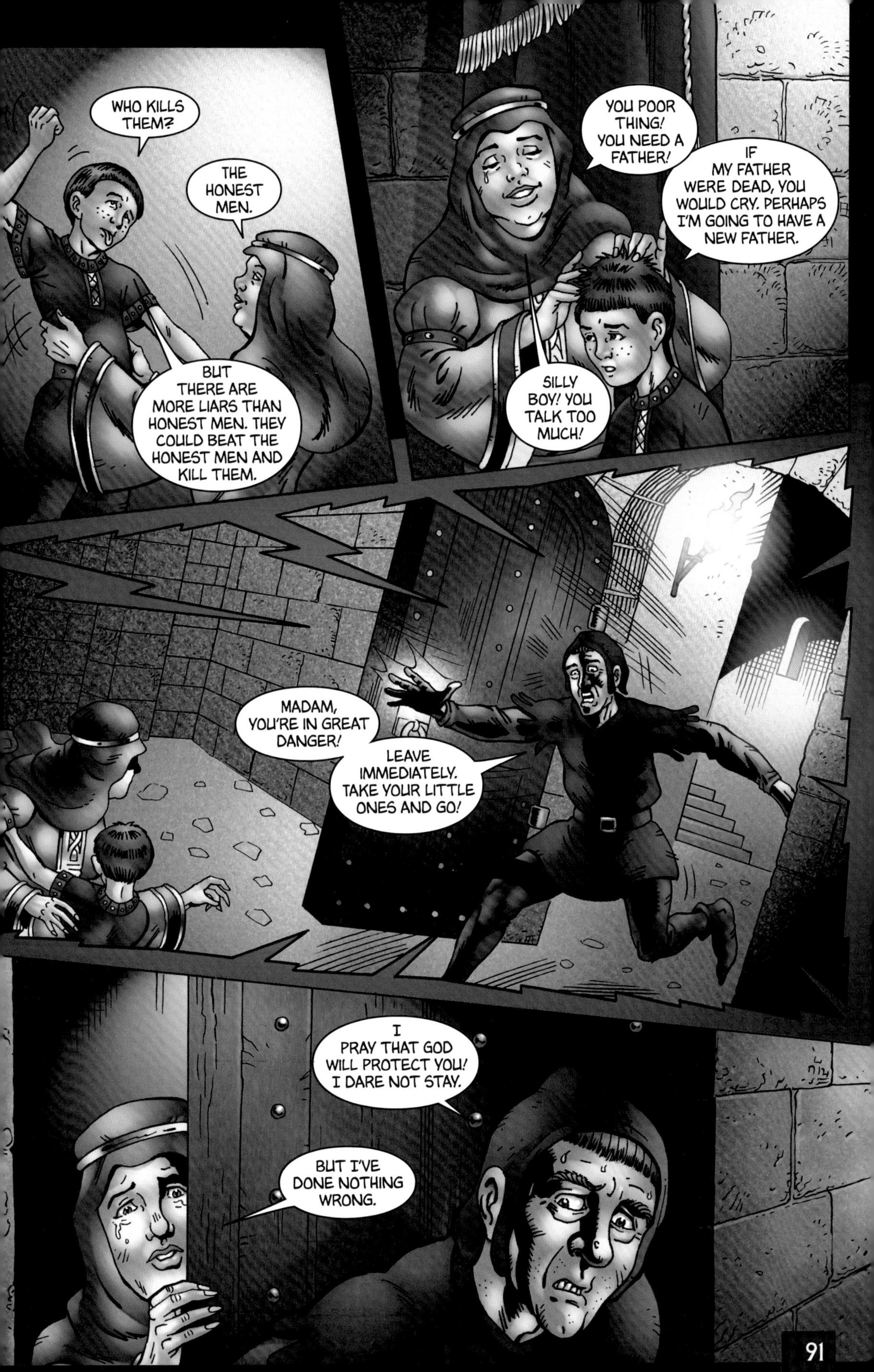
WHO KILLS THEM?
THE HONEST MEN.
BUT THERE ARE MORE LIARS THAN HONEST MEN. THEY COULD BEAT THE HONEST MEN AND KILL THEM.
YOU POOR THING! YOU NEED A FATHER!
IF MY FATHER WERE DEAD, YOU WOULD CRY. PERHAPS I'M GOING TO HAVE A NEW FATHER.
SILLY BOY! YOU TALK TOO MUCH!
MADAM, YOU'RE IN GREAT DANGER!
LEAVE IMMEDIATELY. TAKE YOUR LITTLE ONES AND GO!
I PRAY THAT GOD WILL PROTECT YOU! I DARE NOT STAY.
BUT I'VE DONE NOTHING WRONG.

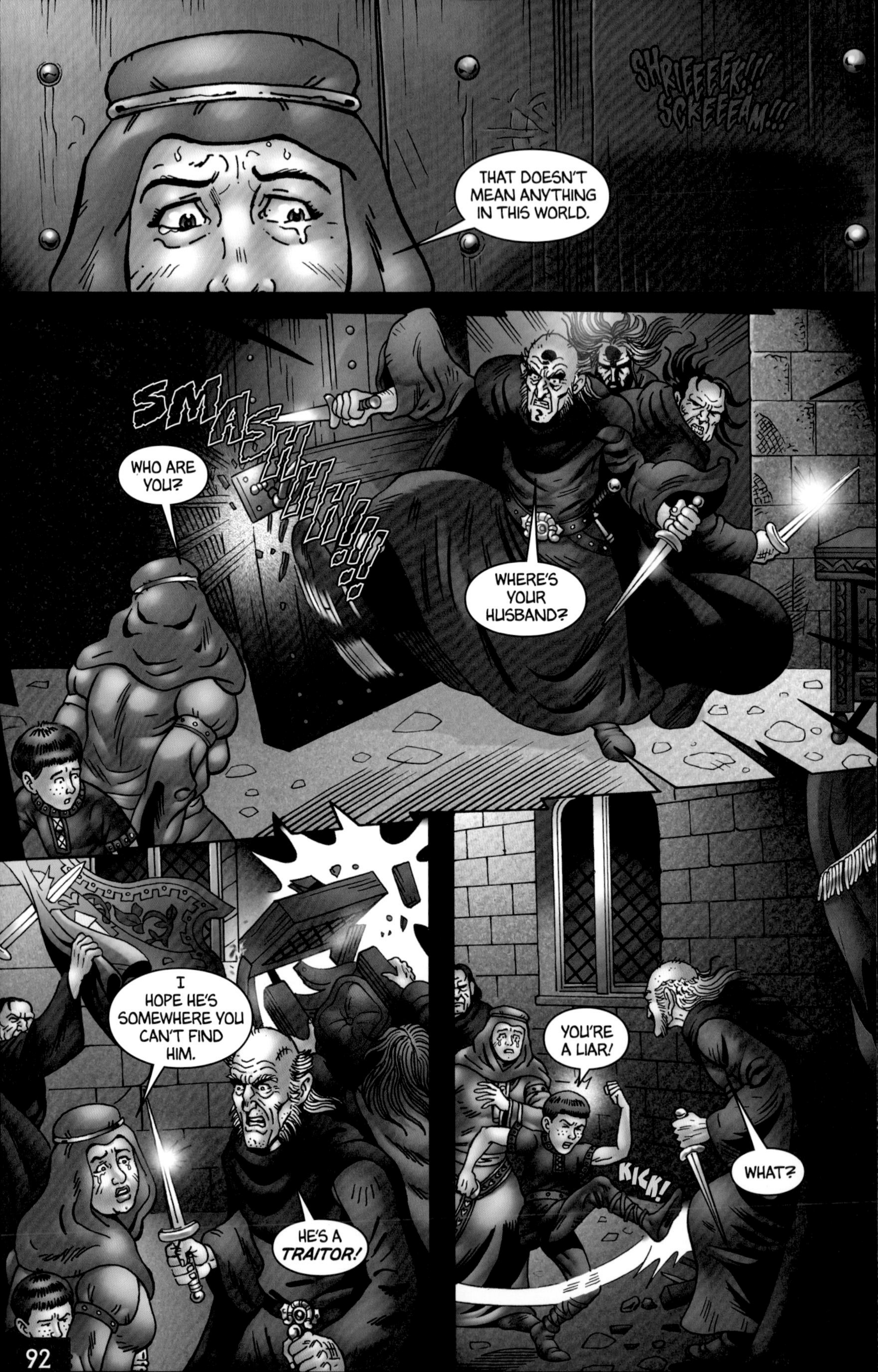
SHRIEEEEK!!!
SCREEEAM!!!
THAT DOESN'T MEAN ANYTHING IN THIS WORLD.
SMASHHHH!!!
WHO ARE YOU?
WHERE'S YOUR HUSBAND?
I HOPE HE'S SOMEWHERE YOU CAN'T FIND HIM.
HE'S A *TRAITOR!*
YOU'RE A LIAR!
KICK!
WHAT?

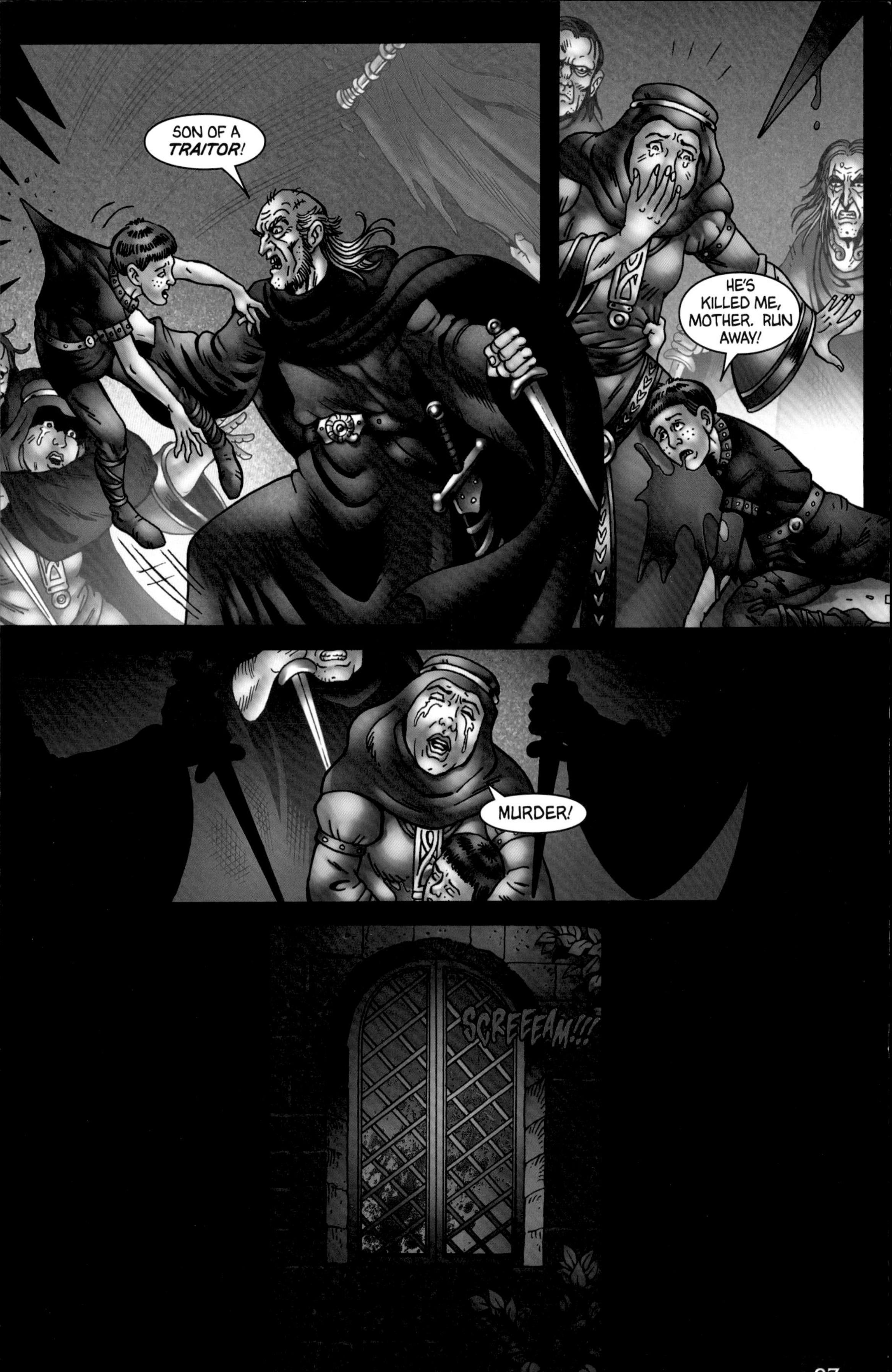
SON OF A *TRAITOR*!
HE'S KILLED ME, MOTHER. RUN AWAY!
MURDER!
SCREEEAM!!!

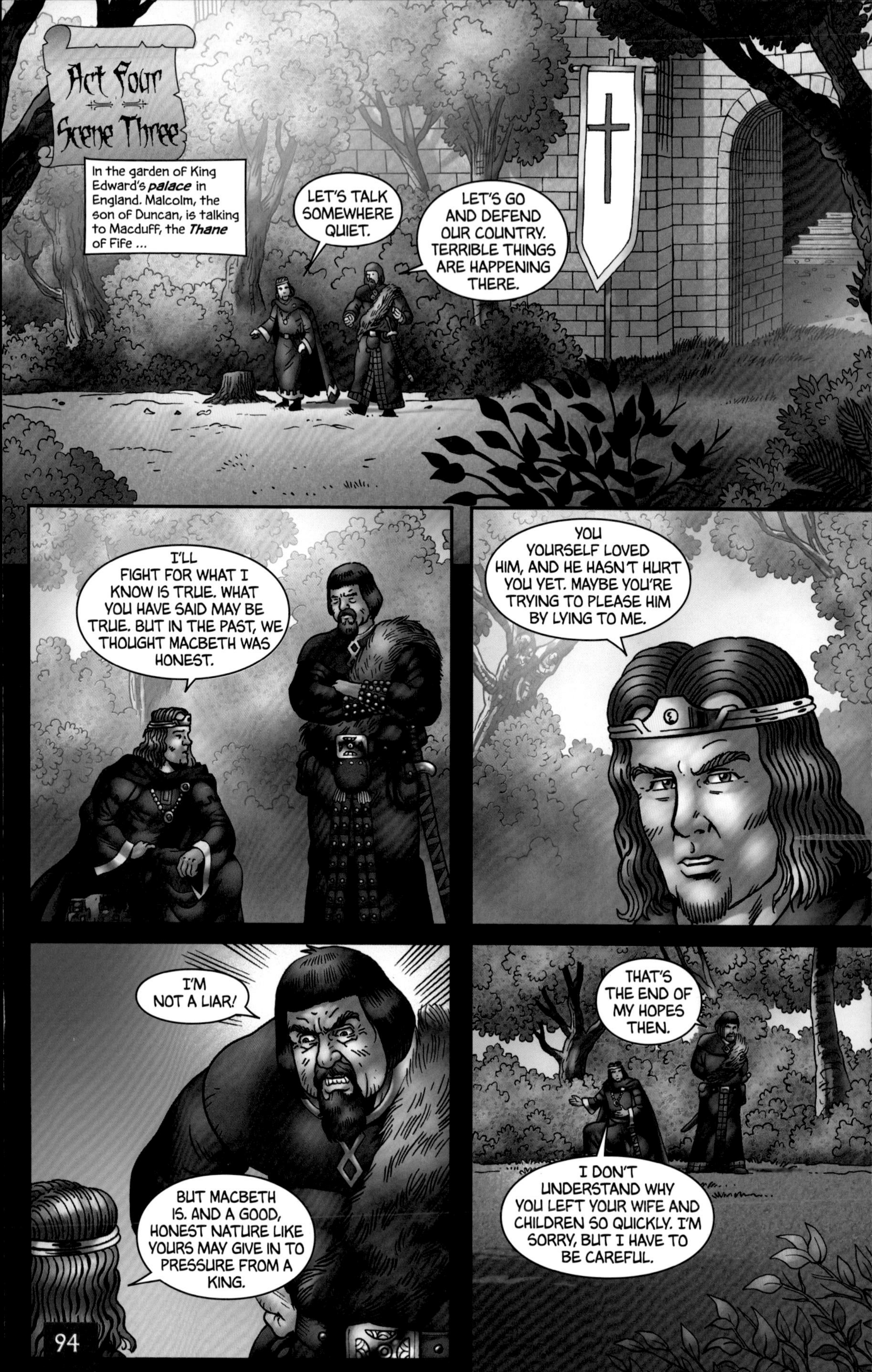
Act Four
Scene Three
In the garden of King Edward's *palace* in England. Malcolm, the son of Duncan, is talking to Macduff, the *Thane* of Fife ...
LET'S TALK SOMEWHERE QUIET.
LET'S GO AND DEFEND OUR COUNTRY. TERRIBLE THINGS ARE HAPPENING THERE.
I'LL FIGHT FOR WHAT I KNOW IS TRUE. WHAT YOU HAVE SAID MAY BE TRUE. BUT IN THE PAST, WE THOUGHT MACBETH WAS HONEST.
YOU YOURSELF LOVED HIM, AND HE HASN'T HURT YOU YET. MAYBE YOU'RE TRYING TO PLEASE HIM BY LYING TO ME.
I'M NOT A LIAR!
BUT MACBETH IS. AND A GOOD, HONEST NATURE LIKE YOURS MAY GIVE IN TO PRESSURE FROM A KING.
THAT'S THE END OF MY HOPES THEN.
I DON'T UNDERSTAND WHY YOU LEFT YOUR WIFE AND CHILDREN SO QUICKLY. I'M SORRY, BUT I HAVE TO BE CAREFUL.

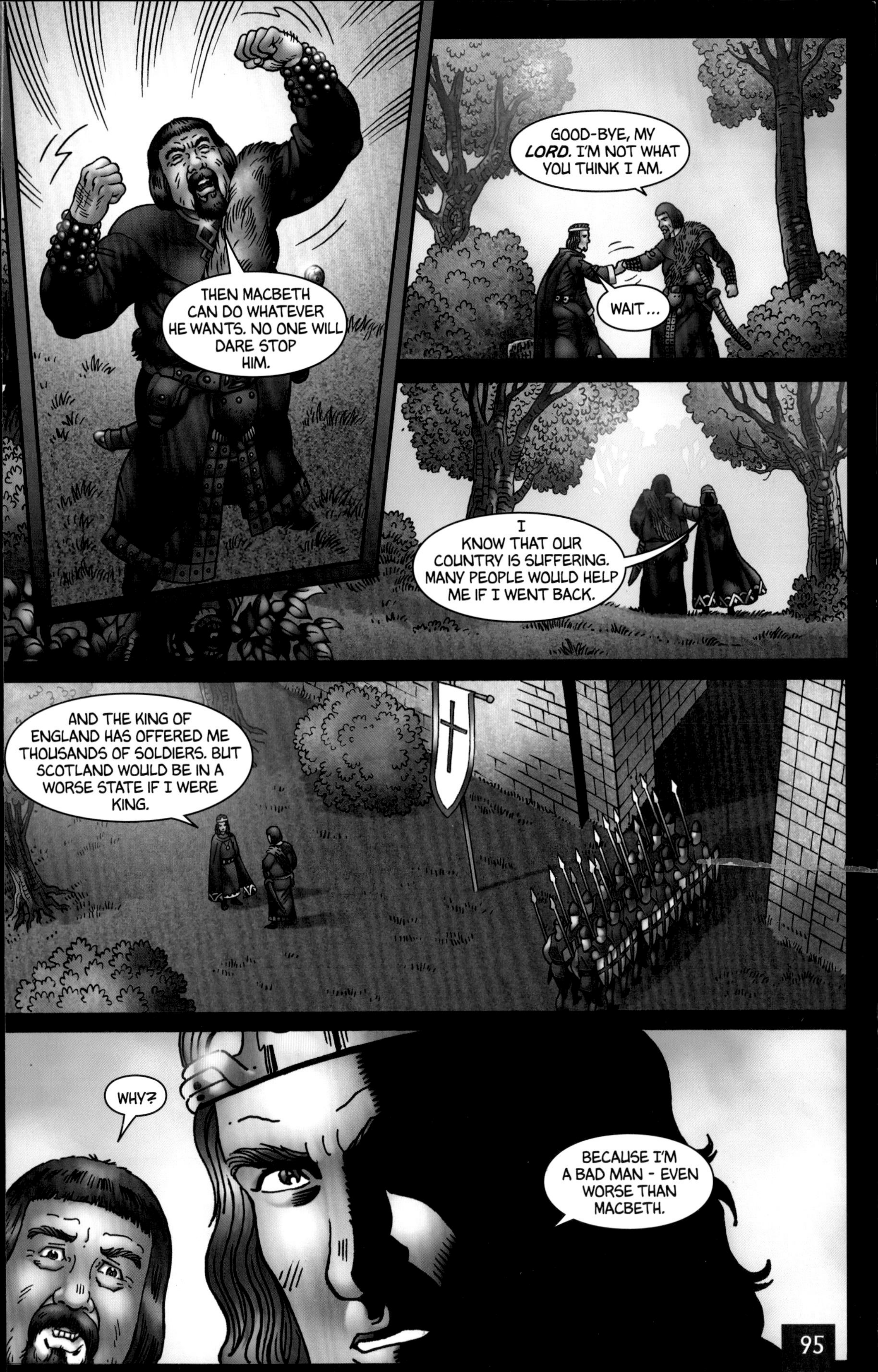
THEN MACBETH CAN DO WHATEVER HE WANTS. NO ONE WILL DARE STOP HIM.
GOOD-BYE, MY LORD. I'M NOT WHAT YOU THINK I AM.
WAIT...
I KNOW THAT OUR COUNTRY IS SUFFERING. MANY PEOPLE WOULD HELP ME IF I WENT BACK.
AND THE KING OF ENGLAND HAS OFFERED ME THOUSANDS OF SOLDIERS. BUT SCOTLAND WOULD BE IN A WORSE STATE IF I WERE KING.
WHY?
BECAUSE I'M A BAD MAN - EVEN WORSE THAN MACBETH.

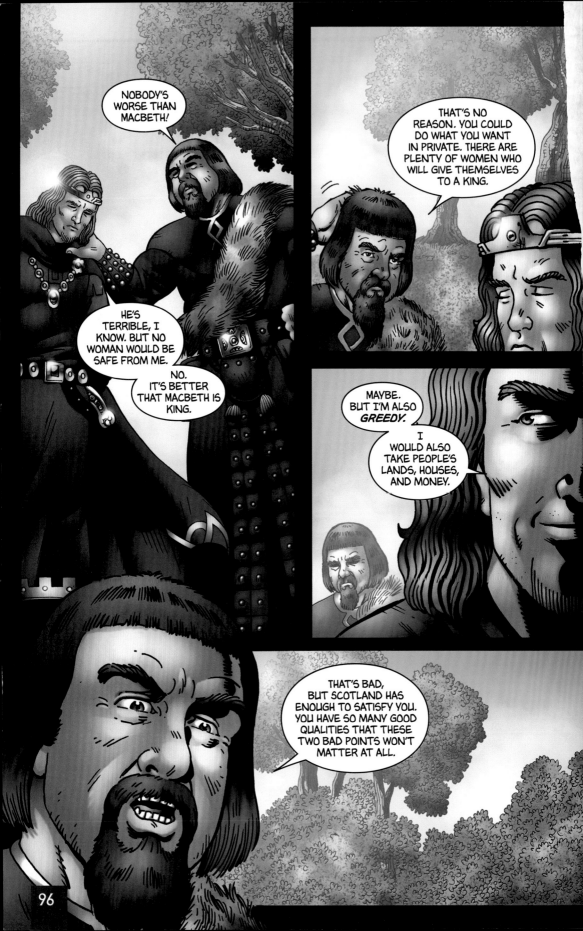

NOBODY'S WORSE THAN MACBETH!

HE'S TERRIBLE, I KNOW. BUT NO WOMAN WOULD BE SAFE FROM ME.

NO. IT'S BETTER THAT MACBETH IS KING.

THAT'S NO REASON. YOU COULD DO WHAT YOU WANT IN PRIVATE. THERE ARE PLENTY OF WOMEN WHO WILL GIVE THEMSELVES TO A KING.

MAYBE. BUT I'M ALSO *GREEDY*.

I WOULD ALSO TAKE PEOPLE'S LANDS, HOUSES, AND MONEY.

THAT'S BAD, BUT SCOTLAND HAS ENOUGH TO SATISFY YOU. YOU HAVE SO MANY GOOD QUALITIES THAT THESE TWO BAD POINTS WON'T MATTER AT ALL.

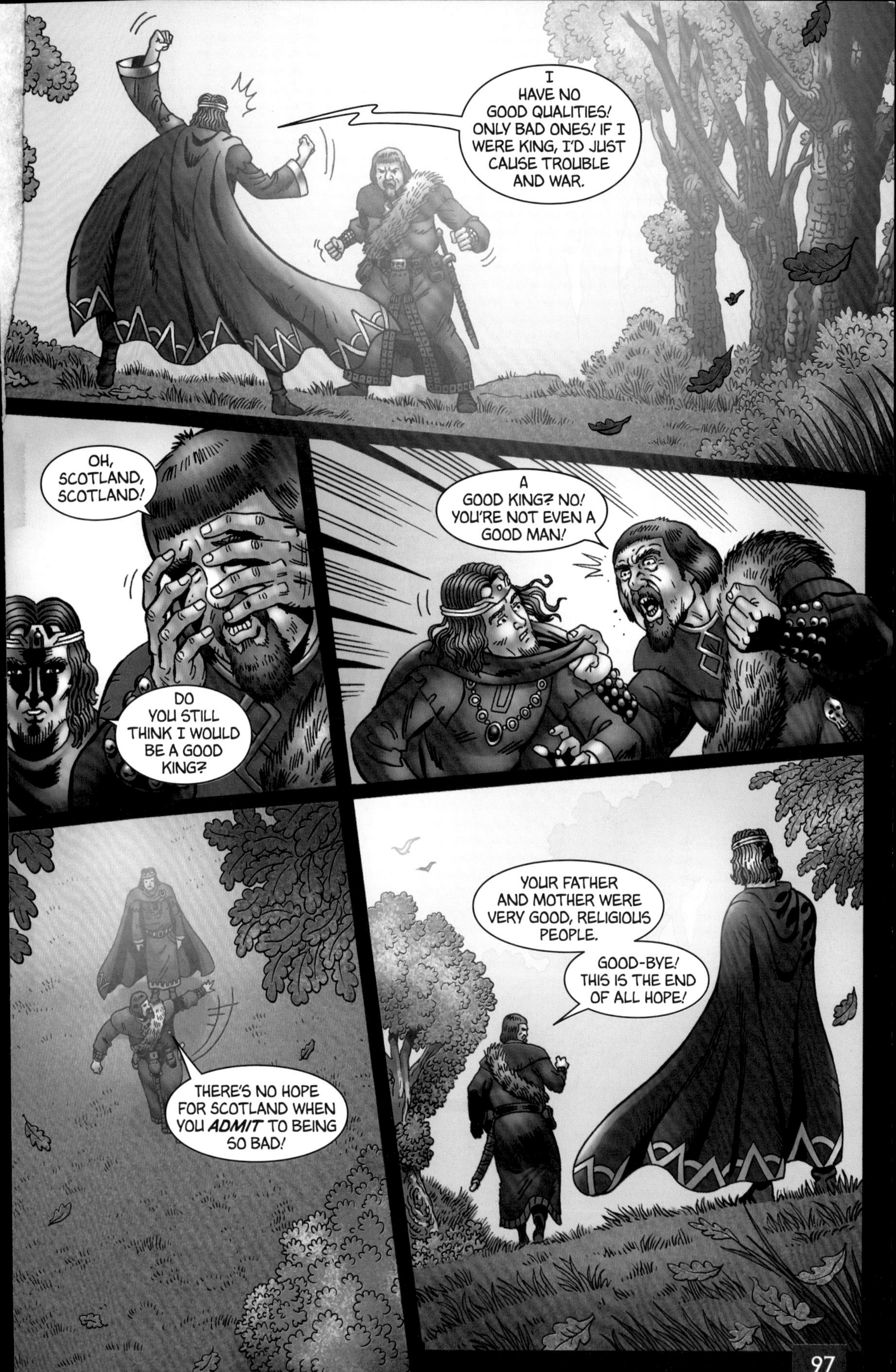
I HAVE NO GOOD QUALITIES! ONLY BAD ONES! IF I WERE KING, I'D JUST CAUSE TROUBLE AND WAR.
OH, SCOTLAND, SCOTLAND!
DO YOU STILL THINK I WOULD BE A GOOD KING?
A GOOD KING? NO! YOU'RE NOT EVEN A GOOD MAN!
THERE'S NO HOPE FOR SCOTLAND WHEN YOU ***ADMIT*** TO BEING SO BAD!
YOUR FATHER AND MOTHER WERE VERY GOOD, RELIGIOUS PEOPLE.
GOOD-BYE! THIS IS THE END OF ALL HOPE!

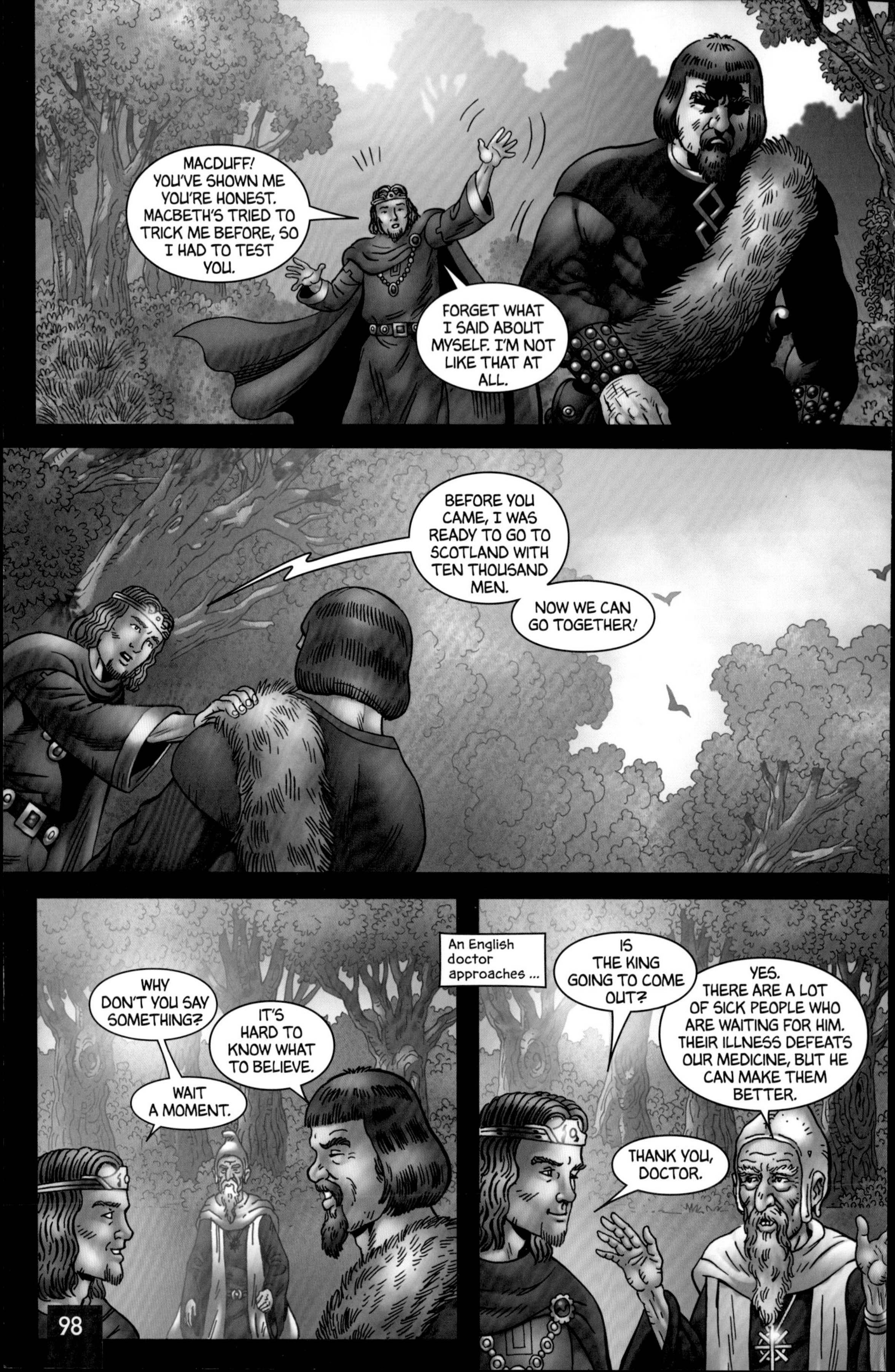
MACDUFF! YOU'VE SHOWN ME YOU'RE HONEST. MACBETH'S TRIED TO TRICK ME BEFORE, SO I HAD TO TEST YOU.
FORGET WHAT I SAID ABOUT MYSELF. I'M NOT LIKE THAT AT ALL.
BEFORE YOU CAME, I WAS READY TO GO TO SCOTLAND WITH TEN THOUSAND MEN.
NOW WE CAN GO TOGETHER!
WHY DON'T YOU SAY SOMETHING?
IT'S HARD TO KNOW WHAT TO BELIEVE.
WAIT A MOMENT.
An English doctor approaches ...
IS THE KING GOING TO COME OUT?
YES. THERE ARE A LOT OF SICK PEOPLE WHO ARE WAITING FOR HIM. THEIR ILLNESS DEFEATS OUR MEDICINE, BUT HE CAN MAKE THEM BETTER.
THANK YOU, DOCTOR.

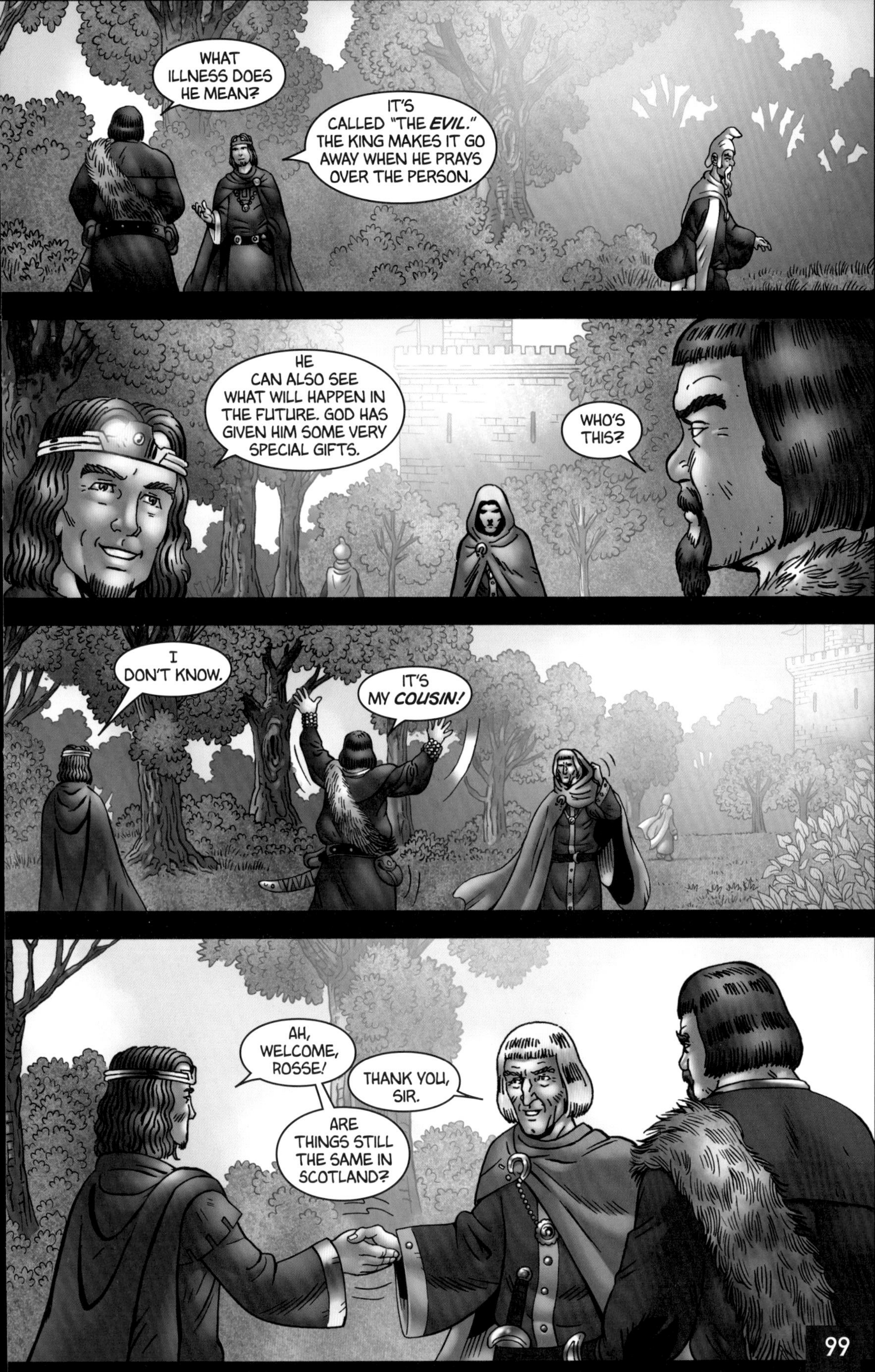
WHAT ILLNESS DOES HE MEAN?
IT'S CALLED "THE *EVIL*." THE KING MAKES IT GO AWAY WHEN HE PRAYS OVER THE PERSON.
HE CAN ALSO SEE WHAT WILL HAPPEN IN THE FUTURE. GOD HAS GIVEN HIM SOME VERY SPECIAL GIFTS.
WHO'S THIS?
I DON'T KNOW.
IT'S MY *COUSIN!*
AH, WELCOME, ROSSE!
THANK YOU, SIR.
ARE THINGS STILL THE SAME IN SCOTLAND?

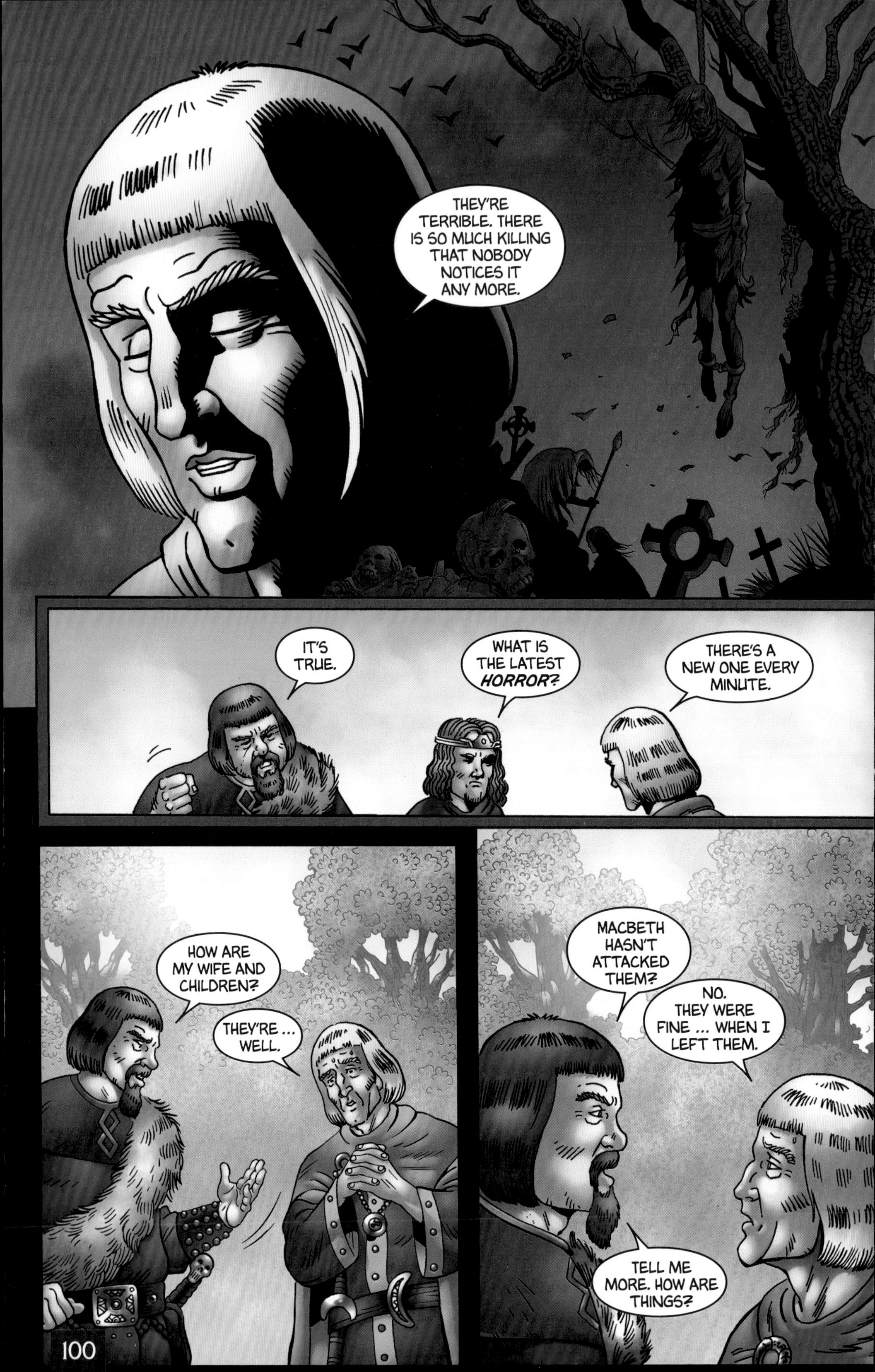
THEY'RE TERRIBLE. THERE IS SO MUCH KILLING THAT NOBODY NOTICES IT ANY MORE.
IT'S TRUE.
WHAT IS THE LATEST HORROR?
THERE'S A NEW ONE EVERY MINUTE.
HOW ARE MY WIFE AND CHILDREN?
THEY'RE ... WELL.
MACBETH HASN'T ATTACKED THEM?
NO. THEY WERE FINE ... WHEN I LEFT THEM.
TELL ME MORE. HOW ARE THINGS?

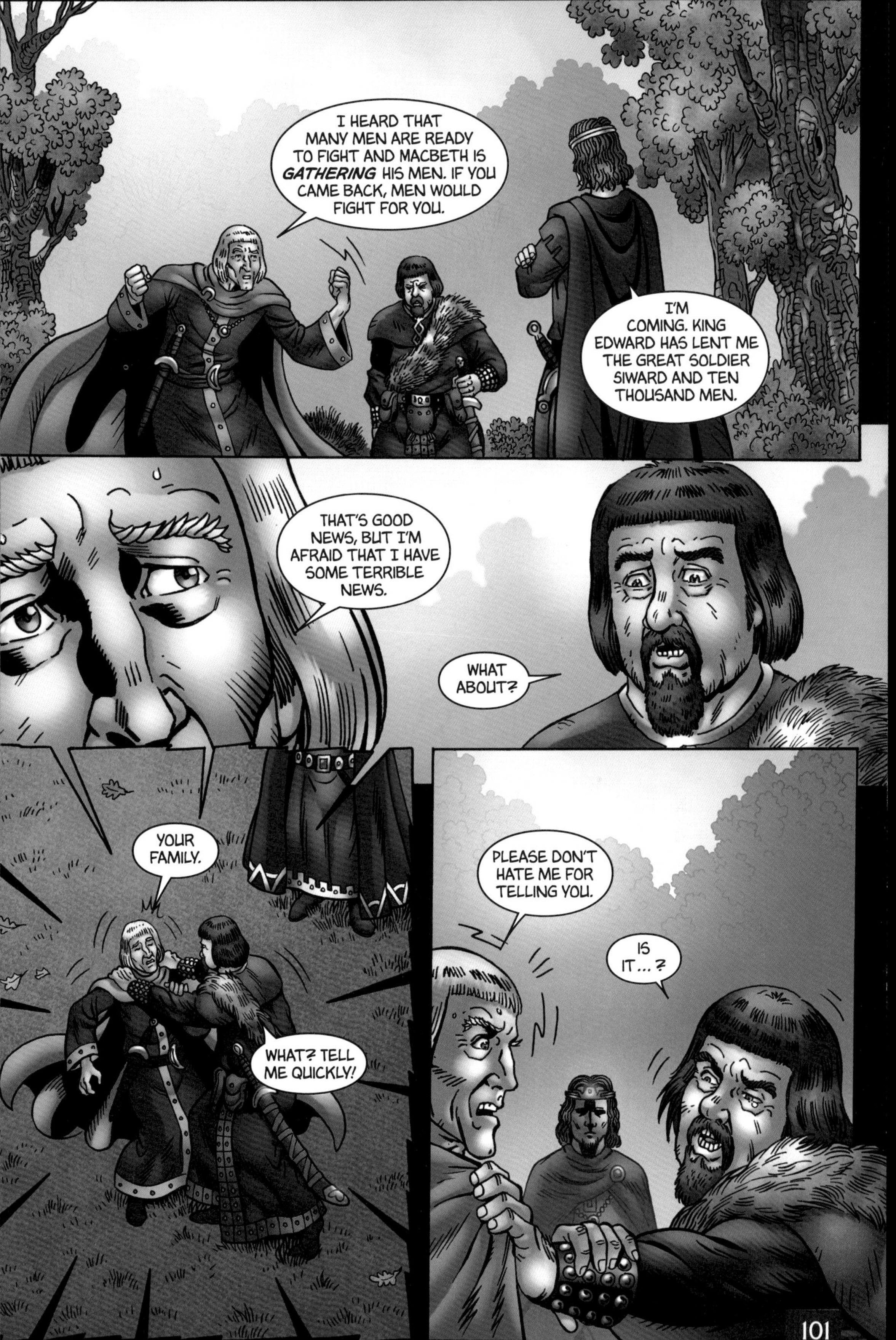
I HEARD THAT MANY MEN ARE READY TO FIGHT AND MACBETH IS *GATHERING* HIS MEN. IF YOU CAME BACK, MEN WOULD FIGHT FOR YOU.
I'M COMING. KING EDWARD HAS LENT ME THE GREAT SOLDIER SIWARD AND TEN THOUSAND MEN.
THAT'S GOOD NEWS, BUT I'M AFRAID THAT I HAVE SOME TERRIBLE NEWS.
WHAT ABOUT?
YOUR FAMILY.
WHAT? TELL ME QUICKLY!
PLEASE DON'T HATE ME FOR TELLING YOU.
IS IT... ?

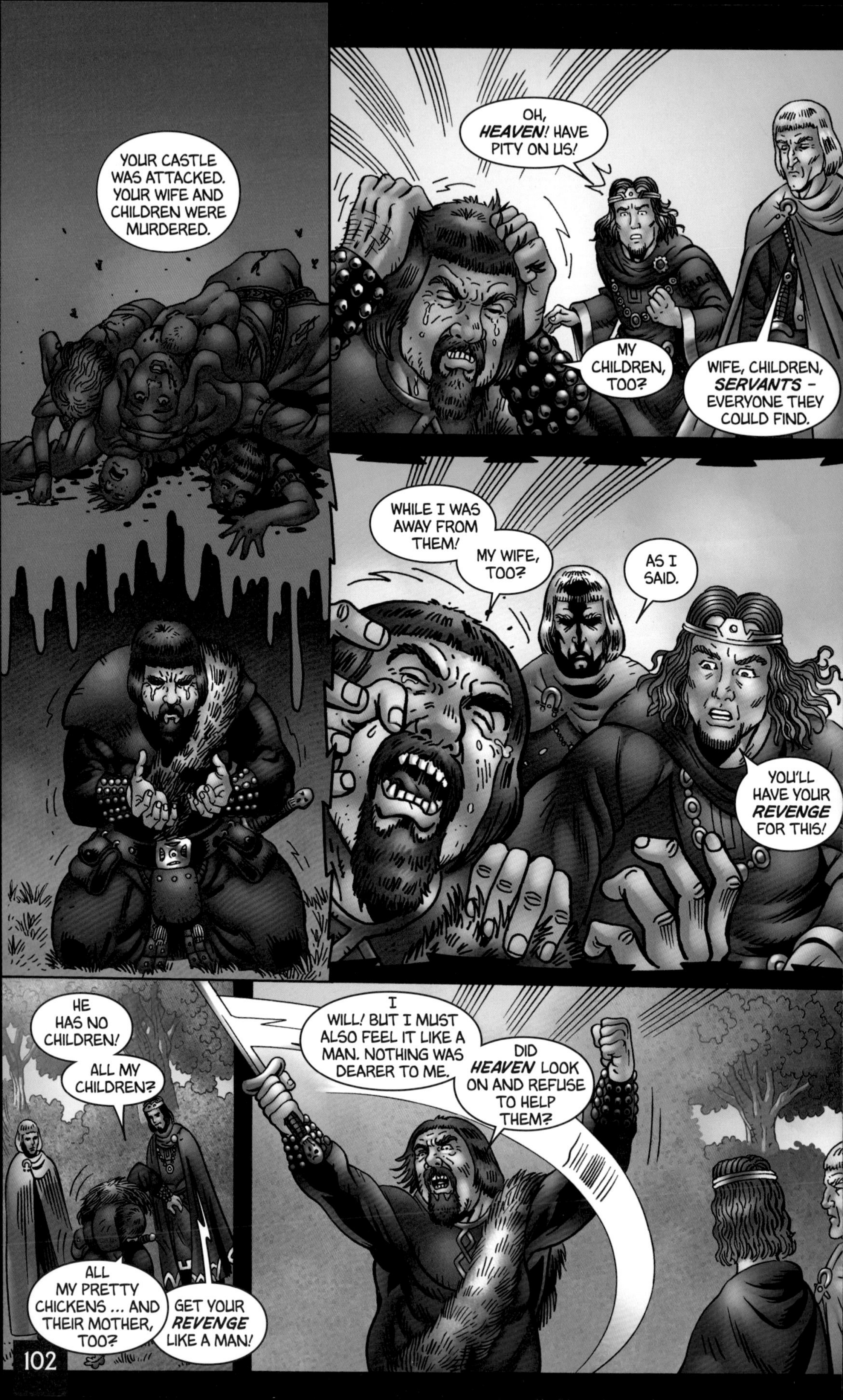
YOUR CASTLE WAS ATTACKED. YOUR WIFE AND CHILDREN WERE MURDERED.
OH, HEAVEN! HAVE PITY ON US!
MY CHILDREN, TOO?
WIFE, CHILDREN, SERVANTS - EVERYONE THEY COULD FIND.
WHILE I WAS AWAY FROM THEM!
MY WIFE, TOO?
AS I SAID.
YOU'LL HAVE YOUR REVENGE FOR THIS!
HE HAS NO CHILDREN!
ALL MY CHILDREN?
ALL MY PRETTY CHICKENS ... AND THEIR MOTHER, TOO?
GET YOUR REVENGE LIKE A MAN!
I WILL! BUT I MUST ALSO FEEL IT LIKE A MAN. NOTHING WAS DEARER TO ME.
DID HEAVEN LOOK ON AND REFUSE TO HELP THEM?

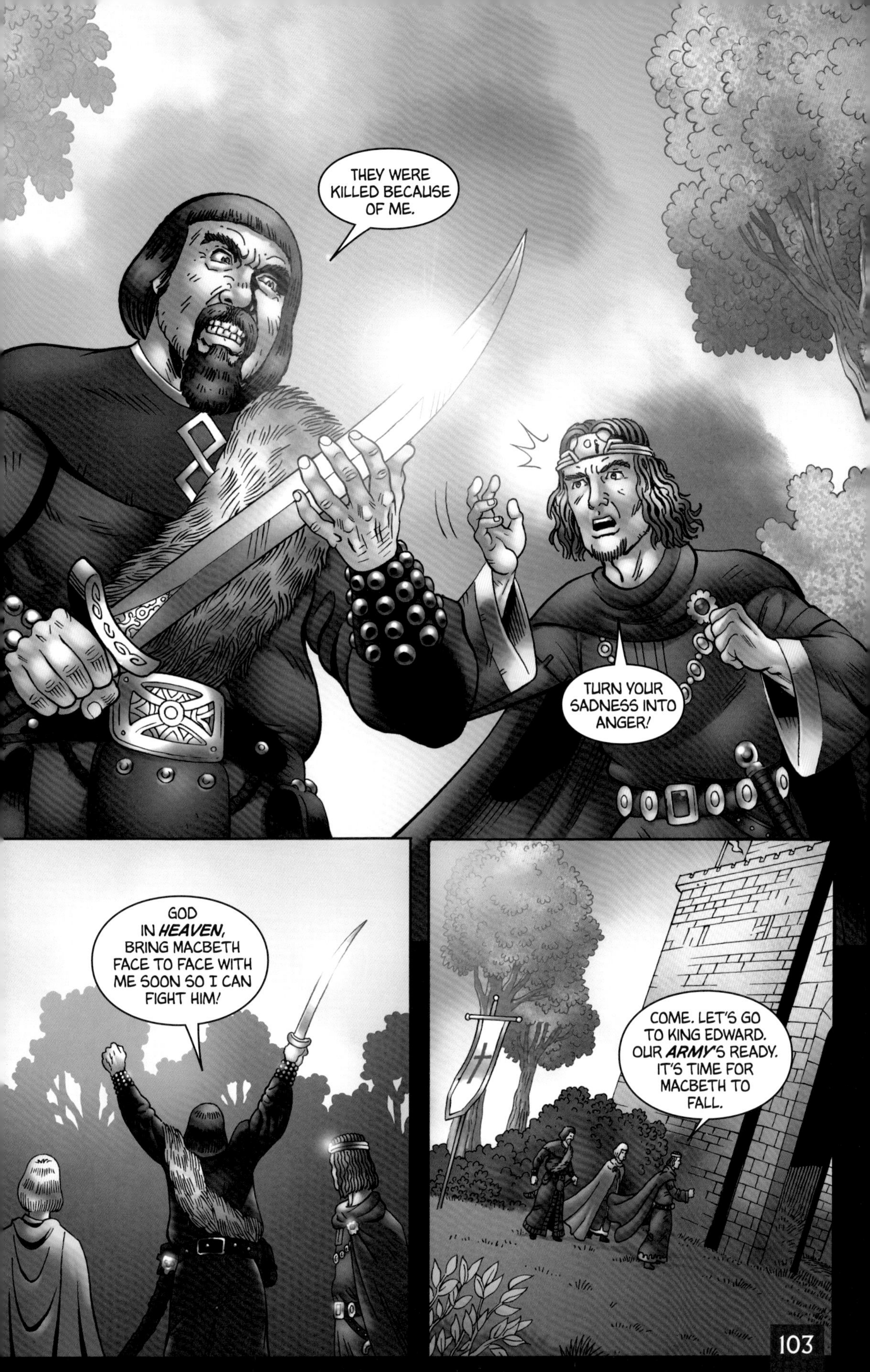
THEY WERE KILLED BECAUSE OF ME.
TURN YOUR SADNESS INTO ANGER!
GOD IN *HEAVEN*, BRING MACBETH FACE TO FACE WITH ME SOON SO I CAN FIGHT HIM!
COME. LET'S GO TO KING EDWARD. OUR *ARMY*'S READY. IT'S TIME FOR MACBETH TO FALL.

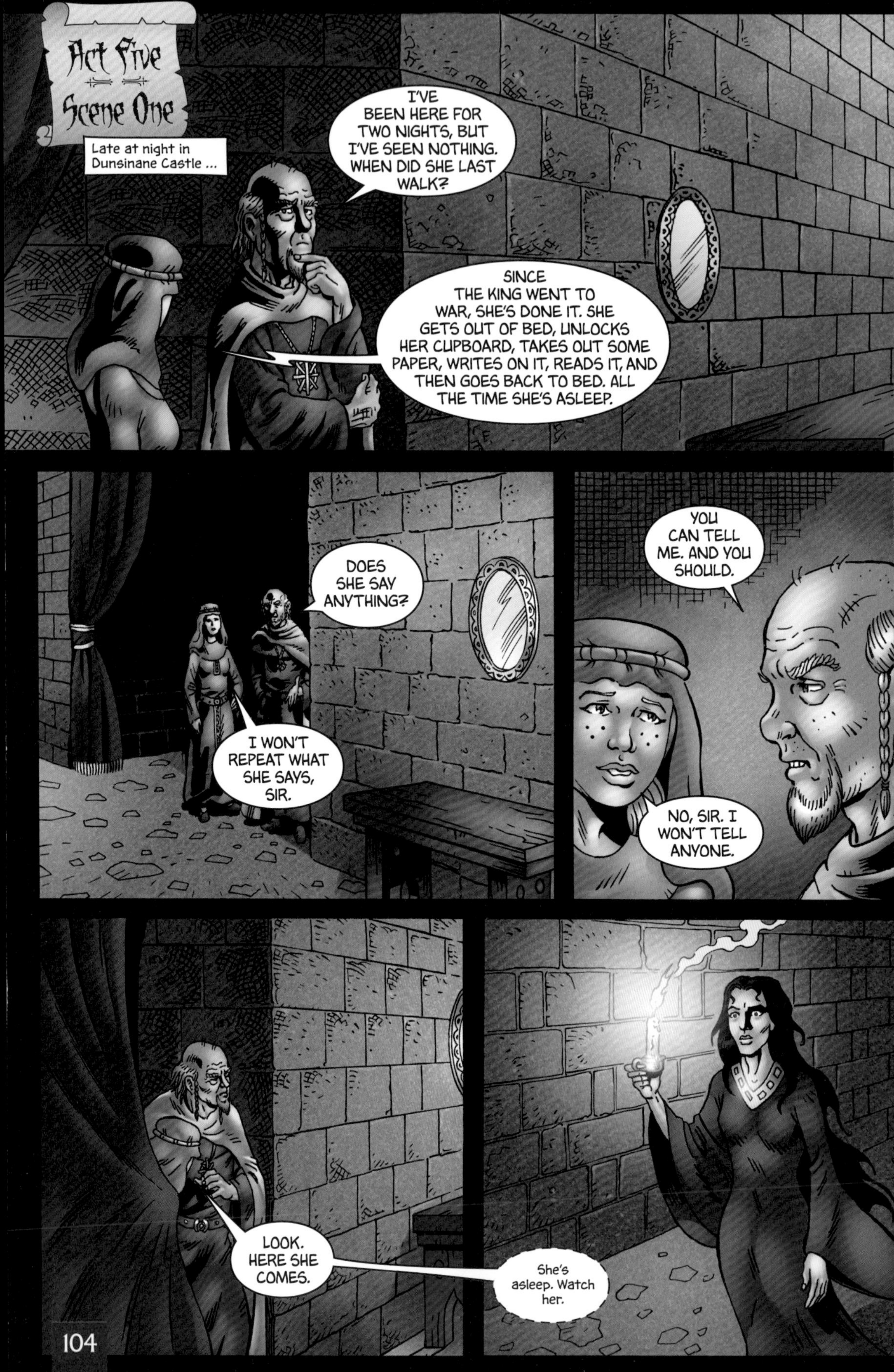

Act Five
Scene One
Late at night in Dunsinane Castle ...
I'VE BEEN HERE FOR TWO NIGHTS, BUT I'VE SEEN NOTHING. WHEN DID SHE LAST WALK?
SINCE THE KING WENT TO WAR, SHE'S DONE IT. SHE GETS OUT OF BED, UNLOCKS HER CUPBOARD, TAKES OUT SOME PAPER, WRITES ON IT, READS IT, AND THEN GOES BACK TO BED. ALL THE TIME SHE'S ASLEEP.
DOES SHE SAY ANYTHING?
I WON'T REPEAT WHAT SHE SAYS, SIR.
YOU CAN TELL ME. AND YOU SHOULD.
NO, SIR. I WON'T TELL ANYONE.
LOOK. HERE SHE COMES.
She's asleep. Watch her.

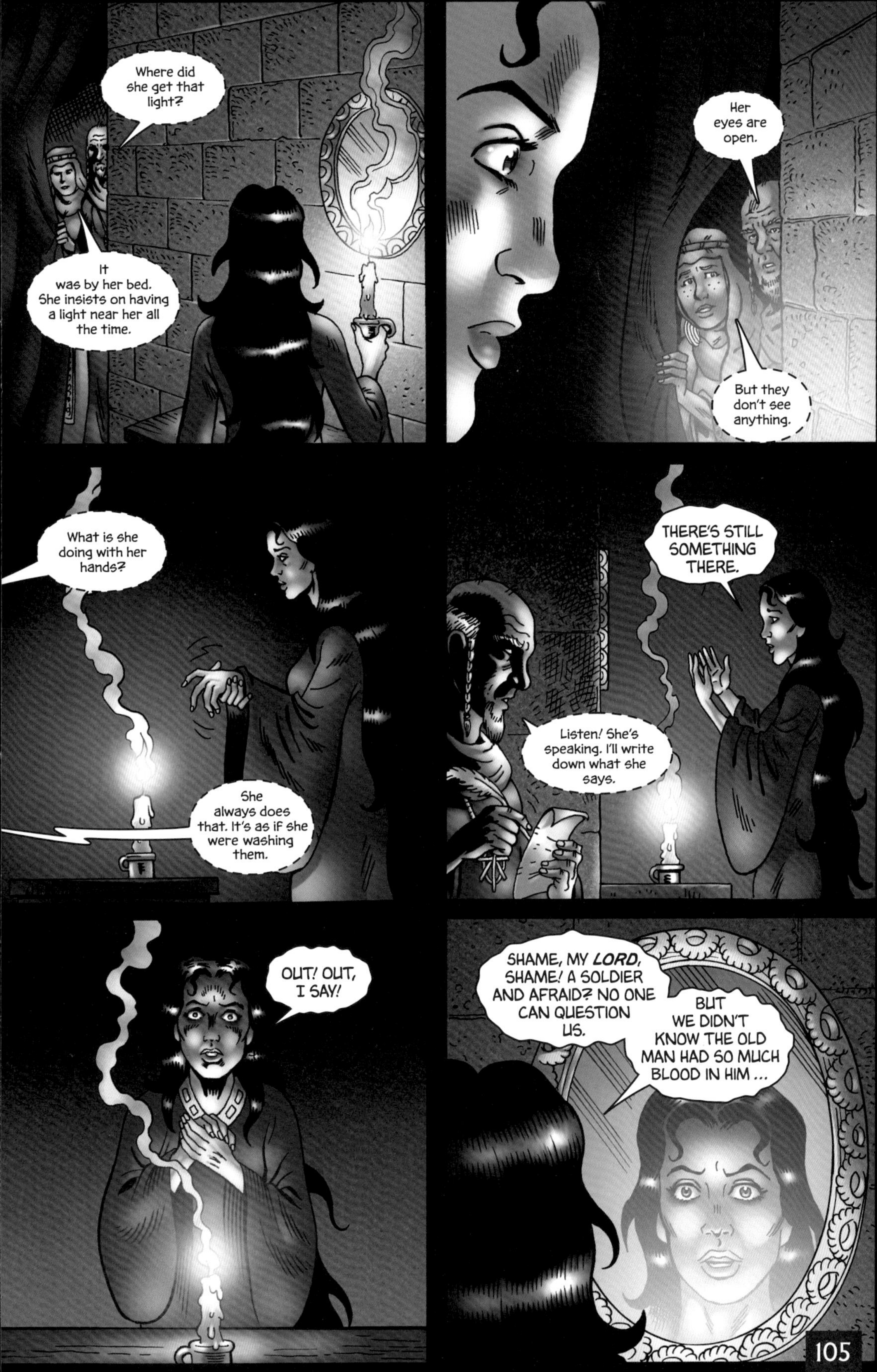
Where did she get that light?
It was by her bed. She insists on having a light near her all the time.
Her eyes are open.
But they don't see anything.
What is she doing with her hands?
She always does that. It's as if she were washing them.
THERE'S STILL SOMETHING THERE.
Listen! She's speaking. I'll write down what she says.
OUT! OUT, I SAY!
SHAME, MY ***LORD***, SHAME! A SOLDIER AND AFRAID? NO ONE CAN QUESTION US.
BUT WE DIDN'T KNOW THE OLD MAN HAD SO MUCH BLOOD IN HIM ...

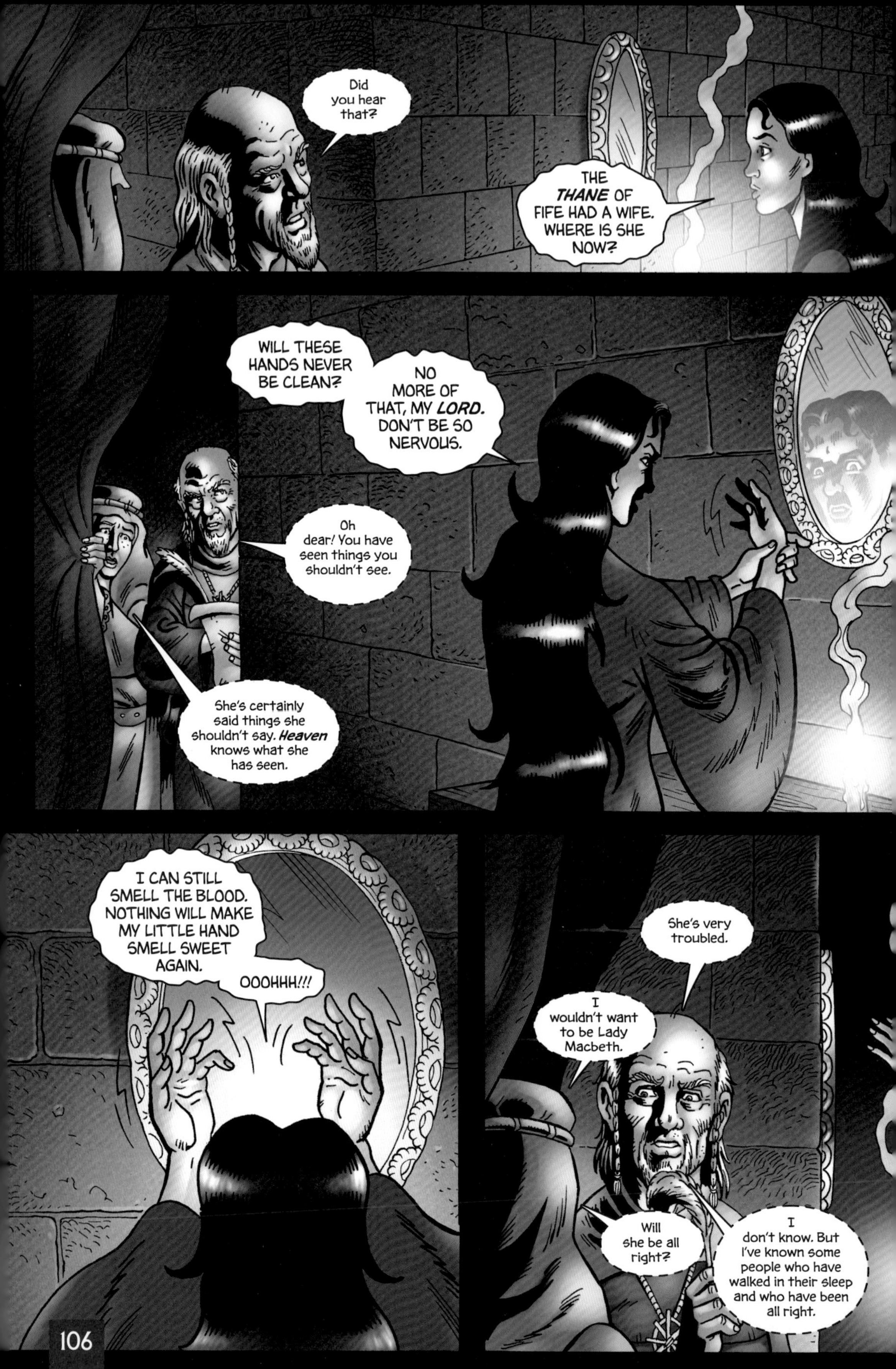
Did you hear that?
THE THANE OF FIFE HAD A WIFE. WHERE IS SHE NOW?
WILL THESE HANDS NEVER BE CLEAN?
NO MORE OF THAT, MY LORD. DON'T BE SO NERVOUS.
Oh dear! You have seen things you shouldn't see.
She's certainly said things she shouldn't say. Heaven knows what she has seen.
I CAN STILL SMELL THE BLOOD. NOTHING WILL MAKE MY LITTLE HAND SMELL SWEET AGAIN.
OOOHHH!!!
She's very troubled.
I wouldn't want to be Lady Macbeth.
Will she be all right?
I don't know. But I've known some people who have walked in their sleep and who have been all right.

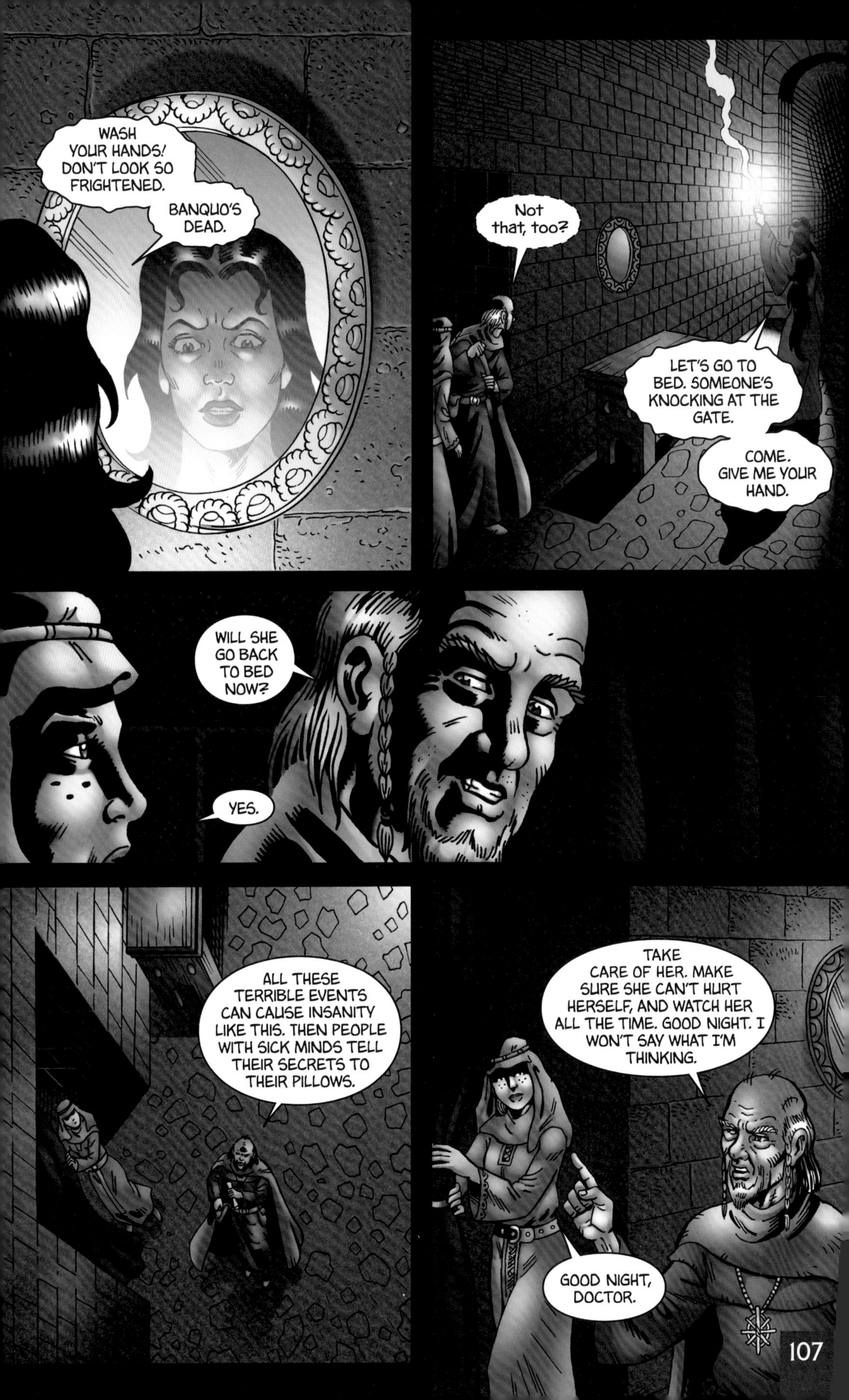
WASH YOUR HANDS! DON'T LOOK SO FRIGHTENED.
BANQUO'S DEAD.
Not that, too?
LET'S GO TO BED. SOMEONE'S KNOCKING AT THE GATE.
COME. GIVE ME YOUR HAND.
WILL SHE GO BACK TO BED NOW?
YES.
ALL THESE TERRIBLE EVENTS CAN CAUSE INSANITY LIKE THIS. THEN PEOPLE WITH SICK MINDS TELL THEIR SECRETS TO THEIR PILLOWS.
TAKE CARE OF HER. MAKE SURE SHE CAN'T HURT HERSELF, AND WATCH HER ALL THE TIME. GOOD NIGHT. I WON'T SAY WHAT I'M THINKING.
GOOD NIGHT, DOCTOR.

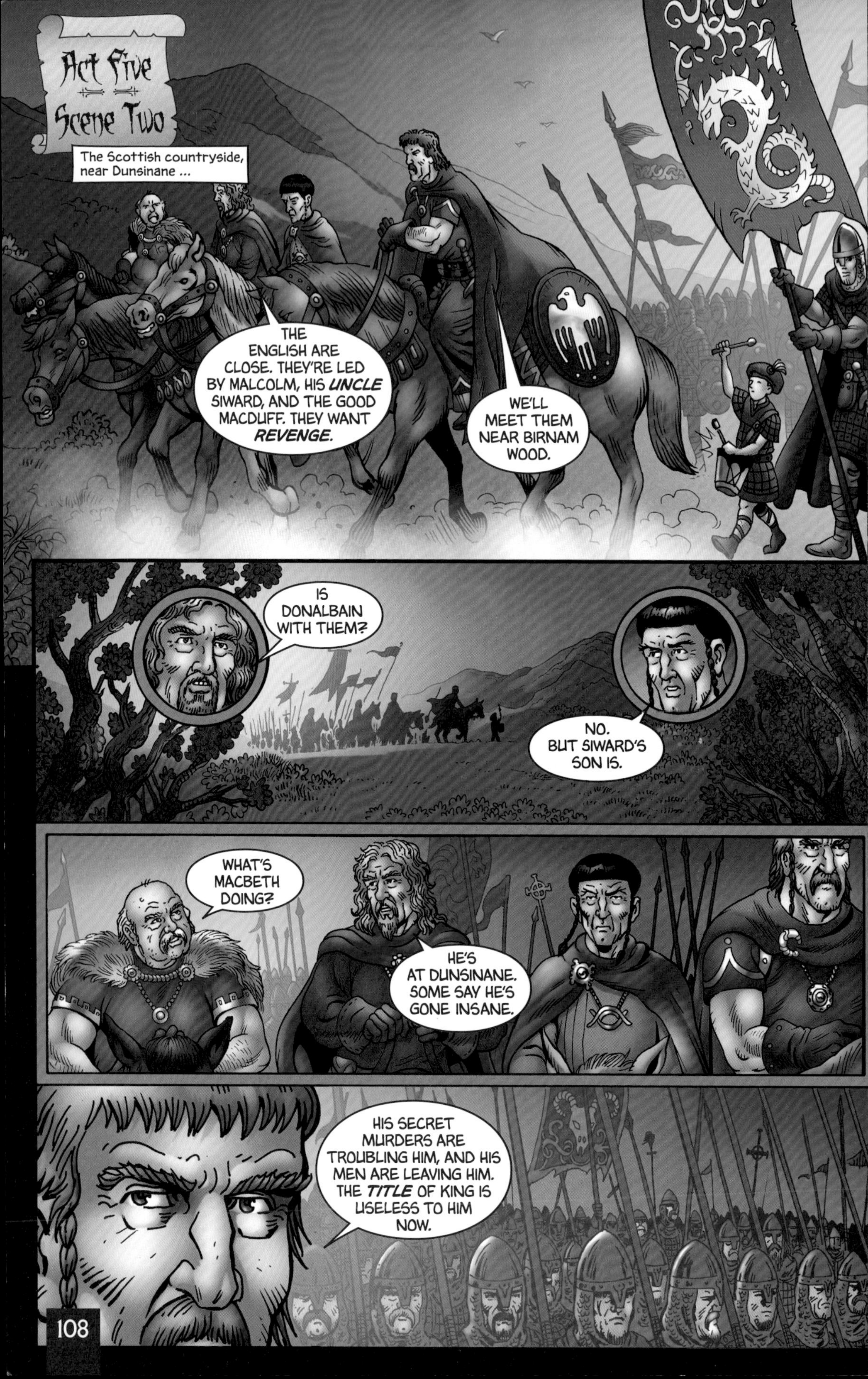
Act Five
Scene Two
The Scottish countryside, near Dunsinane ...
THE ENGLISH ARE CLOSE. THEY'RE LED BY MALCOLM, HIS UNCLE SIWARD, AND THE GOOD MACDUFF. THEY WANT REVENGE.
WE'LL MEET THEM NEAR BIRNAM WOOD.
IS DONALBAIN WITH THEM?
NO. BUT SIWARD'S SON IS.
WHAT'S MACBETH DOING?
HE'S AT DUNSINANE. SOME SAY HE'S GONE INSANE.
HIS SECRET MURDERS ARE TROUBLING HIM, AND HIS MEN ARE LEAVING HIM. THE TITLE OF KING IS USELESS TO HIM NOW.

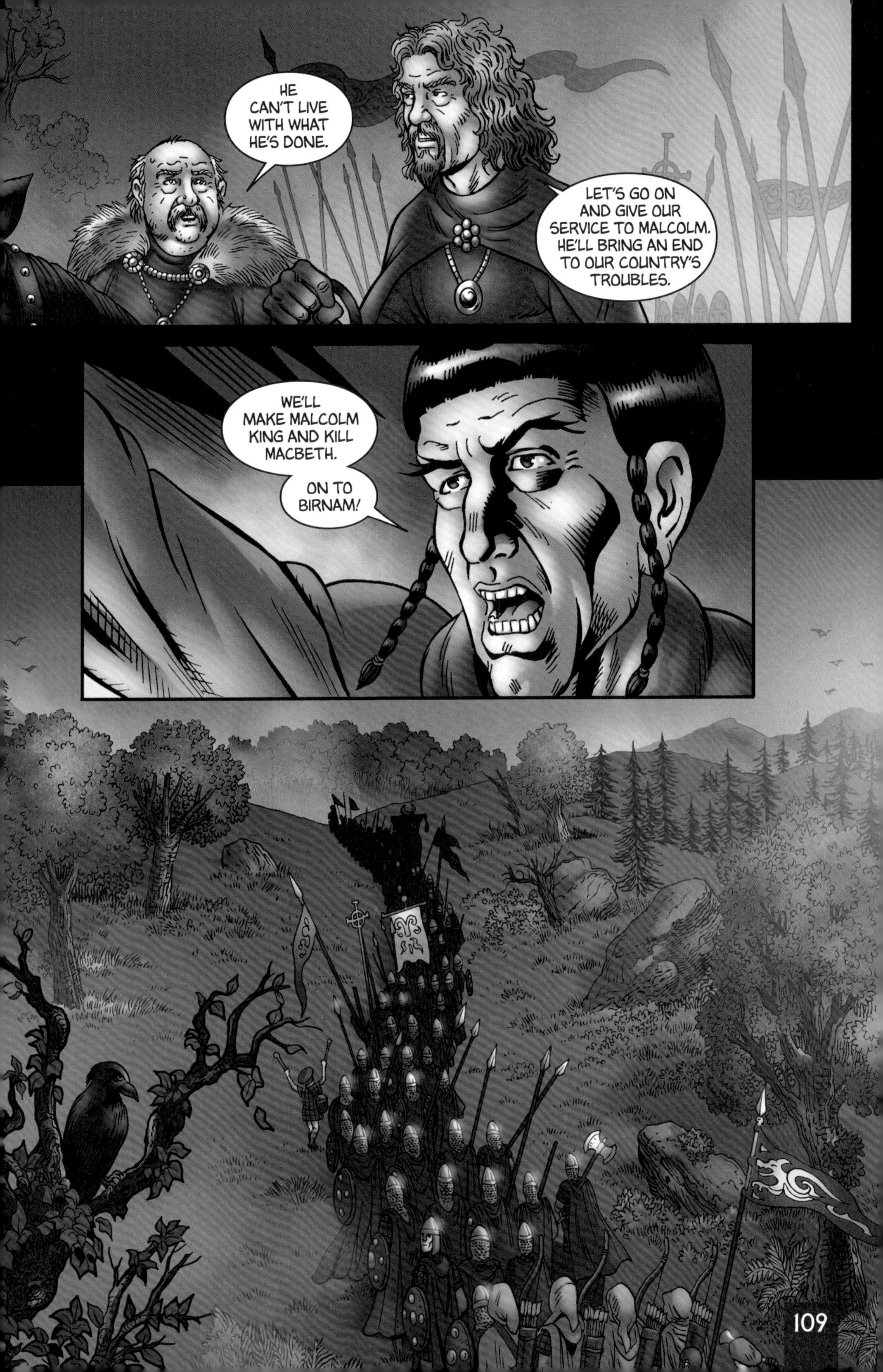
HE CAN'T LIVE WITH WHAT HE'S DONE.
LET'S GO ON AND GIVE OUR SERVICE TO MALCOLM. HE'LL BRING AN END TO OUR COUNTRY'S TROUBLES.
WE'LL MAKE MALCOLM KING AND KILL MACBETH.
ON TO BIRNAM!

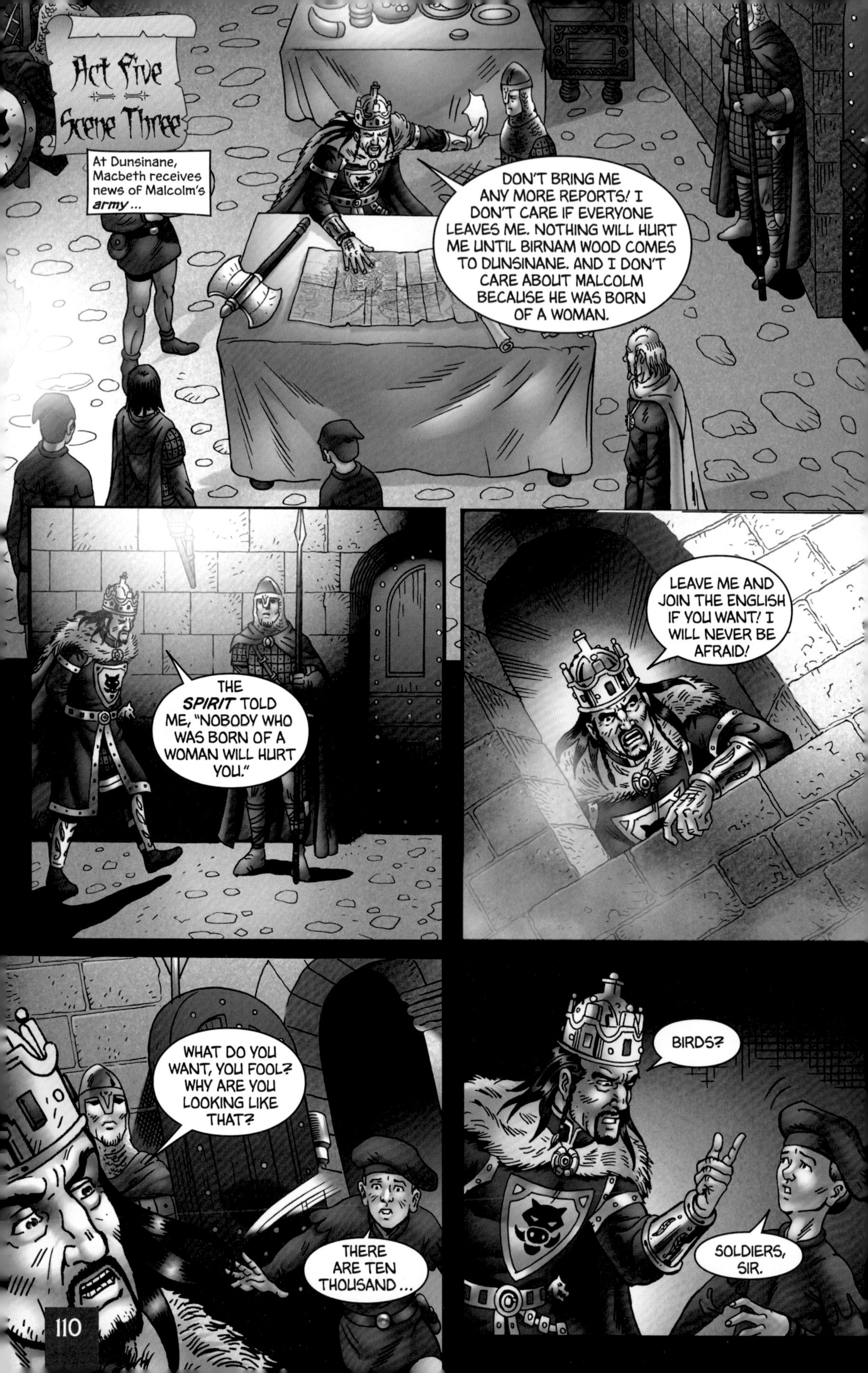
Act Five
Scene Three
At Dunsinane, Macbeth receives news of Malcolm's *army*...
DON'T BRING ME ANY MORE REPORTS! I DON'T CARE IF EVERYONE LEAVES ME. NOTHING WILL HURT ME UNTIL BIRNAM WOOD COMES TO DUNSINANE. AND I DON'T CARE ABOUT MALCOLM BECAUSE HE WAS BORN OF A WOMAN.
THE *SPIRIT* TOLD ME, "NOBODY WHO WAS BORN OF A WOMAN WILL HURT YOU."
LEAVE ME AND JOIN THE ENGLISH IF YOU WANT! I WILL NEVER BE AFRAID!
WHAT DO YOU WANT, YOU FOOL? WHY ARE YOU LOOKING LIKE THAT?
THERE ARE TEN THOUSAND...
BIRDS?
SOLDIERS, SIR.

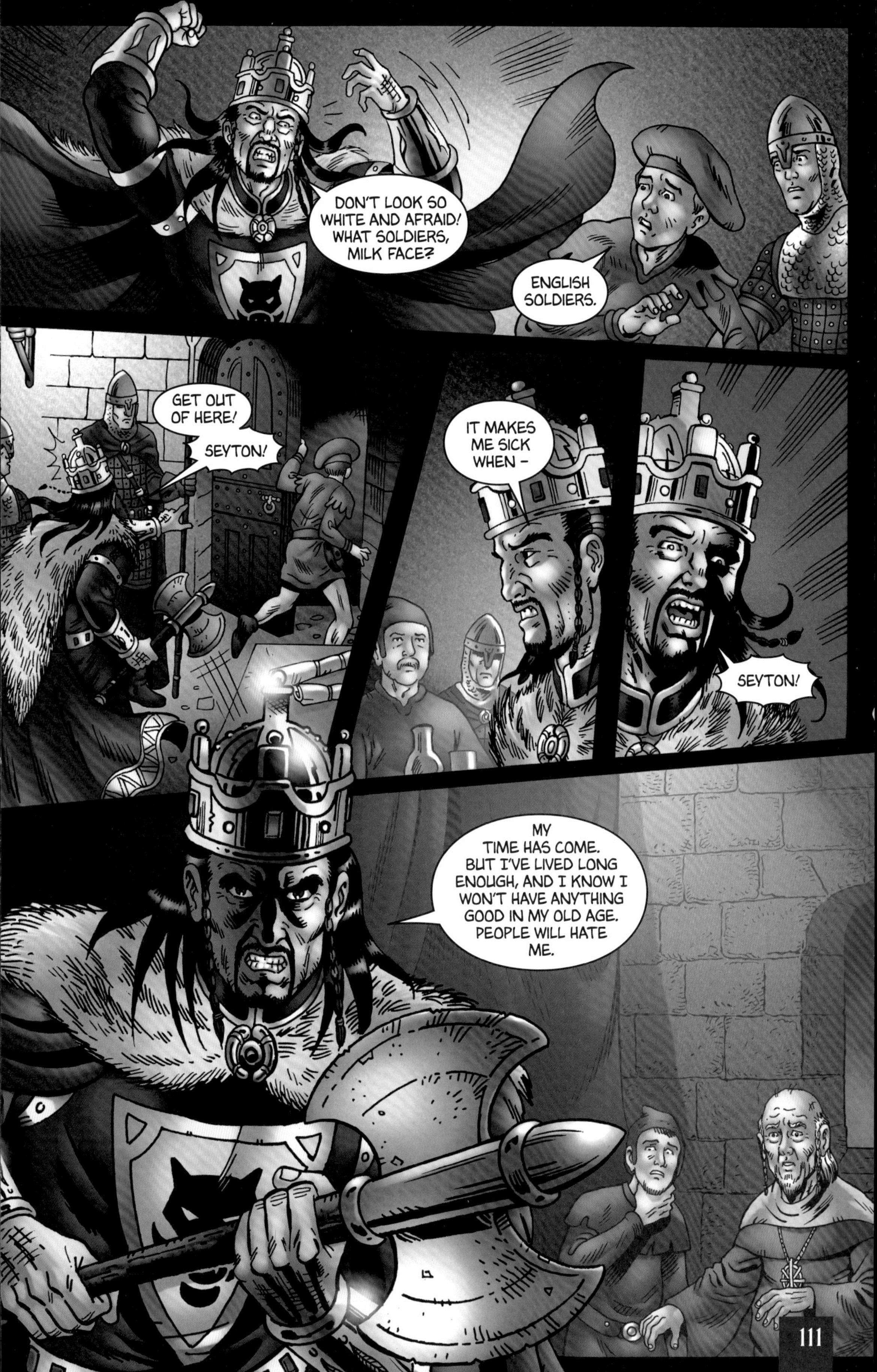
DON'T LOOK SO WHITE AND AFRAID! WHAT SOLDIERS, MILK FACE?
ENGLISH SOLDIERS.
GET OUT OF HERE!
SEYTON!
IT MAKES ME SICK WHEN –
SEYTON!
MY TIME HAS COME. BUT I'VE LIVED LONG ENOUGH, AND I KNOW I WON'T HAVE ANYTHING GOOD IN MY OLD AGE. PEOPLE WILL HATE ME.

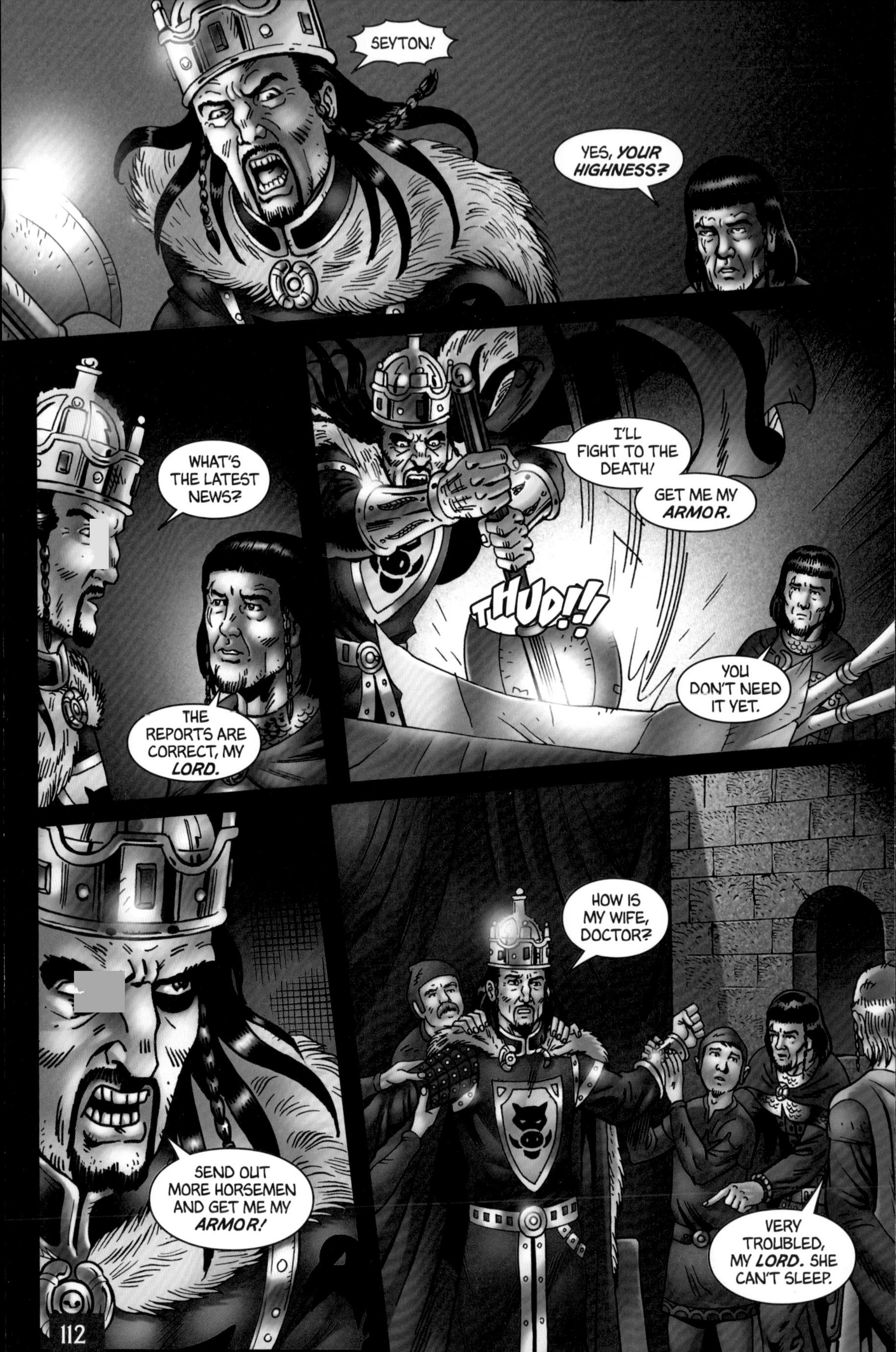
SEYTON!
YES, YOUR HIGHNESS?
WHAT'S THE LATEST NEWS?
THE REPORTS ARE CORRECT, MY LORD.
I'LL FIGHT TO THE DEATH!
GET ME MY ARMOR.
THUD!!
YOU DON'T NEED IT YET.
SEND OUT MORE HORSEMEN AND GET ME MY ARMOR!
HOW IS MY WIFE, DOCTOR?
VERY TROUBLED, MY LORD. SHE CAN'T SLEEP.

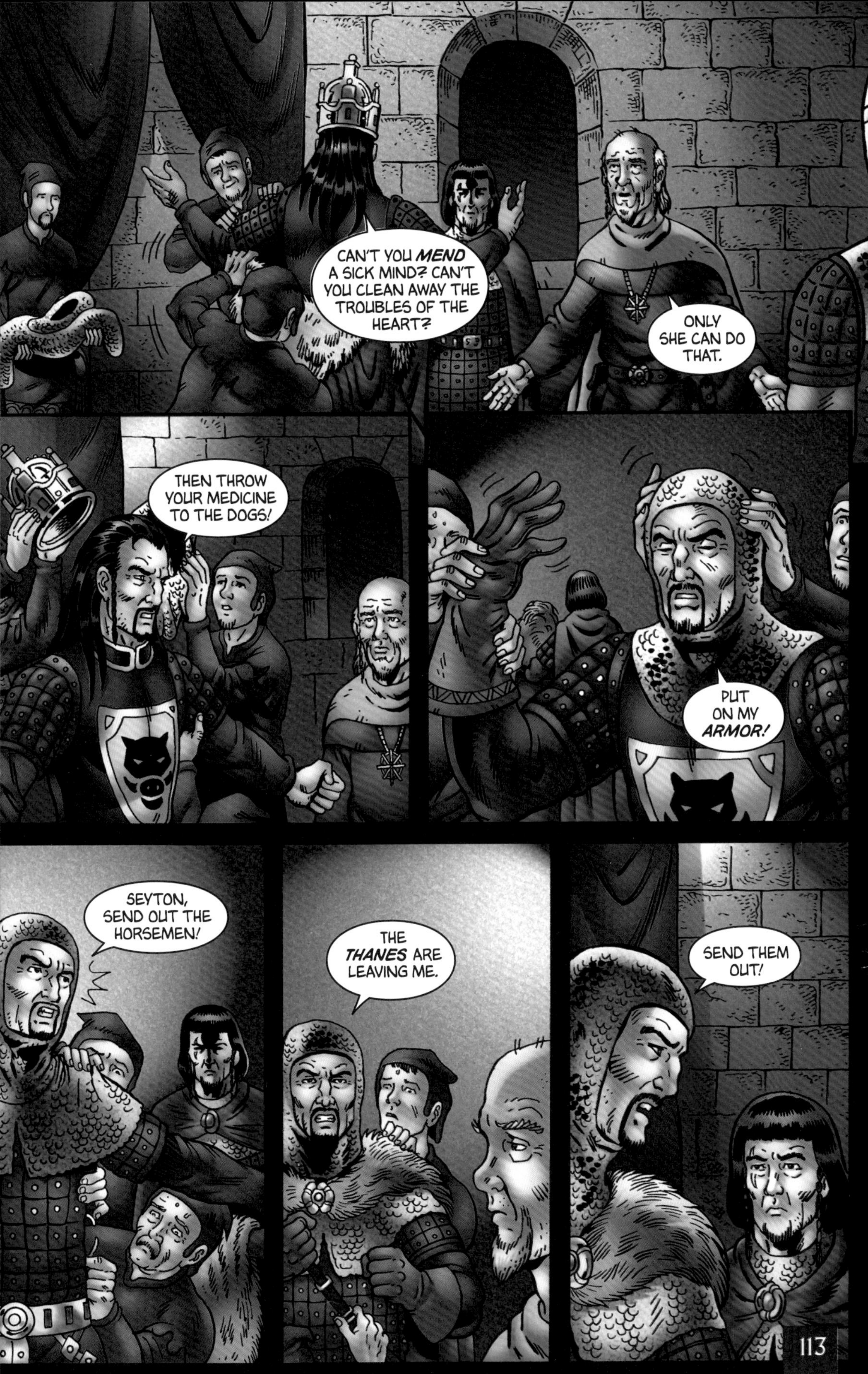
CAN'T YOU *MEND* A SICK MIND? CAN'T YOU CLEAN AWAY THE TROUBLES OF THE HEART?
ONLY SHE CAN DO THAT.
THEN THROW YOUR MEDICINE TO THE DOGS!
PUT ON MY *ARMOR!*
SEYTON, SEND OUT THE HORSEMEN!
THE *THANES* ARE LEAVING ME.
SEND THEM OUT!

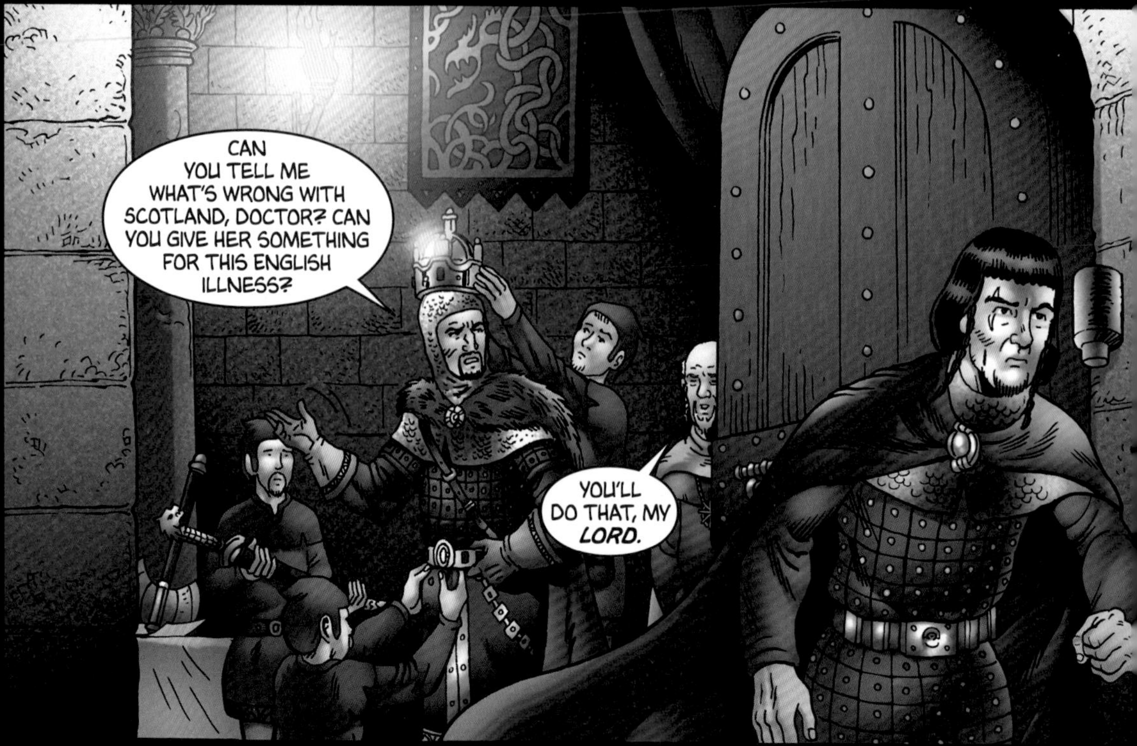
CAN YOU TELL ME WHAT'S WRONG WITH SCOTLAND, DOCTOR? CAN YOU GIVE HER SOMETHING FOR THIS ENGLISH ILLNESS?
YOU'LL DO THAT, MY *LORD.*
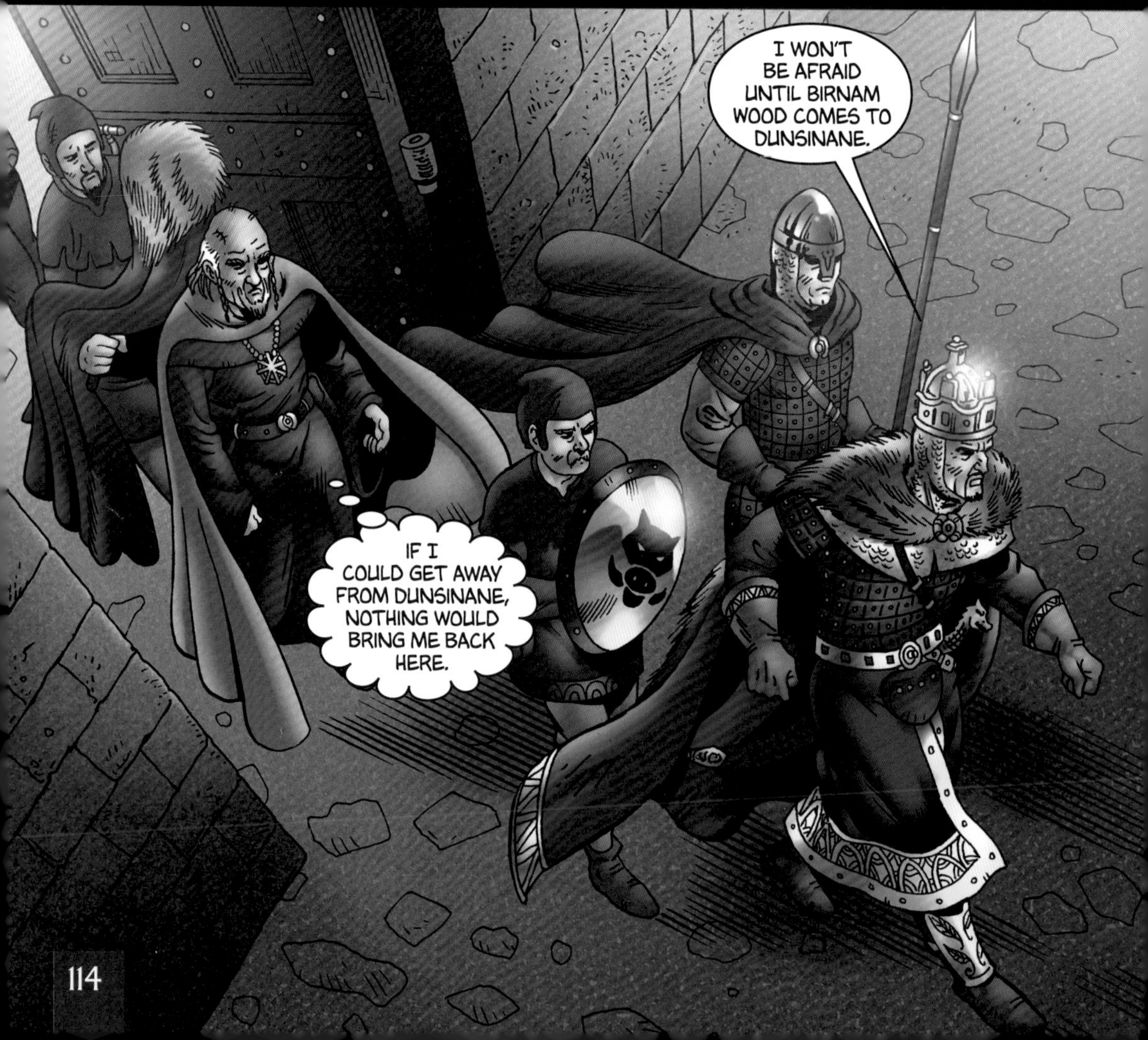
I WON'T BE AFRAID UNTIL BIRNAM WOOD COMES TO DUNSINANE.
IF I COULD GET AWAY FROM DUNSINANE, NOTHING WOULD BRING ME BACK HERE.

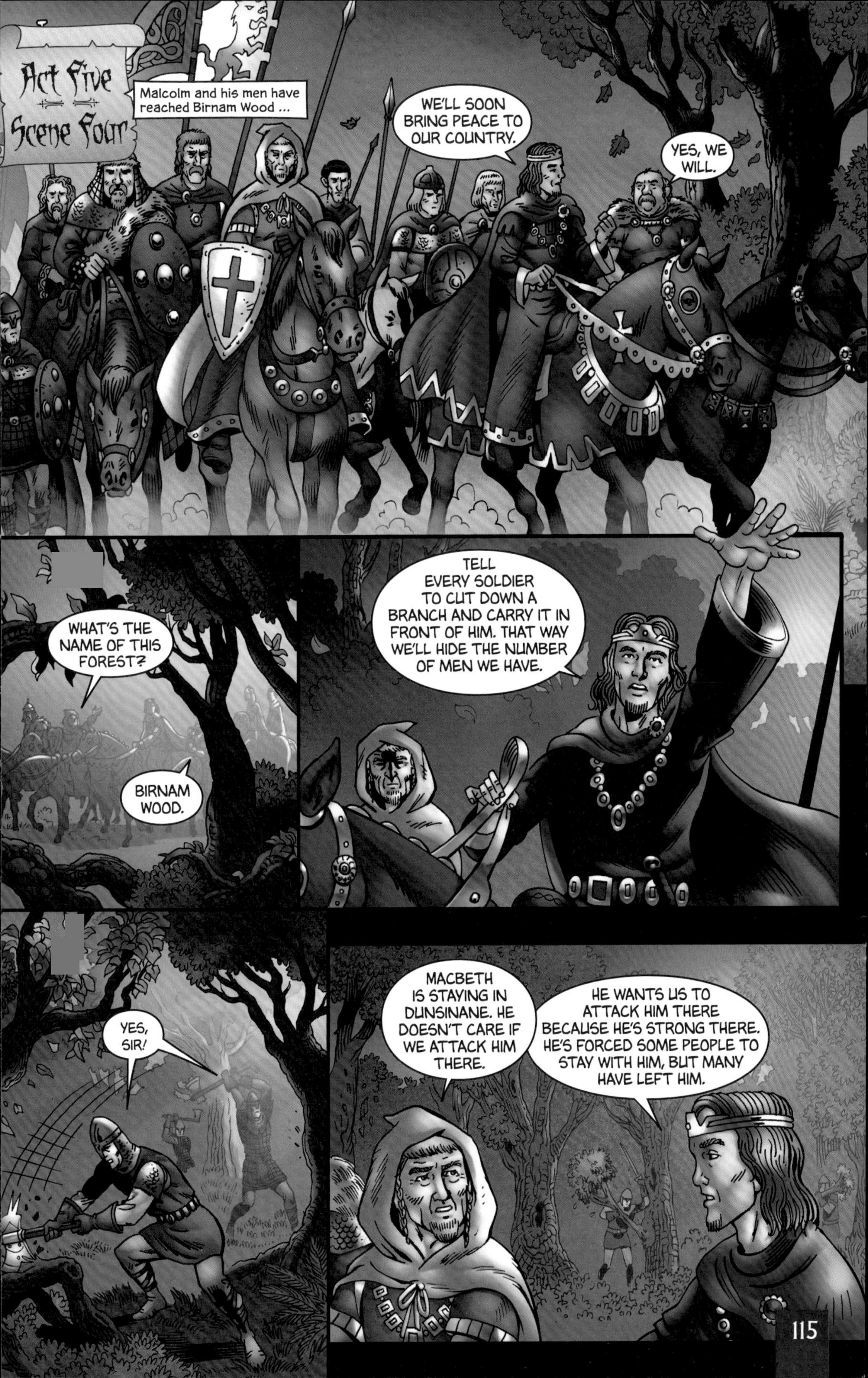

Act Five
Scene Four
Malcolm and his men have reached Birnam Wood ...
WE'LL SOON BRING PEACE TO OUR COUNTRY.
YES, WE WILL.
WHAT'S THE NAME OF THIS FOREST?
BIRNAM WOOD.
TELL EVERY SOLDIER TO CUT DOWN A BRANCH AND CARRY IT IN FRONT OF HIM. THAT WAY WE'LL HIDE THE NUMBER OF MEN WE HAVE.
YES, SIR!
MACBETH IS STAYING IN DUNSINANE. HE DOESN'T CARE IF WE ATTACK HIM THERE.
HE WANTS US TO ATTACK HIM THERE BECAUSE HE'S STRONG THERE. HE'S FORCED SOME PEOPLE TO STAY WITH HIM, BUT MANY HAVE LEFT HIM.

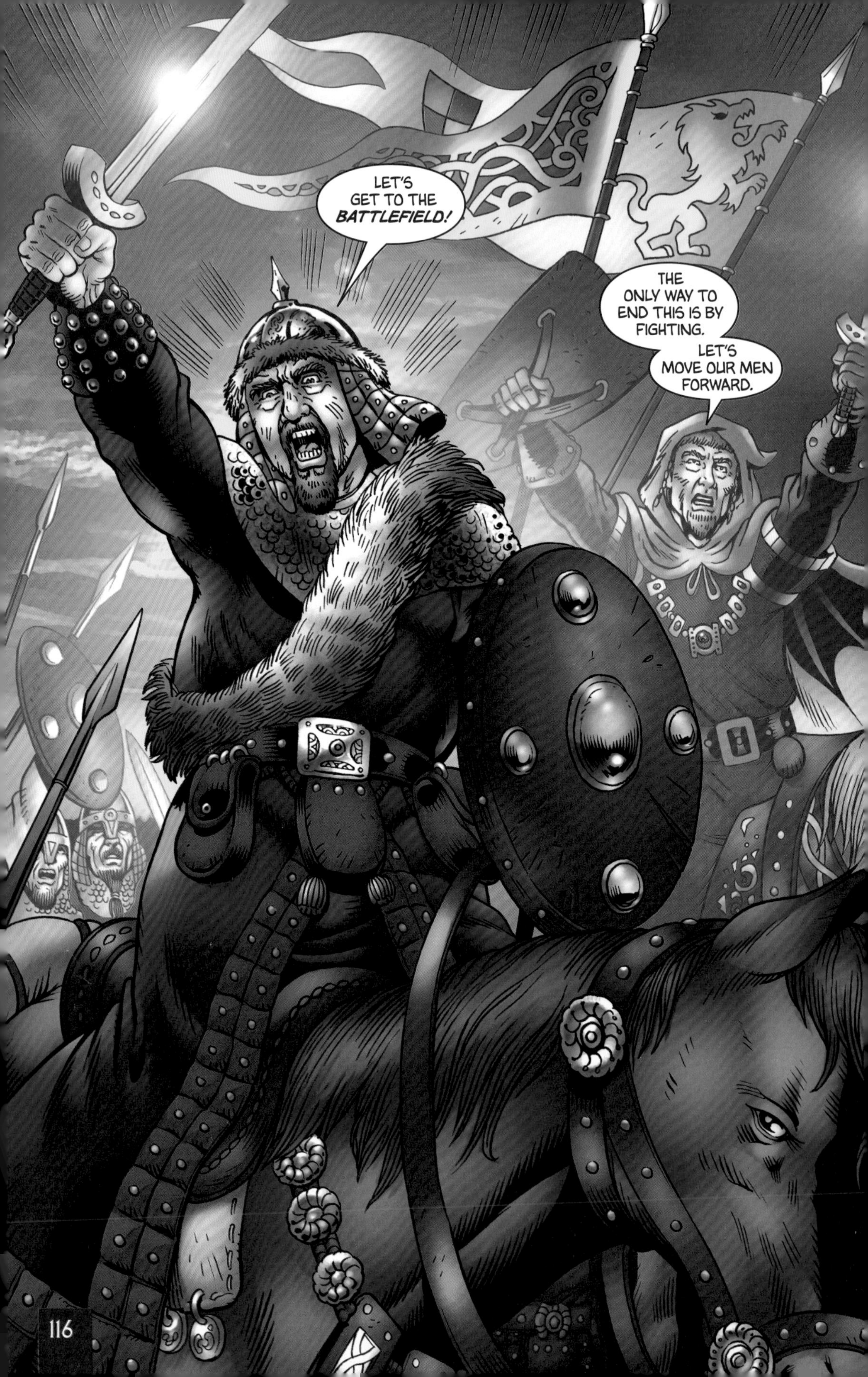
LET'S GET TO THE *BATTLEFIELD!*
THE ONLY WAY TO END THIS IS BY FIGHTING.
LET'S MOVE OUR MEN FORWARD.

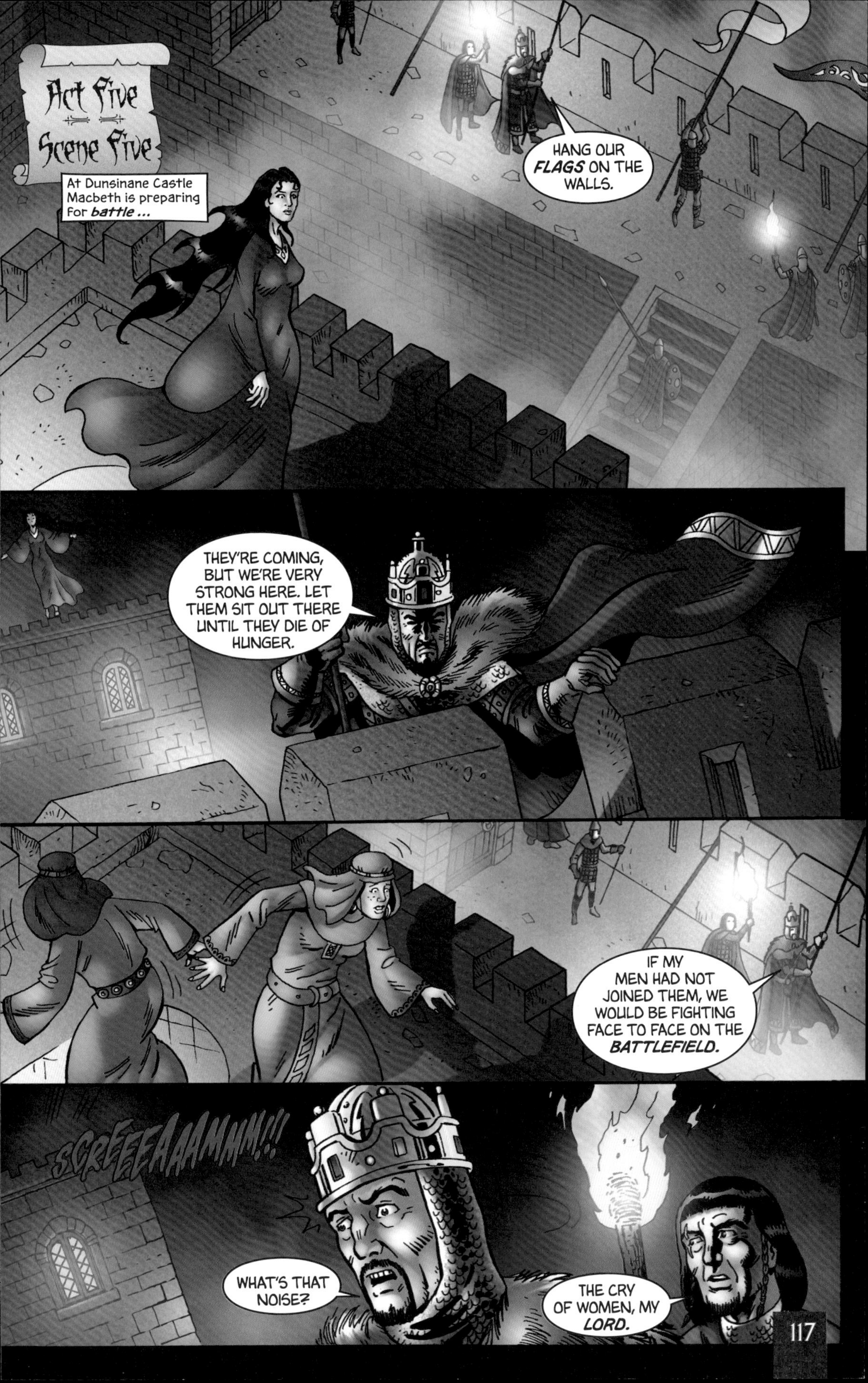
Act Five
Scene Five
At Dunsinane Castle Macbeth is preparing for **battle ...**
HANG OUR **FLAGS** ON THE WALLS.
THEY'RE COMING, BUT WE'RE VERY STRONG HERE. LET THEM SIT OUT THERE UNTIL THEY DIE OF HUNGER.
IF MY MEN HAD NOT JOINED THEM, WE WOULD BE FIGHTING FACE TO FACE ON THE **BATTLEFIELD.**
SCREEEAAAMMM!!!
WHAT'S THAT NOISE?
THE CRY OF WOMEN, MY **LORD.**

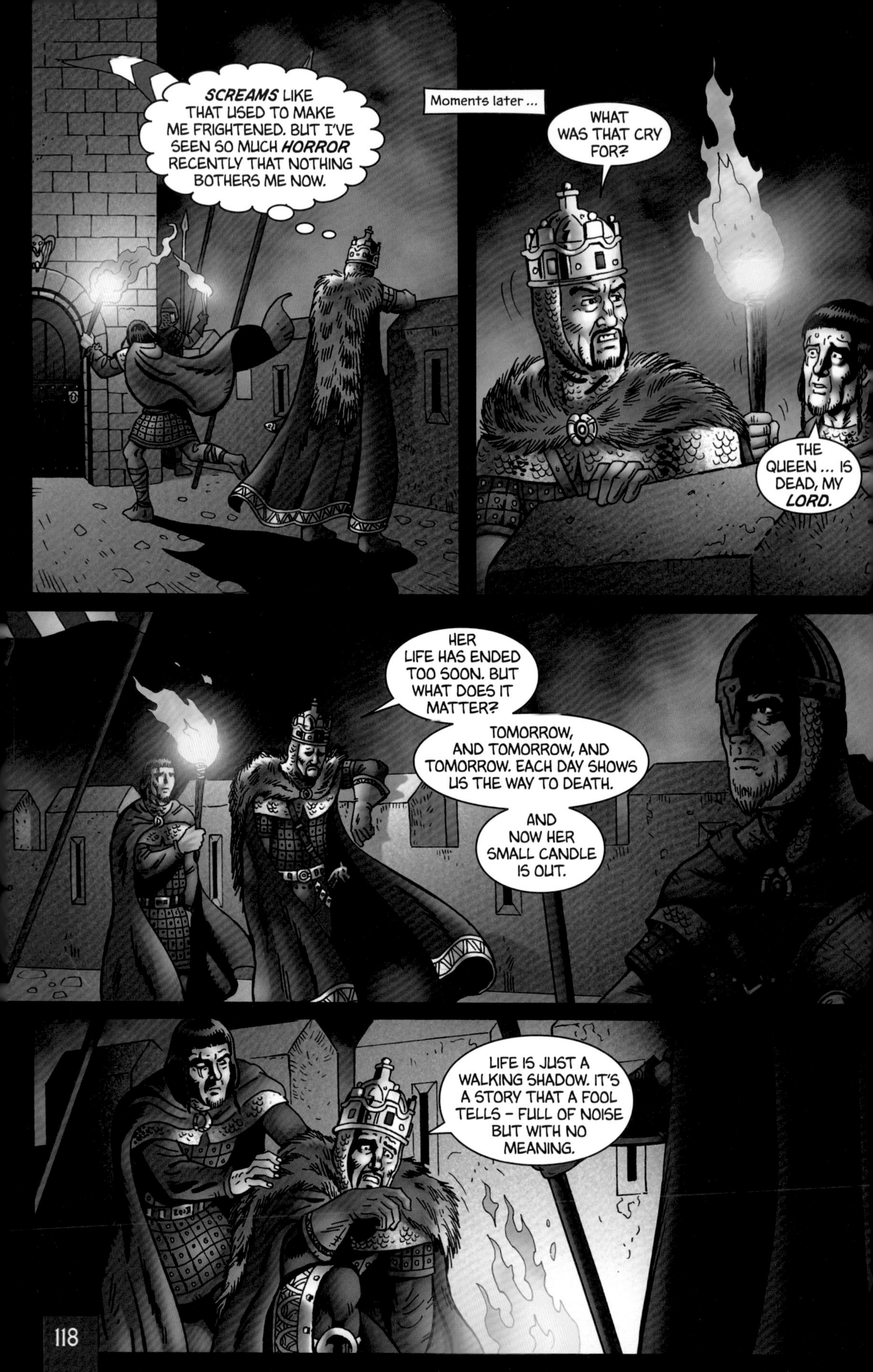
SCREAMS LIKE THAT USED TO MAKE ME FRIGHTENED. BUT I'VE SEEN SO MUCH HORROR RECENTLY THAT NOTHING BOTHERS ME NOW.
Moments later ...
WHAT WAS THAT CRY FOR?
THE QUEEN ... IS DEAD, MY LORD.
HER LIFE HAS ENDED TOO SOON. BUT WHAT DOES IT MATTER?
TOMORROW, AND TOMORROW, AND TOMORROW. EACH DAY SHOWS US THE WAY TO DEATH.
AND NOW HER SMALL CANDLE IS OUT.
LIFE IS JUST A WALKING SHADOW. IT'S A STORY THAT A FOOL TELLS – FULL OF NOISE BUT WITH NO MEANING.

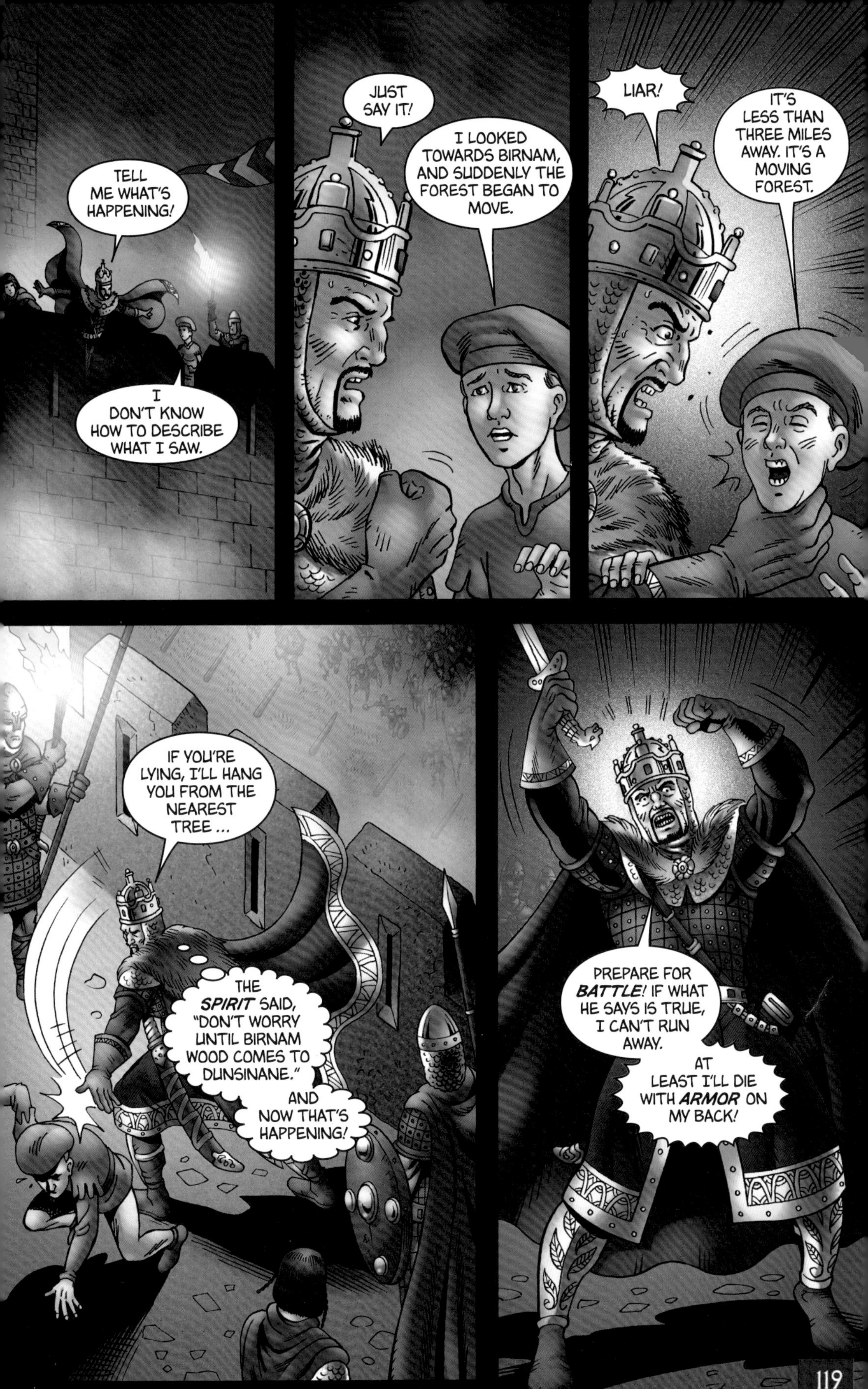
TELL ME WHAT'S HAPPENING!
I DON'T KNOW HOW TO DESCRIBE WHAT I SAW.
JUST SAY IT!
I LOOKED TOWARDS BIRNAM, AND SUDDENLY THE FOREST BEGAN TO MOVE.
LIAR!
IT'S LESS THAN THREE MILES AWAY. IT'S A MOVING FOREST.
IF YOU'RE LYING, I'LL HANG YOU FROM THE NEAREST TREE ...
THE *SPIRIT* SAID, "DON'T WORRY UNTIL BIRNAM WOOD COMES TO DUNSINANE."
AND NOW THAT'S HAPPENING!
PREPARE FOR *BATTLE*! IF WHAT HE SAYS IS TRUE, I CAN'T RUN AWAY.
AT LEAST I'LL DIE WITH *ARMOR* ON MY BACK!

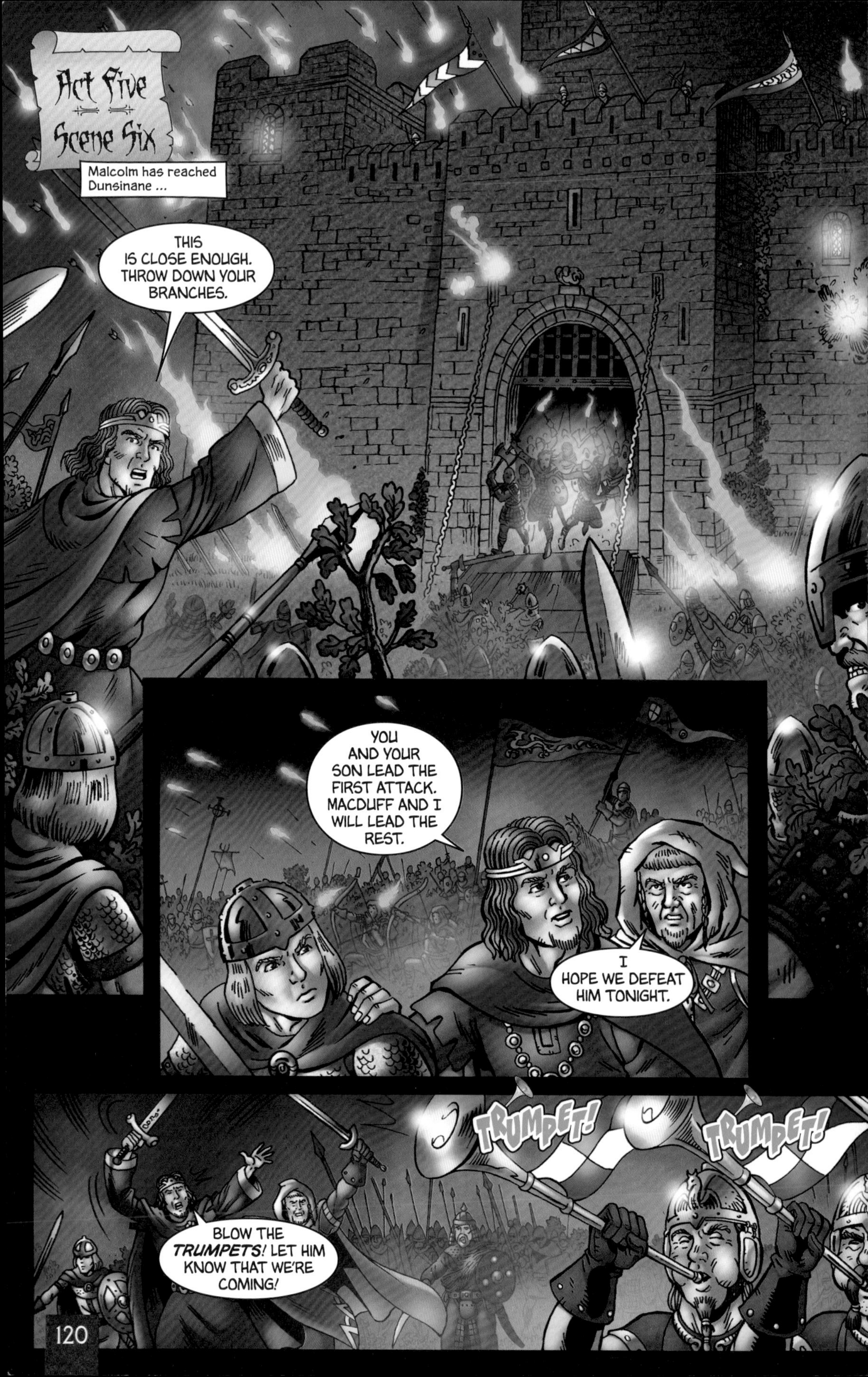
Act Five
Scene Six
Malcolm has reached Dunsinane ...
THIS IS CLOSE ENOUGH. THROW DOWN YOUR BRANCHES.
YOU AND YOUR SON LEAD THE FIRST ATTACK. MACDUFF AND I WILL LEAD THE REST.
I HOPE WE DEFEAT HIM TONIGHT.
BLOW THE *TRUMPETS*! LET HIM KNOW THAT WE'RE COMING!
TRUMPET!
TRUMPET!

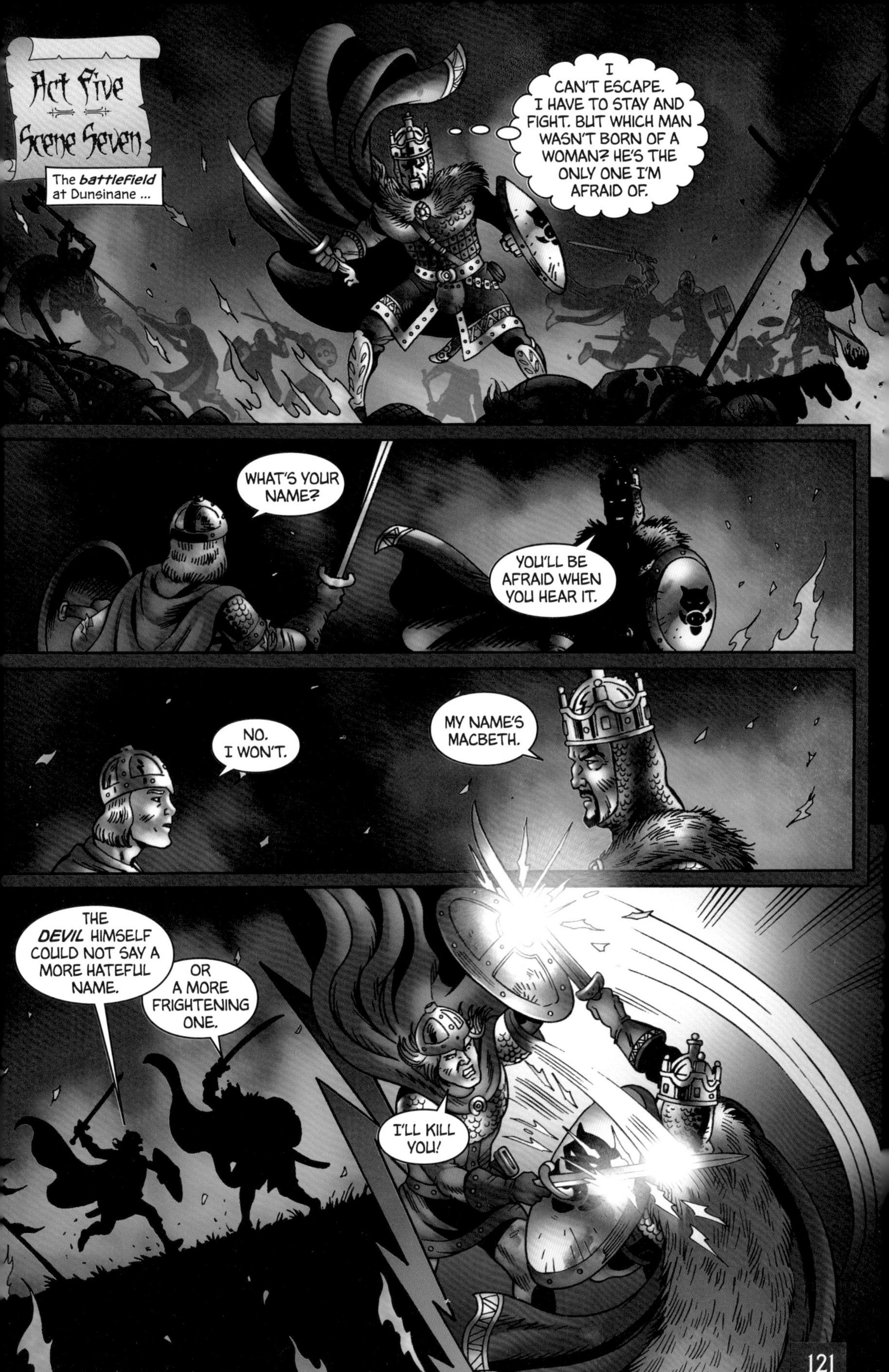

Act Five
Scene Seven
The battlefield at Dunsinane ...
I CAN'T ESCAPE. I HAVE TO STAY AND FIGHT. BUT WHICH MAN WASN'T BORN OF A WOMAN? HE'S THE ONLY ONE I'M AFRAID OF.
WHAT'S YOUR NAME?
YOU'LL BE AFRAID WHEN YOU HEAR IT.
NO. I WON'T.
MY NAME'S MACBETH.
THE DEVIL HIMSELF COULD NOT SAY A MORE HATEFUL NAME.
OR A MORE FRIGHTENING ONE.
I'LL KILL YOU!

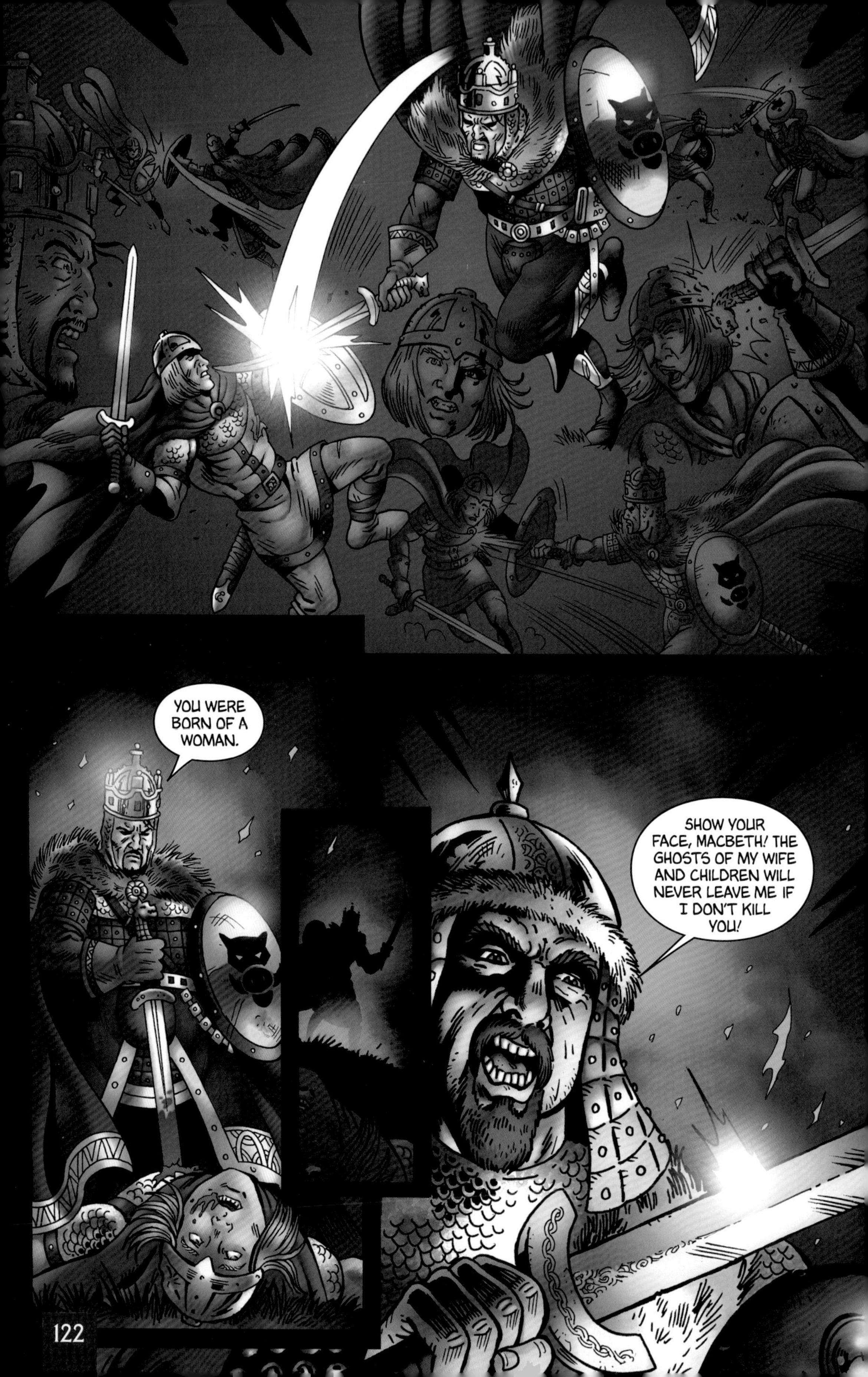
YOU WERE BORN OF A WOMAN.
SHOW YOUR FACE, MACBETH! THE GHOSTS OF MY WIFE AND CHILDREN WILL NEVER LEAVE ME IF I DON'T KILL YOU!

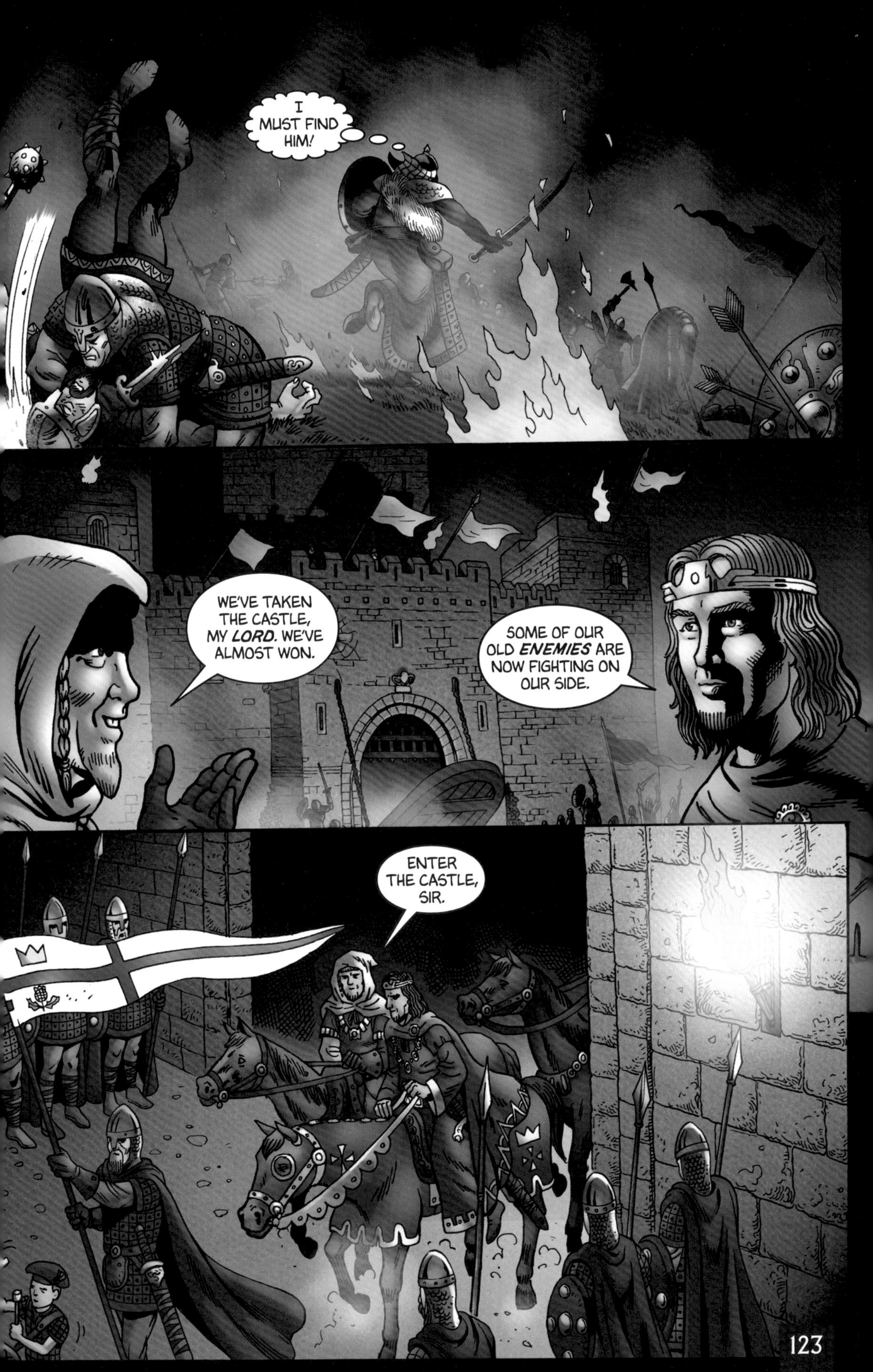
I MUST FIND HIM!
WE'VE TAKEN THE CASTLE, MY LORD. WE'VE ALMOST WON.
SOME OF OUR OLD ENEMIES ARE NOW FIGHTING ON OUR SIDE.
ENTER THE CASTLE, SIR.

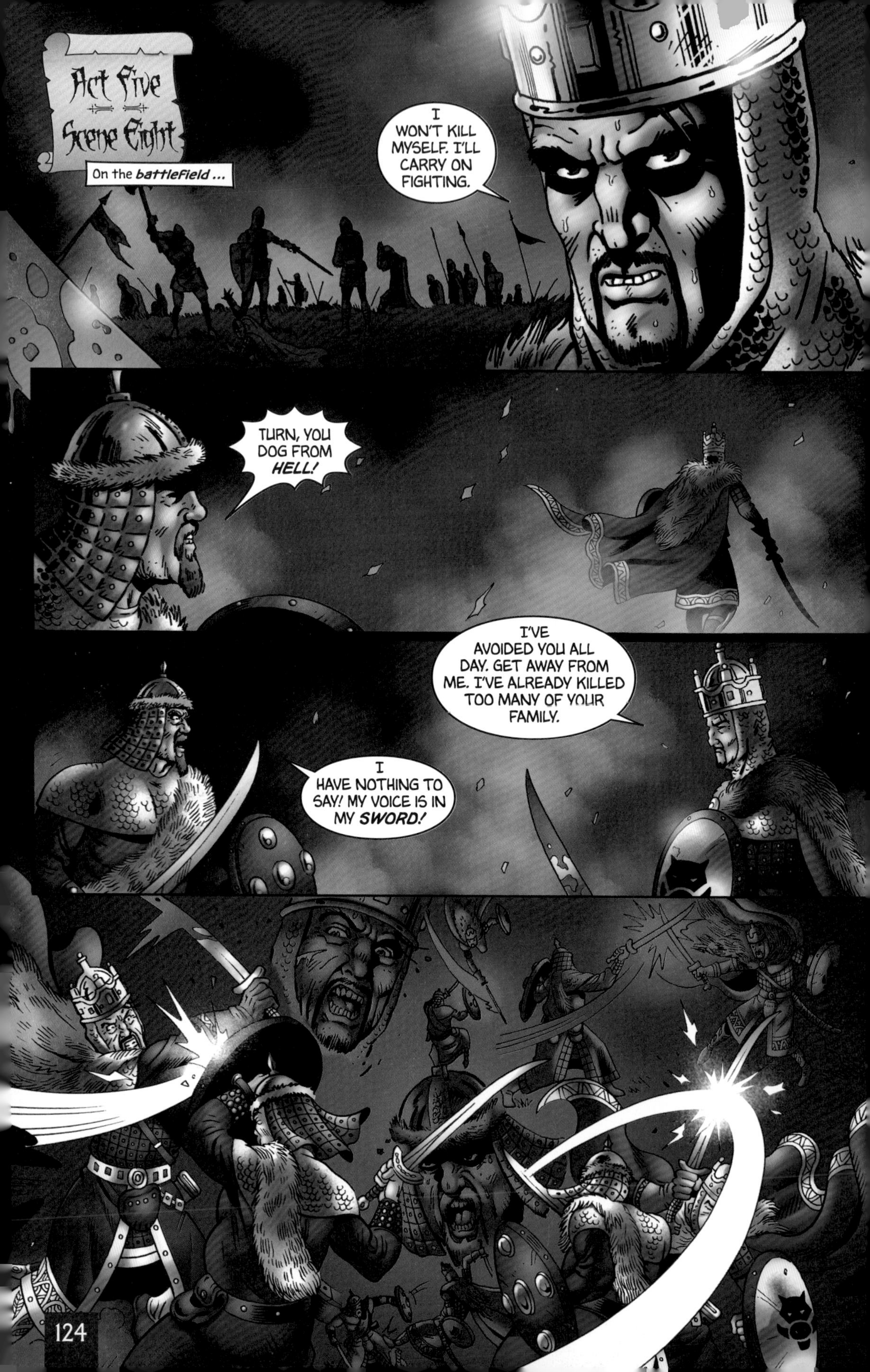
Act Five
Scene Eight
On the battlefield ...
I WON'T KILL MYSELF. I'LL CARRY ON FIGHTING.
TURN, YOU DOG FROM HELL!
I'VE AVOIDED YOU ALL DAY. GET AWAY FROM ME. I'VE ALREADY KILLED TOO MANY OF YOUR FAMILY.
I HAVE NOTHING TO SAY! MY VOICE IS IN MY SWORD!

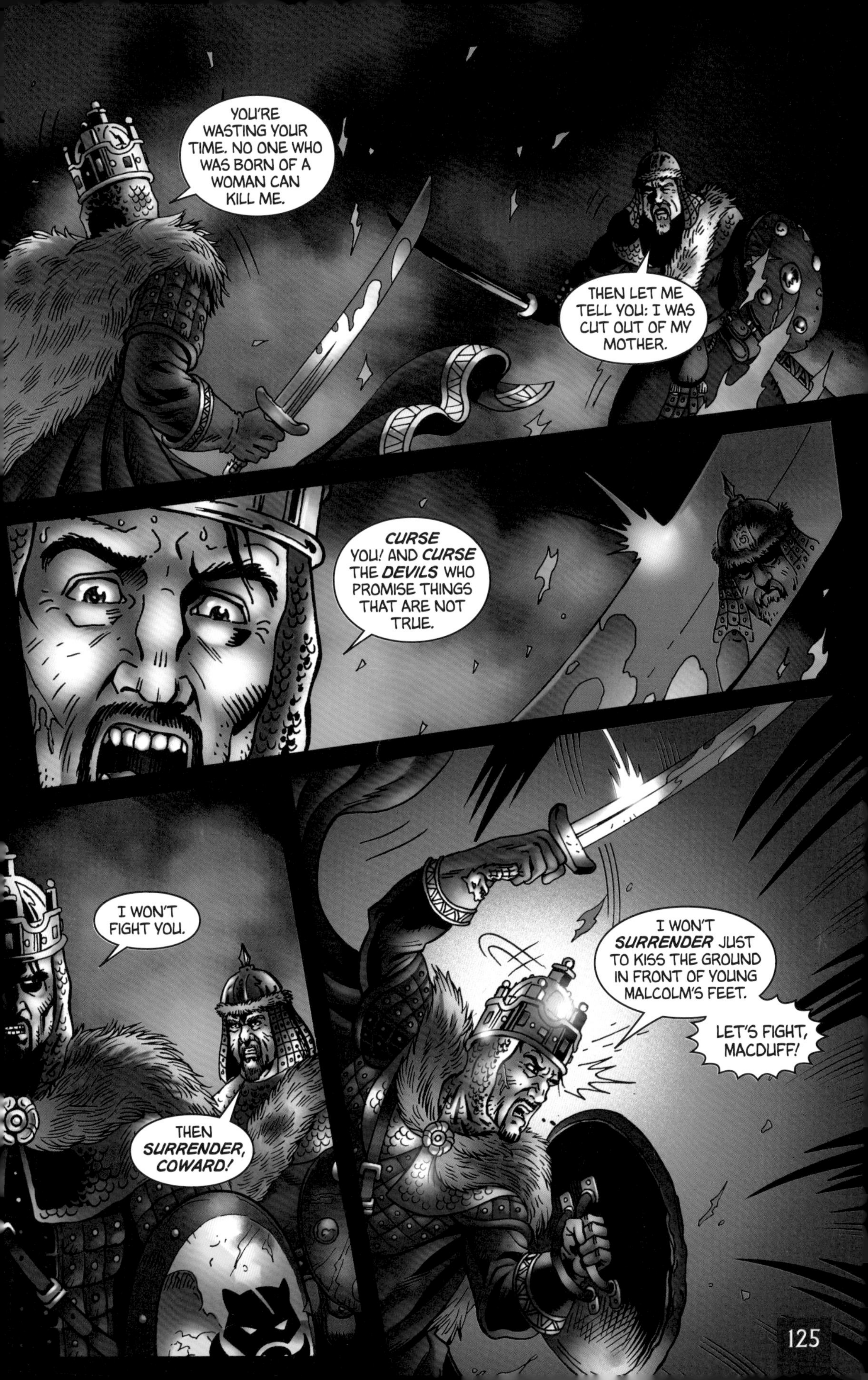
YOU'RE WASTING YOUR TIME. NO ONE WHO WAS BORN OF A WOMAN CAN KILL ME.
THEN LET ME TELL YOU: I WAS CUT OUT OF MY MOTHER.
CURSE YOU! AND CURSE THE DEVILS WHO PROMISE THINGS THAT ARE NOT TRUE.
I WON'T FIGHT YOU.
THEN SURRENDER, COWARD!
I WON'T SURRENDER JUST TO KISS THE GROUND IN FRONT OF YOUNG MALCOLM'S FEET.
LET'S FIGHT, MACDUFF!

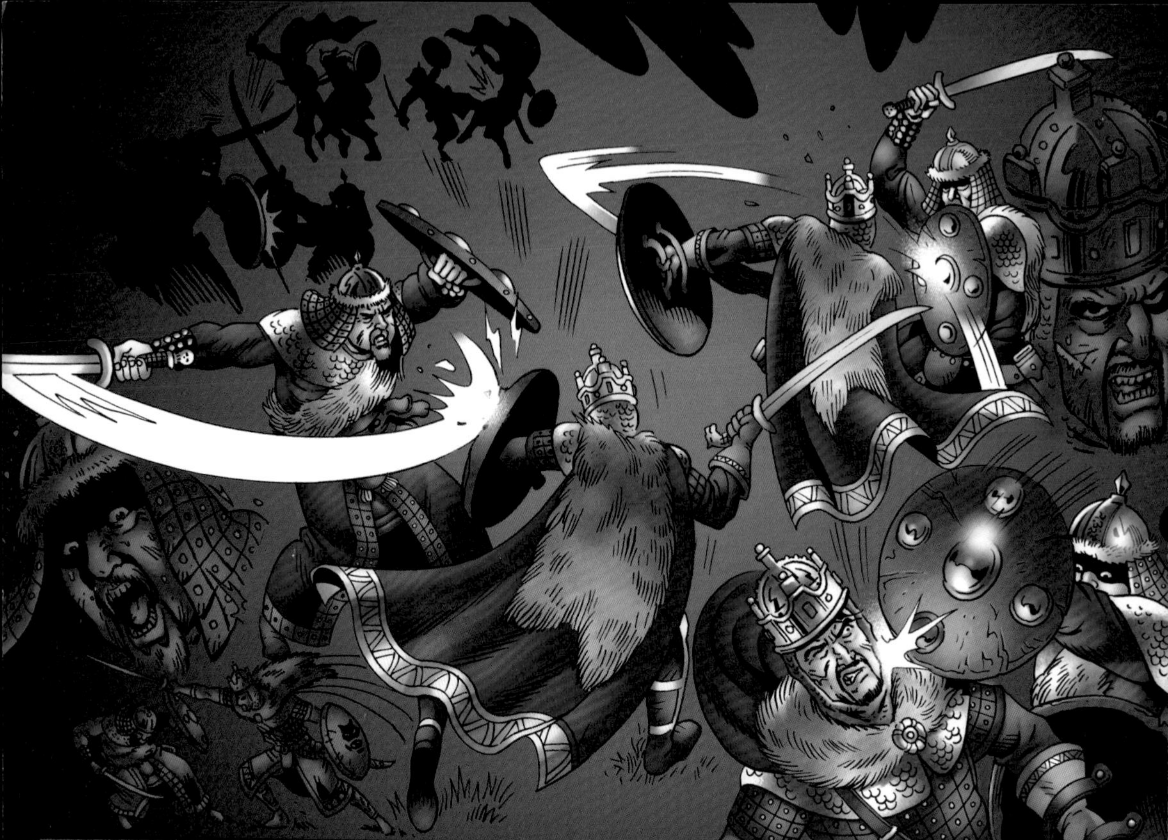

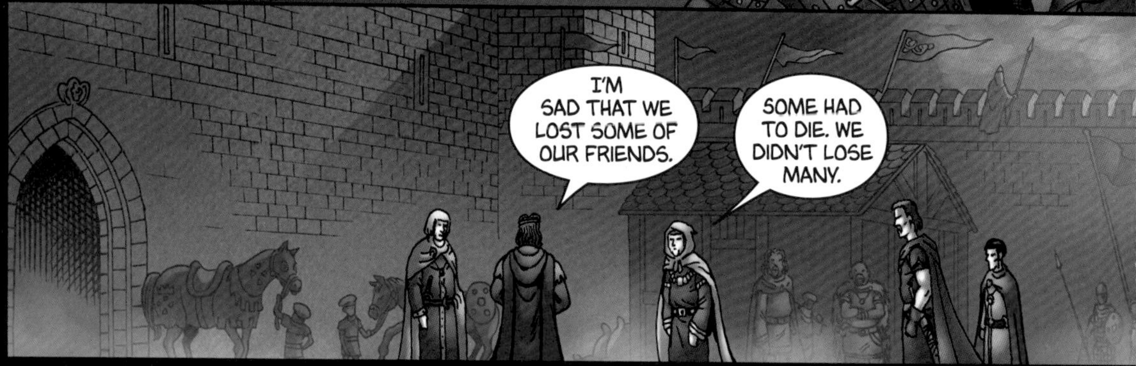
I'M SAD THAT WE LOST SOME OF OUR FRIENDS.
SOME HAD TO DIE. WE DIDN'T LOSE MANY.

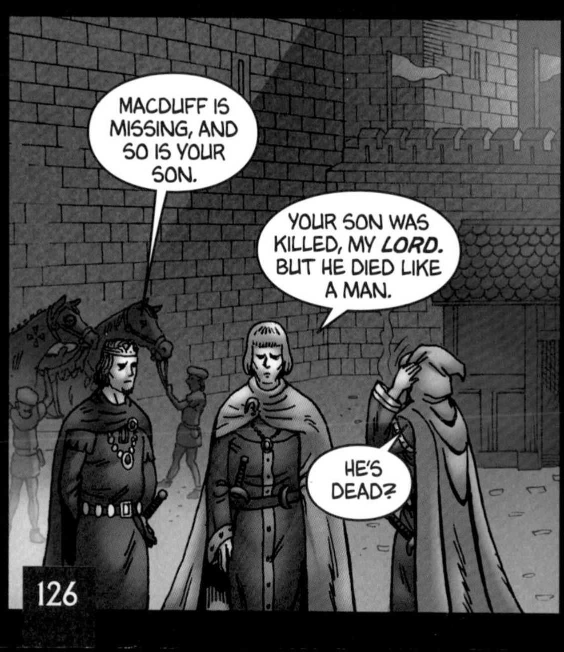
MACDUFF IS MISSING, AND SO IS YOUR SON.
YOUR SON WAS KILLED, MY *LORD.* BUT HE DIED LIKE A MAN.
HE'S DEAD?

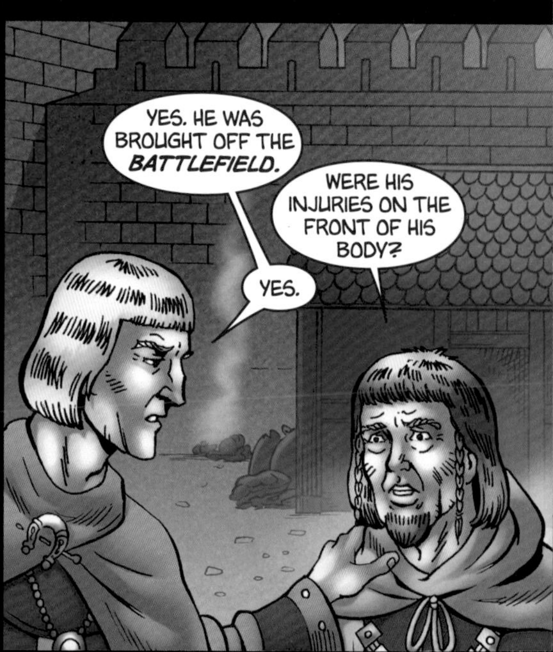
YES. HE WAS BROUGHT OFF THE ***BATTLEFIELD.***
WERE HIS INJURIES ON THE FRONT OF HIS BODY?
YES.

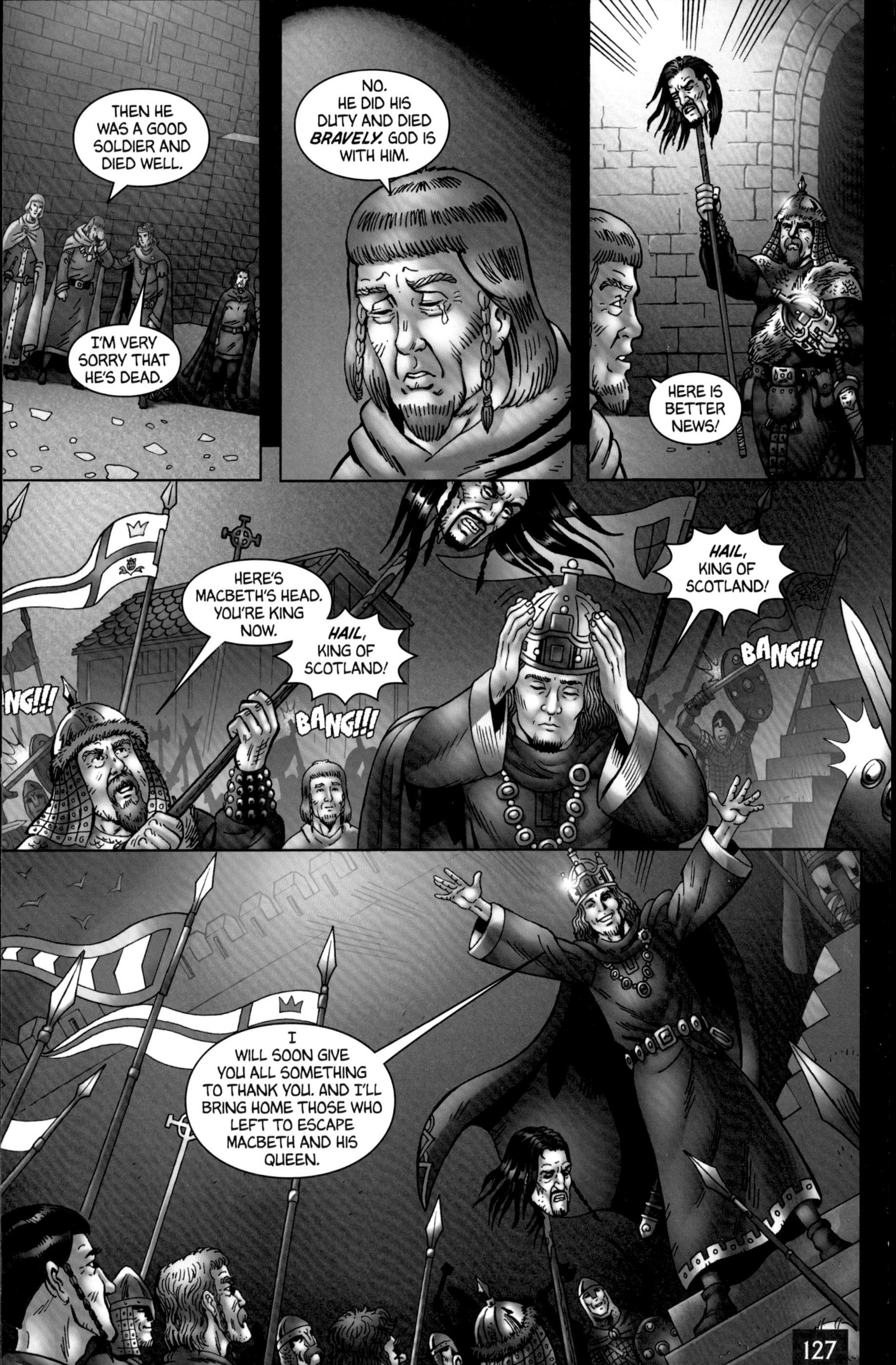
THEN HE WAS A GOOD SOLDIER AND DIED WELL.
I'M VERY SORRY THAT HE'S DEAD.
NO. HE DID HIS DUTY AND DIED BRAVELY. GOD IS WITH HIM.
HERE IS BETTER NEWS!
HERE'S MACBETH'S HEAD. YOU'RE KING NOW.
HAIL, KING OF SCOTLAND!
HAIL, KING OF SCOTLAND!
BANG!!!
BANG!!!
I WILL SOON GIVE YOU ALL SOMETHING TO THANK YOU. AND I'LL BRING HOME THOSE WHO LEFT TO ESCAPE MACBETH AND HIS QUEEN.

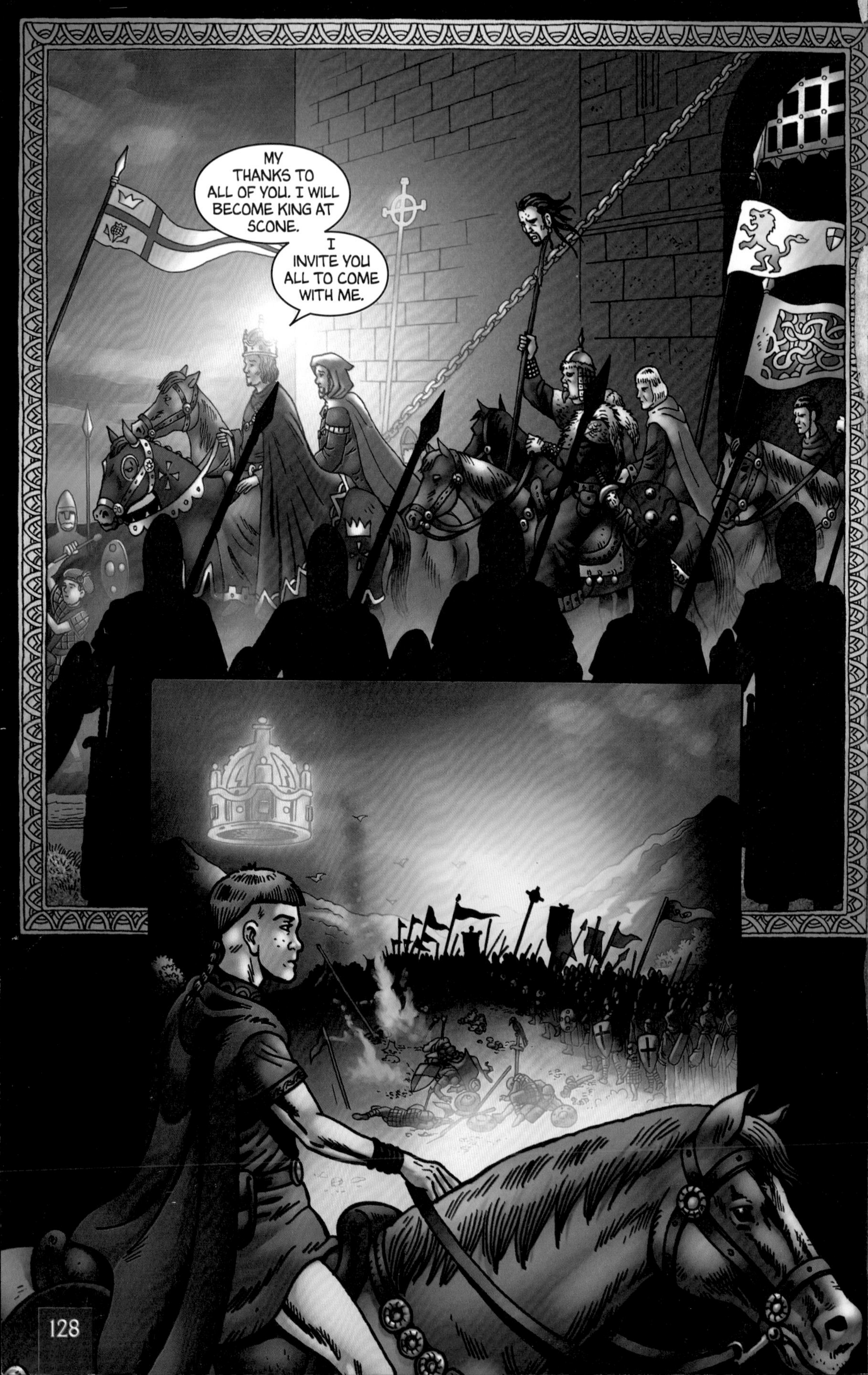
MY THANKS TO ALL OF YOU. I WILL BECOME KING AT SCONE.
I INVITE YOU ALL TO COME WITH ME.

Macbeth

End

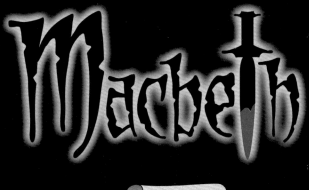

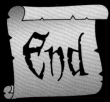

Glossary

A

admit /æd 'mɪt/ — (admits, admitting, admitted) If you admit that something bad, unpleasant, or embarrassing is true, you agree, often reluctantly, that it is true. *He rarely admits to making errors.*

armor /'ar mər/ In former times, armor was special metal clothing that soldiers wore for protection in battle.

army /'ar mi/ — (armies) An army is a large, organized group of people who are armed and trained to fight on land in a war. Most armies are organized and controlled by governments.

B

bang /bæŋ/ — (bangs) A bang is a sudden, loud noise such as the noise of an explosion.

battle /'bæ t°l/ — (battles) A battle is a violent fight between groups of people, especially one between military forces during a war.

battlefield /'bæ təl fild/ — (battlefields) A battlefield is a place where a battle is fought.

bell /bɛl/ — (bells) A bell is a hollow metal object with a loose piece hanging inside it that hits the sides and makes a sound.

betray /bɪt 'reɪ/ — (betrays, betraying, betrayed) If someone betrays their country or their friends, they give information to an enemy, putting their country's security or their friends' safety at risk.

brave /breɪv/ — (braver, bravest) Someone who is brave is willing to do things that are dangerous and does not show fear in difficult or dangerous situations. *She became an extremely brave horsewoman.*

bubble /'bʌ b°l/ — (bubbles, bubbling, bubbled) When a liquid bubbles, bubbles move in it, for example, because it is boiling or moving quickly.

C

cave /keɪv/ — (caves) A cave is a large hole in the side of a cliff or hill or under the ground.

cousin /'kʌ z°n/ — (cousins) Your cousin is the child of your uncle or aunt.

coward /'kaʊ ərd/ — (cowards) A coward is someone who is easily frightened and avoids dangerous or difficult situations.

crack /kræk/ — (cracks) A crack is a sharp sound, like the sound of a piece of wood breaking.

crash /kræʃ/ — (crashes) A crash is a sudden, loud noise. *Two people recalled hearing a loud crash about 1:30 am.*

curse /kɜs/ — (curses, cursing, cursed) If you curse someone or something, you say impolite or insulting things about them because you are angry. *We started driving again, cursing the delay.*

D

dagger /'dæ gər/ — (daggers) A dagger is a weapon like a knife with two sharp edges.

delighted /dɪ 'laɪtɪd/ If you are delighted, you are extremely pleased and excited about something. *Frank was delighted to see her.* Delight is a feeling of very great pleasure.

devil /'dɛ v°l/ — (devils) A devil is an evil spirit.

diamond /'daɪ mənd/ — (diamonds) A diamond is a hard, bright, precious stone which is clear and colorless. Diamonds are used in jewelry and for cutting very hard substances.

dong /dɔŋ/ — (dongs) A dong is the sound a bell makes.

dragon /'dræ gən/ — (dragons) In stories and legends, a dragon is an animal like a big lizard. It has wings and claws and breathes out fire.

drum /drʌm/ — (drums) A drum is a musical instrument consisting of a skin stretched tightly over a round frame.

E

enemy /'ɛ nə mi/ — (enemies) If someone is your enemy, they hate you or want to harm you.

evil /'i v°l/ Evil is used to refer to all the wicked and bad things that happen in the world. *... the battle between good and evil*

F

flag /flæg/ — (flags) A flag is a piece of colored cloth used as a sign for something or as a signal. *.... the Spanish flag*

forgiveness /fər 'gɪv nɪs/ Forgiveness is the act of forgiving. If you forgive someone who has done something wrong, you stop being angry with them and no longer want to punish them. *He fell to his knees and begged for forgiveness.*

G

gather /'gæ ðər/ — (gathers, gathering, gathered) If people gather somewhere or if someone gathers them, they come together in a group. *We gathered around the fireplace.*

gentleman /'dʒɛn təl mən/ — (gentlemen) You can refer politely to men as gentlemen. *This way, please, gentlemen.*

greedy /'gri di/ — (greedier, greediest) If you describe someone as greedy, you mean that they want to have more of something such as food or money than is necessary or fair.

H

hail /heɪl/ — (hails, hailing, hailed) If a person, event, or achievement is hailed as important or successful, they are praised publicly. *US magazines hailed her as the greatest rock 'n' roll singer in the world.*

health /hɛlθ/ Health is a state in which a person is fit and well. *In the hospital they nursed me back to health.*

heaven /'hɛ vən/ — (heavens) In some religions, heaven is said to be the place where God lives and where good people go when they die.

hedgehog /'hedʒ hɔg/ — (hedgehogs) A hedgehog is a small brown animal with sharp spikes covering its back.

hell /hel/ In some religions, hell is the place where the Devil lives and where bad people are sent when they die.

horrible /'hɔ rɪ bəl/ If you describe something or someone as horrible, you mean that they are very unpleasant.

horror /'hɔ rər/ Horror is a feeling of great shock, fear, and worry caused by something extremely unpleasant. *I felt numb with horror.*

hostess /'həʊ stɪs/ — (hostesses) The hostess at a party is the woman who has invited the guests and provides the food, drink, or entertainment.

L

lord /lɔrd/ — (lords) A lord is a man who has a high rank in the nobility, for example, an earl, a viscount, or a marquis.

M

master /'mæs tər/ — (masters) A servant's master is the man that he or she works for.

mend /mɛnd/ — (mends, mending, mended) If you mend something that is damaged or broken, you repair it so that it works properly or can be used. *They mended the leaking roof.*

messenger /'me sɪn dʒər/ — (messengers) A messenger takes a message or package to someone or takes messages regularly as their job. *The document was sent by messenger.*

N

nobleman /'nəʊ bəl mən/ — (noblemen) If someone is a nobleman, he belongs to a high social class and has a title.

nut /nʌt/ — (nuts) The firm shelled fruit of some trees and bushes are called nuts.

P

palace /'pæ lɪs/ — (palaces) A palace is a very large impressive house, especially the home of a king, queen, or president.

porter /'pɔr tər/ — (porters) A porter is a person whose job is to carry things, for example, people's luggage at a train station or in a hotel.

pour /pɔr/ — (pours, pouring, poured) If you pour a liquid or other substance, you make it flow steadily out of a container by holding the container at an angle. *She poured some water into a plastic bowl.*

R

revenge /rɪ 'vɛndʒ/ Revenge involves hurting or punishing someone who has hurt or harmed you. *The other children took revenge on the boy, claiming he was a school bully.*

rule /rul/ — (rules, ruling, ruled) The person or group that rules a country controls its affairs. *Emperor Hirohito ruled Japan for 62 years until his death in 1989.*

S

Saxon /'sæk sən/ — (Saxons) A Saxon is a person belonging to the Germanic people that conquered parts of England in the 5th to 6th century.

scream /skrim/ – (screams, screaming, screamed) When someone screams, they make a very loud, high-pitched cry, for example, because they are in pain or are very frightened. *He screamed, screaming in agony.*

servant /'sɜr vᵊnt/ – (servants) A servant is someone who is employed to work at another person's home, for example, as a cleaner or a gardener.

serve /sɜrv/ – (serves, serving, served) If you serve your country, an organization, or a person, you do useful work for them. *He served the government loyally for 30 years.*

smash /smæʃ/ – (smashes, smashing, smashed) If you smash something or if it smashes, it breaks into many pieces, for example, when it is hit or dropped. *Two or three glasses fell and smashed into pieces.*

spirit /'spɪ rɪt/ – (spirits) A person's spirit is the non-physical part of the person that is believed to remain alive after their death. A spirit is a ghost or supernatural being.

stupid /'stu pɪd/ – (stupider, stupidest) If you say that someone or something is stupid, you mean that they show a lack of good judgment or intelligence and they are not at all sensible. *I made a stupid mistake.*

surrender /sə 'rɛn dər/ – (surrenders, surrendering, surrendered) If you surrender, you stop fighting or resisting someone and agree that you have been beaten. *He surrendered to American troops. / . . . after the Japanese surrender in 1945*

sword /sɔrd/ – (swords) A sword is a weapon with a handle and a long, sharp blade.

T

thane /θeɪn/ – (thanes) A thane is a man ranking between ordinary freemen and nobles and is granted land by the king or by lords for military service.

thud /θʌd/ – (thuds, thudding, thudded) A thud is a dull sound, such as that which a heavy object makes when it hits something soft.

title /'taɪ tᵊl/ – (titles) Someone's title is a word such as "Doctor," "Mr.," or "Mrs." that is used before their own name in order to show their status or profession.

toad /toʊd/ – (toads) A toad is an animal like a frog, but with drier skin.

toil /tɔɪl/ – (toils, toiling, toiled) When people toil, they work very hard doing unpleasant or tiring tasks. *Workers toiled long hours.*

traitor /'treɪ tər/ – (traitors) A traitor is someone who betrays their country, friends, or a group of which they are a member by helping its enemies.

trumpet /'trʌm pɪt/ – (trumpets) A trumpet is a brass musical instrument.

U

uncle /'ʌŋ kᵊl/ – (uncles) Your uncle is the brother of your mother or father or the husband of your aunt.

Viking /'vaɪkɪŋ/ – (Vikings) A Viking is any of the Scandinavian sea pirates who raided and settled in parts of northwestern Europe in the 8th to 11th century.

W

weapon /'wɛ pən/ – (weapons) A weapon is an object such as a gun, a knife, or a missile which is used to kill or hurt people in a fight or a war.

witch /wɪtʃ/ – (witches) In fairy tales, a witch is a woman, usually an old woman, who has evil magic powers.

Your Highness /yɔr 'haɪ nɪs/ – (Highnesses) You use expressions such as Your Highness and His Highness to address or refer to a member of a royal family.

William Shakespeare

(c. 1564 - 1616 AD)

Many people believe that William Shakespeare was the greatest writer in the English language. He wrote 38 plays, 154 sonnets, and five poems. His plays have been translated into every major living language.

The actual date of Shakespeare's birth is unknown. Most people accept that his birth date was April 23, 1564. He died 52 years later on the same date.

The life of William Shakespeare can be divided into three acts. He lived in the small village of Stratford-upon-Avon until he was 20 years old. There, he studied, got married, and had children. Then Shakespeare lived as an actor and playwright (a writer of plays) in London. Finally, when he was about 50, Shakespeare retired back to his hometown. He enjoyed some wealth gained from his successful years of work but died a few years later.

William Shakespeare was the oldest son of tradesman John Shakespeare and Mary Arden. He was the third of eight children. William Shakespeare was lucky to survive childhood. Sixteenth century England was filled with diseases such as smallpox, tuberculosis, typhus, and dysentery. Most people did not live longer than 35 years. Three of Shakespeare's seven siblings died from what was probably the Bubonic Plague.

Few records exist about Shakespeare's life. According to most accounts, he went to the local grammar school and studied English literature and Latin. When he was 18 years old, he married Anne Hathaway. She was a local farmer's daughter. They had three children: Susanna in 1583, and twins Hamnet and Judith in 1585. Hamnet, Shakespeare's only son, died when he was 11.

Shakespeare moved to London in 1587. He was an actor at The Globe Theatre. This was one of the largest theaters in England. He appeared in public as a poet in 1593. Later on, in 1599, he became part-owner of The Globe.

When Queen Elizabeth died in 1603, her cousin James became King. He supported Shakespeare and his actors. He allowed them to be called the "King's Men" as long as they entertained the court.

During 1590 and 1613, Shakespeare wrote his plays, sonnets, and poems. The first plays are thought to have been comedies and histories. He was to become famous for both types of writing. Next, he mainly wrote tragedies until about 1608. These included *Hamlet, King Lear,* and *Macbeth,* which are considered three of the best examples of writing in the English language. In his last phase, Shakespeare wrote tragicomedies, also known as romances. His final play was *Henry VII,* written two years before his death.

The cause of Shakespeare's death is unknown. He was buried at the Church of the Holy Trinity in Stratford-upon-Avon. His gravestone has the words (believed to have been written by Shakespeare himself) on it:

Good friend for Jesus' sake forbear
To dig the dust enclosed here!
Blessed be the man that spares these stones,
And cursed be he that moves my bones.

In his will, Shakespeare left most of his possessions to his oldest daughter, Susanna. He left his wife, Anne, his "second best bed." Nobody knows what this gift meant. Shakespeare's last direct descendant, his granddaughter, died in 1670.

The Real Macbeth

(c. 1005 - 1057 AD)

Macbeth is one of Shakespeare's most famous characters. Yet many people don't know that the story is based on historical events. It is thought that Shakespeare read early historical books which tell the history of England, Scotland, and Ireland. However, he changed these historical events considerably to make his play more entertaining for us, his audience.

Although it is impossible to know all the facts, according to history Mac Bethad (Macbeth) was King of Scotland from 1040 to 1057. The name "Mac Bethad" means "son of life." It is actually an Irish name, not a Scottish name.

Scotland in the eleventh century was a cruel place to live. It had many wars, and mass killings occurred often. Whoever ruled Scotland had to protect his family, his community, and the land from his **enemies**. However, many of a ruler's **enemies** were actually the people closest to him. These **enemies** were usually unhappy and jealous relatives who wanted to be king themselves.

Enemies of the king would form a group and challenge the ruler. This happened because a king could choose the next king. In other words, kings didn't simply pass the rule straight onto their oldest sons or closest relative. In Mac Bethad's time, the king could choose who he wanted to replace him. Many people were murdered by their jealous relatives.

Mac Bethad was born around 1005. He was the son of Findláech mac Ruaidrí who was a High Steward in the north of Scotland. It is thought that Mac Bethad's mother was Donada, the second child of King Malcolm II. This means that Mac Bethad was the grandson of a king.

In 1020, Mac Bethad's father died. It is thought that he was murdered by his brother's son. Mac Bethad's **cousin** became High Steward. Twelve years later, Mac Bethad's cousin was killed as punishment for murdering Mac Bethad's father, and Mac Bethad became High Steward.

Mac Bethad then married his **cousin's** widow, Gruoch (Lady Macbeth). She had one son, named Lulach. Gruoch was the granddaughter of Kenneth III. Their marriage meant that Mac Bethad had a very good claim to the Scottish throne.

However Donnchad mac Crináin (King Duncan I) was the king already. Although Donnchad mac Crináin should have made friends with his unhappy relatives, including Mac Bethad, he didn't. This was a mistake. It meant that Mac Bethad finally killed Donnchad mac Crináin in 1040. One historical tale says that Mac Bethad and Banquo cleverly sent the king a sleeping potion and killed him while he was asleep. Mac Bethad became king.

History states that Mac Bethad was a very good king. His kingdom became more stable and wealthier. Mac Bethad even traveled overseas while he was king, which shows how much confidence he had during his rule.

In 1054, Donnchad's son, Máel Coluim mac Donnchad (Malcolm), opposed Mac Bethad's rule. Máel Coluim and his supporters took control of southern Scotland. Three years later, in 1057, Mac Bethad's **army** finally lost against Máel Coluim's **army**. Mac Bethad was killed in battle. It is thought that he was buried in the graveyard at Saint Oran's Chapel on the Isle of Iona. He is the last of many kings to be buried there.

No one knows what happened to Mac Bethad's wife, Gruoch. In Shakespeare's play, she goes insane and dies, although there is no historical account of what actually happened to her.

Unlike in Shakespeare's play, Mac Bethad's death did not mean that Duncan's son became king. First, Gruoch's son, Lulach, became the Scottish ruler. However, Lulach was a weak king. His people laughed at him for being foolish. He was quickly murdered — and that's when Máel Coluim became king.

The Real Macbeth Family Tree

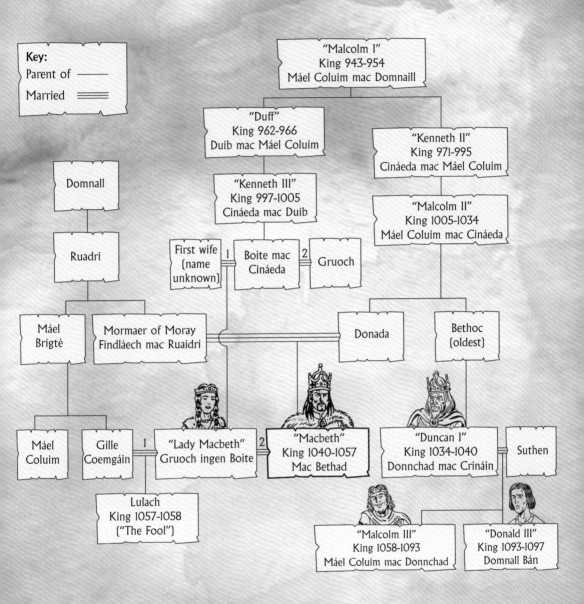

Key:
Parent of ———
Married ═══

"Malcolm I"
King 943-954
Máel Coluim mac Domnaill

"Duff"
King 962-966
Duib mac Máel Coluim

"Kenneth II"
King 971-995
Cináeda mac Máel Coluim

Domnall

"Kenneth III"
King 997-1005
Cináeda mac Duib

"Malcolm II"
King 1005-1034
Máel Coluim mac Cináeda

Ruadri

First wife
(name
unknown) | 1 | Boite mac
Cináeda | 2 | Gruoch

Máel
Brigté

Mormaer of Moray
Findláech mac Ruaidrí

Donada

Bethoc
(oldest)

Máel
Coluim

Gille
Coemgáin | 1 | "Lady Macbeth"
Gruoch ingen Boite | 2 | "Macbeth"
King 1040-1057
Mac Bethad

"Duncan I"
King 1034-1040
Donnchad mac Crináin

Suthen

Lulach
King 1057-1058
("The Fool")

"Malcolm III"
King 1058-1093
Máel Coluim mac Donnchad

"Donald III"
King 1093-1097
Domnall Bán

Summary of the Main Characters in Shakespeare's Macbeth

Macbeth, *Thane* of Glamis

Macbeth is a leader in the king's **army,** but he is not satisfied with this, and his greed makes him want even more success. He becomes the **Thane** of Cawdor after defeating the **Vikings.** The **witches'** predictions and his wife's encouragement lead him to kill Duncan and become King of Scotland. Although **brave** in **battle,** he is an insecure and unfair ruler.

Lady Macbeth, Macbeth's wife

She wants power and wealth more than anything else, and she encourages Macbeth to murder Duncan. In the end, her guilt makes her crazy, and she suffers nightmares, starts sleepwalking, and becomes obsessed with the blood on her hands which no one else can see.

Duncan, King of Scotland

He is a kind and trusting older king. His kindness allows Macbeth to attack him. Macbeth kills him (and his two guards) with a **dagger.** Duncan's death and his sons' escape means Macbeth is made king.

Malcolm and Donalbain, Duncan's sons

These two men are King Duncan's sons. When their father dies, they flee to avoid being murdered themselves. Donalbain escapes to Ireland. Malcolm goes to England where he hopes to build an **army** to take back the kingdom from the **evil** Macbeth. At the end of the play, after Macbeth is defeated, Malcolm becomes king.

Three *Witches*, the Weird Sisters

The three **witches** have a very important role in this play. They tell Macbeth that he will be **Thane** of Cawdor, **Thane** of Glamis, and eventually King. Their predictions lead Macbeth to commit many murders. At the same time, however, they predict that while Banquo may not be king, he will be happier, and his sons will be kings. Later, they predict Macbeth's doom. Macbeth gets very confused by their predictions.

Summary of the Main Characters in Shakespeare's *Macbeth*

Banquo, Leader in the King's *army*

He is a leader in Duncan's **army** along with Macbeth. He's also the subject of one of the **witches'** predictions. Unlike Macbeth, he does not act to fulfill these predictions. Instead, he relies on his better judgment and morals. After Macbeth arranges his murder, Banquo reappears as a ghost, which represents the guilt and anguish Macbeth is feeling over the murder.

Fleance

He is Banquo's son and the first in a line of kings as predicted by the Three **Witches**. He escapes when his father is killed. He represents a future Macbeth cannot bear: a line of kings following Banquo and not his own sons.

Macduff, *Thane* of Fife

He is a Scottish **nobleman** who begins to question Macbeth's unfair rule. Macbeth orders the murder of Macduff's wife and children. Macduff eventually joins Malcolm and the English forces to fight Macbeth and get **revenge** for the murder of his family. The **witches** tell Macbeth that he does not need to fear anyone "born of a woman," however Macduff was cut out of his mother's womb (Caesarian birth) meaning that he wasn't actually born of a woman. He is the man who kills Macbeth.

Siward, Earl of Northumberland

He is the leader of the English **army** and Duncan's brother. He leads an English **army** of ten thousand men against Macbeth. They disguise themselves with branches from Birnam Wood. He loses his son, Young Siward, to Macbeth.

Hecate, The "Queen" *Witch*

She demands loyalty and respect of the Three **Witches**. She makes fun of the Three **Witches** for helping an ungrateful Macbeth. She later commands them to tell Macbeth his future according to her will.

Link Map of Characters in Shakespeare's *Macbeth*

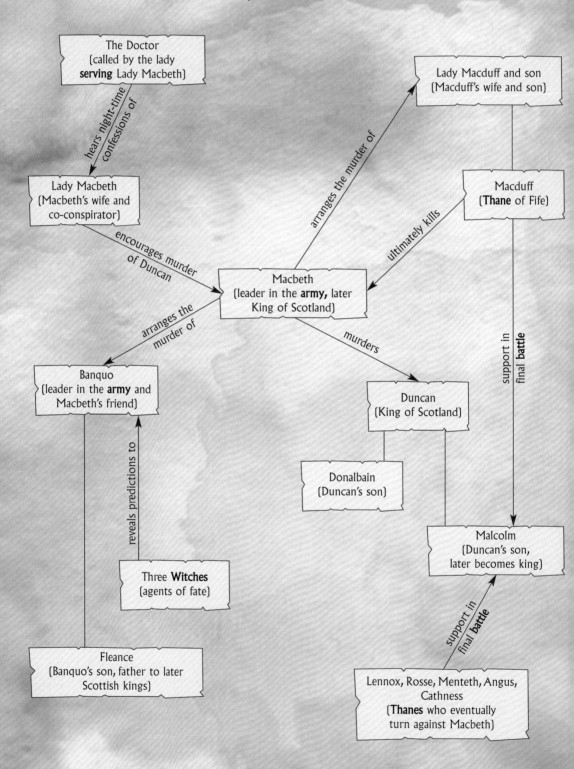

The Doctor
(called by the lady **serving** Lady Macbeth)

hears night-time confessions of

Lady Macbeth
(Macbeth's wife and co-conspirator)

encourages murder of Duncan

arranges the murder of

Banquo
(leader in the **army** and Macbeth's friend)

Macbeth
(leader in the **army,** later King of Scotland)

arranges the murder of

Lady Macduff and son
(Macduff's wife and son)

Macduff
(**Thane** of Fife)

ultimately kills

murders

Duncan
(King of Scotland)

Donalbain
(Duncan's son)

reveals predictions to

Three **Witches**
(agents of fate)

Malcolm
(Duncan's son, later becomes king)

*support in final **battle***

Fleance
(Banquo's son, father to later Scottish kings)

*support in final **battle***

Lennox, Rosse, Menteth, Angus, Cathness
(**Thanes** who eventually turn against Macbeth)

Famous Quotations from Shakespeare's Macbeth

Location	Shakespeare's Original	Adapted Text	Meaning
Act I, Scene I Page 8	"When shall we three meet again? In thunder, lightning, or in rain? When the hurly-burly's done, When the battle's lost and won."	When shall we three meet again? In heavy storm or **pouring** rain? When one side's lost, and the other's won.	The three **witches** say this at the start of the play. They predict when they will meet with Macbeth and Banquo and tell each man of his future. Their meeting will begin the trouble that leads to the multiple murders of this play.
Act I, Scene I Page 8	"Fair is foul, and foul is fair."	Fair is dark, and dark is fair.	The three **witches** say this at the beginning of the play. They tell about the coming events where good and **evil** will be turned upside down, when fair play will be destructive, and destruction will create fairness. Not long afterwards, Macbeth says in Act One, Scene Three that he has never seen such a foul and fair day before (both a good and bad day).
Act I, Scene 3 Page 18	"If chance will have me King, why chance may crown me, Without my stir."	If I'm going to be king, it'll happen by itself.	Macbeth thinks this out loud after hearing the three **witches** predict that he will be made king. He thinks that he doesn't need to do anything but wait, and it will happen. In the end, however, this is what Banquo chooses to do, while Macbeth chooses to take it into his own hands and make it happen by murdering King Duncan.
Act I, Scene 5 Page 20	"Yet do I fear thy nature: It is too full o'the milk of human-kindness."	But you're too kind to do what you have to do to become king.	Lady Macbeth says this as she reads a letter from her husband. In the letter, he tells her that the three **witches** predicted that he will be king. However, Lady Macbeth believes her husband is too weak, too kind, and too gentle to do what he must do to become king: murder Duncan.
Act I, Scene 5 Page 22	"Look like the innocent flower, But be the serpent under't."	You mustn't let people know what you're planning. You must welcome him properly.	Lady Macbeth tells her husband to look sweet like a flower but to really be the snake (serpent) that is underneath the flower. She tells him that he should be very careful and to make sure nobody realizes that he is planning to become king by murder and lies.
Act 2, Scene I Page 31	"Is this a dagger which I see before me, The handle toward my hand?"	Is this a **dagger** I can see? Come here! Let me hold you!	Macbeth thinks he sees a **dagger** in front of him. He feels it is telling him to use it to stab his king. However he fears this **dagger** is not real but just something he imagines is there. As he is thinking all this, he uses a **dagger** to kill King Duncan.
Act 2, Scene 2 Page 36	"Will all great Neptune's ocean wash this blood Clean from my hand? No - this my hand will rather the multitudinous seas incarnadine, Making the green one red."	All the water in the ocean won't wash away this blood from my hands.	Macbeth says this to his wife after he has killed King Duncan. He feels terribly guilty and worries that the guilt will never disappear. His words are echoed later in Lady Macbeth's cries that she has blood on her hands.

Famous Quotations from Shakespeare's Macbeth

Location	Shakespeare's Original	Adapted Text	Meaning
Act 2, Scene 3 Page 45	"There's daggers in men's smiles."	Here there are knives in men's smiles.	Donalbain says this after realizing that his father, King Duncan, and his father's guards have been murdered. He and his brother, Malcolm, are suspicious and do not trust anyone, least of all the people who claim to be helping them get revenge for their father's death.
Act 4, Scene 1 Page 78	"Double, double toil and trouble; Fire burn, and cauldron bubble."	Double, double toil and trouble, fire, burn and make it bubble.	The three **witches** chant this spell as they dance around the potion they are cooking on the fire. They want to double the amount of trouble about to happen. Their words increase the audience's anticipation that the action is about reach a high point.
Act 5, Scene 1 Page 105	"Out, damned spot! Out, I say!"	Out! Out, I say!	Lady Macbeth cries this as she desperately tries to clean her hands. She is sleepwalking and believes her hands are covered in blood. Her guilt causes her to see the blood. The doctor and servant who are watching tell the reader that Lady Macbeth's hands are clean already.
Act 5, Scene 1 Page 106	" ... all the perfumes of Arabia will not sweeten this little hand."	I can still smell the blood. Nothing will make my little hand smell sweet again.	Lady Macbeth continues to talk as she sleepwalks. She says again and again that her hands are stained with blood and truly believes, in her sleep, that she will never be able to wash her hands of their dirty, guilty secret.
Act 5, Scene 5 Page 118	"Out, out, brief candle! Life's but a walking shadow, a poor player That struts and frets his hour upon the stage, And then is heard no more. It is a tale told by an idiot, full of sound and fury, signifying nothing."	Life is just a walking shadow. It's a story that a fool tells — full of noise but with no meaning.	Macbeth says this in sadness and despair when he learns that his wife, the Queen, is dead. He realizes that life is short and often finished before it even begins. It is a bleak and remorseful view, for he now thinks that while life appears to contain much promise, it is actually empty and meaningless.

Notes

Notes

Notes

OTHER TITLES

Henry V

Henry
V

Frankenstein

Frankenstein

Great Expectations

GREAT
EXPECTATIONS

Jane Eyre

Jane Eyre

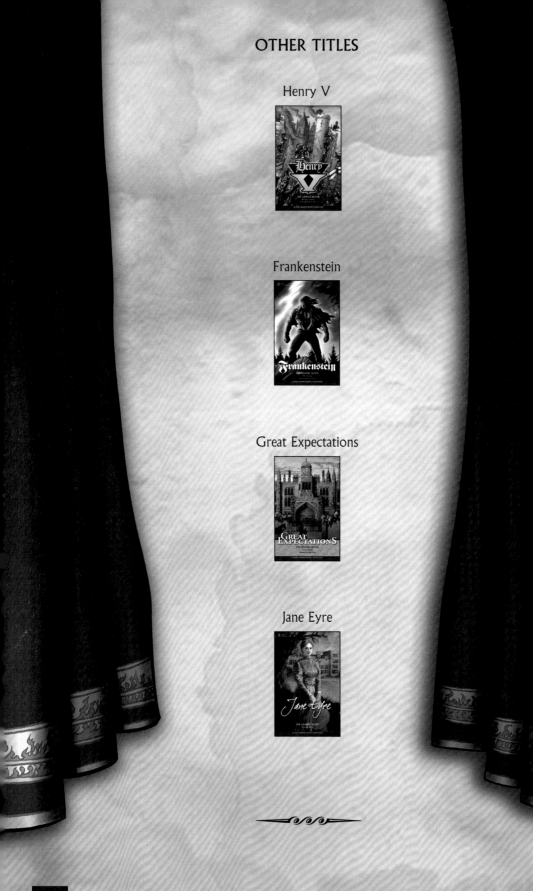

VOLUME IV
SIAM-AMS PROCEEDINGS

Computers in Algebra
and Number Theory

AMERICAN MATHEMATICAL SOCIETY

PROVIDENCE, RHODE ISLAND
1971

PROCEEDINGS OF A SYMPOSIUM IN APPLIED MATHEMATICS OF THE AMERICAN MATHEMATICAL SOCIETY AND THE SOCIETY FOR INDUSTRIAL AND APPLIED MATHEMATICS

HELD IN NEW YORK CITY
MARCH 25–26, 1970

Edited by
GARRETT BIRKHOFF
MARSHALL HALL, JR.

Prepared by the American Mathematical Society under the National Science Foundation Grant No. GP 20418 and U. S. Army Research Office (Durham) Contract No. DAHC04 70 C 0033

International Standard Book Number 0-8218-1323-4
Library of Congress Catalog Number 76-167685
AMS 1970 Subject Classifications. Primary 10-04, 20-04;
Secondary 20DXX, 10EXX

Printed in the United States of America

Contents

vi

Preface

This volume contains the written versions of talks delivered at the Symposium on Computers in Algebra and Number Theory in the Waldorf-Astoria in New York City on March 25 and 26, 1970.

Applications of algebraic ideas to computing are first considered by Garrett Birkhoff and Shmuel Winograd. Their papers devote especial attention to problems of optimizing computer algorithms.

The next five articles are devoted to number theory and combinatorial theory. Those by H. P. F. Swinnerton-Dyer and Bryan Birch are pure number theory, that by Leonard Baumert purely combinatorial. Hans Zassenhaus considers the problem of finding the Galois group of a field extension. J. H. van Lint studies perfect error-correcting codes and applies the effective methods of Alan Baker to related Diophantine problems.

The final section deals with the application of computers to finite groups. Problems on the construction and uniqueness of the new sporadic simple groups have involved heavy use of computers, and in several instances the existence of the groups has not been proved in any other way. The article by Marshall Hall is concerned with problems of existence and construction. The paper by M. D. Hestenes and D. G. Higman is concerned with relations between graphs and permutation groups. The articles by John Conway, John McKay, John Cannon, and Charles Sims deal with problems on the structure and subgroups of groups already known. Joachim Neubüser is concerned with algorithms for detailed analysis of a known group.

MARSHALL HALL, JR.

Pasadena, California
September 17, 1970

The Role of Modern Algebra in Computing[1]

Garrett Birkhoff

1. **Introduction.** This Symposium has as its main theme the applications of digital computers to algebra and number theory; its primary concern is with how such computers can serve "pure" mathematicians. My primary concern will be with the complementary role played by algebra in the science of digital computing, hence with services which mathematicians can render (and have rendered) to computing.

Here by *algebra* I mean the use of *symbol manipulation* in the widest sense, as this seems to describe most accurately its meaning.[2] When the symbols being manipulated stand for real and complex numbers, we have *real and complex algebra*, or algebra in the *classical* sense. When the symbols represent statements, we have the *propositional calculus* (including Boolean algebra), which is the oldest part of symbolic logic. Other interpretations of the symbols lead to group, ring, module, and field theory, and to other parts of *modern algebra* familiar to contemporary "pure" algebraists.

Both classical and modern algebra are important for computing: classical algebra for the highly developed science of *numerical* computation, and modern algebra for the developing science of *nonnumerical* computation (alias "symbol manipulation"). However, the applications of classical algebra to numerical computation involve many ideas from analysis; the resulting science of "numerical algebra" might aptly be called modern applied arithmetic.

Hence I shall say little about real or complex algebra here, but shall concentrate on those modern algebraic ideas and techniques which are most relevant to computing.

Modern algebra. Surprisingly, the aspects of symbolic algebra which are most important for computing are *not* those which received the most

AMS 1969 *subject classifications*. Primary 9430; Secondary 0830.

[1]Report prepared with support from the Office of Naval Research under Contract NR-04-188.

[2][**27**, §1.1]; [**12**, Chapter XXVI]; W. W. Rouse Ball, "A Short History of Mathematics," 3rd edition, Macmillan, 1901, p. 189; see also §4 below.

1

attention in van der Waerden's "Moderne Algebra": Boolean algebras and lattices, binary relations and graphs, and combinatorial algebra play a much greater role in computing than the theory of infinite commutative rings and fields, to which the bulk of van der Waerden's book is dedicated. This inclusion of combinatorics in algebra is in agreement with Tchirnhaus, who claimed already before 1700 that "the combinatorial art stems from algebra," if not with Leibniz, who claimed that combinatorics, as the art of synthesis, included algebra [16a, pp. 287, 297].

To survey the applications of modern algebra to computing in a half-hour requires great oversimplification and superficiality, which I hope you will excuse. To compensate for this superficiality, I shall try to present known facts in a fresh light and mention some unpublished technical results. Throughout, I shall emphasize work done at Harvard ([7]–[10] and [T1]–[T6]), an emphasis which I hope you will also excuse.

Optimization.   Not only has algebra influenced computing, but the problems of computing are influencing algebra. This is especially true of various problems of *optimization* including those of *finding algorithms of minimum "computational complexity"*, say for multiplying together two $n \times n$ matrices or testing a polynomial with integral coefficients for irreducibility over $\mathbf{Z}$; see the papers by Winograd and Zassenhaus in this volume.

The influence on algebra of the concepts of optimization and computational complexity (and computability) can perhaps be best appreciated by analogy. The ancient Greeks took great interest in rationalizing geometry through constructions with ruler and compass (as analog computers), and in correlating the results with numbers. By considering such constructions and their optimization in depth, they were led to the existence of irrational numbers, and to the problems of constructing regular polygons, trisecting angles, duplicating cubes, and squaring circles. These problems, though of minor technological significance, profoundly influenced the development of number theory.

I think that our understanding of the potentialities and limitations of algebraic symbol manipulation will be similarly deepened by attempts to solve problems of optimization and computational complexity arising from digital computing.

A. BINARY ALGEBRA; LATTICES; SEMIGROUPS

2. **Boolean algebra.**   Since most digital computers are constructed from bistable or *binary elements*, it is natural that the algebra of 0 and 1, which I shall refer to as *binary algebra*, should be important for computing. In particular, because human logic is also binary, binary algebra is central to logic design for computers, regardless of whether these are built using relays, vacuum tubes, or semiconductors.

The simplest kind of binary algebra is the *Boolean algebra* of elementary set theory and logic, and especially important is the *free Boolean algebra* with n generators. Already before 1850, Boole showed that this was (in modern notation) 2^{2^n}. More concretely, it is the Boolean algebra of all functions $f: \mathbf{2}^n \to \mathbf{2}$, where $\mathbf{2} = \{0, 1\}$ is the two-element Boolean algebra. If the elements of $\mathbf{2}^n$ are represented as n-vectors $\mathbf{x} = (x_1, \ldots, x_n)$ ("n-bit words"), the generators can be taken as the n functions δ_i: $(x_1, \ldots, x_n) \to x_i$. And in 1913, Skolem[3] showed that the (distributive) sublattice of $\mathbf{2}^{2^n}$, generated by the "evaluation maps" δ_i was $\mathbf{2}^{\mathbf{2}^n}$, the set of all isotone functions f: $\mathbf{2}^n \to \mathbf{2}$ (and the free distributive lattice with n generators).

On the other hand, each function $\mathbf{2}^n \to \mathbf{2}$ can be regarded as a *switching function* which assigns to each "state" of n binary "input" elements a "state" of a specified output element. Hence theorems about Boolean algebras can be reinterpreted as statements about switching circuits. Boole's results make possible the *systematic* design of logic processors for computers from AND-gates, OR-gates, and inverters. Likewise, Skolem's Theorem can be paraphrased as the assertion that precisely the isotone switching functions can be realized by series-parallel networks (using AND-gates and OR-gates, but not inverters).

However, the most important and challenging questions of switching theory concern the most economical or *optimal* logic design for a network which will realize a given Boolean function f: $\mathbf{2}^n \to \mathbf{2}$. Like most questions of optimal design, this question is ambiguous because "cost" assignments are variable; one natural interpretation consists in asking for the *shortest* (fewest-symbol) symbolic expression based on the operations $\wedge$, $\vee$, $'$ which will realize a given f. Although ingenious techniques for shortening Boolean polynomials have been devised by Quine and others, nobody has yet discovered a systematic algorithm for reducing a general Boolean polynomial in 20 variables (say) to *shortest* form, without comparing an impossibly large number of short forms. Therefore, if we define *switching theory* as the branch of modern (i.e., non-numerical) algebra concerned with optimizing logic design, we must admit that the main theoretical problem of switching theory has not yet been solved.[4]

3. **Binary groups.** Also because digital computers are made up of binary elements, codes used with them often make use of properties of elementary Abelian groups of order 2^n, which may properly be called "binary groups." One application of such codes is to synthesize reliable message-transmitting "organisms" (including computers) from unreliable components.[5] The simplest way to accomplish this is by "multiplexing," but modern algebra is needed to achieve optimal or even economical designs.

Specifically, to minimize the probability of error in message transmission

---

[3]Third Scand. Math. Congress (1913), 149–163. For other properties of $\mathbf{2}^{2^n}$, see [**LT3**, Chapter III, §**4**] and H. N. Shapiro, Comm. Pure Appl. Math. **23** (1970), 299–312. (Here and below, **LT***n*] refers to the *n*th edition of [**7**].)

[4]For switching theory, see [**9**, Chapter 6]; also [**26**, Chapter 4]. especially §§1 and 6. For various theoretical difficulties, see J. P. Roth, Trans. Amer. Math. Soc. **88** (1958), 301–326.

[5]See [**38**a, vol. V, pp. 329–378, especially pp. 353–368].

at given cost, encoding-decoding procedures called binary (m, n) *group codes* are often used. In group codes, each m-bit block of the message or "message word" is encoded as a longer n-bit "code word" $(n > m)$. Such n-bit words can be visualized as the vertices of a unit n-cube. The *distance* between two vertices is defined to be the length of the shortest path joining them along edges of the cube (its graph), or, equivalently, the square of the Euclidean distance between them in n-space. In other words, for $\mathbf{x} = (x_1, \ldots, x_n)$ and $\mathbf{y} = (y_1, \ldots, y_n)$:

$$(1) \qquad d(\mathbf{x},\mathbf{y}) = \sum (x_i - y_i)^2, \quad \text{each } x_i, y_i = 0 \text{ or } 1.$$

Also, $d(x,y)$ is the number of coordinates i with $x_i \neq y_i$.

Suppose that a sequence of m-bit message words is to be sent through a *binary symmetric channel* in which, by definition, each bit has a probability p of being correctly received $(0 < p < 1)$. The relevant optimization problem is to *maximize the code rate* $R = m/n$ for a given (very small) probability Q of error when the message has been *decoded*, for fixed p. Shannon proved very early that, for any $\epsilon > 0$, one can make $Q < \epsilon$ and $R > p - \epsilon$ (thus achieving arbitrarily large efficiency), provided long enough code blocks are used. This is a very satisfactory *existence theorem*, but Shannon's construction would require very complicated and costly capital equipment to implement. Algebraic coding theory[6] aims at constructing simpler optimal or near-optimal codes.

Most algebraic codes are binary group codes, in which the code words form a *subgroup* of the elementary Abelian group of order 2^n. Though it is not clear that optimal codes must be group codes, I know of no (m, n) code not a group code which is superior to every (m, n) group code. Moreover systematic decoding is certainly helped by having the group structure built into the code.

Obviously, the chance of confusing two n-bit code words is negligible when the "distance" between them is large. Hence to *optimize* coding, one wishes to know for any n and $l < n$ the maximum number $F(n, l)$ of vertices on an n-cube, such that any two are a distance at least l apart—i.e., such that $\mathbf{x} \neq \mathbf{y}$ implies $d(\mathbf{x},\mathbf{y}) \geqq l$.

For odd $l = 2k+1$, $F(n, 2k+1)$ is the maximum number of disjoint spheres of radius k which can be "packed" in $\mathbf{2}^n$. If one takes the centers of these spheres for *code words*, then one can systematically correct any set of k or fewer errors in transmitting an n-bit message block, by assigning to every received n-bit block which is in one of these spheres the m-bit message block corresponding to the code word at its center.

For this reason, when the hypercube $\mathbf{2}^n$ can be exactly covered by disjoint spheres of radius k, one speaks of a *perfect* packing (or code). This is the case that the obvious inequality

$$(2) \qquad F(n, 2k+1) \leqq \mathbf{2}^n \Big/ \left[1 + \binom{n}{1} + \cdots + \binom{n}{k}\right]$$

[6]See [9] for an elementary exposition, and Berlekamp's article in W. T. Tutte (editor), "Recent Progress in Combinatorics," Academic Press, 1969.

reduces to an equality. As Dr. van List has said, the only known perfect error-correcting codes are the binary Hamming codes [**9**, p. 252] and the two Golay codes [**5**]; there probably are no others. However, the Hamming codes correct only one error ($k = 1, l = 3$ above); the problem of *binary code optimization* is *unsolved* for $k > 1$ [**1**, vol. X, pp. 291–297].

The most powerful known systematic[7] error-correcting codes are the Bose-Chaudhuri-Hocquenghem or BCH-codes [**9**, Chapter 12]. The construction of these uses the properties of finite (Galois) fields of order 2^n, which one may call *binary fields*. A $(2^n-1-(2k+1)n, 2^n-1)$ BCH-code can be designed to correct k errors [**9**, p. 355]; thus a (215,255) BCH-code can correct up to 5 errors with 40 check digits. This is fairly efficient; but each sphere of radius 5 in the hypercube $\mathbf{2}^{255}$ contains only about 8 billion (2^{33}) vertices; hence the "packing" leaves over 99% of all vertices not "covered." Thus, it is far from "perfect"; moreover, $k \ll n$. (Other "good" codes with $k \ll n$ can be based on the Chinese Remainder Theorem.[8])

Finally, for $n = 2^r$ and $l = 2^{r-1}$, I believe that $F(n, l) = F(2^r, 2^{r-1}) = 2r$. Specifically, the r generators δ_i and their r (antipodal in the hypercube $\mathbf{2}^{2^r}$) complements δ_i' are separated by a distance $l = 2^{r-1}$ or (if antipodal) $2l = 2^r$; hence $F(2^r, 2^{r-1}) \geqq 2r$. My conjecture is that equality holds.

Concluding remark. The two unsolved problems in binary algebra which I have described illustrate the fact that *genuine applications can suggest simple and natural but extremely difficult problems*, which are overlooked by pure theorists. Thus, while working for 30 years (1935–1965) on generalizing Boolean algebra to lattice theory, I regarded finite Boolean algebras as trivial because they could all be described up to isomorphism, and completely ignored the basic "shortest form" and "optimal packing" problems described above.

4. **Binary relations and graphs.** The *binary relations* between two sets S and T form a Boolean algebra $\mathbf{2}^{S\times T}$ in an obvious way. If S and T are finite, with elements listed as $s_1, \ldots, s_m$ and $t_1, \ldots, t_n$, then the set of binary relations from S to T is bijective with the set of $m \times n$ matrices $R = \|r_{ij}\|$ with entries 0 and 1: $r_{ij} = 1$ means that s_i and t_j are in the relation R. This illustrates how the binary relations from S to T form a binary algebra under Boolean operations performed componentwise.

When $S = T$, the algebra of binary relations has a richer structure, because the set $\mathbf{2}^{S\times S}$ of all binary relations on a set S also forms a *monoid* under composition. The analysis of the properties of the resulting algebraic system $[\mathbf{2}^{S\times S}; \wedge, \vee, ', \circ]$ forms an important part of the algebra of logic as developed

[7]Especially from the standpoint of efficient implementation (including decoding). The optimal codes to be defined in Part C, like those of negligible redundancy whose existence was established by Shannon, are hard to implement electronically.

[8]See [**1**, loc. cit.]. Also, John Lipson and Erwin Bareiss have important unpublished manuscripts giving other applications of this theorem.

by Boole, Schröder, and Whitehead and Russell. Only since 1940 have the involved algebraic properties of this system been disentangled, and the system identified as a *lattice-ordered monoid* [**7**, pp. 343–345].

Because of the rich algebraic structure of relation algebra and its basic role in logic, I would expect the algebra of binary relations to be useful for computing and computer logic (cf. §10), it is also useful for specifying the zero elements of matrices (cf. Part D). However, I know of no programming language which utilizes this richer structure. Neither do I know of any computer having a "logic unit" (analogous to the "arithmetic unit" implementing approximate addition and multiplication electronically), which utilizes the rich algebraic structure of the algebra of relations.

Graphs.   The binary relations on a set S can also be represented symbolically as *directed graphs*, whose vertices designate the elements of S, with an arrow going from vertex i to vertex j if and only if $r_{ij} = 1$. Such directed graphs are omnipresent in computer science. Graphs appear in flow charts for programs, and in state diagrams for gating (logic) networks.

I maintain that graphs and directed graphs constitute part of algebra in the sense of providing techniques of symbol manipulation, as well as of being connected by a cryptomorphism with the algebra of relations. In support of this view I quote [**24**, pp. 49–50]: "To express . . . system structure symbolically, there has emerged . . . various kinds of flowgraphs . . . evolving into a new kind of notation . . . flowgraphs can be manipulated and "solved" just as . . . conventional algebraic and functional symbols . . . may be manipulated and solved."

Actually, the strictly one-dimensional or *sequential* alphanumeric symbolism of linguistic theory (also preferred by typesetters) is not strictly adhered to even in algebra. Thus one often prefers to manipulate two-dimensional algebraic displays such as matrices or the following:

$$\frac{x^{n+1} - y^{n+1}}{x - y} = \sum_{k=0}^{n} x^{n-k} y^{k}.$$

Moreover, labelled directed graphs are also used in pure algebra, as diagrams for finite posets [**9**, p. 38], and for (very small) categories of mappings. Finally, we shall see in Part D the utility for Gauss elimination of the concepts of the graph and directed graph of a matrix.

Graphs and configurations.   By a *configuration* is meant a system consisting of a set S_0 of "points," a set S_1 of "lines," and an *incidence* relation stating which points are on which lines. It is required that at least two points $p, q \in S_0$ be on each line $L \in S_1$; when there exist exactly two such points, the configuration is called a loop-free *graph*. When no two distinct lines have the same two (incident) points, the graph is called *simple*.[9]

Given any enumeration of the points and lines of a finite graph or other

[9]See [**9**, p. 56] and [**15**, p. 18].

configuration Γ, the incidence matrix of Γ is the relation matrix of its incidence relation as defined above. One can also define a simple loop-free graph, relative to any enumeration of its points, by the *adjacency matrix*. $A(\Gamma) = \|\alpha_{ij}\|$, where $\alpha_{ij} = 1$ if $p_i p_j$ is an edge of the graph and $\alpha_{ij} = 0$ otherwise.

As defined by its adjacency relation, a graph is thus a (homogeneous) "relational system," which brings it within the scope of universal algebra [20, p. 224]; as defined by its incidence relation, it is a heterogeneous relational system.

5. **Lattices.** Although "binary algebras" (i.e., Boolean algebras and binary groups and fields) have a special importance for digital computers, their role is by no means exclusive. Thus, an important role is also played by *lattices*: posets (i.e., partially ordered sets) L, any two of whose elements have least upper bounds and greatest lower bounds in L. Lattices include Boolean algebras as a special case: the case of complemented distributive lattices.

Non-Boolean lattices are important for computer science because not only the subsets but also the *partitions* of the elements of any system (e.g., of the components or states of a machine) form a lattice [23, §2.1]. Moreover, those subsets which are "closed" under specified sets of operations, and those partitions which have some desirable property such as the substitution property for specified operations [23, p. 68], also typically form lattices. In particular, the "state splittings" of a machine are embedded in such a lattice [23, Chapter 5], and this fact makes some aspects of automaton theory (see §§9–10) more understandable.

Closure and dependence. Lattices also arise from closure operations of many kinds; see [LT3, Chapter 5]. Lattices arising from the following three closure operations on vectors are especially important for computing.

DEFINITION. Let $V = V_n(F)$ be any vector space, and let S be the set of *all* vectors of V. By the *linear span* $\lambda(A)$ of a set of vectors $\alpha_1, \ldots, \alpha_r$ of S is meant the set of all linear combinations $\xi = c_1 \alpha_1 + \cdots + c_r \alpha_r$ of the α_i. When $\Sigma\, c_i = 1$, ξ is said to belong to the *affine span* $\beta(A)$ of A. When the scalars belong to an ordered field and all $c_i \geq 0$, as well as $\Sigma\, c_i = 1$, $\gamma = \Sigma\, c_i \alpha_i$ is said to belong to the *convex span* (or hull $\gamma(A)$) of A.

Each of the operations λ, β, γ is a *closure operation* c on the subsets of S, in the sense that [7, Chapter V] $c(X) \supset X$ for all X, $c(c(X)) = c(X)$ for all $X \subset S$, and $X \supset Y$ implies $c(x) \supset c(Y)$. Hence the "closed" subsets (i.e., linear subspaces, affine subspaces, and convex subsets in the three cases of interest here) form a *lattice*, and hence a (homogeneous) algebra in a very precise sense to be discussed in §8.

Given a closure operation c on 2^S, one says that $y \in S$ is *dependent* on a set $X \subset S$ when $y \in c(X)$. The dependence relations so defined from the closure operations λ, β above nave a special *exchange property* due to Steinitz and Mac Lane.

SM.   If neither p nor q is dependent on X, but q is dependent on $p \cup X$, then p is dependent on $q \cup X$.

It follows that the nonvoid linear subspaces and the affine subspaces of any vector space form geometric lattices: the so-called *projective geometry* $P_{n-1}(F)$ and *affine geometry* $A_n(F)$, of lengths $n-1$ and n, respectively; see [7, Chapter IV].

More generally, let S be *any* set of vectors in $V_n(F)$; one can define closure operators λ_S, β_S, and γ_S, consisting of all linear, affine, or affine combinations ξ as above which are in S. This defines (for λ_S and β_S) very large classes of geometric lattices, which may be considered as *subgeometries* of the geometries $P_{n-1}(F)$ and $A_n(F)$ just defined.

Given a *finite* set S of vectors in $V_n(F)$, where F is an ordered field, the convex closures of the subsets of S define what is called a *convex polytope* [20a, p. 31]. The lattice defined in this way satisfies the Jordan-Dedekind Chain Condition, but does not in general have the exchange property. (Instead, it has a weaker "Radon property.")

Three fascinating unsolved problems of lattice theory concern the characterization of those (finite) lattices which arise from the preceding construction, and the ways of *representing* (geometric) lattices as subgeometries of $P_{n-1}(F)$ and $A_n(F)$. In addition, these characterization problems lead to many difficult combinatorial questions.[10]

6. **Combinatorial complexes.**   I now recall a far-reaching generalization of the notion of a graph, essentially due to Poincaré: that of a combinatorial complex [3].

DEFINITION.   An unoriented n-dimensional *combinatorial complex* is a collection of nonvoid sets S_k of k-cells $(k = 0, 1, \ldots, n)$, together with associated *incidence matrices* specifying for each $k = 1, \ldots, n$ which $(k-1)$-cells are incident on which k-cells.

It is usually intended that each n-cell above be a convex polytope in the algebraic sense specified in §5. Since a one-dimensional convex polytope is necessarily just a finite line-segment, a graph is just a one-dimensional complex. It usually also required that two cells meet on at most one face (subcell) of each; this condition holds in "simple" graphs. In applications to the topology of manifolds, moreover, at most two n-cells are allowed to meet on any $(n-1)$-cell or "facet", but the terminology has never become standardized.[11]

A very simple family of two dimensional complexes, that of *rectangular polygons* subdivided by parallels to their sides, is discussed in Appendix A.

---

[10]See for example V. Klee and D. W. Walkup, Acta. Math. **117** (1967), 53–77.

[11]For other definitions of combinatorial complexes, see S. Lefschetz, "Algebraic Topology", Amer. Math. Soc. 1942, p. 89, and the references given there. The definition given here seems closest to that of M. H. A. Newman. The basic reference is E. Steinitz, "Polyeder und Raumeinteilungen," Enz. Math. Wiss. 3AB 12 (1922), 1–139.

Another family of complexes is that of simplicial complexes (in two dimensions, these consist of triangles).

The notion of a combinatorial complex has recently become important for computing, because the *finite element methods* used to solve on computers typical problems of solid mechanics begin by decomposing plates and shells into polygonal "elements." The resulting configuration is an unoriented 2-dimensional combinatorial complex. I shall explain in Part E the importance for computations using "finite element" methods of specifying such complexes carefully. In Appendix A, I shall describe some preliminary ideas for identifying rectangular polygons (up to isomorphism) and assigning addresses to their cells.

In any combinatorial complex whose n-cells are convex polytopes, the k-cells are just the elements of height k, and the incidence relation of the resulting complex (which has one r-cell, the dimension (height) of the span of S) is just the covering relation of the lattice.

Complexes as semilattices. By letting its incidence relation be the covering relation, any unoriented n-dimensional complex can be regarded as a poset P in which (i) all maximal chains have the same length n (implying the Jordan-Dedekind Chain Condition, and (ii) for any maximal element γ, if Γ consists of all elements $x \leqq \gamma$, there is an isomorphism θ from $[\Gamma, \leqq]$ to the set of all "faces" of an n-dimensional convex polytope Π under which $x \leqq y$ holds if and only if $\theta(x) \subset \theta(y)$ in Π).

Conversely, any poset P of finite length is defined up to isomorphism by its *incidence matrix*, the relation matrix of its covering relation. When P is a topological complex, and one enumerates first all its 0-cells, then all its 1-cells, then all its 2-cells,..., one obtains this strictly triangular incidence matrix as the direct sum $\bigoplus \Gamma_k = \Gamma(P)$ of incidence matrices generalizing those for graphs: Γ_k is the relation matrix of covering ("incidence") between k-cells and $(k-1)$-cells. (One has a further direct decomposition of $\Gamma(P)$ into the $\Gamma(P_l)$, where the P_l are the connected components of P.)

In the locally Euclidean case, each $(n-1)$-cell of an n-dimensional complex Γ is incident on at most two n-cells. (Any locally Euclidean graph is a sum of disjoint simple paths and simple cycles.) If one defines the boundary ∂C of a k-dimensional subcomplex C of Γ as the set of $(k-1)$-cells incident on only *one* k-cell, then more generally $\partial(\partial C) = 0$. However relatively "little is known concerning the geometric embeddability of specifically finite-dimensional simplicial complexes in ... Euclidean spaces,"[12] or even about which geometric lattices are convex polytopes over the real field, let alone about the embeddability of complexes in general.

Figures 1a-1b depict the diagrams of posets corresponding to a triangle

[12]See R. A. Duke, Amer. Math. Monthly **78** (1970), 597–603, and references given there. For still other applications of lattices to combinatorial problems see G.-C. Rota and L. H. Harper, Advances in Probability **1** (1971), 171–215.

(2-simplex) and a quadrangle, respectively, when the void set ∅ is included as a "(−1)-cell." Note that they are both lattices (the first is a Boolean algebra). This is a special case of the following result, which applies in particular to simple graphs.[13]

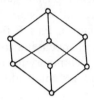

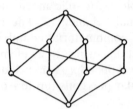

FIGURE 1a   FIGURE 1b

THEOREM 1.   *The closed cells of any combinatorial complex form with the void set ∅ a semilattice of finite length under intersection.*

This semilattice satisfies the Jordan-Dedekind Chain Condition, but is not usually semimodular [7, p. 40]. Its length is the dimension of the complex, plus one.

COROLLARY.   *The points and closed edges of any simple (symmetric) graph form with ∅ a semilattice of length 2.*

By known properties of semilattices [7, p.22], Theorem 1 has a dual.

THEOREM 1'.   *The closed cells of any combinatorial complex form, with an all-element I, a semilattice under join.*

One can also add both the void set ∅ and an all-element I to any complex, getting a lattice. When this is done to graphs, the notion of sublattice gives the usual concept of a "selection subgraph." (We recall that the sublattice concept is also useful when one considers projective geometries as lattices.)

Unfortunately, when graphs are considered as semilattices, the notions of direct product, morphism, and free algebra seem not to be very natural or useful. It seems more natural to consider graphs as "heterogeneous" algebras, and more fruitful to consider them as posets (or "partial lattices"; see §11).

Other applications of (geometric) lattices and posets to computing will be described in §15 and Part E.

7. **Semigroups.**   I do not wish to exaggerate the importance for computer science of lattices (including Boolean algebras), or of binary groups and fields. All of these have a quite special structure. A much more general class of algebraic systems is provided by semigroups, which are indeed basic for a great part of algebra. They may be defined as follows.

---

[13]See [**LT1**, §18], [**LT2**, §10], and [**LT3**, Chapter IV, §11], where a slightly different poset interpretation is given.

DEFINITION. A *semigroup* is an algebra $H = [X, c]$ which consists of a set X of elements combined by a single binary composition operation $c: X^2 \to X$, which is *associative* in the sense that

$$(3) \qquad c(c, x(y, z)) = c(c(x, y), z) \quad \text{for all } x, y, z \in X.$$

Here $c(x, y)$ is commonly written $x \circ y$ or just xy.

Semigroups differ trivially from *monoids*, since every monoid is a semigroup and one can make any semigroup not a monoid into a monoid by adding an identity 1. *Groups* are just monoids in which every element x has an inverse x^{-1}, with $f(x, x^{-1}) = f(x^{-1}, x) = 1$.

Likewise, a semilattice is just a commutative semigroup in which every element is an idempotent. And finite lattices differ trivially from finite semilattices: one need only adjoin an I, or a 0, as the case may be.

Finally, *rings* are just algebras with two binary operations, $+$ and $\cdot$, which are commutative groups under $+$ and semigroups (or monoids according to taste) under $\cdot$, and in which the usual distributive laws are satisfied:

$$x(y+z) = xy+xz \quad \text{and} \quad (x+y)z = xz+yz, \quad \text{all } x, y, z.$$

Semigroups acting on sets. Semigroups arise in computing in many contexts; as we shall see, an especially direct application is to the theory of state machines (see §9) through the following intermediate concept.

DEFINITION. A *left-semigroup acting on a set* S is a triple $\mathscr{L} = \{H, S, \psi\}$, where $H = [X, c]$ is a semigroup, S is a set, and ψ is a mapping $\psi: X \times S \to S$ with the property that

$$(4) \qquad \psi(c(g, h), s) = \psi(g, \psi(h, s)), \qquad \text{all } g, h \in X \quad \text{and} \quad s \in S.$$

A *right-semigroup* $\mathscr{R} = \{H, S, \varphi\}$ is defined similarly, but with $\varphi: S \times X \to S$ and (4) replaced by

$$(4') \qquad \varphi(s, c(g, h)) = \varphi(\varphi(s, g), h).$$

B. AUTOMATA AND UNIVERSAL ALGEBRA

8. **Algebras.** The concept of semigroup provides an excellent introduction to the study of abstract algebra because of its simplicity, generality, and relative concreteness. Moreover it relates to computing through the notion of a "state machine"; see §9. However, it does not include nonassociative loops or quasi-groups; neither does it include most Lie or Jordan algebras.

A much more general class of algebraic systems, which includes Lie and Jordan algebras as well as semigroups, groups, lattices, rings and fields is provided by the following notion of an "algebra." I proposed it around 1935, and it has since gained wide acceptance.

DEFINITION. An *algebra* is a system $A = [S, F]$, where S is a set of *elements* and F is a set of *finitary operations*:

$$(5) \qquad f_i: S^{n(i)} \to S, \qquad n(i) \in N.$$

Universal algebra. In spite of the enormous variety of the systems to which the preceding definition applies, all of them have a substantial number of nontrivial properties in common. Many of these properties concern sub-algebras, (homo)morphisms, congruence relations, direct products, etc. Some of them follow fairly directly from the ideas of the Emmy Noether school, but many others involve Dedekind's concept of a *lattice* which was ignored by this school. These common properties also include some less obvious results about free algebras, identities, and "varieties" of algebras. Moreover, they include still other theorems, trivial for finite algebras, which assert that the complete lattices of subalgebras and congruence relations of any algebra are "algebraic." Finally, an increasing set of recent theorems about general "algebras" invoke the concept of a category (see Example 9 below).

The subject of *universal algebra*[14] is concerned with such theorems about "algebras" in general; it provides the most general context in which a wide range of nontrivial algebraic theorems has so far been proved. By unifying and clarifying the foundations of algebra, in somewhat the same way that symbolic logic has helped to systematize the foundation of mathematics and automaton theory provides a general foundation for the theory of digital computer, universal algebra may be regarded as a further significant step towards fulfilling Leibniz' old dream (see §12) of automating the symbolic method. However, it must be confessed that "universal algebra" has contributed more to the clarification and unification of the foundations of algebra than to the development of powerful new techniques (except for some existence proofs).

Furthermore, to prove general theorems about the existence of free algebras, etc., one must assume that one is dealing with families of algebras defined by axioms stated as "sentences" of rather special logical forms which avoid existential quantifiers and negations. The "universal" proofs do not apply directly even to groups, when defined as monoids in which every element has a left- and a right-inverse, or when defined as semigroups in which any equation of the form $ax = b$ or $ya = b$ has a solution.

To apply the "universal" proofs, one must consider groups as having not only a binary (multiplication) operation, but also a 0-ary operation ("select 1") and a unary operation ("take the inverse a^{-1} of a"), as well as a binary operation. This is because: (i) the notion of "subalgebra" becomes ambiguous with existential quantifiers, (ii) only "positive" sentences are necessarily preserved under epimorphisms, and (iii) only sentences equivalent to "universal Horn sentences" are preserved under direct products.[15]

Cryptomorphisms. We have seen that graphs can be defined in several formally different ways. This is true of many kinds of algebraic systems. Trivial

---

[14]See [2, Part IV]; [7, Chapter VI]; [16]; and P. M. Cohn, "Universal Algebra," Harper and Row, 1965. The name was borrowed from the title of [32]; the technical content was not.

[15]Much of "universal algebra" does not apply to the class of fields, in which division is only a "partial" operation; see §11. For the other statements above, see [20, pp. 226, 281, 285].

examples are provided by the correspondences $\wedge$, $\rightleftharpoons$, $\vee$ in any lattice and $xy \rightleftharpoons yx$ in semigroups. Less trivially, one can convert any Boolean algebra into a Boolean ring by a "compile" transformation which translates I into 1, a' into $\gamma(a') = a + 1$, and $a \vee b$ into $\gamma(a \vee b) = a + b + ab$. Conversely, one can convert any Boolean ring into a Boolean algebra by replacing 1 by I and $a + b$ by $\beta(a + b) = ab' \vee a'b$.

I have proposed [7, p. 154] the word *cryptomorphism* to describe such "compile" methods for translating from one mode of symbolic representation to another.[16] The above example, and the ways of representing graphs as algebraic systems (e.g., by incidence or adjacency matrices, or by circles and arcs), show that two algebraic systems can be "crypto-isomorphic" in very subtle ways.

Note that γ and β are unfortunately not true inverses: neither $\beta(\gamma(E)) = E$ nor $\gamma(\beta(F)) = F$ holds for general expressions. Thus, for example,

$$(6) \qquad \gamma(\beta(a + b)) = ab' + a'b + ab'a'b$$

is not formally the same as $a + b$. One can however obtain inverse "compile" transformations if one introduces also operators δ and δ^* for reducing elements to canonical form in Boolean algebras and Boolean rings respectively. Then the composite operators $\delta^*\gamma$ and $\delta\beta$ are inverse "compilers" for canonical forms.

As a less trivial example, the mapping $xy - yx \mapsto [x, y]$ is a cryptomorphism from any linear associative algebra to a Lie algebra. The right-inverse cryptomorphisms $[x, y] \mapsto xy - yx$ from any Lie algebra L to linear associative algebras determine the representations of L by matrices; and it is known that every Lie algebra is cryptomonomorphic to some linear associative algebra. The cryptomorphisms $[xy + yx]/2 \mapsto \langle x, y \rangle$ share this property, and can even (by definition) be crypto-isomorphisms in the important case of "special" Jordan algebras.

9. **State machines.**[17] Universal algebra applies to computer science through the theory of state machines and (see §10) automata. This is evident from the following definition.

DEFINITION. A *state machine* is an algebra $A = [S, F]$, where S is a set of elements called "states," and F is a set of unary operators acting on S designated by an (input) *alphabet* of "input symbols" $a, b, c, \ldots$. (Typically, $F = \{0, 1\}$ is binary.)

In the theory of automata, the action (effect) of an input symbol $a \in F$ on the state s is usually [9, §3.3] designated by $\nu(a, s)$ instead of $a(s)$. As an application of universal algebra, it is routine to construct the free (homogeneous) state machine $F_X(M)$ generated from the particular state machine of Figure 2a and

---

[16]Cryptomorphisms are closely related to the "algebraic functors" of category theory; cf. F. W. Lawvere, Ph.D. Thesis, Columbia, 1964, where one can also find the remarks about Lie and Jordan algebras made below.

[17]§§9–10 represent joint work with Dr. John D. Lipson, who also collaborated in drafting §17.

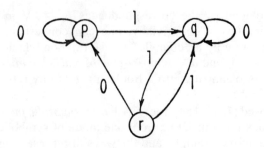

FIGURE 2a.   Machine M.

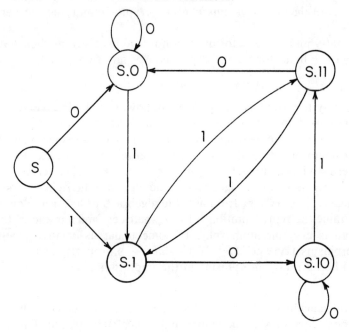

FIGURE 2b.   Free *Homogeneous* Machine $F_X(M)$.

the fixed input alphabet $\{0, 1\}$; the diagram of $F_X(M)$ is shown in Figure 2b.

Although the theory of automata is still too fragmentary and too general to be very useful to machine designers, it has already developed significantly from a purely theoretical standpoint. Thus, the Krohn-Rhodes Theorem [T1][18] represents an ingenious analog of the Jordan-Hölder Theorem. Also, one can define and prove by universal algebra the existence of a unique (up to iso-morphism) *free* automaton with n generators associated with a given machine [10]. Finally, one can show that the usual construction [9, Chapter 3] of the

---

[18]Also Trans. Amer. Math. Soc. **116** (1965), 540–564. See also [**5**, Chapter 5], [**25**, Chapter 9], [**23**], and A. Meyer and C. Thompson, Math. Systems Theory **3** (1969), 110–118, which corrects [**23**].

minimal state machine equivalent to a given (completely specified) finite-state machine applies to *any* ("universal") algebra with only unary operations.

The preceding remarks about state machines have analogs for the automata to be discussed in §10 (these are just state machines with outputs). Whether or not the theory of automata belongs to "applied" mathematics or "pure" computer science, the concept is philosophically exciting because, as the name suggests, it is plausible that a sufficiently fast automaton having enough storage could, *if properly programmed*, simulate many activities of the human brain. Thus, it would fulfill Leibniz' dream of "a new kind of instrument, increasing the power of reason far more than any optical instrument has ever aided the power of reason."[19]

10. **Heterogeneous algebras.** Very recently, John Lipson and I [**10**] have substantially generalized the class of algebras for which the theorem of "universal algebra" can be proved. Our basic definition is the following:

DEFINITION. A *heterogeneous algebra* $\mathfrak{A} = [\mathfrak{S};F]$ is a family $\mathfrak{S}$ of non-overlapping sets S_k called phyla, together with a set F of $n(i)$-ary operations, or functions

$$f_i\colon S_{k(i,1)} \times \cdots \times S_{k(i,n(i))} \to S_{k(i,0)}. \tag{7}$$

Algebras having the same phylum indices i and the same functions $n(i)$ and $k(i,j)$ are said to be of the same *type*.

The class of heterogeneous algebras includes the following important and familiar varieties.

EXAMPLE 1. As in [**10**, Example 1], a *vector space* is a heterogeneous algebra $[A, \Lambda; +, -, \oplus, \ominus, \times, \cdot]$ with two phyla: vectors and scalars. Here $[A; +, -]$ is an additive group with two operations $+\colon A^2 \to A$ and $-\colon A \to A$; $[\Lambda; \oplus, \ominus, \times]$ is a field; and $\cdot : \Lambda \times A \to A$ is a scalar multiplication.

EXAMPLE 2. A *group representation* is a heterogeneous algebra $[G, A, \Lambda; \circ, ^{-1}, +, -,$ etc.], with three phyla: the group elements $g, h, \ldots$; vectors; and scalars. The operations are group composition $\circ$ and inverse formation $^{-1}$; the vector space operations for $\{A, \Lambda\}$ of Example 1; and group action γ. Here $\gamma(g, \mathbf{x}) = g(\mathbf{x}) \in A$ is the effect of $g \in G$ acting on the element $\mathbf{x} \in A$.

The class of heterogeneous algebras also includes *directed graphs*, which may be defined (cryptomorphically) in two ways as follows.

EXAMPLE 3. A directed graph can be interpreted as a heterogeneous algebra $[N, A; \partial^+, \partial^-]$ in the above sense. It has two sets or "phyla" of elements: a set N of *nodes* and a set A of *arcs*; and it has two unary operations $\partial^+\colon A \to N$ and $\partial^-\colon A \to N$.

EXAMPLE 3′. One can also regard a simple directed graph as a (nonverbal) symbolic representation of a *binary relation* on the set N of its nodes,

---

[19]Those interested in the "artificial intelligence" aspects of automaton theory should consult [**31**], [**8**], and the references given there.

and consider it as a heterogeneous algebra $[N, 2; f]$, where 2 is the Boolean set of truth-values $0,1$, and $f: N \times N \to 2$ is a binary operation on N to 2.

The second definition identifies the directed graph with its *relation matrix*; thus the algebra of relations (§4) is applicable to (the adjacency relation) in directed graphs. For algebraic topology, still a third (cryptomorphic) definition is relevant, namely, the following.

EXAMPLE 3″.   A directed graph is a heterogeneous algebra $[A, N, \mathbf{Z}_2; f]$, in which $f: A \times N \to \mathbf{Z}_2$ is defined by:

$$(8) \qquad \begin{aligned} f(a,n) &= \quad 1 \quad \text{if } n \text{ is the final node of } a, \\ &= -1 \quad \text{if } n \text{ is the initial node of } a, \\ &= \quad 0 \quad \text{otherwise.} \end{aligned}$$

Given a chain $C = \Sigma x_i a_i$ $(x_i \in \mathbf{Z}_2)$ in $\mathbf{Z}_2^A$, one can then define $\partial C = \Sigma x_i f(a_i, n_j)n_j \in \mathbf{Z}_2^N$.

Analogs of this definition for higher-dimensional complexes make $\partial(\partial C) = 0$.

Automata.   As was observed in [10], state machines can be defined not only as ("homogeneous") algebras with one phylum as in §8, but also (and more naturally) as heterogeneous algebras. Moreover, automata with output alphabets can also be defined in a natural way as heterogeneous algebras.

EXAMPLE 4.   A (sequential) machine or *automaton* is a *heterogeneous* algebra $M = [\mathscr{S}, F]$ in which $\mathscr{S} = \{S, A, Z\}$ contains three phyla: a nonvoid set S of "states," a nonvoid set A of input symbols (the "input alphabet") and a finite set Z of output symbols (the "output alphabet"). There are two binary operations in F:

$$(9a) \qquad \nu: S \times A \to S \qquad (\text{"change of state"}),$$
$$(9b) \qquad \zeta: S \times A \to Z \qquad (\text{"output functions"}).$$

A *state machine* or *semi-automaton* is obtained as a two-phylum heterogeneous algebra from the above by "forgetting" about the output symbols of Z and the output function ζ. This "forgetful functor" defines a state machine as a heterogeneous algebra $M = [\{S, A\}, \{\nu\}]$.

Both the "heterogeneous" and the "homogeneous" definitions of state machines are in the literature: the heterogeneous in [19] and the homogeneous in [9] and in Minsky[31]. Moreover, the difference between the heterogeneous and homogeneous definitions has basic algebraic consequences (e.g., in [10, §5] compare the two kinds of direct products of state machines). We now discuss these differences, with special reference to *free algebras*.

As in §9, a state machine is also definable as a homogeneous algebra by $M = [S, \{f_a\}]$, where for each letter a of the input alphabet F contains a unary operation $f_a: S \to S$

$$(10) \qquad\qquad f_a: s \mapsto \nu(s, a).$$

In the homogeneous case this input alphabet is *fixed* and plays the role of an

s.yx
x
s.xyx
x
y
y
s.y
s.yy
y
y
x, y
y
s
x
x
x
x
s.xx
s.x
x
x
y
y
s.xyy
s.xy
y

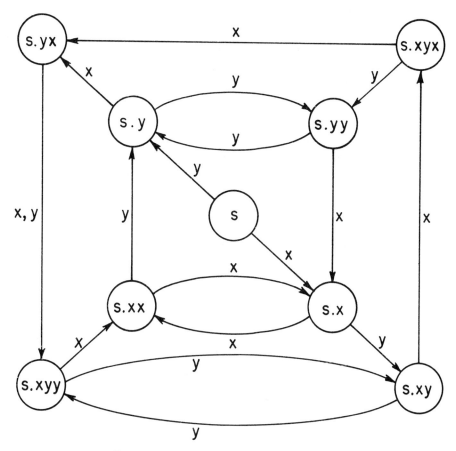

FIGURE 3. Free *Heterogeneous* Machine $F_{\mathfrak{X}}(M)$.

"underlying" structure, analogous to vector space theory where one fixes the underlying field of scalars. To illustrate the contrast, we have displayed in Figure 3 the free *heterogeneous* state machine $F_{\mathfrak{X}}(M)$ generated by one (starting) state letter s and two input letters 0, 1 (i.e., $\mathfrak{X}$ contains $X_1 = \{s\}$ and $X_2 = \{0, 1\}$ as in [**8**, §8]), from the state machine M of Figure 2a. Contrast Figures 2b and 3.

We conclude this section by observing that the proof of Theorem 22 of [7, p. 153] holds with only minor modifications for *heterogeneous* algebras. Consider the class of *all* the algebras $\mathfrak{A} = [\mathfrak{S}; F]$ having given nonvoid phylum-indices k (which we can interpret as the "names" of the phyla), operation-indices i (which we can interpret as the "names" of the operations), and the same *finite* $k(i,j)$ and $n(i)$ in (7). Then for any set of cardinal numbers $r(k)$, one for each phylum, we can define the *free word algebra* $\mathscr{W}_r(F) = [\mathfrak{S}; F]$ of all formal expressions involving the $f_i \in F$ and x_{kl} $(l = 1, \ldots, r(k))$ with $r(k)$ generators in the kth phylum, as in [**10**, §6] and [7, pp. 141–142].

Given $p, q \in \mathscr{W}_r(F)$, define the *polarity*

$$(11) \qquad (p = q)\rho\mathfrak{A} \quad \text{means that} \quad p = q \quad \text{in } \mathfrak{A},$$

that is, no matter what element from the kth phylum of $\mathfrak{A}$ is substituted for each symbol x_{kl}, the equation $p = q$ holds. Then the following is true.

THEOREM 1. *Under the polarity* (11), *the "closed" sets of algebra* $\mathfrak{A}$ *(in the given class) are those closed under the formation of subalgebra, direct product, and epimorphic image; the "closed" sets of identities are the sets* Δ *closed under the following rules of inference:*

(i) *If* $p_h = q_h$ *is in* Δ *for* $h = 1, \ldots, n(i)$, *then* $f_i(p_1, \ldots, p_{n(i)}) = f_i(q_1, \ldots, q_{n(i)})$ *is in* Δ.

(ii) *If* $p = q$ *is in* Δ, *then any substitution of a polynomial* $n(x)$ *for all occurrences of the primitive symbol* x_j *in* p *and* q *is in* Δ.

11. **Partial algebras.**[20] Not only does all of "universal algebra" apply with minor modifications to any heterogeneous algebra, but some fragments of it apply to any partial algebra, defined as follows ([**16**], [**T3**]).

DEFINITION. A *partial algebra* $A = [S, F]$ is a set S of elements, related by a set F of finitary (partial) "operations," each of which is a partial function $f_i: S^{n(i)} \to S$.

EXAMPLE 5. Let $M = [S; 1, \cdot]$ be any *monoid* in which

$$(12) \qquad ax = 1 \quad \text{holds if and only if} \quad xa = 1.$$

Then M is crypto-isomorphic to a unique partial algebra $[S; 1, \cdot, ^{-1}]$ (a "partial group") in which the three conditions $ax = 1$, $xa = 1$, and $x = a^{-1}$ are equivalent.

EXAMPLE 6. Similarly, one can define a *field* as a partial algebra which is a commutative group under addition, a commutative monoid under multiplication, which satisfies the distributive laws, and in which for all $a = 0$, a^{-1} is defined and satisfies $aa^{-1} = a^{-1}a = 1$.

In [**T3**], Vern Poythress has defined *free* partial algebras with the same set F of (partial) operations. A *p-morphism* is a partial function $\varphi: S \to T$ defined on a set X of generators of A such that, for any (n-ary, partial) operation $f \in F$, if $f(b_1, \ldots, b_n)$ is defined in B and $b_i = \varphi_{a_i}$ for $i = 1, \ldots, n$, then we have $f(a_1, \ldots, a_n)$ is defined in A and

$$(13) \qquad \varphi f(a_1, \ldots, a_n) = f(\varphi_{a_1}, \ldots, \varphi_{a_n}) = f(b_1, \ldots, b_n).$$

For A, B fields, a p-morphism is what is called a specialization. Poythress has also shown that the field $Q(x_1, \ldots, x_n)$ of all rational functions over Q in n indeterminates x_i is the *free field* with n generators in the sense of the following definition (taking $\mathscr{C}$ to be the class of all fields).

[20] Vern Poythress helped to write this section; for the notion of "specialization," see O. Zariski and P. Samuel, "Commutative Rings," Van Nostrand, 1960, vol. II, p. 1.

DEFINITION. Let C be a class of partial algebras with a fixed set F of (partial) operations. An algebra $A = [S, F]$ is *C-free* over a subset $X \subset S$ when: (i) X generates A, and (ii) given $B = [T, G] \in C$, any (partial) function $\alpha: X \to T$ extends to a p-morphism $\varphi: A \to B$.

EXAMPLE 7. A *poset* can be considered as a *partial join-semilattice* $P = [S; \vee]$. The binary operation is idempotent, commutative in the strong sense that $y \vee x$ exists and equals $x \vee y$ whenever the latter exists, is associative in the weak sense that $x \vee (y \vee z) = (x \vee y) \vee z$ whenever both exist, and has the property that $x \vee (x \vee y)$ is defined whenever $x \vee y$ is.

Dually, a poset can be defined as a partial meet-semilattice. Or, it can be defined as a *partial lattice* (which is both a join- and a meet-semilattice, in which moreover $y = x \vee y$ if and only if $x = x \vee y$).

It follows that the cells of any topological *complex* can be considered as a partial lattice (excluding φ and the whole manifold). With this interpretation, the *direct product* of any two complexes corresponds to the product subdivision of the Cartesian product complex, as stated in [**LT1**]. In particular, *graphs* (whose importance for computing we have noted) appear as partial lattices of rank two.

EXAMPLE 8. Graphs have a (cryptomorphic) interpretation as *heterogeneous partial* algebras with two phyla: points and lines; and two partial operations $\vee: A_0 \times A_0 \to A_1$ and $\wedge: A_1 \times A_1 \to A_0$; the idea is to write $p \vee q = L$ when the edge L has vertices p and q.

Finally, I want to call your attention to another example (partly because Eilenberg has tried to develop from it new foundations for the theory of automata), and to make a final remark.

EXAMPLE 9. A *small category* $[\mathscr{P}, \mathscr{M}; \partial^-, \partial^+, \circ]$ can be defined as a heterogeneous partial algebra with two phyla: a set $\mathscr{P}$ of *objects* $S, T, U, \ldots$, and a set $\mathscr{M}$ of *morphisms* $f, g, \ldots$. Each $f \in \mathscr{M}$ has a *domain* $\partial^- f \in \mathscr{P}$ and a *co-domain* $\partial^+ f \in \mathscr{P}$; thus as with directed graphs, $\partial^-: \mathscr{M} \to \mathscr{P}$ and $\partial^+: \mathscr{M} \to \mathscr{P}$ are regarded as unary operations. For given $S, T \in \mathscr{P}$, the set of *all* $f \in \mathscr{M}$ with $\partial^- f = S$ and $\partial^+ f \in T$ is denoted $\hom(S, T)$.[21] The *composition* operation is a *partial* binary operation $\circ: \mathscr{M} \times \mathscr{M} \to \mathscr{M}$; $g \circ f$ of which is defined precisely when $\partial^+ f = \partial^- g$. In addition, one postulates the associative law $h \circ (g \circ f) = (h \circ g) \circ f$ and the existence for every $S \subset \mathscr{P}$ of a special $1_S \in \mathscr{M}$ with appropriate properties.

REMARK. One can also interpret many systems as *multi-algebras*, whose operations are *multiple*-valued functions. For example, a directed graph G can be considered as a multi-algebra with a single unary operation, which with each node $n \in V$ the set $f(n) \subset V$ of all nodes which are the tips of arrows originating in n. From this definition one can reconstruct G: its edges are just the pairs $(n, n') \in V \times V$ with $n' \in f(n)$.

---

[21]This definition differs slightly from Mac Lane-Birkhoff, p. 508 ff, where hom is considered as a *multiple*-valued operation $(S, T) \mapsto \hom(S, t)$ with multiple values in $\mathscr{M}$ — i.e., as a heterogeneous partial *multi*-algebra; cf. the following remark.

12. **Mathematical logic.** Although the notion of a (heterogeneous) algebra includes graphs and automata, and has a highly nontrivial theory, it does not cover all applications of the symbolic method to computers. Not even the more general notion of a relational system [**20**, p. 224] seems to be sufficiently general.

Already before 1700, Leibniz had conceived of a much more general "logical calculus," modeled after the then new symbolic algebra of Viète, which would greatly facilitate all reasoning.[22] His starting point was the idea that simple concepts could be designated by letters, complex concepts by algebraic expressions, and assertions by equations, inequalities, and other relational formulas. This idea was stated in his *Fundamenta calculi ratiocinatoris*. In a later version, he proposed assigning to each basic word a "characteristic number," which would detach the word from its meaning.

Around 1880, Frege initiated a new era in symbolic logic, considered as "a language that need not be supplemented by any intuitive reasoning,"[23] It is interesting to note that Frege's symbolic logic made essential use of labelled trees (graphs), and little use of the binary, etc., operations which are so central to my version of "universal algebra."

Symbolic (i.e., algebraic) mathematical logic[24] was developed much further by Peano in his "Formulaire des Mathématiques" (1895–1903). The successes of Boole, Peano, and other mathematicians in developing symbolic treatments of substantial fragments of logic and arithmetic induced Whitehead and Russell to attempt a much more ambitious task in their "Principia Mathematica" (1910–1913). Their goal was to derive all mathematics mechanically from a purely formal *symbolic logic* consisting of: (i) small sets of "primitive propositions" (postulates) intended to characterize various groups of related mathematical concepts, and (ii) well-defined "rules of inference" for manipulating symbolic statements. Although this purely symbolic approach to theorem-proving and mechanical proof-checking is not very efficient for most of mathematics,[25] and Gödel has established the inadequacy of existing systems of symbolic logic (especially for handling quantifiers),—nevertheless symbolic logic has thrown valuable light on the foundations of mathematics.

I think it would be illuminating and most appropriate to formalize "universal algebra" in terms of a revised system of symbolic logic, using techniques like those of Whitehead and Russell, Hilbert-Ackermann, etc. Among other things, this formalization should include the all-pervasive notions of subalgebra and

---

[22]See [**16a**] and G. H. R. Parkinson, "Leibniz: Logical Papers," Oxford, 1966.

[23]See van Heijenoort, "From Frege to Gödel," Harvard University Press, 1967, pp. 2–4. One could mention also E. H. Moore's "General Analysis," which was also written in a Peano-like symbolic notation.

[24]For an excellent modern exposition of symbolic logic see S. C. Kleene, "Introduction to Metamathematics," Van Nostrand, 1952.

[25]More emphasis on efficiency is needed (and less on existence); see L. Wos et al., J. ACM **14** (1967), 698–709.

morphism. Conversely, "universal algebra" should be extended to cover quantifiers.[26] Such a formalization of universal algebra would be appropriate because symbolic logic aims to reduce *all* theorem-proving to a branch of algebra, and because the "automaton" algebras of §§9–10 are simplified versions of the Turing machines invented to mechanize the procedures of "Principia Mathematica." (I have not yet found a satisfactory way to define Turing machines as "algebras," without including **Z** pretty obviously.)

13. **Mathematical linguistics.** Directly related to the theory of automata is another offshoot of symbolic logic: *mathematical linguistics*. This treats printed *statements* as *strings of symbols* from a finite "alphabet," combined by concatenation—which gives a semigroup when done freely, and a monoid if the empty set (a vacuous statement) is allowed. Thus the notion of a programming language is included in the following extremely general definition.

EXAMPLE 10. A "language" is a subset of A^*, the free monoid generated (under a concatenation) by the symbols of some alphabet A. Hence it is a *partial monoid*.

Unfortunately, the concepts of universal algebra (as defined in §8) do not seem to be very fruitful for "languages." Thus, the role of a "sublanguage" is not played by the simple notion of a submonoid or subsemigroup, but rather by the notion of the set of statements generated by so-called *production rules* (given in Backus normal form). These production rules are auxiliary *unary* operations which typically refer to *specified symbols* (letters). Thus, rules like $a \mapsto ab$ or $b \mapsto cbd$ can be considered as production rules, analogous to rules of *grammar* (for which they are intended to substitute), producing grammatical or "acceptable" symbolic "sentences." They do not resemble anything else in the branches of modern algebra most familiar to mathematicians, nor in universal algebra as currently treated.

The original idea of such production rules was similar to that of rules of inference in symbolic logic: they were intended to generate all grammatical and no ungrammatical "sentences," just as the rules of inference in symbolic logic were intended to generate all true and no false mathematical theorems, thus reducing all mathematical theorem-proving to algebraic manipulations according to the specified rules of inference.

Indeed, modern programming languages for computers resemble symbolic logic in their format; and their logical and arithmetic capabilities are reminiscent of these of the formalisms of Boole and Peano. Moreover Newell, Hao Wang, and others have written successful computer programs for mechanical theorem-proving in logic itself.[27] There is no doubt of the close connection between mathematical linguistics and mathematical logic.

There is some interaction between modern algebra and both theorem-

---

[26]So far as the first-order predicate calculus is concerned, this has been done by Tarski and Grätzer [**20**, Chapter 6].

[27]For references to and comments on these achievements, see [**8**, §6.5].

proving and mathematical linguistics; see for example J. ACM **12** (1965), 23–41. Using related ideas, John C. Reynolds has proved that atomic formulas constitute a complete nonmodular lattice.[28] As another application, R. M. Burstall and P. J. Landin[29] use universal algebra based on Cohn's *Universal Algebra* to "prove the correctness of a compiler for evaluating expressions using a stack machine." But on the whole, these connections are exceedingly fragmentary.

Indeed, perhaps the most conspicuous common feature of universal algebra, the theory of automata, symbolic logic, and mathematical linguistics is their extreme generality. Thus, the subject of *mathematical linguistics* is intended to apply to both symbolic logic and to programming languages, and to human ("natural") languages as well. But much as universal algebra by itself seems inadequate for deriving deep results about (say) finite groups, so mathematical linguistics by itself seems to be ineffectual for obtaining deeper results about symbolic logic, programming languages, *or* human languages.

To obtain deeper results, one should probably begin by being less general; it is not clear how much the language of symbolic logic should have in common with programming languages. Thus, most statements of symbolic logic are *declarative* whereas those of programming languages are *imperative*: they are "commands" intended to make an automaton perform certain operations; the appropriate algebraic concept is (as in representation theory) that of a programming language *acting* on an automaton. More specifically, machine languages act on *computers* (whose "outputs" may be arrays of numbers with identifying labels), while higher-level programming languages act on *compilers* (whose "outputs" consist of other computer programs which may be in machine or assembler language).

Indeed, I think the time is ripe for a systematic study of more realistic models of computers than are provided by automata in general. Thus, I think one might well define a *computer* as a special kind of automaton possessing: (i) capabilities for storing addresses, (ii) an integer *arithmetic* unit, (iii) Boolean *logic* capabilities, (iv) a standard *word-length* ("byte") to aid in parsing, and (v) alphanumeric *output* capabilities. One could then consider the matched capabilities of "programming languages" (and compilers!) for *acting* on such a computer, in somewhat the same spirit that one now considers the capabilities of groups for "acting" on given sets (as permutations) or vector spaces (as linear transformations).

If it is any comfort, universal algebra should be applicable to such more complex systems. Thus, likewise, the idea of a programming language for a computing machine can be interpreted as a *heterogeneous partial algebra*, whose "programs" form one phylum (as in Example 10), each member of which consists of a sequence of instructions to be carried out by the automaton of

---

[28]Machine Intelligence **5** (1969), 135–152.
[29]Machine Intelligence **4** (1968), 17–43; see also Landin in ibid. **5** (1969), 99–120.

Example 4 or the state machine of §9 (containing another phylum of "states," including perhaps a "starting state").

C. COMBINATORIAL ALGEBRA

14. **Relevance to computing.**   Many algorithms for digital computers are obviously *combinatorial* in nature. Their description involves labelled directed graphs called "flow charts," which may be designed to handle "stack-like," "tree-like," or "ring-like" (perhaps associative) data structures [27, Chapter 2]. To analyze their efficiency, one often needs to solve *enumeration* problems, also of a combinatorial nature.

Moreover such an analysis, when made from the standpoint of optimization, may lead to unexpected improvements in efficiency. For example, such improvements have recently been made by Stephen Cook and S. Winograd, for the problems of multiplying together two n-digit numbers and two $n \times n$ matrices, respectively.[30]

As a result, attempts to optimize computer algorithms lead to an incredible variety of combinatorial problems (cf. [27]), for which few general techniques of solution are known. During the past decade, Rota and others (cf. [17], [30], [34], etc.) have made increasingly clear the basically algebraic nature of some general techniques. In Part C, I shall try to illustrate these by a few simple examples, taken largely from the work of Rota and some of his students and associates. A characteristic feature of this work is its emphasis on partial orderings and *lattices*.

These notions arise very naturally in enumeration by recursion. This is because in counting complex combinatorial structures, one can often proceed by recursion over a *partial ordering* not a linear ordering, which is often a lattice (e.g., of subsets or partitions).

In Parts D and E, I shall discuss other applications of combinatorial algebra to computing which concern *linear dependence*. As was shown in 1935 by Hassler Whitney [41] and myself, the general theory of linear dependence can be most naturally formulated in terms of the cryptomorphic notions of a combinatorial geometry and a geometric lattice.[31] As has been mentioned in §5, these notions also apply to the theory of affine dependence.

Although typical examples of geometric lattices are furnished by the subspaces spanned by the subsets of a finite set of points in projective space, examples also arise in other combinatorial contexts, apparently unrelated to projective geometry. Thus in [41], Whitney used this algebraic formalism to describe the dependence of circuits in graphs. Again, consider a bipartite

---

[30]See [T0]; also S. A. Cook and S. O. Aanderaa, Trans. Amer. Math. Soc. **142** (1969), 291–314; S. Winograd, J. ACM **14** (1967), 793–802; [27, pp. 258–279]. For inner products and matrix multiplication, see V. Strassen, Numer. Math. **13** (1969), 354–356; S. Winograd, IEEE Trans. C-17 (1968), 693–694.

[31]Formerly called a "matroid" and a "matroid lattice." respectively. See [41], [LT1] and [LT2].

graph representing a relation $R \subset A \times B$. Say that $K \subset A$ is independent when there is a one-to-one subrelation of R (or matching) which is everywhere defined on K. Then the family of all such sets K defines a combinatorial geometry on the set A.

Thus one can apply the properties of linear dependence to disparate combinatorial situations.

15. **Incidence algebras and Moebius functions.** Associated with every poset $P = [X, \leq]$ are its *incidence* function $n: P \times P \to \mathbf{Z}$ and its *zeta* function $\zeta: P \times P \to \mathbf{Z}$, defined respectively by:

(14)
$$n(x, y) = 1 \quad \text{if } x < y, \qquad \zeta(x, y) = 1 \quad \text{if } x \leq y,$$
$$= 0 \quad \text{otherwise}, \qquad\qquad = 0 \quad \text{otherwise}.$$

Relative to any listing (enumeration) of its elements, these functions define the incidence matrix and zeta matrix of P. Figures 4a–4b depict the matrices $N = \|n_{ij}\|$ and $\Xi = \|\zeta_{ij}\|$ for $X = 4$ in its usual ordering; they are strictly triangular and triangular.

$$N = \begin{bmatrix} 0 & 1 & 1 & 1 \\ 0 & 0 & 1 & 1 \\ 0 & 0 & 0 & 1 \\ 0 & 0 & 0 & 0 \end{bmatrix}, \qquad \Xi = \begin{bmatrix} 1 & 1 & 1 & 1 \\ 0 & 1 & 1 & 1 \\ 0 & 0 & 1 & 1 \\ 0 & 0 & 0 & 1 \end{bmatrix}, \qquad \Gamma = \begin{bmatrix} 0 & 1 & 0 & 0 \\ 0 & 0 & 1 & 0 \\ 0 & 0 & 0 & 1 \\ 0 & 0 & 0 & 0 \end{bmatrix}.$$

| FIGURE 4a | FIGURE 4b | FIGURE 4c |

Evidently, N and $\Xi = I + N$ are just the *relation matrices* of the binary relations of strict inclusion and inclusion, respectively. Similarly, one can define the *covering* function $\gamma(x, y)$ and *covering relation* $\Gamma = \|\gamma_{ij}\|$ associated with the covering relation on P. But whereas the values (0 or 1) of these matrices were regarded as *Boolean* in §4, they are here regarded as in $\mathbf{Z}$. (For $P = [X, \leq]$ the poset of a complex, Γ is its incidence relation matrix.)

More generally, we can regard them as in any integral domain D, and refer to the *incidence algebra* and *zeta algebra* of P (over D), meaning by this the *D-module* of all functions having zero values wherever $n(x, y)$ resp. $\zeta(x, y)$ have zero values. Here multiplication is given by the usual rule for multiplying matrices:

(15) $C = AB \quad \text{means} \quad c(x, z) = \sum_{y} a(x, y)b(y, z),$

which is "convolution" for P the semigroup $\mathbf{N}$.

The preceding modules provide useful descriptions of various interesting combinatorial functions. For example, consider the generating function

(16) $1/(I - t\Gamma) = I + t\Gamma + t^2\Gamma^2 + t^3\Gamma^3 + \cdots + t^n\Gamma^n + \cdots;$

the coefficient $\Gamma^n = \|\gamma_n(x,y)\|$ represents the number of *simple paths* of length n from x to y in the directed graph ("Hasse diagram") of the poset P.

As in [7, p. 102], the Moebius function of P is defined from the incidence function of P by

$$\|\mu(x,y)\| = \|I+N\|^{-1} = I - N + N^2 - N^3 + \cdots . \tag{17}$$

Note that when $P = \mathbf{P}$, the ordered set of positive integers, we obtain the classic Riemann zeta function by setting

$$1/\zeta(s) = \sum_{k=1}^{\infty} \mu(k)/k^s, \qquad \mu(k) = \mu(1,k). \tag{17'}$$

Many enumeration problems can be solved by "Moebius inversion" using an appropriate Moebius function;[32] we here give a simple example. First, let $P = \Pi(S)$ be the partition lattice of a set S of n elements [7 p. 95]. Then, if x is a refinement of the partition y (i.e., if $x \leqq y$), and $k(i)$ is the number of blocks of the partition y which are split into i blocks by x, it has been shown by Rota and others that

$$\begin{aligned} \mu(x,y) &= (-1)^l \prod_{r=2}^{n} (r!)^{k(n)} \quad \text{if } x < y \\ &= 0 \quad \text{otherwise,} \end{aligned} \tag{18}$$

where $l = n - \sum k(i)$.

We now use this Moebius function to compute the number of sets E of edges which can be drawn joining the nodes (vertices) of a given set V of n nodes, so as to obtain a simple connected graph. In all, there are $2^{n(n-1)/2}$ ways of drawing in nodes so as to get a graph over V. Every graph on the set of vertices S induces a partition of the set S into connected components. Let $g(y)$ be the number of graphs whose partition is some refinement of the partition y. Then clearly

$$g(y) = \sum_{x \leqq y} f(x), \tag{19}$$

where $f(x)$ is the number of graphs whose partition is precisely the partition x. By applying the Moebius inversion formula we obtain immediately

$$f(y) = \sum_{x \leqq y} \mu(x,y) g(x); \qquad g(x) = 2^{k(1)C_{n,1} + k(2)C_{n,2} + \cdots}, \tag{20}$$

which gives the number of graphs having partition y in terms of the quantity $g(x)$, which is easily computed as above, and the Moebius function. Letting y be the trivial partition with one block, one obtains the desired number of connected simple graphs.

The Moebius function of a partially ordered set (poset) is useful in other contexts, of which we shall only mention one. If one takes a convex poly-

[32]See [**34**]; the example given here was kindly provided by Professor Rota, who also made many other valuable contributions to and criticisms of this paper. In (20), $C_{n,k}$ is simply the number of (connected) blocks of k nodes in the partition x.

hedron in n-dimensional space, one can associate with it an *incidence lattice*, which is obtained by ordering the cells (faces, etc.) of the polyhedron by inclusion. It is an open problem to characterize which lattices are incidence lattices of convex polyhedra. For dimension three this problem was solved by Rademacher and Steinitz. It was recently shown by Rota that a necessary condition for a lattice to be the incidence lattice of a convex polyhedron is that the Moebius function of the incidence lattice take alternatingly the values $+1$ and -1 at successive levels. This result extends the classical Euler identity for the cells of a convex polyhedron. In fact, it implies not only the Euler identity but also the classical Dehn-Sommerville equations [20a, Chapter 9].[33]

Tutte-Grothendieck function. Many other algebraic invariants can be defined on posets, somewhat analogous to those defined from combinatorial complexes in algebraic topology. In this spirit, T. Brylawski[34] has recently imitated the techniques used by Grothendieck in defining the so-called Grothendieck group of an Abelian category. Brylawski succeeded in associating a ring to every hereditary class of combinatorial geometries. A hereditary class of geometric lattices consists of a class of geometric lattices which is closed under the operation of taking subsets on the set in which the geometry is defined, as well as contractions, that is, taking segments of the associated geometric lattice. It was shown by Brylawski that the computation of the characteristic polynomial (21) below, as well as the computation of several other invariant quantities of geometries, such as the numbers of bases, independent sets, spanning sets, etc., could be reduced to simple computations in what he called the Tutte-Grothendieck ring. Among graphs in particular, he has characterized series-parallel networks (cf. §2) by their Tutte-Grothendieck functions.

16. **Critical problems; symmetry.** Moebius inversion also provides an interesting reformulation of the problem of code optimization; generalizing §2, we consider linear group codes over $F = GF(q)$. To be *optimal* among such codes with code word length n correcting l errors, the *subspace of code words must have maximum dimension* among those which are *disjoint* from the subset S of all words (vectors) having fewer than $2l + 1 = d$ nonzero coordinates.

It turns out that the determination of this maximum dimension is connected with Moebius inversion on the combinatorial geometry (geometric lattice) $L = L(n, d)$ of all flats (closed subspaces) of L spanned by points with d nonzero coordinates. Specifically, consider the *characteristic polynomial*

$$(21) \qquad \sum_x \mu(0, x) \lambda^{n-\dim(x)} = p(\lambda),$$

---

[33]See G.-C. Rota, "Möbius function and Euler characteristic," in the Rado Festschrift, Academic Press, 1970, where the result is extended to affine polyhedra.

[34]T. Brylawski, Ph.D. Thesis, Dartmouth, 1970. See also D. A. Smith, Duke Math. J. **34** (1967), 617–633, and **36** (1969), 15–30 and 353–367.

where μ is the Moebius function of L. The required maximal dimension is the first positive integer λ for which $p(\lambda)$ is positive.

The characteristic polynomial defined above can be defined in any geometric lattice, and the problem of finding the first positive integer λ for which $p(\lambda)$ is positive is called by Crapo and Rota the *critical problem*. Clearly, this reformulation of the optimal coding problem as a "critical problem" does not solve it. However, the fact that a host of combinatorial problems are equivalent to critical problems gives some hope of developing general methods for solving them. At least, it should suggest themes for generalizing ingenious special methods successful for individual problems so as to solve groups of related problems.

Symmetry. Many computational problems involve geometrical or other *symmetries*. Typically, these symmetries constitute a *group G acting on a set* S of variables (often unknowns). In order to recognize 0's (see Part D) and to avoid ambiguities and unnecessary duplication of computational effort, it is important that computer programs for treating such problems take account of such symmetries. In enumeration problems, this is done by Pólya's Theorem [**5a**, pp. 144–184].

In many numerical problems, one must recognize "equivalence under the group G" of all such symmetries, when these are applied to polynomial expressions and power series (e.g., generating functions) in the variables of S. Here one has an important *Galois connection* between the lattice of subgroups $H, K, \ldots$ of G and the lattice of partitions $\pi, \pi', \ldots$ of S, defined by the *imprimitivity polarity* ρ:

(22) $$H\rho\pi \quad \text{iff} \quad x\pi y \quad \text{and} \quad \theta \in H \quad \text{imply} \quad \theta(x)\pi\theta(y).$$

The *intransitivity polarity* σ

(23) $$H\rho S \quad \text{iff} \quad \theta \in H \quad \text{and} \quad x \in S \quad \text{imply} \quad \theta(x) \in S$$

is even more important.[35] Moreover a special role is played by the *invariant* polynomials $p(x_1, \ldots, x_n)$ such that $p(x_1, \ldots, x_n) = p(x_1\gamma, \ldots, x_n\gamma)$ for any permutation γ of G; *invariant theory* is concerned with the calculation of a *basis* of such invariant polynomials; I shall consider problems of this type in Part E.

An extremely difficult problem concerns the enumeration of isomorphism-types (i.e., the number of equivalence classes, such as the number of nonisomorphic graphs or groups of a given order). I know of no effective general algebraic or combinatorial techniques for solving this problem. A related and equally difficult problem is that of testing two given graphs or groups for isomorphism.

---

[35]See G.-C. Rota, Bull. Amer. Math. Soc. **75** (1969), 330–334. For other interplays between Galois connections and Moebius functions, see [**34**, Theorem 1] and H. H. Crapo, Archiv Math. (Basel) **19** (1968), 595–607.

In my opinion, the most effective way to attack these problems is through *man-computer symbiosis* [**8**, §22.1], in which theoretical ideas are combined with machine computations analogous to those which have been described by other speakers at this symposium.[36]

17. **Flowgraphs.** Instead of discussing general ideas further, I shall conclude Part C by describing briefly a new kind of heterogeneous algebra, which can be realized by very simple finite-state machines and has been programmed for standard computers, so as to *compute* answers to various combinatorial problems. This will show again how "universal algebra" gives a unified viewpoint which applies to automata, graphs, and other combinatorial structures as well as to the groups, rings, and fields studied in traditional courses on "modern algebra."

This new kind of heterogeneous algebra is the class of flowgraphs. The relevant concept was originated over 15 years ago and applied to circuit design problems by S. J. Mason (see [**20**, Chapter 2]). Its formal definition as a heterogeneous algebra is as follows [**T2**, §2.2][37]; note that, like an automaton, a flowgraph is a *labelled directed graph*.

DEFINITION.   A *flowgraph* in n indeterminates $x_1, \ldots, x_n$ over an integral domain D is a heterogeneous algebra $\mathfrak{F} = [N, A, D; \Phi, \psi]$, where $[N, A; \Phi]$ is a directed graph (Example 3), and $\psi \colon A \to D[x]$ is a function which assigns to each arc $(i, j) \in A$ a "label" or "weight" $\psi(i, j) \in D[\mathbf{x}] = D[x_1, \ldots, x_n]$. The *transmission matrix* of the flowgraph $\mathfrak{F}$ above is $T = \|t_{ij}\|$, where

$$(24) \qquad\qquad t_{ij} = \psi(i, j) \qquad \text{if } (i, j) \in A,$$
$$\qquad\qquad\qquad = 0 \qquad\qquad \text{otherwise.}$$

The *generating function matrix* of $\mathfrak{F}$ is $\Gamma = \|\gamma_{ij}\| = (I - T)^{-1}$.

When there is a preferred starting node s and final node f (as is usually the case), then we call $g = \gamma_{sf}$ the flowgraph *generating function*.

To illustrate the preceding concepts and their applications to combinatorial problems, we solve a specific problem from [**18**, p. 79].

PROBLEM.   Find the number of n-digit binary sequences in which an occurrence of the pattern 010 is (eventually) followed by an occurrence of the pattern 110.

SOLUTION.   *Step* 1.   Construct an automaton $\mathscr{A}$ which recognizes precisely the sequence (of arbitrary length) to be enumerated.

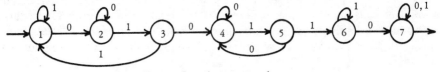

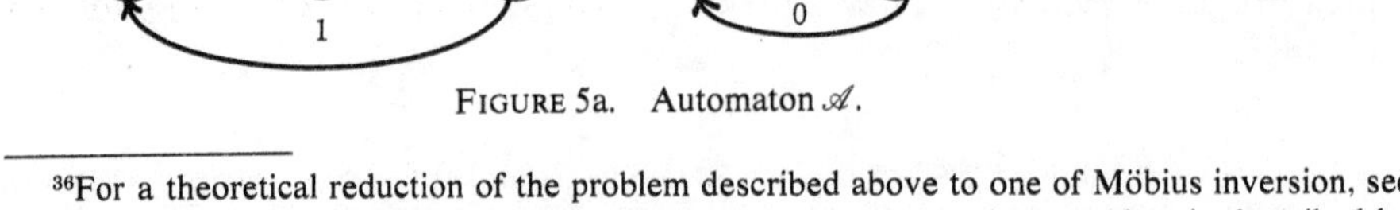

FIGURE 5a.   Automaton $\mathscr{A}$.

---

[36]For a theoretical reduction of the problem described above to one of Möbius inversion, see Rota (op. cit. supra). A machine algorithm for testing graphs for isomorphism is described by D. G. Corneil and C. C. Gottlieb, J. ACM 17 (1970), 51–64.

[37]The rest of this section was kindly adapted by John Lipson from his Thesis [**T2**].

Step 2.   Transform $\mathscr{A}$ into a flowgraph $\mathfrak{F}$ for enumerating paths from the starting state to the final or "accepting" state of $\mathscr{A}$.

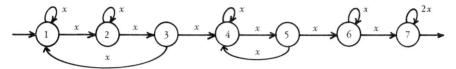

FIGURE 5b.   Flowgraph $\mathfrak{F}$.

Step 3.   Compute the generating function $g = g(x)$:

$$(25) \qquad\qquad g = [(1 - T^{-1}]_{sf}$$

where s is the starting node, f is the final node and $T = \|t_{ij}\|$ is the flowgraph "transmission" matrix. For the above flowgraph $\mathfrak{F}$,

$$(26) \qquad \begin{aligned} g &= x^6/(1 - 6x + 13x^2 - 12x^3 + 4x^4 + x^5 - 3x^6 + 2x^7) \\ &= x^6 + 6x^7 + 13x^8 + 72x^9 + 201x^{10} + 521x^{11} + 1282x^{12} + \cdots . \end{aligned}$$

The coefficient of x^n in the above power series gives the number of sequences (or "strings") of length n having the property specified; thus there are 1282 of them having length twelve.

In the above example the denominator of $g(x)$ can be factored as $(1 - x)(1 - 2x)(1 - 3x + 2x^2 + x^3)$; its smallest root is $x = 1/2$, and so (for large n) the number of acceptable strings of length $n + 1$ is asymptotically twice the number having length n, hence of the order of 2^n.

The transmission matrix of the above flowgraph admits a factorization $T = xA$; such flowgraphs are called unit-delay flowgraphs and have useful special properties. For such flowgraphs:

$$(27) \qquad g(x) = [(I - xA)^{-1}]_{sf} = C_{fs}/|I - xA| = h(x)/d(x),$$

where $d(x)$ is the reciprocal of the characteristic polynomial $c(x) = |xI - A|$, so that $d(x) = x^n c(1/x)$. Writing $g(x) = \Sigma \, g_n x^n$, we have the linear recurrence relation

$$g_{n+1} = 6g_n - 13g_{n-1} + 12g_{n-2} - 4g_{n-3} - g_{n-4} + 3g_{n-5} - 2g_{n-6},$$

from which $g_{13}, g_{14}, g_{15}, \ldots$ are easily computed. In other examples, Bareiss' two-step integer-preserving Gaussian elimination scheme[38] can be used to advantage.

To compute the integral coefficients of the rational generating functions arising in such problems, Dr. Lipson has found modular arithmetic most effective. Thus he showed (using Hadamard's bound on the determinant of a matrix) that on the IBM 360/50 computer (32 bit word length), correct coefficients could be computed by modular arithmetic for any binary input automaton having 20 or fewer states.

---

[38]E. H. Bareiss, Math. of Comp. **22** (1968), 565–578.

An interesting extension of the above method for computing flowgraph generating functions can be based on the following theorem about principal ideal domains.[39]

THEOREM.   *If the elements $m_1, m_2, \ldots, m_k$ are pairwise relatively prime in a principal ideal domain D, then there is an isomorphism φ of rings*

$$(28) \qquad D \bigg/ \left(\prod_{i=1}^{k} m_i \right) \approx \prod_{i=1}^{k} D \bigg/ (m_i),$$

where $\varphi \colon (\prod_{i=1}^{k} m_i) + r \to (m_i) + r, \ldots, (m_k) + r$.

The inverse function φ^{-1} is important from a computational viewpoint. For D the principal ideal domain $\mathbf{Z}$, the computation of φ^{-1} is tantamount to the *Chinese Remainder Algorithm*, an important number theoretic result; while for D the principal ideal domain $F[x]$, the computation of φ^{-1} is tantamount to polynomial interpolation. Both the cases $\mathbf{Z}$ and $F[x]$ are important for symbolic computation: $\mathbf{Z}$ for computing with (large) integers, and $F[x]$ for computing with (large degree) polynomials. Furthermore, both of these situations arise in applications of flowgraphs.

D. LINEAR SYSTEMS

18. **General remarks.**   The rest of my talk will concern the role of *non-numerical* algebra in optimizing the *numerical* solution of systems of N simultaneous linear equations in N unknowns:

$$(29) \qquad \sum_{j=1}^{N} a_{ij} x_j = k_i \quad (i, j = 1, \ldots, N), \qquad \text{or} \qquad AX = K.$$

Nonnumerical algorithms are basic to real algebra because the *real arithmetic of digital computers is only approximate*. Thus one cannot test real (or complex) numbers for equality or real vectors for linear dependence, or real matrices for rank on digital computers; moreover the "real numbers" of digital computers do *not* satisfy such identities as $a + (b + c) = (a + b) + c$, $aa^{-1} = 1$, or $a(b + c) = ab + ac$ [27, vol. 2, pp. 196–204]. Therefore, one must devise *nonnumerical* algorithms to recognize and utilize such exact algebraic identities and relations of linear dependence.

It turns out that many of the deepest questions involved in devising optimal algorithms are basically *combinatorial* (hence purely algebraic); they do not concern roundoff, stability, or the condition number. Only the relation matrix $R(A)$ and directed graph $\mathbf{G}(A)$ of the coefficient-matrix A of (29) are relevant; these are defined as follows:

DEFINITION.   The *relation matrix* $R = \|r_{ij}\| = R(A)$ of $A = \|a_{ij}\|$ is defined by

$$(30) \qquad \begin{aligned} r_{ij} &= 1 \quad \text{if } a_{ij} \neq 0, \\ &= 0 \quad \text{otherwise.} \end{aligned}$$

[39]S. Mac Lane and G. Birkhoff, "Algebra," Macmillan, 1967.

The *directed graph* $G(A)$ of A has for nodes the integers $1, \ldots, n$, and $R(A)$ for its adjacency matrix.

My discussion will refer especially to the linear systems (29) about which I know most: large systems ($N = 100$–$50{,}000$) which arise from elliptic boundary value problems such as the "source" problem described by the DE

$$(31) \qquad -\nabla \cdot [p(x,y)\nabla u] = s(x,y), \qquad p(x,y) > 0.$$

Matrices A arising from such DE's are special: they are highly *sparse, positive definite, symmetric matrices*.

Today, a variety of competing methods are used to obtain approximate solutions to elliptic problems.[40] These fall broadly into three categories

(i) Difference approximations (usually 5-point for (31)) solved by *elimination*, perhaps in double precision arithmetic.

(ii) Difference approximations (usually 5-point) solved by *iterative* methods (variants of SOR and ADI) going back to the 1950's.

(iii) Finite element methods approximations utilizing *variational* principles, leading to systems (29) with somewhat less sparse matrices, usually solved by elimination.

The $64 question is, of course, *which method is best*, and when? Unfortunately, this optimization problem can rarely be solved and is even hard to formulate rigorously. However, it leads to a number of interesting theoretical questions, and these will be the main concern of the rest of my talk.

In Part D, I shall describe the important role played by graph theory in all three of the above kinds of methods. (In this connection, it is a curious historical fact that Frobenius failed to recognize the relevance of graph theory to linear algebra.[41]) In Part E, I shall indicate the special importance of geometric lattices for understanding finite element methods, thus giving additional coherence to my message.

19. **Successive overrelaxation.** I shall begin by pointing out that the graph concept plays an important role even in *iterative* methods for solving large-scale linear systems arising from source problems, and that already Gauss[42] had considered solving real and complex linear systems not only by elimination, but alternatively by *iterative* methods [38]. Indeed, it seems appropriate to mention at this Symposium that Gauss was a truly *pure and applied* mathematician who gladly assumed responsibility for massive astronomical and geodetic calculations, and took a special interest in *numerical methods*. Modern computing owes much to him and to other mathematicians like

---

[40]For a detailed technical discussion of (i)–(iii) from the standpoint of solving elliptic boundary value problems, see my NSF Regional Conference monograph, "Numerical Solution of Elliptic Problems," SIAM Publications, 1971.

[41]See [**28**, pp. 240–241], for complaints by D. König about the cavalier attitude of Frobenius towards graph theory.

[42]See [**38**] and G. Forsythe, MTAC **5** (1951), 255–258.

Jacobi, Cauchy (who introduced the gradient method), L. Seidel, Runge, L. F. Richardson, and other pioneering spirits.[43] Many of their ideas (including perhaps "diakoptik elimination," see §20) are still being explored by research workers today.

I shall now discuss a few algebraic and combinatorial considerations which lead one to solve large linear systems by iterative methods. I shall consider specifically the linear system (29) obtained from the source problem (30) by the usual 5-point difference approximation, using an $n \times n$ array of interior mesh-points. This gives $N = n^2$ equations in n^2 unknowns, whose coefficient-matrix A is *sparse* with about $5n^2$ nonzero entries.

If textbook Gauss elimination is applied blindly to this system, about $n^6/3$ multiplications will be performed, mostly by zero. If multiplications by zero are omitted, and the matrix is given minimal bandwidth (which is nearly achieved if the mesh-points are run through in their natural order by successive rows), the number of multiplications is reduced to about $2n^4$.

If the nondiagonal entries of A are transposed, giving $DX = BX + K$, we can solve *approximately* by the *iterative* Jacobi method:

$$(32) \qquad DX^{(r+1)} = BX^{(r)} + K, \qquad \text{or} \qquad X^{(r+1)} + D^{-1}BX^{(r)} + K_1,$$

where $K_1 = D^{-1}K$. Note that the graph of the nonnegative matrix B, defined to have for nodes the indices $1, \ldots, N$ and edges (i, j) precisely when $b_{ij} \neq 0$, looks just like the graph of mesh-points and mesh-lines. It is bipartite, which is another way of saying that the matrix B is 2-cyclic (has Young's Property A).

This is important for the Successive Overrelaxation (SOR) method, whose properties were first established by David Young in [T6]. With this iterative method, the number of multiplications required to solve (29) to given accuracy can be reduced to $O(n^3)$.

I shall not try to describe the method here, but I do want to emphasize the many ingenious algebraic ideas which its theory utilizes. These include the properties of Stieltjes matrices, the Perron-Frobenius theory of nonnegative matrices, as well as the graph-theoretic ideas mentioned already. If we call the symmetric adjacency matrix of the graph $G(B)$ of B above its *relation matrix*, $R(B)$, then [LT3, pp. 385–386] the mapping $B \mapsto R(B)$ is an *l-epi-morphism* from the *l*-semigroup of nonnegative matrices onto the *l*-semigroup of relation matrices, which carries matrix addition into relation join.

For the preceding source problem, the graph $G(B)$ suggests a physical analogy with a *linear network problem*: the 5-point difference approximation corresponds to a fixed resistivity in each edge or link, i.e., to a potential drop which is a linear function of the flux. Such linear network problems were already studied by Kirchhoff and J. C. Maxwell.[44] Maxwell knew that the

---

[43]Cf. R. von Mises and H. Pollaczek-Geiringer, ZaMM **9** (1929), 58–77 and 152–164.

[44]See G. Birkhoff and J. L. Diaz, Quar. Appl. Math. **13** (1956), 431–443, and G. J. Minty, J. Math. Mech. **15** (1966), 485–520.

equilibrium flow in such a network *minimizes a suitable quadratic function*:

(33) $q(X) = \frac{1}{2}X^{T}AX + K^{T}X + c, \qquad X = (x_1, \ldots, x_N).$

Here A is a real *Stieltjes matrix* [**38**, p. 85], that is, a real symmetric positive definite matrix with negative off-diagonal entries, while K and X are real column vectors. Physically, $q(X)$ represents the rate of dissipation of energy. Mathematically, the minimum of $q(X)$ occurs where $\nabla q = 0$, which is where (29) holds.

This observation makes possible the use of variational ideas which motivate overrelaxation, and which becomes most effective when combined with the techniques which I shall discuss in Part E.

20. **Gauss elimination.** For source problems (31) in a square subdivided by an $n \times n$ mesh, iterative methods become definitely more efficient than Gauss-Choleski elimination with minimum bandwidth $2n + 1$, for the reasons outlined in §19, when n is sufficiently large. Indeed, careful recent experiments[45] indicate that SOR becomes more efficient than elimination for $n > 40$, and hence for $N = n^2 > 1600$.

However, it is not clear that the preceding elimination scheme is *optimal*: though the relevant coefficient-matrix A has only 5 nonzero entries per row, due to the *fill-in* of zero entries by nonzero entries during "elimination," as much arithmetic is done as if there were initially $2n + 1$ nonzero entries per row. Moreover elimination methods have the great attraction (especially for algebraists) of being formally exact and valid over *any field*, including finite fields to which iterative methods are inapplicable. For this and other reasons, there is a great current interest in the problem of *optimizing Gauss elimination* for linear systems (29) having *sparse coefficient-matrices*.[46]

To formulate this problem, it is convenient to rewrite (29) as

(34) $\sum_{S(\sigma)} a_{\sigma\tau}x_\tau = k_\sigma, \qquad \tau \in S(\sigma) \subset S, \quad \sigma \in S.$

Here the subscripts σ, τ refer to *addresses* in the computer where numbers are stored (perhaps in "arrays"). To convert (34) to (29), one needs ordering bijections φ and ψ: from S to $\{1, \ldots, N\}$ specifying substitutions $i = \varphi(\sigma)$ and $j = \psi(\tau)$ for σ and τ; the "fill-in" of zero entries by nonzero entries depends on ψ. The optimization problem is to choose ψ so as to minimize the resulting number of arithmetic operations.

This fact leads to the basic question of *optimal ordering*: how can one list the equations in an order which will minimize the number of arithmetic operations which must be performed in Gauss elimination if (off-diagonal) 0's are omitted?

---

[45]G. J. Fix and K. E. Larsen, unpublished manuscript.

[46]The discussion of optimizing elimination in §§20–22 was written in collaboration with Donald J. Rose, and concerns questions discussed in [**T4**].

Minimum bandwidth. For optimal ordering, an often useful[47] and widely advocated [43] prescription is to so order the rows and columns as to achieve (i) minimum bandwidth — or, alternatively, (ii) minimum bandwidth below the main diagonal, as in a Hessenberg matrix [26, p. 379]. However, as will be shown in §21 by an example taken from [T4], the criterion of minimum bandwidth does not always yield minimum fill-in; moreover the criterion of minimum fill-in is cleanest. Furthermore, potential users should be warned that the problem of finding permutation matrices P and Q such that PAQ has minimum bandwidth is highly nontrivial. Steward [36], and also Harary and Dulmage and Mendelson[48] have solved problem (ii), in the sense of describing an algorithm for finding P and Q such that PAQ is block upper triangular with diagonal blocks of least size. However, no general computer program exists which solves the *optimization problem* of finding a P and Q which *minimize* the bandwidth of PAQ with a *minimum* order of computational complexity. The same is true of minimizing the bandwidth of PAP^T for symmetric A (with least order of computational complexity).

Criteria for optimality. Though I shall concentrate on algorithms for *optimal orderings* of variables for Gaussian elimination here, I want to emphasize that optimal elimination has minimum fill-in as one aspect but, as so often, *any of several different criteria for optimality may be appropriate, depending on the circumstances.*

For example, the optimal algorithm for solving a given linear system $AX = B$ with fewest multiplications need not be the same as that for solving $AX = B_i$ with fixed A and a large number of right-hand sides B_i (see [42, p. 221]).

In general, the solution of linear systems (29) consists in two distinct processes: "triangularization" by a sequence of premultiplications by non-singular quasi-elementary matrices to get

(35) $$UX = E_r E_{r-1} \cdots E_1 A X = E_r E_{r-1} \cdots E_1 B = UB,$$

with U upper triangular, and "back-substitution"

(35') $$LUX = F_s F_{s-1} \cdots F_1 (UX) = LUB$$

with the F_j also quasi-elementary. Note that the multiplication-count and storage-count proceed somewhat differently for (35') than (35).

Real and complex fields. In terminating this part of my discussion, I want to emphasize again that it ignores the major problem of *roundoff.* As Wilkinson [42] and Forsythe and Moler [19] explain, in solving large-scale linear systems (29) on a computer, one must control the *condition number* $\|A\| \cdot \|A^{-1}\|$ (which is the ratio $\lambda_{\max}(A)/\lambda_{\min}(A)$ of the maximum to the minimum eigenvalue of A if A is positive definite symmetric and the Euclidean norm is

---

[47] E. Cuthill and J. McKee, Proc. ACM 23rd Nat. Conf. (1969).

[48] F. Harary, J. Math. and Phys. **38** (1959), 104–111; also "Graph Theory and Theoretical Physics," Academic Press. 1967, p. 167 ff.

used), to limit the amplification of roundoff. One may also want to scale and/or pivot equations (although this is unnecessary if A is positive definite and symmetric).

In practice, a *mixed strategy* which combines elimination and iteration (e.g., by decomposing A into block tridiagonal or block 2-cyclic form) may be more effective than either pure elimination or pure iteration. Furthermore, questions about programming and machine characteristics may also be relevant [39, p. 19]. Moreover, the entries a_{ij} of the matrix $A = \|a_{ij}\|$ in (29) may be specified by a few *formulas* over large sub-arrays, and not stored as *numbers*.

However, the preceding questions relate to numerical analysis and computer science, and not to classical *or* modern algebra; therefore I shall ignore them here.

21. **Symmetric Gauss elimination.** Many matrices A which arise in physical contexts are symmetric. For such matrices, "symmetric Gauss elimination" and the closely related Cholesky method are distinctly preferable to ordinary Gauss elimination and its variants.[49]

Symmetric Gauss elimination and the Cholesky method are usually presented in the context of *real* linear algebra. I shall now show that symmetric Gauss elimination can be applied to "definite" symmetric matrices over *any* field (even one of characteristic two), defined as follows.

DEFINITION. A matrix A over a field F will be called *definite symmetric* when it is symmetric and $XAX^T = 0$ implies $X = 0$.

Note that, over the real field, a symmetric matrix is "definite" in the preceding sense if and only if it is positive definite or negative definite in the usual sense. Hence no diagonal entry a_{ii} of a definite symmetric matrix over any field can be zero, because $a_{ii} = E_i A E_i^T$, where E_i is the ith unit (row) vector, and so the process of symmetric Gauss elimination described below can always be carried out.

Therefore, we can write

$$A = \begin{bmatrix} a & C^T \\ C & M \end{bmatrix},$$

where $a \neq 0$, and apply Gaussian row elimination to the first column and then apply column elimination to the first row. This replaces A at the first step by

$$\begin{bmatrix} a & 0 \\ 0 & M_1 \end{bmatrix},$$

where $M_1 = M - C^T C / a$ remains definite (see Westlake [39, p.21]). Continuing recursively, A is replaced after n such steps by a definite diagonal matrix D,

---

[49]See D. Hartree, "Numerical Analysis," Oxford, 1952, §8, 4; rounding errors amplify less [42].

where

(36) $A = LDL^T$ (L unit lower triangular).

It is moreover easy to compute L in the process, after which one can solve other equations of the same form with variable B by

(37) $X = BA^{-1} = BL^{T-1}D^{-1}L^{-1}.$

   The Cholesky method for real matrices differs from symmetric Gauss elimination as defined above only in that a factor $a^{1/2}$ is applied twice so as to make $D = 1$ and $A = GG^T$. Both Cholesky and symmetric Gauss elimination involve only stable decomposition for positive definite symmetric *real* matrices; see Wilkinson [42], p. 231–232, Equation (44.13).

   REMARK.   It is evident that symmetric Gauss elimination can be generalized to apply to equations of the form $Bx = \mathbf{h}$, for any "diagonally symmetrizable" matrix B of the form $B = DAD$ with $D, \tilde{D}$ diagonal and A symmetric. Furthermore, such diagonally symmetrizable matrices are easily recognized by the property that

$$a_{ij}a_{ik}a_{kl} = a_{lk}a_{kj}a_{ji} \quad \text{for all } i, j, k, l.$$

The proof generalizes an argument of Seymour Parter and J. W. T. Youngs (J. Math. Anal. Appl. **4** (1962), 102–110), and will be omitted.

   Symmetric reordering.   For any permutation matrix P, it is evident that $X \mapsto XP$ carries any definite symmetric matrix A into PAP^T and $q(X) = XAX^T$ into $q_P(X) = (XP)A(XP)^T$: symmetry and definiteness are preserved. So is the *set* of diagonal entries and (for *real* matrices) so are the properties of being diagonally dominant and/or a Stieltjes matrix. Hence it seems appropriate to call such a transformation a *symmetric reordering* (or "pivoting") of the rows and columns of A.

   This is different from "pivoting" in the usual sense ([42, p. 206], [26, p. 2–24]), which can be any transformation $A \mapsto PAQ$, with P, Q arbitrary permutation matrices. Unless $Q = P^T$, such more general pivoting destroys the properties of the preceding paragraph. Hence such general pivoting is not appropriate for symmetric matrices — any more than ordinary Gauss elimination is, relying as it does exclusively on elementary *row* transformations of A.

   For the (positive definite real symmetric) *Stieltjes matrices* [38] arising from linear *network* problems, including systems (29) or (34) arising from the standard 5-point approximation to source problems (30), it seems especially appropriate to use only symmetric reorderings. For, in this case, the ith equation and the ith variable both refer physically to the (potential and current equilibrium at the) ith node of the network. Hence, for network problems, the group of "symmetric pivotings" $A \mapsto PAP^T$ of the matrix A can be interpreted as induced by *reordering nodes*.

   22. **Optimal ordering.**   In [T4], Donald Rose has analyzed carefully the *optimal orderings* of the rows (equations) and columns (unknowns) of a *sym-*

metric matrix; i.e., those "symmetric" orderings (with $\psi = \varphi$ below (34)) which *minimize fill-in* for symmetric Gauss elimination. I shall try to summarize his findings.

Parter[50] has defined the (symmetric) *graph* $G(A)$ of the coefficient-matrix A of the linear system (11) to have nodes $i = 1, \ldots, n$, and edges (i, j) for all i, j with a_{ij} or a_{ji} nonzero. He showed that if A was a Stieltjes or other strictly *diagonally dominant* matrix and $G(A)$ was a *tree* (or forest[51]), fill-in could be entirely avoided by proper "monotone orderings" of the equations.

The basic *degree one algorithm* consists in working from peripheral (or "pendant") nodes inwards. Specifically, call a node "peripheral" when its degree is 0 or 1. Any tree or forest has at least one peripheral node; let x_i correspond to such a peripheral node of $G(A)$. Then the ith equation has the form $a_{ii}x_i + a_{ij}x_j = b_i$; therefore one can eliminate x_i by simply storing the equation

$$(38) \qquad x_i = a_{ii}^{-1}b_i - a_{ii}^{-1}a_{ij}x_j = A_i + B_ix_j,$$

and substituting from (38) into the jth equation which, by definition of $G(A)$, is the only other equation into which x_i enters.

This results in $N-1$ equations in the $N-1$ remaining variables, whose graph is a subgraph of $G(A)$. Since any subgraph of a tree or forest is itself a tree or forest, the algorithm can be repeated $N-1$ times to solve for some x_k. Back-substitution into equations like (38) completes the process, with minimum fill-in (except fortuitously).

Parter's algorithm has been generalized in the *minimum degree algorithm* due to Tinney and others.[52] This eliminates at each step a variable σ (graph node) of minimum (remaining) degree *and* all the adjacent edges. When $G(A)$ is a tree, it gives Parter's algorithm. For systems (29) whose graph is the "snowflake graph" of Figure 6, it is better than the minimum bandwidth algorithm. In this example, the minimum remaining degree never exceeds two, and we can apply the following algorithm.

Degree two elimination algorithm. If i is a node of degree two in $G(A)$, then the ith equation of (29) will be of the form

$$(39) \qquad d_ix_i = a_ix_{\varphi(i)} + b_ix_{\psi(i)} + c_i.$$

The algorithm consists in adding $d_i^{-1}a_{i,\varphi(i)}$ times the ith equation to the $\varphi(i)$th equation, and $d_i^{-1}a_{i,\psi(i)}$ times the ith equation to the $\psi(i)$th equation. This will *eliminate x_i* from the other equations, *without increasing* $\deg \varphi(i)$ or $\deg \psi(i)$.

Triangulated graphs. Parter's ideas have also been significantly extended by Donald Rose in his Thesis [T4], where he has also related them to the concept of a triangulated graph introduced by Berge for other purposes. Namely,

---

[50]See [32]; also A. Jennings, Computer J. 9 (1967), 281–284.

[51]A "forest" is a disjoint sum of trees.

[52]N. Sato and W. F. Tinney, IEEE, PAS (1963), 944–950; W. F. Tinney and J. W. Walker, Proc. IEEE 55 (1967), 1801–1809. For computer experiments, see [43, pp. 25, 35].

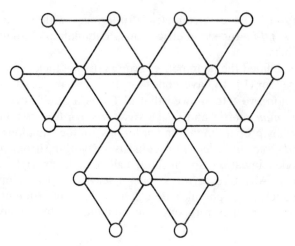

FIGURE 6.   Snowflake Graph.

call a graph G *triangulated* when for every cycle γ of length $l > 3$ there is an edge of G joining two nonconsecutive nodes of γ. For example, the "snowflake graph" of Figure 6 is triangulated. Rose has proved the following basic result [**T4**, p. 3.4].

THEOREM. *Let A be a positive definite symmetric matrix, and let $G = G(A)$ be its graph. Then the following conditions are equivalent:* (i) *G is triangulated,* (ii) *every minimal a, b separator is a clique,* (iii) *there exists an ordering which makes G monotone transitive,* (iv) *with this ordering, symmetric Gaussian elimination minimizes fill-in (is a perfect elimination process).*

Tearing and patching.   A dual approach to the problem of optimizing elimination can be based on the idea of "tearing and patching" networks, whose utility was emphasized by Gabriel Kron[53] in his "diakoptiks." This method depends on finding small *cut-sets S* of the graph $G = G(A)$ of a system (29) or (34). By this is meant [15, p. 17] a set of edges which *separates $G - S$* into two or more nonvoid components T and U joined by no edge of G.

A computer program for "diakoptik elimination" might proceed by first decomposing G into its connected components [9, Chapter 2], then determining all one-node cut-sets, then all two-node cut-sets, and so on.

E. PIECEWISE POLYNOMIAL INTERPOLATION

23. G. D. Birkhoff's problem.   Almost every mathematician is aware of the importance of polynomial and rational functions for numerical computing. Most basic is Lagrange's theorem that, given $n + 1$ distinct points $x_0, x_1, \ldots, x_n$

---

[53]See Steward, Tewarson, and Tinney [**43**, pp. 25–44 and 65–74]; also [**36**] and [**37**]; H. H. Happ, "Diakoptiks and Networks," Academic Press, 1970. Greechie has used similar "tearing and patching" methods to synthesize and decompose orthomodular lattices from their diagrams.

and $n+1$ values $y_0, y_1, \ldots, y_n$, there exists one and only one set of polynomial coefficients $a_0, a_1, \ldots, a_n$ such that, for $i = 0, 1, \ldots, n$:

(40) $$a_0 + a_1 x_i + a_2 x_i{}^2 + \cdots + a_n x_i{}^n = f(x_i) = y_i.$$

Though commonly stated for the real field, the theorem is true over *any field*, because of the formula for the *Vandermonde determinant*.[54]

(41) $$|x_i^{j-1}| = \prod_{i>j} (x_i - x_j).$$

Clearly, this product is nonzero for distinct x_i; hence the transformation $X: \Sigma_{j=0}^n a_j x_i^j \to y_i$ is nonsingular. (In the case $x_i = x_0 + ih$ of equal spaced interpolation, $|x_i^{j-1}| = \prod_{k=1}^{n-1} k^{n-k} h^{n(n-1)/2}$.)

In the limiting case of "coalescent" x_i, Lagrange's Theorem yields *Hermite interpolation*.[55]

(42) $$f^{(k)}(x_i) = \sum_{j=k}^{\nu-k} [j(j-1) \cdots (j-k+1) a_j x_i^{j-k}] = y_i^{(k)},$$

for $i = 0, 1, \ldots, n$, $k = 0, \ldots, K(i)$ and $\nu = \Sigma_{i=0}^n [K(i) + 1]$. The resulting system of ν equations in ν unknowns is also *nonsingular*, over any field whose characteristic $\chi > \text{Max } K(i)$.

When only twenty years old, my father [11] proposed the following algebraic *generalized Hermite interpolation* problem. For which *sets* of pairs (i, k) of nonnegative integers is defined by (42) always (algebraically) possible? This is G. D. Birkhoff's interpolation problem.

The two-point G. D. Birkhoff interpolation problem was given the following solution by Pólya [33].

PÓLYA'S THEOREM. *Let m_k be the number of conditions on the kth derivative (for $i = 0, 1$) and let $J_j = \Sigma_{k=0}^j m_j$. Then the ν equations (42) are always nonsingular if and only if $M_j \leq j+1$ for $0 \leq j \leq \nu - 2$.*

Ferguson [18] has extended Pólya's results as follows. A set of interpolation conditions is said to satisfy the *strong Pólya conditions* when M_j, the total number of interpolation conditions $f^{(k)}(x_i) = y_i^k$ with $k \leq j$, satisfies $M_j \leq j+2$ for $j = 0, \ldots, n-2$. He has proved that G. D. Birkhoff's interpolation problem is well-set for a fixed set of (i, k) and *all complex x_i* if and only if it is a Hermite system or a (two-point) Pólya system.

For further results on this challenging problem I refer you to the literature.[56]

Clearly, G. D. Birkhoff's problem involves both algebraic and combinatorial ideas; and his own interest in it was stimulated by the idea that polynomial *interpolation* was a fruitful source of good *approximation* formulas,

---

[54]Birkhoff-Mac Lane, "Survey of Modern Algebra," 3rd ed., p. 284.

[55]Philip Davis, "Interpolation and Approximation," Ginn, 1963, p. 52.

[56]See I. J. Schoenberg, J. Math. Anal. Appl. **16** (1966), 538–543; A. Sharma and J. Prasad, SIAM J. Numer. Anal. **5** (1968), 864–881; I. M. Sheffer, Amer. J. Math. **57** (1935), 587–614. G. G. Lorentz and K. L. Zeller, SIAM J. Numer. Anal. **8** (1971), 43–48.

useful for computation and for theoretical analysis. Thus, his ultimate goal was to derive mean value theorems for the interpolation *error* (alias "remainder"): to show that very general schemes of polynomial interpolation were not only *algebraically* well-set[57] but also *convergent* (*analytically* well-set)(over the real field), as the mesh-length tended to zero for *fixed* ν.

However, G. D. Birkhoff's problem seems more a fascinating purely mathematical question suggested by computing ("mechanical quadrature") than one which will influence actual computing practice significantly.

24. **Piecewise polynomial interpolation.** Much more important for actual computation is interpolation by *piecewise polynomial* functions, such as cubic and bicubic polynomial splines. In *finite element methods* especially, one commonly deals with such functions, defined by a different polynomial formula in each (polyhedral) cell of a suitable combinatorial *complex* (see §6). *Compatibility* conditions (e.g., of continuous differentiability) across the interfaces between cells lead to many problems concerning *linear dependence* of a kind already hinted at in §6 and §14.

In some cases (e.g., of piecewise linear functions defined on the triangles of a "simplicial" subdivision), these problems have trivial solutions, because strictly *local* interpolation formulas are adequate. More challenging theoretically are the linear dependence problems arising from *global* methods in which the interpolating function of each cell depends on *all* given values.

Univariate splines. The simplest and most widely used global interpolation scheme is provided by *cubic spline* interpolation to values y_i at $n+1$ points x_i with $x_0 < x_1 < \cdots < x_n$, and given end slopes y_0', y_n'. The best way to handle this consists in taking the slopes $y_1', \ldots, y_{n-1}'$ at interior meshpoints as unknowns which, if known, would reduce the problem to one of (local) cubic *Hermite* interpolation of a cubic polynomial in each interval or "cell" $[x_{i-1}, x_i]$ to the four numbers $y_{i-1}, y_i, y_{i-1}', y_i'$. The y_i' can be determined from the given data by the condition of *continuous curvature*, a condition which is equivalent at $x = x_i$ to (for $\Delta x_i = x_i - x_{i-1}$):

$$\begin{aligned} \Delta x_i y_{i-1}' + 2(\Delta_{i-1} + \Delta x_i) y_i' + \Delta x_{i-1} y_{i+1}' \\ = 3[(\Delta x_i \Delta y_{i-1}/\Delta x_{i-1}) + (\Delta x_{i-1} \Delta y_i/\Delta x_i)]. \end{aligned} \tag{43}$$

The coefficient-matrix of the system (43) is always nonsingular over the real field (for distinct x_i).

However, even over the complex field with $n = 3$, the choice $\Delta x_1 = 1$, $\Delta x_2 = i$, $\Delta x_3 = (i+7)/25$ yields a *singular* coefficient-matrix. Therefore, although some interesting work has been done with complex splines,[58] I believe that most of the algebraic theory of "spline" and other global piecewise poly-

[57] In the terminology of Birkhoff and de Boor (cf. H. L. Garabedian, editor, "Approximation of Functions," Elsevier, 1965, pp. 169–170).

[58] J. H. Ahlberg, E. N. Nilson, and J. L. Walsh, Trans. Amer. Math. Soc. **129** (1967), 391–413; [**35**, pp. 1–27].

nomial interpolation schemes is essentially limited to the real field and other ordered fields. One can generalize the notions of "polyhedron" and complex to (perhaps convex) domains in F^n, if F is any such ordered field.

For (univariate) cubic splines, the complex in question is the simple *linear graph* sketched below.

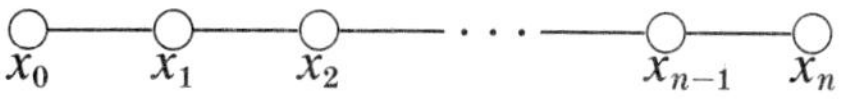
x_0
x_1
x_2
x_{n-1}
x_n

One is interested in the values of $y_i = y_i^0$, $y_i' = y_i^1$, and $y_i'' = y_i^2$ at the $n+1$ mesh-points x_i, giving $3n+3$ numbers in all. By elementary formulas for Hermite interpolation on $[x_{i-1}, x_i]$, we have n (homogeneous linear) dependence relations of each of the forms:

$$(44) \qquad 2y_{i-1}^2 + y_i^1 + 2y_{i-1}^1 \Delta x_i = 3(y_i^0 - y_{i-1}^0),$$

$$(44') \qquad 2y_i^2 + y_{i-1}^1 - 2y_i^1 \Delta x_i = 3(y_{i-1}^0 - y_i^0),$$

where $\Delta x_i = x_i - x_{i-1}$ and $i = 1, \ldots, n$.

From the preceding $2n$ dependence relations, we can obtain the $(n-1)$ "smoothness" conditions (43) by eliminating the $n+1$ y_j^2. Indeed, since the cubic "spline subspace" is $(n+3)$-dimensional and the $2n$ equations (44)-(44′) are linearly independent, *every* true equation between the $3n+3$ variables y_i^k $(k = 0, 1, 2)$ is a linear combination of these $2n$ equation.—Analogous results hold for splines of any odd degree $2m+1$.

Dependence matrix. The $2n$ homogeneous linear compatibility equations $\Sigma\, a_{ki}^j y_i^k = 0$ of (44)-(44′) in the $3n+3$ *interpolation* variables y_i^k can be specified by a $2n \times (3n+3)$ *dependence matrix* $A = \|a_{ki}^j\| = \|a_\lambda^j\|$ $(j = 1, \ldots, 2n)$. Their significance consists in the fact that the $y_i^k = y_\lambda$ cannot be assigned arbitrarily: having specified any subset S of the set $\Lambda = \{y_\lambda\}$ of all interpolation variables y_λ, we have automatically specified all variables which are linearly *dependent* on the y_λ $(\lambda \in S)$.

The mapping $S \mapsto \bar{S}$ from S to the set of variables dependent on the y_λ $(\lambda \in S)$ is a closure operation, and the closed subsets of interpolation variables form a finite *geometric lattice*, the *dependence lattice* of the matrix A above. In (44)-(44′), by Pólya's Theorem with $\nu - 2 = 2$, any four of the six variables y_{i-1}^k, y_i^k except for $\{y_{i-1}^1, y_i^1, y_{i-1}^2, y_i^2\}$ are linearly independent.

25. **Bivariate splines.** Given a subdivided *rectangular polygon* $(\mathscr{R}, \pi \times \pi')$ as in Appendix A, it is interesting to consider the *bivariate spline functions* of degree $2m-1$ in each variable and of class $C^{2m-2}(\mathscr{R})$, as specified by the functionals

$$(45) \qquad \varphi_{ij}^{kl} = \frac{\partial^{k+l} u}{\partial x^k \partial y^l}(x_i, y_j), \qquad k, l = 0, 1, \ldots, m.$$

A complete determination of the linear dependence relations among the φ_{ij}^{kl} is, in general, a formidable task.

Tensor products. In the special case that $\mathscr{R}$ is a rectangle, the resulting dependence lattice is the *direct product* of the lattices of dependence relations of univariate spline functions of degree $2m-1$ on $(\mathscr{L}, \pi)$ and $(\mathscr{L}', \pi')$, respectively. This is due to the underlying *tensor product* construction of bicubic splines. (Likewise, there are important cases, corresponding loosely to cases of "separable variables," in which solution by elimination is greatly facilitated by using the concept of a "tensor product" to solve

$$(46) \qquad\qquad (B \otimes C)u \otimes v = k \otimes l.$$

However, I shall not discuss this technique, which is relevant to Part D, in the present paper.)

Some results concerning the dependence lattice of bivariate spline functions on subdivided rectangular polygons are presented in Appendices B and C of my paper in [35]. In particular, results of Carlson and Hall[59] give bases both of spline functions and for the dependence among the φ_{ij}^{kl} of (45).

Dependence lattice. Letting λ designate a multi-index for (i, j, k, l) in (45), the results of Carlson and Hall therefore give a *dependence matrix* $A = \|a_\lambda^\mu\|$ such that the equations

$$\sum a_\lambda^\mu \varphi_\lambda = 0, \qquad \mu = 1, \ldots, M,$$

span *all* true dependence relations among the φ_{ij}^{kl}. Moreover, if the x_i, y_j are rational numbers, then the a_λ^μ are rational too.

To determine the *geometric lattice* $L(A)$ of all (linearly) closed subsets $\bar{S}$ of φ_λ from this matrix is an interesting exercise in rational arithmetic. I conjecture that (for given L), this $L(A)$ is determined up to isomorphism by the *complex* corresponding to $(\mathscr{R}, n)$.

26. **Lattice structures involved.** For general multivariate interpolation by piecewise polynomial functions in *polyhedral complexes*, at least *three* lattice structures are involved. First is that of the polyhedral complex itself, which I have already discussed from an algebraic standpoint in §6. Even more central are the *paired geometric lattices of functions and linear functionals* to which an index or other identification (e.g., storage address) is assigned in a given computer program. These constitute *paired geometric lattices* in the sense of the following definition.

DEFINITION. Let V be a finite-dimensional vector space of functions f, and W the dual space of linear functionals φ on V. Let $F \subset V$ and $\Phi \subset W$ be *finite* sets of functions f_i and functionals φ_j which span V and W, respectively. Let L and M be the *geometric lattices* of all subsets $S \subset W$ resp. $T \subset \Phi$ which are *closed* under linear combination (in V resp. W). Let $N \subset \Phi \times F$ consist of the pairs (φ_j, f_i) such that $\varphi_j(f_i) = 0$.

Consider the *polarity* defined by the biorthogonality relation $\varphi_j(f_i) = 0$; clearly $T \subset S^*$ implies $\bar{T} \subset S^*$ and $S \subset T\dagger$ implies $\bar{S} \subset T\dagger$. Hence the

[59]R. E. Carlson and C. A. Hall, J. Approx. Theory 4 (1971), 37–53.

subsets closed with respect to the polarity defined by N are also elements in M and L. We can therefore consider biorthogonality as a *polarity* between the geometric lattices L and M.

We will call L and M *biorthogonally paired* when the polarity just defined is a *dual isomorphism* between L and M, which are then necessarily complemented *modular* lattices. (A common case occurs when they are both Boolean algebras, because the f_i and φ_j are linearly independent.) It is interesting to know when the polarity is *onto* in even one direction.

An interesting case arises when we have *patch bases*. In general, given a subset K of the *polyhedral complex* G on which the functions of V are defined, we have an interesting subset of functions with *support* in K. Many $\varphi \in \Phi$ refer, moreover, to individual *cells* of K, and thus annihilate all functions whose support excludes K.

It would be interesting to determine (up to isomorphism) some of the lattices defined by piecewise polynomial functions of given degree with respect to specified sets of functions. We do not completely know these lattices even for the univariate cubic splines of §23.

APPENDIX A. SUBDIVIDED RECTANGULAR POLYGONS

1. **Classification of rectangular polygons.** One of the simplest families of combinatorial complexes in $n > 1$ dimensions is the family of (rectangularly) *subdivided rectangular polygons*. These are moreover especially amenable to the use of bicubic splines and other bivariate piecewise polynomial functions. I shall here discuss some ideas for treating simply connected subdivided rectangular polygons in computer programs (cf. [35, pp. 212–213]).

It is evident (since the sum of the turning angles is 360°) that any simply connected rectangular polygon with J reentrant corners or *notches* must have $J+4$ protruding corners. When $J = 0$, we have a *rectangle*; when $J = 1$, we have an *L-shaped region*.

When $J = 2$, we may have a U-shaped region, a T-shaped region, a doubly notched rectangle, or a 3-step staircase, as shown in Figures 7a–7d.

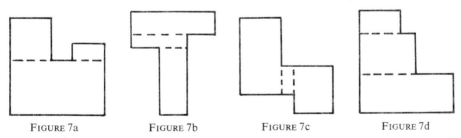

FIGURE 7a   FIGURE 7b   FIGURE 7c   FIGURE 7d

These correspond to the four *cyclic partitions* of the number $J+4 = 6$ into *two* summands, specifying the numbers of protruding corners between successive notches:

$$6+0, \quad 5+1, \quad 4+2, \quad 3+3.$$

For $J = 3$, there are *eight* configurations (inequivalent under the dihedral-symmetric group of all cyclic permutations and reflections) of the sequence of *three* summands in partitions of $J + 4 = 7$. These correspond to the partitions

$$7+0+0, \quad 6+1+0, \quad 5+2+0, \quad 5+1+1,$$
$$4+3+0, \quad 4+2+1, \quad 3+2+2, \quad 3+3+1.$$

For $J = 4$, the dihedral group is not the symmetric group, and there are many possible configurations (inequivalent partitions of $J + 4 = 8$); the most symmetric are *crosses* corresponding to the partition $2+2+2+2$. It is an interesting combinatorial problem to determine for general J the number of different kinds of rectangular polygons with J notches, in the above sense.

2. **Cell addresses.** A *subdivided rectangle* (the case $J = 0$) is easily specified as an *array* of $m \times n = mn$ subrectangles; one can apply to it the tensor product techniques mentioned in §25.

A subdivided L-shaped region can be specified as the sum of the 3 subrectangles into which it is subdivided by extending the edges incident on reentrant corners (notches) until they meet an (opposite) side. Thus, it can be specified as an $m \times n$ subrectangle with abutting $m' \times n$ and $m \times n'$ subrectangles; see Figure 8a. Two such *rectangular L-complexes* specified by integer sequences $(m, m'; n, n')$ and $(\tilde{m}, \tilde{m}'; \tilde{n}, \tilde{n}')$ are *isomorphic* if and only if $m = \tilde{m}, m' = \tilde{m}', n = \tilde{n}, n' = \tilde{n}'$, or $m = \tilde{n}, m' = \tilde{n}', n = m, n' = \tilde{m}'$.

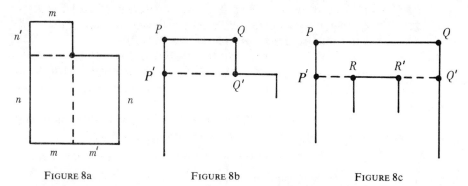

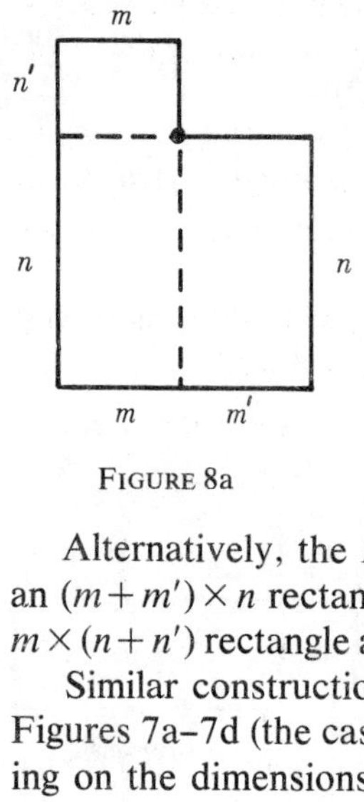

FIGURE 8a 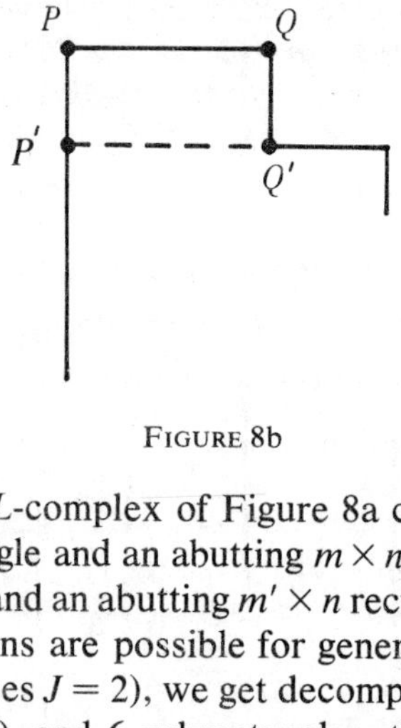   FIGURE 8b 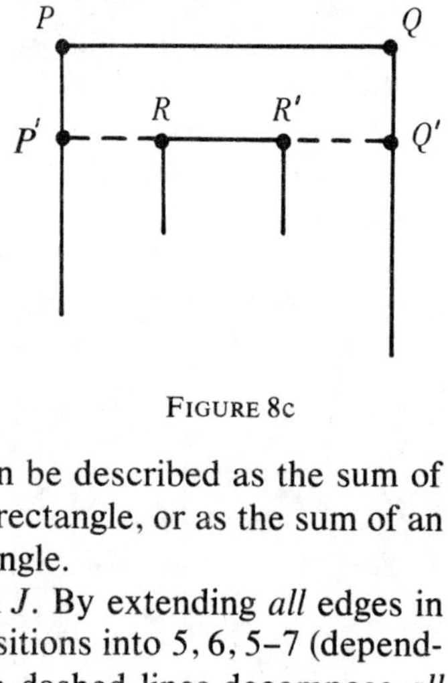   FIGURE 8c

Alternatively, the L-complex of Figure 8a can be described as the sum of an $(m + m') \times n$ rectangle and an abutting $m \times n'$ rectangle, or as the sum of an $m \times (n + n')$ rectangle and an abutting $m' \times n$ rectangle.

Similar constructions are possible for general J. By extending *all* edges in Figures 7a–7d (the cases $J = 2$), we get decompositions into 5, 6, 5–7 (depending on the dimensions), and 6 subrectangles; the dashed lines decompose *all* regions into three subrectangles. In general, we have:

THEOREM 1. *Any connected rectangular polygon with J notches can be decomposed into J + 1 or fewer subrectangles.*

PROOF.   The rectangular $(2J+4)$-gon will have at least $J+1$ pairs of consecutive protruding corners; take the edge PQ joining any such consecutive corners. Translate it inwardly until either: (i) one end P' or Q' of the translated edge coincides with another corner, as in Figure 8b, or (ii) the translated $P'Q'$ falls on another edge, as in Figure 8c. In Case (i), the given $(2J+4)$-gon is decomposed into a subrectangle and a rectangular $(2J+2)$-gon (i.e., a $(2(J-1)+4)$-gon) with one less notch and one less protruding corner. In Case (ii), the given $(2J+4)$-gon is decomposed into a subrectangle and *two* rectangular polygons, having in all *two* fewer notches but two more protruding corners. By induction on J, the resulting $(2K+4)$-gon and $(2L+4)$-gon with $2(K+L)+8 = 2J+4$ can be decomposed into $K+L+2$ subrectangles, where $2(K+L+2)+4 = 2J+4$; hence the original rectangular $(2J+4)$-gon can be decomposed into $K+L+3$ subrectangles where $2(K+L+3)+2 = 2J+4$, which proves that $K+L+3 = J+1$, as claimed.

Consequently, one can specify the cells of any rectangularly subdivided rectangular $(2J+4)$-gon (in Backus normal form) by listing $J+1$ rectangular *arrays*, and cross-addressing *boundary* 0-cells and 1-cells which occur in *two* arrays. If, as in Figure 9, one makes a decomposition into more than $J+1$ subrectangles, reentrant corner 0-cells may lie in *three* subrectangles, hence one may have to cross-address three addresses.

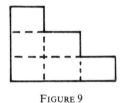

FIGURE 9

REFERENCES

1. Proceedings symposia on applied mathematics, Vols. I-XIX, Amer. Math. Soc., Providence, R. I., 1949–1967.

2. J. C. Abbott (editor), *Trends in lattice theory*, Van Nostrand, Princeton, N.J., 1970.

3. P. S. Aleksandrov, *Combinatorial topology*, OGIZ, Moscow, 1947; English transl., Graylock Press, Albany, New York, 1956. MR **10**, 55; MR **22** # 4056; MR **28** # 3415. See also: D. G. Bourgin, *Modern algebraic topology*, Macmillan, New York, 1963.

4. M. A. Arbib (editor), *The algebraic theory of machines, languages, and semigroups*, Academic Press, New York, 1968. MR **38** #1198.

5. _____, *Theories of abstract automata*, Prentice-Hall, Englewood Cliffs, N.J., 1969.

5a. E. F. Beckenbach (editor), *Applied combinatorial mathematics*, Wiley, New York, 1964. MR **30** #4687.

6. E. R. Berlekamp, *Algebraic coding theory*, McGraw-Hill, New York, 1968. MR **38** #6873.

7. G. Birkhoff, *Lattice theory*, 3rd ed., Amer. Math. Soc. Colloq. Publ., vol. 25, Amer. Math. Soc., Providence, R. I., 1967. MR **37** #2638.

8. _____, *Mathematics and psychology*, SIAM Rev. **11** (1969), 429–469.

9. G. Birkhoff and T. C. Bartee, *Modern applied algebra*, McGraw-Hill, New York, 1970.

10. G. Birkhoff and J. D. Lipson, *Heterogeneous algebras*, J. Combinatorial Theory 8 (1970), 115–133. MR **40** #4119.

11. G. D. Birkhoff, *General mean value theorems with applications to mechanical differentiation and quadrature*, Trans. Amer. Math. Soc. 7 (1906), 107–136.

12. Carl Boyer, *A history of mathematics*, Wiley, New York, 1968. MR **38** #3105.

13. F. H. Branin, *The relation between Kron's method and . . . network analysis*, IRE WESCON Conv. Rec., part 2, 1959, pp. 3–28.

13a. P. Braffort and D. Hirschberg (editors), *Studies in logic and the foundations of mathematics*, North-Holland, Amsterdam, 1967.

14. R. K. Brayton, F. G. Gustavson and R. A. Willoughby, *Some results on sparse matrices*, Math. Comp. **24** (1970), 937–954.

15. R. G. Busacker and T. L. Saaty, *Finite graphs and networks. An introduction with applications*, McGraw-Hill, New York, 1965. MR **35** #79.

16. B. A. Carré, *The partitioning of network equations for block iteration*, Comput. J. **9** (1966), 84–97. MR **33** #3445.

16a. L. Couturat, *La logique de Leibniz*, Paris, 1901.

17. H. Crapo and G.-C. Rota, *Combinatorial geometries*, M.I.T., Cambridge, Mass., 1968. (lithoprinted report).

17a. Irwin Engeler, *Semantics of algorithmic languages*, Springer, New York and Berlin, 1971.

18. D. Ferguson, *The question of uniqueness for G. D. Birkhoff interpolation problems*, J. Approximation Theory **2** (1969), 1–28. MR **40** #599.

19. G. Forsythe and C. B. Moler, *Computer solution of linear algebraic systems*, Prentice-Hall, Englewood Cliffs, N.J., 1967. MR **36** #2306.

19a. L. Fox (editor), *Advances in programming and non-numerical computation*, Pergamon Press, New York, 1966. MR **32** #8540.

20. George Grätzer, *Universal algebra*, Van Nostrand, Princeton, N.J., 1968. MR **40** # 1320.

20a. Branko Grünbaum, *Convex polytopes*, Pure and Appl. Math., vol. 16, Wiley, New York, 1967. MR **37** # 2085. See also *Polytopes, graphs, and complexes*, Bull. Amer. Math. Soc. **76** (1970), 1130–1201.

21. Frank Harary, *Graph theory and theoretical physics*, Academic Press, New York, 1967. MR **37** #6208.

22. _____, *Graphs and matrices*, SIAM Rev. **9** (1967), 83–90. MR **35** # 1501.

23. J. Hartmanis and R. E. Stearns, *Algebraic structure theory of sequential machines*, Prentice-Hall, Englewood Cliffs, N.J., 1966. MR **34** # 4068.

24. W. H. Huggins and Doris R. Entwisle, *Introductory systems and design*, Ginn-Blaisdell, New York, 1968.

25. R. E. Kalman, P. Falb and M. A. Arbib, *Topics in mathematical systems theory*, McGraw-Hill, New York, 1969. MR **40** # 8465.

26. M. Klerer and G. A. Korn (editors), *Digital user's handbook*, McGraw-Hill, New York, 1968.

27. D. E. Knuth, *The art of computer programming*, Addison-Wesley, Reading, Mass., 1968. (7 volumes projected.)

28. D. König, *Theorie der Graphen*, Akademische Verlag, Berlin, 1936; reprint, Chelsea, New York, 1950.

29. N. Levinson, *Coding theory: counterexample to G. H. Hardy's conception of applied mathematics*, Amer. Math. Monthly **77** (1970), 249–258. MR **40** # 8491.

30. C. I. Liu, *Introduction to combinatorial mathematics*, McGraw-Hill, New York, 1968. MR **38** #3154.

31. M. Minsky, *Computations: Finite and infinite machines*, Prentice-Hall, Englewood Cliffs, N.J., 1967.

32. S. Parter, *The use of linear graphs in Gauss elimination*, SIAM Rev. **3** (1961), 119–130. MR **26** #908.

32a. W. W. Peterson, *Error-correcting codes*, M.I.T. Press, Cambridge, Mass.; Wiley, New York, 1961. MR **22** #12003.

33. G. Pólya, *Bemerkangen zur Interpolation und zur Näherungstheorie der Balkenbiegung*, Z. Angew. Math. Mech. **11** (1931), 445–449.

34. G.-C. Rota, *On the foundations of combinatorial theory*. I. *Theory of Möbius functions*, Z. Wahrscheinlichkeitstheorie und Verw. Gebiete **2** (1964), 340–368. MR **30** #4688.

34a. H. A. Schmidt, K. Schütte and H. J. Thiele, *Contributions to mathematical logic*, North-Holland, Amsterdam, 1968.

35. I. F. Schoenberg (editor), *Approximations with special emphasis on spline functions*, Publ. no. 23, Math. Res. Center, U.S. Army, University of Wisconsin, Academic Press, New York, 1969. MR **40** #4638.

36. D. V. Steward, *Partitioning and tearing systems of equations*, J. Soc. Indust. Appl. Math. **2** (1965), 345–365. MR **36** #2307.

37. R. P. Tewarson, *Solution of a system of simultaneous linear equations with a sparse coefficient matrix by elimination methods*, Nordisk Tidskr. Informations-Behandling (BIT) **7** (1967), 226–239. MR **36** #2308.

38. R. S. Varga, *Matrix iterative analysis*, Prentice-Hall, Englewood Cliffs, N.J., 1962. MR **28** #1725.

38a. J. von Neumann, *Collected works*. Vol. V. *Design of computers, theory of automata and numerical analysis*, Macmillan, New York, 1963. MR **28** #1104.

39. J. R. Westlake, *A handbook of numerical matrix inversion and solution of linear equations*, Wiley, New York, 1968. MR **36** #4794.

40. A. N. Whitehead, *Universal algebra*, Cambridge Univ. Press, New York, 1898.

41. H. Whitney, *The abstract properties of linear dependence*, Amer. J. Math. **57** (1935), 509–533; See also: G. Birkhoff, ibid. 801–804.

42. J. H. Wilkinson, *The algebraic eigenvalue problem*, Clarendon Press, Oxford, 1965. MR **32** #1894.

43. R. A. Willoughby (editor), *IBM sparse matrix proceedings*, IBM Report RAI #11707, 1969.

44. A. D. Wyner, *On coding and information theory*, SIAM Rev. **11** (1969), 317–346.

HARVARD DOCTORAL THESES

T0. Stephen A. Cook, *On the minimum computation time of functions*, Trans. Amer. Math. Soc. **142** (1969), 291–314. MR **40** # 2459.

T1. K. B. Krohn, *Algebraic theory of machines*, 1962.

T2. John D. Lipson, *Flow graphs and generating functions*, 1969.

T3. Vern Poythress, *Partial algebras*, 1970.

T4. Donald Rose, *Symmetric elimination . . . and the potential flow network problem*, 1970.

T5. Gary I. Wakoff, *Piecewise polynomial spaces . . .* , 1970.

T6. David M. Young, *Iterative methods for solving differential equations of elliptic type*, 1950.

HARVARD UNIVERSITY

On Performing Group Multiplication by Switching Circuits[1]

Shmuel Winograd

Introduction. The study of the time and the number of components needed to perform various functions by switching circuits was suggested by Kolmogorov. Ofman [**1**], Karetsuba [**2**], and Toom [**3**] investigated the asymptotic rate of growths of the amount of time and the number of components needed to perform addition and multiplication. Under the assumption that the numbers are represented by base 2 representation, they showed that the time required to perform addition or multiplication grows as $\log n$, where n is the number of digits used to represent the arguments.

In this paper we will describe results on lower and upper bounds for the time required to compute various functions. Most of the results have already been described elsewhere [**4**], [**5**], [**6**]. The results on the average time, however, have not been previously reported. We will, therefore, omit the proofs of the theorems, but indicate where they can be found.

In this paper we will deal with the time required to perform the computations by switching circuits. For results about the time required to perform the computations by Turing machines, the reader is referred to [**7**].

The problem. The basic building blocks of switching circuits are the switching elements. Every switching element is described by a set of r input lines (r is called the "fan-in" of the switching element), each of which can carry one of the d signals $0, 1, \ldots, d-1$, and a function $f: \{0, 1, \ldots, d-1\}^r \rightarrow \{0, 1, \ldots, d-1\}$. The function f determines the output signal at time $t+1$ given the input signals at time t. A set of switching elements are connected together to form a *d-valued switching circuit*. Let C be a d-valued switching circuit, given input

---

AMS 1970 *subject classifications*. Primary 68A20.

[1]The research on this report was partially supported by the Office of Naval Research Contract No. N00014-69-C-0023.

configuration i, and the initial configuration s of the output signals of the switching elements, the behavior of C is given by the function $c(s, i, t)$, which describes the output configuration of C at time t. (A precise definition of a d-valued switching circuit is given in [4].)

DEFINITION 1.   Let $f: X_1 \times X_2 \to Y$ be a function. A circuit C is said to be capable of computing f in time t if there exists
(i) a partition of the inputs of C into two classes J_1, J_2,
(ii) mappings $g_k : X_k \to \{0, 1, \ldots, d-1\}^{J_k}, k = 1, 2,$
(iii) a $1 : 1$ function $h : Y \to \{0, 1, \ldots, d-1\}^{O}$ (where O is the set of outputs of C,
(iv) an initial state s_0 such that, for every $(x_1, x_2) \in X_1 \times X_2$,

$$c((g_1(x_1), g_2(x_2)), s_0, t) = h(f(x_1, x_2)).$$

The problem of finding the minimum time required to compute f by a switching circuit can now be formulated as finding the minimum of the set $\{t \mid \exists C \text{ which is capable of computing } f \text{ in time } t\}$.

Results.   Let G be a finite group. Define $f_G : G \times G \to G$ by $f_G(g_1, g_2) = g_1 \circ g_2$. What is the minimum time required to compute f_G by a switching circuit? The first answer to this question was given in [4]. For every group G, we say that $P(G)$ holds if $\cap_{H \leq G; H \neq \{e\}} H \neq \{e\}$. We then define for every group G (which has more than one element) the number

$$\alpha(G) = \min \{|H| (H \leq G, P \cap H)\}.$$

THEOREM 1.   *If C is a switching circuit which is capable of computing f_G in time t, then $t \geq \lceil \log_r 2 \lceil \log_d \alpha(G) \rceil \rceil$, where r is the maximum fan-in of the switching elements comprising C, and $\lceil x \rceil$ denotes the smallest integer $\geq x$.*

The lower bound given in Theorem 1 cannot be much improved when G is abelian, as is shown in the next theorem.

THEOREM 2.   *For every abelian group G, and for every $r \geq 3$, there exists a switching circuit C with maximum fan-in r which is capable of computing f_G in time $t = 2 + \lceil \log_{\lfloor (r+1)/2 \rfloor} 1/(\lfloor r/2 \rfloor) \lceil \log_d \alpha(G) \rceil \rceil$, where $\lfloor x \rfloor = -\lceil -x \rceil$.*

The details of the proof of Theorem 2 (given in [4]) show that even though the results of Theorem 1 allow for three different representations g_1, g_2, and h of the same group G, the result of Theorem 2 can be obtained even if $g_1 = g_2 = h$.

P. Spira [6] showed that for nonabelian groups the results of Theorem 1 do not necessarily give a good lower bound for the time required to compute f_G. He obtained a lower bound for the time which reduces to Theorem 1 in case G is abelian, but may be considerably larger for nonabelian groups.

For each element $g \in G$ ($g \neq e$), we define $\delta(g)$ as the maximal order of a subgroup H of G which does not contain g. For every finite group G, we define $\delta(G) = \min_{g \in G-\{e\}} \delta(g)$. Using this terminology, Spira [6] obtained:

THEOREM 3 (SPIRA). *If C is a switching circuit with maximum fan-in r which is capable of computing f_G in time t, then* $t \geqq \lceil \log_r 2\lceil \log_d |G|/(\delta(G))\rceil\rceil$.

It is easily verified that if G is abelian, then $\alpha(G)\cdot\delta(G) = |G|$, and, therefore, the results of Theorems 1 and 3 coincide.

That the result of Theorem 3 cannot be improved is shown by the next theorem, which is also due to Spira [6].

THEOREM 4. *For every group G, and for every $r \geqq 2$, there exists a switching circuit C with maximum fan-in r which is capable of computing f_G in time* $t = 1+\lceil \log_r \lceil 1/(\lfloor r/2\rfloor)\lceil \log_d |G|/(\delta(G))\rceil\rceil\rceil$.

Examination of the proof of Theorem 4 shows that, unlike Theorem 2, it requires different representation for each of the arguments and for the result; that is, $g_1 \neq g_2 \neq h$.

Specializing the results of Theorem 1 (or Theorem 3), we obtain the following corollaries.

COROLLARY 1. *If C is a switching circuit, with maximum fan-in r, which is capable of adding two integers* mod N *in time t, then* $t \geqq \lceil \log_r 2\lceil \log_d \alpha(N)\rceil\rceil$ *where* $\alpha(N) = \max\{p^i \mid p^i \text{ divides } N\}$.

COROLLARY 2. *If C is a switching circuit, with maximum fan-in r, which is capable of multiplying two integers* mod N *in time t, then*

$$t \geqq \lceil \log_r 2\lceil \log_d \beta(N)\rceil\rceil,$$

where $\beta(N)$ is defined by

(i) $\beta(2) = \beta(4) = 2$, $\quad \beta(2^n) = 2^{n-2}$, $\quad n \geqq 3$,
(ii) $\beta(p) = \alpha(p-1)$, $\quad \beta(p^n) = p^{n-1}$, $\quad p$ *a prime*, $\quad n \geqq 2$,
(iii) $\beta(N_1 \cdot N_2) = \max\{\beta(N_1), \beta(N_2)\}$ *where* $(N_1, N_2) = 1$.

The result of Corollary 1 is obtained immediately by considering $G = Z_N$. The operation of multiplication mod N is not, in general, a group operation. Corollary 2 is obtained by taking for G the group of integers relatively prime to N with multiplication mod N as the group operation.

The importance of the two corollaries lies in the light they shed on the time required to perform two important computer operations—that of addition and multiplication. The operation of (fixed point) addition in a computer is broken into two parts—that of addition mod N (usually $N = 2^n$) and that of determining the overflow, i.e., of computing $\lfloor (x+y)/N \rfloor$. Similarly, the operation of (fixed point) multiplication is broken into two parts—that of multiplication mod N and that of $\lfloor (x\cdot y)/N \rfloor$. Corollaries 1 and 2 consider addition and multiplication mod N. The next two theorems deal with their companion operations. (The proofs of these two theorems are given in [5].)

THEOREM 5. *If C is a switching circuit, with maximum fan-in r, which is capable of computing $\lfloor(x+y)/N\rfloor$ in time t, then*

$$t \geq \lceil\log_r 2\lceil\log_a N\rceil\rceil.$$

THEOREM 6. *If C is a switching circuit, with maximum fan-in r, which is capable of computing $\lfloor(x \cdot y)/N\rfloor$ in time t, then*

$$t \geq \lceil\log_r 2\lceil\log_a \lfloor N^{1/2}\rfloor\rceil\rceil.$$

Comparison of Corollary 1 and Theorem 5 shows that the time required to compute the overflow cannot be less than the time required to compute addition mod N. A detailed examination of the proofs shows that while the prime decomposition of N affects the time required to compute $x+y$ mod N, it is the magnitude of N which is the determining factor in computing $\lfloor(x+y)/N\rfloor$. Similar conclusions can be drawn from a comparison of Corollary 2 and Theorem 6.

Average time. The results discussed so far consider the "worst case" time, that is, the time t by which the switching circuit can finish the computation regardless of what the arguments are. It is every day experience that it is easier to add 0 or two equal numbers than two arbitrary numbers. Similarly, it is easier to multiply by 0 or 1 than by a larger number. This suggests investigating the average time required to compute a function.

DEFINITION 2. Let $f: X_1 \times X_2 \to Y$ be a function. A circuit C is said to be capable of computing f in average time t^a if there exist:

(i) J_1, J_2, g_1, g_2, h, and s_0 as in Definition 1,
(ii) an integer-valued function $t(x_1, x_2)$ satisfying

$$t^a = 1/(|X_1||X_2|)\Sigma_{(x_1, x_2) \in X_1 \times X_2} t(x_1, x_2)$$

such that for every $(x_1, x_2) \in X_1 \times X_2, c((g_1(x_1), g_2(x_2)), s_0, t(x_1, x_2)) = h(f(x_1, x_2))$.

The next theorem shows that the average time required to add two numbers can be much smaller than the "worst case" time.

THEOREM 7. *For every $\epsilon > 0$ and every $r \geq 3$, there exists a 2-valued switching circuit with maximum fan-in r which is capable of computing addition mod 2^n in average time*

$$t_a \leq 2 + \lceil\log_{\lceil(r+1)/2\rceil} Y/\lfloor r/2\rfloor\lceil\log_2 n^{1+\epsilon}\rceil\rceil$$

$$+ \tfrac{1}{2}n^{-\epsilon}(\lceil\log_{\lceil(r+1)/2\rceil} n/(r/2)\rceil - \lceil\log_{\lceil(r+1)/2\rceil} 1/\lfloor r/2\rfloor\lceil\log_2 n^{1+\epsilon}\rceil\rceil).$$

Moreover, the summands as well as the result are represented using base 2 representation.

The result of Theorem 7 shows that the average time for adding two numbers mod 2^n grows no faster than log log n, while Corollary 1 shows that the "worst case" time has to grow as log n.

In order to understand the discrepancy between the average time and the "worst case" time required to add numbers, we should examine Definition 2 more closely. In the case of the "worst case" time, it is known that at time t the output of the circuit represents the sum. In Definition 2 we merely required the existence of time $t(x_1,x_2)$ at which the outputs of the circuit represent the sum; we did not require any mechanism to indicate the time $t(x_1,x_2)$. We will now require that in addition to the condition of Definition 2, the circuit C has an output O_j which has the value 1 only at time $t(x_1,x_2)$.

The next theorem shows that computing this completion signal requires a long time.

THEOREM 8. *Let C be a 2-valued switching circuit of maximum fan-in r which can compute $x + y$ mod 2^n using base 2 representation in average time t^a with completion indicator; then*

$$t^a \geqq \lceil \log_r n^{1/2} \rceil.$$

REFERENCES

1. Ju. Ofman, *On the algorithmic complexity of discrete functions*, Dokl. Akad. Nauk. SSSR **145** (1962), 48–51 = Soviet Physics Dokl. **7** (1963), 589–591. MR **29** # 5686.

2. A. Karatsuba and Ju. Ofman, *Multiplication of multi-digit numbers with computers*, Dokl. Akad. Nauk. SSSR **145** (1962), 293.

3. A. L. Toom, *The complexity of a scheme of functional elements realizing the multiplication of integers*, Dokl. Akad. Nauk. SSSR **150** (1963), 496–498 = Soviet Math. Dokl. **4** (1963), 714–716. MR **27** #6417.

4. S. Winograd, *On the time required to perform addition*, J. Assoc. Comput. Mach. **12** (1965), 277–285.

5. ———, *On the time required to perform multiplication*, J. Assoc. Comput. Mach. **12** (1965), 793–802.

6. P. Spira, *On the computational complexity of finite functions*, Ph.D. Thesis, Stanford University, Stanford, Calif., 1968.

7. S. A. Cook, *On the minimum computation time of functions*, Report #B2-41, The Computer Lab., Harvard University, Cambridge, Mass., 1966.

THOMAS J. WATSON RESEARCH CENTER, YORKTOWN HEIGHTS, NEW YORK

Applications of Computers to the Geometry of Numbers

H. P. F. Swinnerton-Dyer

The simplest and most important of the problems which the Geometry of Numbers deals with are of the following kind. Let D be a given open domain in n-dimensional Euclidean space. Which if any lattices are *admissible* for D — that is, which lattices have no point in common with D except for the origin (if that belongs to D)? In particular, what is the *lattice constant* of D — that is, the lower bound of det Λ for all admissible Λ; and for which Λ if any is this lower bound attained?

Without loss of generality we may assume that D is symmetric about the origin. Nearly all interesting domains D have two further properties:

(i) D contains the origin 0, and hence also a neighborhood of the origin. This implies that there do not exist lattices which are admissible for D and have arbitrarily small lattice vectors; thus with the natural topology on the set of all lattices, the lattices Λ which are admissible for D and have det Λ less than some preassigned bound form a compact set. In particular, the set of values of det Λ for Λ admissible is closed; and if there are any admissible lattices for D then det Λ attains its minimum. Moreover, in looking for lattices Λ admissible for D with det Λ less than some preassigned bound, one need only search through a certain compact set in the space of all lattices.

(ii) D is a star body — that is, if P is any point of D then the entire interval OP lies in D.

D has both these properties if and only if there is a homogeneous function $f(x_1, \ldots, x_n)$ such that D can be written in the form

$$|f(x_1, \ldots, x_n)| < 1.$$

AMS 1970 *subject classifications.* Primary 10-04, 10E05; Secondary 10E25, 10E30, 12A50, 52A30.

For a more detailed account of this background, see for example Cassels [3, Chapter V].

There are some domains D which are of interest because they occur naturally and yet it seems very difficult to find their lattice constants; an obvious example is

$$|x^3 + y^3 + z^3| < 1,$$

for which see Spohn [7]. But there are two types of domain which are interesting both for their own sake and because of possible applications. The first is the n-dimensional ball

(1) $$x_1^2 + x_2^2 + \cdots + x_n^2 < 1.$$

Finding the lattice constant for this is the same as finding the closest lattice packing of n-balls; and, at least for some values of n, the extremal lattices and their automorphism groups are of great interest. (For more details, see Conway's lecture at this Symposium.) For any given value of n, there is a known algorithm which will determine the lattice constant of (1); see for example Barnes [1], where the calculations are carried through by hand for $n = 6$. But it seems very difficult to make this algorithm work on a computer. The lattice constant is known, by other methods, for all $n \leq 8$.

The second type of domain is that given by

(2) $$|x_1 x_2 \cdots x_r (x_{r+1}^2 + x_{r+s+1}^2) \cdots (x_{r+s}^2 + \cdots + x_{r+2s}^2)| < 1$$

whose importance lies in the following theorem:

THEOREM 1. *Let K be an algebraic number field which has r real conjugates and $2s$ complex conjugates. Then any ideal class of K contains an integral ideal whose absolute norm is bounded by $C_{r,s}^{-1}|d|^{1/2}$, where d is the discriminant of K and $C_{r,s}$ is the lattice constant of (2).*

The only known method of finding the class number of a general algebraic number field is based on this theorem, and it is therefore important to find lower bounds for the $C_{r,s}$ which are as large as possible. The first interesting case is when $r = 2$, $s = 0$; and in order to describe what happens it is convenient to rephrase the problem. Let ξ, η be a base for a lattice Λ, so that the general point of Λ is $u\xi + v\eta$ for integers u, v. Then x_1, x_2 are linear forms in u, v, and $x_1 x_2$ is a quadratic form

(3) $$f(u, v) = au^2 + buv + cv^2 = x_1 x_2$$

with discriminant $b^2 - 4ac = (\det \Lambda)^2$, such that

(4) $$|f(u, v)| \geq 1$$

for all integers u, v not both zero. The quadratic forms with not too large discriminant satisfying (4) form a remarkable sequence first investigated by Markoff; for a full account see Cassels [2]. For our present purpose it is enough to state

THEOREM 2.   *There is a sequence $f_1, f_2, \ldots$ of indefinite binary quadratic forms with the following properties*:

(i) *Each f_n has rational coefficients and discriminant $9 - 4N^{-2}$, where N is an integer and $N \to \infty$ with n.*

(ii) *For any n, the minimum value of $|f_n(u, v)|$ for integers u, v not both zero is 1.*

(iii) *If $f(u, v)$ satisfies (3) and is not equivalent to a multiple of any f_n under integral unimodular transformations, then the discriminant of f is at least 9.*

The first few terms of the sequence, in order of increasing discriminant, are

$$u^2 - uv - v^2, \qquad u^2 - 2v^2, \qquad u^2 - \tfrac{11}{5} uv - v^2, \qquad \ldots$$

for which $N = 1, 2, 5, \ldots$. Thus, though in fact the lattice constant of $|x_1 x_2| < 1$ is $5^{1/2}$ we can take $C_{2,0}$ in Theorem 1 as close as we like to 3 at the cost of excepting finitely many fields. In particular, if K is not $Q(2^{1/2})$ or $Q(5^{1/2})$, Theorem 1 holds with $C_{2,0} = \tfrac{1}{5}(221)^{1/2} = 2 \cdot 9732 \ldots$.

In fact Theorem 2 is best proved by means of continued fractions. But it is instructive to see how one would tackle this problem by naive methods with the help of a computer. We look for forms (3) satisfying (4), and we can assume that f is reduced, so that

$$|c| \geqq |a| \geqq |b|, \qquad b^2 - 4ac < 9.$$

Since $ac < 0$ and $|a| \geqq 1$ by (4), we find $|c| \leqq 9/4$; thus the region of search is bounded. The search now proceeds in two steps:

(i) By using (4) for suitably chosen pairs (u, v), we can reject almost all of the region in the (a, b, c)-space as inadmissible.

(ii) We are then left with rather small neighborhoods of known admissible solutions. We cannot, for example, expect the computer to cut down a small neighborhood of the line $a = -b = -c \geqq 1$ to that line itself, if only because one of the reasons why we are left with a neighborhood is the need to allow for round-off error. We therefore need an 'isolation theorem' to tell us that the only admissible points near this line are actually on this line.

Nearly all the effort goes into step (i), so it is important to realize that one cannot expect to bring this work to fruition without a suitable isolation theorem. Indeed, it is almost always wrong to start off on a Geometry of Numbers problem until one has developed the necessary isolation machinery.

Going back to the language of lattices, one can give a general formulation for an isolation theorem. Here D is a domain and Λ_0 a known lattice which is admissible for D.

ISOLATION THEOREM SCHEME.   *Let Λ be a lattice which is in a suitably chosen small neighborhood of Λ_0. Suppose that Λ is admissible for D; then Λ is in a special relationship with Λ_0.*

What the special relationship is must depend on the particular problem. For the domain $|x_1 x_2| < 1$, for example, it would be that Λ can be derived from Λ_0

by a transformation of the form

(5) $$(x_1, x_2) \rightarrow (\alpha_1 x_1, \alpha_2 x_2)$$

for some constants α_1, α_2 close to 1. The transformation (5) is composed from a dilation and an automorphism of D; but this will not always be so. Indeed, some writers have given examples of admissible lattices Λ_0 which they have wrongly claimed are not isolated, because they have used too narrow a definition of 'special relationship'.

Now suppose that D is a star body defined by

$$|f(x_1, \ldots, x_n)| < 1$$

where f is homogeneous, and let Λ_0 be an admissible lattice for D which is such that $\inf |f(P)| = 1$ where the inf is over all points P of Λ_0 other than 0. In other words, if Λ_0 is shrunk it ceases to be admissible. It may be necessary to isolate not merely Λ_0 but also $\lambda \Lambda_0$ for some $\lambda > 1$. This leads one to introduce a 'measure of isolation' defined as the least value of c_0 for which the following statement holds:

Given any $\epsilon > 0$ there is a neighborhood N_ϵ of Λ_0 such that any lattice Λ in N_ϵ either has points other than the origin in $|f| < c_0 + \epsilon$ or is in a special relationship with Λ_0.

Λ_0 is isolated if and only if $c_0 < 1$. We say that Λ_0 is *weakly isolated* if $0 < c_0 < 1$, and *strongly isolated* if $c_0 = 0$; Λ_0 is strongly isolated if and only if $\lambda \Lambda_0$ is isolated for all $\lambda \geq 1$.

It is not hard to prove weak isolation theorems, and indeed even to find the correct value of c_0. Consider for example the domain $|x_1 x_2| < 1$ and write

$$\theta = \tfrac{1}{2}(1 + 5^{1/2}), \qquad -\theta^{-1} = \tfrac{1}{2}(1 - 5^{1/2}),$$

so that the critical lattice Λ_0 has base $(1, 1)$ and $(\theta, -\theta^{-1})$ and for it

$$x_1 = u + \theta v, \qquad x_2 = u - \theta^{-1} v.$$

For any lattice near Λ_0 we shall have

$$|x_1 x_2| = (1 + \epsilon_0)|(L_1 + \epsilon_1 L_2)(L_2 + \epsilon_2 L_1)|$$

where $\epsilon_0, \epsilon_1, \epsilon_2$ are small and $L_1 = u + \theta v$, $L_2 = u - \theta^{-1} v$; and we suppose the 'special relationship' to be defined by $\epsilon_1 = \epsilon_2 = 0$. Suppose therefore $\epsilon_2 \neq 0$ for example, and choose n so that

$$(-1)^n \epsilon_2 > 0, \qquad \theta^{2-2n} \geq |\epsilon_2| > \theta^{-2-2n}$$

which can be done in just one way. For any N we can choose integers u, v such that $L_1 = \theta^N$, $L_2 = (-\theta^{-1})^N$. Do this for $N = n-1, n+1$ and remember that $|x_1 x_2| \geq c_0 + \epsilon$; then we obtain

$$|1 + (-\theta^2)^{n-1} \epsilon_2| \geq c_0 + o(1), \qquad |1 + (-\theta^2)^{n+1} \epsilon_2| \geq c_0 + o(1).$$

After a certain amount of manipulation we obtain $c_0 \leq \tfrac{1}{3} 5^{1/2}$, the critical case being when $(-\theta^2)^n\epsilon_2 = \frac{2}{3}$. To prove that $c_0 = \frac{1}{3}5^{1/2}$ we have therefore to prove that the lattice given by

$$x_1 = u+\theta v, \qquad x_2 = (u-\theta^{-1}v)+\tfrac{2}{3}(u+\theta v) = \tfrac{1}{3}(3-\theta)\{(2+\theta)u+v\}$$

has no points other than the origin satisfying $|x_1x_2| < \frac{1}{3}5^{1/2}$. But at any such point we must have

$$(6) \qquad |u+\theta v| < 1 \qquad \text{or} \qquad |(2+\theta)u+v| < \theta.$$

Assume the first of these; then since

$$x_1x_2 = u^2+uv-v^2+\tfrac{2}{3}(u+\theta v)^2$$

we must have $u^2+uv-v^2 = -1$. But this requires $u+\theta v = \pm\theta^{1-2N}$ for some integer $N > 0$, and in this case

$$|x_1x_2| = 1-\tfrac{2}{3}\theta^{2-4N} \geqq 1-\tfrac{2}{3}\theta^{-2} = \tfrac{1}{3}5^{1/2}.$$

The proof in the second case of (6) is similar.

It is worth noting that the result just obtained is equivalent to saying that the quadratic form $\mu(u^2+uv-v^2)$ is isolated, among forms satisfying (4), if and only if it has discriminant less than 9; and 9 is also the critical discriminant in Theorem 2.

If instead we consider the domain $|x_1x_2x_3| < 1$, the situation changes drastically. The only known way of constructing admissible lattices for this domain is as follows. Let K be a totally real cubic field and let $\alpha_1, \beta_1, \gamma_1$ be a base for K over Q; let $\alpha_2, \beta_2, \gamma_2$ and $\alpha_3, \beta_3, \gamma_3$ be the conjugates of $\alpha_1, \beta_1, \gamma_1$ and write

$$L_i = \alpha_i u + \beta_i v + \gamma_i w.$$

Then $L_1L_2L_3$ is a form in u, v, w with rational coefficients; and it cannot take the value 0 for integers u, v, w not all zero, because none of the L_i can. Hence it is bounded away from zero, and the lattice defined by $x_i = c_iL_i$ is admissible provided only that $|c_1c_2c_3|$ is large enough.

Every such lattice is strongly isolated. The idea of the proof is straightforward; for the tedious details and some more general results see Cassels and Swinnerton-Dyer [**4**]. Suppose for convenience that $c_1 = c_2 = c_3 = 1$ and that $\alpha_1, \beta_1, \gamma_1$ is a base for the integers of K. We have to show that if

$$x_1 = L_1+\epsilon_{12}L_2+\epsilon_{13}L_3$$

and so on, where the ϵ_{ij} are all small and not all zero, then $x_1x_2x_3$ can be made small. The proof divides into twelve cases, according to which of the ϵ_{ij} is largest and what is its sign. Suppose for example that

$$(7) \qquad \epsilon_{12} > 0, \qquad |\epsilon_{12}| = \operatorname{Max}|\epsilon_{ij}|;$$

choose an integer ξ of K such that $\xi_1\xi_2 < 0$ and let η, ζ be a base for the totally positive units of K. Without loss of generality we may assume

$$(8) \qquad \eta_2 > \eta_3 > \eta_1 > 0, \qquad \zeta_2 > \zeta_3 > \zeta_1 > 0$$

because this is merely a matter of suitably choosing the base. Since ϵ_{12} is small, we can choose positive integers m, n such that $-\epsilon_{12}\xi_2\xi_1^{-1}(\eta_2\eta_1^{-1})^m(\zeta_2\zeta_1^{-1})^n$ is close to 1; for this is equivalent to making

$$m \log (\eta_2\eta_1^{-1}) + n \log (\zeta_2\zeta_1^{-1}) + \log (-\epsilon_{12}\xi_2\xi_1^{-1})$$

small, and this is possible by Kronecker's theorem. With these values of m, n choose u, v, w to be the integers such that $\alpha u + \beta v + \gamma w = \xi\eta^m\zeta^n$. In virtue of (7) and (8) each $\epsilon_{ij}L_j$ is small compared to L_i, except that we have just arranged that $\epsilon_{12}L_2$ is almost equal to $-L_1$. Thus

$$|x_1x_2x_3| = o(L_1)o(L_2)o(L_3) = o(\xi_1\xi_2\xi_3) = o(1)$$

which is just the result we need.

It is natural to ask whether there is any analogue to Theorem 2 for this domain. Thirty years ago Davenport [5] showed that the lattice constant of this domain is 7 and the second minimum is 9 — these corresponding to the cubic fields of discriminant 49 and 81 respectively. I have recently programmed Davenport's method for a computer, and have thereby found all the admissible lattices with determinant less than 17. There are nineteen essentially in-equivalent lattices with these properties; they do not appear to form a sensible sequence, and the details of the calculation suggest very strongly that there is no finite limit to the sequence of critical determinants analogous to that of Theorem 2. For a full account see [8]. The same method will in principle extend to the product of n linear forms for any n, though the computations become much longer and there is one additional problem in the programming. The case $n = 4$ is being worked on, and the case $n = 5$ should be practicable also.

The cases of (2) with $s > 0$ are also of considerable interest, though more complicated to attack because of the structure of the isolation theorem. Apart from the trivial case $r = 0$, $s = 1$, all that is known is the theorem of Davenport and Rogers [6] that for

$$(9) \qquad\qquad |x_1(x_2^2 + x_3^2)| < 1$$

the lattice constant is $23^{1/2}$, corresponding to the cubic field of discriminant -23. They conjectured that the second minimum is $31^{1/2}$; but the problem has not recently been attacked, though it is known that the critical lattice is isolated. Let $\theta_1 = 1 \cdot 325$ be the real and θ_2, θ_3 the two complex roots of $\theta^3 - \theta - 1 = 0$, and write

$$L_j = u + \theta_j v + \theta_j^2 w \quad (j = 1, 2, 3).$$

Let Λ_0 be the critical lattice of (9), defined by

$$x_1 = L_1, \quad x_2 + ix_3 = L_2,$$

and let Λ be any lattice near to Λ_0. We can take Λ to be defined by

$$x_1 = (1 + \epsilon_1)(L_1 + \epsilon_{12}L_2 + \bar\epsilon_{12}L_3),$$
$$x_2 + ix_3 = (1 + \epsilon_2)(L_2 + \epsilon_3L_3 + \epsilon_{21}L_1),$$

where ϵ_1 is real and $\epsilon_{12}, \epsilon_2, \epsilon_3, \epsilon_{21}$ are complex. We shall say that Λ is in a special relation to Λ_0 if $\epsilon_{12} = \epsilon_{21} = 0$, and shall prove that Λ_0 is isolated in this sense.

Suppose first that $\epsilon_{12} \neq 0$, and choose n so that

$$1 \geq |2\epsilon_{12}(\theta_1\theta_2^{-1})^n| > |\theta_2\theta_1^{-1}|.$$

For one of $N = n, n-1, n-2$ we also have

$$-\tfrac{9}{20}\pi < \arg\,(-\epsilon_{12}\theta_1^N\theta_2^{-N}) < \tfrac{9}{20}\pi.$$

For this value of N define integers u, v, w by

$$u + \theta v + \theta^2 w = \theta^{-N};$$

then we certainly have $x_2^2 + x_3^2 = (\theta_2\theta_3)^{-N}(1 + o(1))$ and because of cancellation

$$|L_1 + \epsilon_{12}L_2 + \epsilon_{12}L_3| < \theta_1^{-N}\{1 - |\theta_2\theta_1^{-1}|^3 \cos\tfrac{9}{20}\pi\};$$

this is enough to prove isolation in this case.

Similarly if $\epsilon_{21} \neq 0$ we can choose $u + \theta v + \theta^2 w = \theta^M$, where M is so chosen that $\epsilon_{21}L_1$ is comparable with L_2 and works against it. These two calculations together prove that Λ_0 is isolated. If one carries out the argument in full detail, it turns out that the constant of isolation is $c_0 = 1 - 2(\theta_1 - 1)^2 = 0 \cdot 789$.

The most useful way to phrase the special relation $\epsilon_{12} = \epsilon_{21} = 0$ between Λ_0 and any admissible lattice Λ near Λ_0 is to consider u, v, w as new coordinates. Now the condition $\epsilon_{12} = \epsilon_{21} = 0$ says precisely that the plane $x_1 = 0$ and the line $x_2 = x_3 = 0$ are the same for Λ_0 and for Λ. Thus if one is to find the second minimum (or even better the complete sequence analogous to Theorem 2), one needs a partial description of the lattice Λ which only identifies its relationship with the plane $x_1 = 0$ and the line $x_2 = x_3 = 0$, and not its relationship with the entire co-ordinate system given by the x_j.

The natural way to get such a description is by considering the quadratic form

(10) $$\lambda^2 x_1^2 + \lambda^{-1}(x_2^2 + x_3^2)$$

as λ varies from 0 to $+\infty$. For each value of λ, there is a unimodular integral transformation on u, v, w which makes (10) a reduced quadratic form; and the sequence of such transformations as λ varies is precisely the partial description that we need. Of course one has to pay a price for the incompleteness of the description; and the price is that one has no formula for the value of $x_1(x_2^2 + x_3^2)$.

REFERENCES

1. E. S. Barnes, *The complete enumeration of extreme senary forms*, Philos. Trans. Roy. Soc. London Ser. A **249** (1957), 461–506. MR **19**, 251.

2. J. W. S. Cassels, *An introduction to Diophantine approximation*, Cambridge Tracts in Math. and Math. Phys., no. 45, Cambridge Univ. Press, New York, 1957. MR **19**, 396.

3. _____, *An introduction to the geometry of numbers*, Die Grundlehren der math. Wissenschaften, Band 99, Springer-Verlag, Berlin, 1959. MR **28** #1175.

4. J. W. S. Cassels and H. P. F. Swinnerton-Dyer, *On the product of three homogeneous linear forms and indefinite ternary quadratic forms*, Philos. Trans. Roy. Soc. London Ser. A **248** (1955), 73–96. MR **17**, 14.

5. H. Davenport, *On the product of three homogeneous linear forms.* IV, Proc. Cambridge Philos. Soc. **39** (1943), 1–21. MR **4**, 212.

6. H. Davenport and C. A. Rogers, *Diophantine inequalities with an infinity of solutions*, Philos. Trans. Roy. Soc. London Ser. A **242** (1950), 311–344. MR **12**, 394.

7. W. G. Spohn, *On the lattice constant for $|x^3 + y^3 + z^3| \leq 1$*, Math. Comp. **23** (1969), 141–149. MR **39** #2706.

8. H. P. F. Swinnerton-Dyer, *On the product of three homogeneous linear forms*, Acta Arith. (to appear).

TRINITY COLLEGE, CAMBRIDGE, ENGLAND

Approximation to Cubic Irrationals

B. J. Birch

Suppose that α is an irrational number of degree n, so that it satisfies an equation $f(\alpha, 1) = 0$, where $f(x, y)$ is an irreducible form with integer coefficients. Then

(1) $$|f(p, q)| \geq 1 \quad \text{for all integers } (p, q) \neq (0, 0)$$

and this leads immediately to Liouville's theorem, that there is a calculable constant A such that

(2) $$|q\alpha - p| > Aq^{1-n} \quad \text{for all integers } p \cdot q \text{ with } q \neq 0.$$

The first real improvement on Liouville's theorem was obtained by Thué [10] who proved essentially (see [5]) that for every $\epsilon > 0$ there is a $q_0(\epsilon)$ such that $|q\alpha - p| < q^{-n/2 - \epsilon}$ has at most one solution with $q > q_0(\epsilon)$; Thué's theorem was successively improved by various authors until Roth [8] obtained the result with the best possible exponent of q, that $|q\alpha - p| < q^{-1-\epsilon}$ has only finitely many solutions. Unfortunately, Thué's theorem and its successors are ineffective: though one knows that an inequality has only finitely many solutions, one has no information about where they are; so, going back a step in the argument, the theorems of Thué and Roth imply that $|f(p, q)|$ tends to infinity with $|p| + |q|$, but cannot tell one how fast.

Now, there is an effective method. Baker [3] has given an effective method of solving Diophantine equations 'of Thué type', that is, of shape $f(x, y) = m$; Baker's bounds at first appeared stupendously large, but in [4] it was shown that the method was genuinely (as opposed to theoretically!) effective. Very recently, Ellison and collaborators have written an efficient, rapid, and fairly general program, implementing Baker's method for solving equations of Thué type and also of type $y^2 = x^3 + ax + b$. Baker's effective improvement of (1)

AMS 1970 subject classifications. Primary 10F25.

B. J. BIRCH

leads immediately to an effective improvement of (2), essentially $|q\alpha - p| > Aq^{1-n} \exp((\log q)^{1/(n+1)})$, with calculable A.

Unfortunately, this improvement is a tiny one; in this lecture, I want to look at a less sophisticated method that may give better results if only in particular cases. One harks back to Siegel's memoir [9]. Among many other things, he states the principle that if α has a rather thick sequence of rational approximations, then it has no excessively good approximations; it is easy enough to prove this precisely (see [1]):

If $\{p_n/q_n\}$, $n = 1, 2, \ldots$, is an infinite sequence of rational numbers tending to α, in lowest terms so that p_n, q_n are integers with $q_n > 0$ and $(p_n, q_n) = 1$, and if there are fixed real numbers s, t, $0 < s$, $t < 1$, so that $|q_n\alpha - p_n| < \frac{1}{2}q_n^{-s}$, $q_n^t < q_{n-1} < q_n$, then $|Q\alpha - P| > \frac{1}{2}Q^{-1/st}$ whenever P, Q are integers with $Q > q_1^{st}$.

Suppose now that $\alpha = f(x)$, where f is a power series with rational coefficients and $f(0) = 1$, and where x is a rational number with small numerator and large denominator, so that $f(x)$ converges. Then one may find a sequence of pairs of monic polynomials $p_N(x)$, $q_N(x)$ so that $p_N(x) - q_N(x)f(x)$ has no terms of degree $\leq N$, and if N is even p_N, q_N both have degree $\frac{1}{2}N$, while if N is odd p_N has degree $\frac{1}{2}(N+1)$ and q_N has degree $\frac{1}{2}(N-1)$. In general (we avoid power series f for which it is false!) the polynomials p_N, q_N are determined uniquely and have rational coefficients. Write Γ_N for the l.c.m. of the denominators of the coefficients of p_N, q_N and write $P_N = \Gamma_N p_N$, $Q_N = \Gamma_N q_N$. Suppose that $x = u/v$ where u, v are coprime integers with $v > 0$. Then

$$|\alpha - (v^N P_{2N}(x)/v^N Q_{2N}(x))| = O(x^{2N+1}),$$

so we have an infinite sequence of rational approximations to α with error $O(x^{2N+1})$ and denominator $v^N Q_{2N}(x)$. This sequence of approximations will be nontrivial for small enough x if $\log(\Gamma_N)$ is $O(N)$ as $N \to \infty$; and, if we can show this, we will be able to deduce a nontrivial result of the type $|Q - P| > \phi(Q)$ for all integers P, Q with $Q > 0$.

The particular case $f(x) = (1 + x)^{1/R}$ is particularly favourable. The polynomials $p_N(x)$, $q_N(x)$ may be written down as hypergeometric polynomials, explicitly

(3) $$A_N(x) - (1 - x)^{1/R} B_N(x) = x^{2N+1} A_N(1) E_N(x)$$

with

$$A_N(x) = F(-N - 1/R, -N, -2N; x),$$
$$B_N(x) = F(-N + 1/R, R, -N, -2N; x)$$

and

$$E_N(x) = F(N + 1 - 1/R, N + 1, 2N + 2; x)/F(N + 1 - 1/R, 1 + 1/R, 2N + 2; 1);$$

one may prove this by noting that all three terms satisfy the same 2nd order differential equation. Everything is wholly explicit; Γ_N may be calculated; and one may obtain a fairly strong result.

Following Thué, Siegel used this method to show that $|Ax^n - By^n| = 1$ has only one solution, subject to conditions on A, B. The theorem about approximations to $(A/B)^{1/n}$ was proved in a very precise form by Baker [1], [2]. One of the nicest results obtained by Baker by the method I have just been sketching was

$$|2^{1/3} - (p/q)| > C/q^{2.955};$$

to obtain anything as good as this, one has to be very careful indeed over the details of the estimations. Churchhouse recently remarked that in well-chosen cases the earlier "hypergeometric" approximations are actually very good indeed, in the sense that they correspond to very large partial quotients in the continued fraction for $(A/B)^{1/n}$.

Can one apply the method in other cases? One has got a good method of approximating to the roots of the binomial equation $y^n = 1 + x$. The natural case to look at next is trinomial equations; in particular, Nelson Stephens and I have recently been looking at the equation

$$y^3 = y^2 + x.$$

The power series solution of this equation (due to Lagrange [7]) is

$$y = f(x) = 1 + \sum_{n=1}^{\infty} c_n x^n$$

with $c_n = (-1)^{n+1} (3n-2)!/(2n-1)! \, n!$ for $n \geq 1$.

In order to obtain rational function approximations to $f(x)$, it is sensible to work out the continued function; we found

$$f(x) = 1 + \frac{\lambda_0 x}{1} + \frac{\lambda_1 x}{1} + \frac{\lambda_2 x}{1} + \cdots$$

with

(4) $$\lambda_{2N} = \frac{3(6N+1)(3N+2)}{2(4N+3)(4N+1)}, \qquad \lambda_{2N+1} = \frac{3(6N+5)(3N+4)}{2(4N+5)(4N+3)}.$$

Indeed, this is a Gauss continued fraction [6], which standard methods lead us to evaluate as

$$F\left(\frac{1}{6}, -\frac{1}{6}; \frac{1}{2}; -\frac{27}{4}x\right) \Big/ F\left(\frac{1}{6}, \frac{5}{6}; \frac{3}{2}; -\frac{27}{4}x\right);$$

and it is easy to check that this quantity satisfies $y^3 = y^2 + x$.

We obtain a sequence of approximations $p_N(x)/q_N(x)$ to $f(x)$ by $p_0/q_0 = 1/1$, $p_1(x)/q_1(x) = (1+x)/1$, and

(5) $$p_N = p_{N-1} + \lambda_{N-1} x p_{N-2}, \qquad q_N = q_{N-1} + \lambda_{N-1} x q_{N-2} \quad \text{for } N \geq 2.$$

As usual, Γ_N is the l.c.m. of the denominators of the coefficients of p_N and q_N, and we take $P_N = \Gamma_N p_N$, $Q_N = \Gamma_N q_N$. The sequence of approximations $v^N P_{2N}(x)/v^N Q_{2N}(x)$ to y will be useful for small enough rational $x = u/v$ if we can show that $\log \Gamma_N = O(N)$.

Now it is clear from (4) and (5) that

$$\Phi_N = \text{denominator}\left(\prod_1^N \lambda_M\right) \leq \Gamma_{N+1} \leq \prod_1^N \text{denominator }(\lambda_M).$$

The right-hand side increases about as $(2N)!$; on the other hand,

$$\prod_1^{2N} \lambda_M = \frac{(6N+4)!\,(2N+2)!}{(4N+4)!\,(4N+2)!} = \binom{6N+4}{4N+4}\binom{4N+2}{2N+2}^{-1},$$

so Φ_{2N} is bounded by the binomial coefficient $(4N+2\,|\,2N+2) \leq 2^{4N+2}$. One might expect Γ_N to be near the upper bound, dooming the method to failure. However, calculation suggests that Γ_N is nearly the same as Φ_N—for $N \leq 70$, Γ_N/Φ_N never exceeds 30, whereas $\Phi_{70} > 10^{18}$. So it seems to be true that $N^{-1} \log \Gamma_N < 4 \log 2$; unfortunately, we have been unable to prove this. The ratio Γ_N/Φ_N, though small, seems erratic, so it is difficult to guess an explicit formula like (3) which one might then be able to prove.

One may approach the problem by attempting to decide which prime powers p^r divide Γ_N; for fixed p^r, this is doable, and indeed I have accounted for all of our computations on these lines. It is easy to see that if p is a prime with $p^2 > 2N+3$, then $p^2 \nmid \Gamma_N$, and one can predict when p divides Γ_N. If $p^2 \leq 2N+3$, the situation gets more complicated; I *conjecture* that

(6) p^r divides Γ_N only if $p^r \leq 2N+3$.

I have proved (6) for $p^{r-1} < 50$, which is almost as far as we have computational evidence, but I have not proved it in general. As Stephens remarked, (6) would imply $N^{-1} \log \Gamma_N = O(1)$, and so would give an approximation theorem.

NOTE ADDED IN PROOF. Since this lecture was given, I have found a paper by D. K. Faddeev, *On a theorem of Baker*, Sem. Math. V. A. Steklov Inst., Leningrad; translated as Seminars in Math., Vol. 7: Studies in Number Theory, edited by A. V. Malyshev. This seems to imply much of what we were looking for.

REFERENCES

1. A. Baker, *Rational approximations to certain algebraic numbers*, Proc. London Math. Soc. (3) 14 (1964), 385–398. MR 28 #5029.

2. _____, *Rational approximations to $\sqrt[3]{2}$ and other algebraic numbers*, Quart. J. Math. Oxford Ser. (2) 15 (1964), 375–383. MR 30 #1977.

3. _____, *Linear forms in the logarithms of algebraic numbers. IV*, Mathematika 15 (1968), 204–216 (and references therein).

4. A. Baker and H. Davenport, *The equations $3x^2 - 2 = y^2$ and $8x^2 - 7 = z^2$*, Quart. J. Math. Oxford Ser. (2) 20 (1969), 129–137. MR 40 #1333.

5. H. Davenport, *A note on Thué's Theorem*, Mathematika 15 (1968), 76–87. MR 37 #6249.

6. C. F. Gauss, *Disquisitiones generales circa seriem infinitam*, Comm. Soc. Reg. Sci. Göttingen Recentiores II (1813); Werke, Vol. 3.

7. Le Comte J.-L. Lagrange, *Méthode pour résoudre les équations littérales par le moyen des séries*, Mém. Acad. Roy. Sci. Belles-Lettres Berlin 24 (1770); Oeuvres. Tome III.

8. K. F. Roth, *Rational approximations to algebraic numbers*, Mathematika 2 (1955), 1–20; corrigendum, 168. MR 17, 242.

9. C. L. Siegel, *Über einige Anwendungen diophantischer Approximationen*, Abh. Preuss. Akad. Wiss. Phys.-Math. Kl. **1929**, no. 1.

10. A. Thué, *Über Annäherungswerte algebraischer Zahlen*, J. Reine Angew. Math. **135** (1909), 284–305.

Mathematical Institute, Oxford, England

On the Group of an Equation

Hans Zassenhaus

To solve completely a monic algebraic equation

(1) $$f(\xi) = 0, \qquad f(x) = x^n + \alpha_1 x^{n-1} + \cdots + \alpha_n,$$

α_i contained in the ground field F, means to find all its roots.

Let us consider the following interpretations of the task involved:

I. To decide whether there is an element ξ of the field of reference solving (1); if "yes," to exhibit it by means of a construction based on the knowledge of $\alpha_1, \ldots, \alpha_n$ and of the computational rules of F;

II. To construct a field extension of F in which the full factorization

(2) $$f(x) = \prod_{i=1}^{r} (x - \xi_i)^{\nu_i} \qquad (\zeta_1, \ldots, \zeta_r \text{ distinct}, \nu_1 > 0, \ldots, \nu_r > 0)$$

takes place.

Throughout the nineteenth century, the intermediate position:

III. "the coefficients of f are complex numbers; due to the fundamental theorem of algebra, a solution exists and can be computed with any desired degree of accuracy" was taken by the majority of mathematicians who were concerned about solving algebraic equations.

Today we shall test these positions in regard to the deeper problem of finding the group of the equation (1). This is the group $G = G(f, F)$ of all permutations of the ξ_i's that preserve all algebraic equations between $\xi_1, \ldots, \xi_r$ and the elements of F.

Van der Waerden [8] and Fröhlich and Shepherdson [5], [4] have shown that the mere assumption that F is constructive does not suffice to compute G.

I have shown in [10] that if F is constructive then the solution of I implies the knowledge of $G(f, F)$ and thereby also II.

AMS 1969 subject classifications. Primary 6550.

69

On the basis of III the problem at hand becomes solvable if F is an algebraic number field.

Some time ago I gave a method solving the same problem under the less restrictive assumption that F is constructively algebraically ordered or that F is defined in the form $F = F_0(\alpha)$, where F_0 is constructively ordered and α satisfies a given irreducible equation with coefficients in F_0 [8], [9].

Finally I should like to work out an efficient procedure for finding the group of an equation over the rational number field.

In [9], [10] I pointed out that the commutative unital associative F-algebra $A = F[f; \xi_1, \ldots, \xi_n]$ with the defining relation

(3) $$f(x) = \prod_{i=1}^{n} (x - \xi_i)$$

can be explicitly constructed and that the group $\mathfrak{S}_n^A$ of all automorphisms of A over F that permute the ξ_i's is isomorphic to $\mathfrak{S}_n$, so that only the elements of F are fixed by $\mathfrak{S}_n^A$.

Assuming from now on that the polynomial $f(x)$ is separable, i.e. that

$$\mathrm{GCD}\,(f(x), (d/dx)f(x)) = 1$$

it follows that A is a Galois algebra over F.

The method of [10] is as follows: Any homomorphic image B of A is a Galois algebra over F for some subgroup S of $\mathfrak{S}_n^A$. Supposing we have arrived at a constructive presentation of B already, and that we want to test whether there could be an epimorphic image C of B available which is a Galois algebra over F for some maximal subgroup s of S, then we apply the linear mapping

$$\mathrm{tr}_s : B \to B, \quad where\ \mathrm{tr}_s(b) = \sum_{\sigma \in s} \sigma(b) \qquad (b \in B)$$

to an element b of B for which $\mathrm{tr}_s(b)$ does not belong to F, form the minimal polynomial of $\mathrm{tr}_s(b)$ over F and test whether it has a root in F. If there is none, then the test is negative. If there is one, say β, then the ideal $(\mathrm{tr}_s(b) - \beta)B$ of B is proper $\neq 0$. Its factor algebra

$$C = B/(\mathrm{tr}_s(b) - \beta)B$$

turns out to be a Galois algebra for s.

Since there are only finitely many subgroups of $\mathfrak{S}_n^F$ to be tested it follows that after a finite number of steps we shall arrive at an explicit construction of the minimal splitting field of f over F so that its group of automorphisms over F will be known explicitly as a permutation group of the roots of f.

From the logical viewpoint this method is satisfactory. After all if we can find constructively the group of an equation and its minimal splitting field surely it is possible to decide whether f has a root in f and, if the answer is "yes," to find one. But the method is impractical. E.g., in order to solve an equation of the tenth degree we would have to manipulate algebras with 10! basis elements. That is too much even for the most advanced computers.

Reacting to this experience we fall back on interpreting III, say, as follows: It suffices to assume that F is the rational number field. Denoting by N the common denominator of $\alpha_1, \alpha_2, \ldots, \alpha_n$, after substitution of $x = y/N$ in x we obtain the equation $N^n f(x) = g(y)$, where $g(y)$ is a monic polynomial in y with rational integral coefficients. Without loss of generality it suffices to assume that $\alpha_1, \alpha_2, \ldots, \alpha_n$ are in $Z[x]$.

We look at $\xi_1, \ldots, \xi_n$ as complex numbers that are approximated with a certain degree of accuracy. In order to test the assumption that a certain subgroup G of $\mathfrak{S}_n^A$ contains $G(f, \mathcal{Q})$, we form a chain of subgroups

$$G = G_0 \supset G_1 \supset G_2 \supset \cdots \supset G_s = 1$$

such that (possibly after renumbering the ξ_i's) G_i consists of all permutations in G that fix $\xi_1, \ldots, \xi_i$.

We form the rational integer $a(\nu(1), \ldots, \nu(s))$ that is nearest to the G-trace

(4) $$\operatorname{tr}_G(\xi_1^{\nu(1)} \xi_2^{\nu(2)} \cdots \xi_s^{\nu(s)}) = \sum_{\pi \in G} \xi_{\pi(1)}^{\nu(1)} \xi_{\pi(2)}^{\nu(2)} \cdots \xi_{\pi(s)}^{\nu(s)}$$

for all cases in which

$$0 \leq \nu(i) < G_{i-1} : G_i \qquad (1 \leq i \leq s).$$

In order to execute this task it is helpful to remark that among the ξ_j's for each ξ_j also its complex conjugate ξ_j^* occurs so that we can approximate ξ_j^* by $\alpha_j - i\beta_j$ if ξ_j is approximated by $\alpha_j + i\beta_j$ (α_j, β_j real). This implies that the approximation of (4) is real. Furthermore, if our assumption was true it must be possible to approximate the ξ's well enough so as to approximate each of the numbers (4) by a rational integer $a(\nu(1), \ldots, \nu(s))$ with an error of less than a certain positive number ϵ. The number ϵ is determined so that the equation

(5) $$0 = \prod_{\tau} \left(a(\nu(1), \ldots, \nu(s)) - \sum_{\pi \in G} \xi_{\tau\pi(1)}^{\nu(1)} \cdots \xi_{\tau\pi(1)}^{\nu(s)} \right)$$

holds where τ runs through a representative set of the right cosets of $\mathfrak{S}_n^A$ modulo G including 1_G:

$$\mathfrak{S}_n^A = \bigcup_{\tau} \tau G.$$

We don't have to test (5); actually, we only have to make sure that ϵ is less than the reciprocal of the products of the upper bounds for the absolute values of the factors on the right-hand side with $\tau \neq 1_G$. This is because we know from the theorem on symmetric functions that the right-hand side of (4) is a rational integer. It must be zero if its absolute value is less than 1.

The test is conclusive in every case; it enables us after a finite number of applications to find the group of the equation.

If $G = G(f, F)$ then the elements $\xi_1^{\nu(1)} \cdots \xi_s^{\nu(s)}$ occurring above form a $\mathcal{Q}$-basis of the minimal splitting field $E = \mathcal{Q}(\xi_1, \ldots, \xi_s)$ and we have the trace equations

$$\operatorname{tr}_{E/\mathcal{Q}}(\xi_1^{\nu(1)} \cdots \xi_s^{\nu(s)}) = a(\nu_{(1)}, \ldots, \nu_{(s)}) \qquad (0 \leq \nu(i) < G_{i-1} : G_i; \quad 1 \leq i \leq s).$$

In order to know the structure of E completely we need a method of exhibiting any polynomial $P(\xi, \ldots, \xi_s)$ in $\xi_1, \ldots, \xi_s$ with rational coefficients as a linear combination of the $\mathscr{Q}$-basis of E given above. It suffices to do this for the special expressions $\xi_i^{G_{i-1}:G_i}$, since the rest can be done by means of recursively lowering the degrees in $\xi_s, \xi_{s-1}, \ldots, \xi_1$ in P. We know that there hold equations of the form

$$
(6) \qquad \xi_i^{G_{i-1}:G_i} = \sum_{0 \le j(k) < G_{k-1}:G_k; 1 \le k \le i} \alpha(j(1), \ldots, j(i), i)\, \xi_1^{j(1)} \cdots \xi_i^{j(i)}
$$

with unknown rational coefficients $\alpha(j(1), \ldots, j(i), i)$.

We have equations of the form

$$
(7) \qquad \mathrm{tr}_{E/\mathscr{Q}}(\xi_1^{j(1)} \cdots \xi_i^{j(i)}, \xi_1^{\nu(1)} \cdots \xi_i^{\nu(i)}) = \lambda(j(1), \ldots, j(i); \nu(1), \ldots, \nu(i))
$$

$$
(1 \le i \le s),
$$

with rational integers on the right-hand side that are obtained by means of sufficiently accurate approximations of the left-hand side. The theory tells us that the symmetric trace matrices of degree $G:G_i$ formed by the right-hand side of (7) are nonsingular.

Using the same method, we form the rational integers

$$
(8) \qquad \mathrm{tr}_{E/\mathscr{Q}}(\xi_i^{G_{i-1}:G_i}\, \xi_1^{\nu(1)} \cdots \xi_i^{\nu(i)}).
$$

Upon substitution of (6) and (7) we obtain linear equations with integral coefficients for the unknowns $\alpha(j(1), \ldots, j(i), i)$ which have precisely one solution.

In the same manner we also express the roots ξ_k for which $s < k \le n$ as $\mathscr{Q}$-linear combinations of the $\mathscr{Q}$-basis of E given above.

This method is certainly less time consuming than the first method but of far more limited application. Also it may force us to test for many different groups. To reduce the number of groups to be tested, van der Waerden suggested factorizing the polynomial $f(x)$ modulo many prime numbers, say for $p_1 = 2 < p_2 = 3 < p_5 < \cdots < p_N$ so that

$$
f(x) \equiv \prod_{k=1}^{\nu_i} f_{ik}(x) \pmod{p_i} \qquad (1 \le i \le N)
$$

into the product of ν_i mutually prime primary polynomials. For all prime numbers except the divisors of the discriminant $d(f)$ of f the polynomials f_{ik} will be irreducible modulo p_i. If that happens then we conclude that $G(f, \mathscr{Q})$ contains a permutation with a decomposition into commuting cycles of length $[f_{ik}]$ $(k = 1, 2, \ldots, r_i)$ (permutation of type $[f_{i1}] + [f_{i2}] + \cdots + [f_{ik}]$).

Doing this for sufficiently many prime numbers gives us a good idea which permutation types occur in $G(f, \mathscr{Q})$ (see Čebotarev [2]). Actually even the frequency with which each permutation type occurs converges to the ratio of the number of times of its occurrence in $G(f, \mathscr{Q})$ divided by the order of $G(f, \mathscr{Q})$. The estimates implied by Čebotarev are not well worked out yet. However, in practice, up to and including $n = 8$ (see [1], [2], [4], [5]) in most cases the mere collection of permutation types as it emerges from sampling up to N (N large enough) already tells us what the group is, guesswise at least. See also Miller [6], Coxeter and Moser [3]. However, in the case of the regular permutation representations of the quaternion groups Q_8, the dihedral group D_4 and the abelian group $C_2 \times C_4$ of exponent 4 and order 8, the permutation types to be considered are:

> identity permutation, product of four transpositions of disjoint pairs of letters, product of two four-cycles of disjoint quadruples of letters.

Their expectation values are:

Q_8	D_4	$C_2 \times C_4$
$\frac{1}{8}$	$\frac{1}{8}$	$\frac{1}{8}$
$\frac{1}{8}$	$\frac{5}{8}$	$\frac{3}{8}$
$\frac{3}{4}$	$\frac{1}{4}$	$\frac{1}{2}$

which suggests that quite small values of N already may be enough to make an educated guess concerning $G(f, \mathcal{Q})$.

In order to apply the Čebotarev-van der Waerden sampling method of guessing the group of an equation over $\mathcal{Q}^1$ one needs a table of permutation groups of the desired degree. Preferably it should be tabulated according to degree, transitivity behavior, group order, distribution. E.g., up to $n = 5$ we obtain the following

TABLE 1. Permutation groups of less than 6 letters.

Nr	n	Orbits	Type	$\lvert G \rvert$	Description	Distribution
1	1	1	r	1	$\mathfrak{S}_1 = \mathfrak{A}_1 e$	1
2	2	2	$2t, r$	2	$\mathfrak{S}_2$	$1+2$
3		2.1	int	1	$\mathfrak{A}_2 e$	1
4	3	3	$m3t$	6	$\mathfrak{S}_3$	$\mathfrak{A}_3 + 3 \times 2$
5		3	r	3	$\mathfrak{A}_3 e$	$\underline{1} + 2 \times 3$
6		$1+2$	int	2	$\mathfrak{S}_2$	$\underline{1} + 2$
7		3.1	int	1	$\mathfrak{S}_1 e$	$\underline{1}$
8	4	4	$m4t$	24	$\mathfrak{S}_4$	$\mathfrak{A}_4 + 6 \times 2 + 6 \times 4$
9		4	$m2t$	12	$\mathfrak{A}_4 e$	$\mathfrak{R} + 8 \times 3$
10		4	imp	8	Imp	$\mathfrak{R} + 2 \times 2 + 2 \times 4$
11		4	r	4	$\mathfrak{R} = \text{Imp } e$	$\underline{1} + 3 \times 2.2$
12		4	r	4	$\langle(1234)\rangle$	$\underline{1} + 2.2 + 2 \times 4$
13		$1+3$	int	6	$\mathfrak{S}_3$	$\mathfrak{A}_3 + 3 \times 2$
14		$1+3$	int	3	$\mathfrak{A}_3 \, e$	$\underline{1} + 2 \times 3$
15		$2.1+2$	int	2	$\mathfrak{S}_2$	$\underline{1} + 2$
16		4.1	int	1	$\mathfrak{S}_1 \, e$	$\underline{1}$
17		2.2	int	4	Int (2.2)	$\underline{1} + 2 \times 2 + 2.2$
18		2.2	int	2	Int (2.2) e	$\underline{1} + 2.2$

[1] Or, more generally, over a global field.

TABLE 1 (contd).

Nr	n	Orbits	Type	$\|G\|$	Description	Distribution
19	5	5	$m5t$	120	$\mathfrak{S}_5$	$\mathfrak{A}_5 + 10 \times 2 + 20 \times (2t3) + 30 \times 4$
20		5	$1\frac{1}{2}t$	10	$N_5 e$	$S_5 + 5 \times 2.2$
21		5	$m2t$	20	N_5	$N_5 e + 10 \times 4$
22		5	r	5	$S_5 \, e$	$\underline{1} + 4 \times 5$
23		$1 + 4$	int	24	$\mathfrak{S}_4$	$\mathfrak{A}_4 + 6 \times 2 + 6 \times 4$
24		$1 + 4$	int	12	$\mathfrak{A}_4 \, e$	$\mathfrak{K} + 8 \times 3$
25		$1 + 4$	int	8	Imp $(\frac{4}{2})$	$\mathfrak{S} + 2 \times 2 + 2 \times 4$
26		$1 + 4$	int	4	$\mathfrak{K} \, e$	$1 + 3 \times 2.2$
27		$1 + 4$	int	4	$\langle (1234) \rangle$	$1 + 2.2 + 2 \times 4$
28		$2.1 + 3$	int	6	$\mathfrak{S}_3$	$\mathfrak{A}_3 + 3 \times 2$
29		$2.1 + 3$	int	3	$\mathfrak{A}_3 \, e$	$\underline{1} + 2 \times 3$
30		$3.1 + 2$	int	2	$\mathfrak{S}_2$	$\underline{1} + 2$
31		5.1	int	1	$\mathfrak{S}_1 \, e$	$\underline{1}$
32		$1 + 2.2$	int	4	Int (2.2)	$\underline{1} + 2 \times 2 + 2.2$
33		$1 + 2.2$	int	2	Int (2.2) e	$\underline{1} + 2.2$
34		$2 + 3$	int	12	Int $(2 + 3)$	$\underline{\text{Int}} (2+3) \, e + 4 \times 2 + 2 \times (2+3)$
35		$2 + 3$	int	6	Int $(2+3) \, e$	$1 + 2 \times 3 + 3 \times 2.2$
36		$2 + 3$	int	6	$\mathfrak{S}_2 \times \mathfrak{A}_3$	$\mathfrak{A}_3 + 2 + 2 \times (2+3)$

Explanation of symbols used in Table 1:

r The group is a regular permutation group; it is primitive if and only if the order of G is a prime number.

p The group is transitive and primitive; and there are nonidentity permutations fixing two letters.

imp   The group is transitive and imprimitive; if no additional remark is made then there is only one system of imprimitivity of type $n = p \cdot p$ (p a prime number).

$\text{imp} \left(\dfrac{n}{d_1}, \dfrac{n}{d_s}, \ldots, \dfrac{n_n}{d_r} \right)$ The group is transitive and imprimitive in r distinct ways such that the ith system of imprimitivity consists of n/d_i imprimitivity sets of d_i each.

$1\frac{1}{2}t$ The group is transitive, neither regular, nor doubly transitive and any permutation of the group that fixes more than one letter is identity (Frobenius group).

kt The group is k-times transitive, but not $(k+1)$-times transitive; and there is a nonidentity permutation fixing $k + 1$ letters (k an integer > 1).

mkt The group is minimally k-times transitive so that it is k-times transitive and any permutation of the group which fixes k letters is identity (k an integer > 1).

$k\frac{1}{2}t$ The group is k-times transitive, but neither mkt nor $(k+1)$-times transitive such that any permutation of the group that fixes $k + 1$ letters is identity (k an integer > 1).

int	The group is intransitive with a proper partition of n given in the third column as orbit pattern.
S_p	Denotes the p-Sylow subgroup of $\mathfrak{S}_n$ for the prime number p.
N_p	Denotes the normalizer of S_p in $\mathfrak{S}_n$.
$S_p(H)$	Denotes a p-Sylow subgroup of the subgroup H of $\mathfrak{S}_n$.
$N_p(H)$	Denotes the normalizer of $S_p(H)$ in H.
e	After the description of a group indicates that the group consists only of even permutations; moreover, e after any permutation group H of n letters indicates that we have formed the intersection of H with the group $\mathfrak{A}_n$ of all even permutations.
$\mathfrak{S}_n$	The full permutation group of n letters (NB: $|\mathfrak{S}_n| = n!$).
$\mathfrak{S}_m$	Any subgroup of $\mathfrak{S}_n$ which is formed by all permutations of n letters fixing certain $n-m$ letters (NB: $|\mathfrak{S}_m| = m!$).
$\mathfrak{A}_m$	The normal subgroup of $\mathfrak{S}_m$ formed by the even permutations NB: $\mathfrak{S}_m\colon \mathfrak{A}_m = 2$ if $m > 1$, $\qquad\qquad\qquad\qquad = 1$ if $m = 1$.
$\mathfrak{K}$	The Klein's four group consisting of the four permutations $1, (12)(34), (13)(24), (14)(23)$.
$\mathrm{Imp}\left(\dfrac{m}{d}\right)$	The maximal imprimitive subgroup of $\mathfrak{S}_m$ formed by all permutations of $\mathfrak{S}_m$ permuting the members of a partition of the m letters of type $m = (m/d)\cdot d$ $(1 < d < m, d|m)$; (NB: $|\mathrm{Imp}\,(m/d)| = (m/d)^m!(d!)^{m/d})$.
$\mathrm{Imp}\left(\dfrac{m}{d}\right)e$	$\mathrm{Imp}\,(m/d) \cap \mathfrak{A}_m$; (NB: $\mathrm{Imp}\,(m/d)\colon \mathrm{Imp}\,(m/d)\,e = 2$).
$\mathrm{Int}\,(\Sigma_{i=2}^{n}\, a_i\cdot i)$	The maximal intransitive permutation group with orbit length a_i times i (orbit length 1 not being mentioned). (NB: $\mathrm{Int}\,(\Sigma_{i=2}^{n}a_i\cdot i)$ is isomorphic to the direct product of a_i symmetric permutation groups of i letters each for $i = 2, 3, \ldots, n$.)
$k \times \Sigma_{i=1}^{n}a_i \cdot i$	Indicates that the group contains precisely k permutations that have a_i cycles of length i $(1 \leqq i \leqq n)$ in their cycle decomposition. (NB: $\Sigma_{i=1}^{n}\, a_i\cdot i$ is equal to n numerically, but as a rule terms of the form $0\cdot i$ or $a_1\cdot 1$ are dropped from the notation for the partition of n, and a term $1\cdot i$ is replaced by i.)
e	Indicates that $\Sigma_{j=1}^{[n/2]}\, a_{2j} \equiv 0 \pmod 2$ for all partitions $\Sigma_{i=1}^{n}\, a_1\cdot i$ of n occurring in the distribution column, and vice versa.

Direct products   Indicate that the subgroups of $\mathfrak{S}_n$ occurring as direct
                    factors move on disjoint orbits.

If the group of the equation is the symmetric group as happens to be most
probable for random choice of the coefficients the Čebotarev-van der Waerden
method realizes that fact quickly.

Indeed, if $n \equiv 0 \pmod 2$ and $n > 2$ then after sampling about $n+1$ primes
one will run across an $(n-1)$-cycle, and an n-cycle, and a permutation of the
type $2+(n-3)$ and that will be enough to establish $G(f, F) = \mathfrak{S}_n$. If $n \equiv 1$
(mod 2) then one will run across an $(n-1)$-cycle and a permutation of the type
$2+(n-2)$ in about the same time and that will be enough.

The alternating group betrays itself by the squareness of d_f together with
the following occurrence:

degree	Permutation type
$n = 2$	
$n = 3$	3-cycle
$n = 4$	3-cycle
	2^2
$n = 5$	5-cycle
	3-cycle
$n = 6$	5-cycle
	3-cycle
	3^2
$n = 7$	7-cycle, 5-cycle
$n \geq 8$ and $n \equiv 0 \pmod 2$	$(n-1)$-cycle
	$p+(n-1-p)$
	(p the first prime num-
	not dividing n)
$n > 8$ and $n \equiv 1 \pmod 2$	n-cycle
	$p+(n-1-p)$
	(p the first prime num-
	ber not dividing
	$n-1$)

Usually the decision that $G(f, F) = \mathfrak{A}_n$ or $\mathfrak{S}_n$ is reached even after much less
than $n+1$ trials as a consequence of the evolving pattern of permutations
occurring in $G(f, F)$, and the application of known theorems on permutation
groups.

By a method based on III it would take a long time to verify that for a
prime $p \equiv 3 \pmod 4$ $(|p| > 3)$ the group of the polynomial

$$f(x) = x^{|p|} - px^{p-1} - px^{p-2} + 2px^2 + (p-1)x + 2$$

is $\mathfrak{S}_{|p|}$. This is quite easy to see via the congruence method.[2]

---

[2]Modulo p we have $f(x) \equiv x^{|p|} - x + 2$ which is irreducible according to Artin–Schreier.
Modulo 4 we have $f(x) \equiv (x^2 + x + 1)(x^{p-2} - 2)$ which is irreducible times Eisenstein. Hence
there is a p-cycle and a $(2 + (p-2))$-permutation in $G(f, F)$. This implies that $G(f, F) = \mathfrak{S}_p$.

The question arises whether an educated Čebotarev–Van der Waerden guess of $G(f, F)$ happens to be true. For this purpose we could use the method mentioned in the beginning which was based on III. Why not a $\mathfrak{p}$-adic method?

Let F be a finite extension of $\mathcal{Q}$, let $\mathfrak{o}_F$ be the integral closure of $\mathcal{Z}$ in F and let $\mathfrak{p}$ be a prime ideal of $\mathfrak{o}_F$. We assume that f is a monic separable polynomial of $\mathfrak{o}_F[x]$. Determine the factorization

$$(9) \qquad f(x) = \prod_{i=1}^{r} f_i(x)$$

of $f(x)$ into distinct monic irreducible polynomials of $F[x]$. A method to do this was outlined by Zassenhaus [11].

The coefficients of $f_i(x)$ are in $\mathfrak{o}_F$ for $i = 1, 2, \ldots, r$. Furthermore there hold factorizations

$$(10) \qquad f_i(x) \equiv \prod_{k=1}^{r_{i\mathfrak{p}}} \overline{f_{ik\mathfrak{p}}}(x) \quad (\mathrm{mod}\ \mathfrak{p}^{c+1})$$

such that the $\overline{f_{ik\mathfrak{p}}}(x)$ are monic polynomials of $\mathfrak{p}_F[x]$, that there are monic polynomials $f_{ik\mathfrak{p}}(x)$ with coefficients in the $\mathfrak{p}$-adic completion $\mathfrak{o}_{F,\mathfrak{p}}$ of $\mathfrak{o}_F$ satisfying

$$(11) \qquad \overline{f_{ik\mathfrak{p}}} \equiv f_{ik\mathfrak{p}} \quad (\mathrm{mod}\ \mathfrak{p}^{c+1})$$

and that $\overline{f_{ik\mathfrak{p}}}(x)$ is irreducible in the polynomial ring over the $\mathfrak{p}$-adic completion F.[3] The characteristic of $\mathfrak{o}_F/\mathfrak{p}$ is a prime number p. There is a natural number e_0 such that

$$(12) \qquad \mathfrak{p}^{e_0+1} \nmid p$$

and another natural number f_0 such that

$$(13) \qquad \mathfrak{o}_F : \mathfrak{p} = N\mathfrak{p} = p^{f_0}.$$

The polynomial $f_{ik\mathfrak{p}}(x)$ satisfies a congruency

$$(14) \qquad f_{ik\mathfrak{p}}(x) \equiv g_{ik\mathfrak{p}}(x)^{c_{ik}} \quad (\mathrm{modulo}\ \mathfrak{p}),$$

where $g_{ik\mathfrak{p}}$ is monic in $\mathfrak{o}_F[x]$ and irreducible modulo $\mathfrak{p}$.

The least common multiple $f_{E/\mathfrak{p}}$ of the degrees of the $g_{ik\mathfrak{p}}$ is equal to the degree over $\mathfrak{p}$ of any prime divisor of $\mathfrak{p}$ in the minimal splitting field E of f over F.

The congruency

$$(15) \qquad f_{ik\mathfrak{p}}(\xi) \equiv 0 \quad (\mathrm{modulo}\ \mathfrak{p}^{c+1})$$

together with the equation

$$(16) \qquad f(\xi) = 0$$

---

[3] For c we may take the nonnegative integer determined by $\mathfrak{p}^e \mid d_f$, $\mathfrak{p}^{c+1} \nmid d_f$; it suffices to know that $f_{ik\mathfrak{p}}$ is indecomposable modulo $\mathfrak{p}^{c+1}$.

suggests the formation of n distinct π-adic series of the form

$$(17) \qquad\qquad \xi_i = \sum_{j=0}^{\infty} \xi_{ij\mathfrak{v}}\, \pi^j$$

with coefficients $\xi_{ij\mathfrak{v}}$ that are either 0 or which are powers of a primitive $(p^{f_0 f} - 1)$st root of unity ξ. The element π may be chosen as an algebraic integer satisfying a $\mathfrak{p}$-Eisenstein equation of degree $e_{E/\mathfrak{p}}$, where $e_{E/\mathfrak{p}}$ is the ramification index of $\mathfrak{p}$ in E over F and where the norm of π over F is an algebraic integer π_0 of F divisible by $\mathfrak{p}$ but not by $\mathfrak{p}^2$.

The development is done by routine methods beginning with one of the congruencies (15) and keeping in view (16).

In this way $E = F(\xi_1, \xi_2, \ldots, \xi_n)$ is embedded into the algebraic extension $\hat{E} = \mathscr{Q}_p(\zeta, \pi)$. It is not necessary to know all coefficients of the ξ_i's. All that is needed is to know the coefficients up to and including a certain power π^c of π with exponent c obviated by the ensuing construction.

We form the integral domain $\mathfrak{o}_{F,\mathfrak{p}} = \mathfrak{o}_E \mathscr{Z}_p$ generated by the adjunction of π_0 and $\zeta_0 = \zeta^{(p^{f_{E/\mathfrak{p}} \cdot f_0} - 1)/(p^{f_0} - 1)}$ to the ring $\mathscr{Z}_p$ of the p-adic integers.

We form the integral domain $\mathcal{O}$ obtained by the adjunction of $\xi_1, \xi_2, \ldots, \xi_n$, π to $\mathfrak{o}_{F,\mathfrak{p}}$. There is an $\mathfrak{o}_{F,\mathfrak{p}}$-basis $b_1, b_2, \ldots, b_m$ of $\mathcal{O}$. We note that the elements $b_1, \ldots, b_m$ form an $\mathfrak{o}_{F,\mathfrak{p}}$-basis of $\mathcal{O}$ if and only if the residue classes $b_i/\pi_0 \mathfrak{o}_{F,\mathfrak{p}}$ form an $\mathfrak{o}_{F,\mathfrak{p}}/\pi_0 \mathfrak{o}_{F,\mathfrak{p}}$-basis of $\mathcal{O}/\pi_0 \mathcal{O}$.

LEMMA. *There is an exponent c such that a permutation ρ of the indices $1, 2, \ldots, n$ generates an automorphism $\sigma = \sigma_\rho$ of $\mathcal{O}$ over $\mathfrak{o}_{F,\mathfrak{p}}$*

$$\sigma_\rho \xi_i = \xi_{\pi(i)} \qquad (1 \leq i \leq n)$$

if and only if there is a linear mapping τ of $\mathcal{O}$ over $\mathfrak{o}_{F,\mathfrak{p}}$ satisfying the congruencies

$$\tau \xi_i \equiv \xi_{\rho(i)} \pmod{\pi^{c+1} \mathcal{O}}.$$

PROOF. If there is an automorphism σ of E over F for which $\sigma \xi_i = \xi_{\rho(i)}$ $(1 \leq i \leq n)$ then it can be extended to an automorphism of the field $\hat{E}$ generated by E and $\mathscr{2}_p$. It restricts to an automorphism σ_n of $\mathcal{D}$ over $\mathfrak{o}_{F,\mathfrak{p}}$. Conversely, let τ be a linear mapping of $\mathcal{D}$ over $\mathfrak{o}_{F,\mathfrak{p}}$ carrying ξ_i in $\xi_{\pi(i)}$ modulo $\pi^{c+1} \mathcal{D}$ $(1 \leq i \leq n)$.

It follows that

$$\tau(ab) = \tau(a)\tau(b) + t(a, b), \qquad t(a, b) \in \pi^{c+1} \mathcal{D}, \qquad (a, b \in \mathcal{D}).$$

We observe that $\hat{E}$ is separable of characteristic $\mathcal{O}$ over $F = F\mathscr{2}_p$ so that there is a nonnegative integer c^* for which

$$\det(\text{tr}(b_i b_k)) \in \pi_0^{c^*} \mathfrak{o}_{F,\mathfrak{p}}, \qquad \det(\text{tr}(b_i b_k)) \notin \pi_0^{c^*+1} \mathfrak{o}_{F,\mathfrak{p}}$$

Moreover the trace bilinear form

$$f(a, b) = \text{tr}_{\hat{E}/\hat{F}}(ab)$$

of $\hat{E}$ over $\hat{F}$ is nondegenerate and satisfies the conditions

$$f(a, b) = f(b, a), \tag{18}$$

$$f(a_1 + a_2, b) = f(a_1, b) + f(a_2, b), \tag{19}$$

$$f(\lambda a, b) = \lambda f(a, b), \tag{20}$$

$$f(ab, c) = f(a, bc), \qquad (a, b, a_1, a_2 \in E, \lambda \in \hat{F}). \tag{21}$$

There is uniquely defined the dual F-basis $b^{(1)}, \ldots, b^{(m)}$ of $\hat{E}$ by the conditions

$$f(b_i, b^{(k)}) = \alpha_{ik} = f(b^{(i)}, b_k). \tag{22}$$

Setting

$$b_i b_k = \sum \gamma_{ikj} b^{(j)} \tag{23}$$

with γ_{ikj} in $\hat{F}$ we translate (21) to

$$f(b_i b_j, b_k) = f(b_i, b_j b_k).$$

It follows from (22), (23) that

$$\gamma_{ikj} = \gamma_{jki}. \tag{24}$$

Even without using the commutative law of multiplication for the unital hypercomplex system $\hat{E}$ over $\hat{F}$ we assert that the element

$$C(f) = \sum_{i=1}^{m} b_i b^{(i)} = \sum_{i=1}^{m} f^{(i)} b_i$$

($c(f)$ is called the Casimir operator of f) commutes with X elementwise as follows from the equations

$$C(f) b_k = \sum_{i=1}^{m} \sum_{k=1}^{n} b^{(i)} \gamma_{ikh} b^{(h)} = \sum_{i=1}^{m} \sum_{h=1}^{m} \gamma_{khi} b^{(i)} b^{(h)}$$

$$= \sum_{h=1}^{m} \sum_{i=1}^{m} \gamma_{kih} b^{(h)} b^{(i)} = b_k C(f).$$

Since the trace of $C(f)$ is equal to

$$\sum_{i=1}^{m} \operatorname{tr}(b_i b^{(i)}) = \sum_{i=1}^{m} f(b_1, b^{(i)}) = m,$$

it follows that the Casimir operator of f is not zero; furthermore we have $b^{(i)} \in \pi_0^{-c^*} \mathfrak{O}, C(f) \in \pi_0^{-c^*} \mathfrak{O}$.

We choose $c \geqq 2c^* c_{E/\mathfrak{p}}$.

It is our task to show that τ can be modified modulo $\pi^{c+1}\mathfrak{O}$ to a linear mapping $\hat{\tau} = \tau + t$ of $\mathfrak{O}$ into $\mathfrak{O}$ over $\mathfrak{o}_{F,\mathfrak{p}}$ such that

$$t\mathfrak{O} \subseteq \pi^{c+1}\mathfrak{O}, \qquad \tau\xi_i \equiv \xi_{\pi(i)} \pmod{\pi^{c+2}\mathfrak{O}}.$$

If this is achieved then by forming a converging sequence of linear mappings of $\mathfrak{D}$ in $\mathfrak{D}$ over $\mathfrak{o}_{F,\mathfrak{v}}$ we obtain the automorphism of $\mathfrak{D}$ over $\mathfrak{o}_{F,\mathfrak{v}}$ carrying

$$\xi_i \text{ in } \xi_{\pi(i)} \qquad (1 \leq i \leq n).$$

The conditions to be met by t are the congruences

$$\tau(ab) + t(ab) - (\tau(a) + t(a))(\tau(b) + t(b)) \equiv 0 \quad (\pi^{c+2}\mathfrak{D}) \qquad (a, b \in \mathfrak{D}).$$

They can be satisfied if and only if the congruencies

(25) $$t(b_i, b_k) + t(b_i b_k) - \tau(b_i)t(b_k) - t(b_i)\tau(b_k) \equiv 0 \pmod{\pi^{c+2}\mathfrak{D}}$$

can be solved.

On the other hand from the associative law it follows that

(26)
$$\begin{aligned}
\tau(abc) &= \tau(a)\tau(bc) + t(a, bc) \\
&= \tau(a)\tau(b)\tau(c) + \tau(a)t(b, c) + t(a, bc) \\
&= \tau(a)\tau(b)\tau(c) + t(a, b)\tau(c) + t(ab, c) \\
\tau(a)t(b, c) + t(a, bc) &= t(a, b)\tau(c) + t(ab, c) \\
\tau(b_i)t(b_j, b_k) + t(b_i, b_j b_k) &= t(b_i, b_j)\tau(b_k) + t(b_i b_j, b_k).
\end{aligned}$$

Since f is determined by the regular trace of E over F it follows from the near automorphism property of τ that

$$\begin{aligned}
\operatorname{tr} \tau(a) &\equiv \tau(a) \pmod{\pi^{c+1}\mathfrak{D}} \qquad (a \in \mathfrak{D}) \\
f(\tau(a), \tau(b)) &\equiv f(a, b) \pmod{\pi^{c+1}\mathfrak{D}} \qquad (a, b \in \mathfrak{D}), \\
f(\tau(b_i), \tau(b^{(k)})) &\equiv \delta_{ik} \pmod{\pi^{c-e^*+1}\mathfrak{D}}.
\end{aligned}$$

For the dual basis $x^{(i)}, \ldots, x^{(n)}$ of $\tau(b_1), \tau(b_2), \ldots, \tau(b_n)$ we find that

$$f(\tau(b_i), x^{(k)}) = \delta_{ik}, \qquad x^{(k)} = \tau(b^{(k)}) \pmod{\pi^{c-e^*+1}\mathfrak{D}},$$

$$C(f) = \sum_{i=1}^{m} \tau(b_i)x^{(i)} \equiv \sum_{i=1}^{m} \tau(b_i)\tau(b^{(i)}) \pmod{\pi^{c-e^*+1}\mathfrak{D}}.$$

(27)

$$\begin{aligned}
\sum_{k=1}^{m} t(b_j, b_j b_k)\tau(b^{(k)}) &= \sum_{k=1}^{m}\sum_{\nu=1}^{m} t(b_i, \gamma_{jk} b^{(\nu)})\tau(b^{(k)}) = \sum_{k=1}^{m}\sum_{\nu=1}^{m} \gamma_{jk\nu} t(b_i, b^{(\nu)})\tau(b^{(k)}) \\
&= \sum_{k=1}^{m}\sum_{\nu=1}^{m} \gamma_{\nu jk} t(b_i, b^{(\nu)})\tau(b^{(k)}) = \sum_{\nu=1}^{m} t(b_i, b^{(\nu)})\tau(b_\nu b_j) \\
&= \sum_{\nu=1}^{m} t(b_i, b_\nu)\tau(b^{(\nu)})\tau(b_j) = \sum_{\nu=1}^{m} t(b_i, b_\nu)t(b^{(\nu)}, t_j).
\end{aligned}$$

Letting

$$t'(b_j) = \sum_{k=1}^{m} t(b_j, b_k)\tau(b^{(k)})$$

it follows from (24), (25) that

$$\tau(b_i)t'(b_j) + t'(b_i)\tau(b_j) + \nu - 1 = t(b_i, b_j)C(f) + t'(b_i b_j) \pmod{\pi^{2c+2-e^*}\mathfrak{D}}.$$

Let us set

$$t(b_j) = t'(b_j)C(f)^{-1}.$$

The expression

$$t(b_i, b_j) + t(b_i b_j) - \tau(b_i)t(b_j) - t(b_i)\tau(b_j)$$

belongs to $\pi^{2(e+1-e^*)}\mathfrak{O}$ for all i, j, so that the linear mapping t of $\mathfrak{O}$ into $\pi^{e+1}\mathfrak{O}$ determined by setting

$$t\left(\sum_{i=1}^{m} \alpha^{(i)} b_i\right) = \sum_{i=1}^{m} \alpha^{(i)} t(b_i) \qquad (\alpha^{(i)} \in \mathfrak{O} \cap K)$$

does what is required.

Based on the lemma we have the following method of deciding whether the permutation group G of the n letters $1, 2, \ldots$, contains $G(f, F)$.

Firstly let $p \nmid d_f$.

Secondly let G contain the permutation ρ_0 for which $\xi_{\rho_0(i)} \equiv \xi_i^{N\mathfrak{p}} \pmod{\mathfrak{p}}$.

Thirdly let

$$G_{1,2,\ldots,i} = \{\rho \mid \rho \in G \text{ and } \forall j (1 \le j \le i \Rightarrow \rho(j) = j)\},$$
$$G : G_1 = m_1,$$
$$G_{1,2,\ldots,i-1} : G_{1,2,\ldots,i} = m_i \qquad (1 \le i < n).$$

Fourthly choose c so large that the $|G|$ expressions

$$t(i_1, i_2, \ldots, i_n) = \sum_{\rho \in G} \xi_{\rho(1)}^{i_1} \xi_{\rho(2)}^{i_2} \cdots \xi_{\rho(n)}^{i} \qquad (0 \le i_j < m_j, 1 \le j \le n)$$

and their algebraic conjugates are smaller in absolute value then $\frac{1}{2}p^{(c+1)/e_0 e}E/\mathfrak{p} \, n$ (rough bounds c can be obtained without difficulty).

Fifthly the test is negative if one of the $|G|$ expressions defined above does not have its $c + 1$ initial terms congruent modulo π^{c+1} to terms in $\mathfrak{o}_F$.

Sixthly assume that all $t(i_1, i_2, \ldots, i_n)$ have the sum of the $c + 1$ initial terms congruent to an element $\bar{t}(i_1, i_2, \ldots, i_n)$ of $\mathfrak{o}_F$ modulo π^{c+1}. The test fails if $\bar{t}(i_1, i_2, \ldots, i_n)$ cannot be modified modulo π^{c+1} to an element of $\mathfrak{o}$ which has all its algebraic conjugates of absolute value not greater than the bound given above.

Seventhly assume that

$$|\bar{t}(i_1, i_2, \ldots, i_n)| \le \frac{1}{2}p^{(c+1)/c_0 e}E/\mathfrak{p} \qquad (0 \le i_j < m_j, 1 \le j \le n).$$

It follows that

$$t(i_1, i_2, \ldots, i_n) = \bar{t}(i_1, i_2, \ldots, i_n) \qquad (0 \le i_j < m_j, 1 \le j \le n)$$

and that indeed $G \supseteq G(f_1 F)$.

The case that the permutation group $G(f, F)$ is intransitive, corresponds to the reducibility of $f(x)$ in $F[x]$. The orbits of $G(f, F)$ are the sets of roots of the irreducible factors of $f(x)$ in $F[x]$. The extension E is the composite of the normal extension E_i of F obtained by the adjunction of the roots of the irreducible factor $f_i(x)$.

The process of composition can be controlled by the Hensel method or by the earlier method based on III. For example for $n = 6$ we obtain the following table:

TABLE 2.   Transitive groups of 6 letters.

Nr	Type	$|G|$	Description	Distribution
37	$m6t$	720	$\mathfrak{S}_6$	$\mathfrak{A}_6 + 15\times2 + 15\times3\cdot2 + 90\times4 + 120\times6 + 120\times(2+3)$
38	$m4t$	360	$\mathfrak{A}_6\,e$	$\underline{1} + 45\times2\cdot2 + 90\times(2+4) + 40\times3$ $+ 144\times5 + 40\times2.3$
39	$m3t$	120	$\mathfrak{S}_5|N_5(\mathfrak{S}_5)$	$\mathfrak{S}_5|N_5(\mathfrak{S}_5)\ e + 10\times3\cdot2 + 20\times6 + 30\times4$
40	$2\frac{1}{2}$	60	$\mathfrak{S}_5|N_5(\mathfrak{S}_5)\ e$	$\underline{1} + 15\times2\cdot2 + 20\times2\cdot3 + 24\times5$
41	imp $\left(\frac{6}{2}\right)$	48	Imp $\left(\frac{6}{2}\right)$	Imp $\left(\frac{6}{2}\right) e + 3\times2 + 7\times3\cdot2 + 6\times4 + 8\times6$
42	imp $\left(\frac{6}{2}\right)$	24	Imp $\left(\frac{6}{2}\right)\ e$	$\underline{1} + 9\times2\cdot2 + 6\times(2+4) + 8\times2\cdot3$
43	imp $\left(\frac{6}{2}\right)$	24	$\mathfrak{A}_3\!\int\!\mathfrak{S}_2$	$\mathfrak{A}_3\!\int\!\mathfrak{S}_2\,e + 3\times2 + 3\cdot2 + 8\times6$
44	imp $\left(\frac{6}{2}\right)$	24	$\mathfrak{S}_4|\langle(1234)\rangle$	$\mathfrak{A}_3\!\int\!\mathfrak{S}_2\,e + 6\times(2+4) + 6\times3\cdot2$
45	imp $\left(\frac{6}{2}\right)$	12	$\mathfrak{A}_3\!\int\!\mathfrak{S}_2\,e$	$\underline{1} + 3\times3\cdot2 + 8\times2\cdot3$
46	imp $\left(\frac{6}{3}\right)$	72	Imp $\left(\frac{6}{3}\right)$	Imp $\left(\frac{6}{3}\right) e + 6\times2 + 6\times3\cdot2 + 12\times(2+3) + 12\times6$
47	imp $\left(\frac{6}{3}\right)$	36	Imp $\left(\frac{6}{3}\right)\ e$	$\underline{1} + 4\times3 + 4\times2\cdot3 + 9\times2\cdot2 + 18\times(2+4)$
48	imp $\left(\frac{6}{3}\right)$	36	$\langle$Int $(2.3)\ e\ (1425)\,(36)\rangle$	$\mathfrak{S}_2\!\int\!\mathfrak{A}_3 + 18\times(2+4)$
49	imp $\left(\frac{6}{3}\right)$	18	$\mathfrak{S}_2\!\int\!\mathfrak{A}_3$	$\underline{1} + 4\times3 + 4\times2\cdot3 + 3\times3\cdot2 + 6\times6$
50	imp $\left(\frac{6}{3}\right)$	12	$\langle(123)\,(456),(14)\,(25)\,(36),(23)\,(56)\rangle$	$\underline{1} + 2\times2\cdot3 + 3\times2\cdot2 + 4\times3\cdot2 + 2\times6$
51	imp $\left(\frac{6}{2},\frac{6}{3}\right)$	6	$\langle(142536)\rangle$	$\underline{1} + 3\cdot2 + 2\times2\cdot3 + 2\times6$

Explanation of new symbols used in Table 2:

$G|H$ denotes the transitive permutation group consisting of the permutations

$$G|H(x) = \begin{pmatrix} a\,H \\ x\,a\,H \end{pmatrix}$$

of the right cosets of the group G over its subgroup H.

$G \int H$ denotes the wreath product of the permutation group G on m letters over the permutation group H on n letters.

The determination of the group of an irreducible equation (1) over the field of reference F is aided greatly by a knowledge of the set $\mathcal{S}(F,F(\xi_1))$ of the fields X that are intermediate:

$$F \subseteq X \subseteq F(\xi_1).$$

In the sense of Galois theory the set $\mathcal{S}(F, F(\xi_1))$ corresponds to the set $\mathcal{S}(G, G_1)$ of the subgroups S of G that are intermediate to G and the stabilizer G_1 of ξ_1:

$$G > S > G_1.$$

If $\mathcal{S}(G,G_1)$ is empty then the permutation group $G(f,F)$ is said to be *primitive*, otherwise it is *imprimitive*.

In order to decide whether the group $G(f,F)$ is primitive we first of all decide whether f is separable irreducible over F. Suppose "yes" meaning $G(f, F)$ acts transitively on the n distinct roots $\xi_1, \xi_2, \ldots, \xi_n$. Factorize the polynomial $f(x)$,

$$f(x) = (x - \alpha_1) \prod_{i=1}^{s} g_i(x),$$

into the product of $s+1$ distinct separable monic irreducible polynomials of $F(\alpha_1)[x]$ such that

$$[g_1] \leq [g_2] \leq \cdots \leq [g_s], \qquad \sum_{i=1}^{r} [g_i] = n-1.$$

If $s = 1$ then $G(f,F)$ is doubly transitive, hence it is primitive.

Let

$$1 = d_0 < d_1 < \cdots < d_t = n$$

be the $t+1$ positive divisors of n. Form the set $\mathcal{S}([g_1], \ldots, [g_s])$ of all presentations σ of the form:

$$1 + [g_{\beta_1}] + \cdots + [g_{\beta_h}] = d,$$

where

$$1 \leq h \leq s, \qquad 1 \leq \beta_1 < \beta_2 < \cdots < \beta_h \leq s, \qquad 1 < d < n, \qquad d|n.$$

If it is empty then $G(f,F)$ is primitive.

Let $\mathcal{S}([g_1], \ldots, [g_s])$ be nonempty. Let

$$g_i(x) = x^{[g_i]} + \sum_{j=1}^{[g_i]} a_{ij}x^{[g_i]-j},$$

$$(a_{ij} \in F(\alpha_1), \qquad 1 \leq j \leq [f_i], \qquad 1 \leq i \leq r),$$

$$\beta(\sigma) = \alpha_1 - \sum_{i=1}^{h} a_{\beta_i 1} \quad \text{for } \sigma \text{ of } \mathscr{S}([g_2], \dots, [g_s]).$$

Let $t > i > 0$ and assume we know already that there is no extension of F contained in $F(\alpha_1)$ which is of degree greater than n/d_i but less than n over F.

If one of the $\beta(\sigma)$'s for $d = d_i$ satisfies a minimal equation of degree n/d over F, then $G(f, F)$ is imprimitive, a system of imprimitivity being formed by the roots of $x - \alpha_1, g_{\beta_1}, \dots, g_{\beta_g}$.

Suppose now that none of the $\beta(\sigma)$'s for $d = d_i$ satisfies a minimal equation of degree n/d or 1 then there is no extension of F contained in $F(\alpha_1)$ that is of degree n/d or greater than n/d but smaller than n.

Furthermore, let none of the $\beta(\sigma)$'s for $d = d_i$ satisfy a minimal equation of degree n/d but let $\beta(\sigma)$'s be in F for some σ. If for that σ of $\mathscr{S}([g_1], \dots, [g_s])$ we have

$$1 + [g_{\beta_1}] + \cdots + [g_{\beta_h}] = d$$

and if there is no member σ' of $\mathscr{S}([g_1], \dots, [g_s])$ distinct from σ such that

(28) $$[g_{\beta_1}] = [g_{\beta_i}] \qquad (1 \leq i \leq r)$$

then there is a system of imprimitivity of $G(f, F)$ formed by the roots of $x - \alpha$, $g_{\beta_1}, \dots, g_{\beta_h}$.

Furthermore, let none of the $\beta(\sigma)$'s that can be formed for $d = d_i$ satisfy a minimal equation of degree n/d, let one of the $\beta(\sigma)$'s for $d = d_i$ be in F and let there be for each such $\beta(\sigma)$ at least one other $\beta(\sigma')$ for which (28) holds.

The first time this occurs we form the companion matrix A_f of $f[x]$ and the minimal polynomials g_i of $A_f^i (1 < i < n)$.

If any of them is of degree less than n, say $[g_i] < n$ for some i satisfying $1 < i < n$ then we know already that $1 < [g_i]|n$ and that ξ_1^i generates a subfield of $F[\xi_1]$ over F of degree $[j_i]$. Hence $G(f, F)$ has a system of imprimitivity of $n/[g_i]$ letters.

We may assume henceforth that $[g_i] = n \quad (1 < i < n)$.

It follows that there are factorizations

$$g_i(x) = (x - \xi_1^i) \prod_{j=1}^{r} g_{ij}(x),$$

$$g_{ij}(x) = \det(tI_{[f_j]} - A_{f_i}^i)$$

$$= x^{[f_j]} + \sum_{k=1}^{[f_j]} a_{ikj} x^{[f_j]-k}, \qquad a_i k_j \in F(\alpha_1) \quad (1 < i < n).$$

Forming

$$\beta_i(\sigma) = \alpha^i - \sum_{j=1}^{r} a_{i,j}$$

it follows that not for all i the expression $\beta_i(\sigma)$ is in F. If it is not then either

$\beta_i(\sigma)$ generates a subfield of $F(\alpha_1)$ of degree n/d, or 1, $\beta_2(\sigma) \ldots \beta_2(\sigma)^{n/d}$ are linearly independent over F altogether and we test the next σ' of $\mathscr{S}([\beta_1], [\beta_2], \ldots, [\beta_s])$ for $d_i = d$ in the same way until either a subfield of $F(\alpha_1)$ of degree n/d over F is discovered or until all σ's for $d_i = d$ give negative test results so that there is no subfield of $F(\alpha_1)$ of degree n/d over F.

In this way either $G(f, F)$ is found to be primitive or a subfield of $F(\xi_1)$ of highest degree n/d over F with the property that $1 < d < n$, d/n is found.

Iterating the method $\mathscr{S}(F, F(\xi_1))$ can be constructed.

Utilizing the previous methods as well we can break up the task of finding the group of an equation into several primitive steps.

It is necessary for the application of the Čebotarev–van der Waerden method to have tables of the primitive permutation groups. E.g. for $n = 7, 8$.

TABLE 3.   Primitive permutation groups of 7 or 8 letters.

n	Type	$|G|$	Description	Distribution
7	$m7t$	5040	$\mathfrak{S}_7$	Contains 5-cycles
7	$m5t$	2520	$\mathfrak{A}_7$	Contains 5-cycles
7	$2t$	168	PSL(3,2)	$1 + 48 \times 7 + 56 \times 2 \cdot 3 + 42 \times (2+4)$ $+ 21 \times 2 \cdot 2$
7	$m2t$	42	N_7	$N_7 e + 21 \times 7 \cdot 2$
7	$1\frac{1}{2}t$	21	$N_7 e$	$S_7 + 14 \times 2 \cdot 3$
7	$1\frac{1}{2}t$	14	$S_7 \subset G \subset N_7$, not e	$S_7 + 7 \times 7 \cdot 2$
7	r	7	S_7	$1 + 6 \times 7$
8	$m8t$	40320	$\mathfrak{S}_8$	Contains 5-cycles
8	$m6t$	20160	$\mathfrak{A}_8$	Contains 5-cycles
8	$3t$	1344	Hol(GF(2)$^{3\times1}$) e	$1 + 133 \times 4 \cdot 2 + 42 \times 2 \cdot 2 + 168 \times 2 \cdot 4$ $+ 168 \times (2+4) + 224 \times (2+6) + 224$ $\times 2 \cdot 3 + 384 \times 7$
8	$2\frac{1}{2}t$	168	Hol $(N_7(\mathrm{GL}(3,2))\,\mathrm{GF}(2)^{3\times1})$	Hol$(S_7(\mathrm{GL}(3,2))\mathrm{GF}(2)^{3\times1})$ + $56 \times 2 \cdot 3 + 56 \times (2+6)$
8	$2\frac{1}{2}t$	168	PSL(2,7)	$1 + 48 \times 7 + 56 \times 2 \cdot 3 + 42 \times 2 \cdot 4$ $+ 21 \times 4 \cdot 2$
8	$m3t$	336	PGL(2,7)	PSL(2,7) $+ 56 \times 3 \cdot 2 + 112 \times 6$
8	$m2t$	56	Hol $(S_7(\mathrm{GL}(3,2))\,\mathrm{GF}(2)^{3\times1})$	$1 + 7 \times 4 \cdot 2 + 48 \times 7$

Explanation of new symbols used in Table 3:

PGL(n,p^α)   The doubly transitive permutation group formed by all cross ratio preserving collineations of the projective space of dimension $n-1$ over the field of p^α elements (p a prime number). (NB: $|\mathrm{PGL}(n,p^\alpha)| = (p^{\alpha n} - 1)(p^{\alpha n} - p^\alpha) \cdots$ $(p^{\alpha n} - p^{\alpha(n-1)})/(p^\alpha - 1)$.)

PSL(n,p^α)   DPGL(n,p^α) excepting the case $n = 2$, $p^\alpha = 2$, in which PSL(2,2) = PGL(2,2). (NB: $|\mathrm{PSL}| = |\mathrm{PGL}|/(\mathrm{GCD}(n,p^\alpha - 1))$.)

Hol(X,G)   The holomorph of the group X of automorphisms of the group
                     G over G consisting of the permutations

$$\begin{pmatrix} g \\ \alpha(g)+h \end{pmatrix} \Big| g \in G \Bigg) \qquad (\alpha \in \text{Aut } G, h \in G)$$

Hol(G)   Hol(Aut G,G)
                     the holomorph of G

So far we have omitted the use of prime ideal divisors of d_f for the purpose of determining $G(f,F)$. But they can be applied to excellent use as is evidenced by the

THEOREM. *Over the rational number field as ground field the remification groups of the prime ideal divisors of the discriminant of f generate the full automorphism group of the minimal splitting field of $f(x)$.*

This is because the field fixed by the subgroup generated by the inertia groups is unramified over the ground field and by a theorem of H. Minkowski it must coincide with the ground field in case of the rational number field.

The method remains useful over an arbitrary algebraic number field as ground field. Only in general we would have to cope with the finite unramified extensions of an algebraic number field. A theory (mainly due to P. Furt-wängler) exists for solvable unramified extensions. But for nonsolvable un-ramified finite extensions of algebraic number fields little beyond their existence is known.

We obtain e.g. the following

TABLE 4.   Application of the discriminant method to field extensions of degree less than 6.

n	d	Type	Test	Table 1 Nr.
1	1			1
2	nonsquare			2
	square			3
3	nonsquare	irr.		4
		rd.		6
	square	irr.		5
		rd.		7
4	nonsquare	p		8
		imp	$\sqrt{d} \in F(\alpha)$	12
		imp	$\sqrt{d} \notin F(\alpha)$	10
		1+3		13
		2·1+2		15
		2·2		17
	square	p		9

TABLE 4 (contd).

n	d	Type	Test	Table 1 Nr.
		imp		11
		$1+3$		14
		$4\cdot1$		16
		$2\cdot2$		18
5	nonsquare	irr.	$\sqrt{d}$ splits $f/(x-\alpha)$	21
		irr.	$\sqrt{d}$ does not split $f/(x-\alpha)$	19
		$1+4,p_2$		23
		$1+4$, imp$_2$	$\sqrt{d_2} \in F(\alpha_2)$	27
		$1+4$, imp$_2$		25
		$2\cdot1+3$		28
		$3\cdot1+2$		30
		$1+2\cdot2$		32
		$2+3$	$-d_2$ nonsquare	34
		$2+3$	$-d_2$ square	36
	square	irr.	$f/(x-\alpha)$ irreducible in $F(\alpha)$	20
		irr.	$f/(x-\alpha)$ irreducible, but without linear factor in $F(\alpha)$	22
		irr.	$f/(x-\alpha)$ has a linear factor in $F(\alpha)$	23
		$1+4,p_2$		24
		$1+4$, imp$_2$		26
		$2\cdot1+3$		29
		$5\cdot1$		31
		$1+2\cdot2$		33
		$2+3$		35

Explanation of symbols in Table 4:

F a field of reference not of characteristic 2.

f $f(x) = x^n + a_1 x^{n-1} + \cdots + a_n$ a monic separable polynomial of $F[x]$ with derivative $f' = f'(x) = nx^{n-1} + (n-1)a_1 x^{n-2} + \cdots + a_{n-1}$ and with accompanying matrix

$$A_f = \begin{pmatrix} 0 & & & & -a_n \\ 1 & 0 & & & -a_{n-1} \\ & 0 & 1 & 0 & & \cdot \\ & & & \cdot & \cdot & \cdot \\ & & & & \cdot & \cdot \\ & & & 1 & 0 & -a_2 \\ & & & & 1 & -a_1 \end{pmatrix}$$

irr. $f(x)$ is irreducible in $F[x]$

rd. $f(x)$ is reducible in $F[x]$

Type $\Sigma a_i \cdot i$ a proper partition of n indicating that $f(x)$ factorizes into the product of monic polynomials of $F[x]$ exactly a_i of which are of degree i (drop the term $a_i \cdot i$ if $a_i = 0$, but do not drop terms $a_1 \cdot 1$)

f $= f_1 f_2 \cdots f_s$ the factorization of $f(x)$ into monic irreducible factors of $F[x]$, where

$$[f_1] \leqq [f_2] \leqq \cdots \leqq [f_s];$$

refinement of this factorization in a splitting extension of f over F leads to:

$f(x)$ $= \prod_{i=1}^{n} (x - \alpha_i)$

d $d(f) = \prod_{i \neq j} (\alpha_j - \alpha_i) = (-1)^{(n/2)} \prod_{i<j} (\alpha_j - \alpha_i)^2 = \det(f'(A_f))$ discriminant of d

d_i $d(f_i)$

p indicates that f is irreducible and that the field extension $F[\alpha]$ is primitive

imp indicates that f is irreducible but $F[\alpha]$ is imprimitive

p_i indicates 'p' for f_i

imp_i indicates 'imp' for f_i.

References

1. J. E. Burns, *Abstract definitions of groups of degree eight*, Amer. J. Math. **37** (1915), 195–214.

2. N. Čebotarev, *Die Bestimmung der Dichtigkeit einer Menge von Primzahlen, welche zu einer gegebenen Substitutionsklasse gehören*, Math. Ann. **95** (1926), 191–229.

3. H. S. M. Coxeter and W. O. J. Moser, *Generators and relations for discrete groups*, 2nd ed., Ergebnisse der Mathematik und Ihrer Grenzgebiete, Neue Folge, Springer-Verlag, Berlin and New York, 1965. MR **30** #4818.

4. A. Fröhlich and J. C. Shepherdson, *Effective procedures in field theory*, Philos. Trans. Roy. Soc. London Ser. A **248** (1956), 407–432. MR **17**, 570.

5. _____, *On the factorisation of polynomials in a finite number of steps*, Math. Z. **62** (1955), 331–334. MR **17**, 119.

6. G. A. Miller, *Abstract definitions of all the substitution groups whose degrees do not exceed seven*, Amer. J. Math. **33** (1911), 363–372.

7. B. van der Waerden, *Algebra*. Vol. 1, 6th ed., Springer, Berlin, 1964. MR **31** #1292.

8. _____, *Eine Bemerkung über die Unzerlegbarkeit von Polynomen*, Math. Ann. **102** (1930), 738–739.

9. Hans Zassenhaus, *On the fundamental theorem of algebra*, Amer. Math. Monthly **74** (1967), 485–497. MR **36** #2605.

10. _____, *On the group of an equation*, Nachr. Akad. Gött. Math.-Phys. K1. II **1967**, 147–166. MR **37** #5191.

11. _____, *On Hensel factorization*. I. J. Number Theory **1** (1969), 291–311. MR **39** # 4120.

Ohio State University and

University of California, Los Angeles

Nonexistence Theorems for Perfect Error-Correcting Codes

J. H. van Lint

1. **Introduction.** Let p be a prime, $q = p^\alpha$, $F = GF(q)$ and let V be the vector space F^n. For any $x \in V$ we define the *weight* of x to be the number of nonzero components of x. The (Hamming-) distance $d(x, y)$ of two vectors x, y in V is defined to be the weight of $x - y$. If e is a positive integer we define the *sphere* $B_{x,e}$ by

$$B_{x,e} := \{y \in V \mid d(x, y) \leq e\}.$$

A subset C of V is called an *e-error-correcting* code if

$$\forall_{x \in C} \forall_{y \in C} [(x \neq y) \Rightarrow (B_{x,e} \cap B_{y,e} = \emptyset)].$$

If furthermore $V = \bigcup_{x \in C} B_{x,e}$ the code is called *perfect*. In coding theory the vectors of C are called codewords; the dimension n of V is called the *block length* of the code.

The following perfect codes are known:

(a) Trivial perfect codes: If $e = n$ and C_1 consists of one word then C_1 is a perfect code. If $q = 2$, $n = 2e + 1$ and C_2 consists of the words $(0, 0, \ldots, 0)$ and $(1, 1, \ldots, 1)$ then the code C_2 is perfect (repetition-code).

(b) Hamming codes: Perfect codes with $e = 1$. For a description cf. [4].

(c) Golay codes: There are two codes known as Golay codes, one with $e = 2$, $q = 3$, $n = 11$ and one with $e = 3$, $q = 2$, $n = 23$ (cf. [4]).

A necessary condition for the existence of a perfect code with parameters e, q, n is easily established. For each $x \in V$ the cardinality of the sphere $B_{x,e}$ is $\sum_{i=0}^{e} \binom{n}{i} (q-1)^i$. If a perfect code exists this number must be a divisor of the cardinality of V, which is q^n. Hence for some integer β

$$\sum_{i=0}^{e} \binom{n}{i} (q-1)^i = p^\beta.$$

AMS 1970 subject classifications. Primary 10B15, 94A10.

Since $\sum_{i=0}^{n} \binom{n}{i} (q-1)^i = q^n$ we find by subtraction

$$q^n - p^\beta \equiv 0 \pmod{q-1}.$$

This implies that p^β is a power of q. Hence:

(1.1) *If a perfect e-error-correcting code of block length n over* $\mathrm{GF}(q)$ *exists then there is an integer k such that* $\sum_{i=0}^{e} \binom{n}{i} (q-1)^i = q^k$.

A more complicated necessary condition for the existence of perfect codes was found by S. P. Lloyd in 1957 for the case $q = 2$ [10]. This was generalized by F. J. MacWilliams (1962) and later recast by A. M. Gleason (cf. [3]). The condition is:

(1.2) THEOREM (LLOYD, ETC.). *If a perfect e-error-correcting code of block length n over* $\mathrm{GF}(q)$ *exists then the polynomial*

$$P_e(x) := \sum_{i=0}^{e} (-1)^i \binom{n-x}{e-i} \binom{x-1}{i} (q-1)^{e-i},$$

where $\binom{a}{i} := a(a-1) \cdots (a-i+1)/i!$, *has e distinct integral zeros among* $1, 2, \ldots, n-1$.

2. Survey of results on nonexistence of perfect codes.

Several authors have studied perfect codes and proved nonexistence theorems. Nearly all the results are based on (1.1) only. Very often part of the work depended on the use of computers. It has been proved a number of times that $e = 2, q = 2, n = 90$ satisfy the condition in (1.1) but that there is no perfect code with these parameters (cf. [6]). Using known theorems on diophantine equations E. L. Cohen [5] showed that for $e = 2$ and $q < 6$ the equation in (1.1) has no other solutions than the known ones. Also using numbertheoretical methods R. Alter ([1], [2]) treated $e = 2, 7 \leq q \leq 9$ and proved that there are no perfect codes with these parameters except the ones mentioned above. A fairly easy case is: e odd, $q = 2$. For these values the left-hand side of the equation in (1.1) is a polynomial in n which is divisible by $n+1$ and then all solutions are easily found (Shapiro and Slotnick [12]). This has been done for $e < 20$ and no new perfect codes were found.

Computer searches were carried out by E. L. Cohen [5] for $e = 2, 3 \leq q$ (odd) $\leq 125, 3 \leq k \leq 40000$ (parameters in (1.1)); by M. H. McAndrew [11] for $e \leq 20, n \leq 2^{70}$ and in 1968 by this author for $e \leq 1000, q \leq 100, n \leq 1000$ (cf. [7], [8]). In no case was a new perfect code found.

The results mentioned above are complete for binary 2- and 3-error-correcting codes, but not for $e = 4$. The latter were treated by using (1.2) (cf. [7]). The method used was one applied by A. Baker and H. Davenport for a completely different problem in the theory of diophantine equations. It involved over 2 hours of computing time. Exactly the same program was used for the coding theory problem!

Since then the author has found the following theorems (cf. [9]):

(2.1) THEOREM. *For $q = p^\alpha > 3$ there is no perfect 2-error-correcting code over the alphabet $GF(q)$ with block length $n > 2$.*

(2.2) THEOREM. *The only perfect 3-error-correcting codes of block length $n > 3$ over $GF(q)$ are the binary repetition code of block length 7 and the (23, 12)-Golay code.*

The new approach which led to these theorems was combining conditions (1.1) and (1.2). The proofs do not require computer searches.

In the following section we continue these investigations and prove new nonexistence theorems for perfect codes.

3. **New nonexistence theorems.** Since the question of existence of perfect 2- and 3-error-correcting codes has been settled ((2.1) and (2.2)), we restrict ourselves in this section to $e \geq 4$. We shall exclude the trivial case $n = e$ from now on. From (1.1) it then follows that $k < n$ and also $k > e$ (since $\binom{n}{i} > \binom{e}{i}$ for $i \neq 0$). Summarizing, from now on:

$$(3.1) \qquad\qquad n > k > e \geq 4.$$

Now assume that a perfect code with parameters e, q, n exists. Then (1.1) and (1.2) are satisfied. Let x_i ($1 \leq i \leq e$) be the zeros of P_e arranged according to magnitude. By (1.2) we have

$$1 \leq x_1 < x_2 < \cdots < x_e \leq n-1.$$

LEMMA 1. *The zeros of P_e satisfy the relations:*

$$(3.2) \qquad x_1 + x_2 + \cdots + x_e = e(n-e)(q-1)/q + e(e+1)/2,$$

$$(3.3) \qquad x_1 x_2 \cdots x_e = e!\, q^{k_1}, \qquad \text{with } k_1 := k-e,$$

$$(3.4) \qquad x_1 \geq ((n-e+1)(q-1)+e)/((q-1)+e).$$

PROOF. By (1.1) and (1.2) we have

$$P_e(0) = \sum_{i=0}^{e} (-1)^i \binom{n}{e-i}\binom{-1}{i}(q-1)^{e-i} = \sum_{i=0}^{e} \binom{n}{i}(q-1)^i = q^k.$$

The coefficient of x^e in $P_e(x)$ is

$$\sum_{i=0}^{e} (-1)^i \frac{(-1)^{e-i}}{(e-i)!}\frac{1}{i!}(q-1)^{e-i} = \frac{(-1)^e}{e!}\sum_{i=0}^{e}\binom{e}{i}(q-1)^i = \frac{(-1)^e q^e}{e!}.$$

In the same way we find the coefficient of x^{e-1} to be

$$\sum_{i=0}^{e} \frac{(-1)^e (q-1)^{e-i}}{(e-i)!\, i!}\left\{ -\sum_{j=0}^{e-i-1}(n-j) - \sum_{j=1}^{i} j \right\}$$

$$= \frac{(-1)^{e-1}}{e!} q^{e-1}\{e(n-e)(q-1) + \tfrac{1}{2}e(e+1)q\}.$$

From the coefficients of x^e, x^{e-1} and x^0 in $P_e(x)$ the sum and product of the zeros are found, proving (3.2) and (3.3).

To prove (3.4) we first remark that if a is a positive integer then $\binom{a}{i} = (a(a-1)\cdots(a-i+1))/i! \geq 0$ because a negative factor in the numerator occurs only if some other factor is 0. Next we remark that if all terms in the sum defining $P_e(x)$ are zero for some value of x then $n = e$ which we have already excluded. Therefore this sum is an alternating sum with nonnegative terms (assuming that x is an integer). These terms decrease in absolute value if $x < ((n-e+1)(q-1)+e)/((q-1)+e)$. This proves (3.4).

From (3.1) we find as a corollary:

(3.5) $e(n-e) \equiv 0 \pmod{q}$.

LEMMA 2.   *If a nontrivial perfect e-error-correcting code of block length n over $GF(q)$ exists, then*

(3.6) $q \leq e(n-e-1)+1$.

PROOF.   Since by (1.2) the zeros $x_1, x_2, \ldots, x_e$ are different we have $x_1 \leq n-e$. If we combine this with (3.4) then (3.6) follows.

REMARK.   The argument we used to prove (3.4) can also be employed to give a sharper upper bound on x_e which would then lead to a slightly better inequality than (3.6). Much stronger inequalities can easily be proved!

We are now in a position to prove our first theorem.

THEOREM 1.   *If $e \geq 4$, $q = p^\alpha$ with $p > e$, then there is no nontrivial perfect e-error-correcting code over $GF(q)$.*

PROOF.   From (1.1) we find by expanding $(q-1)^i$ in powers of q:

(3.7) $\sum_{j=0}^{e} (-1)^j q^j \binom{n}{j} \binom{n-j-1}{e-j} = (-1)^e q^k$

where $k > e$. Since $p > e$ we find from (3.5) that $q \mid (n-e)$. Furthermore, in the binomial coefficients in (3.7) the factor p does not occur in the denominator but for every $j < e$ the factor $(n-e)$ occurs in the numerator of $\binom{n-j-1}{e-j}$. Since $q \mid (n-e)$ and $p > e$ it follows that $p \nmid (n-i)$ for $0 \leq i < e$. If p^σ is the highest power of p dividing $n-e$ then $p^{\alpha j+\sigma}$ is the highest power of p dividing the jth term on the left-hand side of (3.7) ($j = 0, 1, \ldots, e-1$) whereas $p^{\alpha e}$ is the highest power of p dividing the last term. Since $k > e$ we must have $\sigma = \alpha e$. This implies that the first term on the right-hand side of (3.2) is divisible by q^{e-1} whereas the second term contains a factor p only if $e+1 = p$. It is therefore not possible that all the zeros of P_e are divisible by p^2 and if $p \neq e+1$ then it is even impossible that all the zeros are divisible by p. Hence at least one of the zeros is a divisor of $(e+1)!$ (by (3.3)). It follows that $x_1 \leq (e+1)!$. Since $q^e \mid (n-e)$ we have $n-e \geq (e+1)^e$. Substituting these inequalities in (3.4) we find $(e+1)! \geq 1 + \frac{1}{2}(e+1)^e$ which is false for $e \geq 3$. This completes the proof.

We now consider primes $p \leq e$. Several cases have to be treated separately.

THEOREM 2.   *If* $e \geq 4, q = p^\alpha > e$ *with* $p < e, p \nmid e$ *then there is no non-trivial perfect e-error-correcting code over* $\mathrm{GF}(q)$.

PROOF.   Once again (3.5) implies $q \mid (n-e)$. The quotient of two consecutive terms in (3.7) is

$$-q((n-j)(e-j))/(j+1)(n-j-1)   (0 \leq j \leq e-1).$$

Now, since $p \nmid e$ and $p \mid (n-e)$, i.e. $p \nmid n$, at most one of the terms in the denominator of this quotient is divisible by p and since $q = p^\alpha > e$ and $q \mid (n-e)$ we see that the highest power of p dividing the denominator is less than q if $j \neq e-1$. Again let $p^\sigma \| (n-e)$. Then, since $q \mid (n-e)$ and $q > e$ in

$$(n-1)(n-2) \cdots (n-e+1)/(e-1)(e-2) \cdots 1$$

numerator and denominator are divisible by the same power of p. Therefore $p^\sigma \| \binom{n-1}{e}$. In the same way we see that the last term of the sum in (3.7) is exactly divisible by $p^{\alpha e}$. All the terms of this sum except the last are divisible by a higher power of p than the first term as was shown above. Since the right-hand side of (3.7) is divisible by q^{e+1} we must have $\sigma = \alpha e$. Just as in Theorem 1 we see that if all the zeros of P_e are divisible by a power of p then this power of p is a divisor of $(e+1)$. In the same way as in Theorem 1 this leads to a contradiction, completing the proof of Theorem 2.

In the following case the counting of the number of factors p in numerator and denominator of the binomial coefficients of (3.7) is more difficult. The result is now somewhat weaker.

THEOREM 3.   *Let* $p \mid e$, $q = p^\alpha$ *and let* $q > e$ *if* $p > 2$, $q > 2e$ *if* $p = 2$. *Define*

$$M_p(e) := 2e! + e - 1   \text{if } p > 2,$$
$$:= ((e-1)!)_1 e + e - 1   \text{if } p = 2   (a_1 \text{ denotes the odd part of } a).$$

If a nontrivial perfect e-error-correcting code of block length n over $\mathrm{GF}(q)$ *exists then* $n < M_p(e)$.

PROOF.   Suppose all the zeros of P_e are divisible by a higher power of p than is contained in $\frac{1}{2}e(e+1)$. Then in (3.2) the two terms on the right-hand side are divisible by the same power of p and therefore $p^\alpha \| 2(n-e)$. Assume $p > 2$. Then, just as in the proof of Theorem 2, we see that numerator and denominator of

$$(n-1)(n-2) \cdots (n-e+1)/(e-1)(e-2) \cdots 1$$

are divisible by the same power of p and hence $q \nmid \binom{n-1}{e}$ contradicting (3.7). If $p = 2$ the same reasoning applies because in that case $p^{\alpha-1} \| (n-e)$ and $p^{\alpha-1} = \frac{1}{2}q > e$.

Since we found a contradiction, the original assumption was false, i.e. there is a zero of P_e which is not divisible by a higher power of p than $\frac{1}{2}e(e+1)$. If

$p > 2$ this means that $x_1 \leqq e!$ and if $p = 2$ this means that $x_1 \leqq ((e-1)!)_1(\tfrac{1}{2}e)$. The theorem now follows from (3.4).

REMARK. In the case considered in Theorem 3 the bound on n together with (3.6) gives a bound on q.

The three theorems treated in this section do not cover all possibilities. By treating an example we shall show in the following section that the methods used in the proofs of our theorems are also applicable in the remaining cases. The possibilities left open are covered by the computer search mentioned in §2. Summarizing, the result of our investigation is:

THEOREM 4. *For any e, the values of n and q for which* (1.1) *and* (1.2) *are satisfied can be found by a computer search.*

At the moment we cannot do without the computer search but the investigation is being continued in the hope of ultimately proving that there are no more perfect codes at all besides the known ones.

4. **Nonexistence of perfect 4-error-correcting codes.** As an application of the theorems and methods of §3 we shall now prove:

THEOREM 5. *There is no nontrivial perfect 4-error-correcting code over the alphabet* GF(q).

PROOF. By Theorem 1 it is sufficient to consider $q = p^\alpha$ where $p = 2$ or 3.

If $p = 3$ then by Theorem 2 we need only consider $q = p = 3$. We now proceed by the same method as used in the proofs of the preceding section. By (3.5) we have $n \equiv 1 \pmod 3$. For $j \geqq 2$ the terms in the sum in (3.7) are clearly divisible by 81 and so is the right-hand side. Therefore the sum of the first two terms on the left-hand side of (3.7) must be divisible by 81 which implies $n \equiv 4 \pmod 9$. But then by (3.2) the sum $x_1 + x_2 + x_3 + x_4$ is not divisible by 3 and therefore (3.3) implies that $x_1 \leqq 8$. Then from (3.4) it follows that $n \leqq 25$. In [8] it was shown that for $e = 4$, $q = 3$, $5 \leqq n \leqq 25$ no perfect codes exist.

It remains to consider $p = 2$. The cases $q = 2, 4, 8$ have to be treated separately. If $q = 2^\alpha > 8$ then by Theorem 3 we have $n < 15$ and by (3.6) we find $q \leqq 37$, i.e. $q = 16$ or 32. All these cases were also excluded in [8].

If $q = 8$ then by (3.5) n is even. Therefore all terms in (3.7) with $j > 0$ are divisible by 64 which implies that the term with $j = 0$ must also be divisible by 64. This means that $n \equiv 2$ or 4 (mod 2^8). From (3.2) we see that there must be a zero of P_4 which is not divisible by 4 and from (3.3) we then see that $x_1 \leqq 6$ which together with (3.4) implies $n \leqq 11$, and hence $n = 4$ (trivial code).

If $q = 4$ the reasoning is analogous. From (3.7) we find that $n \equiv 1, 2, 3$ or 4 (mod 16). From (3.2) it then follows that the sum of the zeros of P_4 is $\equiv 1, 4, 7$ or 10 (mod 16). Then by (3.3) we see that $x_1 \leqq 12$ and from (3.4) we find $n \leqq 29$. The cases $e = q = 4$, $5 \leqq n \leqq 29$ were excluded in [8].

We could leave out $q = 2$ since it was treated separately in [8] but we shall show that the reasoning used above is applicable in this case. The first two terms of (3.7) sum to $\frac{1}{24}(n-2)(n-3)(n-4)(7n+1)$ and this number must be divisible by 4. It follows that $n \equiv 2, 3, 4$ or $9 \pmod{16}$. By (3.2) at least one zero is not divisible by 16 and hence by (3.3) $x_1 \leqq 24$. Then (3.4) yields $n \leqq 119$ and once again we can refer to [8].

This completes the proof of Theorem 5.

We have given all the details of the proof of Theorem 5 in order to justify the claim of Theorem 4. We remark that nonexistence of perfect 5- and 6-error-correcting codes can be proved in the same way with no essentially new difficulties. Since the details reveal nothing new and are quite tedious we shall omit them here and publish these separately as a report of the Technological University Eindhoven. (All the T.H.E.-Reports are available on request.)

REFERENCES

1. R. Alter, *On the nonexistence of close-packed double Hamming-error-correcting codes on* $q = 7$ *symbols*, J. Comput. System. Sci. **2** (1968), 169–176. MR **39** # 1227.

2. ———, *On the nonexistence of perfect double Hamming-error-correcting codes on* $q = 8$ *and* $q = 9$ *symbols*, Information and Control **13** (1968), 619–627. MR **39** # 1226.

3. E. F. Assmus, H. F. Mattson and R. Turyn, *Cyclic codes*, Report AFCRL-66-348 of the Applied Research Laboratory of Sylvania Electronic Systems, 40 Sylvan Road, Walthan, Mass. 02154.

4. E. R. Berlekamp, *Algebraic coding theory*, McGraw-Hill, New York, 1968. MR **38** # 6873.

5. E. L. Cohen, *A note on perfect double error-correcting codes on q symbols*, Information and Control **7**(1964), 381–384. MR **29** #5656.

6. M. J. E. Golay, *Notes on digital coding*, Proc. IRE **37** (1949), 657.

7. J. H. van Lint, *On the nonexistence of certain perfect codes*, Proc. Sympos. on Computers in Number Theory, Oxford, 1969.

8. ———, *1967–1969 report of the discrete mathematics group*, Report 69-WSK-04, Technological University, Eindhoven.

9. ———, *On the nonexistence of perfect 2- and 3-Hamming-error-correcting codes over* GF(q), Information and Control **16** (1970), 396–401.

10. S. P. Lloyd, *Binary block coding*, Bell System Tech. J. **36** (1957), 517–535. MR **19**, 465.

11. M. H. McAndrew, *An algorithm for solving a polynomic congruence and its application to error-correcting codes*, Math. Comp. **19** (1965), 68–72. MR **30** # 4612.

12. H. S. Shapiro and D. L. Slotnick, *On the mathematical theory of error-correcting codes*, IBM J. Res. Develop. **3** (1959), 25–34. MR **20** #5092.

TECHNISCHE HOGESCHOOL, EINDHOVEN, THE NETHERLANDS

terms of (7) [illegible] and [illegible] must be divisible by 4. It follows that [illegible] (mod 4) [illegible] zero) are divisible by [illegible] and hence by [illegible]. Then (14) yields [illegible] (19) and once again we can [illegible] to [illegible].

This completes the proof of Theorem [illegible].

We have given all the details of the proof of Theorem [illegible] in order to [illegible] the claim of Theorem [illegible]. We remark that [illegible] of perfect [illegible] and [illegible] correcting codes can be proved in the same way with [illegible] new [illegible]. Since the details reveal nothing new and [illegible] we shall omit them here and [illegible] of the Technological University Eindhoven [illegible]. Reports are available on request.)

References

[illegible]

A Combinatorial Packing Problem[1]

L. D. Baumert, et al.

Introduction. We are concerned with the efficient packing of squares of side two into the $p \times p$ torus. More generally, we are interested in the analogous n dimensional problem: that of packing n dimensional two-cubes efficiently into a $p \times p \times \cdots \times p$ torus. Of course, when p is even, the problem is trivial. (For then, the simplest possible alignment of the cubes completely fills the torus.) Thus, we restrict p to be an odd integer. Further, it should be pointed out that our primary interest is in determining the maximum number $[= \alpha (C_p^n)]$ of cubes which can be packed into the torus and that we are only secondarily concerned with the actual structural details of any particular maximal packing. Figure 1a shows that ($p = 9$, $n = 2$) at least 18 such cubes can be placed in the 9×9 torus. Since an odd number of squares (in particular, at least one square) of each row and column must be vacant in any such packing, it follows that Figure 1a exhibits a maximal packing of the 9×9 torus. That is, $\alpha(C_9^2) = 18$.

The notation $\alpha(G)$ is taken from Berge [1] where it is called the *coefficient of internal stability* of the undirected graph G. That is, $\alpha(G)$ denotes the maximum number of vertices of G, no two of which are adjacent. Another function of interest is

$$\operatorname{cap}(G) = \sup_n \frac{1}{n} \log \alpha(G^n)$$

where G^n denotes a particular n-fold graph theoretic product of G with itself. Cap (G) is called the *capacity* of the graph G and, as its name suggests, is of interest in information theory (see Shannon [2]). The graph C_p is the single

---

AMS 1970 *subject classifications*. Primary 05B40.

[1]This paper presents the results of one phase of research carried out at the Jet Propulsion Laboratory, California Institute of Technology, under Contract No. NAS 7-100, sponsored by the National Aeronautics and Space Administration.

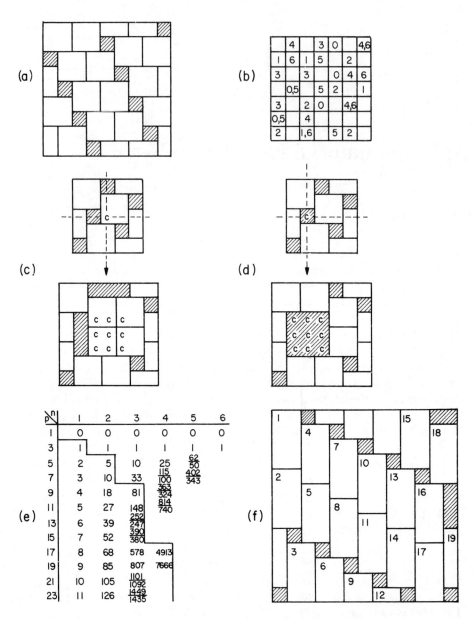

FIGURE 1

cycle graph on p vertices, and the known values of $\alpha(C_p^n)$ provide bounds for cap (C_p). However, cap (C_p) remains unknown for every odd value of $p \geqq 5$.

The work reported below on $\alpha(C_p^n)$ was done over a period of time by several people. These include: L. D. Baumert, R. J. McEliece, Eugene Rodemich, Howard C. Rumsey, Jr., Richard Stanley and Herbert Taylor. In addition it has become clear that some of this work was done independently, indeed previously, by R. Stanton Hales [3].

Some bounds for $\alpha(C_p^n)$ **and an expansion process.** Whenever there is any reason to stress the parameters involved, we shall call the packing cubes, 2^n-*cubes*, and refer to the torus as a p^n-torus. Furthermore, we will use the word *cell* to refer to any n dimensional unit cube.

Let a p^n-torus containing a packing of *size* N_p be given, i.e., a packing which consists of N_p 2^n-cubes. Consider what happens when, with corresponding adjustments in the rest of the torus, an arbitrary preselected cell c is allowed to expand until it becomes a 3^n-cube. That is, when each of the hyperplanes through c perpendicular to a coordinate direction is replaced by three copies of itself. (Figures 1c, 1d give examples of this expansion process applied to the 5^2-torus.) With the convention that every cell created by this process is empty or filled according to whether the cell it is duplicating is empty or filled, this produces a packing of the $(p+2)^n$-torus by 2^n-cubes. Of course, the particular packing obtained depends strongly on the preselected cell c. However, averaging over all the p^n possible expansions (a different expansion for each of the p^n different cells c of the original torus) provides a lower bound on the size of the maximal expansion packing of a $(p+2)^n$-torus derivable from a given packing of a p^n-torus. Thus

THEOREM 1. *If there exists a packing of a p^n-torus of size N_p, then there exists a packing of a $(p+2)^n$-torus of size N_{p+2}, with*

$$N_{p+2} \geqq N_p \cdot ((p+2)/p)^n.$$

PROOF. As noted above, the expansion process takes packings into packings, so only volume arguments need be considered. Expand the p^n-torus in all p^n possible ways getting p^n $(p+2)^n$-tori. Since the expansion process is completely symmetric, each cell of the original p^n-torus will be duplicated the same number of times in this collection of tori. So each cell appears $(p+2)^n$ times, and each time it appears it is filled or vacant according to whether it was filled or vacant in the original packing of the p^n-torus. Thus our collection of $(p+2)^n$-tori contains $N_p(p+2)^n$ 2^n-cubes. So, at least one of them is packed with as many as $N_p((p+2)/p)^n$ such cubes, which completes the proof.

Notice that if (as in Figure 1d) the expansion cell c is empty, it, of course, expands and becomes an empty 3^n-cube, into which one further 2^n-cube can be placed. Since there are $p^n - 2^n N_p$ such vacant cells in any packing of the p^n-torus, our estimate can be increased slightly. That is

COROLLARY 1.

$$N_{p+2} \geqq 1 + N_p (((p+2)^n - 2^n)/p^n).$$

Of course, both estimates, if not already integral, may be replaced by the smallest integer which is larger than them.

COROLLARY 2.

$$\alpha(C_p^n) \geqq 1 + \alpha(C_{p-2}^n) \cdot ((p^n - 2^n)/(p-2)^n).$$

Using the numbers $0, 1, \ldots, p-1$, let us number the p^n-torus in each of its coordinate directions. Thus, each cell of the torus can be designated by an n-tuple with entries from $\{0, 1, \ldots, p-1\}$. A 2^n-cube, then, may be considered to be a set of cells whose coordinates are given by $x+y$, where x is a fixed p-ary n-tuple, y ranges over all 0, 1 n-tuples and the addition is component addition modulo p. Thus x may be considered to be a sort of generalized "upper left-hand corner" for its particular 2^n-cube. It is often convenient to specify packings by designating the cells x which are to be upper left-hand corners in this sense.

Suppose the vectors $x_1, \ldots, x_s$ specify a packing of the p^m-torus and the vectors $y_1, \ldots, y_t$ specify a packing of the p^n-torus. Then the st vectors x_1y_1, $x_1y_2, \ldots, x_1y_t, x_2y_1, \ldots, x_sy_t$ [where the vector x_iy_j is that $(m+n)$-tuple whose first m components are the components of x_i and whose last n components are the components of y_j] specify a packing of the p^{m+n}-torus. This is called a *product packing* of the p^{m+n}-torus. Thus

LEMMA 1. *If a packing of the p^m-torus of size N_p^m and a packing of the p^n-torus of size N_p^n exist, then there exists a packing of the p^{m+n}-torus of size N_p with*

$$N_p \geqq N_p^m \cdot N_p^n.$$

COROLLARY 3.

$$\alpha(C_p^n) \geqq \alpha(C_p^m) \cdot \alpha(C_p^{n-m})$$

for $1 \leqq m \leqq n-1$.

So, by means of Corollaries 2, 3, we have lower bounds on the values taken by $\alpha(C_p^n)$. A study of the known values of $\alpha(C_p^n)$ shows that neither of these lower bounds dominates the other. As far as upper bounds are concerned, consider the following simple volume argument. The percentage of cells vacant in a maximal packing of the p^{n+1}-torus is not less than the percentage of vacant cells in a maximal packing of the p^n-torus. This is because the packing of the p^{n+1}-torus may be considered to be merely the juxtaposition of p packings of the p^n-torus. Allowing for the facts that the 2^{n+1}-cube contains twice as many cells as the 2^n-cube and that packing sizes are integers, yields

LEMMA 2.

$$\alpha(C_p^n) \leqq [p/2 \cdot \alpha(C_p^{n-1})]$$

where, as usual, the square brackets denote the greatest integer function.

COROLLARY 4.

$$\alpha(C_p^n) \leqq (p^n - p^{n-1})/2^n.$$

PROOF. Since $\alpha(C_p) = (p-1)/2$ obviously, the corollary follows by neglecting the possible savings offered by the iterated use of the greatest integer function.

Some maximal packings. Figure 1e tabulates many of the known values of $\alpha(C_p^n)$; these results are established in this section. Where Figure 1e contains two entries, these are lower and upper bounds.

THEOREM 2. *For all integers $n > 0$, $\alpha(C_1^n) = 0$ and $\alpha(C_3^n) = 1$. For all odd integers $p > 0$, $\alpha(C_p) = (p-1)/2$ and $\alpha(C_p^2) = [(p^2-p)/4]$. Here again the square brackets denote the greatest integer function.*

PROOF. The first three assertions are trivial. The first two are only mentioned because they partially illuminate a conjecture made later. Since $\alpha(C_p) = (p-1)/2$, Lemma 2 shows that the theorem will be proved provided packings of the proper size can be displayed for the p^2-torus. Consider the packings specified by the following upper left-hand corners.

Take $(t, 2t+4s)$, $t = 0, 1, \ldots, p-1$, $s = 0, 1, \ldots, a-1$ when $p = 4a+1$. Take $(2s, 2t+s)$, $s = 0, 1, \ldots, 2a+1$, $t = 0, 1, \ldots, a-1$ together with $(2s+1, 2t+s+2a+1)$, $s = 0, 1, \ldots, 2a$, $t = 0, 1, \ldots, a$ when $p = 4a+3$. To verify that these are really packings it is necessary to check in each case that every two vectors of the set differ by as much as 2 modulo p in at least one component; a tedious but straightforward computation which we omit.

THEOREM 3. $\alpha(C_p^n) = (p^n - p^{n-1})/2^n$ *when* $p = k2^n + 1$. $\alpha(C_p^n) = (p^{n+1} - 3p^n + 2^n)/2^n(p-2)$ *when* $p = k2^n + 3$. *In both cases these are the upper bounds provided by Lemma 2.*

PROOF. When $p \equiv 1$ modulo 2^n, it is obvious from Corollary 4 that the upper bound is $(p^n - p^{n-1})/2^n = kp^{n-1}$. When $p \equiv 3$ modulo 2^n, it is necessary to investigate the bound of Lemma 2 more closely. Let B_m denote the upper bound on packings of the p^m-torus. Then $B_1 = (p-1)/2$ and iterating Lemma 2 we see that to determine $B_m (m \leq n)$, it is sufficient to show that

$$p^m - p^{m-1} - 2p^{m-2} - 4p^{m-3} - \cdots - 2^{m-1} \equiv 0 \pmod{2^m}.$$

This follows by summing the left side and remembering that p is odd, i.e.,

$$p^m - \left(\frac{p^m - 2^m}{p-2}\right) = \frac{k \cdot 2^n p^m + 2^m}{p-2} \equiv 0 \pmod{2^m}.$$

So $B_n = (p^{n+1} - 3p^n + 2^n)/2^n(p-2)$ when $p \equiv 3$ modulo 2^n as claimed, and the theorem will be proved provided we exhibit packings of the proper size.

Let $p = k2^n + 1$ first. For $k = 1$, consider the packing given by

$$(x_1, x_2, \ldots, x_{n-1}, x_n) \quad \text{where } x_n = 2x_1 + 4x_2 + \cdots + 2^{n-1}x_{n-1}$$

with $x_1, x_2, \ldots, x_{n-1}$ arbitrary. If x and y represent two 2^n-cubes of this packing, we want to show that they differ by 2 in at least one component. Suppose

$$x - y = (x_1 - y_1, \ldots, x_n - y_n) = (Z_1, \ldots, Z_n)$$

has $Z_1, \ldots, Z_{n-1}$ equal to 0, 1 or -1 modulo p. Let P be the set of indices for which $Z_i = +1$ and let M be the set for which $Z_i = -1$. Then, if $2Z_1 + \cdots + 2^{n-1}Z_{n-1} = 0, \pm 1$ modulo p, we have a congruence of the form

$$\sum_{i \, in \, P} 2^i \equiv \sum_{j \, in \, M} 2^j \quad (\text{modulo } p)$$

where, if necessary, P or M has been extended to include the index 0. But, unless both sums are empty, they represent different integers in the range $[0, 2^n - 1] = [0, p - 2]$ and so cannot be congruent modulo p.

Similarly, for $k > 1$ a maximal packing is given by

$$(x_1 + 2j, x_2, \ldots, x_{n-1}, x_n) \quad \text{where } x_n = 2x_1 + 4x_2 + \cdots + 2^{n-1} x_{n-1}$$

with $x_1, x_2, \ldots, x_{n-1}$ arbitrary and $0 \leq j \leq k - 1$.

When $p = k2^n + 3$, applying Corollary 2 to these results yields

$$\alpha(C_p^n) \geq 1 + k(p-2)^{n-1} \left(\frac{p^n - 2^n}{(p-2)^n} \right) = \frac{p^{n+1} - 3p^n + 2^n}{2^n(p-2)} = B_n.$$

So packings of this size exist, and our proof is complete.

Note that Corollary 2 only tells the average size of the expanded packing. In the proof above this was shown to be equal to the upper bound B_n. Thus, every maximal packing of the p^n-torus, when $p \equiv 1 \pmod{2^n}$, yields, upon expansion about *any* cell c, a maximal packing for the $(p+2)^n$-torus.

THEOREM 4. $\alpha(C_5^3) = 10$, $\alpha(C_5^4) = 25$, $\alpha(C_7^3) = 33$.

PROOF.   Theorem 2 and Corollary 3 show that $10 \leq \alpha(C_5^3)$, whereas Lemma 2 shows that $\alpha(C_5^3) \leq 12$. Exhaustive search shows that $\alpha(C_5^3) \neq 11$, 12. This was established by P. Slepian and independently confirmed by some others. By Corollary 3, it follows that

$$25 = \alpha(C_5^2) \cdot \alpha(C_5^2) \leq \alpha(C_5^4) \leq \tfrac{5}{2} \alpha(C_5^3) = 25$$

this last by Lemma 2. So $\alpha(C_5^4) = 25$.

Similarly Corollary 3 and Lemma 2 show that $30 \leq \alpha(C_7^3) \leq 35$. A computer search, which is discussed in more detail later, showed that $\alpha(C_7^3) \neq 34$, 35 and produced several packings of size 33. One such is indicated in Figure 1b, where the number k in the ith row and jth column indicates that a 2^3-cube has upper left-hand corner (i, j, k).

THEOREM 5.   *Let $p = 4k + 1$ and let $st = k$ be a factorization of k into positive integers s, t with $s \leq t$. There is a one-to-one correspondence between these factorizations and the essentially distinct maximal packings of the p^2-torus.*

PROOF. Since $\alpha(C_p^2) = (p^2 - p)/4$ here, it follows that each row and column of a maximal packing of the p^2-torus contains exactly one empty square. Thus every column contains exactly $(p-1)/2$ 2-cubes. In the jth column i_j of the 2-cubes join with 2-cubes of the $(j-1)$st column to form 2^2-cubes and $(p-1)/2 - i_j$ join with 2-cubes of the $(j+1)$st column. Continuing this all the way around the torus shows (since p is odd) that $i_j = (p-1)/2 - i_j$, i.e., $i_j = (p-1)/4 = k$. So precisely k 2-cubes of each column extend to the right and the remaining k extend to the left.

Let us look at a particular column of this packing. The 2-cubes which are immediately above and immediately below the empty square of this column must extend in opposite directions; for otherwise, some row of the packing would contain two empty squares, a contradiction. So, without loss of generality, we may assume that the 2-cube immediately above the vacant square extends to the right and that the 2-cube immediately below the vacant square extends to the left. Thus, the structure of the packing in any column is determined by a sequence of l's and r's of length $(p-1)/2$ which specifies the direction each 2-cube extends. Suppose this sequence, for column j, consists of m_1 l's, followed by m_2 r's, . . ., followed by m_g r's (g is necessarily even), then (see Figure 2a) the sequence for the next column to the right (column $j+1$) is forced to be m_1 r's, followed by m_2 l's, . . ., followed by m_g l's. If the empty space in column j immediately precedes the m_1 l's of that column, then the empty space in column $j+1$ will be forced to immediately precede the m_2 l's of that column. Thus, of the g blocks of squares only the m_1 block changes rows as we move from column j to column $j+1$ and that block moves up exactly one row. Similarly, moving from column $j+1$ to $j+2$ shifts the m_2 block of squares up one row, etc. Thus going from column j to column $j+g$ raises every block exactly one row. So, in completing the circuit from column j all the way around the torus to column $j-1$ ($=$ column $j+p-1$), the m_1 block is moved up precisely N rows, where N is the least integer greater than or equal to $(p-1)/g$. Similarly, the complete tour from column $j+1$ around to column j lifts the m_2 block exactly N rows. In general then, a complete tour of the torus raises every block of squares precisely N rows. But this can only be the case if g divides $p-1$. On the other hand the m_1 block must be raised at least $2m_1$ rows by the time it moves from column j around to column $j-1$, otherwise there is a conflict in column $j-1$. So $(p-1)/g \geq 2m_1$, whereas $2(m_1 + m_2 + \cdots + m_g) = p-1$, by definition, hence

$$2(m_1 + \cdots + m_g) \geq 2m_1 g.$$

Since there is no loss of generality in assuming that $m_1 = \max m_i$, it follows that $m_1 = m_2 = \cdots = m_g = (p-1)/2g$, with g even. Clearly these conditions are sufficient for they guarantee that all the blocks will mesh properly after completing a tour of the torus.

Thus, for every even divisor g of $(p-1)/2$, there is a maximal packing of the p^2-torus with uniform block size $m_i = (p-1)/2g = s, t = g/2$. That is, a packing

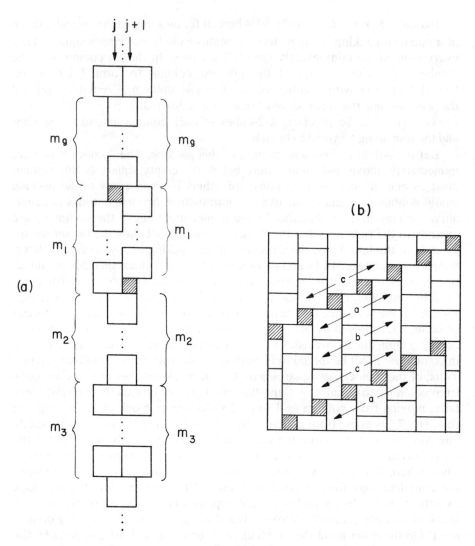

FIGURE 2

which corresponds with the factorization $st = k$. On the other hand, we have seen that in such a packing a particular block of squares only moves up a row once every g columns. This implies that if a packing corresponding to $st = k$ is rotated 90° it yields a packing which corresponds to $s't' = k$ where $s' = t$ and $t' = s$. Thus, all essentially different packings are considered under the requirement $s \leqq t$. So, our proof is complete.

Other packings. Consider the packing of 4×2 rectangles in the 13^2-torus given by Figure 1f. Let the numbered cells designate the upper left-hand corners appearing in the $z = 0$ plane of a 2^3-cube packing of the 13^3-torus.

Further let (x, y, z) with x the row index and y the column index be used to describe the packing. Then the numbered cells of Figure 1f together with the cells derived from them by repeatedly adding $(2, 0, 1)$ modulo 13 provide a packing of the 13^3-torus of size $19 \times 13 = 247$. More generally

THEOREM 6. *Let* $p = 8m + 5$, *then there exists a packing of the* p^3-*torus of size* $(p^3 - p^2 - 4p)/8$.

PROOF. It is only necessary to describe a 4×2 packing of the p^2-torus of size $(p^2 - p - 4)/8$; for such a packing when repeatedly offset by $(2, 0, 1)$ packs the p^3-torus as claimed. For $p = 5$ only two 4×2 rectangles are required and that is easily achieved. Let $p = 8m + 5$ with $m \geq 1$ and let the 4×2 rectangles have upper left-hand corners

$$(4j + s, 2s) \qquad\qquad j = 0, \ldots, m; s = 0, \ldots, 4m + 1,$$
$$(4j + s + 4m + 4, 2s - 1) \quad j = 0, \ldots, m - 1; s = 0, \ldots, 4m + 2.$$

These provide the proper packing. To visualize this, note that Figure 1f consists of 2 bands of 4×2 rectangles, one band being 8 rows wide and the other 4 rows wide. Further, the two bands are offset from each other by one column. The general construction has this same structure with bands of width $4(m + 1)$ and $4m$ respectively.

THEOREM 7. $\alpha(C_7^5) \geq 7^3$.

PROOF. One packing of size 7^3 is given by

$$(x_1, x_2, x_3, 2x_1 + 2x_2 + 2x_3, 2x_1 + 4x_2 + 6x_3)$$

with x_1, x_2, x_3 arbitrary.

LEMMA 3. $\alpha(C_{13}^3) \leq 252$.

(The main point of this lemma is that $\alpha(C_{13}^3)$ does *not* achieve the upper bound $(= 253)$ predicted by Lemma 2. At one time it was considered possible, in view of Theorem 3, that $\alpha(C_p^n)$ achieved the bound of Lemma 2 for all $p \geq 2^n + 1$.)

PROOF. Any packing of the 13^3-torus may be considered to be the juxtaposition of 13 packings of the 13^2-torus. Since at most 39 2^2-cubes fit in the 13^2-torus, this implies that 253 can only be achieved by using twelve packings of size 39 together with one of size 38. Let $P_0, \ldots, P_{12}$ designate these packings where P_{12} is the one of size 38. Any 2^3-cube appears in two consecutive packings P_i, say P_j and P_{j+1}, and is said to *stick up* from P_j and *stick down* from P_{j+1}. Since p is odd, the number of cubes which stick up (or down) from any particular packing P_i is uniquely determined by the sequence of packing sizes. Here, these numbers are alternately 19 and 20 with, of course, exactly 19 cubes of P_{12} going in each direction.

Consider the maximal packing of the 13^2-torus exhibited in Figure 2b. Note that this packing is the union of three diagonals of cubes, the "a," "b," and "c" diagonals, each of which contains 13 cubes. It is a consequence of Theorem 5 that every maximal packing of the 13^2-torus can be so decomposed into diagonals of 13 cubes each. Furthermore, it follows that two such maximal packings have the same slope to their diagonals if and only if one is a translate of the other. If two such packings of differing slopes are compared, we note that they have precisely 9 cubes in common; each diagonal of the one packing meeting each diagonal of the other packing precisely once. Since our packings $P_0, \ldots,$ P_{11} have at least 19 cubes in common with their immediate neighbors, it follows that $P_0, \ldots, P_{11}$ are all (up to translation) the same packing. In fact, by Theorem 5, there is no loss of generality in assuming that they all are, up to translation, the packing of Figure 2b.

Since P_0 and P_1 share 20 cubes, at least one of the diagonals of P_0 has cubes going in both directions. This further necessitates that particular diagonal appearing in all the packings $P_0, \ldots, P_{11}$. Furthermore, this requires certain 2^3-cubes appearing in that diagonal to be shared simultaneously by P_{11}, P_{12} and by P_{12}, P_0, a contradiction. This contradiction establishes the fact that $\alpha(C_{13}^3) \neq 253$, and our proof is complete.

Whenever $p \equiv 5$ modulo 8, exactly this same process can be used to show that $\alpha(C_p^3)$ never achieves the upper bound of Lemma 2. In fact this result can be generalized further to

$$\alpha(C_p^n) \leq [p^{n-1}(p-1)/2^n] - 1$$

whenever $p \equiv 2^{n-1} + 1$ modulo $2^n, n \geq 3$.

A conjecture. As a result of trying to fit a formula to the known data (Figure 1e) using various ad hoc methods, the following rather nice conjecture evolved:

$$\alpha(C_p^n) = \left[\frac{p-1}{2^n}\right] \cdot \left(\frac{p^n - \sigma^n}{p - \sigma}\right) + \alpha(C_{p \bmod 2^n}^n)$$

where σ is the residue of $p - 1$ modulo 2^n.

Note that this formula implies that the first 2^{n-1} entries in each column of Figure 1e are initial conditions which determine the behavior of the function in that column. Thus all the entries above the staircase line of Figure 1e are initial conditions. In these terms then perhaps the nice packings of Theorem 3 are merely reflections of the fact that $\alpha(C_1^n)$ and $\alpha(C_3^n)$ are trivial.

This formula predicts $\alpha(C_{13}^3)$ and $\alpha(C_{15}^3)$ as 247 and 384 respectively.

Computation. The bounds of Corollary 3 and Lemma 2 place $\alpha(C_7^3)$ between 30 and 35. A computer was used to establish that $\alpha(C_7^3) = 33$. The first step was to show that no packing of size 35 could exist. Of course, any packing of the 7^3-torus may be considered as the juxtaposition of 7 packings for the 7^2-torus. Since $\alpha(C_7^2) = 10$, these 7 packings $P_0, \ldots, P_6$ must all be of maximal size in order for their union to constitute a packing of size 35. So a straightforward approach to the problem is merely to list all the maximal packings of the 7^2-torus and try to find 7 of them that fit together properly.

Finding all the maximal packings of the 7^2-torus is not too difficult a project. A few minutes' hand computation shows that, up to the automorphisms of the 7^2-torus, there are only three such packings. Furthermore, the automorphisms of the torus take packings into packings. Thus any automorphism of the 7^2-torus applied to all the packings $P_0, \ldots, P_6$ leads to a problem equivalent to the original one. So P_0 may be assumed to be one of these 3 packings, without loss of generality. However, $P_1, \ldots, P_6$ cannot then be so restricted. Indeed they must be allowed to range over all the maximal packings; there are 980 of these. Again, these are not difficult to generate (inside a computer) for the original 3 packings correspond to 20 which are inequivalent under translations. Thus, it is a simple matter of entering the 20 packings and letting the computer produce the full 980 from these.

Since the sequence of packings sizes corresponding to $P_0, \ldots, P_6$ is $10, \ldots,$ 10 it follows that P_i and P_{i+1} share exactly five 2^3-cubes. A preliminary calculation was performed which showed that relatively few of the 980 packings agreed with any particular one in as many as five cubes. So a fairly simple computer search program was written which first selected five cubes from P_0 and then in turn inserted as P_1 each of the 980 packings having those five cubes. Of course, for any particular P_1, knowing the five cubes shared with P_0 determines the five cubes shared by P_1, P_2, etc. Once P_5 has been selected the structure of P_6 is completely determined, since five of its cubes are determined by P_0 and the remainder are determined from P_5. However, the configuration forced on P_6 at this point never was a 10 packing of P_6 (the cubes coming from P_0 always intersected those coming from P_5). In this manner it was shown that $\alpha(C_7^3) \neq 35$.

If $\alpha(C_7^3)$ were 34 then, without loss of generality, the packing size sequence could be restricted to one of

$$(10, 10, 10, 10, 10, 10, 8), (10, 10, 10, 10, 10, 9, 9),$$
$$(10, 10, 10, 10, 9, 10, 9), (10, 10, 10, 9, 10, 10, 9).$$

Corresponding to each of these sequences is the sequence showing the number of 2^3-cubes shared by P_i, P_{i+1}; these are:

$$(6, 4, 6, 4, 6, 4, 4), (5, 5, 5, 5, 5, 4, 5), (6, 4, 6, 4, 5, 5, 4), (5, 5, 5, 4, 6, 4, 5).$$

Here, again, there is no loss of generality in restricting P_0 to be one of our original three packings. Having picked five or six cubes, as the case may be, from P_0, the computer program proceeded as before, with the added difficulty that the packings of size 9 were not at hand. Where necessary the relevant packings of this size were generated by extending the known partial packing in all possible ways to the proper size. This process allowed the computer to notice the size of the packings it was constructing. In the process of deciding that 34 cubes could not be packed into the 7^3-torus, it produced many packings of size 33. One such is indicated in Figure 1b.

REFERENCES

1. C. Berge, *Théorie des graphes et ses applications*, Coll. Univ. Math., II, Dunod, Paris, 1958; English transl., Methuen, London; Wiley, New York, 1962. MR **21** #1608; MR **24** #A2381.

2. C. E. Shannon, *The zero error capacity of a noisy channel*, IRE Trans. Information Theory **IT-2** (1956), 8–19. MR **19**, 623.

3. R. S. Hales, *On the independence number of product circuit graphs*, Notices Amer. Math. Soc. **15** (1968), 722. Abstract #658-11.

JET PROPULSION LABORATORY, PASADENA, CALIFORNIA

Construction of Finite Simple Groups[1]

Marshall Hall, Jr.

1. **Introduction.** The construction of finite simple groups is a special case of the general problem of construction of groups. The only helpful feature seems to be that any nontrivial representation must be faithful.

Construction methods are closely linked to the kind of presentation used. The most useful presentations have been permutation representations, and the presentation as the automorphism group of some system such as a matrix algebra for Lie groups, a combinatorial design, or a graph. Presentations by generators and relations have been difficult to verify, and this verification has usually been by the method of coset enumeration, which yields permutations from the representations. Presentation by matrices over the complex field or over a finite field have been used. The necessary verifications may be troublesome. There are relatively efficient methods for determining the order of a group generated by a given set of permutations, but I do not know of satisfactory methods for determining the order of a group generated by a given set of matrices over a finite field.

The second section of this paper discusses the known simple groups of orders less than one million. The study of these 56 groups illustrates most of the known construction methods, and for several of these orders this is the first detailed discussion to appear in print.

The third section gives a very brief survey of the known methods and raises some questions for the future. A method which works well for a permutation group on 100 letters may not be practical for a permutation group on 9,606,125 letters.

2. **Known orders less than one million.** There are 56 known simple groups of orders less than one million. Of the classical groups these include groups $L_n(q)$, the projective special linear group of dimension n over $GF(q)$, the

AMS 1970 *subject classifications.* Primary 20D05; Secondary 20G40, 20B25.
[1]This research was supported in part by ONR contract N000 14-67-A0094-0010.

unitary groups $U_3(q)$ of dimension 3 over $GF(q^2)$ for $q = 3, 4, 5$, and sympletic groups $Sp_4(q)$ of dimension 4 over $GF(q)$ for $q = 3$ and 4, and finally the alternating groups A_5, A_6, A_7, A_8, and A_9. Of nonclassical groups there is the first Suzuki group $Sz(2^3)$, three Mathieu groups M_{11}, M_{12}, M_{22}, and two recently discovered "sporadic" groups, the first Janko group of order 175,560 and the Hall-Janko group of order 604,800. Of the orders, 28 of them are of the form $p(p^2 - 1)/2$, p a prime, $p = 5, \ldots, 113$, and by Brauer-Reynolds [4] a simple group of such an order is necessarily $L_2(p)$. The remaining 28 groups, listed by their orders, are

$$\begin{aligned}
360 &= 2^3 \cdot 3^2 \cdot 5, L_2(3^2) \sim A_6 & 58{,}800 &= 2^4 \cdot 3 \cdot 5^2 \cdot 7^2, L_2(7^2) \\
504 &= 2^3 \cdot 3^2 \cdot 7, L_2(2^3) & 62{,}400 &= 2^6 \cdot 3 \cdot 5^2 \cdot 13, U_3(2^2) \\
2520 &= 2^3 \cdot 3^2 \cdot 5 \cdot 7, A_7 & 95{,}040 &= 2^6 \cdot 3^3 \cdot 5 \cdot 11, M_{12} \\
4080 &= 2^4 \cdot 3 \cdot 5 \cdot 17, L_2(2^4) & 126{,}000 &= 2^4 \cdot 3^2 \cdot 5^3 \cdot 7, U_3(5) \\
5616 &= 2^4 \cdot 3^3 \cdot 13, L_3(3) & 175{,}560 &= 2^3 \cdot 3 \cdot 5 \cdot 7 \cdot 11 \cdot 19, \\
& & & \qquad\qquad \text{Janko group} \\
6048 &= 2^5 \cdot 3^3 \cdot 7, U_3(3) & 181{,}440 &= 2^6 \cdot 3^4 \cdot 5 \cdot 7, A_9 \\
7800 &= 2^3 \cdot 3 \cdot 5^2 \cdot 13, L_2(5^2) & 262{,}080 &= 2^6 \cdot 3^2 \cdot 5 \cdot 7 \cdot 13, L_2(2^6) \\
7920 &= 2^4 \cdot 3^2 \cdot 5 \cdot 11, M_{11} & 265{,}680 &= 2^4 \cdot 3^4 \cdot 5 \cdot 41, L_2(3^4) \\
9828 &= 2^2 \cdot 3^3 \cdot 7 \cdot 13, L_2(3^3) & 372{,}000 &= 2^5 \cdot 3 \cdot 5^3 \cdot 31, L_3(5) \\
20{,}160 &= 2^6 \cdot 3^2 \cdot 5 \cdot 7, L_4(2) \sim A_8 & 443{,}520 &= 2^7 \cdot 3^2 \cdot 5 \cdot 7 \cdot 11, M_{22} \\
20{,}160 &= 2^6 \cdot 3^2 \cdot 5 \cdot 7, L_3(2^2) & 604{,}800 &= 2^7 \cdot 3^3 \cdot 5^2 \cdot 7, \text{Hall-} \\
& & & \qquad\qquad \text{Janko group} \\
25{,}920 &= 2^6 \cdot 3^4 \cdot 5, Sp_4(3) \sim U_4(2) & 885{,}720 &= 2^3 \cdot 3 \cdot 5 \cdot 11^2 \cdot 61, \\
& & & \qquad\qquad L_2(11^2) \\
29{,}120 &= 2^6 \cdot 5 \cdot 7 \cdot 13, Sz(2^3) & 976{,}500 &= 2^2 \cdot 3^2 \cdot 5^3 \cdot 7 \cdot 31, L_2(5^3) \\
32{,}736 &= 2^5 \cdot 3 \cdot 11 \cdot 31, L_2(2^5) & 979{,}200 &= 2^8 \cdot 3^2 \cdot 5^2 \cdot 17, Sp_4(2^2)
\end{aligned}$$

(2.1)

The determination of simple groups with specified Sylow 2-groups proves the uniqueness of the simple groups of some of these orders quite directly. We quote the main results we use. Gorenstein and Walter [9] have shown that if a Sylow 2-subgroup $S(2)$ of a simple group G is dihedral, then G is $L_2(q)$ or is A_7. John Walter [26] has shown that if $S(2)$ is Abelian, then

(i) $|S(2)| = 4$ and $G = L_2(q)$, $q \equiv 3, 5 \pmod 8$ as above;
(ii) $S(2)$ is elementary of order 2^n and $G = L_2(2^n)$;
(iii) G is of order 175,560 and is the Janko group, or
(iv) $|S(2)| = 8$ and G is of Ree type, $|G| = q^3(q^3 + 1)(q - 1)$, where $q = 3^{2k+1}, k \geq 1$.

Walter's work does not yield a construction for Janko's group but reduces to Janko's original characterization [19] of his group as a simple group in which the centralizer of an involution t is the direct product of $\langle t \rangle$ and A_5, where t is in the center of $S(2)$.

Alperin, Brauer, and Gorenstein [1] have shown that if $S(2)$ is semidihedral, then either $G = L_3(q)$, $q \equiv 3 \pmod 4$, or $G = U_3(q)$, $q \equiv 1 \pmod 4$ or $|G| = 7920$.

Paul Fong [8] has investigated all groups of order not exceeding 32, and some of order 64 as possible $S(2)$'s in simple groups. The possible $S(2)$'s are

$|S(2)| = 4.$ $S(2)$ elementary.
$|S(2)| = 8.$ $S(2)$ is dihedral or elementary Abelian.
$|S(2)| = 16.$ $S(2)$ is elementary Abelian, dihedral, or quasidihedral.
$|S(2)| = 32.$ $S(2)$ is elementary Abelian, dihedral quasidihedral, or the wreath product $Z_4 \wr Z_2$.

Here the only case not covered by the earlier theorems is the case in which $S(2)$ is $Z_4 \wr Z_2$ and here a result of Brauer [2] may be applied to show that the only orders less than one million which need be considered are 6048, 252,000, 372,000 and 756,000. It can be shown that there is no simple group of either of the orders 252,000 or 756,000.

This leaves the following orders less than one million requiring individual examination.

$$
\begin{aligned}
6048 &= 2^5 \cdot 3^3 \cdot 7, U_3(3), \\
7920 &= 2^4 \cdot 3^2 \cdot 5 \cdot 11, M_{11}, \\
20{,}160 &= 2^6 \cdot 3^2 \cdot 5 \cdot 7, L_4(2) \sim A_8, \\
20{,}160 &= 2^6 \cdot 3^2 \cdot 5 \cdot 7, L_3(4), \\
25{,}920 &= 2^6 \cdot 3^4 \cdot 5, \mathrm{Sp}_4(3) \sim U_4(2), \\
29{,}120 &= 2^6 \cdot 5 \cdot 7 \cdot 13, \mathrm{Sz}(2^3), \\
62{,}400 &= 2^6 \cdot 3 \cdot 5^2 \cdot 13, U_3(4), \\
(2.2) \qquad 95{,}040 &= 2^6 \cdot 3^3 \cdot 5 \cdot 11, M_{12}, \\
175{,}560 &= 2^3 \cdot 3 \cdot 5 \cdot 7 \cdot 11 \cdot 19, \text{Janko group}, \\
181{,}440 &= 2^6 \cdot 3^4 \cdot 5 \cdot 7, A_9, \\
262{,}080 &= 2^6 \cdot 3^2 \cdot 5 \cdot 7 \cdot 13, L_2(2^6), \\
372{,}000 &= 2^5 \cdot 3 \cdot 5^3 \cdot 31, L_3(5), \\
443{,}520 &= 2^7 \cdot 3^2 \cdot 5 \cdot 7 \cdot 11, M_{22}, \\
604{,}800 &= 2^7 \cdot 3^2 \cdot 5^2 \cdot 7, \text{Hall-Janko}, \\
979{,}200 &= 2^8 \cdot 3^2 \cdot 5^2 \cdot 17, \mathrm{Sp}_4(4).
\end{aligned}
$$

For each of these orders there is at least one prime dividing it to exactly the first power and so the methods of Brauer [2] apply to find degrees of characters at least in the principal block for such a prime. With some degrees as a start, consideration of their restriction to a p-normalizer, calculations based on the coefficients of the class-multiplication table, composition of characters, and the orthogonality relations are sufficient in these cases to determine the entire character tables. Almost all of these calculations have been programmed on computers. These methods have been described in some detail by the author elsewhere [11] and full details for the order 604,800 have been given in the joint paper by the author and David Wales [12].

This paper is concerned with the construction and uniqueness of the groups, and we shall assume that the character tables have been constructed. In some cases this enables us to identify the group immediately. For example with $g = 262{,}080 = 2^6 \cdot 3^2 \cdot 5 \cdot 7 \cdot 13$ we are able to show that a 5 normalizer $N(5)$ and 13 normalizer $N(13)$ are the same group of order 130 and that the degree equations for both of the principal blocks $B_0(5)$ and $B_0(13)$ are $1 + 63 - 64 = 0$, 63 being the degree of the exceptional characters. Hence $N(5) = N(13) = H$ is the dihedral group of order 130 and $H = \langle u, t \rangle$ where $u^{65} = 1$, $t^2 = 1$, $tut = u^{-1}$. The group $\langle x \rangle$ has trivial intersection with its conjugates and so Suzuki's theory of exceptional characters [23] is applicable.

The character table of H is

(2.3)

$c(x)$	h	65	65		65	2
$h(x)$	1	2	2		2	65
	1	u	u^2	u^j	u^{32}	t
r_0	1	1	1	1	1	1
r_1	1	1	1	1	1	-1
s_1	2					0
s_i	2		e_{ij}			0
s_{32}	2					0

Here $c(x)$ is the order of the centralizer of x, $h(x)$ the number of conjugates of x. Also $e_{ij} = \eta^{ij} + \eta^{-ij}$ where η is a primitive 65th root of unity. If s_i^* is the character of G induced from the character s_i of H we have from the theory of exceptional characters

(2.4) $$s_i^* - s_j^* = \epsilon(\theta_i - \theta_j), \qquad i \neq j, \quad i,j = 1, \ldots, 32,$$

where $\epsilon = \pm 1$ is independent of i and j and $\theta_1, \ldots, \theta_{32}$ are irreducible characters of G. Since the θ's include the exceptional characters of degree 63 in $B_0(5)$ and $B_0(13)$ they are all of degree 63 and we have a partial character table for G:

(2.5)

$c(x)$	8	65	65		65		65	
$h(x)$	1	4032	4032		4032		4032	
	1	u	u^2	u^j		u^{32}	t	
ρ_0	1	1	1	1		1	1	
θ_1	63							
θ_i	63			$-e_{ij}$				
θ_{32}	63							

Here the restriction of θ_i to H is $r + (s_1 + \cdots + s_{32}) - s_i$ where $r = r_0$ or r_1, and $\theta_i(t) = 1$ or -1. As t is an involution, the requirement that the determinant of the matrix representing t be $+1$ forces $\theta_i(t) \equiv \theta_i(1) \pmod 4$, whence $\theta_i(t) = -1$.

We already know that 5 and 13 do not divide $c(t)$, the order of the centralizer of t and from θ_1 we know that 63 divides $h(t)$. Hence $c(t)$ divides 64 and as $\theta_i(t) = -1$ we know that $c(t) \geq 33$, whence $c(t) = 64$, $h(t) = 4095$. Orthogonality now tells us that θ_1 vanishes for all further conjugate classes of G. An element x of order a power of 2, say 2^m, cannot vanish on a character θ of odd degree, since $\theta(x) \equiv \theta(1)$ (mod $1 - \epsilon$) where ϵ is a 2^mth root of unity. Hence every 2 element is conjugate to the involution t, and so every element of the Sylow 2-group $S(2)$ is of order 2, and $S(2)$ is elementary Abelian. From the results of John Walter [26] we now recognize G as $L_2(2^6)$.

Oyama [20], and independently Graham Higman, have shown that a group with the character table of A_n is necessarily isomorphic to A_n. Thus after the determination of the character tables of simple groups with the same order as A_8 and A_9, these simple groups are then recognized as A_8 and A_9. For the order 20,160 two character tables are found, and one of these is recognized as A_8, while it will be shown below that the other group is $L_3(4)$.

For a simple group of order 6048, the character table turns out to be identical with that for $U_3(3)$. This table appears in [12]. In this there is an element t of order 3 whose centralizer is of order $c(t) = 108$ and index 56. As t is conjugate to t^{-1}, the group $H = N_G(\langle t \rangle)$ is of order 216 and index 28. From the character table the representation of G on the cosets of H must be a doubly transitive group on 28 letters, and H must be the normalizer of a Sylow 3-group $S(3)$ by a cyclic group of order 8 acting faithfully on $S(3)$, and $S(3)$ is the non-Abelian group of order 27 and exponent 3. From this the construction of H as a group on 27 letters and its extension by an involution to the representation of G on 28 letters is relatively straightforward and proves the uniqueness of the group.

Stanton [22] proved the uniqueness of M_{12} for its order by finding its character table and showing that in the representation of degree 11, a variable was fixed by a subgroup of index 12. Once the group was recognized as a permutation group on 12 letters its identification with the quintuply transitive permutation group M_{12} could then be proved. Stanton did the same for the group M_{24}.

David Parrott [21] has shown the uniqueness of M_{11} and M_{22} as simple groups of their orders by first finding their character tables and then determining the structure of the centralizer of an involution. From this, work of Dieter Held [14] leads to a determination of the uniqueness of the groups.

Richard Brauer [3] proved the uniqueness of the simple group of order 25,920 by showing that it had an irreducible representation of degree 5 over GF(3) which had a quadratic invariant. From this it followed that the group must be a subgroup of the orthogonal group $O_5(3)$, which is of order 25,920 and so it must be isomorphic to $O_5(3)$.

The construction of Janko's [19] group of order 175,560 is particularly interesting. Investigation of the principal 11 block showed that his group must have an irreducible representation of degree 7 over GF(11), and the Brauer characters of this representation are known.

A Sylow 2 subgroup $S(2)$ of the group J is elementary Abelian of order 8, $S(2) = \langle t_1, t_2, t_3 \rangle$ and its normalizer $N(2) = H$ is the holomorphic of $S(2)$ by the non-Abelian group of order $21\langle m, n \rangle$ where $m^3 = n^7 = 1, m^{-1}nm = n^2$, and $n^{-1}t_1 n = t_2$, $n^{-1}t_2 n = t_3$, $n^{-1}t_3 n = t_1 t_3$ and $m^{-1}t_1 m = t_1$, $m^{-1}t_2 m = t_3$, $m^{-1}t_3 m = t_1 t_2 t_3$. The representation V^* of degree 7 over GF(11) is an ordinary representation when restricted to H.

Three of the matrices in this representation are

$$(2.6) \qquad T_1 = V^*(t_1) = \begin{bmatrix} -1 & 0 & 0 & 0 & 0 & 0 & 0 \\ 0 & 1 & 0 & 0 & 0 & 0 & 0 \\ 0 & 0 & -1 & 0 & 0 & 0 & 0 \\ 0 & 0 & 0 & -1 & 0 & 0 & 0 \\ 0 & 0 & 0 & 0 & -1 & 0 & 0 \\ 0 & 0 & 0 & 0 & 0 & 1 & 0 \\ 0 & 0 & 0 & 0 & 0 & 0 & 1 \end{bmatrix},$$

$$(2.7) \qquad N_1 = V^*(n) = \begin{bmatrix} 0 & 1 & 0 & 0 & 0 & 0 & 0 \\ 0 & 0 & 1 & 0 & 0 & 0 & 0 \\ 0 & 0 & 0 & 1 & 0 & 0 & 0 \\ 0 & 0 & 0 & 0 & 1 & 0 & 0 \\ 0 & 0 & 0 & 0 & 0 & 1 & 0 \\ 0 & 0 & 0 & 0 & 0 & 0 & 1 \\ 1 & 0 & 0 & 0 & 0 & 0 & 0 \end{bmatrix},$$

$$(2.8) \qquad \begin{bmatrix} 0 & 0 & 0 & 1 & 0 & 0 & 0 \\ 0 & 0 & 0 & 0 & 0 & 1 & 0 \\ 1 & 0 & 0 & 0 & 0 & 0 & 0 \\ 0 & 0 & 1 & 0 & 0 & 0 & 0 \\ 0 & 0 & 0 & 0 & 1 & 0 & 0 \\ 0 & 0 & 0 & 0 & 0 & 0 & 1 \\ 0 & 1 & 0 & 0 & 0 & 0 & 0 \end{bmatrix}.$$

This representation of H can be considered as a representation in the field GF(11) and is irreducible in this field.

The group J contains a further involution t with the properties that $tm = mt$ and $tnt = n^{-1}$. These properties show that the matrix $L = V^*(t)$ must have the form

$$(2.9) \qquad L = V^*(t) = \begin{bmatrix} \gamma & \alpha & \beta & \beta & \gamma & \beta & \gamma \\ \alpha & \beta & \beta & \gamma & \beta & \gamma & \gamma \\ \beta & \beta & \gamma & \beta & \gamma & \gamma & \alpha \\ \beta & \gamma & \beta & \gamma & \gamma & \alpha & \beta \\ \gamma & \beta & \gamma & \gamma & \alpha & \beta & \beta \\ \beta & \gamma & \gamma & \alpha & \beta & \beta & \gamma \\ \gamma & \gamma & \alpha & \beta & \beta & \gamma & \beta \end{bmatrix}.$$

Also $L^2 = 1$ and trace $L = -1$ give the following conditions

$$(2.10) \qquad \beta^2 + \gamma^2 + \alpha(\beta + \gamma) + 3\beta\gamma = 0, \qquad 3\beta + 3\gamma + \alpha = -1.$$

These conditions give 10 possibilities for (α, β, γ). From the structure of $C_J(m)$ it follows that $(t, t)^5 = 1$ and for this only the values $\alpha = -2, \beta = 1, \gamma = 3$ work. Then putting $B = T_1 L, B^5 = 1$ and

(2.11)
$$B = \begin{bmatrix} -3 & 2 & -1 & -1 & -3 & -1 & -3 \\ -2 & 1 & 1 & 3 & 1 & 3 & 3 \\ -1 & -1 & -3 & -1 & -3 & -3 & 2 \\ -1 & -3 & -1 & -3 & -3 & 2 & -1 \\ -3 & -1 & -3 & -3 & 2 & -1 & -1 \\ 1 & 3 & 3 & -2 & 1 & 1 & 3 \\ 3 & 3 & -2 & 1 & 1 & 3 & 1 \end{bmatrix}.$$

Since furthermore $A^7 = 1$, $B^5 = 1$ and J contains no proper subgroup whose order is a multiple of 35 it follows that $J = \langle A, B \rangle$. It was shown by M. A. Ward that $J_1 = \langle T_1, M_1, N_1, L \rangle$ is indeed the desired group of order 175,560 by considering 11 double cosets of $H = \langle T_1, M_1, N_1 \rangle$ with double coset representatives $C_1 = 1, C_2 = L, C_3 = LTL, C_4 = LTLTL, C_5 = LTLNTL, C_6 = (LT)^3 L$, $C_7 = LTLTLN^2TL$, $C_8 = LTLTLN^4TL$, $C_9 = (LT)^3 LN^2TL$, $C_{10} = (LT)^3 LN^5 TL$, and $C_{11} = LTLTLN^4TLTL$. This involved ingenious but extensive calculations showing that the 11 double cosets did indeed form a group J_1, and that J_1 was of order 175,560.

The uniqueness of Suzuki's group of order 29,120 follows from characterizations which he has made, but its uniqueness may also be established by a direct construction, given the character table. It can be shown that a Sylow 2 normalizer $N(2)$ is of order $64 \cdot 7 = 448$, and that this is a Frobenius group in which the element of order 7 acts without fixed points on a non-Abelian 2 group whose center of order 8 is also its Frattini subgroup. This determines $N(2)$ uniquely as a permutation group on 64 letters, and the extension to a doubly transitive group on 65 letters is unique, and this is the group of order 29,120.

The existence and uniqueness of the Hall-Janko group of order 604,800 is given in full detail in [12].

Of the groups listed in (2.2) there remain only four whose uniqueness will be determined here: $L_3(4)$ of order 20,160, $U_3(4)$ of order 62,400, $L_3(5)$ of order 372,000 and $\text{Sp}_4(4)$ of order 979,200.

We shall show first that this group G has a doubly transitive representation on 21 letters, and then that considering these as points and the fixed points of an involution as a line (15 involutions have the same fixed points) we have the projective plane of order 4, and G as a collineation group of this plane must be $L_3(4)$.

In this group G there are 4095 two elements and so at least $4095/63 = 65$ $S(2)$'s. As the number of $S(2)$'s is a divisor of 315 it must be either 315 or 105. If two $S(2)$'s intersect in a group K of order 32 then there will be an odd number of $S(2)$'s in the normalizer of K and so an element of order 3, 5, or 7 will normalize K, but then as $32 - 1 = 31$ such an element of odd order must centralize

Character table of $L_3(4)$

(2.12) $g = 20,160 = 2^6 \cdot 3^2 \cdot 5 \cdot 7$

order	1	7	7	3	5	5	2	4	4	4
$c(x)$	g	7	7	9	5	5	64	16	16	16
$h(x)$	1	2880	2880	2240	4032	4032	315	1260	1260	1260
element x	1	a	a^{-1}	b	c	c^2	d	x	y	z
ρ_0	1	1	1	1	1	1	1	1	1	1
ρ_1	20	-1	-1	2	0	0	4	0	0	0
ρ_2	64	1	1	1	-1	-1	0	0	0	0
ρ_3	45	A	A^*	0	0	0	-3	1	1	1
ρ_4	45	A^*	A	0	0	0	-3	1	1	1
ρ_5	63	0	0	0	B	B^*	-1	-1	-1	-1
ρ_6	63	0	0	0	B^*	B	-1	-1	-1	-1
ρ_7	35	0	0	-1	0	0	3	3	-1	-1
ρ_8	35	0	0	-1	0	0	3	-1	3	-1
ρ_9	35	0	0	-1	0	0	3	-1	-1	3

$$A = (-1 + (-7)^{1/2})/2, \qquad A^* = (-1 - (-7)^{1/2})/2,$$
$$B = (1 + (5)^{1/2})/2, \qquad B^* = (1 - (5)^{1/2})/2.$$

some 2 element. From the character table this is impossible. Hence no two $S(2)$'s intersect in a subgroup K of index 2. In particular since $315 \not\equiv 1 \pmod 4$ we cannot have 315 $S(2)$'s and so there must be 105 $S(2)$'s, and the normalizer $N(2)$ of a Sylow 2-group will be of order $3 \cdot 64 = 192$. A three element in $N(2)$ acts without fixed points on $S(2)$ so that the center $Z(2)$ (which contains only the identity and involutions) has order of the form $1 + 3m$ and so is 4 or 16. But if $Z(2)$ were of order 16, then an element of order 4 such as x, not in $Z(2)$, would have a centralizer of order at least 32, which is not so. Hence $|Z(2)| = 4$ and $Z(2) = \{1, d_1, d_2, d_3\}$ with d_1, d_2, d_3 three involutions. Each of 105 $S(2)$'s contains three central involutions and each of 315 involutions is in the center of an $S(2)$ so that an involution is in the center of an unique $S(2)$. Suppose that an $S(2)$ contains m involutions. Considering the restriction of ρ_1 to S, a particular $S(2)$ we have $(\rho_1 | S, 1_S) = (20 + 4m)/64$ so that $m + 5 \equiv 0 \pmod{16}$. As a 3 element acts on S without fixed points, we have $m \equiv 0 \pmod 3$, whence $m \equiv 27 \pmod{48}$ and so $m = 27$.

Now let $V_1 = \{1, d_1, d_2, d_3\}$ be the center of S, a particular $S(2)$, and let d_4 be a further involution in S, and let $V_2 = \{1, d_4, d_5, d_6\}$ be the center of S^*, the centralizer in G of d_4, where S^* is another $S(2)$. Here $V_1 \subseteq C_G(d_4) = S^* = C_G(V_2)$, and as $d_1 \in S^*$, then $V_2 \subseteq C_G(d_1) = S = C_G(V_1)$. Hence $K = \langle V_1, V_2 \rangle$ is an elementary Abelian 2 group and as no involution is in the center of more than one $S(2)$ it follows that $V_1 \cap V_2 = 1$ whence $|K| = 16$. Since K is Abelian it is in the centralizer of every involution which it contains and as it has 15 involutions, K is contained in at least 5 different $S(2)$'s. As we have observed that two different $S(2)$'s cannot intersect in a group of order 32, it follows that

K is the intersection of any two $S(2)$'s containing it. Now let $K \subset T \subset S$ where $|T| = 32$ and $|S| = 64$ and certainly $K \lhd T$, $T \lhd S$. We wish to show that K is characteristic in T. If this is not so, then T contains a further subgroup K^* which is elementary Abelian of order 16. As $T = \langle K, K^* \rangle$ we then have $|K \cap K^*| = 8$, whence K^* contains 8 involutions not in K. Let T contain r involutions and so $31 - r$ elements of order 4. Then from the restriction of ρ_3 to T we have $(\rho_3 | T, 1_T) = (45 - 3r + 31 - r)/32 = (76 - 4r)/32$, whence $r \leq 19$. But as K contains 15 involutions, there are at most 4 further involutions in T, so that T cannot contain a second elementary Abelian subgroup K^* of order 16, and so K is characteristic in T. As K is characteristic in T and $T \lhd S$ it follows that $K \lhd S$.

Put $H = N_G(K)$. Then H contains at least 5 $S(2)$'s, whence $[G : H]$ is odd and is at most $315/5 = 63$. An element of order 7 cannot normalize K without centralizing one of its nonidentity elements, a possibility excluded by the character table. Hence $[G : H]$ is a multiple of 7 and the only possibilities are $[G : H] = 7, 21, 35, 63$. The character χ of G as a permutation group on the cosets of H consists of ρ_0 of degree 1 and some combination of $\rho_1, \rho_7, \rho_8, \rho_9$ of degrees respectively 20, 35, 35, 35. Hence $[G : H] \equiv 1 \pmod 5$ and the only possibility is $[G : H] = 21$ and $\chi = \rho_0 + \rho_1$ so that G is a doubly transitive permutation group on the 21 cosets of $H = N_G(K)$, and $|H| = 960$.

(2.13)   **The character χ of G on cosets of H is $\chi = \rho_0 + \rho_1$**

$$1 \; a \; a^{-1} \; b \; c \; c^2 \; d \; x \; x \; z$$

$$\chi \quad 21 \; 0 \; 0 \quad 3 \; 1 \; 1 \quad 5 \; 1 \; 1 \; 1$$

Now let us consider χ as a character of H. χ fixes one letter and is transitive on the remaining 20 letters. How many conjugates of an element u does H contain? In general if u has $h(u)$ conjugates in G, and $m(u)$ conjugates in H, then if u is in t_H conjugates of H (i.e. fixes t_H letters in the representation of G on the cosets of H) we have counting incidences of conjugates of u in conjugates of H the rule

(2.14) $[G : H] m(u) = t_H h(u),$

since each of $[G : H]$ conjugates of H contains $m(u)$ conjugates of u, and each of $h(u)$ conjugates of u is in t_H conjugates of H. We may now consider the representation of H as a transitive permutation group on 20 letters, omitting the fixed letter. The character ψ_{20} is

	$m(u)$	1	320	192	192	75	60	60	60
(2.15)	u	1	b	c	c^2	d	x	y	z
	ψ_{20}	20	2	0	0	4	0	0	0.

Here we find $(\psi_{20}, \psi_{20})_H = 3$ so that on the 20 letters H is a transitive group of rank three. Hence in $G_1 = H$ the stabilizer of a further point $G_{12} = W$ has orbits of lengths $1, r, s$ where $r + s = 19$ and r and s are divisors of 48, the order of W.

The only possibility here is orbits of lengths 3 and 16. The subgroup of W fixing a letter of the 16 orbit is of order 3. Hence every 2 element of W moves all 16 letters of the 16 orbit. Thus W contains a group T of order 16, consisting of the identity and 15 involutions, moving the same 16 letters and fixing the same 5 letters.

Let us call the 21 letters moved by G points, and a set of five letters fixed by an involution a line. We have just shown that a set of 15 involutions fixes the same line. Hence there are $315/15 = 21$ lines. As G is doubly transitive there is a line containing any pair of distinct points. There are $21 \cdot 20/2 = 210$ distinct point pairs, and one line contains $5 \cdot 4/2 = 10$ point pairs. Hence a pair of distinct points is on only one line. It now follows that the points and lines form the projective plane of order 4, PG(2, 4), well known to be unique, and as a group of collineations of PG(2, 4), G is necessarily the simple group $L_3(4)$.

For $g = 62,400$, the order of the simple group $U_3(4)$, only part of the character table is needed to provide a base for the construction of the group, proving its uniqueness. Only the eight characters of the principal 13 block and the principal 3 block are needed. They are in (2.16).

(2.16) $g = 62,400 = 2^6 \cdot 3 \cdot 5^2 \cdot 13$

order	1	13	13	13	13	3	2	4	5	5	5	5
$c(x)$	g	13	13	13	13	15	320	16	300	300	300	300
$h(x)$	1	4800	4800	4800	4800	4160	195	3900	208	208	208	208
x	1	a	a^2	a^{-1}	a^{-2}	b	c	d	u	u^2	u^3	u^4

ρ_0	1	1	1	1	1	1	1	1	1	1	1	1
ρ_1	12	-1	-1	-1	-1	0	-4	0	-3	-3	-3	-3
ρ_2	64	-1	-1	-1	-1	1	0	0	4	4	4	4
ρ_3	75	$-A_1$	$-A_2$	$-A_3$	$-A_4$	0	-5	-1	0	0	0	0
ρ_4	75	$-A_2$	$-A_3$	$-A_4$	$-A_1$	0	-5	-1	0	0	0	0
ρ_5	75	$-A_3$	$-A_4$	$-A_1$	$-A_2$	0	-5	-1	0	0	0	0
ρ_6	75	$-A_4$	$-A_1$	$-A_2$	$-A_3$	0	-5	-1	0	0	0	0
ρ_7	65	0	0	0	0	-1	1	1	5	5	5	5

order	5	5	15	15	15	15	10	10	10	10
$c(x)$	25	25	15	15	15	15	20	20	20	20
$h(x)$	2496	2496	4160	4160	4160	4160	3120	3120	3120	3120
x	w_1	w_2	bu	bu^2	bu^3	bu^4	cu	cu^2	cu^3	cu^4

ρ_0	1	1	1	1	1	1	1	1	1	1
ρ_1	2	2	0	0	0	0	1	1	1	1
ρ_2	-1	-1	1	1	1	1	0	0	0	0
ρ_3	0	0	0	0	0	0	0	0	0	0
ρ_4	0	0	0	0	0	0	0	0	0	0
ρ_5	0	0	0	0	0	0	0	0	0	0
ρ_6	0	0	0	0	0	0	0	0	0	0
ρ_7	0	0	-1	-1	-1	-1	1	1	1	1

If $\dfrac{\epsilon^{13}-1}{\epsilon-1} = 0$, $A_1 = \epsilon + \epsilon^3 + \epsilon^9$, $A_2 = \epsilon^2 + \epsilon^6 + \epsilon^5$, $A_3 = \epsilon^4 + \epsilon^{12} + \epsilon^{10}$, $A_4 = \epsilon^8 + \epsilon^{11} + \epsilon^7$.

Let $H = C_G(c)$ where from the table H is of order 320 and index 195, and let χ be the permutation character of G represented on cosets of H. As $H = C_G(c)$, χ vanishes except for those classes $\{x\}$ where $c(x)$ is even.

$$1 \quad c \quad d \quad u \quad u^2 \quad u^3 \quad u^4 \quad cu \quad cu^2 \quad cu^3 \quad cu^4$$

(2.17)

	1	c	d	u	u^2	u^3	u^4	cu	cu^2	cu^3	cu^4
ρ_0	1	1	1	1	1	1	1	1	1	1	1
ρ_2	64	0	0	4	4	4	4	0	0	0	0
ρ_7	65	1	1	5	5	5	5	1	1	1	1
χ	195										

Here since χ is the character of a transitive permutation group we have $(\chi, \rho_0) = 1$. If $(\chi, \rho_2) = s$ and $(\chi, \rho_7) = t$, it follows from inspection of (2.17), since the blanks are nonnegative integers that $s > 0$ and $t > s$, whence $s \geq 1$ and $t \geq 2$. But as $1 + 64s + 65t \leq 195$ we must have exactly $s = 1$, $t = 2$ and $\chi = \rho_0 + \rho_2 + 2\rho_7$.

(2.18)

order	1	2	4	5	5	5	5	10	10	10	10
$m(x)$	1	3	60	16	16	16	16	48	48	48	48
x	1	c	d	u	u^2	u^3	u^4	cu	cu^2	cu^3	cu^4
χ	195	3	3	15	15	15	15	3	3	3	3

In (2.18) $m(x)$ is the number of conjugates of x in H calculated by the rule (2.14). It now follows that H contains only a single $S(2)$ which is therefore normal in H. The involution c is in the center of $S = S(2)$ and c fixes 3 of the 195 letters. An element d of order 4 fixes 3 letters, and if d contains any transpositions then d^2 fixes at least 5 letters, contrary to (2.18). Hence d has 3 fixed letters and 48 4-cycles. But as d commutes with c, d must take the 3 fixed letters of c into themselves. This is possible only if d fixes the same three letters as c. Hence c and 60 elements of order 4 fix the same 3 letters whence the entire $S(2)$ including the two other involutions must fix the same three letters. By a well-known theorem [10, Theorem 5.7.1] the normalizer of $S(2)$ is transitive on these 3 letters.

We have now shown that $N(2)$ is of order a multiple of $64 \cdot 3 \cdot 5$ and so there are at most 65 $S(2)$'s. From (2.16) there are $195 + 3900 = 4095$ 2 elements and so at least $4095/63 = 65$ $S(2)$'s. Hence there are exactly 65 $S(2)$'s, and the representation of G on the cosets of $N(2)$ is doubly transitive, its permutation character being $\psi = \rho_0 + \rho_2$.

The structure of $N(2)$ is now completely determined. The cyclic group $\langle bu \rangle$ of order 15 normalizes $S(2)$ and $\langle b \rangle$ commutes with no 2-element while $\langle u \rangle$ centralizes only $Z(2)$ which consists of the identity and the three involutions in $S(2)$. $Z(2)$ is also the Frattini group $\Phi(2)$.

If d_0 is of order 4, write $d_1 = u^{-1}d_0u$, $d_2 = u^{-1}d_1u$, $d_3 = u^{-1}d_2u$, and $d_4 = u^{-1}d_3u$. Then also as $u^5 = 1$, $u^{-1}d_4u = d_0$. Here u fixes $d_0d_1d_2d_3d_4$, mod $\Phi(2)$, and so $d_0d_1d_2d_3d_4 = c^* \in \Phi(2) = Z(2)$. Replacing d_0 by d_0c^* we now have $d_0d_1d_2d_3d_4 = 1$. Write $d_4^2 = c = c_1$ to determine the involution c. Then $cd_4^{-1} = $

$d_4 = d_0d_1d_2d_3c$ and $c = d_4^2 = (d_0d_1d_2d_3)^2$. Since u centralizes $Z(2)$ we have $d_0^2 = d_1^2 = d_2^2 = d_3^2 = d_4^2 = c$ and also for commutators $(d_i, d_j) = d_i^{-1}d_j^{-1}d_id_j = d_i^2d_j^2(d_i^{-1}d_j^{-1}d_id_j) = (d_id_j)^2$. Furthermore $(d_1, d_0) = (d_2, d_1) = (d_3, d_2) = (d_4, d_3) = (d_0, d_4)$ and $(d_2, d_0) = (d_3, d_1) = (d_4, d_2) = (d_0, d_3) = (d_1, d_4)$. As $(d_i, d_j) = (d_id_j)^2 = d_j^{+1}(d_id_j)^2d_j^{-1} = (d_jd_i)^2 = (d_j, d_i)$ a commutator (d_i, d_j) is equal to (d_1, d_0) or (d_2, d_0). With $i \neq j$, $d_id_j \notin Z(2)$ and so $(d_i, d_j) = (d_id_j)^2 \neq 1$. Now $d_4^{-1}d_3^{-1} = d_0d_1d_2$ and so $(d_4^{-1}d_3^{-1})^2 = (d_4d_3)^2 = (d_4, d_3) = d_0d_1d_2d_0d_1d_2 = d_0^2d_1(d_1, d_0)d_2(d_2, d_0)d_1d_2 = d_0^2(d_1, d_0)(d_2, d_0)(d_1, d_2) = d_0^2(d_2, d_0)$. As $(d_4, d_3) = (d_1, d_0)$ we have $(d_1, d_0) = c_1(d_2, d_0)$ and so if $c_2 = (d_1, d_0)$, $c = c_1 = d_0^2$, then $(d_2, d_0) = c_1c_2 = c_3$.

These relations determine $S(2)$ and the action of u on it completely. Fixing a letter 1, $S(2)$ has its regular representation on 2, . . ., 65 (2 corresponding to the identity of $S(2)$ and u fixes 1, 2, 3, 4, and 5). The permutations for d_0 and u are

$$\begin{aligned} d_0 = {} & (1)(2,6,3,7)(4,8,5,9)(10,24,11,25)(12,22,13,23)\\ & (14,29,15,28)(16,27,17,26)(18,33,19,32)(20,31,21,30)\\ & (34,47,35,46)(36,49,37,48)(38,51,39,50)(40,53,41,52)\\ & (42,54,43,55)(44,56,45,57)(58,64,59,65)(60,62,61,63),\end{aligned}$$

(2.19)

$$\begin{aligned} u = {} & (1)(2)(3)(4)(5)(6,10,14,18,63)(7,11,15,19,62)\\ & (8,12,16,20,65)(9,13,17,21,64)(22,34,42,48,60)\\ & (23,35,43,49,61)(24,36,44,46,58)(25,37,45,47,59)\\ & (26,38,51,33,55)(27,39,50,32,54)(28,40,53,31,57)\\ & (29,41,52,30,56).\end{aligned}$$

Since b is of order 3, permutes with u and $b^{-1}c_1b = c_2$, $b^{-1}c_2b = c_3$, $b^{-1}c_3b = c_1$, b is fully determined as

$$\begin{aligned} b = {} & (1)(2)(3,4,5)(6,43,56)(7,45,55)(8,44,57)(9,42,54)\\ & (10,49,29)(11,47,26)(12,46,28)(13,48,27)(14,61,41)\\ & (15,59,38)(16,58,40)(17,60,39)(18,23,52)(19,25,51)\\ & (20,24,53)(21,22,50)(30,63,35)(31,65,36)(32,64,34)\\ & (33,62,37).\end{aligned} \tag{2.20}$$

Since G is doubly transitive on 1, . . ., 65, there is an involution $t = (1, 2) \ldots$ conjugate to c. Here t normalizes $\langle u\rangle \times \langle b\rangle$ and t takes the fixed letters of u onto themselves. Thus t fixes one letter of 3, 4, 5 and interchanges the other two, and so $tbt = b^{-1}$. Since u and u^{-1} are not conjugate in G it follows that $tut = u$. The orbits of $\langle u\rangle \times \langle b\rangle$ are

(2.21) (1) (2) {(3, 4, 5)

$$\left\{\begin{matrix}(6,10,14,18,63)\\(43,49,61,23,35)\\(56,29,41,52,30)\end{matrix}\right. \left\{\begin{matrix}(7,11,15,19,62)\\(45,47,59,25,37)\\(55,26,38,51,33)\end{matrix}\right. \left\{\begin{matrix}(8,12,16,20,65)\\(44,46,58,24,36)\\(57,28,40,53,31)\end{matrix}\right. \left\{\begin{matrix}(9,13,17,21,64)\\(42,48,60,22,34)\\(54,27,39,50,32).\end{matrix}\right.$$

As t fixes exactly one letter of 3, 4, 5, t must interchange the four orbits of length 15 in pairs. We may replace t by $b^{-1}tb$ or btb^{-1} so that t has a transposition $(6, x)$ where x is one of 7, 11, 15, 19, 62, 8, 12, 16, 20, 65, 9, 13, 17, 21, 64. In each of these 15 cases choose h as the element of $S(2)$ such that $h = \left(\begin{smallmatrix} x & \cdots \\ 2 & \end{smallmatrix}\right)$. Then $td_0tht = m$ is a permutation fixing 1 and so must be an element of $N(2)$. In every case we have 30 values of the permutation t and enough letters of m are determined to identify it. In every case but one there are conflicts, while if $x = 19$, t is completely determined and G is determined uniquely as a doubly transitive permutation group on 65 letters. Here t is given by

$$\begin{aligned} t = {} & (1, 2)(3, 5)(4)(6, 19)(7, 14)(8, 34)(9, 46)(10, 62)(11, 18)(12, 42) \\ & (13, 58)(15, 63)(16, 48)(17, 24)(20, 60)(21, 36)(22, 65)(23, 26) \\ & (25, 56)(27, 40)(28, 54)(29, 37)(30, 59)(31, 50)(32, 57)(33, 49) \\ & (35, 38)(39, 53)(41, 45)(43, 51)(44, 64)(47, 52). \end{aligned} \tag{2.22}$$

For $g = 372{,}000$ only a small part of the character table is needed to show that a simple group G of this order must be a collineation group of the projective plane of order 5 and so necessarily $G = L_3(5)$.

$$g = 372{,}000 = 32 \cdot 3 \cdot 125 \cdot 31$$

order	1	31	3	5	5
$c(x)$	g	31		25	500
$h(x)$	1	12,000		14,880	744
x	1	a^j	b	y_1	y_2
ρ_0	1	1	1	1	1
ρ_1	30	-1	0	0	5
ρ_2	125	1	-1	0	0
θ_i	96	A_{ij}	0	1	-4
φ	124	0	1	-1	-1

For θ_i, $i = 1, \ldots, 10$.
For j, $j = 1, 2, 3, 4, 6, 8, 11, 12, 16, 17$.
A_{ij} is a Gauss sum of 3 31st roots of unity.

These are the characters of the principal 31-block and the principal 3-block. All further characters have degrees which are multiples of 31. A character θ vanishes for all further elements and as θ cannot vanish for a 5-element, the elements y_1 and y_2 are class representatives for all 5 elements.

An $S(5)$ is normal in $C_G(y_2)$ which is of order $500 = 4 \cdot 125$. As $c(y_1) = 25$, an $S(5)$ is its own centralizer and is non-Abelian. Consequently we cannot have 31 dividing the order of $N(5)$, since $31 \nmid (5^2 - 1)(5^2 - 5)$ the order of the group of automorphisms of the Frattini factor group of $S(5)$. Hence the number of $S(5)$'s is of the form $31m$ where m divides 24. As $m \equiv 1 \pmod 5$ we have $m = 1$ or $m = 6$, and G has 31 or 186 $S(5)$'s. As G has $14{,}880 + 744 = 15{,}524 = 126 \cdot 124$ 5-elements, G must have at least 126 $S(5)$'s. Hence G has 186 $S(5)$'s, and $|N(5)| = 16 \cdot 125$. Since $S(5)$ is non-Abelian of order 125, $S(5)$ has exactly 6 subgroups of order 25.

Let P be a particular $S(5)$. Then as is well known the remaining 185 $S(5)$'s fall into conjugate classes under conjugation by P and we have

$$(2.24) \qquad 185 = 5^{a_1} + 5^{a_2} \cdots + 5^{a_s}$$

where there are 5^{a_i} conjugates in the ith class and if P_i is one of the $S(5)$'s in the ith class, then $[P : P \cap P_i] = 5^{a_i}$. As $185 \not\equiv 0 \pmod{25}$ there must be some cases with $[P : P \cap P_i] = 5$, and $P \cap P_i = K$ where K is one of the six subgroups of order 25 in K. As $[P : K] = [P_i : K] = 5$, K is normal in both P and P_i. Here those P_j's containing K are precisely the $S(5)$'s in $N_G(K)$, and so their number is of the form $1 + 5b_K$, including P itself. If we count the incidences of conjugates of K in conjugates of P we have

$$(2.25) \qquad 186 r_K = (1 + 5 b_K)[G : N_G(K)].$$

Here r_K is the number of conjugates of K in P and the left-hand side of (2.25) counts incidences of conjugates of K in the 186 $S(5)$'s while the right counts the $[G : N_G(K)]$ conjugates of K each of which is in $1 + 5b_K$ $S(5)$'s. Now (2.24) takes the form

$$(2.26) \qquad 185 = \sum_K 5 b_K r_K + 25m$$

where in $25m$ we lump together all 5^{a_i} with $a_i \geq 2$. As K is of order 25 and there is no element of order $5 \cdot 31$ we do not have $31 \mid |N_G(K)|$ and so we may write $[G : N_G(K)] = 31h$ and (2.25) becomes

$$(2.27) \qquad 6 r_K - (1 + 5 b_K) h.$$

Since $r_K \leq 6$ we have $(1 + 5b_K)h \leq 36$, and $1 + 5b_K$ is the number of $S(5)$'s in $N_G(K)$. Apart from $1 + 5b_K = 1$ the only possibilities are $1 + 5b_K = 6$ and $1 + 5b_K = 36$. If $1 + 5b_K = 36$ then $r_K = 6$ and in this case all 6 subgroups of P of order 25 are conjugate and here (2.26) becomes $185 = 5 \cdot 7 \cdot 6 + 25m$ a conflict. Hence only $1 + 5b_K = 6$ is possible, $b_K = 1$ and (2.26) becomes

$$(2.28) \qquad 185 = 5 \sum_K r_K = 25m.$$

From this

$$(2.29) \qquad 34 = \sum_K r_K + 5m.$$

As P contains r_K conjugates of K, and P has exactly 6 subgroups of index 5, then $\sum_K r_K \leq 6$ and from (2.29) we have as the only possibility

$$(2.30) \qquad \sum_K r_K = 2.$$

Thus we either have one K with $r_K = 2$ or two K's, each with $r_K = 1$, and in any case $1 + 5b_K = 6$, which says that a K in more than one $S(5)$, is in exactly 6

$S(5)$'s. Now from (2.25) we have

(2.31) $$[G : N_G(K)] = 31 r_K = 31 \quad \text{or} \quad 62.$$

We now show that G has a subgroup H with $[G : H] = 31$. If $r_K = 1$ in (2.31) we may take $H = N_G(K)$. Now suppose that $r_K = 2$ and that $[G : N_G(K)] = 62$, and so G is represented as a transitive permutation group on 62 letters. From Wielandt [27] if G is primitive on $2p$ letters it is either doubly transitive or $2p = r^2 + 1$ for an integer r. Here as $61 \nmid g$, G is not doubly transitive, nor is $62 = r^2 + 1$, and so G is imprimitive on 62 letters, whence there is a subgroup H with $G \supset H \supset N_G(K)$ and here $[G : H] = 2$ or 31 and as G is simple necessarily $[G : H] = 31$.

If χ is the character of G as a permutation group on 31 letters, then necessarily $\chi = \rho_0 + \rho_1$ and G is doubly transitive. As an $S(5)$ is non-Abelian it cannot consist entirely of orbits of length 5, and as $\chi(y_1) = 1$, an $S(5)$ moves 30 of the 31 letters, so that its orbits are 1, 5, 25. $S(5)$ has a subgroup K of order 25 fixing the 5 orbit. Since for no 5-element x is $\chi(x) > 6$, it follows that K is regular and transitive on the 25 letters which it moves.

Let us call the 31 letters of the representation "points" and the six points fixed by K, or a conjugate of K, a "line." Any two conjugates K_1 and K_2 generate a group $\langle K_1, K_2 \rangle$ transitive on the letters they move, and this number cannot be 26, 27, 28, or 29 since no one of these divides g. Hence two distinct points cannot lie on more than one line. As G is doubly transitive there is a line containing any two given distinct points. It now follows that the 31 points lie on 31 lines each containing 6 points, where two distinct points lie on one and only one line. From this the points and lines form the projective plane of order 5, PG (2, 5), which is well known to be unique up to isomorphism. G as a simple group of collineations of this plane is necessarily the simple group $L_3(5)$.

We shall show that G has a subgroup T of order 7200 and index 136, and then construct G as a permutation group on 136 letters.

In this group G, let an $S(5) = S$ contain m elements of the class x_0, and so $24 - m$ elements of classes x_1, x_1^2, x_2, x_2^2. Then

(2.33) $$(\rho_1 | S, 1_S)_S = (90 - 5m)/25$$

whence $m \equiv 3 \pmod 5$. Since x_0, x_0^2, x_0^3, x_0^4 are all conjugate we also have $m \equiv 0 \pmod 4$ and so $m \equiv 8 \pmod{20}$ and as $m < 24$, $n = 8$. As x_0 is centralized by every $S(5)$ which contains it, and as $c(x_0) = 25$, an x_0 is in exactly one $S(5)$. Hence the number of $S(5)$'s is $39,168/8 = 4896$ and so $|N(5)| = 200$.

As $c(x_1) = 300$ and $|N(5)| = 200$, an x_1 is contained in more than one $S(5)$ all of which centralize x_1 and so in a number of $S(5)$'s dividing 12. Thus x_1 is contained in exactly 6 $S(5)$'s and $C_G(x_1)/\langle x_1 \rangle$ is of order 60 and contains 6 $S(5)$'s. It now follows easily that $C_G(x_1) = \langle x_1 \rangle \times A_5$ where A_5 is the alternating group on 5 letters. Restriction of φ_2 to $S(5)$ shows, as in (2.33) that the number of elements of $S(5)$ of classes x_1 and x_1^2 is 8, and so then there remain in $S(5)$

(2.32) $Sp_4(4)$ $g = 979{,}200 = 256 \cdot 9 \cdot 25 \cdot 17$

order	1	17	17	17	17	2	5	5	5	5	5	15	15	15	15	10	10	10	10	3	3	6	6	2	2	4	4
$c(x)$		17				256	25			300		15				20				180		12		3840		32	
$h(x)$		57,600				3825	39,168			3264		65,280				48,960				5440		81,600		255		30,600	
x	a	a	a^3	a^9	a^{10}	b^2	x_0	x_1	x_1^2	x_2	x_2^2	r_1	r_1^2	r_2	r_2^2	s_1	s_1^2	s_2	s_2^2	u_1	u_2	k_1	k_2	v_1	v_2	w	y
ρ_0	1	1	1	1	1	1	1	1	1	1	1	1	1	1	1	1	1	1	1	1	1	1	1	1	1	1	1
ρ_1	18	1	1	1	1	2	-2	3	3	3	3	0	0	0	0	-1	-1	-1	-1	0	5	0	-1	-6	-6	-2	-2
ρ_2	50	-1	-1	-1	-1	2	0	0	0	0	0	0	0	0	0	0	0	0	0	5	4	-1	0	10	10	2	2
ρ_3	256	1	1	1	1	0	1	-4	-4	-4	-4	-1	-1	-1	-1	-1	-1	-1	-1	4	0	0	0	0	0	0	0
θ_1	225	η_1	η_2	η_3	η_4	1	0	0	0	0	0	0	0	0	0	0	0	0	0	0	0	0	0	-15	-15	1	1
θ_2	225	η_2	η_3	η_4	η_1	1	0	0	0	0	0	0	0	0	0	0	0	0	0	0	0	0	0	-15	-15	1	1
θ_3	225	η_3	η_4	η_1	η_2	1	0	0	0	0	0	0	0	0	0	0	0	0	0	0	0	0	0	-15	-15	1	1
θ_4	225	η_4	η_1	η_2	η_3	1	0	0	0	0	0	0	0	0	0	0	0	0	0	0	0	0	0	-15	-15	1	1
φ_1	153	0	0	0	0	-7	3	3	3	3	3	0	0	0	0	-1	-1	-1	-1	0	0	0	-1	9	9	1	1
φ_2	85	0	0	0	0	5	0	5	5	0	0	-1	-1	0	0	0	-1	0	-1	4	-5	0	-1	21	5	-2	-2
φ_3	85	0	0	0	0	5	0	0	0	5	5	0	0	-1	-1	0	-1	0	-1	-5	4	0	-1	5	21	-2	-2
φ_4	34	0	0	0	0	2	-1	4	4	-1	-1	-1	-1	-1	-1	1	-1	1	-1	4	1	1	0	10	-6	-2	-2
φ_5	34	0	0	0	0	2	-1	-1	-1	4	4	-1	-1	-1	-1	-1	1	-1	1	4	1	1	0	-6	10	-2	-2
φ_6	340	0	0	0	0	4	0	-5	-5	0	0	1	1	0	0	-1	1	-1	1	1	-5	-1	1	4	20	0	0
φ_7	340	0	0	0	0	4	0	0	0	-5	-5	0	0	1	1	-1	1	-1	1	-5	1	-1	1	20	4	0	0
φ_8	204	0	0	0	0	-4	-1	D	E	$3A$	$3B$	A	B	0	0	1	1	$-A$	$-B$	3	3	0	0	-4	12	0	0
φ_9	204	0	0	0	0	-4	-1	E	D	$3B$	$3A$	B	A	0	0	1	1	$-B$	$-A$	3	3	0	0	-4	12	0	0
φ_{10}	204	0	0	0	0	-4	-1	$3B$	$3A$	D	E	0	0	A	B	$-B$	$-A$	1	1	0	3	0	3	12	-4	0	0
φ_{11}	204	0	0	0	0	-4	-1	$3A$	$3B$	E	D	0	0	B	A	$-A$	$-B$	1	1	0	3	0	3	12	-4	0	0
φ_{12}	255	0	0	0	0	-1	0	$5A$	$5B$	$5B$	$5A$	$-A$	$-B$	0	0	A	B	0	0	-3	0	0	-3	-17	15	-1	-1
φ_{13}	255	0	0	0	0	-1	0	$5B$	$5A$	$5A$	$5B$	$-B$	$-A$	0	0	B	A	0	0	-3	0	0	-3	-17	15	-1	-1
φ_{14}	255	0	0	0	0	-1	0	0	0	0	0	0	0	$-A$	$-B$	0	0	A	B	0	-3	B	A	15	-17	-1	-1
φ_{15}	255	0	0	0	0	-1	0	0	0	0	0	0	0	$-B$	$-A$	0	0	B	A	0	-3	A	B	15	-17	-1	-1
φ_{16}	51	0	0	0	0	3	1	$3+A$	$3+B$	$-3A$	$-3B$	A	B	0	0	$-B$	$-A$	A	B	3	0	-1	0	-13	3	-1	-1
φ_{17}	51	0	0	0	0	3	1	$3+B$	$3+A$	$-3B$	$-3A$	B	A	0	0	$-A$	$-B$	B	A	3	0	0	-1	-13	3	-1	-1
φ_{18}	51	0	0	0	0	3	1	$-3B$	$-3A$	$3+A$	$3+B$	0	0	A	B	A	B	$-B$	$-A$	0	3	-1	0	3	-13	-1	-1
φ_{19}	51	0	0	0	0	3	1	$-3A$	$-3B$	$3+B$	$3+A$	0	0	B	A	B	A	$-A$	$-B$	0	3	0	-1	3	-13	-1	-1

$r_1 = x_1 u_1$, $s_1 = x_1 v_1$, $k_1 = u_1 v_1$, $\eta_i =$ Gauss sums of 17th roots of unity,

$r_2 = x_2 u_2$, $s_2 = x_2 v_2$, $k_2 = u_2 v_2$,

$A = (1+(5)^{1/2})/2$, $B = (1-(5)^{1/2})/2$, $D = -3+4A$, $E = -3+4B$.

8 elements of classes x_2 and x_2^2. Hence the six subgroups of an $S(5)$ are of types $\langle x_0 \rangle, \langle x_0' \rangle, \langle x_1 \rangle, \langle x_1' \rangle$ and $\langle x_2 \rangle, \langle x_2' \rangle$, and so are conjugate in three pairs.

Since the skew symmetric product of ρ_1 with itself is φ_1, it follows that the square of an element of order 4 (conjugate to w or y) is in the class b^2. The elements x_1 and x_1^{-1} are conjugate and so there is a two element t such that $t^{-1}x_1 t = x_1^{-1}$. As t^2 commutes with x_1, it follows that t cannot be in the classes of w or y and so t is an involution. Since $t^{-1}C_G(x_1)t = C_G(t^{-1}x_1 t) = C_G(x_1^{-1}) = C_G(x_1)$ it follows that $\langle x_1 \rangle \times A_5 = t^{-1}(\langle x_1 \rangle \times A_5)t = \langle x_1 \rangle \times t^{-1}A_5 t$ so that $t^{-1}A_5 t = A_5$. Thus $\langle A_5, t \rangle$ is of order 120. If it is isomorphic to S_5, then an involution in A_5 is the square of an element of order 4 and so conjugate to b^2. But this conflicts with the fact that an involution in A_5 commutes with x_1 whereas $c(b^2) = 256$. Hence $\langle A_5, t \rangle = \langle t^* \rangle \times A_5$ where $t^* = tt_1 = tt$ and t_1 is an involution in A_5. Thus $t^* x_1 t^* = tx_1 t = x_1^{-1}$. We may assume that our choice of t was such that $t = t^*$. Let z be an element of order 5 in A_5. Then the subgroups of the $S(5)$ contained in $\langle x_1 \rangle \times A_5$ are $\langle x_1 \rangle, \langle z \rangle, \langle x_1 z \rangle, \langle x_1^2 z \rangle, \langle x_1^3 z \rangle, \langle x_1^4 z \rangle$. As $tx_1 zt = x_1^4 z$ and $tx_1^2 zt = x_1^3 z$ and the six subgroups are conjugate in three pairs the remaining two subgroups $\langle x_1 \rangle$ and $\langle z \rangle$ are also conjugate. Since $S(5)$ is Abelian, elements conjugate in $S(5)$ are conjugate in $N(5)$. Choose $x_1' \in \langle z \rangle$ where x_1 and x_1' are conjugate.

We can now determine the structure of $N(5)$. Let us take x_1 and x_1' as a basis for $S(5)$. Then every automorphism of $S(5)$ takes $\langle x_1 \rangle$ and $\langle x_1' \rangle$ into themselves or interchanges them. Let us choose the exponent j so that $x_1(x_1')^j \in \langle x_0 \rangle$. As x_0, x_0^2, x_0^3, x_0^4 are all conjugate, there is an automorphism γ such that $(x_1(x_1')^j)\gamma = x_1(x_1')^{2j}$. But if $(x_1)\gamma = x_1^r$, $(x_1')\gamma = (x_1')^s$, then $x_1^r(x_1')^{js} = x_1^2(x')^{2j}$ whence $x_1^r = x_1^2$. $(x_1') = (x_1')^2$. But x_1 and x_1^2 are not conjugate. Hence $(x_1)\gamma = (x_1')^r$, $(x_1')\gamma = x_1^s$ and so $x_1^2(x')^{2j} = (x_1')^r x_1^{sj}$, and $x_1^2 = x_1^{sj}$, $(x_1')^{2j} = (x_1')^r$. Here $sj \equiv 2 \pmod 5$ and $r \equiv 2j \pmod 5$ and so $rsj \equiv 4j \pmod 5$ whence $rs \equiv 4 \pmod 5$. If we now write $\bar{x}_1 = (x_1')^r$, the automorphism takes the form $(x_1)\gamma = \bar{x}_1$, $(\bar{x}_1)\gamma = x_1^{rs} = x_1^{-1}$ and we find $(x_1 \bar{x}_1^{-2})\gamma = \bar{x}_1 x_1^2 = (x_1 \bar{x}_1^{-2})^2$ and so $x_0 = x_1 \bar{x}_1^{-2}$. Also $(x_1 \bar{x}_1^2)\gamma = \bar{x}_1 x_1^{-2} = (x_1 \bar{x}_1^{-2})^3$ so that $x_1 \bar{x}_1^2$ is also conjugate to x_0. Hence the two subgroups conjugate to $\langle x_2 \rangle$ will be $\langle x_1 \bar{x}_1 \rangle$ and $\langle x_1 \bar{x}_1^{-1} \rangle$. The four elements conjugate to x_1 in $S(5)$ are $x_1, x_1^{-1}, \bar{x}_1, \bar{x}_1^{-1}$ and x_1 is taken into these by the powers of γ. As $N(5)/S(5)$ is of order 8 and acts faithfully on $S(5)$, there is a further automorphism β of order 2 fixing x_1 and so $(x_1)\beta = x_1$, $(\bar{x}_1) = \bar{x}_1^j \neq \bar{x}_1$ whence $(\bar{x}_1)\beta = \bar{x}_1^{-1}$. Thus $\langle \beta, \gamma \rangle$ is the group of automorphisms induced in $S(5)$ by conjugation in $N(5)$. If we put $\alpha = \beta\gamma$, then $(x_1)\alpha = \bar{x}_1$ and $(\bar{x}_1)\alpha = x_1$ and $\alpha^2 = 1$. Thus there is an involution s in $N(5)$ such that $sx_1 s = \bar{x}_1$, $s\bar{x}_1 s = x_1$. Since s commutes with the 5 element $x_1 \bar{x}_1$ it is a conjugate of v_1 or v_2.

Now we consider the groups $H = \langle x_1 \rangle \times A_5$ and $K = \langle x_1, \bar{x}_1, s \rangle$. Here $H \cap K = \langle x_1, \bar{x}_1 \rangle = S$. When ρ_2 is restricted to these subgroups of G we have

(2.34)

$h(x)$	1	20	15	124	80	60
$H:$ x	1	u	s	x_j^i	$x_1^i u$	$x_1^i s$
ρ_2	50	5	10	0	0	0

(2.35)

$$K: \quad \begin{array}{c|c|c|c|c} h(x) & 1 & 5 & 24 & 20 \\ \hline x & 1 & s & x_n^i & x_j^i s \\ \rho_2 & 50 & 10 & 0 & 0 \end{array}$$

(2.36)

$$S: \quad \begin{array}{c|c c} h(x) & 1 & 24 \\ \hline x & 1 & x_m^i \\ \rho_2 & 50 & 0. \end{array}$$

Hence $(\rho_2 \mid H, 1_H) = 1$, $(\rho_2 \mid K, 1_K) = 2$, and $(\rho_2 \mid S, 1_S) = 2$ and as $1 + 2 > 2$ it follows that the space of dimension 2 fixed by $H \cap I = S$ in the representation ρ_2 is also the space fixed by K, and the space of dimension 1 fixed by H is a subspace of it, so that $T = \langle H, K \rangle$ fixes this space and so is a proper subgroup of G.

Now we determine the group T. T contains $H = C_G(x_1) = \langle x_1 \rangle \times A_5$ and also an involution s with $sx_1s = \bar{x}_1$ where $\bar{x}_1$ is a 5-element in A_5. Hence T also contains $\bar{H} = sHs = C_G(\bar{x}_1) = \langle \bar{x}_1 \rangle \times \bar{A}_5$ where x_1 is a 5-element in $\bar{A}_5$. In A_5 there is an involution v with $vx_1v = x_1$, $v\bar{x}_1v = \bar{x}_1^{-1}$, so that conjugation of the $S(5) = S = \langle x_1, \bar{x} \rangle$ by v gives the automorphism of S denoted by β above. As conjugation of S by the involution s gives the automorphism $\alpha = \beta\gamma$, it follows that v and s generate the full group of automorphisms of S in G, so that $N(5) = \langle S, v, s \rangle$, and $N(5) \subseteq T$. Thus $|T| = 200 (1 + 5k)$ where T has $1 + 5k$ $S(5)$'s and since H is a subgroup of T, $3 \mid 1 + 5k$. The 6 $S(5)$'s in H all contain $\langle x_1 \rangle$, and the 6 $S(5)$'s in $\bar{H}$ all contain $\langle \bar{x}_1 \rangle$ so that $1 + 5k > 6$. The possible values of $1 + 5k$ are 36, 96, 51, 306, or 816 and $[G : T]$ is correspondingly 136, 51, 96, 16, or 6. Now G is not faithful on 6 or 16 letters. On 96 letters an $S(17)$ fixes $11 + 17m$ letters and this number must divide $|N(17)|$, which is as $|N(17)| = 68$. On 51 letters the permutation character would be $\rho_0 + \rho_2$, but this is impossible as $\rho_0(y) + \rho_2(y) = -1$. Hence the only possibility is $[G : T] = 136$ and $|T| = 7200$.

We have now shown $|T| = 7200$ and $[G : T] = 136$. Here T contains 36 $S(5)$'s. As $H = C_G(x_1) = \langle x_1 \rangle \times A_5$ is a subgroup of T, and $|H| = 300$, T contains exactly 24 conjugates of x_1 and as x_1 and x_1^{-1} are conjugate, exactly 12 subgroups conjugate to $\langle x_1 \rangle$. A_5 contains 6 of these and $\bar{A}_5$ also contains 6 of these. $H \cap \bar{H}$ centralizes both $\langle x_1 \rangle$ and $\langle \bar{x}_1 \rangle$ and so $S = \langle x_1 \rangle \times \langle \bar{x}_1 \rangle$. Hence $H \cap \bar{H} + S$. Hence $A_5 \cap \bar{A}_5 = H \cap \bar{H} \cap A_5 \cap \bar{A}_5 = (S \cap A_5) \cap (S \cap \bar{S}_5) = \langle \bar{x}_1 \rangle \cap \langle x_1 \rangle = 1$. As A_5 and $\bar{A}_5$ are disjoint, the twelve conjugates of $\langle x_1 \rangle$ in T are precisely the 6 in A_5 and the 6 in $\bar{A}_5$. Let $\langle x_1^* \rangle$ be a conjugate of $\langle x_1 \rangle$ in A_5. Like $\langle x_1 \rangle$ it is in 6 $S(5)$'s and each of these contains a second subgroup $\langle x_1'' \rangle$ conjugate to $\langle x_1 \rangle$. Since $\langle x_1^* \rangle$ does not commute with the other conjugates of $\langle x_1 \rangle$ in A_5, the group $\langle x_1'' \rangle$ must be contained in $\bar{A}_5$, and so the six $S(5)$'s containing $\langle x_1^* \rangle$ contain the six different conjugates of $\langle x_1 \rangle$ in $\bar{A}_5$. But as these generate $\bar{A}_5$ it follows that $\langle x_1^* \rangle$ centralizes $\bar{A}_5$. But then every 5 element in A_5 centralizes $\bar{A}_5$, so that also A_5 centralizes $\bar{A}_5$. We conclude that $\langle A_5, \bar{A}_5 \rangle = A_5 \times \bar{A}_5$ and finally

(2.37) $$T = \langle A_5 \times \bar{A}_5, s \rangle$$

for $A_5 \times \bar{A}_5$ is of order 3600 and, as $sA_5s = \bar{A}_5$, $s\bar{A}_5s = A_5$, that $\langle A_5 \times \bar{A}_5, s \rangle$ is of order 7200, whence this is the entire group T.

The permutation character χ of G on the 136 cosets of T is necessarily $\rho_0 + \rho_2 + \varphi_2$ or $\rho_0 + \rho_2 + \varphi_3$ from the degree alone but as T does contain elements $x_1 u_1$ of order 15, it must be $\rho_0 + \rho_2 + \varphi_3$. The character is given here, and $t(x)$ is the number of conjugates of x in T

(2.38)

order	1	17	17	17	17	2	5	5	5	5	5	15	15
$t(x)$	1					225	288	24	24	144	144	480	480
x	1	a	a^3	a^9	a^{10}	b^2	x_0	x_1	x_1^2	x_2	x_2^2	r_1	r_1^2
ρ_0	1	1	1	1	1	1	1	1	1	1	1	1	1
ρ_2	50	-1	-1	-1	-1	2	0	0	0	0	0	0	0
φ_3	85	0	0	0	0	5	0	0	0	5	5	0	0
χ	136	0	0	0	0	8	1	1	1	6	6	1	1

order	15	15	10	10	10	10	3	3	6	6	2	2	4	4
$t(x)$			360	360	720	720	40	400	600	1200	30	60	900	
x	r_2	r_2^2	s_1	s_1^2	s_2	s_2^2	u_1	u_2	k_1	k_2	v_1	v_2	w	y
ρ_0	1	1	1	1	1	1	1	1	1	1	1	1	1	1
ρ_2	0	0	0	0	0	0	5	5	1	1	10	10	2	-2
φ_3	-1	-1	0	0	1	1	-5	4	-1	0	5	21	1	1
χ	0	0	1	1	2	2	1	10	1	2	16	32	4	0

Following D. G. Higman [15] G is a rank 3 group and if the orbits are $\{a\}$, $\Delta(a), \Gamma(a)$ of lengths $1, k, l$ and λ, μ are defined by

(2.39)
$$|\Delta(a) \cap \Delta(b)| = \lambda \quad \text{for } b \in \Delta(a),$$
$$= \mu \quad \text{for } b \in \Gamma(a),$$

then the following relations hold:

(2.40) $\mu l = k(k - \lambda - 1)$, $d = (\lambda - \mu)^2 + 4(k - \mu)$ is a square, and

(2.41) $f_2, f_3 = (2k + (\lambda - \mu)(k + l) \mp d^{1/2}(k + l))/(\mp 2d^{1/2})$

where $1, f_2, f_3$ are the degrees of the irreducibles making up χ. As f_2, f_3 are 50 and 85 in this case we have

(2.42) $k = 60$, $l = 75$, $\lambda = 24$, $\mu = 28$.

A convenient representation for T is as a permutation group on 10 letters where $\bar{A}_5$ is the alternating group on 1, 2, 3, 4, 5, A_5 is the alternating group on 6, 7, 8, 9, 10 and we take

(2.43)
$$x_1 = (1, 2, 3, 4, 5), \quad u_1 = (3, 4, 5), \quad s = (1, 6)(2, 7)(3, 8)(4, 9)(5, 10).$$

The stabilizer W of the 60 orbit is a group of order 120, which from (2.38) contains a 5-element of class x_2, a 3-element of class u_2 but no element of order

15. Hence W contains an A_5^* which is a subdirect product of A_5 and $\bar{A}_5$. Since x_2 is not conjugate to x_2^2 W is not isomorphic to an S_5 and so is isomorphic to a direct product $A_5^* \times \langle \tau \rangle$ where τ is an involution and $W = C_T(\tau)$. No involution in $A_5 \times \bar{A}_5$ commutes with a subdirect product of A_5 and $\bar{A}_5$ so that $\tau = y_1 y_2 s$ with $y_1 \in A_5$, $y_2 \in \bar{A}_5$. As $1 = \tau^2 = y_1 y_2 s y_1 y_2 s = y_1(y_2 u_1^s) y_2^s = (y_2 y_1^s)(y_1 y_2^s)$, as $y_2^s \in A_5$ and $y_1^s \in \bar{A}_5$ we have $y_2 y_1^s = 1$ so that $y_2 = (y_1^{-1})^s$. But now $\tau = y_1(y_1^{-1})^s = y_1 s y_1^{-1}$ so that τ is conjugate to s. Taking a conjugate of W as our stabilizer, we may choose $W = C_H(s)$. Here $W = \langle s, yy^s \rangle$ for all $y \in A_5$.

We must now determine the stabilizer V of the 75 orbit where V is of order 96. V contains a Sylow 2-group of T which without loss of generality we may take as generated by the following elements, using the 10 letter representation of T:

$$
\begin{aligned}
s = &(1, 6)\,(2, 7)\,(3, 8)\,(4, 9)\,(5, 10),\\
&(2, 3)\,(4, 5),\\
&(2, 4)\,(3, 5),\\
&(2, 5)\,(3, 4),\\
&(7, 8)\,(9, 10),\\
&(7, 9)\,(8, 10),\\
&(7, 10)\,(8, 9).
\end{aligned}
$$

(2.44)

In addition V contains a 3-element which from (2.38) is of class u_2 and so of the form $(a, b, c)\,(d, e, f)$ with a, b, c from $1, 2, 3, 4, 5$ and d, e, f from $6, 7, 8, 9, 10$. If such an element u_2 moved either 1 or 6, V would contain an element of order 5. Hence the u_2 fixes both 1 and 6, and by conjugation by the elements in (2.44) may be assumed also to fix both 2 and 7. Hence $u_2 = (3, 4, 5)\,(8, 9, 10)$ or $u_2 = (3, 4, 5)\,(8, 10, 9)$ or u_2 is the inverse of one of these two elements. In the first case $u_2 s$ is an element of order 6 of the type $u_2 v_2$ and is in $C_H(s) = W$. But for such an element from (2.38) $x(u_2 v_2) = 2$ and as it fixes the 1 orbit and a letter in the 60 orbit it cannot also fix a letter in the 75 orbit. This excludes the first choice for u_2 (and of course also the inverse of this element). Hence the second choice $u_2 = (3, 4, 5)\,(8, 10, 9)$ (for which $u_2 s$ is of order 2) must be an element of V. We conclude that

(2.45) $V = \langle s(2), (3, 4, 5)\,(8, 10, 9) \rangle$

with $s(2)$ generated by the elements of (2.44).

We take $\{1\}, \{2, \ldots, 61\}, \{62, \ldots, 136\}$ as the letters of the three orbits of lengths 1, 60, 75 respectively. The permutations for x_1, u_1, s are

(2.46)

$x_1 = (1)\,(2, 3, 4, 5, 6)\,(7, 8, 9, 10, 11)\,(12, 13, 14, 15, 16)\,(17, 18, 19, 20, 21)\,(22, 23, 24, 25, 26)$
$(27, 28, 29, 30, 31)\,(32, 33, 34, 35, 36)\,(37, 38, 39, 40, 41)\,(42, 43, 44, 45, 46)\,(47, 48, 49, 50, 51)$
$(52, 53, 54, 55, 56)\,(57, 58, 59, 60, 61)\,(62, 63, 64, 65, 66)\,(67, 68, 69, 70, 71)\,(72, 73, 74, 75, 76)$
$(77, 78, 79, 80, 81)\,(82, 83, 84, 85, 86)\,(87, 88, 89, 90, 91)\,(92, 93, 94, 95, 96)\,(97, 98, 99, 100, 101)$
$(102, 103, 104, 105, 106)\,(107, 108, 109, 110, 111)\,(112, 113, 114, 115, 116)$
$(117, 118, 119, 120, 121)\,(122, 123, 124, 125, 126)\,(127, 128, 129, 130, 131)$
$(132, 133, 134, 135, 136),$

$u_1 = (1)(2,7,12)(3,17,22)(4,15,32)(5,25,9)(6,35,119)(8,37,42)(10,45,14)(11,23,39)$
$(13,47,34)(16,43,49)(18,52,57)(20,60,24)(21,33,54)(26,58,41)(27,38,61)$
$(28,51,46)(29,59,55)(30,44,40)(31,53,48)(36,50,56)(62,87,112)(63,113,88)$
$(64,115,66)(65,91,89)(67,92,117)(68,118,93)(69,120,71)(70,96,94)(72,97,122)$
$(73,123,98)(74,125,76)(75,101,99)(77,102,127)(78,128,103)(79,130,81)(80,106,104)$
$(82,107,132)(83,133,108)(84,135,86)(85,111,109)(90,116,114)(95,121,119)$
$(100,126,124)(105,131,129)(110,136,134).$

$s = (1)(2)(3,6)(4,5)(7,12)(8,19)(9)(10,32)(11,22)(13,35)(14,25)(15)(16,17)(18)$
$(20,36)(21,26)(23,34)(24)(27)(28)(29)(30)(31)(33)(37,49)(38,57)(39,42)(40,56)$
$(41)(43,47)(44,60)(45)(46,54)(48,52)(50)(51,58)(53,61)(55)(59)(62)(63,67)(64,72)$
$(65,77)(66,82)(68)(69,73)(70,78)(71,83)(74)(75,79)(76,84)(80)(81,85)(86)(87)$
$(88,92)(89,97)(90,102)(91,107)(93)(94,98)(95,103)(96,108)(99)(100,104)(101,109)$
$(105)(106,110)(111)(112)(113,117)(114,122)(115,127)(116,132)(118)(119,123)$
$(120,128)(121,133)(124)(125,129)(126,134)(130)(131,135)(136).$

Since there is only one orbit of length 60, it is self-paired, and so **[27]** it follows that G contains an element $t = (1, 2)\cdots$. Replacing t by an odd power of itself, we may take t to be a 2-element and so of order 2 or 4. By conjugation 5 must induce an automorphism in $G_{1.2} = W$, the stabilizer of 1 and 2 determined above. As $W = \langle s \rangle \times A_5^*$, t must commute with s and induce an automorphism in A_5^*. Since a 5-element in A_5^* is of class x_2 or x_2^2 and is not conjugate to its square, the automorphisms generated in A_5^* by t and itself do not include automorphisms isomorphic to S_5. Thus t induces an inner automorphism in A_5^*, and multiplying t by an involution in A_5^* if necessary, we may now assume that t centralizes A_5^* and so all of W.

The orbits of W are

$$\begin{aligned}
&\{1\}, \{2\},\\
&\{3, 6, 38, 39, 42, 43, 47, 48, 52, 53, 57, 61\},\\
&\{4, 5, 8, 10, 14, 16, 17, 19, 23, 25, 32, 34\},\\
&\{7, 11, 12, 13, 20, 21, 22, 26, 35, 36, 37, 40, 44, 46, 49, 51, 54, 56, 58, 60\},\\
(2.47)\quad &\{9, 15, 18, 24, 27, 28, 29, 30, 31, 33, 41, 45, 50, 55, 59\},\\
&\{62, 68, 74, 80, 86, 87, 93, 99, 105, 111, 112, 118, 124, 130, 136\},\\
&\{63, 66, 67, 69, 73, 75, 79, 81, 82, 85, 89, 90, 95, 96, 97, 101, 102, 103, 108, 109\},\\
&\{64, 65, 70, 71, 72, 76, 77, 78, 83, 84, 113, 116, 117, 119, 123, 125, 129, 131, 132, 135\},\\
&\{88, 91, 92, 94, 98, 100, 104, 106, 107, 110, 114, 115, 120, 121, 122, 126, 127, 128, 133, 134\}.
\end{aligned}$$

Since $\lambda = 24$ from (2.42) this means

$$(2.48)\qquad |\Delta(1) \cap \Delta(2)| = 24.$$

Here $\Delta(1)$ and $\Delta(2)$ are respectively the 60 orbits of G_1 and G_2 and their intersection is taken into itself by $W = G_{12} = G_1 \cap G_2$. Hence the 24 letters of (2.48) are the two twelve orbits of W in (2.47) namely those including 3 and 4. Hence t must interchange the two 15 orbits, namely those containing 9 and 62, and the 20 orbit containing 7 with one of the last three orbits.

Since t^2 belongs to $G_{12} = W$ then t^2 fixes at least $15+15+20+20 = 70$ letters, and so we have

$$(2.49)\qquad t^2 = 1.$$

Since t centralizes W, if t fixes a letter in one of the orbits of (2.47) it fixes all of them. As t fixes 8, 16, or 32 letters from (2.38) the only possibility is 32. This also follows from the fact that $C_G(x_2) = \langle x_2 \rangle \times A_5$ and so t, as an involution centralizing $x_2 = x_1(sx_1s)$ is conjugate to s. Thus t must fix the letters of one of the 12 orbits in (2.47) and one of the last three 20 orbits. The fixed letters of $x_2 = x_1(sx_1s)$ are (1), (2), (3), (4), (5), and (6) and t must take these into themselves. Hence

$$(2.50) \qquad t = (1, 2)\,(3)\,(6)\,(4, 5) \cdots \quad \text{or} \quad t = (1, 2)\,(3, 6)\,(4)\,(5) \cdots.$$

Since from (2.46) $s = (1)\,(2)\,(3, 6)\,(4, 5) \cdots$ replacing t by st if necessary we may take $t = (1, 2)\,(3)\,(6)\,(4, 5)$. Since t centralizes $W = \langle s, x_1s_1x_1s_1, u_1s_1x_1u_1 \rangle$, this is enough to determine the action of t on the two 12 orbits in (2.47):

$$(2.51) \quad \begin{aligned} t = {}& (1, 2)\,(3)\,(6)\,(38)\,(39)\,(42)\,(43)\,(47)\,(48)\,(52)\,(53)\,(57)\,(61) \\ & (4, 5)\,(8, 19)\,(10, 32)\,(14, 25)\,(16, 17)\,(23, 34) \cdots. \end{aligned}$$

It now follows that

$$(2.52) \qquad tx_1 tsx_1 tx_1^{-1} = (1)\,(2)\,(3)\,(4)\,(5)\,(6)\,(38, 42, 47, 52, 61) \cdots$$

and this element, belonging to W, must be $(x_1sx_1s)^3$. We now have a relation on t:

$$(2.53) \qquad\qquad\qquad tx_1 tsx_1 t = (x_1sx_1s)^3 x_1.$$

The fixed letters of $u_2 = u_1(su_1s)$ in W are (1) (2) (7) (12) (63) (67) (88) (92) (113) (117). As t interchanges the 20 orbit containing 7 in (2.47) with one of the last three 20 orbits, and as t takes the fixed letters of u_2 into themselves t must contain one of the transpositions (7, 63), (7, 67), (7, 88), (7, 92), (7, 113), or (7, 117). The three choices (7, 63), (7, 88), and (7, 113) all lead to conflicts in the relation (2.53), but the three choices (7, 67), (7, 117), (7, 92) lead to a complete determination of t from (2.53) and the fact that t centralizes W. But there is a permutation z (not an element of G) such that z fixes $1, \ldots, 61$ and

$$(2.54) \quad \begin{aligned} z = {}& (62, 112, 87)\,(63, 113, 88)\,(64, 114, 89)\,(65, 115, 90)\,(66, 116, 91) \\ & (67, 117, 92)\,(68, 118, 93)\,(69, 119, 94)\,(70, 120, 95)\,(71, 121, 96) \\ & (72, 122, 97)\,(73, 123, 98)\,(74, 124, 99)\,(75, 125, 100)\,(76, 126, 101) \\ & (77, 127, 102)\,(78, 128, 103)\,(79, 129, 104)\,(80, 130, 105) \\ & (81, 131, 106)\,(82, 132, 107)\,(83, 133, 108)\,(84, 134, 109)\,(85, 135, 110) \\ & (86, 136, 111). \end{aligned}$$

By conjugation z fixes x_1, u_1, and s and permutes the three solutions for t among themselves. Hence all three solutions for t give the same group G and we have proved the uniqueness of the simple group G of order 979,200 which must therefore be $Sp_4(4)$.

The value of t with the transposition $(7, 67)$ is

$t = (1, 2) (3) (4, 5) (6) (7, 67) (8, 19) (9, 86) (10, 32) (11, 75) (12, 63) (13, 85)$
$(14, 25) (15, 74) (16, 17) (18, 80) (20, 69) (21, 66) (22, 79) (23, 34) (24, 28)$
$(26, 82) (27, 124) (28, 112) (29, 130) (30, 118) (31, 136) (33, 62) (35, 81)$
$(36, 73) (37, 101) (38) (39) (40, 103) (41, 87) (42) (43) (44, 96) (45, 105)$
$(46, 89) (47) (48) (49, 109) (50, 93) (51, 102) (52) (53) (54, 97) (55, 111)$
$(56, 95) (57) (58, 90) (59, 99) (60, 108) (61) (64) (65) (70) (71) (72)$
$(76) (77) (78) (83) (84) (88, 92) (91, 107) (94, 98) (100, 104) (106, 110)$
$(113) (114, 122) (115, 127) (116) (117) (119) (120, 128) (121, 133)$
$(123) (125) (126, 134) (129) (131) (132) (135).$

3. **General construction methods.**   In problems on the uniqueness of simple groups, it is sometimes possible to find a presentation of the group G so that it is then easy to identify. In proving the uniqueness of $L_2(p)$ as the only simple group of order $p(p^2 - 1)/2$, Brauer and Reynolds [4] use modular theory and finally are able to show that G has an irreducible representation of degree 3 over $GF(p)$. With G as a subgroup of $SL_3(p)$, its identification becomes elementary. Again Brauer [3] using a 5-dimensional representation of a simple group of order 25,920, was able to show this to be a subgroup of the known simple group $O_5(3)$ of the same order and so identify it. These are instances of characterizing and identifying known groups. An unsolved problem of this kind is that of showing (if it is true) that the Ree-type groups are indeed the Ree groups, and could be resolved if it could be shown that the groups in question have 7-dimensional representations over the appropriate $GF(3^{2n+1})$.

If we have a group G defined by generators and relations, then if we choose an appropriate subgroup H, we may consider the permutation representation of G on the cosets of H. An elementary method described by Coxeter [6] shows how to use the relations to find the permutation representation of G. This method lends itself to numerical analysis, and is known as coset enumeration. In practice this is most effective if G can be considered as the amalgam of known subgroups. Thus with Janko's simple group of order 50,232,960, Graham Higman and John McKay [17] took a subgroup H of order 8160, which was the extension of $L_2(16)$ by an outer automorphism of order 2, and a further subgroup L of order 2880, L being the split extension of an elementary group of order 16 by $GL(2, 4)$. Here $H \cap L$ is of order 480. Hence G is an amalgam of H and L, but not, of course, the infinite free amalgam. They were able to show that in the amalgam of H and L in G certain relations had to hold, specifically three relations relating elements of H and L in addition to those defining H and L separately. Coset enumeration by John McKay on the computer in the Atlas Laboratories showed that these relations defined G as a group on 6156 cosets of a the subgroup H of order 8160. From Janko's character table of G, John Thompson was able to prove the existence of the subgroup H. The existence of L was a consequence of Janko's conditions on the centralizer of an involution. In this way both the existence and uniqueness of the simple group G were shown.

The new simple group of order $4{,}010{,}387{,}200 = 2^{10} \cdot 3^3 \cdot 5^2 \cdot 7^3 \cdot 17$ due to Held [13] is particularly interesting. Held considered simple groups in which the centralizer H_0 of an involution was isomorphic to that in M_{24}. He showed that such a group was one of three possible groups: $L_5(2)$, M_{24}, or a new group G of the order above. In this paper Held is able to show that G has 34 conjugate classes of elements, and describes the centralizer of a representative element exactly. From this information John Thompson was able to construct the character table of G. Then a test of the character table by John McKay showed that G might have a subgroup H of index 2058, and presumably H would be the extension of $Sp_4(4)$ by an outer automorphism of order 2. Taking this as an assumption, Graham Higman and John McKay were able to find defining relations sufficient to define the group, as was verified by a coset enumeration. More recently it has been shown by Graham Higman and John Thompson independently that Held's group must have such a subgroup H, thus proving the uniqueness of a simple group satifying Held's hypotheses.

A powerful method in construction is to construct a graph which has G as an automorphism group. If G is representable as a transitive permutation group on a set of n letters, consider these letters as points, and let $\Delta^i(b)$ be the ith orbit in the stabilizer G_b. If Δ^i is a self paired orbit [27, p. 45] then c is a letter of $\Delta^i(b)$ if and only if b is a letter of $\Delta^i(c)$. Hence joining an arbitrary point b to every point of $\Delta^i(b)$ gives an undirected graph Γ which has G as an automorphism group. If Γ can be constructed directly then G is a subgroup of the full group of automorphisms of Γ, and in practice G is either $A(\Gamma)$ the full group of automorphisms of Γ or a subgroup of index 2 in $A(\Gamma)$. This approach is of no value if G is doubly transitive, for then Γ is the complete graph on n points and $A(\Gamma)$ is the symmetric group S_n. In this way the Higman-Sims [16] group of order 44,352,000 was constructed as a rank 3 group on 100 letters, the stabilizer of a letter being M_{22} with orbits of lengths 1, 22, 77. In this case as in others, the graph is originally determined in terms of orbits of the stabilizers in such a way that the subgroup of $A(\Gamma)$ fixing a point (1) is clearly isomorphic to G_1. The difficulty consists in proving that $A(\Gamma)$ is transitive on the points of Γ. This approach has been used by McLaughlin and by Suzuki [23] in the construction of their simple groups. B. Fischer [7] constructs groups generated by 3-transpositions, meaning a class $T = \{t\}$ of involutions such that any two involutions of T which do not commute have a product of order 3. Fischer represents his groups G as permutation groups by conjugation of the involutions in T. He can show that if $H = C_G(t)$, $t \in \Gamma$, then the involutions $\{t_i\}$ permuting with t, $t_i \neq t$, are conjugate in H, and those $\{t_j\}$ not permuting with t are a further conjugate class in H. Hence G is in a natural way a rank 3 group on the involutions and Γ is defined by joining a pair of commuting involutions by an arc.

In the construction of the Hall-Janko group, and in the construction of

$Sp_4(4)$ in section two of this paper, a stabilizer $H = G_1$ of a permutation representation of G was constructed and an involution t adjoined to make $G = \langle H, t \rangle$. Once we have found t, we may find permutations x_i, $i = 1, \ldots, n$ such that $x_i = (\begin{smallmatrix} 1 \cdots \\ i \cdots \end{smallmatrix})$. If a, b, t, $\ldots$ are generators of G and if $x_i a = (\begin{smallmatrix} 1 \cdots \\ j \cdots \end{smallmatrix})$ then it is necessary that $x_i a x_j^{-1} \in H = G_1$. From the Schreier theory the group $G^* = \langle a, b, t, \ldots \rangle$ will have as its stabilizer the group $G^* = \langle \ldots x_i a x_j^{-1} \ldots, x_i b x_s^{-1} \ldots \rangle$ and it is necessary to prove that $G_1^* = H$. If G has n cosets and r generators G_1^* has nr generators and it must be verified that these are in H. These nr verifications (300 for the Hall-Janko group) are redundant, and future methods should reduce the number of verifications.

It should be possible in the future to devise procedures for working directly with double cosets. Current work with permutations and coset enumeration is near the storage capacity of the known or projected computers. A challenging case is the pseudo-group of Richard Lyons which if it exists should have a permutation representation on 9,606,125 letters, but with only 5 double cosets.

REFERENCES

1. J. Alperin, R. Brauer and D. Gorenstein, *Finite groups with quasi-dihedral and wreathed Sylow 2-subgroups*, Trans. Amer. Math. Soc. 151 (1970), 1–261.

2. R. Brauer, *On groups whose order contains a prime number to the first power*. I, II, Amer. J. Math. 64 (1942), 401–440. MR 4, 1; MR 4, 2.

3. _____, *On simple groups of order $5 \cdot 3^a \cdot 2^b$*, Bull. Amer. Math. Soc. 74 (1968), 900–903. MR 38 # 4552.

4. R. Brauer and W. F. Reynolds, *On a problem of E. Artin*, Ann. of Math. (2) 68 (1958). 713–720. MR 20 #7064.

5. A. Bryce, *On the Mathieu groups M_{23}* (to appear).

6. H. S. M. Coxeter and W. O. J. Moser, *Generators and relations for discrete groups*, Springer-Verlag, Berlin, 1957, MR 19, 527.

7. B. Fischer, *Finite groups generated by 3-transpositions*, Lecture Notes, Mathematics Institute, University of Warwick.

8. Paul Fong, *Sylow 2-subgroups of small order*. I, II (to appear).

9. D. Gorenstein and J. H. Walter, *The characterization of finite groups with dihedral Sylow 2-subgroups*. I, II, III, J. Algebra 2 (1965), 85–151, 218–270, 354–393. MR 31 #1297a.

10. Marshall Hall, Jr., *The theory of groups*, Macmillan, New York, 1959. MR 21 #1996.

11._____, *A search for simple groups of order less than one million*, Computational Problems in Abstract Algebra, Pergamon Press, Oxford and New York, 1970, pp. 137–168.

12. Marshall Hall, Jr. and David Wales, *The simple group of order* 604,800, J. Algebra 9 (1968), 417–450. MR 39 # 1544.

13. Dieter Held, *The simple groups related to M_{24}*, J. Algebra 13 (1969), 253–296. MR 40 # 2745.

14. _____, *Eine Kennzeichnung der Mathieu-Gruppe M_{22} und der alternierenden Gruppe A_{10}* (to appear).

15. Donald G. Higman, *Finite permutation groups of rank 3*, Math. Z. 86 (1964), 145–156. MR 32 # 4182.

16. Donald G. Higman and C. Sims, *A simple group of order* 44,352,000, Math. Z. 105 (1968), 110–113. MR 37 # 2854.

17. Graham Higman and John McKay, *On Janko's simple group of order* 50,232,960, Bull. London Math. Soc. **1** (1969), 89–94; correction, ibid. 219. MR **40** #224.

18. _____, *On Held's group* (to appear).

19. Z. Janko, *A new finite simple group with Abelian Sylow 2-subgroups and its characterization*, J. Algebra 3 (1966), 147–186. MR **33** #1359.

20. T. Oyama, *On the groups with the same table of characters as alternating groups*, Osaka J. Math. **1** (1964), no. 1, 91–101. MR **29** #3529.

21. David Parrott, *On the Mathieu groups M_{22} and M_{11}* (to appear).

22. R. G. Stanton, *The Mathieu groups*, Canad. J. Math. **3** (1951), 164–174. MR **12**, 672.

23. M. Suzuki, *Applications of group characters*, Proc. Sympos. Pure Math., vol. 1, Amer. Math. Soc., Providence, R.I., 1959, pp. 88–99. MR **22** #5687.

24. _____, *A new type of simple groups of finite order*, Proc. Nat. Acad. Sci. U.S.A. **46** (1960), 868–870. MR **22** # 11038.

25. David Wales, *Uniqueness of the graph of a rank three group*, Pacific J. Math. **30** (1969), 271–276. MR **40** #216.

26. John H. Walter, *The characterization of finite groups with Abelian Sylow 2-subgroups*, Ann. of Math. (2) **89** (1969), 405–514. MR **40** #2749.

27. H. Wielandt, *Finite permutation groups*, Lectures, University of Tübingen, 1954/55; English transl., Academic Press, New York, 1964. MR **32** #1252.

CALIFORNIA INSTITUTE OF TECHNOLOGY

Groups, Lattices, and Quadratic Forms

J. H. Conway

I shall in fact talk about quadratic forms, lattices, and groups, in that order.

By an integral quadratic form I understand a function $Q(x_1, \ldots, x_n) = \Sigma Q_{ij}x_i x_j$ in which (Q_{ij}) is a symmetric matrix with integral entries, and we are primarily interested in the values of the form at integral values of $x_1, \ldots, x_n$. Two such forms are *integrally equivalent* if they are related by an *integral unimodular* change of base,

$$Q_1(y_1, \ldots, y_n) = Q(\Sigma a_{1i}x_i, \ldots, \Sigma a_{ni}x_i)$$

where the matrix (a_{ij}) has integral entries and determinant ± 1. Two matrices Q and Q_1 correspond to equivalent forms if and only if there is an integral matrix A with $Q_1 = A'QA$ and $\det(A) = \pm 1$.

The problem of classifying the integral equivalence classes of forms is an old and difficult one, but it is now essentially solved. For indefinite forms in three or more variables the forms are classified by an invariant called the *spinor genus*, and for any value of the determinant we have a formula for the number of inequivalent forms. For indefinite forms in two variables there is a classical theory of Gauss — there is a notion of *reduced form*, and the reduced forms fall naturally into a system of *cycles*, two forms being equivalent if their reduced forms fall into the same cycle.

So we are left with the problem of classifying positive definite quadratic forms. Here there is also a classical notion of reduced form (a form is reduced if and only if it is referred to a basis $V_1, \ldots, V_n$ of vectors such that for each i, V_i is chosen so that $Q(V_i)$ is minimal subject to $V_1, \ldots, V_i$ forming part of a basis), and for small dimensions this gives a practicable complete solution.

AMS 1970 subject classifications. Primary 10E25, 20D05; Secondary 20–04.

But for large dimensions and small determinants the following geometrical method seems more fruitful.

If we allow transformations with real coefficients any positive definite form is equivalent to $y_1^2 + \cdots + y_n^2$, and we have Theorem 1 below, giving the connection with lattices.

THEOREM 1. *If Q is a positive definite quadratic form in n variables, then there exist n vectors $V_1, \ldots, V_n$ in n-dimensional Euclidean space R^n such that $Q(x_1, \ldots, x_n)$ is just the squared length of the vector $x_1 V_1 + \cdots + x_n V_n$.*

Now for integral values of $x_1, \ldots, x_n$ the vectors $x_1 V_1 + \cdots + x_n V_n$ form a *lattice* in R^n, and it should be obvious that two quadratic forms Q_1 and Q_2 are integrally equivalent if and only if the corresponding lattices L_1 and L_2 are geometrically congruent, the transformation having determinant $+1$ or -1 according as the congruence is direct or opposite. So we have

THEOREM 2. *We can classify all positive definite integral quadratic forms of determinant n if and only if we can classify all integral lattices of determinant n.*

(A lattice L is *integral* if every scalar product $x \cdot y \, (x, y \in L)$ is integral. The determinant of the lattice is n if and only if L has one point per $n^{1/2}$ units of volume.)

Kneser has pursued this geometrical approach to the problem with great success, and recently his student H. V. Niemeier has made an outstanding contribution soon to be described. Now when I said the problem was essentially solved, this was a euphemism meaning only that it was solved to just about the extent that any reasonable mathematician would want it to be solved, as we shall soon see. First let us enquire about the connection with groups.

It is a sound empirical principle that solutions of "tight" geometrical problems are likely to be symmetrical. The reason is that the restrictions which apply to one part of the solution are the same as those which apply elsewhere, so that the solution should look the same from many points of view. Now the problem of constructing an integral quadratic form with given properties gets tighter as the determinant gets smaller, for then we are packing more points into a given volume, while still demanding that all scalar products be integral.

So we should expect unimodular integral lattices (those with determinant 1) to have high symmetry, at least in small dimensions. (In high dimensions, space gets more roomy!) There is a further natural restriction we can impose, namely that all squared lengths be even, that is, that L be an *even lattice*. At first sight it seems impossible for the quadratic form defined by a square matrix (Q_{ij}) of determinant 1 to represent only even integers, but on reflection we see that this is equivalent to demanding that the diagonal entries be even. Of course some off-diagonal entries will be odd, and these correspond to scalar products $x \cdot y \, (x \neq y)$. We can tighten the problem still further by demanding that all the lattice vectors be longer than some given lower bound, but with one point per unit volume there is obviously a limit to the bound we can impose.

In some cases we can elevate the empirical symmetry principle into a provable theorem. The so-called Mass-formula, of Minkowski and Siegel, enables us to compute the sum of the reciprocals of the orders of automorphism groups of all the lattices of certain types. For instance, we can do this in any dimension for all the lattices of any given determinant, or for all the even lattices with that determinant. If this turns out to be a very small number, we know that all the groups involved must be large, even if we do not know what they are.

[This opens up an interesting possibility. One of the central problems of finite group theory is the classification of all nonabelian simple groups. For a long time the only ones known, with a few exceptions, were the alternating groups and the so-called Chevalley groups, for instance the projective special linear groups over finite fields. Recently the number of exceptions has grown, and there are probably 19 exceptions known at the moment. Are there really infinitely many of these "sporadic" simple groups, and are they really "sporadic" or merely part of a pattern of which a lot remains to be discovered? It has always seemed impossible that one could prove that there were infinitely many groups of some kind without organising them into natural infinite families like the alternating and Chevalley groups, but perhaps something like the Mass-formula could be used in such a proof. But I myself believe that if there are infinitely many new simple groups to be found, they will form a natural family with a sensible structure.]

It has long been known that the dimension of an even unimodular quadratic form (or lattice) must be divisible by 8. In 8 dimensions, there is just one lattice, and the order of its symmetry group can be read off from the Mass-formula. The lattice is spanned by the permutations of $(\pm 1, \pm 1, 0, 0, 0, 0, 0, 0)$ and $(\pm\frac{1}, \pm\frac{1}{2}, \pm\frac{1}{2}, \pm\frac{1}{2}, \pm\frac{1}{2}, \pm\frac{1}{2}, \pm\frac{1}{2}, \pm\frac{1}{2})$ (with an even number of signs in the second case), or, in a more convenient notation $((\pm 1)^2, 0^6)$, $((\pm\frac{1}{2})^8)$. These 240 points are the vertices of Gosset's polytope 4_{21}, and the lattice is the root lattice of the Lie Algebra E_8. It is also known to give the densest lattice packing of spheres in 8 dimensions, and its group is an 8-dimensional orthogonal group over the field of order 2, and essentially a simple group.

In 16 dimensions, there are just two even unimodular lattices, one of which is the direct sum of two copies of this 8-dimensional lattice. In 24 dimensions, it was known to Witt that there were at least 11 such lattices, and Niemeier's work has given us the complete list of 24 lattices, all of which must have large groups, since the mass-constant is about 10^{-14}. In 32 dimensions, however, the mass-constant is about 10^8, and no reasonable mathematician would want to list 10^8 forms, especially since there seems to be no regular structure even in the 24-dimensional case. Niemeier's result enables us to classify forms for which the sum of determinant and dimension is at most 25, with the even-ness requirement when it is exactly 25, and this seems altogether a very happy stopping point.

All but one of Niemeier's lattices are obtained by a certain 'glueing' process from very simple lattices. The exception is the remarkable 24-dimensional lattice discovered by John Leech as giving an extremely dense lattice packing of spheres (in which 196560 spheres touch any given one!), and is the unique one of the 24 having no vector of squared length 2.

It was obvious to Leech that his lattice was of group-theoretic interest, since its construction involved the Mathieu group M_{24}, the most famous of the classical exceptions, and it seemed to have additional symmetries. In fact from the Mass-formula it *must* have additional symmetries, and I was able to prove that its group, when factored by a centre of order 2, is a new simple group which in various senses includes many of the other exceptional groups. I now sketch Leech's construction.

We first select 759 subsets (called *octads*) of 8 of the 24 coordinates to form a *Steiner system* $S(5, 8, 24)$, which means that every 5-element subset of the coordinates is to be contained in just one of the octads. It was proved by Witt that this system is unique to within permutations of the coordinates, and that the group of permutations of the 24 coordinates leaving the system fixed is the Mathieu group M_{24}.

The Leech Lattice is now spanned by the permutations of the vectors of form $c(4^2, 0^{22})$, $c(2^8, 0^{16})$, $c(-3, 1^{23})$ which are such that the 8 distinguished coordinates in the second case form an octad. The scale factor c is $8^{-1/2}$ — we omit it in what follows. The lattice is obviously invariant under the group M_{24} of permutations fixing the set of octads, and it turns out also that it is invariant when we change the sign of any octad of coordinates. These sign-changes generate a group of order 2^{12}, and applying them to the spanning vectors we find $2^2 \cdot 276$ vectors $((\pm4)^2, 0^{22})$, $2^7 \cdot 759$ vectors $((\pm2)^8, 0^{16})$, and $2^{12} \cdot 24$ vectors $(\mp3, (\pm1)^{23})$ which are all the 196560 shortest vectors of the lattice.

In addition to these symmetries I was able to show that the matrix with five 4×4 blocks $I - \frac{1}{2}U$ and one block $\frac{1}{2}U - I$ (where U is the 4×4 matrix with every entry 1) is a symmetry of the lattice if the blocks are so chosen that the union of any two is an octad, and that these symmetries generate the entire group of order

$$2^{22}3^95^47^211 \cdot 13 \cdot 23 = 8,315,553,613,086,720,000.$$

We obtain one simple group by factoring out the obvious centre (±1) of order 2, and others, including the Mathieu groups and the simple groups of Higman and Sims and of McLaughlin and two further new groups, by stabilising various sublattices of small dimension.

The Suzuki simple group arises in a slightly different way. If we take in the big group an element ω of order 3 with no fixed point, then ω (as a matrix) satisfies $\omega^2 + \omega + 1 = 0$, and if we define $(a + b\omega)X = aX + b(\omega(X))$ for every lattice vector X, we have changed the lattice into a 12-dimensional lattice over the ring of complex numbers $a + b\omega$. The Suzuki group is the symmetry group of the lattice when equipped with this complex structure, if we factor by the centre of order 6 consisting of the elements $\pm\omega^i$.

There is a striking analogy between the original real lattice and the new complex one, in which 2 is everywhere replaced by $\theta = \sqrt{-3}/-3$. Thus in a suitable complex coordinate system, and ignoring factors of $\pm\omega^i$, the minimal vectors have the shapes $((-3)^2, 0^{10})$, and $(\theta^6, 0^6)$, and $(1+3, 1^{11})$, corresponding to $(4^2, 0^{22})$, $(2^8, 0^{16})$, $(1-4, 1^{23})$ in the real case, and the distinguished hexads in the second class form the Steiner system $S(5, 6, 12)$, whose automorphism group is the Mathieu group M_{12}. The group of sign changes of order 2^{12} is replaced by a group of diagonal matrices of order 3^6 $(= \theta^{12})$, and the group of coordinate-permutations becomes M_{11}, or a group $2M_{12}$ if we allow ourselves to take complex conjugates as well.

Even the additional symmetry fits the pattern—it has 3×3 blocks with entries $1/\theta$ instead of 4×4 blocks with entries $\frac{1}{2}$, the union of any two blocks corresponding to a special hexad. The Suzuki group contains another of the new simple groups, the Hall-Janko group, corresponding to a complex 6-dimensional lattice.

This is about all I have to say on the connection between the sporadic simple groups and lattices and quadratic forms, but it will be as well to point out that several of the groups not directly involved with the Leech Lattice seem nevertheless to be intimately connected with the rest. I mention the Fischer groups, built around a group $2^{12}M_{24}$ which seems closely related to the distinct group $2^{12}M_{24}$ of permutations and sign changes in my own big group, Held's group, which is closely related to M_{24}, and the new group, if it exists, of Richard Lyons, in which an element of order three is centralised by a perfect extension of McLaughlin's group.

Where do computers come in? In the complicated calculations which were necessary to prove the existence of some of the groups (not mine!), and in the construction of their character tables, from which one can read off a vast amount of information about the groups. While this conference was proceeding, the Titan computer in Cambridge finished calculating the table for my group. Hanging on the wall of my office, it is a 'square' matrix measuring nearly four feet by eight!

SIDNEY SUSSEX COLLEGE, CAMBRIDGE, ENGLAND

[illegible] of complex [illegible]. The [illegible] group [illegible] of the [illegible] which [illegible] with [illegible] structure [illegible] centre of order 3 [illegible] of the [illegible].

The [illegible] striking analogy between [illegible] real lattice and [illegible] complex one [illegible] in which [illegible] In [illegible] complex coordinate [illegible] and [illegible] factors [illegible] the shape [illegible] and [illegible] one case [illegible] distinguished [illegible] the second class [illegible] group is the Mathieu group [illegible] group of [illegible] changes of order [illegible] placed [illegible] of diagonal [illegible] and the group of coordinate permutations [illegible] to take complex conjugates as well.

Even [illegible] with [illegible] blocks with entries [illegible] blocks with [illegible] corresponding [illegible] [illegible] -dimensional lattice.

[illegible] group [illegible] and [illegible] out that [illegible] the groups [illegible] nevertheless to be intimately connected with the [illegible] the Fischer groups built around a group $2^{24}M$ which seems closely related to the [illegible] group [illegible] of permutations and sign changes [illegible] group. Fischer's group which is closely related to M_{24} and the new group [illegible] consists of [illegible] in which [illegible] order [illegible] perfect [illegible]

[illegible] the complex [illegible] which [illegible] were [illegible] connect [illegible] of a vast number of [illegible] was [illegible] the [illegible] Cambridge [illegible] counting the [illegible] group [illegible] and [illegible] measuring [illegible] four feet by eight!

[illegible] Sidney Sussex College [illegible]

Rank 3 Groups and Strongly Regular Graphs[1]

M. D. Hestenes and D. G. Higman

This paper contains an exposition of the first parts of the general theory of rank 3 permutation groups of even order as initiated in [4], based on consideration of the associated strongly regular graphs. Where possible we deal with strongly regular graphs without assumptions on their automorphism groups, a primary reason being that such graphs arise in connection with groups of higher rank. The purposes of the paper are (a) to provide a convenient self-contained reference for basic facts used in theoretical and computational work on rank 3 groups, (b) to present the material in §5 developing Sims' [14] idea of studying the 4-vertex subgraphs, and (c) to give another proof (in §6) of the classification of strongly regular graphs with minimum eigenvalue -2 published by J. J. Seidel [12].

1. **Graphs and permutation groups.** Associated with a relation $f \subseteq X \times X$ in a set $X \neq 0$ there is a *graph* $\mathscr{G}_f = (X, f)$ having X as vertex set and f as edge set. By the term *graph* we will always mean a graph of this type. We shall say that such a graph is *oriented* or *ordinary* according as f is strictly nonreflexive and strictly nonsymmetric or strictly nonreflexive and symmetric. In the ordinary case we identify (x, y) and (y, x). By a *subgraph* we mean a subset of the vertex set together with all edges joining pairs of vertices in the subset. A *t-vertex subgraph* is one involving exactly t vertices. The matrix $A_f = (\alpha_{x,y})$, where the rows and columns are indexed by X and $\alpha_{x,y} = 1$ or 0 according as $(x,y) \in f$ or $(x,y) \notin f$, is called the *matrix* of f or the *adjacency matrix of* $\mathscr{G}_f$. The *complement* of a graph $\mathscr{G}_f$ is the graph $\overline{\mathscr{G}}_f = \mathscr{G}_{\bar{f}}$, where $\bar{f} = X \times X - (f \cup I)$, $I = \{(x, x) | x \in X\}$.

AMS 1970 *subject classifications*. Primary 05C25, 20B05, 20B25; Secondary 20D05.

[1]Research supported in part by the National Science Foundation.

The graph $\mathscr{G}_f$ is *connected* if there is a *path* (of length n) from any one vertex x to any other vertex y, i.e., a finite sequence $x_0 = x, x_1, \ldots, x_n = y$ of vertices such that $(x_i, x_{i+1}) \in f, i = 0, 1, \ldots, n-1$.

For a given vertex x, the number of vertices in the set

$$f(x) = \{y \mid (x,y) \in f\}$$

of vertices *adjacent* to x is called the *valence* of x. A graph is called *regular* if every vertex has the same valence; this of course means precisely that A_f has constant row sum.

An *m-clique* in an ordinary graph is an m-vertex subgraph in which any two vertices are adjacent, and a *m-claw* is an $(m+1)$-vertex subgraph such that one of the vertices is adjacent to all the rest, which are all mutually nonadjacent.

Let G be a transitive permutation group on a set X, and denote the action of G on X by $x \to x^g$, $x \in X$, $g \in G$. The number of G-orbits in $X \times X$ (under componentwise action), the number of G_x-orbits in X for a fixed $x \in X$, and the number of (G_x, G_x)-double cosets in G are all equal. For the maps $\Delta \to \Delta(x) \to \{g \in G \mid x^g \in \Delta(x)\}$, for Δ a G-orbit in $X \times X$ and x a fixed element of X, are bijections. We call the G-orbits in $X \times X$ *orbitals* and refer to their number as the *rank* of G.

If Δ is an orbital then $\Delta(x)^g = \Delta(x^g)$ for all $x \in X$ and $g \in G$. Moreover, the converse $\Delta^{\smile} = \{(y, x) \mid (x, y) \in \Delta\}$ of Δ is again an orbital, so $\Delta \to \Delta^{\smile}$ is a pairing on the set of orbitals [15, §16]. An orbital is either *symmetric* ($\Delta = \Delta^{\smile}$) or *strictly nonsymmetric* ($\Delta \cap \Delta^{\smile} = \emptyset$). Note that $\Delta^{\smile}(x) = \{g \in G \mid x^{g^{-1}} \in \Delta(x)\}$ so that the (G_x, G_x)-double coset corresponding to $\Delta^{\smile}$ is the inverse of that corresponding to Δ.

(1.1) [15, p. 45] *G has a symmetric orbital $\neq I$ if and only if $|G|$ is even.*

PROOF. Take $x \in X$. G has a symmetric orbital $\neq I$ if and only if $G_x g G_x = G_x g^{-1} G_x$ for some $g \notin G_x$, and this is possible if and only if $|G|$ is even.

As is well known (cf. [15])

(1.2) *The matrices A_Δ constitute a basis of the centralizer ring of the permutation representation.*

In particular, the rank of G is equal to the dimension of this centralizer ring, and so to the length (ρ, ρ) of the permutation character ρ.

An orbital $\Delta \neq I$ is strictly nonreflexive and, as we remarked above, either symmetric or strictly nonsymmetric. Hence the graph $\mathscr{G}_\Delta$ is either ordinary or oriented.

(1.3) [5, p. 26] *G is primitive if and only if $\mathscr{G}_\Delta$ is connected for all $\Delta \neq I$.*

PROOF. Let Δ be an orbital $\neq I$. For $x \in X$ let $\Sigma_\Delta(x) = \{y \in X \mid$ there exists a path in $\mathscr{G}_\Delta$ from x to $y\}$. Then $\Sigma_\Delta(x)^g = \Sigma_\Delta(x^g)$ for all $x \in X$ and $g \in G$, and for $y \in \Sigma_\Delta(x)$, $\Sigma_\Delta(y) \subseteq \Sigma_\Delta(x)$, so that $\Sigma_\Delta(y) = \Sigma_\Delta(x)$. Hence $\Sigma_\Delta(x)$ is an imprimitive block, so, if G is primitive, then $\Sigma_\Delta(x) = X$ and $\mathscr{G}_\Delta$ is connected. On the other hand, if G is imprimitive and Σ is a nontrivial imprimitive block, then for $x \in \Sigma$, $\Sigma = \{x\} + \Delta(x) + \ldots$, a union of G_x-orbits with at least one $\Delta \neq I$ occurring. If $y \in \Delta(x)$, then $y = x^g$ for some $g \in G$, and $\Delta(y) = \Delta(x^g) = \Delta(x)^g \subseteqq \Sigma^g = \Sigma$. Hence $\Sigma_\Delta(x) \subseteqq \Sigma$ and $\mathscr{G}_\Delta$ is not connected.

2. **Rank 3 groups and strongly regular graphs.** Let G be a rank 3 permutation group on X with orbitals I, Δ, and Γ. For $x \in X$, the G_x-orbits in X are $I(x) = \{x\}$, $\Delta(x)$ and $\Gamma(x)$. The numbers $1 = |I(x)|$, $k = |\Delta(x)|$ and $l = |\Gamma(x)|$ are called the *subdegrees* of G, and $n = 1 + k + l$, where $n = |X|$ is the *degree* of G. Assume that $|G|$ is even, so that one, and hence both, of Δ, Γ is symmetric. The ordinary graph $\mathscr{G}_\Delta$ is regular, each vertex having valence k. The *intersection numbers* λ, μ of G [**4**] are defined by

$$
\begin{aligned}
|\Delta(x) \cap \Delta(y)| &= \lambda \quad \text{if} \quad y \in \Delta(x), \\
&= \mu \quad \text{if} \quad y \in \Gamma(x).
\end{aligned}
$$

In $\mathscr{G}_\Delta$, λ is the number of 3-cliques (i.e., triangles) containing a given edge (x, y) and μ is the number of 2-claws containing a given nonedge, and these numbers are independent of the choice of edge or nonedge respectively. This means that the graphs $\mathscr{G}_\Delta$ and $\mathscr{G}_\Gamma$ are a pair of complementary *strongly regular graphs* [**1**]. Such graphs will be considered in some detail in §§4–6.

A strongly regular graph arising in this way from a rank 3 permutation group, i.e., a strongly regular graph whose automorphism group has rank 3 on the points will be called a *rank* 3 *graph*.

3. **Theorems from matrix theory**. In this section we cite some results about matrices which play an essential role in our discussion of strongly regular graphs.

Let A be a real symmetric matrix of degree n with spectrum $\lambda_1 \leqq \lambda_2 \leqq \cdots \leqq \lambda_n$. It is well known that

(3.1) *If B is a principal submatrix of A, then*

(a) *the spectrum of B is contained in $[\lambda_1, \lambda_n]$, and*

(b) *if λ_j, $j = 1$ or n, is an eigenvalue of B, y is an eigenvector of B with eigenvalue λ_j, and z is an eigenvector of A with eigenvalue $\neq \lambda_j$, then y is perpendicular to the projection of z onto the subspace corresponding to B.*

By the *spectrum* of a graph $\mathscr{G}$ we mean the spectrum of its adjacency matrix A. If $\mathscr{G}$ is ordinary, then A is symmetric, so (3.1) implies at once

(3.2) *Let $\mathscr{G}$ be an ordinary graph. Assume that $\mathscr{G}$ is regular, with each vertex having valence $k > 0$, and let λ_1 be the minimum eigenvalue of $\mathscr{G}$. If $\mathscr{G}_0$ is a subgraph of $\mathscr{G}$, then the spectrum of $\mathscr{G}_0$ is contained in $[\lambda_1, k]$. If λ_1 is an eigenvalue of $\mathscr{G}_0$, then any eigenvector of $\mathscr{G}_0$ with eigenvalue λ_1 has coordinate sum zero.*

A 3-claw $[P;Q_1,Q_2,Q_3]$ is the graph

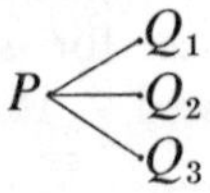

$$P \diagdown \begin{matrix} Q_1 \\ Q_2 \\ Q_3 \end{matrix}$$

Using (3.2), A. J. Hoffman [8] showed

(3.3) *If an ordinary graph $\mathcal{G}$ with minimum eigenvalue -2 contains a 3-claw $[P;Q_1,Q_2,Q_3]$, then each vertex $R \neq P$ adjacent to Q_1 and Q_2 is adjacent to P but not to Q_3.*

The last result of this section is in a sense dual to (3.1). Once more, let A be a real symmetric matrix of degree n with spectrum $\lambda_1 \leq \lambda_2 \leq \cdots \leq \lambda_n$. Given a partition $\{1, 2, \ldots, n\} = \Delta_1 + \Delta_2 + \cdots + \Delta_m$, with $|\Delta_i| = n_i > 0$, consider the corresponding blocking $A = (A_{ij})$, so that A_{ij} is an $n_i \times n_j$ block. Let e_{ij} be the sum of the entries in A_{ij} and put $\hat{A} = (e_{ij}/n_i)$. As pointed out by Sims, an argument similar to the standard proof of (3.1) gives

(3.4) (a) *The spectrum of $\hat{A}$ is contained in $[\lambda_1, \lambda_n]$, and*

(b) *if λ_1 is an eigenvalue of $\hat{A}$, y is an eigenvector of $\hat{A}$ with eigenvalue λ_1, and z is an eigenvector of A with eigenvalue $> \lambda_1$, then $\sum_{i=1}^{m} \sum_{\alpha \in \Delta_i} z_\alpha y_i = 0$.*

This result will be applied to the adjacency matrix of an ordinary graph $\mathcal{G}$ with $\Delta_1, \ldots, \Delta_m$ being a partition of the vertex set. Then e_{ij} is the number of directed edges from Δ_i to Δ_j.

4. **Strongly regular graphs.** A *strongly regular graph* [1] is an ordinary graph $\mathcal{G}$ with n vertices such that

(1) $\mathcal{G}$ is regular with valency $k, 0 < k < n-1$,

(2) the number λ of 3-cliques (i.e., triangles) in $\mathcal{G}$ containing a given edge is independent of the choice of edge, and

(3) the number μ of 2-claws containing a given nonedge is independent of the choice of nonedge.

Let $\mathcal{G}$ be a strongly regular graph, Δ the set of edges in $\mathcal{G}$ and Γ the set of nonedges. Then $\mathcal{G} = \mathcal{G}_\Delta$, $\bar{\mathcal{G}} = \mathcal{G}_\Gamma$, $\Delta(x)$ is the set of vertices adjacent to x, so that $|\Delta(x)| = k$, and $\Gamma(x)$ is the set of vertices $\neq x$ and not adjacent to x. Put $l = |\Gamma(x)|$, so that $n = 1 + k + l$. From the definition,

(4.1) $0 \leq \lambda \leq k-1, \quad 0 \leq \mu \leq k \quad and \quad k-\mu \leq l-1$.

The adjacency matrices $A = A_\Delta$ of $\mathcal{G}$ and $B = B_\Gamma$ of the complement $\bar{\mathcal{G}}$ of $\mathcal{G}$ satisfy

          (i) $I + A + B = J$,

(4.2)   (ii) *A has row sum k and B has row sum l, and*

          (iii) $A^2 - (\lambda - \mu)A - (k-\mu)I = \mu J$,

where J denotes the matrix of all 1's.

PROOF. The first two of these statements are immediate from the definitions. Since the (x,y)-entry in A^2 is the number of paths of length 2 in $\mathcal{G}$ from x to y, we have $A^2 = \lambda A + \mu B + kJ$, and (iii) follows from this by (i) and (ii).

It is easy to see that a (0,1)-matrix with row sum k, $0 \leqq k < n-1$, having all diagonal entries 0 and satisfying an equation (iii) with $0 \leqq \lambda \leqq k-1$ and $0 \leqq \mu \leqq k$ is the adjacency matrix of a strongly regular graph.

From the definitions,

(4.3) *$\mathcal{G}$ is connected if and only if $\mu \neq 0$, and*

(4.4) *The complementary graph $\overline{\mathcal{G}}$ is strongly regular with*

$$\bar{n} = n, \quad \bar{k} = l, \quad \bar{l} = k, \quad \bar{\lambda} = l-k+\mu-1$$

and

$$\bar{\mu} = l-k+\lambda+1.$$

The number of edges in $\mathcal{G}$ is $nk/2$; hence

(4.5) *At least one of k, l is even.*

The number of triangles with a given vertex is $k\lambda/2$ and the total number of triangles is $nk\lambda/6$; hence

(4.6) $$2|k\lambda \quad \textit{and} \quad 3|nk\lambda, \quad \textit{and dually}, \quad 2|l\bar{\lambda} \quad \textit{and} \quad 3|nl\bar{\lambda}.$$

The number of 2-claws containing a given edge (x,y) is $k-\lambda-1$ and the number containing a given nonedge (x,z) is μ. Hence the number containing x is

(4.7) $$k(k-\lambda-1) = \mu l.$$

From (4.6) and (4.7),

(4.8) $$2|\mu l \qquad \textit{and} \qquad 2|\bar{\mu}k.$$

From (4.3), (4.4) and (4.7),

(4.9) *$\overline{\mathcal{G}}$ is connected if and only if $\mu \neq k$.*

We shall say that $\mathcal{G}$ is *primitive* if $\mathcal{G}$ and $\overline{\mathcal{G}}$ are connected.

(4.10) *$\mathcal{G}$ is primitive if and only if $\mu \neq 0, k$.*

By (4.7),

(4.11) *If $\mathcal{G}$ is primitive, then $(k,l) \neq 1$.*

By (4.2), A satisfies the polynomial

(4.12) $$(x-k)(x^2-(\lambda-\mu)x-(k-\mu)) = 0.$$

Thus the spectrum of $\mathcal{G}$ consists of k and the two eigenvalues

(4.13) $$\begin{Bmatrix} r \\ s \end{Bmatrix} = \frac{\lambda-\mu\pm d^{1/2}}{2}, \qquad d = (\lambda-\mu)^2+4(k-\mu) \neq 0.$$

The eigenvalues $\{^r_s\} = (\lambda - \mu - 2 \pm d^{1/2})/2$ of $\bar{\mathscr{G}}$ are related to those of $\mathscr{G}$ by

(4.14) $r + \bar{s} = s + \bar{r} = -1$

as can be seen directly from the explicit formulas or by simultaneously diagonalizing A and B.

If $\mathscr{G}$ is connected, then A is irreducible so k has multiplicity 1 by the Perron-Frobenius Theorem. If $\mathscr{G}$ is not connected, then $\{^r_s\} = \{^k_{-1}\}$. The eigenvalues r and s are distinct and their respective multiplicities f and g (with the appropriate interpretation in case $\mathscr{G}$ is not connected) are determined by

$$n = 1 + f + g,$$
$$0 = k + rf + sg \quad (\text{trace } A = 0),$$

to be

(4.15) $f = \dfrac{(n-1)s + k}{s - r}$ $\quad$ and $\quad$ $g = \dfrac{(n-1)r + k}{r - s}$.

That is

(4.16) $\begin{Bmatrix} f \\ g \end{Bmatrix} = \dfrac{(k+l)(\lambda - \mu) + 2k \mp d^{1/2}(k+l)}{\mp 2d^{1/2}}$.

Note that $\bar{f} = g$ and $\bar{g} = f$ are the respective multiplicities of $\bar{r}$ and $\bar{s}$ as eigenvalues of $\bar{\mathscr{G}}$.

We refer to the 9-tuple $(n, k, l, \lambda, \mu, r, s, f, g)$ as the *parameter set afforded by* $\mathscr{G}$.

The matrix $C = B - A$ (the so-called $(-1, 1, 0)$-adjacency matrix of $\mathscr{G}$, cf. [11]) has eigenvalues $\rho_0 = l - k$ (its row and column sum), $\rho_1 = -(2r+1)$ and $\rho_2 = -(2s+1)$ of multiplicities $1, f$ and g respectively. From the equations

$$A = -\tfrac{1}{2}(B-A) - \tfrac{1}{2}I + \tfrac{1}{2}J, \quad B = \tfrac{1}{2}(B-A) - \tfrac{1}{2}I + \tfrac{1}{2}J,$$
$$A^2 = (\lambda - \mu)A + (k - \mu)I + \mu J, \quad B^2 = (\mu - \lambda - 2)B + (k - \lambda - 1)I + \bar{\mu}J$$

and

$$AB = -2(k - \lambda - 1)A - 2(k - \mu)B,$$

we get that

(4.17) $C^2 - (\rho_1 + \rho_2)C + \rho_1\rho_2 I = (n - 1 + \rho_1\rho_2)J$.

Since f and g are positive integers we see by (4.16) that

(4.18)   [4, Lemma 7] *One of the following holds*:

   (I) $k = l = 2\mu = 2(\lambda + 1)$, or
   (II) $d = (\lambda - \mu)^2 + 4(k - \mu)$ *is a square and*
   (i) *if n is even,* $d^{1/2}$ *divides* $2k + (\lambda - \mu)(k + l)$ *while* $2d^{1/2}$ *does not, and*
   (ii) *if n is odd, then* $2d^{1/2}$ *divides* $2k + (\lambda - \mu)(k + l)$.

If $f = g$, then case (I) holds. In case (II) the eigenvalues of $\mathscr{G}$ are integers. Cases (I) and (II) are not mutually exclusive. $\mathscr{G}$ belongs to case (I) or (II) according as $\bar{\mathscr{G}}$ belongs to case (I) or (II).

In case (I),

$$n = 1+4\mu, \quad d = n^{1/2}, \quad \begin{Bmatrix} r \\ s \end{Bmatrix} = \frac{-1 \pm n^{1/2}}{2} \quad \text{and} \quad f = g = k.$$

The only examples of such strongly regular graphs that we know are the rank 3 graphs of Singer type [7], together with three examples having $n = 7^2, 23^2$ and 47^2 respectively associated with certain exceptional solvable imprimitive rank 3 groups. J. J. Seidel has observed the following useful result.

(4.19) *If $\mathscr{G}$ is strongly regular with $k = l = 2\mu = 2(\lambda+1)$, then n is a sum of two squares.*

PROOF. We put

$$D = \begin{bmatrix} 0 & j \\ j^T & C \end{bmatrix},$$

where $j = (1, 1, \ldots, 1)$ and $C = B - A$. By (4.17), $D^2 = nI$. Since D is a symmetric rational matrix of degree $\equiv 2 \pmod 4$, it follows at once from the theory of rational congruences that n is a sum of two squares.

Suppose that $\mathscr{G}$ is connected and imprimitive, so that $\mu = k$ and $\lambda = k - l - 1$, and hence

$$\begin{Bmatrix} r \\ s \end{Bmatrix} = \begin{Bmatrix} 0 \\ -(l+1) \end{Bmatrix}$$

and

$$\begin{Bmatrix} f \\ g \end{Bmatrix} = \begin{Bmatrix} \dfrac{nl}{l+1} \\ \dfrac{k}{l+1} \end{Bmatrix}.$$

In particular

(4.20) *If $\mathscr{G}$ is imprimitive, then $l+1 \mid k$ or $k+1 \mid l$ according as $\mathscr{G}$ is connected or not.*

Alternatively, we can see (4.20) by observing that when $\overline{\mathscr{G}}$ is not connected, the connected components are the sets $\{x\} + \Gamma(x)$. If G is an imprimitive rank 3 group (and hence necessarily of even order) with, say, $\mathscr{G}_\Gamma$ not connected, then there is just one imprimitive decomposition of $\mathscr{G}$, the blocks being the sets $\{x\} + \Gamma(x)$. G is doubly transitive on the set of blocks and the stabilizer of a block is doubly transitive on the block.

(4.21) *If $\mathscr{G}$ is primitive and $n \neq 5$, then $r \geqq 1$ and $s \leqq -2$.*

PROOF. By (4.18), $r \geqq 1$ and $\bar{r} \geqq 1$, and hence $s \leqq -2$ by (4.14).

Choose a vertex x, and let $\Delta_1 = \{x\}$, $\Delta_2 = \Delta(x)$, and $\Delta_3 = \Gamma(x)$ and put

$$e_{ij} = \text{the number of directed edges from } \Delta_i \text{ to } \Delta_j$$

so that

$$(e_{ij}) = \begin{bmatrix} 0 & k & 0 \\ k & k\lambda & k(k-\lambda-1) \\ 0 & \mu l & (k-\mu)l \end{bmatrix}.$$

The matrix $\hat{A}(x) = (e_{ij}/n_i)$, $n_i = |\Delta_i|$, is called the *intersection matrix* for $\mathscr{G}$. We see that

$$\hat{A}(x) = \begin{bmatrix} 0 & k & 0 \\ 1 & \lambda & k-\lambda-1 \\ 0 & \mu & k-\mu \end{bmatrix}$$

is independent of the choice of x and has the same eigenvalues k, r, s as A. Moreover

(4.22) *For* $\theta \in \{k, r, s\}$ *the vector* $(k, \theta, \rho)^T$, *where*

$$\rho = \frac{\theta^2 - \lambda\theta - k}{k-\lambda-1} = \frac{\mu\theta}{\theta - k + \mu},$$

is an eigenvector of $\hat{A}(x)$ *with eigenvalue* θ.

Forming $\hat{B}(x)$ from B with respect to the same partition of the vertices, so that $\hat{B}(x)$ is the intersection matrix of $\overline{\mathscr{G}}$, we have $I + \hat{A}(x) + \hat{B}(x) = \hat{J}$, where every row of $\hat{J}$ is equal to $(1,k,l)$. From the general theory of intersection matrices ([**5**] and [**6**]) we know that $\{I, A, B\}$ and $\{I, \hat{A}(x), \hat{B}(x)\}$ are bases of isomorphic matrix algebras.

5. **4-vertex subgraphs.** Let $\mathscr{G}$ be an ordinary graph. We say that two subgraphs of $\mathscr{G}$ are of the *same type with respect to a pair* (x,y) *of distinct vertices* if both contain x and y and there exists an isomorphism of one onto the other mapping x to x and y to y. For example, if (x,y) is an edge, the possible types of 3-vertex subgraphs of $\mathscr{G}$ with respect to (x,y) are

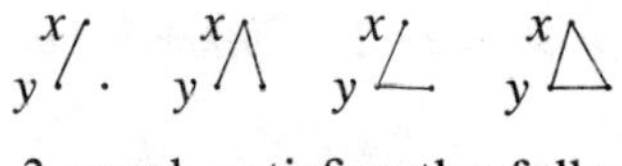
x
y
x
y
x
y
x
y

It is clear that a rank 3 graph satisfies the following condition, which we refer to as the *t-vertex condition*, for all $t \geqq 2$: The number of t-vertex subgraphs of a given type with respect to a given pair (x,y) of distinct vertices depends only on whether (x,y) is an edge or not.

If $\mathscr{G}$ satisfies the t-vertex condition for some t, so does $\overline{\mathscr{G}}$. The t-vertex condition is vacuous for $t = 1$ and automatically satisfied for $t = 2$ in any ordinary graph $\mathscr{G}$. If $\mathscr{G}$ is not the complete graph or its complement, the 3-vertex condition holds in $\mathscr{G}$ if and only if $\mathscr{G}$ is strongly regular; in this case the number of 3-vertex subgraphs can be obtained from the intersection matrices for $\mathscr{G}$ and $\overline{\mathscr{G}}$. We are now interested in the 4-vertex subgraphs of a strongly regular graph, following a method due to Sims. In particular, (5.21), (5.22) and (5.23), as well as the method of applying (3.4) are due to Sims.

Assume that $\mathcal{G}$ is strongly regular, take an edge (x, y), and define $\Delta_i \equiv \Delta_i(x, y)$ by

$$\Delta_1 = \{x\}, \quad \Delta_2 = \{y\}, \quad \Delta_3 = \Delta(x) \cap \Delta(y),$$
$$\Delta_4 = \Delta(x) \cap \Gamma(y), \quad \Delta_5 = \Delta(y) \cap \Gamma(x) \quad \text{and} \quad \Delta_6 = \Gamma(x) \cap \Gamma(y).$$

The numbers of vertices in these sets are respectively

$$n_1 = n_2 = 1, \quad n_3 = \lambda, \quad n_4 = n_5 = k - \lambda - 1 \quad \text{and} \quad n_6 = \bar{\mu}.$$

As in §3 we let $e_{ij} \equiv e_{ij}(x, y) =$ the number of directed edges from Δ_i to Δ_j so that

$$(5.1) \qquad 0 \leqq e_{ij} = e_{ji} \leqq n_i(n_j - \delta_{ij})$$

and

$$(5.2) \qquad \begin{gathered} e_{11} = e_{15} = e_{16} = e_{22} = e_{24} = e_{26} = 0, \\ e_{12} = 1,\ e_{13} = e_{23} = \lambda, \quad \text{and} \quad e_{14} = e_{25} = k - \lambda - 1. \end{gathered}$$

We put

$$\alpha \equiv \alpha(x, y) = \text{the number of 4-cliques in } \mathcal{G} \text{ containing } x \text{ and } y,$$

so that $e_{33} = 2\alpha$, and compute the remaining e_{ij} in terms of $k, \lambda, \mu, \bar{\mu}$ and α.

To carry out the computation we put $e(S, T) =$ the number of directed edges from S to T for any two sets S and T of vertices, so that $e_{ij} = e(\Delta_i, \Delta_j)$, and observe that

(5.3) *For* $z \in \Delta_i$,

$$\begin{aligned} e(z, \Delta(x)) &= k, \quad \textit{and} \quad e(z, \Gamma(x)) = 0, & i &= 1, \\ &= \lambda, & = k - \lambda - 1, \quad i &= 2, 3 \text{ or } 4, \\ &= \mu, & = k - \mu, \quad i &= 5 \text{ or } 6, \end{aligned}$$

and

$$\begin{aligned} e(z, \Delta(y)) &= k, \quad \textit{and} \quad e(z, \Gamma(y)) = 0, & i &= 2, \\ &= \lambda, & = k - \lambda - 1, \quad i &= 1, 3 \text{ or } 5, \\ &= \mu, & = k - \mu, \quad i &= 4 \text{ or } 6. \end{aligned}$$

Furthermore,

(5.4) *For* $z \in \Delta_i$,

$$n_i e(z, \Delta(x)) = e_{i2} + e_{i3} + e_{i4} \quad \textit{and} \quad n_i e(z, \Gamma(x)) = e_{i5} + e_{i6},$$
$$n_i e(z, \Delta(y)) = e_{i1} + e_{i3} + e_{i5} \quad \textit{and} \quad n_i e(z, \Gamma(y)) = e_{i4} + e_{i6}.$$

Combining (5.1) through (5.4) we obtain

$$(5.5) \qquad \begin{aligned} e_{33} &= 2\alpha, \\ e_{34} &= e_{35} = \lambda(\lambda - 1) - 2\alpha, \\ e_{36} &= e_{44} = e_{55} = \lambda(k - 2\lambda) + 2\alpha, \\ e_{45} &= (\mu - 1)(k - \lambda - 1) - \lambda(\lambda - 1) + 2\alpha, \\ e_{46} &= e_{56} = (k - \lambda - \mu)(k - \lambda - 1) + \lambda(\lambda - 1) - 2\alpha, \\ e_{66} &= \bar{\mu}(k - \mu) - (k - \lambda - \mu)(k - \lambda - 1) - \lambda(\lambda - 1) + 2\alpha. \end{aligned}$$

We see than any one of the e_{ij}, $i \geq 3, j \geq 3$, determines the rest. Moreover, the number of 4-vertex subgraphs of each given type with respect to (x, y) determines and is determined by one of these e_{ij}. Hence

(5.6) *If the number of 4-vertex subgraphs of $\mathscr{G}$ of one type with respect to (x, y) is independent of the choice of the edge (x, y), then so is the number of 4-vertex subgraphs of each type with respect to (x, y).*

We note that

(5.7)   *The number of 3-claws*

in $\mathscr{G}$ is

$$\tfrac{1}{2}\{(k - \lambda - 1)(k - 2\lambda - 2) + \lambda(\lambda - 1) - 2\alpha\}.$$

For this number is $\tfrac{1}{2}\{n_4(n_4 - 1) - e_{44}\}$.

Assume now that $\mathscr{G}$ is primitive and $\lambda \neq 0$, that is, assume that all the n_i are $\neq 0$. By (4.22), (5.3) and (5.4) we see that for $\theta \in \{r, s\}$, the matrix

$$\hat{A}(x, y) = (e_{ij}/n_i)$$

has $(k, \theta, \theta, \theta, \rho, \rho)^T$ and $(\theta, k, \theta, \rho, \theta, \rho)^T$ as eigenvectors with eigenvalue θ, with ρ as in (4.22). Since this gives four linearly independent vectors, r and s each have multiplicity at least 2 as eigenvalues of $\hat{A}(x, y)$. Since k is an eigenvalue of multiplicity 1 as the row sum, we have that

$$t = \operatorname{trace} \hat{A}(x, y) - (k + 2(r + s))$$

is an eigenvalue of $\hat{A}(x, y)$. By (5.2) and (5.5),

$$\operatorname{trace} \hat{A}(x, y) = \frac{2\alpha}{\lambda} + 2\lambda - 2\,\frac{\lambda(\lambda - 1) - 2\alpha}{k - \lambda - 1}$$

$$+ k - \mu - \frac{(k - \mu - \lambda)(k - \lambda - 1) + (\lambda(\lambda - 1) - 2\alpha)}{\bar{\mu}}.$$

Using, e.g., $\bar{\mu}k = l(k - 1)$ and $r + s = \lambda - \mu$, we obtain

(5.8) $$t = 2\left\{\frac{1}{\lambda} + \frac{2k - \mu}{(k - \lambda - 1)(k - \mu)}\right\}\alpha + \frac{k\lambda(\mu - 2\lambda + 2) - 2\mu\lambda}{(k - \lambda - 1)(k - \mu)}.$$

Now we repeat the above procedure, this time starting with a nonedge $(a, b) \in \Gamma$ and considering the sets $\Gamma_i \equiv \Gamma_i(a, b)$ defined by

$$\Gamma_1 = \{a\}, \qquad \Gamma_2 = \{b\}, \qquad \Gamma_3 = \Delta(a) \cap \Delta(b),$$
$$\Gamma_4 = \Delta(a) \cap \Gamma(b), \qquad \Gamma_5 = \Gamma(a) \cap \Delta(b) \qquad \text{and} \qquad \Gamma_6 = \Gamma(a) \cap \Gamma(b)$$

consisting of

$$m_1 = m_2 = 1, \qquad m_3 = \mu, \qquad m_4 = m_5 = k - \mu \qquad \text{and} \qquad m_6 = \bar{\lambda}$$

vertices respectively. We let

$$f_{ij} \equiv f_{ij}(a, b) = e(\Gamma_i, \Gamma_j)$$

so that

(5.9) $$0 \leqq f_{ij} = f_{ji} \leqq m_i(m_j - \delta_{ij})$$

and

(5.10) $$f_{11} = f_{12} = f_{15} = f_{16} = f_{22} = f_{24} = f_{26} = 0,$$
$$f_{13} = f_{23} = \mu \quad \text{and} \quad f_{14} = f_{25} = k - \mu.$$

Further, we put

$\beta \equiv \beta(a, b) = $ the number of subgraphs of $\mathscr{G}$ of the form

$$a \quad\qquad b$$

so that $f_{33} = 2\beta$, and compute the remaining f_{ij} in terms of $k, \lambda, \bar{\lambda}, \mu$, and β. The method is the same as for the e_{ij}, so we omit details. The results are

(5.11)
$$f_{33} = 2\beta,$$
$$f_{34} = f_{35} = \mu\lambda - 2\beta,$$
$$f_{36} = \mu(k - 2\lambda - 2) + 2\beta,$$
$$f_{44} = f_{55} = (k - \mu)\lambda - \mu\lambda + 2\beta,$$
$$f_{45} = (k - \mu)\mu - \mu\lambda + 2\beta,$$
$$f_{46} = f_{56} = (k - \mu)(k - \lambda - \mu - 1) + \mu\lambda - 2\beta,$$
$$f_{66} = (k - 2\mu)\bar{\lambda} + \mu(k - 2\lambda - 2) + 2\beta.$$

Here again we see that any one of the f_{ij}, $i \geqq 3, j \geqq 3$, determines the rest. Since the number of 4-vertex subgraphs of each type with respect to (a,b) determines one of these f_{ij} and conversely can be obtained from it,

(5.12) *If the number of 4-vertex subgraphs of $\mathscr{G}$ of one type with respect to (a,b) is independent of the choice of the nonedge (a,b), then so is the number of 4-vertex subgraphs of each type with respect to (a,b).*

Combining (5.6) and (5.12) we see that

(5.13) *If $e_{ij}(x, y)$ is independent of the choice of $(x, y) \in \Delta$ for some $i \geqq 3$, $j \geqq 3$ and $f_{pq}(a,b)$ is independent of the choice of $(a,b) \in \Gamma$ for some $p \geqq 3$, $q \geqq 3$, then $\mathscr{G}$ satisfies the 4-vertex condition.*

Note that

(5.14) *The number of 3-claws* $\;\underset{a}{\overset{\nwarrow\!\!\nearrow b}{\big|}}\;$ *in $\mathscr{G}$ is* $f_{36} = \mu(k - 2\lambda - 2) + 2\beta$.

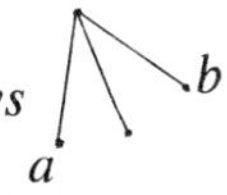

By (5.7), (5.13) and (5.14),

(5.15) *The following statements are equivalent.*
(a) $\mathscr{G}$ *has no 3-claws.*

(b) $\alpha(x,y) = \frac{1}{2}\{(k-\lambda-1)(k-2\lambda-2)+\lambda(\lambda-1)\}$ *for all* $(x,y) \in \Delta$.

(c) $\beta(a,b) = -\frac{1}{2}\{\mu(k-2\lambda-2)\}$ *for all* $(a,b) \in \Gamma$.

(d) $\mathcal{G}$ *satisfies the* 4-*vertex condition and* α *and* β *have the values given in* (b) *and* (c).

Assume once more that $\mathcal{G}$ is primitive, and this time, that $\bar{\lambda} \neq 0$, so that all the m_i are $\neq 0$. By the same argument as before we see that

$$u = \operatorname{trace} \hat{A}(a,b) - (k+2(r+s))$$

is an eigenvalue of the matrix

$$\hat{A}(a,b) = (f_{ij}/m_i).$$

By (5.10) and (5.11),

$$\operatorname{trace} \hat{A}(a,b) = \frac{2\beta}{\mu} + 2\lambda - 2\frac{\mu\lambda - 2\beta}{k-\mu} + k - 2\mu + \frac{\mu(k-2\lambda-2)+2\beta}{\bar{\lambda}}.$$

Hence

$$u = 2\left\{\frac{k+\mu}{\mu(k-\mu)} + \frac{1}{\bar{\lambda}}\right\}\beta - \frac{2\mu\lambda}{k-\mu} + \frac{\mu(k-2\lambda-2)}{\bar{\lambda}}. \tag{5.16}$$

Assuming that $\mathcal{G}$ is primitive and $\lambda \neq 0$, we take an edge $(x,y) \in \Delta$, i.e. a nonedge in $\bar{\mathcal{G}}$, and we consider the corresponding partition $\Delta_1, \ldots, \Delta_6$ of the vertices as before, so that

$$\operatorname{trace} \hat{A}(x,y) = k + 2(r+s) + t.$$

But this is precisely the partition from which we compute $\bar{u}$ for the nonedge (x, y) in $\bar{\mathcal{G}}$, that is, if $\hat{B}(x, y)$ is obtained from B using this partition, then

$$\operatorname{trace} \hat{B}(x,y) = l + 2(\bar{r}+\bar{s}) + \bar{u}$$

where $\bar{u}$ corresponds to u and is given by (5.16) on barring the parameters occurring, $\bar{\bar{\lambda}} = \lambda$. Since $I + \hat{A}(x,y) + \hat{B}(x,y) = \hat{J}$, where the rows of $\hat{J}$ are all equal to $(n_1, n_2, \ldots, n_6)$, we see on taking the trace that

$$t + \bar{u} = -1. \tag{5.17}$$

By §3 we know that $s \leqq t$ and $\bar{s} \leqq \bar{u}$. Hence

$$s \leqq t \leqq r \text{ if } \mathcal{G} \text{ is primitive and } \lambda \neq 0. \tag{5.18}$$

In the same way we see that

$$u + \bar{t} = -1 \quad \text{and} \quad s \leqq u \leqq r \quad \text{if } \mathcal{G} \text{ is primitive and } \bar{\lambda} \neq 0. \tag{5.19}$$

Counting the total number of subgraphs of the form

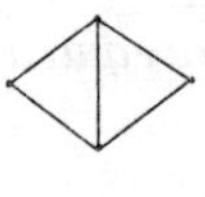

in $\mathcal{G}$ in two ways we get the equation

$$\sum_{(x,y) \in \Delta} [n_4(n_4-1) - e_{44}(x,y)] = \sum_{(a,b) \in \Gamma} f_{44}(a,b)$$

which reduces to

(5.20) $$nk\binom{\lambda}{2} - \sum_{(x,y) \in \Delta} \alpha(x,y) = \sum_{(x,y) \in \Gamma} \beta(x,y).$$

In particular

(5.21) *If $\mathcal{G}$ satisfies the 4-vertex condition, then*

$$k\left\{\binom{\lambda}{2} - \alpha\right\} = l\beta.$$

The analogous counts of the total numbers of 4-vertex subgraphs of other types all give the same result (5.21).

The total number of 4-cliques in $\mathcal{G}$ containing a vertex x is $\frac{1}{3}\sum_{y \in \Delta(x)}\alpha(x, y)$ and the total number of 4-cliques is $\frac{1}{12}\sum_{(x,y) \in \Delta}\alpha(x,y)$. In particular,

(5.22) *If $\mathcal{G}$ satisfies the 4-vertex condition then $3|k\alpha$ and $4|nk\alpha$, and dually, $3|l\bar{\alpha}$ and $4|nl\bar{\alpha}$.*

For in this case the respective numbers of 4-cliques are $k\alpha/3$ and $nk\alpha/12$. As usual, the bar denotes the corresponding parameter for $\bar{\mathcal{G}}$, so $\bar{\alpha}(a,b) = \binom{\bar{\lambda}}{2} - f_{66}(a,b)/2$ for $(a,b) \in \Gamma$ and $\beta(x,y) = \binom{\mu}{2} - e_{66}(x,y)/2$.

By (5.1) we know that $0 \leq \alpha \leq \binom{\lambda}{2}$. Suppose that $\alpha = \binom{\lambda}{2}$, i.e., that $\beta = 0$. Then for a given vertex x, the sets $\{y\} + (\Delta(x) \cap \Delta(y))$ with $y \in \Delta(x)$ are $(\lambda+1)$-cliques partitioning $\Delta(x)$. Moreover, the sets

$$\{x,y\} + (\Delta(x) \cap \Delta(y)), \qquad (x,y) \in \Delta$$

are $(\lambda+2)$-cliques and each edge is contained in exactly one of these. Hence their total number is

$$\frac{nk}{2}\binom{\lambda+2}{2}^{-1} = \frac{nk}{(\lambda+1)(\lambda+2)}.$$

Thus

(5.23) *If $\mathcal{G}$ satisfies the 4-vertex condition and $\alpha = \binom{\lambda}{2}$, then $\lambda+1|k$ and $\lambda+2|nk$.*

Finally we remark that using (5.21), (5.8) reduces to

(5.24) *If $\mathcal{G}$ is primitive, $\lambda \neq 0$ and $\mathcal{G}$ satisfies the 4-vertex condition, then*

$$t = \frac{2\alpha}{\lambda} - \left\{\frac{4}{\mu} + \frac{2}{k(k-\mu)}\right\}\beta + \frac{\lambda\mu}{k-\mu}.$$

6. Strongly regular graphs with minimum eigenvalue -2. To illustrate the methods of §§4 and 5 we give another proof of the following result (Seidel [12]).

(6.1) *If $\mathscr{G}$ is a strongly regular graph with minimum eigenvalue -2, then one of the following holds*:

(I) $n = 2m, \quad k = \mu = 2(m-1), \qquad (m \geqq 2)$.
(II) $n = m^2, \quad k = 2(m-1), \quad \mu = 2, \quad (m \geqq 3)$.
(III) $n = \binom{m}{2}, \quad k = 2(m-2), \quad \mu = 4, \quad (m \geqq 5)$.
(IV) $n = 10, \quad k = 3, \quad \mu = 1$.
(V) $n = 16, \quad k = 10, \quad \mu = 6$.
(VI) $n = 27, \quad k = 16, \quad \mu = 8$.

The graphs with these parameters are known:

Case (I). $\mathscr{G}$ is (isomorphic with) the complement of the *ladder graph* (cf. [**11**]).

Case (II). The *lattice graph* $\mathscr{L}_2(m)$ of order m is the unique graph for $m \neq 4$, and for $m = 4$ there is exactly one graph not isomorphic with $\mathscr{L}_2(4)$, [**13**]. This graph has 3-claws, does not satisfy the 4-vertex condition, and does not have a transitive automorphism group.

Case (III). The *triangular graph* $\mathscr{T}(m)$ of order m is the unique graph for $m \neq 8$. For $m = 8$ there are exactly three exceptional graphs ([**2**], [**3**] and [**8**]), all of which have intransitive automorphism groups.

Case (IV). The unique graph is the so called *Peterson graph* [**9**] which is the complement of $\mathscr{T}(5)$.

Case (V). The unique graph is the *Clebsch graph* corresponding to the 16 lines on the Clebsch quartic surface [**12**, p. 295]. This graph does admit a rank 3 automorphism group.

Case (VI). The unique graph is the *Schafli graph* corresponding to the 27 lines on a cubic surface [**12**, p. 296]. This graph admits $U_4(2) \approx O_6(-1, 2)$ as a rank 3 automorphism group.

Our proof is quite different from Seidel's [**12**] which deals with the larger class of *strong graphs*. A proof of (6.1) up to a finite list of cases, using Ray-Chaudhuri's characterization of line graphs [**10**], has been given by Sims [**14**].

PROOF OF (6.1). Assume that $\mathscr{G}$ is a strongly regular graph with $s = -2$. By (4.13),

(1) $$k = 2\lambda - \mu + 4 \quad \text{and} \quad r = \lambda - \mu + 2.$$

If $\mu = 0$, then by (1) and (4.7), $k = 2\lambda + 4 = \lambda + 1$ which is impossible. Hence

(2) $$\mu > 0 \quad \text{and} \quad l = k(\lambda - \mu + 3)/\mu,$$

and by (4.15)

(3) $$f = k(2\lambda - \mu + 6)/\mu(\lambda - \mu + 4).$$

The formulas (1), (2), and (3) will be used repeatedly without explicit reference.

Since $l - k = k(\lambda - 2\mu + 3)/\mu$,

(4) $$k \leqq l \text{ if and only if } 2\mu \leqq \lambda + 3.$$

If $\mathscr{G}$ is imprimitive, then $\mu = k$ by (4.10), so $\mu = \lambda + 2$ and $l = 1$. Hence n is even by (4.20), so

(5)   *If $\mathscr{G}$ is imprimitive, then* (I) *holds.*

If $\mu = 1$, then $f = (2\lambda + 3)(2\lambda + 5)/(\lambda + 3)$, giving $\lambda = 0$, so

(6)   *If $\mu = 1$, then* (IV) *holds.*

From now on we assume that $\mathscr{G}$ is primitive with $\mu \geq 2$. Putting $m = \lambda + 2$ we see that

(7)   *If $\mu = 2$ or 4, then* (II) *or* (III) *holds respectively.*

Our next step is to show that

(8)   *If $\mathscr{G}$ has 3-claws, then either* (II) *with $m = 4$ or* (III) *with $m = 8$ holds.*

PROOF.   Let $[P; Q_1, Q_2, Q_3]$ be a 3-claw. By (3.3) we know that each of the $\mu - 1$ vertices $\neq P$ adjacent to two of the Q_i is adjacent to P but not to the third Q_i. This accounts for $3 + 3(\mu - 1)$ vertices adjacent to P. Of these, $2(\mu - 1)$ are also adjacent to Q_1, so $2(\mu - 1) \leq \lambda$. The remaining $\lambda - 2(\mu - 1)$ vertices adjacent to Q_1 and P are adjacent to neither Q_2 nor Q_3 and the analogous statement holds for any permutation of $\{1, 2, 3\}$. Hence we have at least

$$3 + 3(\mu - 1) + 3\{\lambda - 2(\mu - 1)\} = 3(\lambda - \mu) + 6$$

vertices adjacent to P, that is, $k \geq 3(\lambda - \mu) + 6$. Hence $0 \leq k - 3(\lambda - \mu) - 6 = 2(\mu - 1) - \lambda$, so $\lambda \leq 2(\mu - 1)$, and therefore $\lambda = 2(\mu - 1)$. Hence $k = 3\mu$ and $f = 3(3\mu + 2)/(\mu + 2)$ giving $\mu = 2, 4$ or 10.

The first two cases are the ones listed in (8). In the third case we have $n = 64$, $k = 30$, $\lambda = 18$, $\mu = 10$, $r = 10$ and $s = -2$. By (4.17) the matrix $C = B - A$ satisfies the equation $C^2 - 18C + 63 = 0$, and, with suitable ordering of the rows and columns, the matrix ECE, where

$$E = \begin{bmatrix} I_{31} & 0 \\ 0 & -I_{33} \end{bmatrix},$$

has the form

$$\begin{bmatrix} 0 & -j \\ j^T & D \end{bmatrix}, \qquad j = (1, \ldots, 1),$$

and satisfies the same equation. Hence $D^2 - 18D + 63 = -J$, and since D has row sum -18, it follows that there exists a strongly regular graph with $n = 63$, $k = 40$, $\lambda = 28$, $\mu = 20$, $r = 10$ and $s = -2$. This graph has no 3-claws and so satisfies the 4-vertex condition, as does its complement. For the complement we have $\bar{k} = 22$, $\bar{\lambda} = 1$ and $\bar{\mu} = 11$, so by (5.21), $\alpha = \beta = 0$ and by (5.16), $\bar{u} = -2 + 99/14 > 1$ contrary to $\bar{r} = 1$ by (5.19).

From this point on we assume that $\mathcal{G}$ has no 3-claws. Then by (5.15)

(9) $\mathcal{G}$ *satisfies the 4-vertex condition with*

$$\alpha = \tfrac{1}{2}\{(k-\lambda-1)(k-2\lambda-2)+\lambda(\lambda-1)\} \quad and \quad \beta = -\tfrac{1}{2}\mu(k-2\lambda-2).$$

Let P and Q be nonadjacent vertices. Then $\Delta(P) = \Delta + \Lambda$ with $\Delta = \Delta(P) \cap \Delta(Q)$ and $\Lambda = \Delta(P) \cap \Gamma(Q)$. Let m be the number of vertices adjacent to P, Q and X for some $X \in \Delta$. Since there are no 3-claws, each of the $k-2$ vertices $\neq P$, Q adjacent to X is adjacent to either P or Q. Hence $k-2 = m+2(\lambda-m) = 2\lambda - m$, and therefore $m = \mu - 2$, that is,

(10) *For each $X \in \Delta$ there is a unique $\bar{X} \in \Delta$ such that X is not adjacent to $\bar{X}$. In particular, μ is even.*

Now take $X \in \Delta$ and $A \in \Lambda$. Since there are no 3-claws, A must be adjacent to one of X, $\bar{X}$. On the other hand, P, Q and the $\mu-2$ vertices $\neq X, \bar{X}$ in Δ are all adjacent to X and $\bar{X}$, accounting for all μ vertices adjacent to both X and $\bar{X}$. Hence

(11)   *Each $A \in \Lambda$ is adjacent to exactly one of $X, \bar{X}$ for $X \in \Delta$.*

(12)   *If $k > l$, then either $k = 2\mu$ or $\bar{\lambda} = 0$.*

PROOF. Assume that $k > l$ and $\bar{\lambda} \neq 0$. The subgraph on the set $\Gamma(P) \cap \Gamma(Q)$, where P and Q are nonadjacent vertices, has $\bar{\lambda}$ vertices and is regular with valence $k-2\mu$. If there are two nonadjacent vertices in $\Gamma(P) \cap \Gamma(Q)$, then the absence of 3-claws implies that all μ vertices adjacent to both lie in $\Gamma(P) \cap \Gamma(Q)$. Hence in this case $\mu < k-2\mu$, or $2\mu < \lambda+2$, contrary to (4). This means that our subgraph is a clique, i.e., that $k-2\mu = \lambda-1$, so that by (4.7), $\mu(4\lambda - 5\mu + 10) = k(\lambda - \mu + 3)$,   whence $(\lambda+3-2\mu)(2\lambda+4-3\mu) = 0$, i.e., $(\lambda+3-2\mu)(k-2\mu) = 0$. Hence $k = 2\mu$ by (4).

(13)   *If $k = 2\mu$, then one of (II), (III) or (VI) holds.*

PROOF. If $k = 2\mu$, we have $3\mu = 2(\lambda+2)$ and $f = 8(\mu+1)/(\mu+4)$, giving $\mu = 2, 4, 8$ or 20. In the first two cases (II) and (III) hold respectively, and the third case is (VI). In the last case the parameters are $n = 63$, $k = 40$, $\lambda = 28$, $\mu = 20$. This case was shown to be impossible in the proof of (8).

(14)   *If $\bar{\lambda} = 0$, then (II), (III) or (V) holds.*

PROOF. If $\bar{\lambda} = 0$, then the subgraph on $\Gamma(P)$ is a clique and hence $\Lambda = \Gamma(Q) - \{P\}$ where Q is not adjacent to P and we are using the notation of (10) and (11). For $A \in \Lambda$, $\Delta(A) \cap \Delta(P)$ consists of $\mu/2$ vertices in Δ, by (10), and the $l-2$ vertices $\neq A$ in Λ. Hence $\lambda = l-2+\mu/2 = 2\lambda - 3\mu/2 + 3$, giving $3\mu = 2\lambda + 6$. Hence $k = 2\mu - 2$ and

$$f = 8(\mu-1)/(\mu+2)$$

so that $\mu = 2, 4, 6, 10$ or 20. In the first three cases we have (II), (III), and (V) respectively. Using (9) and (5.8) we obtain for the last two cases

n	k	λ	μ	α	t
28	18	12	10	46	$-10/3$
64	42	30	22	325	$-22/3$

contrary to (5.18).

To complete the proof of (6.1) we show that

(15) $\qquad$ *If $\bar{\lambda} \neq 0$ and $k \leq l$, then* (II) *or* (III) *holds.*

PROOF. By (7) and (11) it suffices to show that $\mu \leq 4$. For a given vertex Q, the subgraph $\mathcal{G}_0$ on $\Gamma(Q)$ is regular with valence $k - \mu$. Since $\bar{\lambda} \neq 0, \mathcal{G}_0$ is not a clique, and the absence of 3-claws in $\mathcal{G}$ implies that all μ paths of length 2 joining two nonadjacent vertices in $\Gamma(Q)$ lie in $\Gamma(Q)$. Let P and A be adjacent vertices in $\Gamma(Q)$, so that $A \in \Lambda = \Delta(P) \cap \Gamma(Q)$. By (11), exactly $\mu/2$ of the λ vertices adjacent to P and A lie in $\Delta = \Delta(P) \cap \Delta(Q)$, so exactly $\lambda - \mu/2$ are in $\Gamma(Q)$. This means that $\mathcal{G}_0$ is a strongly regular graph with parameters $k_0 = k - \mu$, $l_0 = \bar{\lambda}, \lambda_0 = \lambda - \mu/2$ and $\mu_0 = \mu$. Since $k_0 = 2\lambda_0 - \mu_0 + 4, -2$ is an eigenvalue of $\mathcal{G}_0$, and by (3) the multiplicity of the other eigenvalue $\neq k_0$ is

$$f_0 = 8(\lambda - \mu + 2)(\lambda - \mu + 3)/(2\lambda - 3\mu + 8).$$

Assume that $\mu > 4$ and write $\mu = 2t + 4, t > 0$. Then

$$f_0 = 2(\lambda - 2t - 2)(\lambda - 2t - 1)/(t + 2)(\lambda - 3t - 2)$$

from which we have that

$$\lambda - 3t - 2 | t(t + 1) \quad \text{or} \quad 2t(t + 1)$$

according as t is even or odd. On the other hand

$$f = 2(\lambda - t)(\lambda - t + 1)/(t + 2)(\lambda - 2t)$$

giving that $\lambda - 2t | t(t + 1)$ or $2t(t + 1)$ according as t is even or odd. Since $(\lambda - 2t, \lambda - 3t - 2)|t + 2$ and $(t + 2, t(t + 1))|2$ it follows in any case that

$$(\lambda - 2t)(\lambda - 3t - 2)|2t(t + 1).$$

On the other hand, since $k \leq l$, we have $2\mu \leq \lambda + 3$ by (4), i.e., $\lambda \geq 4t + 5$, which gives a contradiction. This completes the proof of (15), and hence of (6.1).

(6.2) *Let $\mathcal{G}$ be a strongly regular graph with parameters as in* (II) *or* (III) *of* (6.1) *with $m \geq 2$ or $m \geq 3$ respectively. Then the following are equivalent.*

(a) *$\mathcal{G}$ satisfies the 4-vertex condition.*

(b) *$\mathcal{G}$ has no 3-claws.*

(c) *$\mathcal{G}$ is isomorphic with a lattice graph $\mathcal{L}_2(m)$ of order m for some $m \geq 2$ or a triangular graph $\mathcal{T}(m)$ for some $m \geq 3$.*

PROOF.   (a) $\Rightarrow$ (b). By (8) above, the only possibilities for the existence of 3-claws are case (II) with $m = 4$ and case (III) with $m = 8$. In the first of these cases we find $\alpha = 1$ by (5.21), and hence there are no 3-claws by (5.15). In the second we find $\alpha = 0$, 5, 10 or 15. By (5.23), $\alpha \neq 15$, and by (5.8) we get $t = -12$ or $-16/3$ according as $\alpha = 0$ or 5 respectively. Hence $\alpha = 10$ by (5.18), and there are no 3-claws by (5.15).

(c) $\Rightarrow$ (a) since the graphs $\mathscr{L}_2(m)$ and $\mathscr{T}(m)$ admit rank 3 automorphism groups.

(b) $\Rightarrow$ (c). Assuming the nonexistence of 3-claws we show that the set Σ of all cliques consisting of $k/2 + 1$ vertices each has the properties that (I*) each vertex lies in exactly two members of Σ, and (II*) each edge lies in exactly one member of Σ. Given a vertex P, let Q be a vertex not adjacent to P, put $\Delta = \Delta(P) \cap \Delta(Q)$, $\Lambda = \Delta(P) \cap \Gamma(Q)$ and for $X \in \Delta$, write $\bar{X}$ for the unique vertex in Δ not adjacent to X—this is the notation of (10) above which is applicable since there are no 3-claws. The absence of 3-claws implies that $\Delta(X) \cap \Lambda$ is a clique, and Λ is a disjoint union of the two cliques $\Delta(X) \cap \Lambda$ and $\Delta(\bar{X}) \cap \Lambda$ of $(k - \mu)/2$ vertices each. For $Y \in \Delta - \{X, \bar{X}\}$, $\Delta(Y) \cap \Lambda = \Delta(X) \cap \Lambda$ or $\Delta(\bar{X}) \cap \Lambda$. Otherwise there exists $A \in \Delta(Y) \cap \Delta(X) \cap \Lambda$ and $B \in \Delta(Y) \cap \Delta(\bar{X}) \cap \Lambda$ and we have three mutually adjacent vertices P, A and Y in $\Delta(X) \cap \Delta(B)$, contrary to (10) since $\mu \leq 4$. Now fix $X \in \Delta$ and put $K_1 = \{P\} \cup (\Delta(X) \cap \Lambda) \cup \{Y \in \Delta | \Delta(Y) \cap \Lambda = \Delta(X) \cap \Lambda\}$ and $K_2 = $ the same thing with $\bar{X}$ in place of X. Then K_1 and K_2 are cliques consisting of $k/2 + 1$ vertices each such that $K_1 \cup K_2 = \{P\} + \Delta(P)$ and $K_1 \cap K_2 = \{P\}$. If K is a third clique $\neq K_1, K_2$ containing P and at least $k/2 + 1$ vertices altogether, then we can assume that $|K \cap K_1| \geq k/4 + 1$ and $K \cap K_2$ contains a vertex $A \neq P$. Then $\Delta(P) \cap \Delta(A)$ contains at least $k/4$ vertices $\neq P$ in $K \cap K_1$ and all $k/2 - 1$ vertices $\neq P, A$ in K_2, so that $\lambda \geq 3k/4$, which is not possible in cases (II) or (III). Hence the set Σ of cliques consisting of $k/2 + 1$ vertices each has the properties (I*) and (II*). Consequently, by Theorem (6.2) of Bose's paper [1], $\mathscr{G}$ is the graph of a partial geometry with parameters $(2, m, 1)$ or $(2, m - 1, 2)$ according as (II) or (III) holds. It is known [1] (and very easily verified) that the partial geometries with these parameters are uniquely determined.

REFERENCES

1. R. C. Bose, *Strongly regular graphs, partial geometries and partially balanced designs*, Pacific J. Math. **13** (1963), 389–419. MR **28** #1137.

2. L. C. Chang, *The uniqueness and nonuniqueness of the triangular association scheme*, Sci. Record **3** (1959), 604–613. MR **22** #7950.

3. ———, *Association schemes of partially balanced block designs with parameters $v = 28$, $n_1 = 12, n_2 = 15$ and $p_{11}^2 = 4$*, Sci. Record **4** (1960), 12–18. MR **22** # 7951.

4. D. G. Higman, *Finite permutation groups of rank 3*, Math. Z. **86** (1964), 145–156. MR **32** # 4182.

5. ———, *Intersection matrices for finite permutation groups*, J. Algebra **6** (1967), 22–42. MR **35** # 244.

6. ———, *Coherent configurations*. I, Rend. Sem. Mat. Univ. Padova **44** (1970), 1–26.

7. ———, *Solvability of a class of rank 3 permutation groups*, Nagoya Math. J. **41** (1970).

8. A. J. Hoffman, *On the uniqueness of the triangular association scheme*, Ann. Math. Statist. **31** (1960), 492–497. MR **22** #7949.

9. A. J. Hoffman and R. R. Singleton, *On Moore graphs with diameters 2 and 3*, IBM J. Res. Develop. **4** (1960), 497–504. MR **25** #3857.

10. D. K. Ray-Chaudhuri, *Characterization of line graphs*, J. Combinatorial Theory **3** (1967), 201–214. MR **35** #4119.

11. J. J. Seidel, *Strongly regular graphs of L_2-type and of triangular type*, Nederl. Akad. Wetensch. Proc. Ser. A **70** = Indag. Math. **29** (1967), 188–196. MR **35** # 88.

12. ———, *Strongly regular graphs with $(-1, 1, 0)$ adjacency matrix having eigenvalue 3*, Linear Algebra Appl. **1** (1968), 281–298. MR **38** # 3175.

13. S. S. Shrikhande, *The uniqueness of the L_2 association scheme*, Ann. Math. Statist. **30** (1959), 781–798.

14. C. C. Sims, *On graphs with rank 3 automorphism groups*, J. Combinatorial Theory (to appear).

15. H. Wielandt, *Finite permutation groups*, Lectures, University of Tübingen, 1954/55; English transl., Academic Press, New York, 1964. MR **32** #1252.

MICHIGAN STATE UNIVERSITY

UNIVERSITY OF MICHIGAN

[illegible] Nagoya Math. J. [illegible]
[illegible] Math. [illegible] MR 27 [illegible]
[illegible] MR 26 [illegible]
[illegible] MR 28 [illegible]
11. [illegible] Nederl. Akad. Wetensch. Proc. Ser. A [illegible] Math. 29 (1967), [illegible]
12. [illegible] Algebra [illegible] MR 38 [illegible]
13. [illegible] 30 [illegible]
14. [illegible]
15. [illegible]

MICHIGAN STATE UNIVERSITY
[illegible]

Computing Local Structure of Large Finite Groups[1]

John J. Cannon

1. **Introduction.** The subgroup lattice and automorphism group programs of Neubüser[3], [4], [6] have demonstrated that it is possible to compute fairly complete information about the structure of groups of order up to 20,000. However, group theorists studying simple groups are often interested in obtaining some information about the structure of much larger groups. So we shall take this opportunity to describe some techniques which can be used to compute information about groups whose orders lie in the range 10^4 to 10^8. In particular, techniques for finding centralizers, Sylow subgroups, the Fitting subgroup, elementary subgroups and the normal subgroup lattice of groups of order up to 10^8 are given. In addition, we shall describe methods for finding normalizers, the derived series and the lower central series of groups of somewhat smaller order.

In §2 a number of constructions which are basic to this work are described while in §3 we show how these techniques are used to compute the subgroups listed above. §4 contains a very brief indication of possible applications of this work to the study of large groups. §5 describes some of the more important features of a program developed at Sydney in which many of the algorithms described here have been implemented. The paper concludes with a description of an application of this program to the determination of the Sylow structure of the simple group $Sp_4(3)$, of order 25,920.

For background information and an extensive list of references see Cannon[1].

AMS 1970 *subject classifications*. Primary 20–04; Secondary 20D20, 20D25, 20D30.

[1]This research was supported in part by a grant from the Australian Research Grants Committee.

JOHN J. CANNON

Notation

$\{x_1, \ldots, x_n\}$	the set consisting of elements $x_1, \ldots, x_n$,
$\langle x_1, \ldots, x_n \rangle$	the group generated by elements $x_1, \ldots, x_n$,
$|X|$	cardinality of X,
$\emptyset$	null set,
$X \times Y$	direct product of groups X and Y,
x^y	$y^{-1} xy$,
$N(X)$	normalizer of X,
$C(X)$	centralizer of X,
$Z(X)$	centre of X,
$[G:H]$	index of subgroup H in group G,
$[X, Y]$	$\langle x^{-1} y^{-1} xy \mid \forall\, x \in X, \forall\, y \in Y \rangle$,
$[x, y]$	$x^{-1} y^{-1} xy$,
$[n]$	the ceiling of n, •
$\leftarrow$	"becomes": the identifier on the left of this symbol becomes the name of the object defined by the expression on the right of the symbol.

2. **Basic constructions.**   Throughout much of this paper it will be assumed that both a presentation and faithful representation of the group G are known. It will also be assumed that the elements of G can be ordered in some way.

2.1 *Coset representatives.*   Given an arbitrary subgroup H of G we shall often require a set of coset representatives for H in G. If a presentation for G is known one may use the Todd-Coxeter process to enumerate the cosets of H and then find a set of coset representatives from the resulting coset table. The success of this method depends on the given presentation and the size of the index of H in G, $[G : H]$. Recently the author enumerated the 18,468 cosets of a subgroup in a covering group of the Hall-Janko-McKay group and it is probably possible to enumerate cosets of subgroups of index up to 50,000 in favorable situations.

In situations where it is not possible to use the Todd-Coxeter algorithm one may use the given faithful representation of G to compute the coset table of H directly. In this process the most time consuming operation is checking whether a newly generated coset has been found previously. To facilitate this operation we choose the smallest element lying in a coset to be the canonical representative of that coset. Generally all the elements of $H = \{h_1, \ldots, h_r\}$ are stored during this process. Then it is usually possible to see that an element $h_i g$ of the cost Hg cannot be the canonical representative of Hg by examining only the first few components of the product $h_i g$. To determine whether a newly generated coset has been found previously one merely checks whether its canonical representative occurs among the canonical representatives of the known cosets.

A partial set of coset representatives for subgroup H can be found from a partial coset table constructed by either of the above methods.

2.2 Generation of group elements. Suppose

$$I = H_1 < H_2 < \cdots < H_n < H_{n+1} = G$$

is a chain of subgroups of G. The elements of G are generated by constructing coset representatives for H_i in H_{i+1}, $i = 1, \ldots, n$. There is a one-to-one correspondence between the elements $g \in G$ and the vectors $(j_1, \ldots, j_n), j_i = 1, \ldots,$ $[H_{i+1} : H_i]$. Let us call the vector corresponding to g the indexing vector of g.

If G is a group of permutations of the integers $1, \ldots, n$ we take H_{n+1-i} to be the stabilizer of $1, 2, \ldots, i$. It is then an easy matter to write down a set of coset representatives for H_i in H_{i+1}. A set of generators for H_i is obtained from a set of generators of H_{i+1} and the coset representatives of H_i in H_{i+1}, by applying Schreier's theorem. Once the sets of coset representatives of the adjacent terms of this chain of subgroups are known it is a simple matter to write down the indexing vector of a permutation $g \in G$. Thus one may determine whether a permutation is an element of G without actually generating the elements of G. For details of this method of generating permutation groups see Sims[7].

In the general case the user has to specify a suitable chain of subgroups and the sets of coset representatives are found using the methods of the previous section. Here, if one wishes to use the Todd-Coxeter algorithm, one must supply presentations for $H_{n+1}, H_n, \ldots$ etc. as far down the chain as possible.

This method of generating a group has the drawback that it is often not feasible to find the indexing vector associated with an arbitrary element of the group because of the large amount of computation that is involved. We suppose that the coset representatives chosen for H_i in H_{i+1}, $i = 1, \ldots, n$, are the canonical representatives of §2.1. The nth component of the indexing vector is found by determining the canonical representative g_n of the coset $H_n g$ and noting the position of g_n among the canonical representatives of H_n. The process is now repeated with element gg_n^{-1} and subgroup H_{n-1} to obtain the $(n-1)$th component etc. An element g belongs to G if and only if the canonical representative of $H_n g$ occurs among the canonical representatives of H_n.

The Felsch-Neubüser algorithm [3] is used whenever all the elements of a a small group are required.

2.3 Centralizer. Let H be a subgroup of order approximately the square root of the order of G. The subgroup H is usually obtained from among the chain of subgroups used to generate the elements of G. Let $H = \{h_1, \ldots, h_r\}$ and suppose it is required to find the centralizer, $C(x)$, of $x \in G$. Note that x does not necessarily lie in H.

The centralizer procedure begins by forming the conjugates $h_1^{-1} xh_1, \ldots,$ $h_r^{-1} xh_r$. The set of h_i such that $h_i^{-1} xh_i = x$ will be denoted by $C_H(x)$, while the complement of $C_H(x)$ in H will be denoted by $\tilde{C}_H(x)$. Those conjugates $h_i^{-1} xh_i$ not equal to x are stored in a list L and the distinct elements of L are sorted so as to form an ordered list L.

Let $y_1, \ldots, y_r$ be a set of coset representatives for H in G. Now if $y_i x = xy_i$, i.e. if $y_i \in C(x)$, then $C_H(x)y_i \in C(x)$ but $\tilde{C}_H(x)y_i \notin C(x)$. However, if $y_i \notin C(x)$ then $C_H(x)y_i \notin C(x)$ but some elements of $\tilde{C}_H(x)y_i$ may centralize x. If $h_j \in C_H(x)$ the element $h_j y_i$ centralizes x if and only if

$$h_j^{-1} x h_j = y_i x y_i^{-1}.$$

So if $y_i \notin C(x)$, we may quickly determine which elements of $\tilde{C}_H(x)y_i$ centralize x by doing a binary search of L with the element $y_i x y_i^{-1}$.

The process involves computing $|H| + [G:H]$ conjugates, $|C(x)|$ products and making about $[G:H][\log_2 |H|]$ comparisons of group elements. As computing a conjugate is the most expensive operation we make $|H| + [G:H]$ as small as possible by choosing H so that its order is about the square root of $|G|$. To take a numerical example, if $|G| = 10^6$ and $|H| = 10^3$, the process involves computing about 2,000 conjugates and making about 10,000 comparisons of group elements.

In the case of permutation groups Sims [8] has developed techniques for constructing centralizers which are applicable to groups of considerably larger order than the more general method described above.

2.4 *Normalizer.* Suppose the normalizer, $N(H)$, of a subgroup H of G is required. If the index of H in G is sufficiently small so that the cosets of H in G can be enumerated then the following procedure can be used to compute $N(H)$. Let H be generated by the elements $h_1, \ldots, h_r$. In the following algorithm R and S are sets of group elements.

(i) $R \leftarrow \{h_1, \ldots, h_r\}$.

(ii) Enumerate the m cosets of subgroup $\langle R \rangle$, $i \leftarrow 2, S \leftarrow \emptyset$.

(iii) Find a coset representative g_i for the ith coset of $\langle R \rangle$. If $g_i^{-1} h_j g_i \in H$ for $j = 1, \ldots, r$ then $S \leftarrow S \cup \{g_i\}$; otherwise S is unchanged.

(iv) If $S \neq \emptyset, R \leftarrow R \cup S$, and go to (ii).

(v) $i \leftarrow i+1$. If $i \leq m$ go to (iii).

(vi) $N(H) \leftarrow \langle R \rangle$.

As $[G:H]$ is often too large in practice to do a complete coset enumeration, the above process may be modified so that initially it attempts to find normalizing coset representatives from partial coset tables constructed by either of the methods of §2.1. When $[G:\langle R \rangle]$ is sufficiently small so that the cosets of $\langle R \rangle$ can be enumerated we do a complete coset enumeration and check to see if all of $N(H)$ has been found. At the present time we are unable to give a satisfactory method for computing normalizers of subgroups of large index. However, there are methods available which sometimes turn out to be useful in practice. Suppose that H is generated by elements x and y, where x is of prime order, and suppose further that by coset enumeration or otherwise, it is possible to find a set of coset representatives for $C(x)$ in G. Constructing $C(x)$ as in §2.3 we find the normalizer of x, $K = N(x)$, by the coset method. Let $z_1, \ldots, z_r$ be a set of coset representatives for $N(x)$ in G and put $K = N_k(H) \cup \tilde{N}_K(H)$ where $N_K(H)$ is the normalizer of H in K and $\tilde{N}_K(H)$ is the complement of $N_K(H)$ in K. Then it may be shown that the normalizer $N(H)$ of H in

G consists of the complete sets $N_K(H)z_i$, where $z_i \in N(H)$, and possibly some elements of the sets $\tilde{N}_K(H)z_i$, where $z_i^{-1} xz_i \in H, z_i^{-1} yz_i \notin H$.

If the order of $N(H)$ is known then we know that H has $[G:N(H)]$ distinct conjugates. So if elements $y_1, \ldots, y_r$ can be found such that $y_1^{-1} Hy_1, \ldots, y_r^{-1} Hy_r$ is the complete conjugacy class of H then $\{y_1, \ldots, y_r\}$ is a set of coset representatives for $N(H)$ in G. Using Schreier's theorem it is then a simple matter to write down a set of generators for $N(H)$. If the order of $N(H)$ is unknown but $[G:N(H)]$ is small we can keep conjugating H and its conjugates by the generators of G until nothing new is obtained to get a set of coset representatives for $N(H)$.

In order to be able to determine rapidly whether a newly generated conjugate subgroup has already been found each subgroup of the class is characterized by a canonical set of generators in the following way. Let $\bar{x}$ denote the smallest element generating the cyclic subgroup $\langle x \rangle$. Suppose $H = H_1 = \langle a_1, b_1 \rangle$. Then $\{\bar{a}_1, \bar{b}_1\}$ is taken to be the canonical generating set for H_1. If $x_i^{-1}H_1x_i = H_i, i > 1$, then

$$H_i = \langle x_i^{-1}\bar{a}_1x_i, x_i^{-1}\bar{b}_1x_i \rangle = \langle a_i, b_i \rangle$$

where $a_i = x_i^{-1}\bar{a}_1x_i$, $b_i = x_i^{-1}\bar{b}_1x_i$, and $\{\bar{a}_i, \bar{b}_i\}$ is the canonical generating set for H_i. To determine whether H_i is a new conjugate of H it is simply necessary to see if $\{\bar{a}_i, \bar{b}_i\}$ occurs among the known canonical generating sets. Although the same procedure can be used when H is generated by more than two elements it is desirable to use a small as possible generating set for reasons of efficiency.

If an efficient algorithm for enumerating double cosets was available then one could exploit the fact that either all the elements of HxH normalize H or none do. As the number of double cosets of H is quite small this would appear to be a very effective method of computing normalizers.

2.5 *Normal closure.* If H is a subgroup of G, let H^* denote the smallest normal subgroup of G containing H (the normal closure of H). The index of H^* in G may be found by adding the words generating H as additional relators to a presentation of G and enumerating the cosets of the identity in this group.

When $[G:H]$ is sufficiently small so that the cosets of H in G can be enumerated, a set of generators for H^* may be computed as follows: Suppose H is generated by elements $h_1, \ldots, h_m$.

(i) Using the coset algorithm of the last section, find the normalizer $N(H)$ of H. Let $y_1, \ldots, y_n$ denote a set of coset representatives for $N(H)$ in G. $M \leftarrow H, i \leftarrow 0, k \leftarrow 0$.

(ii) $i \leftarrow i+1$. If $i > n$, finish. Else $j \leftarrow 0$.

(iii) $j \leftarrow j+1$. If $j > m$, go to (ii). Else if $y_i^{-1} h_j y_i \in M$, go to (iii). Otherwise,

(iv) $k \leftarrow k+1, z_k \leftarrow y_i^{-1} h_j y_i, M \leftarrow \langle M, z_k \rangle$. Go to (iii).

Now H^* is generated by the elements $h_1, \ldots, h_m, z_1, \ldots, z_k$.

Note that if M is generated by one of the techniques of §2.1 then it is often possible to avoid storing all the elements of M in order to determine whether $y_i^{-1} h_j y_i \in M$ in step (iii).

2.6 *Classes.* The centralizer algorithm can be used to determine the size of the conjugacy class of an element x. If a set of coset representatives $y_1, \ldots, y_n$ for $C(x)$ can be computed then the class of x consists precisely of the elements $y_1^{-1} x y_1, \ldots, y_n^{-1} x y_n$. If it is not possible to find a set of coset representatives for $C(x)$ then the class of x is found by repeatedly conjugating x by the generators of G until $[G : C(x)]$ distinct conjugates have been obtained.

Centralizers corresponding to several different classes can often be obtained simultaneously by looking for a cyclic subgroup Z of large order and constructing the centralizer of an element, x say, of Z having small order. Then the centralizers of all those elements of Z whose powers include x are contained in $C(x)$. For example if $|Z| = 12$, and x is the element of order 2 in Z, then $C(x)$ contains the centralizers of the elements of orders 4, 6 and 12 lying in Z.

The conjugacy class of a subgroup H consists precisely of the subgroups $y_1^{-1} H y_1, \ldots, y_n^{-1} H y_n$ where $y_1, \ldots, y_n$ are coset representatives for the normalizer $N(H)$ of H in G. If $N(H)$ is not available but the class of H is not too big then the conjugates of H may be found directly using the method of canonical generating sets described in §2.4.

Sims [8] has developed highly efficient techniques for finding conjugacy classes in large permutation groups.

2.7 *Subgroup lattice.* In this study the cyclic extension method of constructing subgroup lattices (Neubüser [3], [6]) was programmed. As it stands this method constructs only the solvable part of the lattice so that in the case of a nonsolvable group a more general extension procedure must be employed to find perfect subgroups. Having found all the perfect subgroups, the remaining nonsolvable subgroups are constructed as cyclic extensions of the perfect subgroups.

The extension procedure used to construct the perfect subgroups is based on the following result (pointed out to me by J. N. Ward). If H is a subgroup of G and

$$G = H x_1 H \cup \cdots \cup H x_n H,$$

then all subgroups of G minimal with respect to containing H occur among the subgroups

$$\langle H, x_1 \rangle, \ldots, \langle H, x_n \rangle.$$

Although this fact could be used to construct the complete subgroup lattice of a group, the resulting algorithm would appear to be less efficient than the cyclic extension method.

If the group G is nonsolvable but not perfect then the search for perfect subgroups can be shortened by noting that all the perfect subgroups of G must be contained in the stationary term of the derived series for G.

It appears possible to compute subgroup lattices of groups of order up to 20,000 if this algorithm is implemented as described in Neubüser [6].

3. **Construction of special subgroups.** In this section we will show how the basic constructions described above can be used in practical situations to compute certain interesting subgroups of groups of moderately large order.

3.1 *Centralizer of an involution.* The construction of the centralizer of an element of order 2 of G is a direct application of the centralizer algorithm of §2.3. Provided the degree of the representation of G is not too large it is possible to compute the centralizer of an involution in groups G of order up to 10^8.

3.2 *Sylow subgroups.* A Sylow p-subgroup of G is constructed by successively extending a p-subgroup by p-elements. Suppose we wish to find a set of generators $x_1, \ldots, x_r$ of the Sylow p-subgroup $S(p)$ of G where $S(p)$ is of order p^m.

 (i) Look through the elements of G until a p-element, x_1 say, is found. $i \leftarrow 1, P \leftarrow \emptyset$.

 (ii) $P \leftarrow \langle P, x_i \rangle$. If $|P| = p^m$ then $S(p) \leftarrow P, r \leftarrow i$, and $S(p) = \langle x_1, \ldots, x_r \rangle$. Otherwise,

 (iii) $i \leftarrow i+1$. Find a p-element x_i such that

  (a) $x_i \notin P$.

  (b) $x_i^{p^\alpha} \in P$, where $\alpha \geq 1$.

  (c) $x_i \in N(P)$, i.e. $x_1^{x_i}, \ldots, x_{i-1}^{x_i} \in P$.

Go to (ii).

The crucial step in this algorithm is, of course, the location of suitable p-elements in step (iii). If the order of G is quite small then one can simply run through all the elements of G looking for p-elements. However, as the order of G increases this becomes impractical. If the classes of G are at hand then one immediately has available all the p-elements of the group. In the case where G is large and its classes are not available we exploit the following theorem on p-groups: If K is a nontrivial normal subgroup of the p-group P, then $K \cap Z(P) \neq 1$. If we put $S_i = \langle x_1, \ldots, x_i \rangle$ in the above algorithm then $S_i \lhd S_{i+1}$ and the theorem tells us that there is at least one element in $Z(S_i)$ which is centralized by S_{i+1}. So in step (iii) one must find a suitable x_i if one runs through the p-elements lying in the centralizers of the elements of order p in $Z(S_i)$.

Note that as one constructs a generating set for $S(p)$, one can simultaneously construct a presentation for $S(p)$.

3.3 *Elementary subgroups.* An elementary subgroup is a subgroup which is a direct product of a cyclic group and a p-group for some prime p. The importance of elementary subgroups arises from Brauer's characterization theorem which states that every character of G is an integral linear combination of characters of G induced from linear characters of elementary subgroups of G. An element x of G is said to be p-regular if p does not divide the order of x. It is easily seen that an elementary subgroup of G is the direct product of a cyclic group generated by a p-regular element of G and a p-subgroup of G.

The elementary subgroups of G are constructed as follows. Let $\{x_1, \ldots, x_n\}$ be a full set of representatives of the classes of cyclic subgroups of G and let $X_i = \langle x_i \rangle$ be the cyclic subgroup generated by x_i. Then for each x_i and for each prime p such that x_i is p-regular we construct the subgroups $Z_{ij} = X_i \times Y_j$ where Y_j is a Sylow p-subgroup of the centralizer $C(x_i)$ of x_i. Note that some subgroups of the set $\{Z_{ij}\}$ may be conjugate.

3.4 *Fitting subgroup.* The Fitting subgroup $\mathscr{F}(G)$ of G is the union of all the nilpotent normal subgroups of G. Let K_p denote the intersection of all the Sylow p-subgroups of G. Then $\mathscr{F}(G)$ is generated by the set

$$\bigcup_{\text{all } p \mid |G|} K_p.$$

Alternatively, if the normal subgroup lattice of G is known, $\mathscr{F}(G)$ may be obtained as follows. Pick out those normal subgroups of G of prime power order p^m such that there is no normal subgroup of order a higher power of p. Denote these subgroups by $F_1, \ldots, F_s$. Then

$$\mathscr{F}(G) = F_1 \times F_2 \times \cdots \times F_s.$$

3.5 *Normal subgroup lattice.* A normal subgroup of G is a union of conjugacy classes of G. In this section we describe an algorithm for finding the normal subgroup lattice of G which uses the class multiplication constants. This algorithm, which was developed jointly with J. N. Ward, consists of two parts. First, all normal subgroups generated by one or two classes are found. Then, using the fact that the set of normal subgroups of G form a modular lattice, the remaining normal subgroups are found by forming unions of existing normal subgroups until nothing new is obtained. The construction of the normal subgroup lattice directly from the classes is also discussed by McKay [5].

Suppose C_i, C_j and C_k denote classes of elements of G. Then the class multiplication constants, c_{ijk}, are defined by the relations

$$C_i C_j = \sum_{k=1}^{r} c_{ijk} C_k, \qquad i, j = 1, \ldots, r,$$

where r is the number of classes of G. If $S = \{i_1, \ldots, i_s\}$ is a subset of the integers $1, \ldots, r$ such that

$$c_{i_u i_v k} = 0 \quad \text{for all} \quad i_u, i_v \in S, \quad k \notin S,$$

then the set

$$N = \bigcup_{j \in S} C_j$$

is a normal subgroup of G. This fact is used as the basis of an algorithm which finds all the normal subgroups generated by one or two classes. The algorithm transforms the table of class multiplication constants as it proceeds so that these normal subgroups can be easily read off.

The class constants, c_{ijk}, i, j fixed, $k = 1, \ldots, r$, are stored in the form of a binary vector by replacing all nonzero constants by 1. The notation c_{ijk} will be retained when referring to the kth component of such a vector. An arbitrary normal subgroup N will be represented by a set of integers indicating the classes it contains. Let $N_{i,j}$ denote the normal subgroup generated by classes C_i and C_j.

(i) $i \leftarrow 0$.

(ii) $i \leftarrow i+1$. If $i > r$ finish. Otherwise $j \leftarrow i$.

(iii) $j \leftarrow j+1$. If $j > r$ go to (ii).

(iv) $U \leftarrow \{k \mid c_{ijk} = 1\}$, $V \leftarrow \{k \mid \text{for some } l \in U, c_{ilk} = 1\}$. If $V \not\subseteq U$ go to (vi). Else,

(v) $V \leftarrow \{k \mid \text{for some } l \in U, c_{jlk} = 1\}$. If $V \subseteq U$, $N_{i,j} = \{k \mid c_{ijk} = 1\}$ and go to (iii). Else,

(vi) For $k = 1, \ldots, r$, $c_{ijk} \leftarrow 1$ if $k \in V$. Go to (iv).

The remaining normal subgroups are obtained by the following procedure which exploits the result that the normal subgroups of G satisfy the Jordan-Dedekind condition, i.e. any two normal subgroup chains have the same length. If N is a normal subgroup and t is an integer, let $\langle N, t \rangle$ denote the normal subgroup generated by N and class t, i.e.

$$\langle N, t \rangle = \bigcap_{\substack{S \subset \{1, \ldots, r\} \\ N \subset S, t \in S \\ i,j \in S \Rightarrow N_{i,j} \subset S}} S.$$

We shall use script capitals to denote sets of normal subgroups and italic capitals to represent individual subgroups. Ω is a set of integers.

(i) $\Omega \leftarrow \{j \mid j > 1, N_{1,j} \neq N_{1,t} \text{ for any } t < j\}$, $i \leftarrow 1$, $\mathcal{M}_i \leftarrow \{N_{1,j} \mid j \in \Omega\}$.

(ii) $\mathcal{L}_i \leftarrow \{N \mid N \in \mathcal{M}_i, N \text{ is minimal in } \mathcal{M}_i \text{ with respect to inclusion}\}$. $\mathcal{L}_i$ is the ith layer of normal subgroups and we either store them or output them.

(iii) $i \leftarrow i+1$, $\mathcal{M}_i \leftarrow \{\langle N, t \rangle \mid N \in \mathcal{L}_i, t \in \Omega - N\}$. If $\mathcal{M}_i = \emptyset$, finish. Otherwise go to (ii).

A normal subgroup N is represented as an r bit binary number, $K(N)$ say, where the ith bit of $K(N)$ is set to 1 if N contains the ith class and set to zero otherwise. We ascertain whether subgroup N_1 is contained in subgroup N_2 by testing

$$K(N_1) \wedge K(N_2) \overset{?}{=} K(N_1)$$

where "$\wedge$" denotes bitwise logical AND.

If the character table of G is already known then it is cheaper to compute the normal subgroups directly from the character table. As the character table of a group can often be computed using relatively few class constants it may sometimes be cheaper to compute the normal subgroups from the character

table rather than computing them directly from the class constants. For details as to how the character table of G may be constructed from the class
constants see Dixon [2] or McKay [5]. The normal subgroups of G are found
from the table of ordinary characters using an algorithm suggested by J. D.
Dixon.

As before we represent a normal subgroup as a set of integers indicating
which classes are contained in the subgroup.

(i) Let $\mathscr{K}_1 = \{K_1, \ldots, K_r\}$ be the set consisting of the distinct nontrivial
kernels of the ordinary irreducible characters of G. $k \leftarrow 1, \mathscr{L}_k \leftarrow \mathscr{K}_k, \mathscr{K}_0 \leftarrow \emptyset$.

(ii) Let $\mathscr{K}_k = \{L_1, \ldots, L_s\}$ consist of the distinct nontrivial elements of $\mathscr{L}_k$.
If $\mathscr{K}_k = \mathscr{K}_{k-1}$, finish. Otherwise, $k \leftarrow k+1$.

(iii) $\mathscr{L}_k \leftarrow \{K_i \cap L_j \mid i = 1, \ldots, r; j = 1, \ldots, s\}$. Go to (ii).

The normal subgroups of G are the elements of the set

$$\mathscr{K}_1 \cup \mathscr{K}_2 \cup \cdots \cup \mathscr{K}_k.$$

3.6 *Lower central series and derived series.* The lower central series of a
finite group G is the sequence of subgroups

$$G = G_0 \supseteq G_1 \supseteq \cdots \supseteq G_r$$

where $G_i = [G_{i-1}, G]$, while the derived series of G is the sequence of subgroups

$$G = G^{(0)} \supseteq G^{(1)} \supseteq \cdots \supseteq G^{(s)}$$

where $G^{(i)} = [G^{(i-1)}, G^{(i-1)}]$. The subgroups G_i and $G^{(i)}$ are normal. The
terms of either of these series can easily be computed inductively using an
algorithm based on the following observation. Given a normal subgroup M
generated by $x_1, \ldots, x_m$ and a normal subgroup N generated by $y_1, \ldots, y_n$, the
subgroup $[M, N]$ is the smallest normal subgroup containing the commutators,
$[x_i, y_j], i-1, \ldots, m, j = 1, \ldots, n$. Thus $[M, N]$ can be found by the method of
§2.5.

Small terms towards the ends of these series may be computed directly to
avoid having to enumerate cosets of subgroups of large index. Here we use the
fact that $[M, N]$ is generated by the commutators $[x_i, y_j], i = 1, \ldots, m; j = 1,
\ldots, n$; and their conjugates.

3.7 *Centre.* The centre of a group G is found by constructing the centralizer $C(x)$ of an element x having relatively large composite order and picking
out those elements of $C(x)$ which commute with the generators of G. Although
the centre of G must lie inside the centralizer of any element, an element of
relatively large composite order is chosen in the expectation that it will have a
relatively small centralizer.

4. **Applications.** The structure of centralizers of involutions, Sylow subgroups and the normalizers of Sylow subgroups play an important role in
current attempts to classify finite simple groups and to determine their properties. Having computed a set of generators for any of the above subgroups of a

group G using the methods of the last two sections, we may then use the machine to investigate the structure of this subgroup.

For example, if the subgroup H is a Sylow subgroup of G it is trivial to determine whether H is cyclic, elementary abelian, otherwise abelian or metacyclic. By computing the lower central series we may find the class of H and if H is a Sylow 2-subgroup of maximal class, to further determine whether H is generalized quarternion, generalized dihedral, semidihedral etc. by looking at the order of the first term of the Ω-series of H.

In general one can determine whether a local subgroup H of G is nilpotent, supersolvable, solvable or p-normal and construct either special subgroups of H, its normal subgroup lattice or, provided the order of H is relatively small, its complete subgroup lattice.

We mention here only three of the many applications that are possible once a Sylow p-subgroup P of G is known. If P is p-normal then the p-part of the Schur multiplier of G is isomorphic to the p-part of the multiplier of $N(Z(P))$. It is a simple matter to compute $SCN_t(P)$, the set of maximal abelian normal subgroups of P having rank equal to or greater than t. Finally, let $A(P)$ be the set of abelian subgroups of P of maximal order and define

$$J(P) = \langle A \mid A \in A(P) \rangle.$$

Part of the importance of $J(P)$ arises from the Glauberman-Thompson theorem which states that if p is an odd prime then G has a normal p-complement if and only if $N(Z(J(P)))$ has a normal p-complement. In fact if p is a prime such that $p \geqq 5$ then G has a normal p-complement if and only if $N(J(S))/C(J(S))$ is a p-group.

5. **A program.**   At Sydney University an on-line interactive group theory program capable of doing fairly sophisticated group computations has been implemented. This program allows the user to study the structure of a particular group in a real-time environment with relatively little programming effort on his part.

The heart of the system consists of a large collection of group theoretic subroutines ranging from a routine which multiplies two permutations to a routine which finds the subgroup lattice of a group. Included among these routines are implementations of many of the algorithms described above. The routines are coded in English Electric KDF9 machine language but the user is provided with a set of commands which enable him to call any of the functional routines without his having to know the details of how the system is organized. By stringing together appropriate sequences of commands he is able to program a variety of group theoretical constructions. The range of constructions presently permitted is much too restrictive and work is proceeding on the design of a much more sophisticated group theory language.

The program is designed so that it is to a large extent independent of a particular type of group representation. Only the multiplication and some associated routines need know how a particular group is represented in the machine. While computing the structure of a group G one may wish to take a subgroup or factor group of G and work with that for a while before returning to the original group. Associated with each group G in the machine there is usually a varying amount of information which is used by many different sub-routines. This information may include a presentation for G, a set of permuta-tion or matrix generators for G, and its elements stored as abstract words and/ or as permutations or matrices. If there are several groups in the machine simultaneously there cannot be a unique location for a block of information of one of the above types. So with each group G present in the machine we associate a table, the state table of G, which summarizes what information is known about G and where this information is located in the machine. All routines operating on this common data base obtain the location of a particular piece of information associated with G from G's state table.

The state table belonging to the group G currently being worked on is always stored in the same place in the machine so that when one switches to another group G' its state table must first be copied into this region of store. If one wishes to return to G at some later stage a copy of its state table must be preserved somewhere else in the machine. In this way one can switch back and forth between different groups even though their elements may be represented quite differently.

The commands may be executed singly or in blocks. After a command or block of commands has been executed and any output printed, the machine calls for a new command. The entire machine state generated by a command is preserved so that the next command operates on this machine state. This command-by-command execution allows the user to exercise close control over his computation by enabling him to use the output of his last command to help decide his next step. For example, a user may compute the normal sub-groups of a fairly large group G and then pick out certain of these normal sub-groups which he thinks may give rise to interesting factor groups. To help him recognize a particular factor group he may ask the machine to compute its subgroup lattice.

As the normal subgroups of G are preserved until the user indicates they are to be deleted, he may take a new factor group at any time without either having to output them at some stage or recompute them. This interactive mode of operation is of particular importance when outputing results because of the vast amount of information such a program can generate. Instead of the user having to specify in advance the output he requires he is able to repeatedly interrogate the machine about the results of a particular piece of computation and thus only output information relevant to his particular problem.

Whenever possible the machine keeps a summary of whatever information it may have already discovered concerning a group G. This is done because the user does not always know what he may want to do at some later stage and recomputation is expensive. For example, if the classes of G have been com-puted but the space they occupy is required for something else, instead of deleting all information concerning the classes, the machine retains some information about each class including a representative x of the class and a set of generators for the centralizer of x. The existence and whereabouts of such information is noted in G's state table. Any command requiring information about G which may have been computed earlier first checks the state table to see if this information is already known. Also any "global" properties of G (e.g. exponent, whether nilpotent, solvable, etc.) which happen to be discovered are noted for possible future use. Thus as the computation proceeds more and more information is assembled about G.

One of the assumptions behind the design of the program is that a group theorist using a machine to study a group often knows a good deal about the group already and if some of this knowledge can be conveyed to the machine the computations can be done much more efficiently. If a large group is to be generated in terms of sets of coset representatives of some chain of subgroups then it is usually much easier for the user, rather than the machine, to locate a suitable chain of subgroups. Knowing the total number of conjugacy classes of G, the number of classes of elements of a particular order, or representatives from some classes can often be of considerable help to a class finding routine. So in certain circumstances the program allows the user to input pieces of information he may already know about G. It turns out in practice that this facility is very important and work is proceeding on ways of extending the machines ability to make use of the user's knowledge of a particular group.

6. **An example.** We shall conclude the paper with a simple example in which the machine determined the structure of the Sylow subgroups of the simple group $Sp_4(3)$ of order $25,920$ (the subgroup of index 2 in the group of 27 lines on a cubic surface).

Beginning with the presentation

$$a^3 = b^3 = c^2 = d^2 = (bc)^3 = (cd)^3 = (bd)^2 = 1,$$

$$e^{b^{-1}} = f, \quad e^{bcb^{-1}} = g, \quad g^{dc} = h, \quad b^a = fb, \quad c^a = fc, \quad e^a = fcf,$$

$$hbecb^2 = aha, \quad d^{(adcba)^{-1}} = d^{cb},$$

which is due to Dickson, the machine enumerated the cosets of the subgroup $\langle b, c, d, e \rangle$ to obtain the following faithful permutation representation of $Sp_4(3)$ on 27 letters:

$a = (1\ 2\ 3)\,(4\ 17\ 14)\,(5\ 13\ 12)\,(6\ 7\ 20)\,(8\ 23\ 21)(9\ 26\ 18)\,(10\ 11\ 22)\,(15\ 25\ 24)$
$\quad\quad (16\ 27\ 19),$
$b = (5\ 6\ 15)\,(7\ 13\ 23)\,(9\ 10\ 16)\,(11\ 26\ 17)\,(12\ 20\ 19)\,(18\ 22\ 24),$
$c = (4\ 5)\,(6\ 15)\,(8\ 9)\,(10\ 16)\,(12\ 14)\,(13\ 26)\,(17\ 23)\,(18\ 21)\,(19\ 20)\,(22\ 24),$
$d = (2\ 4)\,(3\ 8)\,(6\ 15)\,(10\ 16)\,(11\ 12)\,(13\ 23)\,(17\ 20)\,(19\ 26)\,(21\ 27)\,(22\ 24),$
$e = (6\ 10)\,(7\ 25)\,(11\ 27)\,(12\ 21)\,(13\ 23)\,(14\ 18)\,(15\ 16)\,(17\ 26)\,(19\ 20)\,(22\ 24),$
$f = (5\ 9)\,(6\ 10)\,(7\ 13)\,(11\ 26)\,(12\ 20)\,(14\ 24)\,(17\ 27)\,(18\ 22)\,(19\ 21)\,(23\ 25),$
$g = (4\ 8)\,(5\ 9)\,(7\ 27)\,(11\ 25)\,(12\ 14)\,(13\ 17)\,(18\ 21)\,(19\ 22)\,(20\ 24)\,(23\ 26),$
$h = (2\ 3)\,(4\ 8)\,(7\ 18)\,(11\ 12)\,(13\ 22)\,(14\ 25)\,(17\ 19)\,(20\ 26)\,(21\ 27)\,(23\ 24).$

Using this representation the machine found the Sylow subgroups of $Sp_4(3)$:

Sylow 2-subgroup Order 64
Presentation

$a^2 = 1,$
$b^2 = 1, \quad a^b = a,$
$c^2 = 1, \quad a^c = a, \quad b^c = b,$
$d^2 = c, \quad a^d = ac, \quad b^d = bc, \quad c^d = c,$
$e^2 = abc, \quad a^e = ac, \quad b^e = bc, \quad c^e = c, \quad d^e = abd,$
$f^2 = bc, \quad a^f = ac, \quad b^f = b, \quad c^f = c, \quad d^f = abd, \quad e^f = ace.$

Generators

$a = (4\ 5)(6\ 15)(8\ 9)(10\ 16)(12\ 14)(13\ 26)(17\ 23)(18\ 21)(19\ 20)(22\ 24),$
$b = (4\ 6)(5\ 15)(7\ 11)(8\ 10)(9\ 16)(12\ 19)(14\ 20)(17\ 23)(18\ 24)(21\ 22),$
$c = (4\ 8)(5\ 9)(6\ 10)(7\ 11)(12\ 18)(13\ 26)(14\ 21)(15\ 16)(17\ 23)(19\ 24)(20\ 22)(25\ 27),$
$d = (4\ 5\ 8\ 9)(6\ 16\ 10\ 15)(7\ 26\ 11\ 13)(12\ 19\ 18\ 24)(14\ 22\ 21\ 20)(17\ 27\ 23\ 25),$
$e = (1\ 3)(7\ 13)(11\ 26)(4\ 14\ 16\ 24)(5\ 18\ 10\ 20)(6\ 22\ 9\ 12)(8\ 21\ 15\ 19)(17\ 25\ 23\ 27),$
$f = (1\ 3)(7\ 17)(11\ 23)(4\ 21\ 10\ 20)(5\ 12\ 16\ 24)(6\ 22\ 8\ 14)(9\ 18\ 15\ 19)(13\ 25\ 26\ 27).$

Sylow 3-subgroup Order 81
Presentation

$a^3 = 1,$
$b^3 = 1, \quad a^b = a,$
$c^3 = 1, \quad a^c = a, \quad b^c = b,$
$d^3 = ab^2, \quad a^d = c^2, \quad b^d = a^2bc^2, \quad c^d = a^2b^2c^2.$

Generators

$a = (5\ 6\ 15)(7\ 13\ 23)(9\ 10\ 16)(11\ 26\ 17)(12\ 20\ 19)(18\ 22\ 24),$
$b = (1\ 2\ 3)(4\ 25\ 21)(5\ 17\ 20)(6\ 11\ 19)(7\ 24\ 10)(8\ 27\ 14)(9\ 23\ 22)(12\ 15\ 26)(13\ 18\ 16),$
$c = (1\ 27\ 21)(2\ 14\ 4)(3\ 8\ 25)(5\ 12\ 11)(6\ 20\ 26)(8\ 25\ 3)(15\ 19\ 17),$
$d = (1\ 24\ 6\ 3\ 13\ 12\ 2\ 9\ 17)(4\ 7\ 11\ 21\ 16\ 15\ 25\ 22\ 20)(5\ 8\ 10\ 19\ 14\ 18\ 26\ 27\ 28).$

Sylow 5-subgroup Order 5
Presentation

$a^5 = 1.$

Generator

$a = (2\ 4\ 5\ 6\ 15)(3\ 8\ 9\ 10\ 16)(7\ 19\ 14\ 11\ 23)(12\ 26\ 13\ 20\ 17)(18\ 22\ 24\ 27\ 21).$

At this stage the subgroup lattices of the Sylow 2-subgroup and Sylow 3-subgroup were computed. However, for reasons of space we shall only reproduce the classes of subgroups for the Sylow 3-subgroup. In the following table, the generators of a subgroup i of G are printed in one of two ways:

(a) If i is a cyclic subgroup then we print $\langle k \rangle$ in the column headed Subgroup Definition, where k is the number of an element of G that generates i.

(b) If i is noncyclic, nonperfect then we print $\langle j, k \rangle$, in the column headed Subgroup Definition, where i is the cyclic extension of subgroup j by element k.

The presentation of a subgroup is printed so that the letter a corresponds to the first generator of the subgroup, the letter b to the second generator and so on. In case (b) only those relations involving k are printed.

Subgroup Classes of Sylow 3-subgroup of $\mathrm{Sp}_4(3)$

Layer Number	Subgroup Number	Subgroup Definition	Order	Class Order	Presentation
1	1	$\langle 8 \rangle$	3	1	$a^3 = 1$
1	2	$\langle 2 \rangle$	3	3	$a^3 = 1$
1	5	$\langle 20 \rangle$	3	9	$a^3 = 1$
1	14	$\langle 7 \rangle$	3	3	$a^3 = 1$
1	17	$\langle 5 \rangle$	3	3	$a^3 = 1$
1	20	$\langle 10 \rangle$	3	3	$a^3 = 1$
2	23	$\langle 71 \rangle$	9	3	$a^9 = 1$
2	26	$\langle 1, 2 \rangle$	9	3	$b^3 = 1, \quad a^b = a$
2	29	$\langle 1, 62 \rangle$	9	1	$b^3 = 1, \quad a^b = a$
2	30	$\langle 1, 77 \rangle$	9	3	$b^3 = 1, \quad a^b = a$
2	33	$\langle 56 \rangle$	9	3	$a^9 = 1$
2	36	$\langle 2, 79 \rangle$	9	3	$b^3 = 1, \quad a^b = a$
2	39	$\langle 2, 24 \rangle$	9	3	$b^3 = 1, \quad a^b = a$
2	42	$\langle 14, 62 \rangle$	9	3	$b^3 = 1, \quad a^b = a$
3	45	$\langle 23, 62 \rangle$	27	1	$c^3 = 1, \quad a^c = a, \quad b^c = ab$
3	46	$\langle 26, 79 \rangle$	27	1	$c^3 = 1, \quad a^c = a, \quad b^c = b$
3	47	$\langle 29, 77 \rangle$	27	1	$c^3 = 1, \quad a^c = a, \quad b^c = ab$
3	48	$\langle 29, 31 \rangle$	27	1	$c^3 = a, \quad a^c = a, \quad b^c = ab$

ACKNOWLEDGMENT.   I would like to thank Miss Kim McAllister for her excellent work in implementing a large part of the Sydney system.

REFERENCES

1. J. J. Cannon, *Computers in group theory; A survey*, Comm. ACM **12** (1969), 3–12.

2. J. D. Dixon, *High speed computation of group characters*, Numer. Math. **10** (1967), 446–450. MR 37 #325.

3. V. Felsch and J. Neubüser, *Ein Programm zur Berechnung des Untergruppenverbandes einer endlichen Gruppe*, Mitt. Rh.-W. Inst. Math. Bonn 2 (1963), 39–74.

4. _____, *Über ein Programm zur Berechnung der Automorphismengruppe einer endlichen Gruppe*, Numer. Math. **11** (1968), 277–292. MR 37 #3801.

5. J. K. S. McKay, *The construction of the character table of a finite group from generators and relations*, Computational Problems in Abstract Algebra, Pergamon Press, Oxford and New York, 1970, pp. 89–100.

6. J. Neubüser, *Computing moderately large groups: Some methods and application*, SIAM-AMS Proceedings, vol. 4, Amer. Math. Soc., Providence, R.I., 1971.

7. C. C. Sims, *Computational methods in the study of permutation groups*, Computational Problems in Abstract Algebra, Pergamon Press, Oxford and New York, 1970, pp. 169–183.

8. _____, *Determining the conjugacy classes of a permutation group*, SIAM-AMS Proceedings, vol. 4, Amer. Math. Soc., Providence, R.I., 1971.

BELL TELEPHONE LABORATORIES, MURRAY HILL, NEW JERSEY

Subgroups and Permutation Characters[1]

John McKay

1. In the course of recent investigations into the structure of finite simple groups with a given property, such as containing a specific centralizer of an involution, a character table is constructed, and one is led to try to deduce the existence (or otherwise) of a group with such a character table. A start to a theoretical examination of this question has been made by Brauer [1] and Harris [2]. Some computational techniques which have proved of value in this situation are described here.

We use the notation:

G is a group of order g with conjugacy classes C_i containing h_i elements, $i = 1, 2, \ldots, r$ ($C_1 = 1$) and $C_{i'} = \{x \mid x^{-1} \in C_i\}$.

$\chi_{ij}, i,j = 1, 2, \ldots, r$ is the character table of G; it is the value of the character of the irreducible representation R_i of degree d_i ($= \chi_{i1}$) on an element of class C_j.

$\omega_{ij} = h_j \chi_{ij}/d_i, i,j = 1, 2, \ldots, r$.

$c_i = \Sigma_{x \in C_i} x, i = 1, 2, \ldots, r$ are the class sums which form a basis for the class algebra (the center of the group algebra).

To check the character table we use the orthogonality relations in the form

$$(1) \qquad U^*U = UU^* = I, \quad \text{where} \quad [U]_{ij} = u_{ij} = (h_j/g)^{1/2} \chi_{ij}$$

and * denotes complex conjugate transpose. It is convenient to work with unitary matrices to avoid unnecessary difficulties with overflow. An independent check is to compute the structure constants a_{ijk} of the class algebra

$$(2) \qquad c_i c_j = \sum_{k=1}^{r} a_{ijk} c_k, \qquad i,j = 1, 2, \ldots, r,$$

AMS 1970 *subject classifications*. Primary 20D05, 20–04.
[1]Partially supported by ONR contract N00 014-67-A 0094-0010.

by means of the equations

$$(3) \qquad a_{ijk} = \left(\frac{gh_ih_j}{h_k}\right)^{1/2} \sum_{s=1}^{r} \frac{u_{si}u_{sj}\bar{u}_{sk}}{d_s}, \qquad i,j,k = 1,2,\ldots,r.$$

The structure constants are nonnegative rational integers and satisfy the matrix equations

$$(4) \qquad A^{(i)}\boldsymbol{\omega}^s = \omega_{si}\,\boldsymbol{\omega}^s, \qquad i,s = 1,2,\ldots,r,$$

where $[A^{(i)}]_{jk} = a_{ijk}$ and $\boldsymbol{\omega}^s = (\omega_{s1}, \omega_{s2}, \ldots, \omega_{sr})^t$.

If the above checks are satisfied then there is a commutative associative algebra associated with the a_{ijk} as defined by (3). To see this, note that the condition that an algebra with structure constants a_{ijk} be associative is that

$$(5) \qquad \sum_{k=1}^{r} a_{isk}a_{kjt} = \sum_{k=1}^{r} a_{sjk}a_{ikt}, \qquad i,j,s,t = 1,2,\ldots,r,$$

which is the condition that $A^{(i)}$ and $A^{(j)}$ commute since the first two suffixes of the structure constants commute from (3). From (4) the $A^{(i)}, i = 1,2,\ldots,r$, are diagonalizable by a common set of eigenvectors $\boldsymbol{\omega}^s$, $s = 1,2,\ldots,r$, and so commute.

A useful check for character irrationalities is that $\frac{1}{2}(\chi^2(x) \pm \chi(x^2))$ are both characters. This follows from the decomposition with respect to the general linear group of the square of a character into its symmetric and skew-symmetric parts.

2. To each subgroup $H \subseteq G$ there occurs a transitive permutation character φ of G on the cosets of H. Necessary conditions for such a character to exist are given below. It will be seen that they are most easily tested when $[G:H]$ is small.

(a) $\varphi(1) \mid g$,
(b) $\varphi(x) = 1 + \Sigma_{i=2}^{r} a_i\chi_i(x), 0 \leqq a_i \leqq \min(\chi_i(1), \varphi(1)/\chi_i(1))$,
(c) $\varphi(x) \geqq 0$ is a rational integer,
(d) $h_j\varphi(x)/\varphi(1)$ is a rational integer if $x \in C_j$,
(e) $\varphi(x^k) \geqq \varphi(x)$ for integers $k \geqq 0$, and
(f) if $\varphi(x) > 0$ then $(\varphi(1) \cdot |\langle x\rangle|) \big| g$.

The only condition requiring comment is (d). The number of cosets of H fixed by x is $\varphi(x)$, thus

$$Hx_ix = Hx_i \quad \text{for } \varphi(x) \text{ distinct cosets } Hx_i.$$

The number n of distinct conjugates of x in H is given by

$$(6) \qquad n = |H| \cdot \varphi(x)/|C_G(x)| = h_j\varphi(x)/\varphi(1).$$

All the techniques for searching for a character φ of G with the above properties use the rational character table of G. Since φ assumes only rational integral values, it will contain all algebraic conjugates of an irrational irreducible character with the same multiplicity. We replace each character by the sum of its algebraic conjugates. Removing duplicated rows and columns we obtain a table whose columns are indexed by classes of conjugate cyclic subgroups and whose t rows are indexed by rationally irreducible characters.

Firstly, we prepare a table of factors of g by generating the factors from the prime decomposition of g and sorting them into increasing order of magnitude. These factors are, by (a), the only candidates for the degree $\varphi(1)$ of φ. The necessary conditions given for φ to be a transitive permutation character may be checked in full generality for increasing values of the degree. In this way we obtain an upper bound to the order of any proper subgroup of G, as well as obtain candidates for permutation characters.

Secondly, we bound the multiplicities a_i above by k and examine all $(k+1)^{t-1}$ choices for suitable φ. Taking $k = 1$ we obtain the multiplicity-free characters. Although it is in general not true that permutation characters on the cosets of maximal subgroups are multiplcity-free, this property frequently holds for at least one maximal subgroup of a simple group.

Thirdly, we search for candidates by the number s of distinct rationally irreducible characters occurring as constituents of φ. Searching for multiplicity-free characters means examining $\binom{t-1}{s-1}$ characters.

The above methods are all bounded in utility by the time they take. For a group with many (say > 50) large rationally irreducible characters, only the third method seems feasible. There is a method suggested by Dr. Shen Lin which should prove useful in computing multiplicity-free characters which is bounded not by time but by storage considerations. It consists of constructing a table of t rows and n columns where n is the largest degree of a permutation character being sought. Each entry is either a zero or a one and so can be stored as a bit in the computer. Row i is associated with a rationally irreducible character of degree d_i and $d_i \le d_{i+1}, i = 1, 2, \ldots, t-1$. The only nonzero entry in the first row is a 1 in the first column. The other rows are given entries according to the scheme

(7) $$\text{row}_i = \overset{\to (d_i - d_{i-1})}{\text{row}_{i-1}} \cup \overset{\to d_i}{\text{row}_{i-1}}, \qquad i = 2, 3, \ldots, t,$$

where $\to k$ denotes a shift of k columns to the right. Degrees of the largest constituents of a character of degree j ($\le n$) will be found from the rows in which there is a 1 in column j. To each constituent there will correspond one or more decompositions. The set of next largest constituent degrees is found from the rows containing 1 in column $j - d_i$ where d_i is the largest constituent; and so on. One further remark is that occasionally one may know of a principal indecomposable character which occurs as a constituent thus enabling one to extend the range of a search.

3.   Let us assume that we have obtained a candidate for the character φ satisfying (a) to (f) of §2. We have from (6) the distribution in H of the elements

of G. Sometimes a counting argument will eliminate φ at this stage. If $\varphi(1)$ is sufficiently small one can attempt to construct, by restriction to H, the character table of H. If we have a faithful representation of G we may attempt to construct H. This has been done [3] for the simple subgroups $PSL(2, p), p = 17$, 19, of the large Janko group J_3 of order $50{,}232{,}960 = 2^7 3^5 5 \cdot 17 \cdot 19$ which will be used as an illustration of the method. $PSL(2, p)$ is a factor group of the group

$$\langle x, y \rangle : x^2 = y^3 = (xy)^p = 1.$$

It is constructed by picking elements x, y from the appropriate conjugacy classes such that the product $xy \ (=z)$ lies in a class of elements of period p. The probability that a pair of elements $x \in C_i, y \in C_j$ should be chosen at random from their classes so that $xy \in C_k$ is given by $p_{ijk} = a_{ijk} h_k / h_i h_j$. Alternatively we could choose at random elements to satisfy $zy^{-1} = x$ or $x^{-1}z = y$. The three probabilities are p_{ijk}, $p_{kj'i}$ and $p_{i'kj}$. To find which of these probabilities is largest we need to examine the constants a_{ijk}. How many solutions (x, y, z) are there to the equation $xyz = 1$ where $x \in C_i, y \in C_j$ and $z \in C_k$? This is seen to be the number of times we can represent $z^{-1} \in C_{k'}$ by xy where $x \in C_i$, $y \in C_j$ and is therefore $a_{ijk'} h_{k'}$. The classes commute and the number of solutions (x, y, z) to $xyz = 1$ is the same as the number of solutions to $z^{-1} y^{-1} x^{-1} = 1$, hence the terms $a_{ijk'} h_{k'}$ are invariant under permutation of classes and simultaneous inversion of all three classes. The numerators of the three probabilities have the same value and so (provided that $a_{ijk} \neq 0$) we maximize our chances by minimizing the denominator. Let this denominator be $h_i h_j$. In J_3 there is a unique class C_i of involutions and these have a centralizer of order 1920. There are two classes of elements of order 3, but examination of permutation characters on the cosets of the two subgroups reveals the class C_j to be that of elements centralized by the Sylow 3-subgroup of J_3 of order 243. Elements of order 17 and 19 are self-centralizing. From computed class structure constants we find that there are 119 ordered pairs (x, y), $x \in C_i, y \in C_j$ such that xy is a fixed element of period 17. For a product of period 19 the corresponding figure is 95. The probability of a random pair (x, y), $x \in C_i, y \in C_j$ being chosen such that xy has period 17 is found to be $42/323$ and for period 19 it is $30/323$. These probabilities take into account that for both periods 17 and 19 there are two classes of elements, an element not being conjugate to its inverse.

The probabilities are upper bounds on the probability of generating the subgroups since further relations have to be checked, and it may be that the whole group is generated and the further relations are never satisfied. Since the subgroups we seek are simple it is sufficient to find elements satisfying the further relations; in the more general case it would be necessary to show that the elements do not generate a factor group of the subgroup sought.

A "random" element is computed by forming the word w_{i+1} from the word w_i ($w_0 = 1$) by multiplying it by one of the two generators of J_3 chosen with equal probability. In this case the generators have periods 12 and 15 so we may expect few repetitions in the sequence we generate. In fact it is not the elements

x and y of the product xy which are conjugated at random. One of the elements can be conjugated at random with the same effect.

Using a permutation representation on the smallest index subgroup of J_3 of index 6156, generators for the two subgroups were obtained in two minutes using a computer of cycle time 1.5 μ secs. As far as I know this is the only proof available that PSL(2, 17) and PSL(2, 19) are subgroups of J_3.

REFERENCES

1. R. Brauer, *On pseudo-groups*, J. Math. Soc. Japan **20** (1968), 13–22. MR **37** # 324.

2. M. E. Harris, *A note on pseudo-groups*, J. Fac. Sci. Tokyo **16** (1969), 256–272.

3. J. McKay and G. Higman, *On Janko's simple group of order* 50,232,960, Bull. London Math. Soc. **1** (1969), 89–94; correction, ibid. 219. MR **40** # 224.

CALIFORNIA INSTITUTE OF TECHNOLOGY

Computing Moderately Large Groups: Some Methods and Applications

J. Neubüser

1. **Introduction.** For a start the terms in the title need some explanation. By "computing a group" a rather detailed analysis of its structure is meant, in which, e.g., the lattice of subgroups is produced by methods applicable to rather wide classes of groups without use of special features of a specific group to be investigated. It is clear that such a capability of a program can only be bought at the price of restrictions to be imposed, e.g. on the order of the group and the number of its subgroups. This is meant by the term "moderately large groups"; some details on the restrictions imposed by the methods and computers in use will be given later.

A good deal of the methods have been described in technical papers and survey articles [5], [15], so in this paper only some general remarks about present progress and future possibilities are presented; knowledge of some of the older papers, in particular of the surveys, will be assumed.

In the last section a brief report on some application is given – again described in detail elsewhere [2], [3], [17] – which shows that programs of the kind described here are capable of producing mathematical results which otherwise could not easily be obtained. It is quite obvious, however, that – in contrast to some other group theoretical programs – these ones are of no direct use in helping to investigate very big groups like those studied now in the search for new simple groups of composite order.

2. **Generating a group.** Throughout we assume that the group to be investigated is finite and given by a finite set of generators, which may either be abstract generators with a finite set of defining relations or elements from a faithful representation (i.e. matrices or permutations). The first task then is to determine the order of the group and a list of its elements.

AMS 1970 *subject classifications*. Primary 20–04.

In case a finite presentation of a finite group is given, the Todd-Coxeter algorithm may be applied and will — in theory — eventually determine the order of the group [13] and a faithful representation by permutations which can then further be used. A number of different versions and implementations of this algorithm has been described, see e.g. [12]. It is only in case of special relations — like the ones described for soluble groups below — that one can use these directly.

In case the generators are given in a faithful representation a list of all elements may be found by a simple algorithm [14]. However, before producing it, it is worthwhile to ask what use will be made of such a list, if it is not computed for some direct inspection. There are two ways this list is used in subsequent programs like the one for the determination of all subgroups:

(a) It is searched through linearly, e.g. in order to sort out all cyclic subgroups of a given order. For such a purpose however it is not necessary that the list is physically present in store or even in core-store. An algorithm that generates each element once and only once at little cost of time (i.e. that is much faster than the algorithm [14] referred to above) would do as well. We shall see in a moment that it is possible in various ways to find such algorithms which need rather little store to retain information necessary for their execution.

(b) It is used to store information already obtained about the elements in parallel lists. For this purpose however it is much more efficient to have a way of numbering the elements of a group G of order $|G|$ by the integers $1, \ldots, |G|$ in such a way that for any element $g \in G$ that may e.g. be obtained by multiplication of other elements, its number $n(g)$ can be computed at little cost of time. Again such "natural numberings" are possible in various ways. If moreover the numbering also allows obtaining the elements from their numbers easily, then this numbering also solves the first problem in a very elegant way.

A list of elements of a larger group may take a great amount of store; the applicability of further programs can be extended considerably, if such techniques can be used. We shall discuss now three different methods by which both requirements can be met.

2.1.   Let G be a soluble group and

$$\langle 1 \rangle = N_0 < N_1 < \cdots < N_r = G$$

be a subnormal series with cyclic factors, i.e. $N_{i-1} \triangleleft N_i$ for $i = 1, \ldots, r$ and N_i/N_{i-1} a cyclic group of order n_i, and let elements $g_1, \ldots, g_r \in G$ be chosen such that $N_{i-1}g_i$ is a generating coset of N_i/N_{i-1}. Then each element $g \in G$ is uniquely expressible in the form

$$g = g_1^{\alpha_1} \cdots g_r^{\alpha_r}, \qquad 0 \leq \alpha_i < n_i, \quad i = 1, \ldots, r.$$

So, if the element g is given the number

$$n(g) = 1 + \alpha_1 + \alpha_2 n_1 + \alpha_3 n_1 n_2 + \cdots \alpha_r n_1 \cdots n_{r-1},$$

the elements of G are numbered by the integers $1, \ldots, |G|$. In terms of the generators $g_1, \ldots, g_r$ the group G can be defined by a set of defining relations of the form

$$g_1^{n_1} = 1, \qquad g_i^{n_i} = g_1^{v_{i,1}} g_2^{v_{i,2}} \cdots g_{i-1}^{v_{i,i-1}}, \qquad i = 2, \ldots, r,$$

$$g_j^{-1} g_i g_j = g_1^{\mu_{i,j,1}} \cdots g_{j-1}^{\mu_{i,j,j-1}}, \qquad i = 1, \ldots, r-1, \quad i < j \leq r.$$

A program generator can be written [11], which generates from such defining relations a rather efficient program that obtains from the numbers $n(g)$ and $n(h)$ of two elements g and h in G the number $n(gh)$ of their product gh. Once this "multiplication program" has been generated, no further information need be stored.

2.2.   Let G be a group of permutations of the integers $1, \ldots, r$ and let a chain of stabilizers

$$G = G_0 \geq G_1 \geq \cdots \geq G_{r-1} = \langle 1 \rangle$$

be defined by

$$G_0 = G, \qquad G_i = \{g \mid g \in G_{i-1}, ig = i\}, \qquad i = 1, \ldots, r-1.$$

By computing the orbit of 1 under G from the given generators one finds the coset representatives of G_1 in G. From these and the generators of G, generators of G_1 are obtained by Schreier's technique, see e.g. [9]. The process can be repeated with G_1, etc. It works efficiently since for each i the rather large number of generators of G_i obtained by the Schreier process from the generators of G_{i-1} and coset representatives of G_i in G_{i-1} can in general be substantially reduced before applying the Schreier process for the next step. This technique was first used by C. C. Sims [16] and P. Swinnerton-Dyer to determine the order of big permutation groups. An implementation of it within a system of group-theoretical programs is described in [8].

Once coset representatives of the cosets of G_i in G_{i-1} are stored for each $i = 1, \ldots, r-1$, one assigns to each element $g \in G$ a "natural number." This is done in the following way: A coset of G_i in G_{i-1} consists of all elements in G fixing all k, $0 < k \leq i-1$, and mapping i to a certain fixed integer, say j. Denote by C_{ij} the coset thus characterized by the integers i and j and by r_{ij} a representative of it. Let the $n_i = G_{i-1} : G_i$ cosets of G_i in G_{i-1} be numbered by the integers $0, \ldots, n_i-1$ in a fixed way and denote for each element $h \in G_{i-1}$ by $\mu_i(h)$ the number of the coset of G_i to which it belongs.

To define the "natural number" $n(g)$ for an element $g \in G$ first a sequence $g_1, \ldots, g_{r-1}$ of elements of G is defined by:

$$g_1 = g; \qquad \text{if} \quad g_i \in C_{ij} \quad \text{then} \quad g_{i+1} = g_i r_{ij}^{-1}.$$

Then we define

$$n(g) = \mu_1(g_1) \cdot n_2 \cdots n_{r-1} + \mu_2(g_2) \cdot n_3 \cdots n_{r-1} + \cdots + \mu_{r-1}(g_{r-1}) + 1.$$

To compute $n(g)$ from g or g from $n(g)$ only the list of the representatives and a listing of the numbering functions μ_i are needed, which do not require much

store. Also the time needed for such computations is short, and the method has
been used successfully in the program described in [**8**].

2.3.   While the method of §2.1 is applicable only to soluble groups and the
method of §2.2 only to permutation groups, the following, proposed by J.
Cannon [**6**], is not restricted to a particular kind of group. It may be introduced
in the following way:

Let $v: g \to gv$ be a numbering of the elements of a group G by the integers
$1, \ldots, |G|$ and let the regular representation π of G on the set $\{1, \ldots, |G|\}$
be defined by

$$\pi : g \to g\pi = \begin{pmatrix} hv \\ (hg)v \end{pmatrix}.$$

If for a set $g_1, \ldots, g_r$ of generators of G the permutations $g_1\pi, \ldots, g_r\pi$ are
known, then finding the number of the product gg_i of an element $g \in G$ with
a generator g_i from the number gv simply means looking up the image of gv in
the permutation $g_i\pi$:

$$(gg_i)v = (gv)(g_i\pi).$$

So, if in addition to the regular representation of the generators $g_1, \ldots, g_r$ for
each element $g \in G$ an expression as a word in these generators is known,
then the multiplication of two elements g and h can be performed by using
this expression for h, say $h = g_{i_1} g_{i_2} \cdots g_{i_s}$, and forming

$$(\cdots (((gv)(g_{i_1}\pi))(g_{i_2}\pi)) \cdots)(g_{i_s}\pi).$$

As explained, for this method regular representations for the generators and
words for all elements have to be stored. The latter can be done in the form of
a backwards linked list, connecting as a tree each element to the identity by a
chain of generators. The necessary data can as well be obtained from a finite
presentation via the Todd-Coxeter procedure as from a faithful representation
by direct calculation. It certainly enables rather fast multiplication; however,
the store required is no longer negligible, although certainly in many cases
smaller than a list of elements in faithful representation would be.

3. **Computing the lattice of subgroups.**   Methods of the kind mentioned in
the last section enable us to circumvent storage problems at the level of
handling the elements of a group. A next problem is to find all subgroups. None
of the combinatorial methods that have been implemented has worked efficiently further than up to groups of order a few hundred. There exists a
proposal of C. C. Sims [**16**], [**15**] which has not yet been implemented, so that
nothing can be said about its efficiency. The most successful method so far has
been to use as far as possible the cyclic extension method [**14**] and to supple-
ment it by special routines for each of the nonabelian simple groups that may
occur as composition factors. As the list of simple groups is known completely
at least up to order 20000 — probably further in view of present investigations

[10] — this method works at least for groups up to order 40000, which at present still seems to be a practical upper bound for such computations. What will be discussed here is an improvement of the cyclic extension method which allows us to reduce the amount of information that must be kept in (fast-access) store during the computation. To explain this, let us just recall the simple idea of the method:

The subgroups of a group G are ordered into "layers," the layer Σ_i consists of all subgroups $U \leq G$, such that $|U|$ is the product of i primes (different or not).

If a subgroup V in Σ_i is nonperfect, i.e. is different from its derived group, then it can be obtained as a cyclic extension of a subgroup in Σ_{i-1}; more precisely, for each such V there exists a subgroup $U \in \Sigma_{i-1}$ and an element $g \in N_G(U)$ such that $\langle U,g \rangle = V$. The element g may be chosen from a set containing one generator for each cyclic subgroup of prime power order of G. Moreover, if with a group V in Σ_i all its conjugates are determined by conjugation, it suffices to form cyclic extensions of representatives of the classes of conjugate subgroups in Σ_{i-1} only. An algorithm using this idea may be described as follows:

Let $U_1, \ldots, U_n$ be a set of representatives of the classes of conjugate subgroups in Σ_{i-1} and let $g_1, \ldots, g_r$ be a set of elements consisting of one generator for each cyclic subgroup of prime power order of G.

For each $k = 1, \ldots, n$ and for each $j = 1, \ldots, r$ it is tested if
1. $g_j \notin U_k$ (or equivalently $\langle g_j \rangle \nleq U_k$),
2. $g_j \in N_G(U_k)$ (or equivalently $\langle g_j \rangle \leq N_G(U_k)$),
3. $g_j^p \in U_k$ (or equivalently $\langle g_j^p \rangle \leq U_k$) where p is the prime, a power of which is the order of g_j,
4. $\{g_j\} \cup U_k \nsubseteq V$ for all subgroups $V \leq G, V \in \Sigma_i$, that have been found.

If the answer to all four tests is affirmative, the extension $\langle U_k, g_j \rangle$ and all conjugates of this group are formed and added to the list of subgroups in Σ_i. Otherwise the "next" pair U_k, g_j is tested.

For an implementation of this method it is necessary to store subgroups rather compactly in a way that allows fast execution of the tests 1, 2, 3, 4. As a subgroup is uniquely determined by the set of those cyclic subgroups of prime power order of G that are contained in it, it can be represented by its characteristic function on the set of all cyclic subgroups of prime power order of G. If such a characteristic function is stored as a bit-string in the machine, the test for inclusion of one subgroup in another amounts to comparison of the corresponding bit-strings that can be implemented with very few logical operations.

If the bit-strings thus representing $\langle g_j \rangle$, $\langle g_j^p \rangle$, U_k, $N_G(U_k)$, and all already known $V \in \Sigma_i$ are present in core-store, the tests 1, 2, 3, 4 can be executed very rapidly. So this way of storing the subgroups ideally suits the requirement mentioned above and has indeed been used several times in implementations of the cyclic extension method.

However, when going to bigger groups a certain bottleneck is noticed: Towards the end of the construction of Σ_i the whole list of characteristic functions of subgroups in Σ_i, so far determined, has to be kept in core-store, as it is again and again searched through in testing condition 4. Storage shortage at this point was in fact the main obstacle in using the existing programs for the investigation of groups with more than a few thousand subgroups.

To overcome this difficulty, rather recently [8] the implementation of the cyclic extension method has been varied. Let us introduce for each of the representatives $U_k, k = 1, \ldots, n$, of the classes of conjugate subgroups in Σ_{i-1} a second characteristic function on the set of cyclic subgroups of prime power order of G, which we may call the extension characteristic. At the beginning of the computation of Σ_i for all U_k each of those $\langle g_j \rangle$ are marked in the extension characteristic of U_k which fulfills conditions 1, 2 and 3 with respect to U_k. As soon as a new subgroup $V \in \Sigma_i$ is found, either by cyclic extension or by conjugation, all the extension characteristics that are still relevant are altered according to condition 4. After this has been done, using of course the characteristic function of V, the characteristic function of V is no longer needed in core-store and may be transferred to secondary store.

With this revision of the cyclic extension method the number of transfers to backing store is rather small, and the storage space needed in core-store considerably reduced. On a comparatively small computer (64K cells of 27 bits core, cycle time 2.5 μ sec) the soluble subgroups of the symmetric group S_7 have been computed as a test for this method. It has been found that there are 11065 soluble subgroups in S_7, the time needed was about $2\frac{1}{2}$ hours of total run time (not time of the central unit). With a faster and bigger computer, groups with some 50,000 subgroups should not be out of reach.

Although it has not yet actually been reached, the next bottleneck can be foreseen, even if one forgets about the increase of computing time brought about by further increase of the actual number of subgroups: with the increase of the group order the length of the bit-strings representing characteristic functions grows. Storing lots of them may become a problem even on secondary store like drums and disks (tapes are rather unsuited for this kind of algorithm). Even more forbidding however is the increase of time needed for the comparison of two such bit-strings. While so far in all implementations of the cyclic extension method (in contrast to the situation with combinatorial methods) storage space has been more restrictive than computing time, it has to be expected that this will no longer be the case. It would be a major progress therefore if the characteristic functions on the set of cyclic subgroups of prime power order of G could be replaced by something more compact, still meeting, or even better meeting, the requirement that a fast comparison of subgroups is possible.

4. **An application.**   Although it has been known for a long time [1] that for each n there are only finitely many classes of finite integral $n \times n$-matrix groups under integral equivalence, the actual number of these classes and representa-

tive groups for them had been determined only for $n \leqq 3$ until recently, see e.g. [4]. For $n = 4$ such a determination was made possible by a paper of E. C. Dade [7] who proved that there are 9 integral classes of maximal finite groups of integral 4×4 matrices, and determined representatives of these classes. The rest was then—as Dade remarked in the introduction of his paper—a job for computers. In fact the programs mentioned in the last sections have been used in doing this job.

The order of the 9 Dade groups varies from 96 to 1152; to find all their subgroups needs in fact a computer. For the purpose of the integral classification it suffices to list one representative for each of the classes of conjugate subgroups. It turned out that there are 1361 such representatives which then had to be sorted into integral equivalence classes. This sorting, which for higher n would be a very difficult problem, is still possible by rather elementary means for $n = 4$ and yields 710 integral classes [2].

Using these and again the subgroup relations known from the computation of the Dade groups, it was further possible to show that there are 64 Bravais-types of 4-dimensional lattices and to determine quadratic forms representing these. A report on the methods and detailed listings are in print [3], [17].

References

1. L. Bieberbach, *Über die Bewegungsgruppen der euklidischen Räume*, Math. Ann. **70** (1911), 297–336; ibid. **72** (1912), 400–412.

2. R. Bülow and J. Neubüser, *On some applications of group-theoretical programmes to the derivation of the crystal classes of R_4*. Computational Problems in Abstract Algebra, Pergamon Press, Oxford and New York, 1970, pp. 131–135.

3. R. Bülow, J. Neubüser and H. Wondratschek, *On crystallography in higher dimensions* II, Acta Cryst. (in print).

4. J. J. Burckhardt, *Die Bewegungsgruppen der Kristallographie*, Basel, Stuttgart, 1966. MR **34** #2708.

5. J. Cannon, *Computers in group theory: A survey*, Comm. ACM **12** (1969), 3–12.

6. _____, *Computation in finite algebraic structures*, Thesis, University of Sydney, 1969.

7. E. C. Dade, *The maximal finite groups of 4×4 integral matrices*, Illinois J. Math. **9** (1965), 99–122. MR **30** #1192.

8. P. Dreyer, *Ein Programm zur Berechnung der auflösbaren Untergruppen von Permutationsgruppen*, Diplomarbeit, Kiel, 1970.

9. M. Hall, *The theory of groups*, Macmillan, New York, 1959. MR **21** # 1996.

10. _____, *On the construction of finite simple groups*, SIAM-AMS Proc., vol. 3, Amer. Math. Soc., Providence, R. I., 1971.

11. H. Jürgensen, *Calculation with the elements of a finite group given by generators and defining relations*, Computational Problems in Abstract Algebra, Pergamon Press, Oxford and New York, 1970, pp. 47–57.

12. J. Leech, *Coset enumeration*, Computational Problems in Abstract Algebra, Oxford and New York, 1970, pp. 21–35. MR **40** # 7343.

13. N. S. Mendelsohn, *An algorithmic solution for a word problem in group theory*, Canad. J. Math. **16** (1964), 509–516; correction, ibid. **17** (1965), 505. MR **29** #1248.

14. J. Neubüser, *Untersuchungen des Untergruppenverbandes endlicher Gruppen auf einer programmgesteuerten elektronischen Dualmaschine*, Numer. Math. **2** (1960), 280–292. MR **22** #8713.

15. _____, *Investigations of groups on computers*, Computational Problems in Abstract Algebra, Pergamon Press, Oxford and New York, 1970, pp. 1–19.

16. C. C. Sims, *Computational methods in the study of permutation groups*, Computational Problems in the Study of Abstract Algebra, Pergamon Press, Oxford and New York, 1970, pp. 169–183.

17. H. Wondratschek, R. Bülow and J. Neubüser, *On crystallography in higher dimensions.* III, Acta Cryst. (in print).

RHEINISCH WESTFÄLISCHE TECHNISCHE HOCHSCHULE AACHEN, FEDERAL REPUBLIC OF GERMANY

Determining the Conjugacy Classes of a Permutation Group

Charles C. Sims

The purpose of this paper is to describe some computer techniques used by the author to determine the conjugacy classes of Suzuki's simple group, a permutation group of degree 1782 and order 448,345,497,600. These techniques can be applied to any primitive permutation group of degree up to 2000, since all that is required is that the group not have many elements fixing a large number of points. Most of the notation used here is taken from [1].

1. **Definitions**. Let G be a permutation group on the set Ω. A *base* for G is a sequence $X = \alpha_1, \ldots, \alpha_k$ of points such that the only element of G fixing all of the α_i is the identity. Thus an element of G is determined by the image of X under that element. Suppose $X = \alpha_1, \ldots, \alpha_k$ is a base for G and let $G^{(i)}$ be the stabilizer of $\alpha_1, \ldots, \alpha_{i-1}$. Then $G^{(1)} = G$ and $G^{(k+1)} = 1$. A *strong generating set* for G relative to X is a subset Z of G such that $G^{(i)}$ is generated by $Z \cap G^{(i)}$, $1 \leq i \leq k$. Let U_i be a set of right coset representatives for $G^{(i+1)}$ in $G^{(i)}$. In [1] a method was given for storing the group G on a computer in the case $\Omega = \{1, \ldots, n\}$ and $X = 1, \ldots, k$ by storing the sets U_i. This method can be modified to fit the case of an arbitrary base. If the degree is large, then rather than storing each element x of each U_i explicitly we store just enough information to allow x to be reconstructed easily as a product of elements of $Z \cap G^{(i)}$. Thus we may assume that given any sequence of points $\beta_1, \ldots, \beta_r$, $r \leq k$, we may decide easily whether or not there is a g in G such that $\beta_i = (\alpha_i)^g$, $1 \leq i \leq r$, and find one such g, if it exists.

2. **Changing the base**. Suppose we are given a set Z of permutations on a set Ω and a sequence X of points in Ω. Let G be the group generated by Z. The problem of deciding if X is a base for G and, if so, whether Z is a strong generat-

---

AMS 1969 subject classifications. Primary 2020; Secondary 2029.

ing set for G relative to X is not in general an easy one. The algorithm outlined in [1] can be used, but for groups of degree more than a few hundred the running time is quite long. However, if we are given a strong generating set Z for a group G relative to some base X, then for any other sequence of points X' we can easily decide if X' is a base for G and, if so, find a strong generating set for G relative to X'. We shall refer to this process as changing the base of G.

Any change of base may be accomplished by a sequence of steps in which a given base $X = \alpha_1, \ldots, \alpha_k$ is changed to one of the following bases:

(a) $X' = \alpha_1, \ldots, \alpha_k, \beta$, for some point β,

(b) $X' = \alpha_1, \ldots, \alpha_{k-1}$, provided this is a base,

(c) $X' = \alpha_1, \ldots, \alpha_{i-1}, \alpha_{i+1}, \alpha_i, \alpha_{i+2}, \ldots, \alpha_k, 1 \leq i < k$.

In cases (a) and (b) a strong generating set for G relative to X is also a strong generating set relative to X'. Thus we only need consider changes of type (c). For simplicity we describe the change from $X = 1, 2, \ldots, k$ to $X' = 2, 1, \ldots, k$. Let Z' be the strong generating set relative to X' to be constructed. We begin by putting $Z'' = Z \cap G_{1,2}$ into Z'. Next we must find elements of G which together with Z'' generate G_2. Let Δ be the G-orbit containing the point 1. For each $G_{1,2}$-orbit Γ on Δ choose a representative β in Γ. Choose g in G such that $1^g = \beta$. We next determine whether or not there is an h in G_1 such that $2^h = 2^{g^{-1}}$. If such an h exists, then we add hg to Z'. Finally we need additional generators which together with that part of Z' which we now have will generate G. These are found by choosing a representative β from each G_2-orbit on the G-orbit containing 2 and adding to Z' an element taking 2 to β.

3. **Centralizers.** Let G be a permutation group on $\Omega = \{1, 2, \ldots, n\}$ and let x be an element of G. The job of calculating the centralizer $C_G(x)$ of x in G can be made considerably easier if we have a strong generating set Z for G relative to a base $X = \alpha_1, \ldots, \alpha_k$ which is *compatible* with x in the sense that x has a cycle decomposition

$$x = (\alpha_1, \ldots, \alpha_r)(\alpha_{r+1}, \ldots, \alpha_s) \ldots (\ldots, \alpha_k, \ldots) \ldots.$$

For any permutation g of Ω the set $g^{-1}Zg$ is a strong generating set for $g^{-1}Gg$ relative to the base X^g. Thus after conjugation and a change of base if necessary we may assume that $X = 1, 2, \ldots, k$ and that X is compatible with x. We now order the elements g of the symmetric group S_n lexicographically by the sequences $1^g, 2^g, \ldots, n^g$.

LEMMA. *An element g in S_n is the first element in its right coset Gg if and only if for each i, $1 \leq i \leq k$, $i^g \leq j^g$ for every j in the $G^{(i)}$-orbit containing i.*

PROOF. Suppose that there is an h in $G^{(i)}$ such that $(i^h)^g = i^{hg} < i^g$. Then since h is in G and $j^g = j^{hg}$ for $1 \leq j < i$, we have that hg is an earlier element of Gg than g. Conversely, suppose that for some h in G the element hg comes before g. Let i be the first integer such that $i^{hg} \neq i^g$. Then $i \leq k$, h is in $G^{(i)}$ and $(i^h)^g < i^g$.

The fact that we have a strong generating set for G relative to the base $X = 1, 2, \ldots, k$ makes it easy to apply the criterion of the lemma.

A strong generating set for $C_G(x)$ relative to X may be constructed as follows:

(a) Set $K = \langle x \rangle$ and $T = 1$. In general K will be that subgroup of $C_G(x)$ which we know at any particular time and T will be a sequence $\alpha_1, \ldots, \alpha_r$ of $r \leq k$ points which are to be thought of as the image of $1, 2, \ldots, r$ under some element in $C_G(x)$ but not in K. We assume that a strong generating set for K relative to X is known.

(b) Go to step (d) if any one of the following hold:

1. There does not exist an element g in G such that $j^g = \alpha_j, 1 \leq j \leq r$.

2. There exists $j < r$ such that r is in the $K^{(j)}$-orbit containing j and $\alpha_r < \alpha_j$.

3. The cycle of x containing α_r does not have the same length as the cycle containing r.

4. There exists $j \leq r$ with $m = j^x \leq r$ and $(\alpha_j)^x \neq \alpha_m$.

(c) If $r = k$, then go to step (f). If $r < k$, then let β be the first element in Ω and not in $\{\alpha_1, \ldots, \alpha_r\}$ and replace T by $\alpha_1, \ldots, \alpha_r, \beta$. Go to step (b).

(d) Let β be the first element in Ω and not in $\{\alpha_1, \ldots, \alpha_r\}$ which is greater than α_r. If $\alpha_i = i, 1 \leq i < r$, then we require that β be the first point in its K-orbit. If no such β exists, then go to step (e). Replace T by $\alpha_1, \ldots, \alpha_{r-1}, \beta$ and go to step (b).

(e) If $r = 1$, then we are done. Otherwise, replace T by $\alpha_1, \ldots, \alpha_{r-1}$ and go to step (d).

(f) Find the unique g in G such that $i^g = \alpha_i, 1 \leq i < k$. If $gx \neq xg$ or $g = 1$, go to step (d). If $g \neq 1$ and $gx = xg$, then add g to K and replace T by $\alpha_1, \ldots, \alpha_s$, where s is the smallest integer such that $\alpha_s \neq s$, and go to step (d).

Several comments should be made about the algorithm presented above. The FORTRAN program actually written combines several of the steps; in particular test 4 of step (b) is combined with step (c). All of the tests in step (b) can be very quickly applied. The base X does not really have to be compatible with x but if it is not, then test 4 of step (b) is not very useful. The algorithm works fastest if the largest cycles of x are put first, that is, if the cycles of x containing $1, 2, \ldots, k$ are long. Typical running time with G the Suzuki group is 5–8 minutes, including the required change of base, on an IBM 360/67 computer. Finally, with suitable modifications to tests 3 and 4 of step (b) and to step (f) the same basic algorithm can be used to find the automorphism group of a graph or block design or to find the normalizer in a group G of some given subgroup of G.

4. **Conjugacy classes.** In this section we discuss the problem of finding representatives for the conjugacy classes of a permutation group G on $\{1, 2, \ldots, n\}$ for which we assume we have a strong generating set relative to some base. To each element g of G let cyc(g) be the cycle decomposition of g in

which the first cycle starts with 1 and each new cycle starts with the first point not occurring in any previous cycle and let seq(g) be the sequence of points obtained by removing the parentheses from cyc(g). Thus if $n = 7$ and $g = (2, 4)$ $(5, 7)$, then cyc(g) = (1) (2, 4) (3) (5, 7) (6) and seq(g) = 1, 2, 4, 3, 5, 7, 6. We order the elements of any conjugacy class of G by saying that g comes before h if one of the following holds:

(a) For some i and all j, $1 \leq j < i$, the jth cycle of cyc(g) has the same length as the jth cycle of cyc(h) but the ith cycle of cyc(g) is longer than the ith cycle of cyc(h).

(b) For each i the ith cycle of cyc(g) has the same length as the ith cycle of cyc(h) but seq(g) comes before seq(h) in the lexicographic order.

This ordering was chosen because the centralizer program works most efficiently when long cycles occur at the beginning of cyc(g).

We wish to describe an algorithm for determining the first element in each conjugacy class. For example, if $G = S_4$, then the representatives sought are

$$(1)\,(2)\,(3)\,(4)$$
$$(1, 2)\,(3)\,(4)$$
$$(1, 2)\,(3, 4)$$
$$(1, 2, 3)\,(4)$$
$$(1, 2, 3, 4).$$

The algorithm is still in the developmental stage but a version of it has been coded in FORTRAN and the results are promising.

Only relatively minor additions to the tests in step (b) of the centralizer program are necessary to create a program which will decide for a given element g of G whether or not g is first in its conjugacy class. What is required is a procedure for constructing a subset of G which contains the first element of every class and is as small as possible. Using the method for changing bases described above, we may determine the orbits of G on ordered k-tuples for the first few values of k, in the case of the Suzuki group for k at least as large as 5 or 6, and determine for each orbit A the lexicographically first element of A. Given a k-tuple T which is the first element in its G-orbit, we consider elements g of G for which seq(g) begins with T by looking at the various ways of introducing parentheses into T to get the initial segment of cyc(g). Ideally one would like to have orbits on k-tuples for large enough k such that once parentheses are introduced into T there is at most one element g of G for which cyc(g) has the given initial segment. For groups as large as the Suzuki group this is probably not possible. However, a group like M_{11} can be handled in a few seconds and the program was used to look for 2-elements in the Suzuki group.

5. **Classes of the Suzuki group.** Let $\mathscr{G}$ be the Suzuki graph with 1782 vertices and valence 416, let $\bar{G} = \text{Aut}(\mathscr{G})$ and let G be the simple subgroup of index 2 in $\bar{G}$. Explicit generators of $\bar{G}$ have been constructed and the conjugacy classes in $\bar{G}$ of those elements lying in G have been determined. A sum-

mary of these even classes of $\bar{G}$ is given in Table 1. The numbering of the classes is in increasing order of the elements and otherwise arbitrary. An asterisk after the number of a class indicates that the class splits into two classes in G. The symbol $C(x)$ denotes the centralizer of x in $\bar{G}$.

TABLE 1

No.	$|x|$	$|C(x)|$	Cycle structure
1	1	896690995200	1^{1782}
2	2	6635520	$1^{54}\, 2^{864}$
3	2	322560	$1^{42}\, 2^{870}$
4	3	6480	$1^{18}\, 3^{588}$
5	3	19595520	$1^{162}\, 3^{540}$
6	3	69984	3^{594}
7	4	92160	$1^{30}\, 2^{12}\, 4^{432}$
8	4	3072	$1^2\, 2^{26}\, 4^{432}$
9	4	6144	$1^6\, 2^{24}\, 4^{432}$
10	4	576	$2^{21}\, 4^{435}$
11	5	3600	$1^{12}\, 5^{354}$
12	5	600	$1^2\, 5^{356}$
13	6	6912	$1^{18}\, 2^{72}\, 3^{12}\, 6^{264}$
14	6	144	$1^6\, 2^6\, 3^{12}\, 6^{288}$
15	6	864	$3^{18}\, 6^{288}$
16*	6	1296	$3^{18}\, 6^{288}$
17	7	168	$1^4\, 7^{254}$
18	8	384	$1^6\, 2^{12}\, 4^6\, 8^{216}$
19	8	64	$2\, 4^{13}\, 8^{216}$
20	8	128	$1^2\, 2^2\, 4^{12}\, 8^{216}$
21*	9	54	9^{198}
22	10	40	$1^2\, 5^8\, 10^{174}$
23	10	80	$1^4\, 2^4\, 5^{10}\, 10^{172}$
24	11	22	11^{162}
25	12	576	$1^6\, 2^6\, 3^8\, 4^{36}\, 6^2\, 12^{132}$
26	12	96	$1^2\, 2^8\, 4^{36}\, 6^6\, 12^{132}$
27	12	48	$3^2\, 6^8\, 12^{144}$
28	12	72	$2^3\, 4^3\, 6^6\, 12^{144}$
29	12	144	$3^{10}\, 6^4\, 12^{144}$
30*	13	13	$1\, 13^{137}$
31	14	56	$2^2\, 7^6\, 14^{124}$
32	15	30	$1^2\, 5^{32}\, 15^{108}$
33*	15	45	$1^3\, 3^3\, 5^3\, 15^{117}$
34*	18	18	$9^6\, 18^{96}$
35	20	40	$2^2\, 4^2\, 5^6\, 10^2\, 20^{86}$
36*	21	21	$1\, 3\, 7^{23}\, 21^{77}$
37	24	48	$2^3\, 3^2\, 4^3\, 6^3\, 8^{18}\, 12\, 24^{66}$

REFERENCES

1. C. C. Sims, *Computational methods in the study of permutation groups*, Computational Problems in Abstract Algebra, Pergamon Press, Oxford and New York, 1970, pp. 169–183.

RUTGERS UNIVERSITY

Subject Index